HALLEY'S GATHERING

Halley's Gathering

a novel by

William Overstreet

WRp
North Adams, Massachusetts

First published in 2025 in the United States of America

Map and cover artwork and design by Alison Kolesar

Publisher's Cataloging-in-Publication Data

Names: Overstreet, William.
Title: Halley's gathering/ William Overstreet.
Description: [North Adams, MA] :William Overstreet, 2025
Identifiers: LCCN:2024926619|ISBN 9798992216400 (pbk.) |
    ISBN 9798992216417 (ebook)
Subjects:LCSH:Trading posts – Fiction.|Women– West (U.S.) –
    Fiction. | Navajo Indians– Fiction. |Navajo Indian Reserva-
    tion – Fiction.|Southwestern States – Fiction.|BISAC: FIC-
    TION / Westerns.|FICTION / Historical / 19th Century /
    General.|FICTION / Indigenous / General.
Classification:LCC PS3615.V47 H35 2025|DDC813 O--dc23
LC record available at https://lccn.loc.gov/2024926619

ISBN 979-8-9922164-2-4

eISBN 979-8-9922164-1-7

CONTENTS

HALLEY'S GATHERING

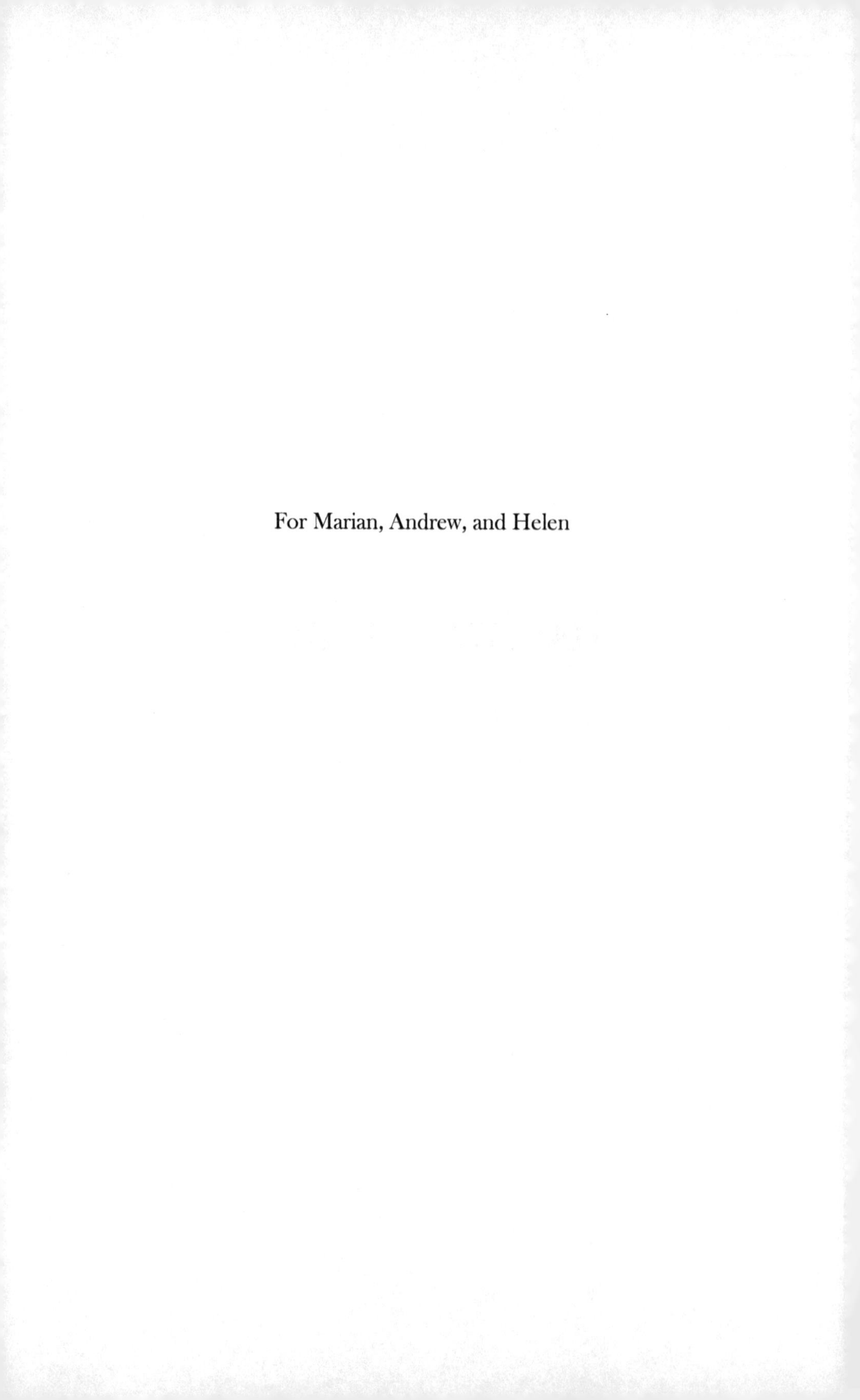

For Marian, Andrew, and Helen

My life is not an apology, but a life. It is for itself and not for a spectacle. I much prefer that
it should be of a lower strain, so it be genuine
and equal, than that it should be glittering and
unsteady.

—Ralph Waldo Emerson

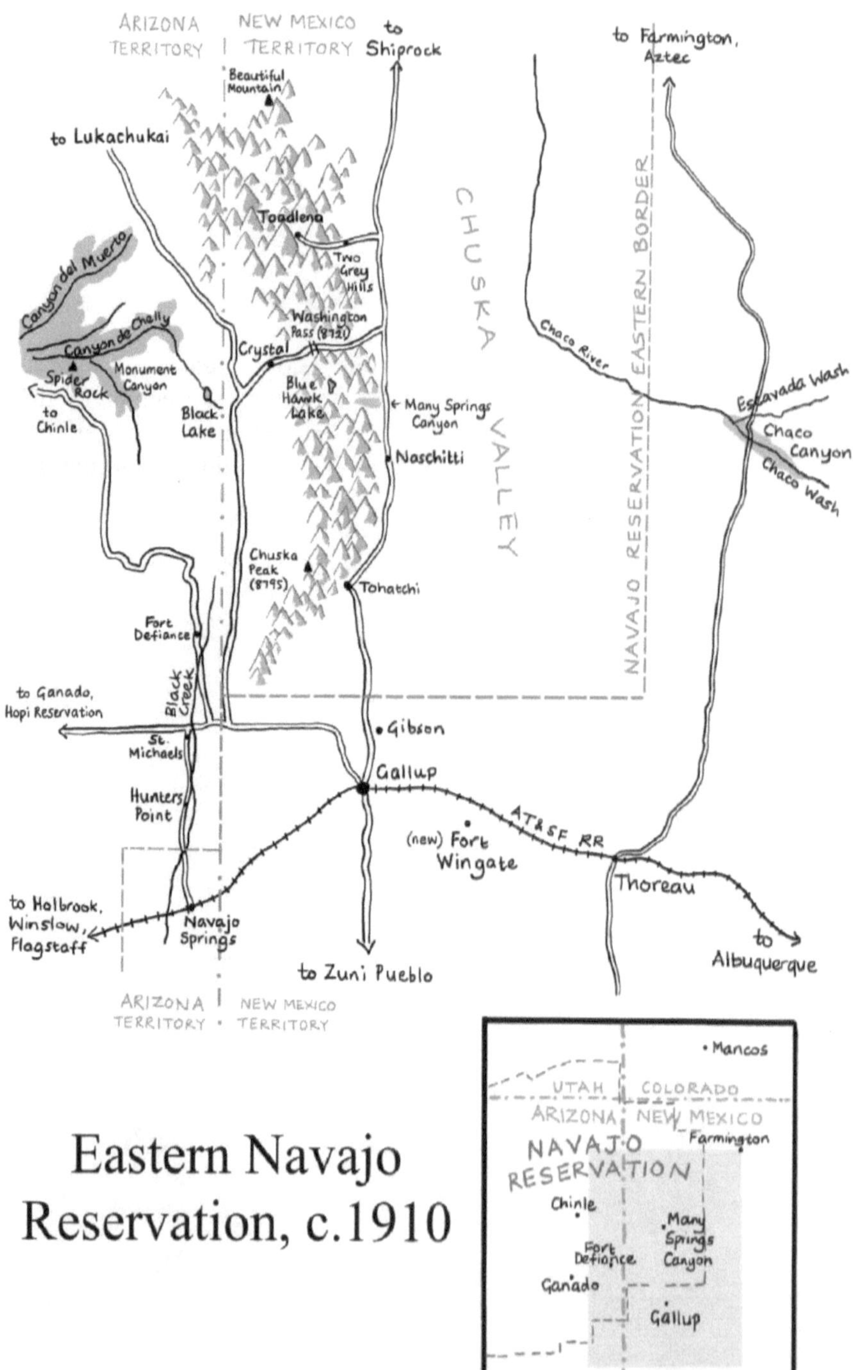

Eastern Navajo Reservation, c. 1910

PART I: ARRIVING

They might not need me—yet they might—
I'll let my Heart be just in sight—
A smile so small as mine might be
Precisely their necessity—

—Emily Dickinson

CHAPTER ONE: Rescue

Julia Halley flung another piece of firewood into the stove and then, holding the spiral handle in her apron, slammed the cast iron door shut. The long, narrow room was already much warmer than she usually kept it, especially before deep winter dragged itself into February, when her fortitude always faded and not even two sweaters would keep her comfortable in the evening unless she kept fires going in both the kitchen stove and this small box stove, in the area she called her parlor. It was only November, but outside the temperature had plunged well below freezing, with the wind-whipped snowfall from the surprise storm swirling into deep drifts. Owen Rouse must surely be in serious trouble by now, and she could only hope that Clement Yazzie and Pete Pietrowski managed to find him soon.

Nearly two hours earlier, as the worsening weather brought an early end to the late afternoon light, Julia had sent Pete, grumbling, to collect Owen from his tent on the other side of the wash. She was standing in the kitchen stirring her stew when Pete returned and told her that the wind had pulled up the tent anchors and that he'd found the canvas draped in the lower branches of a nearby pinyon. Owen's meager possessions—those few that Pete could see despite the driven snow—were scattered across the campsite. There was no sign of Owen Rouse.

She'd set down her spoon and looked at Pete, her expression grim. "We have to try and find him," she said.

"Can't he make his own way back here?" Pete asked, but he didn't remove his derby and coat.

"He isn't well." She didn't elaborate. She moved quickly toward her coat, gray wool, full-length, hanging on a shaker peg beside the door. Before she could get there, however, the door flew open, startling her. Clement Yazzie stepped inside and shut the door behind him with a grunt.

"Bad wind," he said.

"Have you seen Owen?"

Yazzie's brown, weather-worn face frowned. "No. I came down to check on the windmill. Then I thought I should see if you needed anything."

"He's missing. I haven't seen him since this morning." From his arrival in September, Owen had been exploring in the Chuska Mountains, beyond the canyon and up through the ponderosa forest, along the ageless Indian trails, sometimes taking his surveying equipment but sometimes just a field notebook and a bagged lunch.

"He passed by my place," Yazzie said. "But I didn't see him return. Maybe I missed him."

"No," Julia said, reaching for her coat, "he's still up there."

"Wait," Yazzie said.

Julia had learned long ago that Yazzie did nothing rashly. He wasn't a tall man, nor broad, nor powerful to the eye, and he never prattled on, and maybe that was why he commanded attention when he meant to.

"You have a gun?" Yazzie asked Pete.

"In my wagon."

"Best get it. Search between here and my place." Yazzie and his sister, Johanna, lived half a mile deeper into the canyon. "Shoot once if you find him. I'll do the same."

"Huh," Pete said. He didn't much like Yazzie, never had, and the feeling was mutual—Pete's drinking and cutting humor ran counter to Yazzie's way. Julia knew that they tolerated each other for her sake, and only for her sake.

"Don't go beyond the lower meadow," Yazzie said. "I don't want two of you getting lost."

A scowl darkened Pete's blunt face.

"What should I do?" Julia asked. Years before, she'd learned to rely on Yazzie's advice in a crisis, without question.

"Stay here," Yazzie said. "Get your rifle." Julia owned two guns, a rifle that she kept in her wardrobe and a loaded handgun hidden under the counter in the trading post even though, in eleven years, she'd never needed to reach for it, nor had her Navajo clerks, Carmelita and Tom Gorman. "Fire twice if he turns up."

Julia wanted to be out there, searching, but staying behind made more sense. "In this storm, I don't know if you'll hear it, if you're up in the high meadow."

"I will hear," Yazzie said. He turned, opened the door, and left, leaving behind a thin veil of wind-blown flakes that melted when they settled to the floor.

"I don't much like being ordered around," Pete said.

"I'm not going to stand here and discuss it with you." Julia was already moving toward her bedroom to retrieve her rifle, which she hadn't fired in many months, since a coyote went after her hens one night.

Pete left without another word and Julia, needing distraction, went to the kitchen. But there was nothing to do there. Just an hour ago she'd made a fresh pot of coffee, which now sat on the side shelf of the kitchen stove, beside a muslin-draped plate of biscuits. A serving dish of mutton stew, a dinner intended for Pete and herself that had yet to be touched, warmed in the oven. What else? Set the table. But for how many? What shape would Owen be in? They would find him, of course they would. Would Yazzie stay? Was there enough stew if he did? What was she thinking? People could fend for themselves, raid the larder. Maybe hot water for tea, yes, she could do that. She pumped her tea kettle full and carried it to the cook plate of the squat box stove in the parlor. She adjusted the draft and then turned, crossed the room, and opened the door to the spare bedroom—the outward flow of cold air felt good on her face, which was flushed, partly from tending the stove and partly from a combination of fury and worry. She lifted two folded wool blankets from the foot of the bed, which she kept neatly made, white sheets tucked around the tick mattress, even though no one had slept there since the previous spring, when another freakish storm, sleet and freezing rain, had stranded her friend Harry Whitaker, the doctor from the Tohatchi clinic. Julia left the door wide open so that the sparsely furnished room—chest of drawers, wardrobe (she pulled two white towels from the shelf), nightstand, kerosene lantern—might warm a bit, and returned to her parlor. She laid the folded blankets and the towels on the stove's stone hearth.

She stood there, waiting for the water to boil, for an invisible inch of steam to materialize into a cloud of vapor above the kettle's spout. This little stove was one of the first purchases, and certainly the wisest, she and Will had made after arriving in Many Springs: it had become quickly apparent, even in that early autumn, that the kitchen stove, at the other end of the large, open room—beyond the dining table, around the corner—couldn't adequately heat the entire space, at least not for them; they didn't possess pioneer constitutions. Julia, in particular, had lived her childhood in relative comfort. Though far from prosperous, her family had never wanted for secure shelter or enough coal and wood and wool blankets to keep the New England cold at bay. Now, after a decade in New Mexico's high desert, she tolerated winter more easily than she had at first; tending the animals, chopping through the ice in the trough in subzero weather . . .

How much time had passed? It would have taken Yazzie, mounted, in this weather, maybe fifteen minutes, past the pond, across the low meadow, to reach his hogan; another few minutes to enlist Johanna, who wouldn't have bothered to saddle her horse, relying on bridle and reins alone; and for the two of them, taking different tracks, to enter the high meadow, where the canyon opened out, nearly a mile wide, the meadow nearly a mile deep before giving way to tree cover, which meant they would never find Owen in time, if he was above their homestead, unless he'd paid attention to the coming storm and either stayed in the shelter offered by the hemlocks and pines or retreated there at the first flakes . . .

She heard the boom of a gunshot, far away, and its echo off the canyon walls. There wasn't anything else she could do, was there, except wait? She stood with her left hand clasped over her mouth, the thumb resting on her cheekbone and the fingers gripping her jaw line. The water in the kettle began its boil. She pulled her favorite chair, a lattice-back rocker, closer to the hearth. Then she left the parlor, her sanctuary, again, this time reentering her own bedroom, adjacent to the spare room. She pulled the down-filled quilt off her bed and took that, too, to the parlor, where she draped it over the back of the rocking chair.

And sat and rocked. A quarter of an hour, half an hour.

The latch on the kitchen door lifted, and the heavy door, impelled both by the wind and Clement Yazzie's kick, slammed against the wall, breaking free a piece of the painted plaster that filled the chinks between the horizontal logs. The Navajo, his arms encircling Owen Rouse's lower legs, stumbled backward through the doorway. Pete Pietrowski held Owen under the arms; Owen's bare head lolled against Pete's chest. Snow clung to the three of them—Yazzie's and Pete's hats and the shoulders and arms of their coats, Owen's hair and coat and pants.

"Put him in the rocker," Julia said, passing them and shoving the outside door closed. She recrossed the room as they settled Owen into the chair.

He was beyond shivering, but he was still alert enough to look up at her and murmur, "Sorry." His frame didn't fill the chair; she was sure that if she stripped off his coat and shirt she'd see more rib than flesh. His arms and legs were also far too thin, but his face was that of a handsome boy: high forehead, blue eyes beneath fine, near-blond eyebrows, pronounced cheek bones, a smooth knob of chin. His wheat-colored hair, plastered with wet, fell roughly to his collar. Past pale in the lantern light, his tight lips nearly blue, he looked dazed.

Julia began drying his hair with one of the warm white towels.

"Lost," Owen said.

"No fooling," Pete said, shedding his coat and dropping it on a chair by the hearth. His thick black mustache trickled snow melt down his chin, and he swiped at it with a shirt sleeve.

"Help me with his coat," Julia asked Pete, who unfastened the row of buttons while she dried Owen's face and neck. They each pulled a sleeve off an arm, and she dropped the soaked coat; in the stove's heat the snow was quickly melting into the cotton fabric. At least his flannel shirt was passably dry, unlike his corduroy pants.

"Sister found him a few hundred yards up from our corral," Yazzie said in his scratchy monotone.

"Where's Johanna now?" Julia asked.

"Home."

Owen's teeth had begun to chatter, almost as if his lower jaw was in spasm.

"He said he couldn't feel his feet," Yazzie said.

"Let's pull off these shoes," Julia said. "We need to check for frostbite." She and Pete, on their knees, set to work on the ice-caked laces, which, for some reason, had been loosely tied under the tongues, which hung limp.

"What's this, the latest fashion back East?" Pete asked.

Owen, struggling to sit more upright, pulled his foot from Julia's grip. "Don't. I'm all right."

"Maybe he doesn't want us to see the holes in his socks," Pete said.

"Pete," Julia said sharply. He was her oldest friend out here and the one who visited her most often, from Gallup, fifty miles to the south, where he had his photography studio. He was also the friend who annoyed her the most, with his smart mouth and his drinking—he kept a bottle in his wagon; she wouldn't let him drink in her presence—but when he approached the line between banter and injury, she made her displeasure apparent, and he, from experience, knew enough to temper his words or, better yet, as now, to shut up.

"You're not all right," Julia said to Owen, grabbing his right foot again and yanking the ankle-high shoe off. Then she worked the wet, heavy wool sock down. She was surprised to find his foot wrapped in several layers of gauze dressing, which, also soaked through, circled his instep and arch and heel. She let the bandage be for the moment. His toes were bluish, the skin like ice. She pinched the tip of the middle toe as hard as she could and asked, "Can you feel that?"

He turned his face away; he shook his head.

"I warned you about the treacherous weather this time of year, didn't I—that you needed to be prepared?" She'd seen it happen once before this early in November, a storm rising up over the Chuskas and falling into Many Springs Canyon like an avalanche. It wouldn't last long, and in two days the snow would be melted, but that didn't lessen the immediate dangers, including temperatures that could drop forty degrees in an hour.

She went at the bandage next—a nod of her head told Pete, sitting back on his haunches, to do likewise with the other foot—and, unwrapping its layers, uncovered a series of fiercely red, weeping sores, one on the instep so deep that she could see the slick white bone beneath the thinnest, transparent tissue. There were other ulcers, on his heel and aside the ball of his foot. "My God," she said, "how did you even walk?" She glanced at the other unwrapped foot. "How long have your feet been this way?"

Owen didn't answer her question. He looked down at his feet, as if studying foreign objects.

"What now?" Pete asked.

"The trousers. They're soaking wet."

"I'm not about to take another man's pants off, certainly not in front of a woman."

Julia glared at him and yanked the quilt from the back of the chair. Then she draped it over Owen; it hung from shoulders to ankles.

"Can you manage yourself?" she asked him.

Owen nodded, and she turned away. "Mr. Yazzie?" The Navajo had yet to remove his coat but had shaken the snow from his broad-brimmed hat and returned it to his head, and he now stood with folded arms, watching. "Would you take the bowl of stew from the oven and ladle out a cup of broth? We should get something hot into him."

Yazzie nodded and headed to the kitchen. Julia unfolded one of the blankets she'd warmed on the hearth, and when Owen was done removing his trousers, she kicked them aside, knelt down, and wrapped the blanket loosely around his bare feet. Owen's eyes were beginning to close.

"Stay awake!" she snapped, and he startled.

"S-s-sorry," he said.

"It's all right. Don't pay me any mind. I'm just relieved that Johanna found you when she did. You'll be fine now, you'll be fine," she added in a whisper, as much to convince herself as to reassure him.

OWEN ROUSE HAD SHOWN UP unannounced at the Many Springs Canyon Trading Post two months before, in mid-September 1909. Julia was sitting in the shade in a slant-backed chair on the veranda (as she liked to think of it) that wrapped around the east-facing storefront to her living quarters: three rooms, the kitchen facing south, where the window caught more of the fall and winter sun. She was stripping the final, overgrown pole beans off the vines that she'd pulled up that morning. She intended to dry some and save the seeds for next year, and the rest she would can; although a little woody, they would hold up well when added to a winter stew or soup.

She could see all the way down the trail, so she noticed the approaching figure a long ways off on this warm, cloudless day. Midafternoon, and the sun still rode high enough to fill the length of the canyon in front of her with golden light. Less than a quarter of a mile wide here at the trading post, Many Springs Canyon opened up in the direction of her view, until the towering red rock walls, with their stratified cuts and notches, petered out half a mile on, where the road between Gallup and Shiprock, a dust-brown ribbon against the openness of scrubland, ran the length of the Chuska Valley, north and south.

Even at a distance, she suspected that the figure walking up the trail toward her, carrying a rucksack, his thumbs anchored under the heavy shoulder straps, was no Navajo. He'd tipped the flattened brim of his bowler hat to shade his eyes from the sun, so she couldn't see his face in the resultant half-shadow. He walked deliberately; no meandering about him. He carried himself like an adult, but he had the build of an adolescent, maybe five-foot-five, and very slender, wearing no coat. As he drew closer she could see that his blue cambric shirt was buttoned at the collar even though the sweat stains under his arms and at the middle of his narrow chest suggested that he'd been walking for some time. He took off his hat, revealing a full head of blond hair plastered down by sweat, and wiped his brow with a red handkerchief that he pulled from a pants pocket.

"Are you Mrs. Halley?" he asked, smiling shyly.

"I am indeed," Julia said as she continued to yank green beans off the last of the plants and drop them into a canning kettle; a knee-high pile of tangled leaves and vines lay beside her chair. "What can I do for you?"

"My name is Owen Rouse," he said. "Richard Wetherill sends his regards." He pulled his brown canvas rucksack off his shoulders and set it down on the veranda.

"And how is Mr. Wetherill?" she asked. Richard Wetherill and his family had a ranch and ran a trading post in Chaco Canyon, a good forty-five miles east of Many Springs. "I haven't seen him since his brother Win sold the store at Two Grey Hills. I guess that was five years ago now."

"He's well, as are Marietta and their children." The visitor's eyes were a sharp blue, and a splash of reddish-brown freckles crossed his cheeks and the bridge of his nose.

"You look like you could use something to drink. I can offer you coffee or English tea."

"Something cool?" he asked.

"Well, the coldest thing I can give you is water right from the well."

"That would be wonderful," he said.

Julia dropped the final beans into the kettle, wiped her hands on her well-worn white apron, and stood up. "Then come in."

He grabbed his rucksack, climbed the three steps to the wide-planked veranda, and followed her through the door and into the store.

Except for a circle around the Franklin stove, where Navajo men would gather to chat, joke, and smoke free tobacco, the large, rectangular room was crammed with merchandise: displayed on every counter and shelf, hung from nearly every beam, and taking up so much floor space that customers often had to sidle around barrels of nails in common gauges and weights, and sacks of dried beans, red winter wheat flour, hominy, cane sugar, ground oats, corn meal. In this, the Many Springs Trading Post was much like every other small reservation store, where the intent was to provide the Navajos with as great a variety of what they might need as possible. To Julia's way of thinking, that was the trading post's only purpose, and any thought of decoration or presentation beyond an orderliness and basic cleanliness—the floor was scrubbed at least twice a week, and more often in mud season—was superfluous.

Floor-to-ceiling shelves behind the main trading counter were filled with cans of corn, peas, tomatoes, baked beans, and other consumables. Off to the left, stacked (and much-coveted) Pendleton-style Indian blankets offered splashes of color amid more numerous and less costly gray wool blankets, while the lower shelves were piled high with readymade work pants and shirts and union suits and the like, and broad-brimmed hats nested inside each other, from large to small. Along the front of the store, on either side of the entrance, additional shelving held bolts of cloth, aniline yarns, spools of cotton thread, notions, and, by comparison with men's clothing, relatively few finished women's garments, for most Navajo women preferred making their own long-sleeved blouses, pleated cotton or velvet skirts, and shawls. To the right of the trading counter sat boxes of hardware fixtures (brackets, hinges, drain cocks . . .); simple hand tools, from hammers to chisels and saws; metal dishes and pans; and, mounted individually on thick dowels, a dozen unadorned saddles. At the end of the room, farthest to the right, a second, shorter counter with a glass top displayed pawn, mostly silver and turquoise jewelry but also knives and handguns; a rack of rifles, with a locked chain running through the trigger guards, was bolted to the wall behind the pawn counter, beneath which drawers contained boxes of ammunition in assorted calibers. Throughout the store, suspended from hooks screwed into ceiling beams and unfinished square posts, hung kerosene lanterns, bridles and harnesses, saddle bags, belts, baskets, buckets, coiled rope and similar goods. Animal feed and some of the larger items in Julia's inventory—wash tubs, for example—were kept in the trading post's rear storage room, along with items purchased from her customers, primarily Navajo rugs and other weavings, typically in exchange for store credit. One of these days, Julia intended to partition the storeroom and create a proper rug room, where she could display the work of her best weavers and thereby, she hoped, sell more of them at better prices to the—as yet—small number of business travelers and off-the-beaten-track tourists who ventured by.

Julia led Owen Rouse through a connecting door into her home, furnished sparsely, immaculately clean and uncluttered, with white painted interior walls and a pale grey ceiling and polished plank floor—a marked and deliberate contrast to the overstuffed, dim store.

"Have a seat," Julia said, nodding toward a large rectangular dining table that separated the kitchen area from the rest of the room. She proceeded to the sink, where she seized the pump handle and with a few strong strokes produced a gusher of water. Owen sat down facing the kitchen. He put his rucksack on the floor and thanked her when she handed him the glass. He drank it down and she returned to the sink to fill it again.

"Where are you from?" Julia asked, handing him the glass a second time.

"New Hampshire, originally."

"I'm from Western Massachusetts, myself." Julia dried her hands on her apron.

"Really?" He laughed. "Do you know Leominster?"

She smiled in turn. "I've never been there, but I know where it is, more or less. It's not that far from my hometown, Pittsfield—what, maybe a hundred miles?"

"That sounds about right." He set the half-empty glass on the table. "I was living in Leominster until a few months ago."

"In the time I've been out here, you'd be surprised how many Massachusetts people have passed through, most of them from Boston, of course." She folded her arms across her chest and took a good look at her visitor. "Can I offer you something to eat?"

"Oh no, thank you," Owen said. "Just the water."

Julia sat down. "You obviously didn't just wander up the trail, so what brings you here?"

"I'm hoping you'll let me pitch a tent for a few weeks. I could pay you a little for the privilege."

"Why here?"

"That's rather a long story," Owen said.

"Well, it's a Sunday afternoon, the trading post is closed, and I have the time to listen," Julia said. "First, let me get my pan of beans."

She returned from the veranda with the canning kettle, which she placed on another chair before retrieving from a kitchen shelf a large metal bowl. She sat down again with the kettle at her elbow and began snapping the beans into inch-long pieces and dropping them in the bowl.

"If you'd like," Owen said, "I'd be happy to give you a hand with those."

Julia lifted her eyebrows, but then she reached into the canning pot and deposited a heap on the table in front of him. He began snapping them, following her example. "Do you mind if I crunch on a few?" he asked.

"You like them raw?"

"I do."

"Then help yourself. You're sure I can't find you something more substantial to eat?"

"No no, this is fine."

"So you were about to tell me how you ended up here."

He'd been staying at Chaco Canyon since June, he said. Richard Wetherill, in his spare time, had been giving him hands-on lessons in exploring the enormous Pueblo Bonito ruin and the other Chaco sites, certainly the most impressive collection of pre-Columbian dwellings in the United States, next to the cliff houses in Mesa Verde, which, as he was sure Julia knew, Richard and other members of his family had stumbled on in the late 1880s when they were ranching in Colorado's Mancos Valley. In fact, Owen said, it was the prospect of seeing Mesa Verde that had drawn him west, and from there it seemed like a natural course to follow Wetherill to his current home in Chaco Canyon.

Julia had visited Chaco Canyon once (though never Mesa Verde), back when the Wetherill outpost was little more than a three-room shack thrown up adjacent to the multistory Pueblo Bonita, and with stone walls constructed from the collapsed remnants of another ruin and with ceiling beams cadged from Pueblo Bonito itself. She hadn't much liked the stiff, standoffish Wetherill—that's how he struck her, anyway, though she refrained from saying so to Owen—but had found his lively wife, Marietta, much more welcoming. As for the half-buried ruins themselves, which stretched for quite a distance along the Chaco Wash, she considered it remarkable that an ancient race had managed, maybe a thousand years ago, to build structures so large and so remote without the aid of the wheel or beasts of burden.

"And how did you become so interested in Anasazi ruins?" Julia asked Owen.

He'd first read about the cliff dwellings, and then went to see the Southwestern artifacts at the Peabody Museum in Boston, when he was in college, he told her. He came from a farming family and had attended the New Hampshire College of Agriculture and the Mechanic Arts in Durham, which was where he learned what became his trade, surveying. At the time, he thought he might someday like to work for the U.S. Geological Survey. He'd spent most of his three months at Chaco Canyon—the Wetherills generously had offered him a bed in their bunkhouse—surveying the ruins, plotting their precise dimensions and locations. He also dug about—carefully, with a hand trowel and a fine brush, as Wetherill had instructed him—looking for clues as to when and why the structures had been built and then abandoned.

"And that somehow led you here?" Julia asked.

He chewed on a woody bean for some time before responding: He thought there might be interesting outliers—small, unexplored Anasazi settlements, offshoots from Chaco Canyon—in the vicinity. "Richard's brother John," he went on, "found another cliff village just last month in Arizona, up in Tsegi. They're calling it Betatakin, which I gather means 'House on a Ledge' in Navajo."

"I hadn't heard about it. Do you plan to go visit it?"

"Maybe, when I'm done here." He somewhat shyly added, "That's assuming you let me camp out."

"You're quite welcome to stay," Julia said, "but if you're looking to find something grand, I'm afraid you'll be disappointed. Not that there aren't scattered ruins here and about, though nothing in the canyon itself. But most are *very* small—a few rooms, just the remnants, a bit of wall and some scattered pottery shards and charred wood. As for anything bigger, well . . ." She trailed off with a shake of her head. "The Chuska Mountains have been pretty well traveled by Navajos for generations."

"I know." He shrugged, and snapped the last of his beans. Then he cast a weak smile in her direction. "I don't have any great ambition but—no offense intended—I've learned a bit about what signs to look for, things that most people would quite naturally overlook."

Julia couldn't argue with that. She decided that she'd pressed him enough and saw no reason to risk giving offense. There was a gentleness about him, a diffidence, a self-effacing quietness in his voice. Not her typical Anglo visitor: drummers, buyers, freight haulers as well as fortune-seekers, wanderers, life's passers-through; always men, almost never accompanied by women, and frequently full of themselves. Many returned periodically, especially the teamsters and the salesmen making the rounds of the trading posts, because she always offered a hot meal and a place to sleep. For that purpose, as well as to provide shelter for the odd Navajo customer or family who might be stranded by mishap or a surprise storm, there was a guest hogan opposite the corral. She liked best the family men who spoke warmly of their wives and children and joked in the usual manner about in-laws: their wives' sharp-tongued mothers and the lazy brothers who'd never worked an honest day in their lives. To be sure, some she found dodgy or unctuously dangerous and made sure they didn't linger, but a surprising number proved unexpectedly learned or delightful in the course of an evening's conversation.

It occurred to Julia that she might offer Owen Rouse the use of the guest hogan. She wouldn't charge him much—it was hard to tell from his appearance if he had much money, but she suspected not. Still, she could always use a bit more cash income.

"I could let you stay in the guest hogan for a nominal sum. It isn't much—two pallets, a small table, a stove, a dirt floor, and you might have to share it now and then. "

"I appreciate the offer," he said, "but a tent will do me fine."

"Well," Julia said, rising from her chair, "stay as long as you want. Just keep things tidy around your campsite and douse your fire when you're not around. The rainy season is over, and the brush gets very dry this time of year."

"What shall I pay you?"

"Oh, there's no charge, but if you can do a little cash business at the trading post for day-to-day supplies, I'd appreciate it. There's an outside pump and a wash tub around back that you can use anytime. And an outhouse at the back of the garden. I don't mean to be coarse about it, but I'd rather you not use the bushes. Just watch out for black widows—they congregate inside where it's warm when the season turns."

He laughed. "Then it's a timely warning."

"I don't like spiders in general," Julia said, "but black widows"—she shook her head—"the bite won't kill you, but the pain is fierce."

"You've been bitten?"

"I haven't had that particular pleasure," she said, and he laughed again.

"I can also offer you regular meals, but those you have to pay for—a quarter for breakfast, fifty cents for dinner. I tend to eat on the early side, but I can always keep a plate warm for you. And if you don't mind my saying, it looks to me like you could use a decent meal."

He blushed. "Mrs. Wetherill said the same thing."

"My guess is that Marietta runs a better kitchen than I do. Most days I only have to please myself. She has to feed that whole ranch crew."

"Again, I appreciate the offer, but I have peculiar tastes."

"Suit yourself, Mr. Rouse."

"Owen."

"Very well, Owen. And one other thing. If I were you, I wouldn't plan on staying *too* long. We could have a hard frost any night now. The days will stay warm for quite a while yet, but by the end of October you may not want to be camping out."

"Thank you for the advice and the hospitality, Mrs. Halley." He stooped to retrieve his rucksack. "Would you mind if I filled my canteens?"

"Help yourself. The well's always full, even in a dry year."

"I gathered that there's a reason why they call this Many Springs Canyon."

"Indeed. In that, I'm very fortunate." She watched him filling his canteens. "Where are you headed now?"

"To Gallup. I plan to buy a tent and a few supplies. Then I'll head back in this direction."

Julia frowned. "How are you getting to Gallup?"

"Shanks' mare."

"I can rent you a horse for four dollars, including a saddle and tack."

"I'm in no particular hurry. Besides, horses and I tend not to get along."

"It's a hard country to get around in if you don't ride," Julia said.

"True. I just choose to avoid horses if I can. But when I get back, maybe I'll take you up on your offer. I'll need to collect my surveying instruments and a few other things that I left with the Wetherills." Owen paused. "There's one other matter that I'd like your advice about."

"Of course."

"I didn't think it'd be wise to go walking about the countryside with my pockets full of money, so I'll need to find a bank in Gallup. I have a statement from my bank in New Hampshire and a letter of reference from Richard, but he conducts his business through Farmington, not Gallup. He said that if I run into a problem, I should contact his brother Al at the post office, but I'm wondering if you might have a recommendation."

"I'd try the First National Bank, if I were you. I have no idea what arrangements the McKinley County Bank might have for dealing with accounts outside the territory, and the only other bank, the Commercial Bank of Gallup, doesn't provide personal services unless you have a business account there."

"Very good," Owen said. "The First National Bank will be my first stop."

"There's something else you should know," Julia said, frowning. "Al Wetherill is well liked—everyone knows him, he's been the postmaster for several years—but Richard isn't universally loved." She hesitated before continuing. "Some say his dealings with the Navajos haven't always been to their benefit. Let me leave it at that."

Owen screwed his mouth to one side. "I see."

"I don't mean to offend," Julia said. "You clearly admire him, and I'm in no position to judge." She was sure that at Chaco Canyon Owen had heard more than an earful about her own status, if not from Wetherill himself, then from the ranch hands, most of it borrowed from a web of gossip whose strands included thin air, idle curiosity, and simple meanness of spirit.

"Let me write you another quick note," Julia said. She went to retrieve paper, pen, and ink from a roll-top desk near the doorway to the store. She sat down and dipped her pen in the ink. "I have a very good friend in Gallup, Alberto Rodriguez. He owns the Furniture Emporium on Railroad Avenue, but he's also a director of the commercial bank. You can take this to him if you have difficulty."

"You're very thoughtful," Owen said.

She continued writing. "Are you sure you don't want to rent a horse?"

"Thank you again, but I'll keep to my original plan."

"You'll be sleeping beside the road tonight."

"I don't mind. I have a good blanket roll and enough food in my rucksack. Besides, I like walking. I notice things I'd miss if I were traveling faster."

It took a few more minutes for her to finish the letter. She rose from the desk, shaking the sheet of paper to dry the ink. "About eight miles down the trail you'll come to Naschitti. If you change your mind and want a roof over your head, ask for Tom Gorman. He and his wife Carmelita and their elder son, Johnny, work for me, and they'll gladly put you up for the night. Another eighteen miles on, you'll reach Tohatchi. Harry Whitaker runs the clinic there, and he'll do likewise. From there, it's another twenty-five miles to Gallup. You'll be passing near several coal mining camps down that way. Some of the miners can be a rough lot, so watch yourself." Julia folded the letter and handed it to him. "Will you be done with your business by early Thursday?"

"I should be."

"Johnny Gorman should be heading back this way with a buckboard of supplies. There'll be room for your things if you want to hitch a ride. I'll tell him to ask around for you. Gallup's a small town."

"Well, I'll certainly consider that. Thank you again."

"You aren't a drinker, are you?"

Clearly taken aback, he said, "I never developed the taste."

"Good for you."

Julia walked him to her kitchen door, which opened onto the shorter side—the sunnier side at this time of day—of her veranda. They went out, and he stopped for a moment, basking in the warm light with his eyes closed. She could see the small veins in his eyelids, and the fair lashes.

"I've never been out of New England before," he said.

He struck her as *so* young, but she hid her smile. He spoke as if he had no time to spare. Ah, youth! Julia thought; they either think they have all the time in the world or no time at all.

"And you decided to see something different?"

"Yes. Different." He nodded and looked away, down the canyon, the colors deepening now—purple, red, gold, tufts of gray-green—in the settling light.

It was late Thursday night, four days later, when Julia heard the wagon and the brace of horses coming up the trail and then pulling into the yard by the corral. She was already in bed, reading a month-old Chicago newspaper; her younger sister Penelope faithfully packaged up and shipped to her not only local newspapers, but also magazines and books that were all the rage or that her friends in Chicago were reading. Julia rose from her bed, went to the window, and pulled the muslin curtain aside. By moonlight she could see Johnny Gorman starting to unhitch the horses, and Owen Rouse hopping down from the bed of the wagon. Ordinarily, Johnny would have spent the night in Naschitti and finished the trip in the morning. He must have continued on in deference to Owen. Julia returned to bed and finished reading an article about the delivery of the first military flyer to the Army Signal Corps, for which Wilbur and Orville Wright had been paid $30,000. For one aeroplane! Certainly an ungodly sum, but flying had fascinated her ever since she'd read about the Wright brothers' first flight in 1903. If she ever had the opportunity to be a passenger, she'd do it without hesitation.

After extinguishing the lamp on her bedside table, she lay quietly listening. She heard Johnny move the horses to the stable. Time passed, but she didn't fall asleep. She went to the window again. She could see the wagon, about twenty yards away. Then she noticed that the door of the guest hogan was open. Thin shadows moved through a weak light before the door was closed.

During the rest of September she saw Owen Rouse most often at a distance, although he did visit the store irregularly. (Early on, he bought a 25-pound sack of oatmeal, the only size she carried, and ten pounds of coffee beans, and he seemed to fancy canned hams.) Mostly, he kept to himself. He had pitched his good-sized tent—how he would have hauled it from Gallup if he hadn't hitched a ride with Johnny, she didn't know—on the other side of Many Springs Wash, well below the shed where the best wool was scoured after shearing. He went off each day, most often heading up the trail past the Yazzies' place and carrying various surveying instruments. By nightfall he'd usually be back, although sometimes he'd be gone overnight and the next day she'd see him coming up the trail from below, which led her to conclude that he'd ventured farther, following one of the interwoven mountain footpaths along the eastern side of the Chuskas to Pine Bluff or Black Butte and then circling down and around, returning via the Gallup road.

Some evenings he visited her on the veranda or, later in October, as the nights began to get colder, he'd knock on her kitchen door, and he'd show her what he'd found that day: pottery shards of various colors and textures—brown or blue shale corrugated, black-on-white from the Chuska Valley, white clay painted with red or black geometric markings—arrowheads and stone blades, bits of woven sandals; nothing surprising, and nothing she hadn't seen before. Sewing or knitting, sitting in her parlor, she'd nod and listen to him talk about the probable ages of the things he'd found and about how the Anasazi farmed and hunted hundreds of years before the Navajos arrived in the Southwest—she cautioned him about saying that to Navajos, many of whom wouldn't take kindly to a *bilagáana,* a white man, revising their history for them. For the Navajo, this land, Dinétah, between the four sacred mountains, had always been their home, ever since their emergence from below, through the hard-shell sky of their previous world.

Julia and Owen quickly developed an easy way of talking, a bantering that demanded nothing more than an attentive ear, a quick mind, and self-deprecation. Still, she was aghast that he had no interest in literature or music or current affairs.

"What *did* they teach you at college?" Julia asked one unusually warm evening. She was sitting on the veranda in her usual slant-backed, Westport chair. She had two of them, thanks to her sister, who'd seen them for sale while on an Adirondack vacation with her husband and had the pieces shipped west by the manufacturer.

Owen was perched on the veranda's railing with one leg up, his back against a post. "Biology. Organic chemistry. Soils. Animal husbandry. Agricultural machinery. Horticulture. Statistics. Mechanical engineering. Crop rotation—my father asked me about that one: he wanted to know if it had to do with how rocks move from field to field all on their own."

She herself could benefit from a course in animal husbandry. Of necessity, she knew a little about horses and dairy cows and chickens, and over the years she'd learned considerably more about sheep, which were far more numerous and far more profitable than cattle on the reservation.

"So your education was very practical."

"Appropriately so. I'm a very practical person," Owen said, "and dull as a stump."

On the contrary, she thought. Dull, practical people didn't pack their bags and come out West scouring for traces of ancient Indians.

"I just read a newspaper article that recommended raising pigs. What do you think?" Julia asked, only half in jest. "They eat just about anything and enrich the soil. Or so the article said."

"Anything you add to this soil has to help it," Owen replied. "It's either sand or clay. As for pigs, my father raised a couple every year. They're very smart, you know. We had neighbors that kept a sow as a pet. She slept right in the bedroom with them."

She caught the glint in his eye. "Did she now?"

"You know New England farmers—they get notions."

"She probably helped keep the room warm in the winter," Julia said with a straight face.

"Maybe, but that wasn't the reason."

"No? Then it must have been for the elevated level of conversation."

"Ah," he said, "you *do* know New England farmers."

Julia invited him to join her for dinner several times before he finally accepted. She was stewing a chicken and had also invited her clerks, Carmelita and Tom Gorman, who often stayed for an early dinner with her on Saturday, a short workday for everyone. On this particular occasion they were also joined by a Santa Fe rug buyer named Wendell Sterling, who was making the rounds of area trading posts—Crystal, Two Grey Hills, Toadlena, Coyote Canyon as well as Many Springs Canyon—on his way north to Shiprock and Farmington. Carmelita and Tom, never voluble in the presence of Anglo visitors, said very little. Sterling, who'd visited Many Springs Canyon several times before (and who bought only middling weavings because he refused to pay top dollar for the best), dominated the conversation with talk about statehood and his prosperous life in Santa Fe. Carmelita and Tom ate and left as quickly as they could for home. Owen, meanwhile, mostly listened to the rug dealer's monologue and ate some chicken and farm cheese, but not the canned tomatoes from Julia's garden or the dumplings or baked beans or apple brown betty. She wasn't offended, just curious that a man could be such a picky eater.

When Sterling, looking more porcine than usual, finally pushed himself away from the table and, bidding adieu, headed off toward Two Grey Hills, where he planned to spend the night, Julia invited Owen into her parlor. She sat in her rocker, he in a deep armchair upholstered with a bright Mexican fabric of greens and blues.

"That was a man who's full of himself," Owen said.

"And of my dumplings," Julia added. "Believe it or not, Mr. Sterling isn't the worst of the rug dealers. Some take great pleasure in cheating Navajo women, buying low and then selling high to Santa Fe tourists."

"How do you know what's a fair price?" Owen asked.

"When I first came out here, I spent some time at the Hubbell Trading Post, in Ganado. That was my introduction to everything about the trading business. As for Navajo rugs, even today most are still bought and sold by the pound. The weavers understand and respond accordingly. They know that if all they can get is pennies, they'll weave as fast as they can, and as you'd expect, the quality suffers. I've seen rugs made from wool that hasn't even been washed properly. The more lanolin and the more dung left on the wool, the heavier the rug. So I won't buy rugs like that anymore. I've lost some regular customers as a result, but the good weavers appreciate that I try to compensate them fairly for their time and effort. And lately some of us—Lorenzo Hubbell, Ed Davies up at Two Grey Hills, George Bloomfield at Toadlena, J. B. Moore at Crystal—have been trying to convince the weavers to use natural colors and vegetal dyes, and to spend more time improving their skill so that the rugs are more marketable."

The conversation lagged, and Julia could see that Owen was fidgety. He had a nervous twitch in his right leg, and his eyes kept darting around the room.

"It's getting chilly," she said. "It's time for a fire." She kept a pile of old newspapers, a wicker basket of kindling, and a small pyramid of split pinyon near the box stove.

"Don't do it on my account," Owen said.

She rose to light the fire anyway. "Is something troubling you?" she asked. "You're not your usual self."

"I feel I owe you an apology."

"For what?"

"For my poor manners at dinner."

Poor manners? She stopped feeding kindling into the stove and, straightening up, turned toward him. "You owe me nothing, Owen. You give me your company, which I thoroughly enjoy, and that's enough."

"You know I feel the same. It's been a great pleasure to sit with you in the evenings."

He said it as if their time together had reached its end.

"But this isn't about that," he went on.

"Then what?"

"I'm afflicted with diabetes."

She held her expression.

"I assume you know what that is," he said.

"I do." A death sentence. Julia turned back to the stove, adjusted the draft, and lit the newspaper. "How long have you known?"

"Since April, but I may have had it for some time before that. It can creep up on you undetected, until it lays you low."

"And that's why you've turned down my dinner invitations until today." The kindling was already snapping. She fed two pieces of pinyon into the flames and closed the iron door before facing him again.

"It's embarrassing," he said, his face flushed.

"Because you have to limit what you eat?"

"Because I can never sit and have a normal meal with friends or anyone else. Whether they know or not. And if they do know, they're bound to be uncomfortable."

"That isn't necessarily so, Owen. If they're truly your friends—" She stopped short and then with considerable concern said, "What I served today—"

"Was fine. A little meat is all right. The chicken was a real treat."

"What do you usually eat?"

"Oatmeal, butter, and eggs," he said, looking up at her.

"That's all?"

"It's a special diet. A German doctor came up with it. Oatmeal, butter, and egg whites."

She screwed up her face. "Separately or together?"

He couldn't help smiling. "Your expression—it's too bad your friend Pete isn't here to photograph it." He'd met Pete Pietrowski just once, briefly, during one of Pete's weekend visits. "If you really want to know, the recipe calls for three cups of oatmeal boiled into a slurry, half a pound of butter, and three egg whites."

"Dear God," she said. That explained the eggs she'd been letting him collect from her hens whenever he wanted—what should she have done, charged him a penny apiece?—and the butter he insisted on paying her for.

"But I've discovered that if you use less water, cook it for a shorter time, and let it cool, you can cut it into bricks for easy transport."

She began to laugh in little bursts, trying to hold the laughter back, appalled at herself. This was no laughing matter.

"Oh, Owen," she said. What else could she say? That she was sorry? *Sorry.* What did that even mean? He'd told her, one evening, that he was twenty-four. Only twenty-four, and he was going to die.

"It's only half as bad as it sounds, the oatmeal recipe," he said. "Besides, no one could live on just that for long. Most diabetics only keep to it for a week or two, to get through a medical crisis. I'm supposed to eat a little something five or six times a day—no big meals. I don't really mind it. A couple times a day I'll eat something else."

"Canned ham."

"Usually." He shrugged. "Or a handful of nuts. I bought a sack when I was in Gallup." He paused. "I should have told you before about all this. The time never seemed right."

Julia sat down in her rocker. "Is there anything I can do?"

"No. Don't trouble yourself about it."

"Don't *trouble* myself?"

Owen leaned his head back against his chair and folded his hands on his stomach. His shirt fell loosely from his shoulders, and the belt around his waist bore a series of roughly awled extra holes.

"Wouldn't you be better off back home?" Julia asked. "In New Hampshire or Massachusetts?"

"I could ask you the same," he said.

"Me? Not at all. There's no comparison. This is the life I've chosen," she said. "It suits me."

"It suits you?"

"Yes, it does, quite apart from my . . . circumstances."

He'd never asked about her marriage—wisely, for it would have put her off—and she'd volunteered very little beyond mentioning that she and Will Halley had come out here after a short time in St. Louis. She'd added, as an afterthought, that until her marriage she'd generally been regarded as an old maid not only by years, but also by temperament—she'd left it to Owen to conclude for himself that she didn't suffer fools lightly.

Unlike her sister, Penny, no one had ever called her a beauty. A full head of soft light-brown hair suited her hazel, copper-flecked irises, but an unremarkable nose and a shallow Cupid's bow, above a fuller lower lip, though not unattractive, had failed to contribute to either prettiness or allure. In the mirror, her cheeks were too chubby, her chin too shallow, and her figure had always tended toward the flat and trim rather than the shapely. And now, of course, every exposed inch of skin was deeply tanned, and she fully expected that in not too many more years her face would resemble creased leather. There was nothing to be done about that, nor about her hands, which had lost their slender elegance to physical demands. (She could still picture them as they once were, poised above a piano keyboard, the slender fingers and the blue veins beneath the white skin, pink nails neither too long nor too short.) Minus the coarse complexion, if she were back in Massachusetts she imagined that she'd now be seen, at thirty-nine, as having aged into that unenviable, dismissible category, the well-kempt woman.

"You're aware of my marital situation?" she asked Owen.

"Of course." Then, as if fearing he sounded too presumptuous, he attempted to correct himself: "I mean, in general—not in its . . . specifics." His gaze shifted from her.

"But you were courteous enough not to inquire."

"I'm your *guest*," he said. That in itself, he seemed to be saying, was sufficient explanation, regardless of any natural curiosity about her marriage. "You've been very kind, letting me camp here, inviting me into your home in the evening, feeding me—"

"Trying to feed you," Julia interrupted.

"Yes, well, you aren't the first."

They listened to the low whistle of fire from within the box stove. They had safely circled around the uncomfortable subject of *her* status, and returned once again to the more immediate issue, *his* status.

When Owen finally spoke again, it was with a measured diffidence: "The easiest thing has been to avoid talking about my prospects. Revealing anything conveys a burden, and it's not fair."

"Oh, 'fair,' " Julia said with a sigh. "Little in life is 'fair,' Owen. No one should have to bear such things alone."

"Well, I guess that's what I've chosen to do."

"Maybe you should reconsider."

The parlor had warmed now, but the afternoon light had failed. Julia rose and lit an oil lamp in a mirrored sconce on the wall behind them, between the doors to the two bedrooms.

"You read about soldiers coming home from war with horrible injuries," Owen said after a while, "injuries that they've somehow survived but that make a normal life impossible, and you wonder how they go on. But most of them do." He shook his head. "I know it isn't a fair comparison."

That word again—"fair"—but she left it alone. She returned to the rocking chair. "It seems to me that you've been dealing with this quite admirably."

"Oh, I don't know." He slumped in the armchair. "It might be best if I moved on."

"Why is that?" Soon enough, when the weather turned, he'd be gone, Julia thought. What would he do? Where would he go?

"I've imposed enough."

"Owen, you haven't imposed at all."

"It's kind of you to say."

"I'm not being *kind.*" She thought for a minute before saying, "I can't deny what I know, Owen, but if you decide to stay a bit longer, I shall do my very best to continue on just as we have these past few weeks."

He seemed to brighten a bit. "Well, the weather's held so far, so maybe I will."

"In that case, you should pay a visit to my friend Harry Whitaker in Tohatchi."

"The Indian doctor?"

"He ministers to all," Julia said.

"Then I'll do that," Owen said, "if there's ever a need."

SHE EXAMINED OWEN'S thin hands, the blue veins, the prominent knuckles, but at least his fingers were red, perfused. Such foolishness, not to know enough to head back, from wherever he was, when the thick gray clouds lowered onto the mountain peaks above him. She knelt down again and unfolded the blanket from around his feet, which she'd propped on a hassock. They did not look good; at their centers the ulcers were the color of peeled red plums. She couldn't tell about the frostbite; she knew that it could be a day or two before telltale blisters formed or, at worst, the flesh turned hard and black.

Clement Yazzie and Pete Pietrowski had seated themselves at the dining table, helping themselves to the mutton stew and biscuits.

"These sores," she said quietly enough so that only Owen could hear her, "are they because of your diabetes?"

Exhausted but warmed, and once again conversant, he answered, "I imagine so. Bad circulation." He'd finished the cup of broth, and now he was picking at a bowl of stew.

"The doctors warned you?"

He shrugged. "They warned me about a lot of things. Too many." He said it in a way that told her, not that he couldn't comprehend them all, but that to attend to them all would restrict his life beyond what he could bear.

"I don't understand how you can walk from your tent, let alone hike those trails."

"If I watch how I step, I'm usually all right. Some of the feeling's gone in my feet."

Pete brought a final biscuit and a cup of steaming coffee to the parlor, where he claimed his favorite chair. "How's the patient?" he asked.

"Doing better," Owen said.

"As soon as the trail looks passable," Julia said to Owen, "I'm going to send Mr. Yazzie for Harry Whitaker."

"You shouldn't bother him," Owen objected. "Not for simple frostbite."

"I'm more concerned about the sores than the frostbite." She rose and turned to face Pete. "And maybe Tóya should come with him."

"I thought she won't treat Anglos," Pete said.

"If I ask, she'll make an exception," Julia said, hoping she was right. Tóya was a dear friend but not an easy woman.

"Who's Tóya?" Owen asked.

Julia explained that Tóya was a hand trembler, a traditional Navajo diagnostician, but also a herbalist who'd been helping at the Tohatchi clinic since shortly after it opened in 1898. As a young woman, she'd survived the horrific Long Walk, when most of the Navajo nation was rounded up in 1864 and interned for four years at Bosque Redondo, outside Fort Sumner, in eastern New Mexico.

"If anyone around here has a way to heal those sores, it's Tóya," she said.

"Yazzie should take him down to Tohatchi by wagon," Pete said.

"A wagon would get bogged down when the snow starts melting," Julia said, and then to Owen, "Besides, I think we should keep you warm."

Pete muttered something, his voice dropping into his barrel chest.

"Was I meant to hear that?" Julia said.

"No."

"The situation could be worse," Julia said to Owen. "*Pete* could be the patient."

"But Julia," Pete said, "I'd be the most docile and obedient of invalids."

"I'm not an invalid," Owen said, trying to lift himself from the rocking chair.

"Keep your feet raised," Julia said. She turned to Clement Yazzie, who'd followed Pete to the parlor and now stood nearby. "Maybe we should move Owen to the spare bedroom."

"No," Owen said, "I'm not going to be a burden. This isn't what I want." His ragged hair had dried in the heat from the stove—pale curls circled behind his ears and across the crown of his head—and his cheeks were flushed.

"Then you need to be more careful, don't you?" Julia turned and asked Yazzie, "Can you manage him?"

"For God's sake, I can walk that far," Owen said.

"You stay off those feet," Julia ordered.

Yazzie moved to the side of the rocking chair and paused. "You aren't going to fight me, are you?" he asked Owen in a flat voice.

"No," Owen said quietly.

Yazzie bent from the knees, slipped his left arm under Owen's legs and his right between his back and the chair, taking care not to dislodge the quilt from his lap. Owen swung his left arm across Yazzie's shoulders, and the Navajo lifted him easily. He carried him across the room and into the spare bedroom. Julia followed with the other blanket that she had placed on the stove's hearth. Yazzie deposited Owen on the side of the rope bed, which creaked and sagged. Owen lay back and Yazzie lifted his legs onto the mattress. Julia straightened the quilt, covering him neck-high, and also draped the second warmed blanket over his lower legs and feet. Then she raised the milk glass globe of the bedside lantern, struck a match, held it to the wick, adjusted the flame higher, and lowered the glass back into place.

Yazzie pulled the muslin curtain aside from the single-paned window and looked out into the yard between the building and the stable. "The snow's dying down," he said. "I can leave at first light."

"Do you need anything?" Julia asked Owen.

He rolled his head from side to side.

"Then I'll be back to tend you in a few minutes." She and Yazzie left the room but didn't return to the parlor, where Pete's head was nodding, his eyes closed. Instead, they went to the kitchen and stood by the cooker. As she spoke, she tended the fire; she would keep both stoves going all night instead of letting the flames die back. "How long will you be?" she asked.

"It'll be slow. I can make better time in the snow than in mud," Yazzie answered. "If the ground stays cold enough, we can start back in the light."

"No," Julia said, placing her hand on his arm after considering his answer. "Spend the night in Tohatchi. Fifty miles around would be too much. You'll ruin your horse."

"The brown's strong. He'll do fine."

"Stay with Harry overnight. Twelve hours won't matter." Owen's toes would regain feeling and circulation or they wouldn't, but the possibility of blood poisoning from the open sores was another matter.

Yazzie walked to the door, grabbing his coat from where he'd draped it over the back of a dining chair.

"One other thing," Julia said. "Be sure to tell Harry that Owen has diabetes."

Yazzie turned back to her. " *'Ats'íístah 'áshįįh łikan nanit'ą' silįį'*?"

"*Aoo'*," she confirmed. The Navajo language had no predecessor, no Greek or Latin or Anglo-Saxon, to mine when confronted by foreign terms and concepts, and thus Navajo renderings of English were often literal. Julia rarely gave it a second thought now that she spoke Navajo fluently, but sometimes the Navajo version was, as in this instance—"sugar that becomes hidden within the body"—suitably graphic.

As Yazzie closed the door behind him, Julia caught sight of the white sifting down beyond the veranda. The wind had died.

Pete was gently snoring now, his large hands folded across his stomach, which rose and fell peacefully.

Julia returned to the spare bedroom carrying a chair from the dining area. She placed it beside the bed and sat down. Owen was wide awake. "Are you in pain?" she asked.

"Not really. There's some burning."

"That's probably a good sign. Have you ever had frostbite before?"

"My fingers, when I was a boy, but it wasn't bad."

"The burning will go away."

"Oh, I know."

She reached over and lowered the flame in the lantern, and the shadows went soft. "You should get out of the rest of your clothes, at least whatever is still damp. Let me help with your shirt."

With a sigh, he pushed himself up and then leaned back on his forearms as she worked at the buttons. She slid his thin arms from the sleeves. He lay back down and, under the quilt, began removing his union suit. She stepped to the window and looked out; there was nothing to see but snow falling from the blackness and into the ellipse of light from the room. She left him and, carrying a lantern, went through into the store, where she took from various shelves a full set of clothes for him. Having returned and placed the clothing on the foot of the bed, she said, "In the morning we'll gather what we can of your things—the things that haven't been blown half way to Mexico."

He grunted.

She sat down beside him again.

"I have to find my field journals first," he said, "before the snow melts and they get wet. They were in a box under my cot."

"I'll look first thing."

"And my surveying instruments."

"Of course."

In a while he drifted into a fitful sleep.

"Julia?"

She turned in the chair. Pete was framed by the doorway.

"I'm going out to the hogan now." Unless winter weather drove him inside, he preferred to sleep on a bearskin in his enclosed wagon, which he'd meticulously outfitted for his frequent travels.

"It'll be cold. I didn't think to start a fire in the hogan's stove," Julia whispered. "Stay here if you'd like."

"At present, the bed seems to be occupied."

"I won't be using mine. Sleep there." She turned back toward Owen.

"He's not that bad off. There's no need to be a mother hen. You'll want your bed when the tiredness hits." Pete didn't move from the doorway. "I suppose we could try it together."

"Pete," she said with a sigh.

"I know, you're in no mood for my nonsense." He waited a moment but Julia didn't say anything else. "As soon as the road is passable, I should head back to Gallup. I have wedding portraits that I should finish up."

"Why don't you stay at least until Harry and Tóya arrive? We haven't had a little gathering in a while."

"I suppose I could do that. If you aren't sick of me."

"You know you're always welcome, Pete. Even if you exasperate me to no end."

"Well, I guess that can't be helped. So I'll just say goodnight."

She heard him shuffle toward the outside door, which then opened and closed.

CHAPTER TWO: Julia (The Past)

1. Away

The first time she saw Wilford Halley, in 1897, he was sitting by himself in the rear pew of her father's church. The service had concluded, and she'd moved from the first pew and into the aisle, and was following her father toward the exit, where she was expected to stand a deferential half step back, at his right elbow, while he greeted his departing parishioners—all thirty-nine of them, on this particular Sunday.

Her father, a tall, gaunt man with a gray mien and grayer hair brushed straight back from his high forehead, shook each offered hand, nodded, and smiled his peculiar smile, with the right side of his face rising as the left threatened to dip into a frown. His departing flock repeatedly praised his sermon as inspirational or "to the point." What point? Julia wondered, since she'd heard him deliver the same message on every Pentecost for years. In this church, the Third Congregational, there was speaking only by one tongue, and that was her father's.

Julia waited with interest for the stranger to emerge from the church; he was the last to do so. She guessed that he was several years younger than she. His thick, dark brown hair, parted in the middle, had recently been trimmed, and his razor had left no sign of stubble on his rather square, handsome face. Of moderate height and build, he was impeccably dressed in a stylish dark grey wool suit that suggested a certain sophistication, something that none of the few other male parishioners, all over the age of forty, ever exhibited. Apart from her sister Penelope, who'd stayed at home with the sniffles—her father had no patience with coughs, sneezes, or nose-blowing during services—he'd be the youngest member of the congregation, if he joined.

Gray bowler in his left hand, the young man reached out with his right and vigorously shook her father's. "I quite enjoyed your sermon, Reverend," he said, flashing a set of even teeth.

Julia, standing with her hands folded in front of her, barely succeeded in suppressing a groan, because she knew what she was in for: the Adjectival Correction.

"And you are?" her father asked.

"Wilford Halley, sir."

"You must call me Mr. Marshall," her father began. "We're all equals in this congregation. Besides, Mr. Halley, the word 'reverend' is never properly a noun, but an adjective. You'll notice on the church sign"—he slowly turned and pointed toward the placard mounted beside the plain door—"that I'm identified as 'The Reverend Mr. Joseph Marshall.' I've given up trying to correct the local newspapers, however, which continue to refer to me as 'Reverend Marshall,' although I've yet to see them reference Mayor Hawkins as 'Honorable' Hawkins, which would be a comparable error."

Halfway through the lecture, Halley's blue eyes drifted toward Julia's and lingered for several seconds before sliding back to her father. "I see what you mean, Mr. Marshall," Halley replied.

"I suppose it's just an eccentricity of mine," her father said.

"Not at all. In my line of work precision matters greatly. Precision in the measuring and sewing of a cuff, precision in the fit of a collar, precision in the pricing of a French perfume"—his eyes darted briefly to Julia, as if hinting that she was worthy of the finest fragrance—"so that costs are recovered and a reasonable profit made. And, of course, always, precision in the ledgers."

"Your business is . . ." Her father cocked his head to the right, as if to better hear Halley's reply, although, as Julia could attest, his hearing remained acute.

"I'm presently an assistant floor manager at England Brothers Department Store."

"Ah, I see. May I introduce my daughter Julia?" Her father touched her left elbow and she took a half-step forward.

"How do you do, Mr. Halley?" she said, extending a gloved hand.

He took her hand gently in his own and bowed slightly. "Miss Marshall."

"Will we be seeing you at future services?" her father asked.

"I believe so," Halley replied. "I prefer an intimate congregation."

"Quite so," Mr. Marshall said, and Halley, with a nod, turned and left, still carrying his hat in his hand.

All the other parishioners had drifted away. Her father pursed his lips as his eyes followed Halley down the street. "And what do you think?" he asked Julia, unnecessarily sotto voce.

"Of Mr. Halley? He's presentable."

Her father cleared his throat and the two of them walked back into the dimly lit church, which had been built in the 1850s as a noncirculating social library; the opening of a new public library, the Berkshire Athenaeum, in 1876 had quickly led to its closing. For the next twenty years the building housed municipal records, but then it was shuttered and put on the market. Mr. Marshall had rented the premises from the new owner in the fall of 1895, after being forced out of his previous ministry by the governing council of the Second Congregational Church. The book stacks were removed and replaced by second-hand pews—not enough of them to fill the hall, but enough to hold out the false promise of a growing parish.

"He'll be back," Mr. Marshall said as he and Julia began collecting hymnals from the dozen rows of pews, "but I suspect his preference for an intimate congregation is secondary."

Julia made no reply. Her father had been a minister for four decades, during which he'd encountered all the seemingly wily strategies employed by unattached young men to inject themselves into church society in an effort to find suitable wives. Often, they didn't have even the slightest religious inclination. It was, he said, the curse of the new mercantile class, all of these mobile young men with a modicum of education—some had even spent time at college—finding it necessary to market themselves. In general, they weren't confidence men or charlatans. Most were quite sincere. The Rev. Mr. Marshall sympathized because, as he saw it, they'd probably constitute the principal counter to a future oligarchy of inherited wealth, which he saw as a looming social ill. Nevertheless, some of these self-promoters were far too clever for his tastes. As Julia finished collecting the hymnals, she suspected that Wilford Halley, with his apparent expertise in French perfumes, would ultimately fall into that category.

Twice before, Julia had been courted. She was nineteen when the first prospective suitor made his appearance at the much larger Second Congregational Church, where her father had ministered to over five hundred members for more than a decade. Julia had already assumed many of the duties previously performed by her mother, whose neurasthenia had become more pronounced by then. The suitor was pleasant enough, able, a law clerk, but she felt nothing but a vague boredom in his presence and so discouraged his irritating enthusiasm. He soon turned his attentions to the daughter of another congregant, and a year later the Rev. Mr. Marshall performed their wedding ceremony.

John Sewell made his appearance when Julia was twenty-two. An engineer, he worked for the Stanley Electric Manufacturing Company and traveled frequently to moderate-size towns throughout New England that were considering municipal electrification. While away, he wrote her the most detailed letters, almost daily, describing the attractions and the merits of the various communities—he always managed to find something uniquely positive about each place—as well as the practical problems he had to solve. She wrote him frequently but always felt that her letters must disappoint him: so little of her daily life merited being put to paper, certainly not the specifics of her mother's increasing debilitation after years of fatigue, headaches, palpitations, torpor; nor her household and congregational chores; nor her uneasy but resolute efforts to raise her much-loved sister Penelope, fourteen years younger than she. Discussing humdrum tasks and the problems of an eight-year-old schoolgirl didn't strike Julia as likely to increase a young man's affection—which she most certainly wanted to do, for she'd fallen in love with John virtually from their first casual meeting at a church supper. So she wrote to him about the books she read—Dickens, Hawthorne, Tennyson, George Eliot, Howells—and the news of the day and about how much she missed their conversations.

After her mother's heart seizure and quick, merciful death, the character of their too-infrequent meetings and their letters changed to a greater intimacy. At the same time, Julia began noticing that certain women parishioners fell silent or turned away when she approached them at a tea or other social function. She assumed her relationship with John had become the subject of gossip. Except for their letters, the courtship had been entirely public, if one discounted the lovers' moments stolen in a walk-in pantry or in the dark corners of her home's side porch, where John's hands had sometimes tried to venture under her clothing and where, on one occasion, she'd done nothing to discourage him, more out of curiosity than passion.

And then John was offered a position in Schenectady, New York, with the General Electric Company, heir to the Edison Electric Company and the employer of Charles Steinmetz, a hunchbacked genius whose theoretical work, John asserted, surpassed even Edison's and Nikola Tesla's. John asked her to think about their future and what this would mean, because he dearly loved her but couldn't turn down such an opportunity. Shortly after, he pressed his case again, this time in a letter.

She went to her father's study with the letter in hand and, for the first time, let him read what John had written.

"So he hasn't proposed," her father said, setting the letter down on his desk.

"He hasn't, not in so many words," Julia said, her face flushed with an anticipation that she couldn't have hidden even if she'd wanted to.

"Because it would be highly improper, not to mention disrespectful to your mother, so soon after her death."

"Father, it's been six months."

"I don't need to be reminded." Her father cleared his throat and drummed his fingers on the edge of his desk. "He must wait at least a full year before even proposing a . . . proposal." Her father rarely stumbled over words. "And he must speak to me first."

"And if I were to write that in reply?"

He twisted in his swivel desk chair; the metal spindle squealed harshly. His lips were drawn tight, and his lower jaw shifted from side to side. "Penelope would be lost without you. You've just started a new book—what's the title?" Each evening the sisters would curl up together on a settee in the parlor and read to each other.

"*Jo's Boys.*"

"Yes. Precisely. A new book." He propped an elbow on the desktop, and, head tipped, he repetitively ran the palm and thin fingers around his crown. His eyes focused on a corner of his desk. "You must wait."

"And if we can't?"

He looked up. His pomaded hair was mussed, stiffly projecting from the back of his head. "How would Penelope respond if I never let you into this house again?"

Julia was shocked. "You wouldn't do that!"

His prominent Adam's apple pumped up and down before he spoke again. "Another six months until mention of an engagement. A further year until the marriage."

"Father," Julia said, trying to reason with him, "I'm about to turn twenty-three. John is twenty-five. We aren't children."

"That's precisely what you are, inconsiderate children."

She saw no point in angering him further. If she allowed him time to accustom himself to the idea, he might relent, so she said, "I'll write to John tonight and tell him what you . . . propose."

"I'll tell him myself. Write down his address." He handed her a pencil and a torn envelope that had been sitting on his desk. (The envelope was from the Pittsfield Electric Company—a bill for the church, she assumed; the congregation had recently installed electric lights in place of gas lamps.) Julia did as he requested. Without another word she retrieved John's letter and left the room.

She meant to write her own letter to John that night, but she was so desolate that she feared her emotions would overwhelm him. She waited two days, as a consequence of which their letters crossed in the mail:

My Dear, Dear John,

By the time this letter arrives, you'll already have received my father's conditions regarding our future together. Although I find his exercise of paternal authority unreasonable, I must put Penelope's needs before my own for this bit of time....

Your beloved,
Julia

Dearest Julia,

I received your father's letter in today's post. I find his demands disagreeable and very self-serving. As upsetting as this is to me, I accept that, having lost her mother so recently, Penelope would be disconsolate without your full attention at this vulnerable time.

I have decided to take the position in Schenectady and intend to immerse myself in work. We must hold firm in our affection and together (although apart) count down the long weeks and the longer months until we can see each other again.

With all my love,
John

Julia read the letter several times—"the long weeks and longer months until we can see each other again"?—before she went to her father. Once again, she found him behind his cluttered desk.

"What did you write to him?" she demanded. "Did you say that we shouldn't see each other?"

"Six months is nothing."

"Nothing to you!"

"True affection bears the test of time—"

"Oh, please!" she cut him off.

"—and after six months, you have my permission to see each other. Trains run regularly between Schenectady and Pittsfield."

She tried to remember the phrasing of her own letter. Could John believe from reading it that she'd agreed to this six-month moratorium on his visits? She wrote to John again, feverishly assuring him that she'd known nothing about this; her father had deceived him, if his letter had implied her knowledge and acceptance. John's response was cool, measured. He had no desire to drive a wedge between father and daughter, he wrote. They could outlast her father if they held firm. Adverse circumstances often parted lovers for longer than six months, and nothing prohibited the two of them from corresponding as often as they wanted.

Yes, cool and measured. Perhaps a little too cool, Julia thought.

The day before John's move to Schenectady, her father relented and allowed a last visit for Sunday dinner. Her father's part-time cook, Mrs. Palmer, had prepared roast beef with Yorkshire pudding, and Julia did her best to eat bits of undercooked beef and crust, but everything—the disgusting food, the strained atmosphere—felt poisoned. Poor Penny, who understood nothing of what underlay the tension around the oak dining table, tried to act as if she were sixteen instead of a child, flirting with John, giggling when a spot of gravy fell from his fork and stained his jacket, talking utter rubbish about her friends at school despite glares from Julia. Her father, seemingly oblivious to the spectacle, let Penny prattle on until Julia, who was tempted to throw her napkin across the table, sharply told her to behave herself. Penny, tears in her eyes, didn't say another word.

After dinner, Julia spent an unsatisfying hour with John, while the Rev. Mr. Marshall, seated at the other end of the room, read Charles Monroe Sheldon's *In His Steps, or What Would Jesus Do?* At one point her father, bored with his book, insisted that she play something on the piano. Julia told him she'd rather not. Her father responded by slamming his book shut. John cast a pleading look at her, and she acquiesced.

Trying to calm herself, she sat down on the piano bench and closed her eyes. For many years Julia's mother had supplemented the family income by giving piano lessons to parishioners' children, and although Julia resisted at first, she too had become a pupil, learning her scales and the circle of fifths before she even understood what she was doing. Playing the piano was the hallmark of an educated young lady, according to her mother, who resolutely resisted teaching popular music, preferring Mozart and Bach and especially Chopin. Although Julia had come to like the piano, in part because her hour of practice each day was time spent alone with her own thoughts, from the age of twelve she'd been forced to play the church harmonium during services, and she loathed the harmonium.

Julia knew her limitations at the keyboard. She selected one of the less-difficult Chopin nocturnes, No. 20 in C-sharp minor; she especially loved the conclusion, the melody lifting and cascading several times, flowing in common time to a final ascending ritardando. John, smiling, applauded, but her father interrupted, asking with displeasure, "Why do you always play in the minor?"

"I don't," she protested, though later, when she thought about her favorite pieces, almost all were indeed in minor keys.

"It's your melancholic nature," her father said.

When John left, Julia could only wonder why he'd even think of involving himself in such a catastrophe of a family. She went to her room and made for herself, slowly, meticulously, a cloth-bound diary small enough to fit in an apron pocket. Each of the forty-five pages represented four days, labeled by number and then date. Six months; 180 days.

On Day 44 Julia turned twenty-three; from John, who had timed the mails perfectly, she received a beautiful card and two letters.

On Day 78 Julia finally realized that the object of the rumors and hushed comments among the gossiping congregants wasn't her relationship with John, but her father's relationship with one of their own. A robust woman in her mid-forties with two grown sons, Mrs. Edna Blaine had been among the handful of particularly attentive parishioners in the months after the death of Mrs. Marshall. Furthermore, Mrs. Blaine had recently filed for divorce from her contemptible (by all accounts) but wealthy husband of twenty-six years, Edward. On Day 78 Julia chanced upon her father and Mrs. Blaine sitting in the parlor, where the drapes had been closed. They were holding hands, and Mrs. Blaine's head was on her father's shoulder. They were both weeping. Julia turned and left the room.

On Day 122 Julia received a brief letter from John, his first in over a week, explaining that he'd been so busy with work that he'd not had the time to write.

On Day 127 the Council of the Second Congregational Church failed to renew the contract of the Rev. Mr. Marshall.

On Day 135, having not heard from John since Day 122, Julia wrote her final letter to him, releasing him from their nonengagement, and then shredded her calendar with pinking shears.

WILFORD HALLEY—WILL, AS HE preferred to be called—became an active member of the Third Congregational Church. At about the same time, her father announced his intention to remarry. He and Mrs. Edna Blaine, who had moved to Albany, New York, after her husband's timely death—that is, before the divorce proceedings could be concluded—had been "in correspondence" for some time and had decided that there were no longer any impediments to their marrying. Edna, a woman of some means now, had recommended, and he'd agreed, that in the fall Penelope should enroll at the Troy Female Seminary, a highly regarded institution founded by the renowned educator Emma Willard. Furthermore, her father would retire from the ministry.

"True affection bears the test of time," Julia said in response to the news of her father's engagement.

"Quite right. Quite right." Her father ran a forefinger between his clerical collar and a band of ruddy flesh. He'd taken to wearing his collars until they frayed, and French wine had long since disappeared from the dinner table. Lately, when Julia looked in his eyes, as she did now, she often discovered an unexpected vacancy, a sense that his black pupils were no longer windows to his soul, but craters. Even now, as angry and as bitter as she'd ever felt toward him, it distressed her.

"Of course, Julia, you'll have your own rooms."

Not *a* room; *rooms.* "In Albany."

"Yes."

"In Mrs. Blaine's house."

"Mr. and Mrs. Marshall's house," he corrected her.

"Have you said anything to Penny?"

"I thought we might best do that together."

"You and Mrs. Blaine?"

"You and I."

"I see."

"I thought that if Penelope sees that we—Mrs. Blaine and I—have your support, she might be less . . ."

"Upset."

"Quite right. At our move. Of course the change will be all to the good, but we can't expect her to fathom that. She is, after all, still a child."

"Will she be a boarding student?"

He opened his hands. (Sermon-like benevolence, Julia thought.) "We think it best."

It all seemed quite straightforward, didn't it?

Outwardly, Julia gave Penelope's preparations for boarding school and the family's pending relocation her fullest attention. Now thirteen, a delicate beauty with cascading ringlets of strawberry blonde hair, her sister innocently succumbed to her father's bribes—a fashionable new wardrobe, a walnut and cedar hope chest, tailored curtains for her room in Albany— whenever she voiced concerns, and shed tears, about leaving all her friends behind in Pittsfield. Julia reproached her father more than once about all these promises, which she feared would spoil her sister, but he ignored her.

Meanwhile, there was Will Halley, a man with ambitions, and he made her laugh. As she'd suspected, he didn't possess a scintilla of true religious feeling, and he made little effort, with her at least, to pretend otherwise. He confessed that on that first Sunday morning he happened to be passing the Third Congregational Church and ventured in only because he heard someone playing the harmonium. It must have been, he said, a momentary fit of nostalgia for his days in an orphanage in Boston, where for years he'd been subjected to hymns poorly played on a similar instrument.

"So," Julia asked—they were conversing across a table during the once-monthly after-church refreshments of coffee and crumb cake for which her father insisted she play hostess—"you have a passion for the harmonium?"

Looking over his shoulder to be sure no one else would hear, Will said, "I absolutely loathe the harmonium."

Julia laughed out loud, attracting several glances. "At least we have that in common," she said.

"But you play it so well," Will said.

"I *do*. It takes considerable skill not to be overshadowed by the choir."

"But there isn't any choir."

"Then I must be mistaken," Julia said, and it was his turn to laugh.

There was a cruelty about their humor, targeting, as it often did, her father's pretensions and his church. It wasn't as if she'd never before questioned what her father preached: God's heavenly promise for the afterlife, and Satan's unyielding perversity, which could not be distinguished from man's own failings and perversity. She kept returning, in her private contemplation, to a supposedly benevolent God's mysterious inattention to the world's sorrows and why her father's theology even needed Satan when Man was sufficiently evil in and of himself. But what irked her most about the institution of the church was the venality of so many parishioners, which her father, advising her not to be so judgmental, dismissed as human nature and therefore common to every church and sect. Look for the good, he told her; if a clergyman tried to intervene in every little squabble, his life would descend into the slough of despair. She could see the wisdom in this piece of advice, but too often in her role as social stand-in for her father, various ladies of the parish would seek support for their petty grievances and she'd be left to mouth platitudes or smile benignly when what she really wanted to do was slap them.

Will brought a different approach to the church. He regarded it as a business, he told her. He didn't say this at first, of course—not until they'd had numerous brief conversations and he'd received her father's permission "to step out with her," as Will put it with a charming smile that blended satisfaction and irony. The church sold people the goods that they wanted, he said, including brimstone, a small dose of which, delivered from the pulpit, could leave a pleasant whiff in the air, not unlike an extinguished match.

"Why do you even attend services?" Julia asked him on one Saturday excursion to an ice cream parlor.

"It's expected," Will answered, scraping his fluted metal dish with a delicate spoon.

"Do you even believe in God?"

"At times," he said, winking.

"I don't know how to take comments like that," Julia said, done with her own dish.

"Take them for what they're worth," Will said.

"You're impossible."

"No, I'm not," he said. "I'm very doable."

He was too sure of himself, too slick, too charming, but she wanted him to kiss her anyway, to feel his hands cupping her shoulder blades, fingers digging into the muscle. Was it even possible that he felt the same toward her? She was twenty-seven, a minister's daughter (though inwardly, secretly, neither prim nor proper), an old maid.

"What do you want from me?" she asked.

He clearly was neither surprised nor put off by her directness. He leaned forward and covered one of her hands with his. "I want to know if I'm right—if you really have spirit. Or if you've already decided to sour on life." He withdrew his hand. "In which case I won't trouble you again."

Her jaw stiffened. "You're very insolent."

"I am. But you've known that all along. You had me pegged from the first."

"And have you had me pegged from the first?"

"That remains to be seen," he said.

Her father had used her badly, that couldn't be denied. First, by forcing her to serve as her mother's surrogate, during her mother's prolonged illness, at an age when her friends had no more serious responsibilities than washing dinner dishes and minding their younger siblings. Even worse, he'd made her leave school at sixteen; she'd watched her friends advance and leave her behind, the dutiful churchly daughter. Had she also been his shield? Had her presence, following her mother's death, eased the way for Mrs. Blaine and him to meet? And now, as his remarriage drew closer, was she wrong in perceiving that he wanted her gone?

She went to him one afternoon and told him of her and Will's plans to marry and move to St. Louis, where he'd been offered a position.

"This isn't what I expected," her father said. "I have to say that I'm rather surprised that you can't see through his intentions. You don't honestly think he's enamored, do you?"

"There's a certain . . . affection."

"He smells the prospect of money, Julia." She knew very well what her father meant: a little piece of the future Mrs. Marshall's wealth. Her father took off his glasses and rubbed his eyes with thumb and forefinger, bringing them together at the bridge of his nose, red where the glasses had perched. He wasn't used to them yet; he'd had perfect vision until quite recently. "Everything else is . . . window dressing."

Her eyes suddenly burned with anger and shame, that her own father would compare her to department store commodities on display for the public.

"The only question for Mr. Halley is, how much money?"

"I'd like my inheritance," Julia said, controlling the tremor in her voice.

"Your inheritance?"

"I know Mother left Penelope and me a bit. She told me before she died that she'd put aside money that had come to her unexpectedly, from a relative whom she hardly knew."

"And why haven't you ever mentioned this before?" her father asked.

"No one has proposed before. At least not recently."

"What else did your mother tell you?"

"She said that every woman should bring to her marriage her virtue, although that would always be secondary to a man's pecuniary interests."

Her father hesitated. "Did she really say that—about marriage?"

"She did." It was of course a bald-faced lie. "So I'd like to claim my inheritance, however much it is."

"You don't know? She didn't say?"

"No."

He returned his glasses to the bridge of his nose and looked out the window. Julia studied his profile; his pendulous ear lobes, his wattled neck. "Your . . . venture will cost how much?"

"Travel and a month's rent and other living expenses, until Will receives his first pay."

"Julia, this is *lunacy.*" Her father's voice broke and water welled in his eyelids, but he tightened his lips and held firm.

She raised her eyebrows and then let them fall, but she said nothing. Lunacy? To marry a man she hardly knew, a man who replied to an advertisement in a newspaper and, virtually overnight, accepted a job as floor manager in a downtown department store in St. Louis, a thousand miles away? Lunacy would be a sufficient explanation.

"Honor thy father and thy mother!" her father exploded. He thumped his fist on the desk, and the vibration toppled the top half of an untidy stack of papers. They slid in a fan across the wide boards of the bare floor.

Thy shalt not covet thy neighbor's wife, Julia thought.

Her father quickly contained his anger. He sat with his eyes closed for several minutes, his elbows propped on the arms of his chair, his long forefingers pressed together at the apex of a triangle, his thumbs horizontal, crossed.

Here is the church, here is the steeple, open the doors and see— He's calculating, she thought. He knows exactly what our mother left, but he's trying to gauge how little he can get away with giving me.

Maybe it had been a mistake to say that she didn't know how much her mother had put aside, but she couldn't very well pull a figure out of the aether. For all she knew, the money had long been spent, invested in his new church or used to keep dinner on the table.

The Rev. Mr. Marshall opened his eyes, which were bloodshot from trying to adjust to the new glasses, and looked straight at her. "Your share of your mother's money is $2,500."

She had to grab the back of a chair to stay upright. *Two thousand five hundred dollars!* She'd had no idea; she'd hoped for a few hundred. How was this even possible? Oh, if she had only known—

"I'll agree to dispense that entire amount," her father said, leaning forward, "but only if you accept two conditions. First, you and I will go down to the bank tomorrow and open an account that will be in your name only. I will transfer $1,000 into that account, but you must promise me that you will never tell Mr. Halley that that account exists. That money is for you alone. And for your children, if you have any. Do you agree?"

Her emergency fund. Sufficient for her to flee an intolerable situation. And at least in this, he understood her: she wasn't so foolish that she would object.

"Second, I will deliver into your hands $1,500 in whatever form you and Mr. Halley desire. Spend it as you wish—throw it away, if you want. In return, you will *never* ask me for another penny to support your . . . escapade." The word dripped with distaste.

Is that what this was, an escapade? He could think so if he wanted. To her, it was more an escape.

But she wasn't done with him quite yet.

"Will you perform the ceremony?" she asked.

"I will not," he said.

"Then city hall will have to do." She turned to leave the room.

"There are other ministers. I'll speak to someone."

"Do as you wish," Julia said. "I'm sure God will understand when I decline."

"Marriage has always been a perverse market—I assume you've read Jane Austen? The seller has to pay the buyer to take the female off his hands. Maybe that's why the lower classes never bothered with marriage until society began forcing it upon them. It's a historical fact."

Edna Blaine sat stiffly in a straight chair in the Marshall living room. Julia sat across from her, on the settee. She was somewhat intimidated by this "new" Mrs. Blaine. She remembered Mrs. Blaine as an unimposing woman with a sharp nose, no sense of fashion, and an off-putting subservience; when the divorce scandal became common knowledge, she wore her injury like a protective garment. In contrast, this new Mrs. Blaine, proudly displaying an off-putting haughtiness, was wearing a very smart tan skirt and matching jacket with wide, dark brown velvet lapels, a ruffled white blouse, a brown velvet hat with pinned pheasant feathers, and a beautiful red fox stole—two pelts sewn together, the nose of each fox attached to the base of the other's luxurious tail. Mrs. Blaine had indeed come into money.

Julia was enduring this meeting—this dressing down, as she saw it—at her father's insistence. The sun was still bright outside, behind the drawn drapes. Tomorrow, she and Will Halley were to be married in the Third Congregational Church. Mrs. Blaine would be attending, sitting on the bride's side of the aisle.

"I know nothing about your mother's bequest, but I believe that the sum your father has offered you—"

"He didn't 'offer' anything—the money is mine."

Mrs. Blaine ignored the interruption: "—is in line with what your mother intended, despite the fact that he has found it necessary, now and again, to tap into those funds to support you and Penelope."

"Then what about Penny's share?"

Mrs. Blaine had the annoying habit of letting her eyelids fall briefly before making a pronouncement. "You needn't worry about Penelope. She'll be well provided for. She's a lovely young lady, and even given her fundamental nature, her desire to please, which undoubtedly made the task easier, you've done admirably as a substitute for your dear mother. I give credit where credit is due. Penelope is bright, polite, and charming."

"All of which I'm not."

"I would never say you aren't bright," Mrs. Blaine said. "As for Penelope, you're leaving her in good hands. She'll go off to boarding school, and even perhaps on to college."

Penny wasn't even speaking to Julia at the moment. She wasn't upset because Julia was marrying, though she disliked Will Halley, but because they'd be leaving the following day for St. Louis. "College? Where she'll meet some fine, steady young man, and they'll be happily married when he graduates?"

"I fail to see an issue."

"And if she decides that isn't what she wants?"

Mrs. Blaine ignored the question. "And what do *you* want?"

"I don't owe you an answer."

"True. We owe each other nothing, except perhaps civility."

Julia, perhaps for the last time, took in the room around them. Empty packing crates—she could smell the fresh pine, an anomalous scent in this room that she knew so well—were piled chest-high along one wall, at the ready. The move to Albany would be accomplished within the month. Julia would not be attending *that* wedding.

"You seem to know considerably more about my father's finances than I do," Julia said. "He never discussed our expenses with me, not even when I asked."

"I suppose he thought he was protecting you from the ugly truth. It's something that men continue to do, but it's a profound mistake."

"I assume your first marriage taught you that."

"Not my marriage, dear. My truncated divorce—which, I needn't tell you, was initially very distressing, until I 'toughened up,' as they say. But it taught me so *very* much about business and accounting and the legal profession and how the masculine world works, which is why your father has decided to put his affairs in my hands. I was of course fortunate that Randolph died when he did, not only because the seamier aspects of his personal life weren't revealed in open court, but also because, as his wife, I inherited the assets he wanted to deny me. As a result, my dear, I am the best possible thing that could happen to your father at this point in his life."

"Financially speaking."

"Quite."

"So he'll be entirely dependent on your . . . largess?"

Edna leaned forward, though she kept her hands folded on her lap. "If you think you're going to offend me or put me off my mission, you're wrong, so stop trying." She leaned back. The eyelids dropped, almost a flutter. "I shall provide your father with everything he needs."

"Why my father?" Julia asked.

"I assume you mean, why have I pursued him?" Mrs. Blaine didn't even try to suppress her laugh. "Because I love him, of course! But that isn't something I expect you to understand. When my marital difficulties became public fodder, your father stood by me. He refused to believe malicious rumors. He *listened* to me. I shall never forget that. Above all else"—accenting each word—"*I am loyal.*"

The implied criticism forced Julia to reply, "I've been loyal to a fault. If not, why have I stayed with him and tried my best to raise Penelope as my mother would have, had she been able?"

"The difference, my dear, is that you resented every minute of it."

Edna Blaine was too much for her, especially today, the day before she intended to bind herself—the most imprudent thing she'd ever contemplated—to Will Halley. So she turned to another matter, one that the two of them might be able to discuss with less animosity:

"I don't think my father has been himself lately, even before my leaving became an issue."

"Your father is getting old, Julia. Some men age well, but your father is no Benjamin Franklin. You needn't worry," she said again. "I'll take care of him."

"You aren't at all the woman I remember from before," Julia said. She intended it as a half-compliment.

"You were young."

"Not that young."

Mrs. Blaine began putting on her tan doeskin gloves, signaling that as far as she was concerned, the interview was reaching its conclusion. Then came the half-flutter. "It's the money, dear. Money allows you to say what you want and do as you wish. Randolph grew up knowing that but I didn't, and he preferred to keep me chained financially. Money untempered by a sense of morality—"

Julia had heard quite enough and she interrupted: "My father lost his ministry at the Second Congregational Church because of you."

Mrs. Blaine held up a gloved hand. "Stop right there."

Julia's anger nearly choked her. "You deny it?"

"I do," Mrs. Blaine said. "Oh, there were rumors. Your father and I tried to keep our special friendship a secret, but such efforts always fail eventually, don't they? I was still married, after all, and for the church gossips that made the situation particularly . . . juicy."

Julia recoiled at the word. The room was hot; she felt a rivulet of sweat run down her spine.

"Nevertheless, your father and I never did anything improper, either before your poor mother's death or after. Our intimacy simply grew." She added, imperiously, "As sometimes happens with maturity."

Julia had to admit—to herself, not to Mrs. Blaine—that she'd never witnessed anything to contradict Edna's version of propriety, not even the tearful episode in the parlor.

Mrs. Blaine continued, "The Second Congregational Church chose not to renew your father's contract because its finances were not in order. It was simple mismanagement, not malfeasance. You might say it was the church council's own fault—for years they refused to employ a proper bookkeeper."

She sits on her chair, Julia thought, like a great horned owl on its perch.

"One other thing, Julia. I need to be perfectly clear about this. Your father has stated unequivocally that should your marriage fail, I am *not* to rescue you financially."

"He's already made his feelings clear to me."

"Very well." Mrs. Blaine paused. "This wouldn't be my preference, Julia. You shouldn't have to pay for the rest of your life because of one lapse in judgment. But unless your father changes his mind, I'll strictly honor his wishes."

"So in your opinion my marriage is a 'lapse in judgment.' "

"I was referring to the likelihood that your move to the West will present unanticipated difficulties."

"They're of a piece, aren't they—my marriage and the move?"

"Not necessarily, but—forgive me—if I were at Saratoga right now and this were a match race, I wouldn't place a bet on either horse."

Neither would I, Julia thought. "Are we done?"

"Quite," Mrs. Blaine said.

2. St. Louis

"BUT THEY PROMISED YOU the position," Julia said. They'd arrived in St. Louis four days ago, on a Thursday. Today Will had shown up at Wilcox & Sons to begin his new job.

"They did," Will said, "and now they've reneged."

"I don't understand—can they do that?"

"They can do what they want. At the last minute, they found someone better qualified. The husband of the owner's niece." He laughed scornfully.

"Then why did they let you travel all the way out here?"

"They claim that they sent me a telegram."

"Do you think it's true?"

"It doesn't matter, does it? We're here. Besides, they've offered me another position." He laughed again. "Stock boy."

From floor manager to stock boy. She didn't even ask what the job paid. They could never manage on a stock boy's salary. "Did you accept?"

"I said I needed to speak with you. They told me to hurry up, there's a waiting list."

So there was no time to think, to plan. "Then take it until you find something better. And I can start looking for work, too."

"We could go back to Pittsfield."

"Never," she said vehemently.

"That's my girl." He gathered her into his arms. "Besides, we have your mother's money."

She pulled back against his strength. "We agreed not to spend any more of that."

He released her. "I meant, if we need a bit to tide us over." He kissed the top of her head. "We'll be fine. There are other, bigger stores. Scruggs, Vandervoort, and Barney. Stix, Baer, and Fuller over on Washington Avenue. Barr's Dry Goods. We should go apply together. They can hire both of us. You can help old ladies try on corsets." His hands slipped down to her uncorseted ribs.

She looked over his shoulder: their little domain. A double bed with an iron frame and stained mattress (which she had double-sheeted). A dresser and wardrobe with well-chipped and scratched varnish. A marble wash stand; above it, a framed print of a sailing ship. An armchair with a loose right arm that Will said he could fix with a couple of nails. A small table and two straight chairs beneath a double window. A narrow fireplace with a coal insert. (No cooking allowed—they were expected to take their meals elsewhere.)

They'd planned to save what they could from Will's salary for three or four months and then move to a nicer location, one with a kitchen. And her mother's money? They would wait. They would do something with it that would significantly better their lives. They would be patient.

On Wednesday, Will's first day as a stock boy, Julia went looking for work. She had no experience, no references; she'd never handled money except at church socials. No one would hire her, at least not to do anything she considered respectable. She wouldn't even venture into saloons with help wanted signs for "girls"; she wouldn't wash the linens and personal items of weekly renters at a men's boarding house—the list of jobs she couldn't or wouldn't take ran long and often scraped the city's underbelly.

But she didn't give up. She began visiting the St. Louis Public Library, located on the sixth and seventh floors of the Board of Education Building at Locust and Ninth streets. She exchanged pleasantries with the elevator operator, an elderly black man who soon recognized her. In the main reading room she checked the employment advertisements in the newspapers.

Soon, she was waking up in the morning more tired than when she fell asleep at two or three o'clock. Often, her heart would be racing and she could feel a lump in the back of her throat. The sensation came and went during the day. She saw a doctor, who told her to gargle twice a day with warm salt water. He also advised her to have a child.

She thought she might be losing her mind.

She continued to write cheerful letters to Penelope, who seemed to be enjoying boarding school.

Will worked through the winter. He kept them in food and coal, but his inability to find a better position soon left him morose and uncommunicative. Still, he remained parsimonious with their money except for a payday visit with his coworkers to a local tavern. Though Julia could smell the beer on his breath when he came home, she didn't begrudge him, and he never drank to excess. Julia used her mother's bequest only to pay their rent.

One evening Julia returned from the library and placed on the windowsill above their table a piece of paper on which she'd copied a classified advertisement from the *Post-Dispatch*. Will arrived home late—it was a payday—and they ate a cold dinner of leftover ham hock and fatty greens that she had surreptitiously cooked the previous day. When they were finished, she handed him the copied advertisement.

He took it in, and then he scratched his head. Julia noticed, not for the first time, that his hairline was beginning to recede. "What am I supposed to make of *this*?" he asked.

"It's been in the newspaper for several weeks."

"St. Louis isn't what we'd hoped, but at least it's a city." He read, " 'Address inquiries to A. Rodriguez, c/o the Commercial Bank of Gallup, Gallup, New Mexico Territory.' Is Gallup a city? It sounds like what you yell at a horse. Do people like you and me even live in New Mexico? Do they speak English?"

"I assume Mr. Rodriguez does," she said, her mouth drawn small.

"Where is this place"—he checked the paper again—"Many Springs Canyon?"

"In New Mexico, on an Indian reservation."

Will stared at her across the table. "I don't even know what to say. Are you serious?"

"There's no harm in replying to Mr. Rodriguez."

"You want to go live with the *Indians*? I mean, Julia—"

"It's foolish," she said, throwing her hands in the air and abruptly rising from her chair, nearly tipping it over. "I know. It was just a thought. I have hours and hours to think."

"A *trading post*? Pardon me, Jule, but what in God's name do we know about running a trading post?"

"You're right, of course you're right." Julia took the piece of paper back from him and folded it in quarters. "I just thought . . . it would be our own business. We'd be our own bosses. We'd make our own life." *Foolish, foolish*, she thought, but she pressed on: "Even if things get better and you find a decent job, how many years do you think it'll take before we can do that in St. Louis?"

Will rose from the table and retrieved his pouch of tobacco and rolling papers, but he didn't return to the table immediately. Julia, her eyes downcast, began clearing the table of the meager meal.

"It doesn't even mention money," Will said.

" 'All reasonable offers considered,' " Julia quoted the listing.

"And how are we supposed to know what's a reasonable offer?"

"I don't know," Julia said, giving up. "It was just an idea."

"A damn silly one."

The subject disappeared from their conversation, just as the advertisement soon disappeared from the newspaper, and Julia gave it no more thought.

For the first time she thought seriously about a return to Pittsfield. Perhaps Will could even get his old job back at England Brothers, and she could certainly find something productive to do, couldn't she? Maybe she could tutor children. She'd always been an avid reader, and she'd long ago discovered that, given sufficient time, she could master almost any subject if she found the proper book, one that presented the material logically and clearly. Even now, in her frequently heightened emotional state, she found that when she picked up a book that she'd once rejected as too deep for her—even Mr. Emerson's essays, which her father had regularly praised and which, as a result, she'd been too quick to dismiss—she could begin to appreciate the argument and thus the mind that lay behind it. In the case of Mr. Emerson, perhaps she now understood more than her father, whose admiration, coming despite the writer's lack of religious orthodoxy, she unkindly attributed to her father's having once shaken the great man's hand after an 1867 lecture delivered in Pittsfield. Such books—in truth, any book, from Emerson and Thoreau to *A Romance of Wastdale* to the scandalous *The Woman Who Did*—were her escape now, from a life mired in dreariness and her husband's ill humor.

When Will returned home early one afternoon and announced that he'd been fired, Julia immediately proposed that they go home to Pittsfield.

This time, it was Will who wouldn't hear of it. He'd been fired for insubordination by the very man, the gloating bastard, who'd taken his promised job. Fortunately, a fellow worker's meatier arm had restrained Will; Julia suspected that even a glancing blow would have given the manager reason enough to summon the police. Now, pacing their room, Will was in no mood to consider any reasonable option. Julia didn't care what it would cost them to abandon St. Louis there and then, to pack whatever their suitcases would hold and go directly to Union Station. No, no, Will told her. He was owed money—half a week's pay—and he intended to collect it. The money was a pittance, but she knew Will wouldn't let it go. Nor would he forget that he'd been fired, humiliated, in front of the men he'd been working with.

"Will, if we leave, you'll never see any of those people again. Forget about them." She took his hand and pressed it to her breast. "We should just *go*."

His handsome face turned stony. "If we'd gone back to Pittsfield right away, right after we got here, I could've joked about what a hellhole St. Louis is unless you like Lemp Beer and Germans, and everybody would've laughed with me. But after all this time, everybody will see it for what it is, failure, and nobody will be laughing with me. They'll be laughing behind my back." He moved into her. "Or they'll say you blubbered about coming home to the Reverend Daddy Marshall, and I let you lead me back by my—"

"Don't," she said sharply.

"We're here until I decide otherwise," he said.

"And I have no say in the matter?" She backed up a step and folded her arms across her chest. Although Will had never raised a hand against her, St. Louis had revealed flashes of resentment and anger, and a moody coolness toward her when she challenged him.

"It seems to me that you're having your say right now."

"And if *I* choose to go back to Pittsfield?"

"I don't suppose I'd stop you."

Everything they said pushed them further apart; they'd had spats, but not like this, a heated test of wills, of nature and resolve. *She* didn't want this. Did *he*?

"Will," she said, softening her voice, "don't go back to the store. Nothing good can come of it. You know that. A few dollars isn't worth trouble."

And he in turn softened, letting his shoulders drop and running a hand back through his lank hair. "I won't go back to Pittsfield."

"No, of course not," she said, solicitous. She went to him again, placing the side of her head on his shoulder, her hands to his back.

"I don't know," he said, shaking his head. "I just don't know."

After that, he went looking for day work every morning. Sometimes he succeeded. He came home one evening and told her that he'd nearly been killed when a hoist in a metal fabrication plant broke and crashed to the concrete floor not a yard away from where he was standing. Once he was hired for a week to help dig a trench for a new sewer line. On the second morning he could barely struggle out of bed, but he stuck it out for the full six days, at the end of which the contractor couldn't be found; everyone on the job went home empty handed. Meanwhile, he tried applying for more permanent positions at the city's other department stores, but the word had spread that he was unreliable and a troublemaker. Or so he was told by the one prospective employer who deigned to interview him.

There was something admirable and something mad in Will's refusal to submit to their tenuous reality. Julia held her silence, knowing that she couldn't prevail over his stubbornness and pride; he would have to find his own path forward, and then she would have a decision of her own to make. Waiting, waiting, she went out and bought a second-hand sewing machine with a bit of her mother's money. With the assistance of a kindly German woman who lived a floor below them, after only a week of practice she could cleanly hem in several desirable stitches and, like her tutor, began taking in piecework, finishing ladies' handkerchiefs for half a cent each. On a very good day she could make a dollar-fifty, but good days were infrequent, and if Will failed to find day work and returned to their room, his ill-temper and his hovering made it impossible for her to accomplish anything, and so they would often go out together to a park or to Julia's favorite haunt, the library. Once there, they often went their separate ways, although some days they both preferred the periodical room, where they could browse through magazines or newspapers from across the country. Also shelved in the room, at one end, beneath hanging ceiling lights and overhead heating pipes, were various atlases and gazetteers, in which Will took a particular interest. A nearby high table with an angled top and raised lip permitted the substantial volumes to be examined in comfort.

Julia had her favorite chair, which, once she was ensconced, she was loath to leave for fear someone else might occupy it. One day, however, Will dragged her away from *Weldon's Ladies' Journal.* He'd spread out on the map table two volumes as well as a recent edition of the *Post-Dispatch.*

"Look at this article," he said.

"Santa Fe RR Plans Expansion," the headline began, and in smaller type, "New Lines to Link Boom Towns," and in small caps, "MINING AND

Transport Key to Prosperity." Will directed Julia to a map that accompanied the article. "Do you see that? There's going to be a rail line built from Durango, in Colorado, south through Gallup to Clifton, Arizona. Here." He put his finger on the dot.

"Gallup?" she said, confused. She remembered Gallup. And A. Rodriguez. What was this about?

"Look at this." She heard the sharp excitement in Will's voice. He directed her to *W. S. Lesherton's Color Atlas of the United States*, which was open to a map of the states and territories west of the Mississippi River. "Most of the existing rail routes run east-west, like the one through Albuquerque and Gallup in New Mexico and Winslow in Arizona and on, all the way to California. There are other lines farther north that do the same thing, east-west." His forefinger sped over the map. "But the farther west you go, there aren't many connecting routes, north-south. The nearest one is from Albuquerque to near Santa Fe and then to Denver."

"Nearest one?"

"To the planned line."

"Why to"—she went back to the newspaper article, the small map— "Clifton?"

"Copper," Will said. "Probably the biggest copper deposit in the country. They're going to link up the mines in the Southern Rockies—gold, lead, silver, zinc, in Leadville and Silverton and Ouray and Telluride, here, north of Durango—with Clifton."

"But Clifton looks like it's in the middle of nowhere."

"Nowhere is in the middle of nowhere," he said, "not anymore, not if you build a rail line from there to a port—San Diego or the Gulf coast. That would mean they could ship the ore to refineries or mills by sea, which is a lot cheaper than overland. But here's the point," he said, his enthusiasm displayed by the finger that repeatedly tapped the map in the atlas. "A new rail line between Durango and Gallup has to go through the Chuska Valley, and what's right there in the middle? Many Springs Canyon. The railroad will need the water."

So this *was* all about the advertisement for the trading post. "But what about this river?" Julia placed her finger a bit to the east.

"The Chaco?" Will laughed. "Just because they call it a river doesn't mean it's a river like you and I know. I looked it up. Most of the year you can wade across the Chaco River and not even get your ankles wet. This is what they call high desert," he said, circling his finger around the hypothetical route. "High in elevation, so it doesn't look like what you usually think of as desert, but it's a desert still. Water is at a premium."

"All right," Julia said, seeking to tamp his enthusiasm, "but you can't assume just because of the name 'Many Springs' that there's water to spare."

"Of course not, but doesn't it seem likely?"

"And besides, I threw away that notice about the trading post weeks ago. If that's what this is all about."

"Here," he said, taking from his pocket a page torn from an older edition of the newspaper.

She took it from him. "It must have sold by now."

"It's more likely that it hasn't."

She went back to the atlas. She ran her finger south from the Colorado border through the Chuska Valley, tracing the proposed rail route. "This is all Navajo Reservation land, isn't it? Why would the Indians let the rail line go through here?"

"You think that anybody cares what the Indians think?" The twist in his mouth told her how very naïve he thought she was being. "If the railroads need the land, they'll get their hands on it, you can be damn sure of that. They'll spread their money around Washington, and next thing you know—presto."

"I suppose you're right about that," Julia said. But even in her ignorance, the folly of the whole thing was so apparent that she couldn't understand why Will didn't see it. Everything could slip through their fingers like a crumbled clod of dirt. Julia sat down, placed her hands on her knees.

"If we have a going business, we could get a contract to supply water and whatever else the construction and rail crews need—food, clothing, tobacco, medicinals, liquor." Neither of them knew at the time that traders were prohibited from selling alcohol. They didn't even know that purchase of a trading post business and buildings did not include land, not even the land on which the buildings stood, nor any rights to the water beneath the surface, all of which was held by the tribe as a whole.

"When is the railroad going to do this?" Julia asked.

"The railroad isn't going to tell anybody anything until it's ready to move."

"Then this is all . . ."

"A gamble? Haven't you ever gambled?" he asked, irritated.

"No."

"Of course not. Not in the Reverend Daddy Marshall's house."

"I wish you wouldn't call him that."

Will's mouth turned down in what she could only describe as a pout, an expression that did him no service.

"If this is such a good idea," she said, "why hasn't somebody else figured it out ahead of us?" Or maybe someone had, and they were too late. If they were lucky.

"You were keen on this not so long ago," he said.

"I was never *keen* on it," she said. "I was desperate."

"Are we any less desperate now? Sometimes you have to gamble, Jule. You've got to take a chance. We played it safe, didn't we? I had a job lined up, we were going to start a new life, and luck turned against us, for no good reason." He waited for a response, but when none came he went on: "I've been good, Julia. I haven't asked you for any of your mother's money beyond what we need just to get by. Now that we're married, it's as much mine as yours." He paused. "Some would say that as your husband, it's all mine, to do with as I want."

She was appalled. "Do you really think that?"

"No, of course not," he backed off. "That'd be no better than thievery."

Maybe, but they kept coming back to the subject of her mother's money, didn't they?

"Think of it as an investment," he said. "If things don't work out, we sell everything, take back our money, and try something else."

He couldn't be that simple-minded, could he? Surely, most of the money would be lost.

She stood up and looked at the maps again.

Maps, geography in general, had never much interested her. She had no innate sense of distance. The farthest her family had ever ventured from Pittsfield was to Boston when she was nine years old, and after the initial excitement of boarding the train, she soon grew jaded by the interminable length of the trip, through gray and white winter countryside and the uninviting gateways—bleak rail yards and belching smokestacks beside filthy rivers—that announced Springfield and Worcester and finally Boston. Not even the much longer journey to St. Louis had enlightened her, for she'd spent most of it sleeping away the night between Albany and Chicago.

Now, looking at Lesherton's atlas, turning first to the immediately preceding and more familiar map of the Eastern United States—minus the northern wilds of Maine and peninsular Florida, both truncated and boxed on a later page—she committed a child's mistake: she failed to account for scale. Because the western map matched in size the eastern, she intuitively equated the territory of the two and therefore concluded that the New Mexico Territory was only two or three times larger than Massachusetts—whereas in fact New Mexico was closer to twelve times larger—and thus that a trip from Many Springs Canyon to Gallup and back would be an afternoon jaunt by horse and buggy, not a 100-mile circuit through vacant wilderness.

Years later, looking back, she wondered if the half-comforting thought of a nearby town, even one named Gallup, had really made that much of a difference in her capitulation. She hated St. Louis. Anything had to be an improvement.

Will wrote to Mr. A. Rodriguez that night, inquiring as to the status of the Many Springs Trading Post and seeking additional information.

The reply from Alberto Rodriguez, on Commercial Bank of Gallup letterhead, arrived much sooner than they'd anticipated. The trading post had not yet been sold. Yes, water was plentiful; one well, already functional, easily supplied all that the trading post needed. Obtaining a trading license was largely pro forma as long as the prospective licensee(s) had no criminal record. (The license did, however, require a $10,000 surety bond against criminal liability, but such bonds could be obtained through any number of surety agencies for roughly $25 a year.) All prospective employees would require character references.

Mr. Rodriguez also made it clear that he personally had no stake in the Many Springs venture but, as a favor to the Taskins of Las Cruces, New Mexico, family friends, he was acting as agent. One of the Taskin brothers, Abner, had operated the trading post for several years before encountering health issues that required him to return to Las Cruces. Sale would include all buildings, including the stable and corral, and a hogan—a one-room house common to the Navajos—that had been built in 1896 to accommodate overnight passersby or salesmen. The principal building, the combined trading post and residence, dated from 1890. Photographs of the buildings and surrounding canyon were enclosed. As agent, Rodriguez would of course relay any offer to the Taskins, all of whose other business ventures were located far to the south.

"They want to get rid of it," Will said. "At this point, they'll probably take anything we offer."

Julia scanned the photographs. Other than a sink and stove, the main living area was bare of everything except a square table and two rickety chairs and a large, unevenly laid rug, decorated with diamonds and crosses, that covered the floor beneath the table and extended well beyond. Abner Taskin had obviously used one of two small side rooms as his bedroom; a photograph showed a cot, a chest of drawers, and a single straight chair. The other small room was empty; either Taskin hadn't used it, or it had been cleared out.

If the residence could best be described as meagerly furnished, the store, in contrast, was crammed full, from floor to ceiling, with trade goods in barrels, on shelves, on a counter, strung from the rafters, nailed to posts, stacked on the floor. Julia thought there was hardly room to breathe, let alone move, except for a vacant circle around a central stove. She couldn't remotely see herself standing behind that counter. There were no people in the photographs, which was probably just as well. Dark-skinned men, their long hair, their dirty work clothes, sidearms in slung holsters, broad-brimmed hats; dark-skinned, silent women wearing dusty skirts and blankets around their shoulders—she felt faint at the mere thought. She imagined the grime on her skin, the dirt in her hair and under her nails and working its way beneath her layers of clothing. She'd never feel clean again—she might sweep and dust and scrub and sweep again and *nothing* would ever be clean.

First tears came, and then relentless sobbing; she was scarcely able to breathe.

Will knelt down beside her and took her in his arms. "Shh, Jule," he said, stroking her hair, "shh, it'll be all right. We'll do it together or we won't do it at all."

"I can't," she managed to say, her tears wetting the shoulder of his shirt.

"I know, I know. I feel the same way."

"You do?" she murmured.

"It's all so different. That's it, isn't it?" He lifted her chin and looked into her eyes, red and watery.

"Yes." She nodded.

"Unfamiliar."

"Yes."

"Well, maybe we should look at it a different way. At how we could make it familiar. Here, let me take those." He gathered the photographs from her lap and arranged them neatly in an arc on the floor in front of her. "This is the living quarters."

"Don't call it that," Julia said, wiping her eyes. "It makes it sound like a . . . like a fort in the wilderness."

"All right," Will said, smiling. "The residence. This is the kitchen—the stove, the sink, the shelves; we'll need more of those—and here's where the dining room table will be, and this room, over here, this is our bedroom, and beside it, maybe a nursery."

"A nursery."

"Well," he said, a bit hesitant, "that's what we want, isn't it?"

"Yes."

He hurried on: "We can put a door between the bedroom and the nursery. That'd be easy. And out here, outside the bedroom and nursery, this will be our parlor. It's a bit narrow, but it's quite long, and—"

"There's no ceiling," Julia said. "Just the log roof."

"A ceiling," he said. "Of course. The beams are already there. We lay planks above them, and you have your ceiling, and even an attic of sorts. What color should we paint the ceiling?"

"I don't know."

"What else? Here, the wall at the far end of the parlor, I'll build you bookcases, one on either side of the window, filling the wall."

"They would have to be white," she said. "The parlor must be so dark, with just the one window."

"We'll paint it bright white, the brightest, shiniest white we can find. And as I said, we'll put up more shelving in the kitchen, and a low cabinet for your pots and pans and a counter above it. And we'll put up normal inside walls everywhere. I can hammer some studs into the logs from floor to ceiling, and then lath, and we can plaster the whole damn thing, and you can paint it whatever color you want. Or buy wallpaper."

"White," she said, "the walls have to be white."

"And if you want, we can put up a new wall to separate the parlor from the kitchen and dining area. A wall with a door—or French doors, if you want."

She had to laugh at that. French doors in a log cabin.

"And we'll splurge and buy a nice dining room table so you're not embarrassed to have guests, and a hutch for your dishes."

"I don't have any dishes," she said.

"You will." He picked up her hand and kissed her palm, ran his tongue in an arc around the meat at the base of her thumb.

Later, after they'd made love, they dressed and went out to dinner at a neighborhood restaurant where the owner, an Irishman who'd taken a liking to them, allowed them to share a thick veal chop with extra fried potatoes and red cabbage.

That night, Julia rose in her thin nightgown despite a chill in the air and, having lit a single lamp, looked again at the photographs. Not the interior views. No, the exterior views of the trading post and the canyon, including one taken from what could only be a vantage point part way up a canyon wall, looking down on the roof of the building and, beyond, the corral and stable and nearly round hogan, and then farther west, a widening of the canyon to what appeared to be sparse grazing land, and, farthest off, a blurry line that she took to be tall trees, the edge of a forest: the sunshine and the shadows, slanting from the northwest in the afternoon, the world cut into shards of light and dark.

Still, she wavered, irritating Will to no end, until the day two policemen came to their door. The preceding week, in the middle of the night, Wilcox and Sons had burned to the ground, a clear case of arson, and the police had begun questioning all former employees. The visit lasted no more than ten minutes because, yes, she could vouch for her husband, that on the night in question they'd retired together and neither had left their room until the following morning. No, of course no one else could verify that.

The next morning, as Will was dressing in his work clothes to go and stand in the rain with the other day laborers, Julia said, "I'd like you to tell me you had nothing to do with that fire."

Indignant, he said, "How could I? You know I was right here."

"There could be other ways," she said.

He pulled a work boot on and slammed the heel into the floor, driving his foot home, and then bent over to tie the shoestring. "If I said I wasn't involved, would you believe me?"

"I know that some of what you've told me, about the orphanage and your past, probably isn't true, not completely. But you've never lied to me about anything that mattered to *us*."

"Would you know if I had?" The second boot; an identical *thunk.*

"I think I would."

"Then I'll tell you this once," looking up as his fingers tied the string, "and you're never to ask me again. I had *nothing* to do with that fire. It served them right, but I don't know anything about it."

"It didn't serve their employees right, nor their families."

He stood up. "Have we settled this?"

"We have," Julia said.

3. *Fear and Beauty*

ALBERTO RODRIGUEZ PERSONALLY met their train at Gallup. Tall, brown-skinned, and elegantly dressed in a gray wool business suit, fashionable shoes, and a homburg that he doffed, revealing a full head of black hair as neatly trimmed as his mustache, he struck Julia as a man of carefully studied manners. Having arranged for their bags to be taken to a nearby hotel where they would spend the night, he took them directly to the Commercial Bank, where the final paperwork for their trading license awaited and where they intended to open a business account. He introduced them to the bank manager, a Mr. Walter Martin—a weaselly looking man, Julia thought—and brought them into a small side office, where everything they needed to verify and sign had already been laid out on the desk.

While Will read through the papers, Julia said to Mr. Rodriguez, "I'm not sure exactly what your position here at the bank is."

"I'm a member of the board of directors," he said.

"Then you're not a banker?" Julia asked, somewhat surprised.

"No," Rodriguez replied. "I own a furniture store, the Emporium."

"Oh, we passed it on the way here," Julia said. The Emporium couldn't be missed; the store was nearly half a block long, with wide plate glass windows and a stone façade. "Have you been in Gallup long?"

"Ten years. My family is from Albuquerque, but my brothers and I branched out. My father continues to run the original store."

"Are you all in furniture?"

"For the most part."

"So, you don't generally handle real estate transactions?"

"Not at all."

"Then Many Springs must have been something of a nuisance for you."

Rodriguez smiled, revealing two rows of perfectly even teeth. "Doing a favor for friends of the family should never be described as a nuisance."

Which Julia interpreted as a "yes."

"Everything seems to be in order," Will said, looking up from the paperwork.

"You'll see," Mr. Rodriguez said for Julia's benefit, "that my typist has identified both of you as licensees operating under the name Many Springs Trading Post."

Julia reached across the desk, turned the application around, and saw that she was listed simply as J. M. Halley. She also saw that the typist had filled in the name of the bond holder, the Metropolitan Surety Company of New York, and the names of Thomas and Carmelita Gorman as employees, the expectation being that the husband and wife, who lived down the road from Many Springs Canyon, in Naschitti, would resume the positions they'd held under Abner Taskin, pending a favorable meeting with the new owners. Mr. Rodriguez had himself offered a testimonial as to the "fair character" of the Gormans and their "fitness" to be in Indian country—rather an absurdity, Julia thought, since both were Navajo. According to Mr. Rodriguez, the Office of Indian Affairs would almost certainly issue the license with alacrity.

In the morning Julia would be heading west, to Ganado in Arizona Territory, where—once again thanks to Alberto Rodriguez, who'd extended himself far beyond any familial duty—she had been invited to spend time with the Hubbell family at their store, her introduction to Indian trading. Meanwhile, Will would go north to Many Springs, bringing with him, in addition to cartons and sacks of food essentials, a wagonload of lumber and other building supplies to start work on making their home commodious. Mr. Rodriguez had found an experienced handyman, Rodrigo Peña, to assist. Tom Gorman would also be stopping by to lend a hand when he could; since Ab Taskin's departure from Many Springs, Gorman had found work at a company store in one of the mining communities just north of Gallup.

So they had a plan—as much of a plan as they could. And underpinning that plan lay Julia's determination, once Will and she had made the final decision to move forward, that she would reconsider nothing. Taking Mr. Emerson's advice, she would not "antedate experience." She was determined to see each new vista with fresh eyes, without judgment; to reject society's definition of appropriateness whenever and wherever it conflicted with her own experience; to face each new object in their path, hers and Will's, as a challenge surmountable by the application of natural intelligence and self-reliance. What should she fear? Discomfort? Discomfort was nothing but a futile complaint against the physicality of the world, and she could reject it by force of will and action: change her dress or remove her shoes in the heat or don a coat against the cold, shield her eyes against the sun, wrap a scarf across her mouth and nose to protect against wind-blown grit or sleet, wash the sweat and grime of labor from her face and neck and hands. Should she fear the unknown or illness or accident or even death? That amounted to worthless speculation. Should she fear embarrassment? No. Why should she concern herself with the opinion of someone whom she might meet in passing on the train or in the street? With people who came to know her, understanding would follow, as might permissible laughter at her foibles and faux pas—far removed from the pitiable pain of embarrassment. Should she fear failure? Dear Mr. Emerson had his answer for that: "Whatever course you decide upon, there is always someone to tell you that you are wrong. There are always difficulties arising which tempt you to believe that your critics are right. To map out a course of action and follow it to an end requires courage."

She hadn't wavered. Not when Will and she boarded the train in St. Louis. Not when they came down out of the Rocky Mountains and the forests and saw the bare plateau and the first red rock cliffs. Not when they stepped onto the station platform in Gallup, nor when, pressing her new broad-brimmed straw hat tight to her head and, having said goodbye to Will, she climbed into the wagon that, behind four brown horses, would carry her and assorted sundries and the mail across the fifty-five open miles between Gallup and Ganado.

JULIA'S TIME WITH JOHN LORENZO and Lina Hubbell certainly proved informative. Her first surprise was how little of their trading post business, the oldest on the reservation, involved cash and how much of it involved wool. Julia already knew, of course, that trading posts provided local herders—practically every Navajo family kept sheep—with a convenient place to sell their wool, but she'd thought of the process as an uncomplicated, once-a-year venture, a way for her and Will to make a little extra money by, in turn, selling the wool to a wholesaler. She hadn't realized that most Indians bought on credit and then used their spring income from the shearing to pay off—or at least pay into—their outstanding accounts.

Julia's second realization was that fifty years after the Mexican War, and despite the approach of the twentieth century, most Navajos still couldn't speak English. She was hardly surprised that the oldest generation knew only Navajo, but the same held true even for Indians her own age. Many relied on their sons and daughters to translate for them, but a significant percentage of children didn't speak English either. So she and Will would definitely have to learn Navajo. She knew from overheard conversations in the trading post that it wouldn't be easy; Navajo didn't sound like any other language she'd ever heard, and it had no written form that she could study on the page.

"And Spanish would come in handy," Lina told her. The daughter of Mexican parents, Lina was fluent in Spanish, as was J. L., the son of an Anglo father and Mexican mother. "But I don't suppose you speak Spanish?"

They were both sitting outside the Hubbell kitchen, peeling potatoes in the shade. The youngest of Lina's four children, Roman, seven, sat cross-legged on the ground by their feet, attempting to peel carrots.

"No," Julia said, "but I can speak schoolgirl French."

Lina didn't pause in her task, but Julia read Lina's sideways glance as one more indication that her skills, such as they were, didn't match the task ahead. (Julia had already realized that her newly adopted Emersonian philosophy bore no relation to the everyday practicalities, and she, respectfully, had packed away her travel volume of Emerson's essays.) Lina, quiet, unfailingly polite, said, "I think we've had one or two Frenchmen pass through. Scandinavians and Germans are more common."

"Really?"

"They come to see the old Indian ruins."

"There are ruins here?" Julia asked.

"Nearby," Lina said. "They're scattered all over, dozens of them. Most are small, just a few rooms tucked away in the rocks. But then there's

Hawikuh, down on the Zuni Reservation, south of Gallup. They say that's where Coronado's Spanish army first met Indians on this side of the Colorado River, and where the legend of the Seven Cities of Gold got its start. And closer by, west of here, there's Awatovi, on the Hopi Reservation. The Hopis themselves destroyed Awatovi two hundred years ago because the people living there had abandoned the old ways and converted to Catholicism. And nearest to where you'll be, there's Chaco Canyon. Richard Wetherill has moved his family down from Colorado and started up a trading post right there in the ruins."

As a schoolgirl Julia had learned a bit about Coronado's quest, but listening to Lina reinforced Julia's conviction that by education, experience, and temperament she herself was without doubt the most unsuited individual ever to try and run a trading post. She'd be better off sitting here peeling potatoes for the rest of her life—peeling potatoes and teasing Roman, who'd taken a shine to her, about how much longer she was going to have to wait for a raw carrot to gnaw on.

As if sensing Julia's troubled thoughts, Lina smiled. With her pretty face and high forehead and large brown eyes and plump cheeks and chin, Lina's smile seemed wide enough for both of them. "I wouldn't worry too much. People are people. The Navajos have their peculiar ways, but at the end of the day they're just like the rest of us. They want a good meal, a safe place to raise their children and rest their heads at night, and a little comfort in their old age."

"Have you always felt safe out here?" Julia asked.

"Well now, J. L. bought this place twenty years ago, when he was still on his own, before we met down in St. Johns. I didn't spend much time here in our first years together, but not because I didn't feel safe." She paused and looked at Julia, "The nervous types don't stay. You're not the nervous type, are you?"

"I've had my moments," Julia said, "but no, I wouldn't say so."

Lina continued: "Before too long I had Lala and then Barbara and then Lorencito to care for, and to my way of thinking this just wasn't a fit place to be raising them, although for a time J. L. had a partner, C. N. Cotton, and he and his wife and family made this their home. The children and I spend more time here now, even though we have a second home in Albuquerque. Lala—Adele—I should stop calling her Lala now that she's a young lady—anyway, she's there now, and Lorenzo Jr. is at school in Indiana, which he hates. He wants to be back here, but he has to finish his education first, just like his sisters did." She paused and frowned. "I never had the chance."

The family's Mexican cook opened the kitchen door, stuck his head out, and asked Lina a question in Spanish. Lina answered, "*Sí*," and he collected the potatoes from Lina and Julia and returned to the kitchen. Roman, having given up on the mangled carrot, ran off. He was something of a hellion. Lina brushed a stray peel from her voluminous lap. "Once the new barn is finished, J. L. plans to build us a new house, something that will make the winters here less of a trial, and I expect I'll do less traveling back and forth." Lina's thoughts seemed to drift off, and Julia let the silence linger.

In the next two weeks Julia learned that J. L. Hubbell—thin, angular, distinguished, with a drooping mustache and steel-rimmed glasses—was first and foremost a businessman, one who didn't pay too much attention to the niceties when he was in his store but who nevertheless freely indulged his wife and children. In the 1880s he'd served two terms as Apache County sheriff, and he'd also been elected to the Arizona Territorial Legislature. He seemed to treat his Navajo customers fairly, although she did wonder about the metal tokens he handed out as payment for pelts, weavings, pawn, and the other items brought to the trading post. Unfamiliar with the concept of credit, some of the Navajo clearly thought the tokens were as good as money, even though the Hubbell tokens could only be redeemed for goods from the Hubbell store. Apparently, the use of tokens was fairly common at the larger trading posts. More than once the federal government, viewing the practice as akin to counterfeiting, had tried to stop it.

On just her third day, J. L. had put Julia behind the counter, next to a Mexican fluent in English, Navajo, and Spanish. "If you want to learn the business, talk to the customers, not me," J. L. told her. "When you run into trouble, Luke here will help you out."

So began her life as a trader to the Navajo. At first, she hung back, though Luke Moreno—mostly Mexican but part Anglo, and handsome, with dark eyes and slicked-back hair—was never more than a few strides from her side. Luke, speaking Navajo, would ask her to retrieve items from the shelves—*gohwééh* (coffee), *áshįįh łikan* (sugar), *naa'olí* (canned beans)—and she'd repeat (or try to) the Navajo word as she handed the requested item to him. Fairly often her pronunciation would evoke a titter from the customer, but sometimes an exchange of smiles would follow. By the end of the week, however, Julia had enough confidence to tend to her own customers, with Luke's intervention as needed, and to venture out from behind the counter. Most of the Indians who approached her were women, which was probably why she didn't feel intimidated.

The Navajo women. Well. What did she think of them? She had no experience with other races, discounting the one negro family that had attended the Second Congregational Church during her father's tenure as minister. (Her contact with Jeremiah and Susan Gilpin had amounted to formulaic greetings as parishioners filed from the church after Sunday services, and the occasional handshake at a church supper, her own pale flesh against dark, which had always disconcerted her.) And now here she was, surrounded by another race. Race*s*, some would say, scanning the brown faces of the Mexicans-by-birth—the Hubbells, Luke Moreno, many of the other hands at the trading post—as well as the browner faces of the Navajo. She, Julia, was the oddity here, confronted by these women, whose lives she could barely imagine, their long hair pulled back and twisted into a distinctive bun, the *tsiiyéél*, tied with strands of colorful yarn: the grandmothers, nearly toothless, stooped, breasts flattened from long-ago nursings and covered by soft velveteen and by wool blanket shawls, knowing exactly what they wanted and the value of each token in their hands, faces worn, carved by decades of exposure; and these grandmothers' daughters, mothers themselves, dressed much alike in skirts and deeply dyed blouses and wraps, except for those who still chose to wear the traditional wool blanket dress with bared arms, some of this younger generation buying, in addition to flour and coffee and sugar and beans, a new skillet or notions or a yard or two from a bolt of cotton cloth, a bit of tobacco for their husbands and a stick of candy for a child, having already concluded negotiations with J. L. or his buyer on prices for their latest weavings; and *their* daughters, a third generation, their nut-brown faces still smooth, unpocked by disease or age, more able to speak English but also more visibly suspicious of this white woman—all three generations displaying distinctive bracelets of thick silver and turquoise nuggets, and elaborate necklaces unlike anything Julia had ever seen before, weighty with blue-greenish stones in silver settings and with silver beads and flowers and crescents.

And then the men, most of them too wary to approach her. What they wore told two tales, one of tradition—head scarves and the tsiiyéél, and simple shirts and pants and blankets draped over their shoulders, and on their feet moccasins—and the other of the newer West, flat-brimmed hats and loose neck scarves and loose-collared shirts and leather vests, and well-worn store-bought pants and cowboy boots, and gun belts slung with holsters and six-shooters. The men intimidated her, with their fathomless stares. She didn't know what they were seeing: an alien creature to be shunned, or a woman so out of place as to be laughable, or a woman no different (except for that white face, those white hands) than the Mexican women they were accustomed to by now? In a very short time men such as these would be her own customers, and somehow she'd need to learn how to read them.

In the evenings J. L. and Julia often talked about the vagaries of the trading business. He would answer her questions, relate how things were in his early days, give advice, including, one evening, that she should always have a man around when the store was open for business—someone who could handle himself but who wouldn't fly off the handle if provoked.

"You're going to have dissatisfied customers," he told her. "Not many and not often, but some. And I hate to say it, but now and then a drunken

Indian—liquor's a curse, I've never touched it myself, not once. Traders all have their stories, so you'd best be prepared." Then he added, "And learn how to shoot."

The juxtaposition of topics gave Julia pause. "You mean, to defend myself? In the store?"

"No, no, leave that to the men. I meant that you should take up the rifle for when the coyotes try to take your hens. Or for the odd rattlesnake."

Relieved, Julia asked, half in jest, "Are there any other creatures I need to watch out for?"

"Bears," Lina said, jumping into the conversation. The three adults and the Hubbell's younger daughter, Barbara, seventeen and deep in a volume of Dickens, were sitting together in the living room of the Hubbells' modest adobe house. There were books aplenty—in addition to Dickens, complete sets of Poe, Hawthorne, Bulwer-Lytton, Scott, many others—but Julia had never seen Lina open one. She suspected that her friend, for that was how she'd come to regard the gentle, unaffected Lina, could neither read nor write. "They come down from the mountains. But there's no need to shoot them. They'll wander off on their own. Yelling and banging pots and pans helps. They don't like that."

"My wife is a pacifist," J. L. said. "I'm not."

Julia's thoughts kept returning to J. L.'s admonition about always having a man nearby. She pictured Will behind the counter. Had he ever handled a gun? Even if he had, he wouldn't always be there.

"Do you know Tom Gorman?" she asked J. L. "He and his wife used to work for Abner Taskin."

"I don't believe I do," J. L. said.

"Alberto Rodriguez said they were interested in helping us out. I gather that Mr. Gorman's mother, but not his father, is Navajo. And his wife is part Mexican. According to Mr. Rodriguez, they're fervent Christians."

J. L. seemed to ponder this. "Up where you're headed, there aren't many Anglos and even fewer Mexicans. As for the Gormans, all I can say is that Alberto Rodriguez is a fair-minded man. But there are honest Christians and unreliable hypocrites, just as there are honest Navajos and thieving Navajos. If it was always easy to tell the one from the other, all our lives would be the better for it." He left it at that.

On their last evening together, Lina and Julia, wrapped against the chill, were sitting outside. J. L., having already said his farewell to Julia, was away, tending to his warehouse down in St. Johns. The two women were discussing the day, the coming fall—Lina and Barbara would be leaving for

Albuquerque right after the first frost—when Lina suddenly said, "Mr. Hubbell is my second husband. Did you know that?"

"I had no idea," Julia said, taken aback.

"Most people don't know, and of the ones who do, out of respect for J. L. they don't bring it up."

A bit embarrassed by the revelation, Julia didn't know what to say.

"My first husband married me when I was eleven."

"*Eleven?*" Julia said.

"He was a ne'er-do-well, a drinker and gambler and worse."

Eleven. How was that even possible?

"J. L. is the one who insisted that I get a divorce. This was in 1884, and J. L. and I already had three children. People thought we'd gotten legally married back in 1879. I didn't want to do it. I didn't want to get a lawyer and go to court, and bring it all up—it was just too terrible." She fidgeted with a button on her blouse. "I know how it must seem to you, being from the East and being a minister's daughter and all."

"Not a very good daughter, I'm afraid."

"Well, even if that's true, I'm not one to judge." After a while Lina said, "I married J. L. for the children, not so much for myself."

"Do they know?' Julia asked.

"Just Lala. I told her myself. She's eighteen, with a good head on her shoulders."

"I'd like to meet her. And Lorenzo Jr., too." It seemed like an appropriate thing to say.

After a while Lina ventured, "I suppose you're wondering why I've said so much."

"You don't owe me an explanation. It's I who owe *you*." And the sudden flush of feeling—sympathy, compassion, admiration, tenderness—almost overcame her. She took one of Lina's plump hands and pressed it between her own.

"I'm sure terrible things happen where you're from, too," Lina said, "but I'm guessing you've been spared most of it."

"Yes, I suppose you're right," Julia said. Even with regard to Edna Blaine—Edna Marshall, now—and her vile first husband, she'd been spared the full details, if not the public rumors. As for what she saw, or suspected she saw, in the streets of St. Louis, she kept all that at a remove.

"If you stay out here," Lina said, laying her free hand over Julia's, "you're not going to be spared anything. Those days are over." After a bit she went on, "A couple months ago a woman showed up with her son and asked to see J. L. She's Apache, but she's married to a Navajo from Kinlichee. She told J. L. that she feared her husband was going to kill both of them. Her son's back was scarred and freshly raw from being whipped with a belt buckle. J. L. had one of his hands take them down to her people in Whiteriver."

"And the husband?" Julia asked.

"He's probably already found another woman to beat."

Julia withdrew her hands from Lina's, folded them in her lap, and looked down.

"Another time, three or four years ago, an Indian girl who lives just up the trail from here ran into the store terribly upset. Her brother had been out chopping wood and maybe something distracted him, I don't know. The axe bit into his leg, high up, and cut through an artery. He was outside in their wagon with his mother, but there wasn't anything I could do. He died right there in front of me. I was kneeling in his blood."

Julia didn't want to hear any more stories.

"J. L. and I have made a good life despite everything, but it isn't a life most people take to, Julia. Better for you if you figure that out now rather than later. You run up against the weather. The distances. The loneliness. Human nature. There are times . . ." Lina shook her head. "J. L. used to be a terrible gambler until I put a stop to it." (Years later, Julia would learn that J. L. Hubbard was also a notorious womanizer who'd fathered a number of children by Navajo women.) Lina sighed. "And sometimes you just have to decide not to look."

The next morning, Luke Moreno and Julia set out by carriage for the Day family's trading post at Cienega Amarilla, not far from the New Mexico border. After a night as guest of Sam and Anna Day, she was to be driven south to the depot at Navajo Springs, where she could board an eastbound train for the short trip into Gallup.

Lina Hubbell had packed Julia and Luke a lunch of pigeon, cornbread, dried fruits, and corn roasted with olive oil, salt, cumin, and bits of hot red pepper, a dish that had been a revelation to Julia's tongue the first night it was served at the Hubbell table—she couldn't get enough of it. Lina also sent along a bottle of tea for her (the ever-thoughtful Lina!) and a larger container of water. "Drink, even when you're not thirsty," Lina had told her. "The dry air and altitude can do you in if you aren't careful."

At midday Julia and Luke stopped and ate in the shade of tall pines that grew on the southern expanse of the Defiance Plateau. On the trail they'd passed the time speaking Navajo. Or trying to, in Julia's case. Working beside Luke in the trading post, she'd picked up several dozen expressions—"Trader Navajo," Luke called it—as well as many additional words, and today he was doing his best to improve her vocabulary, pointing out and giving name to various natural features and high desert plants.

The back curtain as well as the roof of the carriage offered protection from the sun, but the afternoon was still hot and the ride tiring, and conversation lagged. They came to the eastern edge of the plateau and the vista opened up, and Julia asked Luke to stop so she could stretch her legs. Luke, seeking some privacy, wandered off in one direction; she chose the opposite, taking with her the nearly empty bottle of tea but first wetting her kerchief from the water bottle and wiping the dust off her face and neck. As she walked, she drank what remained of the tea, slowly, a mouthful at a time.

The sky lay open. Five or six clouds, tufts of cotton, floated above her. How far could she see? East, maybe ten miles—she was still flummoxed by distances—across the width of the Black Creek Valley below, to near the territorial border; to red rock walls and stone formations that looked like haystacks, and beyond them, much farther, the western slopes of the Chuska Mountains. Northward, several sharp, black volcanic flumes stood stark against the valley floor, which in that direction gradually rose into the widening curve of the plateau.

She suddenly realized that she was looking at something else that she'd never seen before: the complete shadow cast by each overhead cloud on the plain beneath. Of course she'd seen clouds passing against the mountains back home, but their shadows had always been rippled or distorted by outcroppings or cloves and the textured green or autumn colors or bare trees of the hillsides. Here, each shadow replicated its cloud, shape and path, sky to scape.

Tired, Julia sat down on the hard-packed ground, which had been stripped of any excess sand by the winds that regularly flowed down off the plateau. She pulled her legs up to her chest, wrapped her arms around her shins, rested her forehead on her knees, and closed her eyes.

She'd lost weight in St. Louis. She knew by the fit of her clothes, the looser stretch of her dress across her back and shoulders. She'd never felt a need to be tightly corseted, but now she easily did without. The inch or two of excess had disappeared. Will, his hands on her hips, had noticed, and he'd teased her that he didn't like his women too skinny. But he was also slimmer now. She could feel it in his waist when he was stretched above her.

Three days ago she'd received a letter from him. She didn't know why it had taken so long to reach her. Someone had mailed it for him from Gallup. The letter said that the trading post had been stripped bare of all the trade goods before he arrived. Someone had broken in through the door to the rear storeroom, but something didn't look right. He suspected that the Taskins and Rodriguez had cheated them.

Julia hadn't said anything to J. L. or Lina. She didn't want J. L. to think she was asking for his help. This wasn't his problem, and she'd already imposed on him enough. She had no idea how much it would cost to re-stock the store, but she knew this much: they could only do it if she used some of the reserve money that Will knew nothing about and that she'd promised her father she'd keep for her own needs. Her escape money. If she mentioned it now, Will would want to know where it came from, and she would have to lie about its purpose and its true amount. Or she could tell him the truth, doubly breaking the promise she'd made to her father. But the difficulty involved more than that, because she didn't *want* Will to know. Mention it now, and he would always wonder what else she hadn't told him.

They could return to Pittsfield. (How many times in the last months had she considered and rejected that idea?) They could build their new life in a place they knew. She could visit Penny whenever she wanted to—at the thought of seeing her sister again, Julia felt her eyes flooding—but to do *that*, she would first have to repair relations with her father, to whom she'd written from St. Louis, announcing that Will and she had an opportunity to start their own business in New Mexico Territory. The letter provided no details, and certainly not that the business was a trading post on the Navajo Reservation. She would send them the new address, she wrote, after Will and she arrived.

She hadn't lied, but her message had been couched to suggest that they'd done very well for themselves in St. Louis. If they now returned to the East, her father would be suspicious. A number of diplomatic, pleasantly social visits to Albany would be required. She would tell amusing tales about misadventures in St. Louis; she would laugh about how New Mexico turned out to be a complete folly, how unsuited she and Will were to the Wild West, although she wouldn't have missed the experience for anything—

There would not be an ounce of sincerity in her performance. Her father would suspect it. Edna would know it. They would assume she wanted more money. They would expect obeisance. They would expect fealty. And she would go to hell before she gave it.

Julia opened her eyes and looked around for Luke. Every muscle in her body jumped: to her left, less than three feet away, a tarantula was creeping toward her, one bent leg at a time. It was the size of her palm. She didn't like spiders. She'd already encountered her first black widow, in a corner of the Hubbell Trading Post's storeroom; it was a vile creature, with its messy web and long front legs and shiny back. She'd also run into her first scorpion, which she'd crushed into the ground without compunction. And now, moving slowly toward her shoe, a hairy black tarantula.

Could it smell the fear running down her sides and wetting the back of her dress? Could it hear her heart beating? She could pick up the empty bottle by her side and kill it, but the thought of the smashed mess glued to the glass made a bubble of acid rise into her throat. Those two clawlike things by its mouth, for pushing food in—she couldn't recall what they were called. But she did remember—she'd read something in school—that the tarantula wasn't poisonous. And that it had poor vision despite its multiple eyes.

The first black leg touched her shoe. Slowly, she raised the skirt of her dress above her ankles and wrapped the fabric tightly around her legs. Her foot was merely an obstacle in the tarantula's way; the spider mounted the side of the dusty brown shoe and proceeded across the toe.

The world didn't care. The fear was inside her, it was all hers.

She held out her hand, fingers spread wide, and with her middle finger quickly touched the back of the creature, which immediately ceased all motion. Julia reached out again. This time she stroked it. Several times. No response. One minute passed. Another. And then the tarantula moved on, just as slowly, fixed on its path.

No, the world didn't care, but she would not be its victim.

"*K'adísh hasht'e'ádiinilyaa?*" said Luke, who'd come up to her from behind. She turned and looked up at his smile. He'd asked a double question, the first, implicit one being, Do you understand what I said?

It took her a moment to frame her reply: "*Aoo', k'ad hasht'e'ádiish-yaa.*" Yes, I'm ready now.

THE FOLLOWING EVENING, suitcase in hand, Julia approached the Rodriguez residence, a modest but pleasant stuccoed house with a roof of orange clay tiles, a flagstone walkway bordered by well-tended native plants—various ornamental grasses, globe-mallow, thorny ocotillo, blue barestem larkspur, red penstemon (though she didn't know any of their names at the time)—and a front porch just wide enough for two high-backed cane chairs and a side table. She rang the green-patinated bell hung beside the carved oak door. A gray-haired Mexican woman wearing a white apron over a black dress opened the door. Julia introduced herself and said she wished to see Mr. Rodriguez.

The maid looked at her slightly askance and, speaking with a thick Mexican accent, inquired as to the reason.

"A business matter," Julia said.

"Mr. Rodriguez doesn't conduct business at home," the maid said. "He can be found at his store in the morning." She started to close the door.

"Please inform Mr. Rodriguez that Mrs. Halley wishes to speak to him."

"Mr. and Mrs. Rodriguez are dining," the maid said. A small dark-haired girl in a flowery dress appeared by her side.

"Who's that?" the girl asked the maid.

"Hello," Julia said, bending down and smiling. "My name is Julia Halley. What's yours?"

"Please leave now," the maid said, once again beginning to close the door.

"Elena," said the girl.

The maid spoke a few sharp words to Elena in Spanish.

"Please tell Mr. Rodriguez that he'll see me now or I'll be right here when he leaves for work in the morning. I can make do quite nicely in one of these lovely chairs until then."

"Roberta, is she going to sleep on our *porch*?" Elena whispered to the maid.

"Please wait here and I'll speak to Mr. Rodriguez," Roberta said. She closed the door and Julia waited.

Despite the Days' hospitality, which had included a comfortable bed, she hadn't slept well the previous night. She hadn't been able to settle her mind, thinking about Will and the empty trading post and how, at the very least, someone had taken advantage of them. She'd decided there and then to confront the only person she could—Alberto Rodriguez—about the theft or deceit or whatever it was that had left them with a store but no inventory to sell.

The door opened to reveal Alberto Rodriguez, who said, "Won't you come in, Mrs. Halley?" Roberta and Elena hovered in the background.

"Thank you, Mr. Rodriguez," Julia said, stepping across the threshold.

"I see you've already met my daughter."

"Papa," Elena said, "she wants to sleep on our porch!"

"I don't think that's what Mrs. Halley would prefer to do," Alberto said. "Why don't you go with Roberta now and get ready for bed?"

Roberta took Elena by the hand and led her away.

"Please," Alberto said, "leave your bag there for the time being. Come and meet my wife." He led Julia down a short hallway and into the dining room, where a very short, very pregnant woman rose from the table after wiping her lips on a white linen napkin. With light brown hair, pale skin, and blue eyes, she obviously was neither Mexican nor Indian.

"Mrs. Halley, may I introduce you to Matilda; Matilda, may I present Julia Halley."

"How very nice," Matilda said, but venom dripped from her eyes.

"It's my pleasure," Julia said. Now that she was here, she wished she'd waited until the morning and gone to the furniture store. "I apologize for interrupting your dinner."

"Not at all," Alberto said. "Why don't you join us? Matilda, dear," he said, turning to his wife, "ring for Roberta and we'll have her set another place."

"Oh no," Julia said, "I couldn't. I'm not even properly dressed." Rodriguez was wearing a well-tailored dark blue suit, stiff white wing collar, and tie. Matilda, in a rose-pink silk dress, reached for a little silver bell by her wine glass and gave it a sharp ring.

"That's no matter," Rodriguez said. "We don't stand on formality, and you've obviously been traveling. From Ganado?" He pulled out a chair for her while Matilda spoke quietly in Spanish to Roberta, who'd entered from an adjoining room.

"From Cienega Amarillo. The Day family kindly accommodated me last night after my stay with the Hubbells."

Rodriguez returned to his side of the table, opposite Julia; Matilda sat at the head, between them. No one spoke while Roberta set dishes, silverware, and glassware before Julia. Matilda, playing hostess, picked up Julia's plate and began filling it from several elegant bowls and a platter. Roberta poured wine and a goblet of water before departing.

"This is very generous of you both," Julia said, attempting a smile. "I shouldn't have come so . . ."

"Late in the day?" Matilda offered as she set Julia's plate down.

"What can I do for you?" Rodriguez said, and then, gesturing, "Please, eat."

Julia picked up her dinner fork and lifted a bite of pilaf to her lips. "I don't know if my husband has written to you regarding the state of the Many Springs Trading Post when he arrived."

"No, he hasn't," Rodriguez said, "but I heard from the workman he hired, Mr. Peña, that the store had been broken into."

"So it would appear," Julia said. "Everything is gone."

"Yes?" He said it as if it came as no surprise, and that he was waiting for her to go on.

"And you also understand that we agreed to purchase the trading post based partly on the photographs you sent us?"

He waited for a moment before replying. "I had a local photographer take them because I thought a prospective buyer would find them useful, but they weren't intended to supplement the contract. Surely, your lawyer knew that and explained that the sale involved fixed assets only. The Taskins sold the contents to a wholesaler for cents on the dollar. The trading post had been on the market for some time, and they didn't think they would receive any offers. They therefore saw no reason to keep the contents."

Julia took a sip of wine and a bite of veal cutlet. She wasn't going to tell him that Will and she had foregone the expense of a lawyer.

"I regret any misunderstanding. I'm sure the Taskins would have been delighted to sell you and your husband the inventory at a very reasonable price if you had made your offer for the trading post earlier." He paused. "That said, I must add that I regret my involvement in the whole matter. It isn't something I'd do again."

"Perish the thought," Matilda said. "The Taskins simply wanted to avoid paying a broker's commission."

Fixed assets, she thought. *So that's what it means.* The term had appeared somewhere in the contract, but Will and she had thought it meant everything in the store. They hadn't given it a second thought. How utterly stupid.

"This leaves my husband and me in a rather difficult position," Julia said. "We thought we had a business that we could open immediately, and now we find that we have nothing to sell."

"I understand," Rodriguez said. His sympathy seemed genuine.

"I hope the food is to your liking," Matilda interrupted. "Being from Massachusetts, you may find our table a bit . . . simple."

"Not at all. Everything is delicious." Veal glazed in its own juices, rice pilaf with pine nuts, sautéed summer squashes and cherry tomatoes, pears poached and sliced, complementing the veal. Julia hadn't eaten this well in so very long. Still, hostesses seeking compliments had always annoyed her, and Matilda Rodriguez was no exception.

Roberta appeared at the door again and spoke to Alberto in Spanish.

"You'll have to excuse me for a moment," he said, rising from the table. "Elena insists that I tuck her in. It's our little ritual."

"Of course," Julia said, smiling. Now she'd have to make small talk with Matilda, when what she really wanted to do was finish her meal and leave. She'd embarrassed herself enough.

Matilda had stopped eating. She sat there turning her wine glass in circles on the tablecloth. "My husband is a generous man, and very forgiving," she said without looking directly at Julia. "People attempt to take advantage of him."

"I don't know Mr. Rodriguez very well, but he doesn't strike me as a man who's easily deceived." Julia laid down her knife and fork. "But I'm afraid my intrusion has ruined your appetite."

Matilda lifted her chin and placed a hand on her round middle. "Not at all. With Elena I enjoyed everything. This time we're"—she patted her stomach—"not so easily pleased. I find *many* things that I can't stomach."

Everything out of Matilda's mouth felt like a backhanded slap. There wouldn't be any pleasing her. So be it, Julia thought. She picked up her utensils and resumed eating. By the time Alberto returned to the table, she'd cleaned her plate.

"I had to reassure Elena that you won't be sleeping outside her window tonight," Alberto said.

"Where *are* you staying?" Matilda asked.

"A hotel, just for the night." She hadn't made arrangements for tomorrow's trip to Many Springs; she hoped she could hire a buggy and driver at a livery stable.

"Nonsense," Matilda said. "You must stay with us."

What? Julia thought. This was certainly unexpected.

"Of course," Alberto said. "I'll have Roberta put your suitcase in our spare room."

"We insist," Matilda said before Julia could object.

"And in the morning," Alberto said, "we can walk down to the Emporium."

"That really isn't necessary," Julia said. "I've imposed enough, and I certainly don't intend to trouble you any more about the . . . misunderstanding."

"Actually, I was going to suggest that you pick out a few essentials for your new home."

Buying new furniture was out of the question. The money they had put aside for that would have to be spent on stocking the store. She smiled politely. "Maybe once Will and I get settled."

"Don't forget," Alberto said, "I saw those photographs, too. You can't possibly settle in if all you have is the cast-offs that Ab Taskin left. Unless, of course, you're shipping things from St. Louis?"

"No," Julia said.

"You really must take advantage of my husband's generosity," Matilda said, which, to Julia's ears, but almost certainly not to her husband's, took on a jaundiced meaning in view of what Matilda had said not ten minutes before.

"You should pick out what you need," Alberto continued, "and I'll sell it to you at cost. Pay as your finances permit. There's no hurry. Think of it as my personal apology for whatever part I played in your difficulties."

"Yes, you must," Matilda said, all disingenuous warmth and cheer.

"I don't think my husband would approve," Julia said.

"What man doesn't enjoy nodding off in a comfortable armchair?" Matilda said. "Besides, the home is the woman's domain. Once the husband crosses the threshold, he should have no say whatsoever. The wife sets the rules." She laughed and touched Alberto's arm possessively.

And how many of your rules have I already violated? Julia wondered.

* * *

Julia spent most of the night rolling from side to side in the Rodriguez's spare bed, bouncing between embarrassed self-recrimination and tearful surrender to her misfortunes, and only shortly before dawn had she settled herself down enough to decide, despite the weariness enveloping her, that she'd rather be taken for a harpy than for a simpleton.

By late morning, Julia and Sam Bosco, a voluble teamster who worked for Alberto Rodriguez (and who had an unfortunate fondness for the darkest chewing tobacco), were ready to head north in a wagon full of furnishings: two armchairs, a lattice-back rocking chair, a dining table and six straight chairs, a small desk, a hutch for her new dishes, a bed and dresser and wardrobe for the bedroom, a simple second bed for visitors.

Before leaving Gallup behind, Julia asked Sam to make one short stop: at the studio of the photographer who'd taken the Many Springs photographs.

Pete Pietrowski turned out to be a disheveled mess of a man, but the work hanging haphazardly on his studio's walls confirmed her impression that he knew his business. He grumbled a bit, but Mr. Pietrowski agreed to take a new series of photographs, each showing Julia posed with her wagonload of new furniture. In truth, she didn't care a whit about the photographs themselves. No, she cared about conveying a very particular message, for the story of the disappearing goods and the green, foolish Easterners who thought they could run a reservation trading post would spread—if it hadn't already—and become even more ridiculous in the retelling, and the only way to ameliorate the damage would be to offer an even better story: that of a woman, an Easterner to be sure, who had the *unmitigated gall* to show up on the Rodriguez doorstep at dinnertime and *demand* entrance, who had filled a wagon with the Emporium's furniture *without laying down a single dollar,* and who had roused Pete Pietrowski from his bed at the ungodly hour of eleven o'clock in the morning and *ordered* him to photograph her and her furniture *right there in the street*—in short, a woman to be reckoned with.

After an exhausting, dust-choked afternoon on the trail, Julia and Sam spent the night in Tohatchi, where Mrs. Emma de Vore and her sister, Mrs. June Haskell, ran a school for Navajo children and welcomed visitors traveling between Gallup and the north. At first light Julia and Sam started out again, intent on reaching Many Springs Canyon as early as possible in the afternoon.

To the east stretched the Chuska Valley, dry, predominantly flat, but far from featureless: countless dips and rises; scrub, sand hillocks, and even green expanses of ground cover. Farther off, she knew, lay the Chaco River, into which the many trail-crossing washes fed their spring melt and the runoff from summer cloudbursts. To the west of the trail lay the Chuska Mountains, a ragged wall and broken buttes of grayish-brown sandstone, variegated layers above and slopes of crumbled stone below. As they proceeded northward Julia began to see deposits of reddish brown sandstone capping the others. Beyond the collection of hogans (and little else) called Naschitti the cliffside became less and less sallow and gray, more and more saturated with color, and Julia's anticipation rose. Miles farther on, following in the ruts left behind by a thousand preceding wheels, the wagon descended into the shallow Many Springs Wash. The mud in the center of the channel sucked at the wheel rims. Sam snapped the reins and the team of four put their broad shoulders to the traces, and the wagon, swaying enough that Julia instinctively grabbed the seat rail tightly and planted her feet against the toe board, crossed and then climbed up the other side of the wash.

The side trail into the canyon curved with the wash. A scattering of deciduous trees, the leaves not yet turning, held back the banks. A hundred feet above—and then gradually much, much higher as they moved deeper into the canyon—at either side of the gap, north and south, stunted evergreens and low-growing brush could be seen where the uppermost layers of sandstone, defined by erosion and color—paler tan, deeper red—receded step by step to the crest, with a cloudless blue above. In places, streaked panels of stone were cut randomly by cross-fractures that sometimes produced thin ledges or marked the transition to more irregular strata. In partial shade, the variations of the south wall stood out, while the sun's glare off the light-bleached north wall was almost too painful.

Gradually, the canyon opened up. Ahead on the left, in the lee of the higher north wall, stood the trading post.

"There she is," Sam said. "Home."

4. Many Springs Canyon

THAT FIRST NIGHT, overtired but still unable to fall asleep, Julia rose in her nightdress without disturbing Will—she could hear Sam Bosco snoring in the adjacent room, where he occupied Ab Taskin's old cot—and walked outside. Even on the clearest nights in Pittsfield the smoke from factories and foundries and forges and homes obscured so much. Here, above, in the moonless night—such a panoply! Suddenly, her head began to swim, and to keep from falling she sat down roughly on the ground. She pressed her palms into the bare dirt, and then she lay back. With her view framed by the walls of the canyon on either side, she had the oddest sensation of falling upward into an endlessness, empty except for the stars, their flawless clarity. The feeling was both dreadful and exhilarating, sending shivers in waves through her limbs. She inhaled deeply. She could smell the pinyon smoke from the cook stove's chimney, and a hint of something else as well, a coarser texture, like creosote.

She'd hated St. Louis not because of its unmanageable size—she'd lived within a narrow urban rectangle far smaller than her hometown—but because, among so *many* people, the rich, the shabby, the blinkered businessmen hurrying to their offices, the women dressed in all manner poor and prosperous, the motley children bumping and teasing their way home from school, the negroes both unexpectedly refined and careless, so many streets thronged with multiplicities—

She'd hated St. Louis because she didn't belong. On a typical day she talked to no one except Will and maybe a grocer or shopkeeper or, later, the German woman who'd helped her with her sewing. Even her conversations with Will had slowly shed words and tenderness as their separate resentments festered. Until, united by folly, they began to construct whole-cloth a life entirely different from anything either had ever imagined.

And now here she was under the stark, starry sky, flat on her back, as if rooted to the place they'd imagined. But not really, not that imagined place, for this was *real*, this dry, sandy ground (so different from the East's familiar moist grassy green!), here beneath her head and shoulder blades and spine and limbs, where she lay between the raw rock walls with their fractures and outcroppings that might slough off slabs or release stony rubble down upon her at any time. And though her husband lay asleep just yards away, within the sound of a cry, she felt all *herself*: by herself, of herself, the dread, the exhilaration, alone with nothing to hold her fast but whatever gravity she could find within her own contrary nature.

Two days later, Julia and Will were scrubbing down the floor of the back storage room when Tom and Carmelita Gorman arrived.

"We waited outside," Tom said, hat in hand. "After a while, we thought we should just come on in." He spoke English slowly, in a flattened register that Julia had already come to identify as typically Navajo.

"Of course," Julia said, drying her hands on an apron. "We didn't expect you quite so soon."

"We can come back another time," Tom said, looking around the empty, windowless room. Julia and Will had been working in the light that entered through the two open doorways, one to the store and the other, newly repaired, to the loading dock. Julia turned away and lifted her apron to wipe the sweat from her face.

"Certainly not," Will said, extending his hand. Julia felt the awkwardness in the ensuing round of limp handshakes.

"I'm sure I look a sight," Julia said, shaking the skirt of her plain cotton dress to dislodge the dust. When the intended pleasantry elicited no response, she continued, "Why don't we go over to our residence, where we can sit down and be comfortable." She led the Gormans through the store and the connecting door.

Neither Gorman was quite what Julia had expected. Tom, wiry, of indeterminate middle age, offered a shy smile; unlike most Navajo men, he wore his straight, black hair cut short. Carmelita, a bit darker-skinned and bearing what Julia would soon recognize as a perpetual frown, was dressed not in the standard Navajo garb of pleated skirt and deeply hued velveteen blouse, but a high-necked russet cotton dress. Her black hair was pulled back in a tight bun. Husband and wife wore no jewelry except their wedding rings.

Julia offered them coffee, which both the Gormans took black, and hastily opened a package of soda crackers and a jar of store-bought strawberry preserves. Arranging the crackers on a plate and scooping jam into a small bowl, she explained, a bit embarrassed, that she hadn't quite succeeded in mastering the wood-fired oven yet and therefore couldn't offer them something baked in her own kitchen. And again, neither Gorman responded.

The four settled at the new oak dining table. Most of the other pieces of furniture from the Rodriguez store were crowded together in a corner of the room, awaiting completion of the various construction projects Will had barely started. The plank ceiling was half-finished. Studs had been erected against the long log wall that separated the store and living space, but the lath remained stacked at the far end of the room . . . When she had asked Will—diplomatically, without implying fault—how he had filled his days during the two and a half weeks she'd spent at the Hubbell Trading Post, he'd said that without her there to bolster his spirits, he'd fallen into a terrible, paralyzing funk, the likes of which he'd never experienced before. He couldn't explain it, really. The strangeness of the landscape; the realization, each time he opened the door to the empty store, that they'd been cheated or lied to or otherwise victimized; resultant worry that their remaining funds would certainly be depleted by restocking the store; a recurrent notion that they would be better off getting back on the train and going to someplace civilized, California maybe; and of course her absence, his aching for her . . .

"Have you always lived on the reservation?" Will asked Tom.

"Pretty much," he answered, "except for the time I spent at the Carlisle Indian School."

"When was that?" Julia asked as she filled his cup with coffee. She'd read about Carlisle, in Pennsylvania, the first off-reservation Indian boarding school.

"Eighteen-eighty," Tom answered, "but I only stayed for two years."

"It must have been very hard," Julia said. The Indian schools all did their utmost to—in the infamous words of Capt. Richard Pratt, Carlisle's founder—"Kill the Indian, and save the man." Students were forced to speak only English and abandon all vestiges of native religion, dress, and conduct.

"Until I found the Lord," Tom said.

Before leaving for Gallup, Sam Bosco, who knew the Gormans from when they worked for Ab Taskin, had warned Julia that husband and wife practiced Christianity with missionary zeal and had rejected all traditional Navajo beliefs and practices as pagan and therefore sinful. "They're reliable, but it don't make them any easier to get along with. Especially that Carmelita. She's a tough one," Sam had said.

"I'm glad you managed to find another job when Taskin closed the trading post," Will said, changing the subject and permitting Julia a sigh of relief. She had no wish to venture into religion.

"I've been working in the company store in Gibson," Tom said. Along with Catalpa and Clarkville, Gibson was one of the larger coal camps servicing the Gallup, Weaver, Otero, and Thatcher mines. "But I can't say much for it."

"Why's that?" Will asked.

Tom scratched his chin. He glanced at Carmelita, as if gauging how much to reveal. "I'd guess there's about six hundred miners. They work twelve-hour shifts and live in company housing. Most shop in the company store, even though the prices are too high."

"So they stick close to the mine?" Will said.

"Except when they want to drink and carouse," Carmelita interjected with obvious disapproval. "They go to Gallup for that." She spoke English with great fluidity.

"Oh," Tom said, "some of the fellows are all right. They have wives and kids and are just trying to make a living."

"Many Navajos?" Will asked.

"Some, but more Mexicans and foreigners—Austrians and Eye-talians mostly."

"You don't approve of foreigners?"

"Oh," Tom said, "I don't hold it against them. I guess they're happy for the work, even though most of them end up with nothing."

"Why is that?" Julia asked.

"What they owe to the store comes right out of their pay, along with their rent money."

"It must be a challenge communicating with people from so many different places," Julia said.

"Well," Tom said, "everybody has at least a smattering of English."

"Do you speak Spanish?" Will asked.

"*Sí*," Carmelita jumped in. "*Nosotros dos. Es usted?* "

Julia didn't need a translation. Nor did she miss the intent: the Gormans were not the ones with language issues.

"Unfortunately, no." Julia moved on: "So you'd like to come back and work here?"

"We might," Carmelita answered. She peered at Julia, who suspected that Carmelita, though she'd let her husband do most of the talking thus far, was a woman of firm opinions.

"You know," Will said, making an attempt to ease matters, "when I asked Alberto Rodriguez whose help we could use once the trading post is up and running, he named you right away."

"Well, we're very grateful to him for that," Tom said.

"So you see," Julia said, looking directly at Carmelita, "your reputation precedes you, which gives us something of an advantage. I'm sure you must have questions for us."

Carmelita sat erectly in the dining chair, her hands in her lap. She'd only taken one sip of the coffee, which apparently wasn't to her liking. Throughout the conversation Julia had felt Carmelita's eyes taking her measure, trying to figure out why this white woman from the East was even here. Now, rather than asking a question, she said, "There are some traders who charge too much in the store and pay too little for the wool the People bring in. Some have scales that cheat. I know this for a fact. We won't work for a trader like that."

Who was interviewing whom? Julia wondered. She exchanged glances with Will, who was trying to contain his irritation. What had they expected from the Gormans? Deference, at the very least.

"Mrs. Gorman," Julia said, summoning a smile, "my husband and I came all the way out here so we could run our own business as we see fit. That doesn't include cheating anyone. I was raised as a good Christian myself. My father is a minister, and before Will and I married I spent much of my time tending to the needs of his church, especially after my mother died."

Julia waited to see how Carmelita would respond, but the Navajo woman's expression didn't change.

"Mrs. Gorman meant no offense," Tom said.

"Certainly not," Julia said.

Will cleared his throat and asked, "You worked for Abner Taskin for how long?"

"Going on three years," Tom said.

"And what did you think of him?"

When Tom hesitated, Carmelita said, "He was a drinker. After it got the better of him, he hardly ever came into the store."

"Mr. Taskin treated us fine," Tom, the conciliator, said, "and we tried to do right by him."

"So, in effect, you ran the business?" Julia asked.

"Well," Tom said, "I wouldn't go that far—"

"We did," Carmelita interrupted. "We tended the store and kept the inventory and ordered supplies, and he showed us how to handle the accounts."

"But you didn't pay the bills," Will said. He obviously thought Carmelita Gorman was a bit too uppity.

"I guess you're right about that," Tom said. "Mr. Taskin had to sign his name."

"May I ask what Mr. Taskin paid you?" Julia asked.

"Well," Tom said, collecting his thoughts, "we worked Monday through Friday and a half day on Saturday, and Mr. Taskin paid me four dollars a week, and another two dollars for Mrs. Gorman. And he let us have whatever supplies we needed to feed our family—flour, sugar, and the like."

"And dry goods at cost," Carmelita added.

"I think we can do better than that," Julia said.

"I don't know," Will quickly cautioned. "If we decide to hire you, we might start you there and see how business develops."

"I guess that'd be fair," Tom said.

"I think right off we could raise Mrs. Gorman's pay a bit," Julia said. Another dollar wouldn't bankrupt them. Their immediate problem was filling the shelves, not the pittance Carmelita Gorman would earn.

Will cleared his throat again. "Let's put the question of compensation aside for now. There's something else I'd like to ask you about. When Mrs. Halley and I agreed to buy the trading post from the Taskins, we thought the store was fully stocked, but before we arrived there was a break-in."

"Will," Julia cut in, "this isn't something we need to trouble the Gormans about." She'd told him what Alberto Gonzalez had said, that the Taskins sold the contents to a wholesaler, as was their right, but Will had continued to dwell on the smashed door to the storeroom. Now Will ignored her and went on:

"Do you have any idea who might've broken in?"

Carmelita visibly stiffened, the creases of her frown deepening.

Tom, mirroring his wife's frown, his eyes cast down, slowly shook his head. "Can't say that I do. By then, I was already working down in Gibson, so I don't know what went on up here."

"You didn't hear anything? Rumors?"

"It wasn't Navajos," Carmelita said.

"You're sure?"

"Will, maybe we should just let it be," Julia tried again.

"Why not Navajos?" Will was smiling, but it was a false smile.

"A smart Navajo would take what he wanted," Carmelita said, "and then burn the place down to hide the thievery."

Julia, shocked by Carmelita's view of her own people, shifted uncomfortably in her chair.

"I think that what the missus means," Tom said, once again the conciliator, "is that no one from around here could steal trade goods and try to sell them without drawing attention. Word would get out."

"I can see that," Will said, nodding. Then he quickly added, "I wasn't suggesting that you were involved in any way."

"No," Tom said, looking to his wife, "we didn't think that, did we, Missus?"

Julia felt helpless. Tom Gorman's polite response was predictable. Carmelita's countenance, however, with her small, hard chin lifted high, reflected the tacit insult: the implication that as Navajos, even if not complicit, they couldn't be fully trusted. Julia half-expected Carmelita to rise from the table and walk out the door. But she didn't. The Gormans wanted to come back to work at the trading post. Otherwise, why would they even be here?

"Would anyone like more coffee?" Julia asked.

"I can think of someone who probably knows something," Carmelita said.

"Now, Missus," Tom said in mild reproach.

"And who's that?" Will asked Carmelita.

"Him," Carmelita said with scorn, tossing her head toward the west, the upper canyon.

"Him?" Will asked.

"Clement Yazzie."

"Now, Missus," Tom repeated, "you can't go accusing people."

"There are bad stories about him," Carmelita said.

"So I've heard," Will said. He'd already encountered Clement Yazzie, Julia knew, the morning after finding the empty store. He'd been standing outside the kitchen door, drinking a cup of coffee and trying to put his anger aside and sort out what he should do about the theft, when he saw an Indian coming down the trail, leading two horses. He recalled Alberto Rodriguez's mentioning that a Navajo family lived farther up the canyon. As the Navajo drew closer, Will, observing that he wasn't carrying a sidearm, relaxed. Without so much as a hello, the Indian tied the horses' leads to the corner post of the veranda. Will held out his hand and introduced himself.

"These horses are yours," the Navajo said.

Will withdrew his hand. "I don't know anything about any horses."

"They were Taskin's. Before he left he asked me to look after his animals until someone came for them. But no one came."

"I didn't buy his horses," Will said. He expected that the Indian would next ask to be reimbursed for his trouble, and he had no intention of paying so much as a cent.

"You'll need a team."

"They aren't mine."

The Navajo looked away, leaving the clear impression that he couldn't care less what Will said. "There's also a milk cow. Come and get it if you want it. It's in my corral." He started to go but then added, "Taskin also had some chickens. When no one showed up, we ate them."

Will had taken an immediate dislike to the man. "Sounds fair enough," he said.

Later that morning, after thinking the matter over, he'd asked Rodrigo Peña to go and collect the cow.

"From Yazzie?" Peña had asked.

"I believe that's his name."

Peña shook his head. "I don't want anything to do with him."

"Why not?"

"Mr. Rodriguez didn't tell you about him?"

"No."

"They say Yazzie killed a man in cold blood a few years back. Then he strung him up by the heels and left him hanging for his family to find. Some say he did even worse."

Will hadn't asked for details. Nor did he go to fetch the cow.

Julia now asked the Gormans, "You don't get along with Mr. Yazzie?"

"I wouldn't put it that way," Tom said.

"Did he do business at the store?" Will asked.

"He did."

"And did he cause trouble?"

"No, I can't say that he did," Tom said. "He always paid what he owed, unlike some."

"There were delinquent accounts?" Julia asked. For a moment she wondered if she and Will would now, as the owners of the trading post, be able to collect on them. But no, she was sure there was nothing in the contract about that, and anyway, they had no record of what had transpired between Ab Taskin and his customers. Another foolish thought.

"Some," Tom said.

Julia caught Carmelita's eye, which told a different tale.

"And what did Mr. Taskin do about them?" Will asked.

"Well, you can't expect everyone to settle up," Tom said, which didn't answer the question.

"The Taskins told Rodriguez that about two hundred families rely on the trading post," Will said. He'd begun nervously drumming his fingers on the table.

"People are scattered out here," Tom said. "It's hard to say."

"You must have some idea," Will pressed him.

Tom looked at his wife. "More like a hundred?"

Julia's stomach sank.

"Aoo'," Carmelita said.

Tom quickly added, shifting in his chair, "Not counting the people who come in now and then or are just passing through."

"And how many squared their accounts regularly?" Julia asked.

"I'd have to think about that," answered Tom, whose disposition obviously favored avoiding unpleasantness.

Once again, Carmelita didn't say anything immediately. Julia, her elbows on the table, her hands folded in front of her mouth, suspected that the Navajo woman's calculation had little to do with numbers, and more to do with how Will and she would respond to the truth.

"Maybe forty," Carmelita said.

Will blanched. "Jesus God," he muttered.

Carmelita flinched at the blasphemy.

"We were also led to believe," Julia said, hoping to salvage a future—something—from this conversation, "that with good management the store could make a reasonable profit."

"Well," Tom said in his laconic voice, "I guess I'd agree with that." He was plainly uncomfortable answering so many unanticipated questions.

"Is that also your opinion, Mrs. Gorman?" Julia asked.

"It depends on the wholesale market for wool and how much of each grade gets brought in."

"I see," Julia said.

"And you can make a bit from selling weavings and hides and dead pawn, too," Tom offered.

"The Hubbell Trading Post in Ganado seems to be doing quite well," Julia said.

Carmelita clicked her tongue. "The Hubbells own land and run their own stock. And many people live near Ganado, so the store is always busy."

"Then what you seem to be saying," Will said, looking back and forth between the Gormans, "is that this store—putting the wool business aside—has consistently run a deficit."

"People are poor," Tom said flatly, as if nothing more needed to be explained.

"What if we stocked better merchandise?" Will said. "That could bring in more customers."

"I think," Julia said quietly, "no one could afford to buy it." She didn't know what else to say, and the silence that followed told her that neither did Will. He slouched, one hand still drumming. She suspected that they were thinking similar thoughts, that they'd invested their money (her mother's money) in a high-desert sinkhole. Why even pretend, she thought, that they had so much as an inkling about how to run a trading post? She couldn't imagine why the Gormans or anyone else would want to be in their employ when the whole enterprise was so certainly doomed to fail.

"What we said is not what you wanted to hear," Carmelita broke the silence.

Her candor surprised Julia, who replied, "I suspect that the same is true for what you've heard from us."

The four of them sat and studied the unblemished surface of the new table, which, Julia thought, she'd ask Alberto Rodriguez to take back, along with the other new furniture.

Tom, with a deep sigh, was the first to look up, taking his hat in hand and running his fingers along the sweat-stained brim, preparing to leave. "Well," he drawled, and nothing more. Then Carmelita spoke:

"We told you the truth," her eyes looking steadily across the table at Julia, "and I tell you this, too. You can do better than Abner Taskin did. I don't know why he ever bought this place. All he cared about was his drink."

"Now, Carmelita," Tom said, "be charitable."

"And no one ever reported it to the Indian agent?" Will asked. Their license had clearly outlined the penalties for possessing, let alone selling, alcohol on the reservation.

"I can't rightly say," Tom answered. "Mr. Taskin never sold drink, so maybe no one ever told the agent. Or maybe the agent didn't care to be bothered."

Julia had no interest in Abner Taskin's drinking habits—her gaze was still focused on Carmelita Gorman. Unless she was mistaken—*You can do better*—Carmelita was offering their help, hers and Tom's. The Gormans knew the customers who'd return as soon as the trading post opened its doors. They knew the best suppliers. They knew what inventory—goods and quantities—would be needed and what could be dispensed with, at least at first. And Carmelita had given considerable thought, Julia was sure, to how they might attract new customers, from south of Naschitti and from up through Washington Pass, and from the Chuska Valley to the east.

In a just world, Julia thought, Tom and Carmelita Gorman would be the proprietors of the Many Springs Trading Post. They possessed everything that the business needed . . . except money. And maybe the political influence that could assure them a license to run a trading post on their own reservation.

Did Will see what she saw? Did he see that they were sitting across the table from the very people, two Indians, who just might save them from ruin?

"I suppose we've kept you long enough," Will said, placing his hands flat on the table and rising. "I'll let you know what we decide as soon as we've thought it through."

"It would be very discourteous of us," Julia said to Will, "not to invite Mr. and Mrs. Gorman to stay for dinner. Assuming your children don't need you at home?" she asked Carmelita.

Will, perplexed, folded his arms and stared down at her.

"I wish we had better to offer you, something I made from scratch myself, but—"

"Trouble with the woodstove," Carmelita said.

"Yes, the woodstove." And Julia hurried on, hoping that something she and Carmelita shared, the necessity of putting food on the table, would overcome the awkwardness. "I can't seem to make a decent loaf of bread for the life of me. The dough rises nicely, and then I pound it down, and do everything else I've always done, but yesterday and again today it came out of the oven like a brick."

"Tsk," Carmelita said, clicking her tongue. "Yeast bread."

"Yes?"

"You're using too much yeast and not enough water. The altitude makes a difference. I can't be bothered with yeast. Too much trouble. I make soda bread. Do you have baking powder and baking soda?"

"I do," Julia said.

"Then I'll show you." Carmelita rose from the table and walked into the kitchen.

Will, still standing, and Tom, still with hat in hand, both slack jawed, followed her with their eyes.

The pantry held little but sacks and cans, but with Carmelita's guidance Julia managed to put on the table a decent meal. When Julia sliced into the warm soda bread, the aroma nearly brought her to tears—which were instead released by the main course, a casserole of canned tomatoes, canned corn, and canned baked beans with a corn bread crust, all spiced by chile hot enough to set lips, tongue, and membranes afire. While the bread was baking, Carmelita had led Julia outside to a square of land, adjacent to the corral, that had been Ab Taskin's garden, though it was Carmelita who'd tilled, sowed, and tended it. Once planted with tomatoes, corn, beans, squash, and chiles, the small square was now partly denuded by drifted sand and partly overgrown with patches of desert grass and weeds that Julia couldn't begin to identify. Carmelita turned her attention to the weeds, bending over, brushing them aside, picking up small desiccated pods with thumb and forefinger and then rubbing them between her palms.

"See," she said to Julia, "chile seeds," and then to Julia's quizzical look responded, "dried seeds hold the flavor."

And the heat. Eating the casserole, Julia, wiping her watering eyes, began to laugh, and before long the other three had joined her.

"This is real Mexican food," Tom said. "It takes some getting used to. When I was growing up my mother thought salt and chiles were all anybody ever needed to add to a cook pot."

"Where are your parents now, Tom?" Julia asked. They'd all, with cautious politeness, begun using first names.

"Well," Tom said, "I hope they're with the Lord in heaven, but I doubt it. I tried to lead them to the path, but a fever took them first."

"I'm sorry to hear that they've passed on," Julia said. Tom apparently no longer felt the general Navajo distaste for speaking of the dead—one of the first things she'd learned from the Hubbells about the Navajos—nor the fear that doing so might call up their *chindi*, the ghosts of whatever evil the departed may have left behind. But she no more wanted to address that than she did his impassioned Christianity.

Tom struck her as patient, practical, and trustworthy; a man of even temperament. His wife was also practical and trustworthy but not so patient, and a woman of irritating confidence in the rightness (and righteousness) of her opinions. Behind the counter, Julia speculated, Carmelita would brook no nonsense from her fellow Navajos.

Julia had lost the gist of the conversation.

"Why don't we pay a bit more for the wool—beat the other traders' price," Will was saying. "If the families on this side of the reservation are as savvy as you say when it comes to negotiating, they'll take our offer. That way, we can more than make up in volume what we lose per pound."

"Well," Tom said, "it isn't for me to say, but the other small traders would come down hard on you. Everyone pretty much agrees on what they'll offer. A price war could put just about everybody out of business."

"You mentioned something before," Julia said, "about different grades of wool."

"The better the wool," Carmelita said, "the higher the wholesale price."

"I understand that, but isn't the wool from all the flocks similar?"

"Mostly," Tom said, "but not always."

"Then who would you say has the best?"

"That would be Clement Yazzie." Tom nodded toward the upper canyon.

"And why's that?" Will asked.

"It's the mother's doing," Carmelita said. "From way back, she never let other breeds mix with her churros."

"What's so special about churros?" Will asked.

"The breeds the government gave out after the Long Walk aren't suited to the land and the weather. Most people didn't care. They just wanted to increase the size of their herds. But not her."

The Long Walk: something else Julia had learned about from the Hubbells. During the Civil War much of the Navajo nation was rounded up by the Union army, marched to eastern New Mexico, and forced to live in desperate conditions near Fort Sumner. A treaty in 1868 permitted the return to their homeland of those who had survived the ordeal, and also included government promises of support, many of which were soon abandoned.

"The People have herded churros for a long time," Carmelita continued. "Every spring Yazzie's mother culled any mixed-breed lambs. Other herds ended up bigger but they produced less wool."

Tom added, "In a good year churros will give you a second shearing in the early fall. The other breeds don't."

"Does Yazzie have a large herd?" Will asked.

"Not the largest, but a good size," Tom said.

"Have you met his mother?" Carmelita asked.

"No," Julia said. "but yesterday afternoon I saw an older woman riding past, going up the canyon."

"No, that wasn't her," Carmelita said. "She's sick and can't get around anymore. You probably saw 'Asdzáán Bítóyiszééyiztał, an old friend of hers from Tohatchi."

"I've also seen two boys," Julia said. They were riding a single horse bareback when she saw them, the older with his arms around the much younger, both obviously curious about the new owners of the trading post, judging by the number of times they passed by. "Are they Mr. Yazzie's sons?"

Tom nodded. "I expect so."

"So it's Mr. Yazzie, his mother, his wife, and his two boys living in the upper canyon?" Julia asked.

"No wife," Carmelita said. "She died right after the youngest was born."

"Oh," Julia said. "Did you know that?" she asked Will.

"No," he said, "but I've seen another woman that I assumed was his wife. One afternoon she was sitting up above here, where the wash flattens out, for a good hour."

"That would be Johanna, Yazzie's younger sister. She lives with him," Carmelita said.

"She sticks close to home, too," Tom added.

"She can't talk," Carmelita said, rubbing her throat.

"You mean, she's mute?" Julia asked.

"Mute, yes. And weak up here," pointing to her forehead.

"Oh, Johanna's all right," Tom said. "She used to come by the store and just sit. No one paid her a nevermind. More than once I heard Mr. Taskin say she was the smartest one around because she knew when to keep her mouth shut."

Will alone laughed.

"When he was drinking," Carmelita said, "that's when he talked non-sense."

It occurred to Julia that for some time now they'd been talking around the subject of the disreputable Clement Yazzie—speaking of his possible complicity in the break-in, speaking of his sheep, of his family, all without directly confronting if his worrisome presence in the canyon threatened her and Will's safety.

While the talk at the table, mainly between Will and Tom, continued, Julia rose and began collecting the empty dishes; the four of them had finished off everything. When Carmelita also stood up, Julia said, "Absolutely not, Carmelita. We have you to thank for this meal, and besides, I won't have a guest clearing the dishes from my table. Please, sit down." Julia carried the dishes to the sink. Above it, a small window looked out beyond the side veranda to the dusty bare ground and, fifty yards away, the shallow wash; farther on, stunted aromatic bushes and pinyon dotted the canyon bottom until it reached the south sandstone wall, which rose a good three hundred feet before encountering the iridescent sky. Julia lingered for a moment at the window, enjoying the afternoon light, before returning to the table.

"Have you heard anything about the railroad?" Will asked the Gormans.

Tom looked quizzical. "The railroad?"

"We read in St. Louis about plans to build a line from Durango south through Gallup to southern Arizona."

Tom looked at Carmelita. "Why would the railroad want to do that?" he asked.

"I imagine," Will said, "to haul ore from the mines in southern Colorado down toward the Gulf of Mexico so that it can be shipped east at lower cost."

"Well," Tom said, "I suppose that could make sense."

"But you haven't heard anything about it?"

" 'Fraid not."

"Apparently, they've already surveyed the route, just east of here."

"We haven't seen any surveyors, have we, Missus?"

"No," Carmelita said, shaking her head, and then to Tom, "We should be getting home. Johnny will be wondering what's keeping us." She added, for Julia and Will's benefit, "Johnny's our oldest. He's watching his sister and brother, Annie and Jimmy."

"Of course," Julia said. Will, with a blank stare, was drumming his fingers on the table again. The Gormans looked at each other but didn't get up from the table. Of course not, Julia thought, realizing that nothing had been made explicit about the jobs they'd come for. Should she say something or should she defer to Will, who at the moment seemed oblivious to anything but his own thoughts?

Finally, Julia said, "Before you go, I believe I can speak for my husband as well as myself. If you want to work for us, you're hired."

"And the wages?" Carmelita asked.

Will jumped in, "Starting pay of four dollars a week for you, Tom, and"—he glanced at Julia—"two-fifty for Carmelita. Plus everything else you received from Ab Taskin, whatever store goods you need."

"Well," Tom said, relieved and pleased, "that sounds just fine."

But Carmelita wasn't quite done. As pleasant as dinner had been, business was business, her manner announced. "We need to be paid cash money every week."

Julia could see by the way Will was working his jaw that he'd heard more than enough from Carmelita Gorman. And in truth, so had she, but they needed the Gormans (whose names, she remembered, were already on the license application).

"All right. Is there anything else?" Julia asked.

"We won't work on the Sabbath, never. And in the store, in front of customers, I'd like to be called Mrs. Gorman."

"Just as we expect to be called Mr. and Mrs. Halley, also as a sign of respect."

"I'd say that's your due," Tom offered. He and Will both rose from the table.

Julia remained seated, waiting for Carmelita's response.

" 'So in everything, do to others what you would have them do to you,' " Carmelita said, narrowing her gaze.

It was a test that Julia, many years of her father's sermons behind her, easily passed: "Matthew 7:12," she said.

Carmelita nodded, satisfied by the conclusion of the conversation.

Later, Julia was brushing her hair, getting ready for bed.

"I don't like it," said Will, sour since the departure of the Gormans. He watched Julia's nighttime ministrations from the doorway to their bedroom. "That Yazzie, he can't be trusted. He's probably the one who broke in."

"You can't accuse him," Julia said. "He lives here. We have to try and get along."

"He probably stole what he could before the Taskins sold everything else out from under us. He's a smart one. I could tell that right away."

What more could she say to Will so that he'd let it be? She couldn't prove that nothing had been stolen, though she wondered why, if he was so dishonest, Clement Yazzie didn't just keep the horses that he'd brought down the canyon to Will. Would anyone have challenged him if he said they were his?

"And *Mrs.* Gorman," Will said, abruptly changing his target, "if we're paying her we should be able to call her whatever we damn well please."

"And what would that be?" Julia asked.

He ignored her question. "You made it pretty clear that we don't know what we're doing."

She put down her brush and turned to face him; she didn't like that he seemed to be blaming her for their situation. "Was there any point in trying to pretend otherwise?"

"You can't command respect if your employees look down on you."

"But they didn't ask for anything unreasonable, did they?"

He said nothing.

"And they were certainly forthcoming, wouldn't you say? Or do you doubt their honesty?"

"I doubt everybody's honesty," Will said, tapping a fist against the door frame, "until they prove otherwise. And even then . . ." He suddenly lashed out, slamming the wide-open door into the wall with a swift kick that startled Julia. "What in hell have we gotten ourselves into?"

SATURDAY MORNING, A WEEK later, Julia was waiting for Will to return from Gallup. He might be back by nightfall or, less likely, he might decide to spend the night in Naschitti with the Gormans. So she was alone, had been since Thursday morning, when Will and Tom set off. She hadn't seen a soul in the interim, which, truth be told, she didn't mind. She had plenty of work to do.

She and Will had already finished replacing the crumbling mud-and-newspaper chinking on the inside of the storeroom's outer walls. Anticipating a slow, messy process as they gained experience working adobe between the logs, they'd started on the storeroom, where the end result would be least visible. Simultaneously, Tom Gorman, working at twice their combined speed, had set about repairing the exterior.

The more time Julia spent around Tom, the more she appreciated him. In addition to being a steady and uncomplaining worker, he took their ignorance of so many things, especially Navajo ways, in stride. Although a day didn't pass without his quoting the Bible or noting the ever-present gifts of the Lord—the sunshine or the cooling shade of passing clouds, the dry weather as well as the relief offered by a single passing thunderstorm, the bountiful food (Julia rolled her eyes) they shared—a religious commentary that Julia either acknowledged with a nod and smile or ignored when doing so wouldn't give offense—she sensed in him an innate, unpretentious kindness. She was very glad to have him around.

On Thursday, after Will and Tom's departure, she'd decided to tackle the mess Will had made impetuously trying to plaster the long wall between the residence and the store. She couldn't stand looking for one more day at that disaster.

Something had told her, even before Will began plastering, that it was a bad idea. Will insisted that he'd seen it done and could do it well enough himself. With a third of the lath nailed in place, Julia convinced him to try the first coarse coat of plaster—water, sand, lime, and horsehair—on just the first two bays, to see how well it set. Will accomplished the task quite handily, and while waiting for it to dry, proceeded with nailing lath to additional studs.

His confidence wasn't justified. Perhaps he waited too long to scour the rough plaster, or maybe he didn't wait long enough for the keyed plaster to set firmly between the laths. Most probably, he was also wrong in assuming that he could go straight to a finish coat of slaked lime. In the end, they watched the lime drip, sag, and soak into the underlying coarse coat, some of which collapsed, reexposing patches of lath. Will's silence did nothing to hide his fury.

Finally, Julia said, "I'm sorry, Will. It's my fault." It wasn't, but what else could she say? "I don't know what I was thinking. We don't need a New England parlor. This was a terrible idea."

"So it appears," he said, scraping drops of lime from his bare forearms with a thumbnail.

Keenly aware that her patience was slipping, Julia took a silent, deep breath. Should she pretend to be sympathetic? Should she wait out his mood? Why, lately, had she found herself often trying to anticipate his responses and adjusting her own preferences and actions to what she thought might generate the least friction? Was this what marriage inevitably evolved into when each other's character and temperament were truly exposed, their interactions scripted by habit and without any remaining surprises or even irritating quirks to be discovered—teeth picked at the table, dried snot deposited on the inside of a pillow case, book pages dog-eared—and only the most private mysteries left, the ones never to be revealed. What a disappointment for both, wife and husband, to unearth so little worth knowing! And yet people, marriages, continued on, mixing irreconcilability and consolation.

"Pine boards, that's what we need," she said, nodding toward the long wall in front of them. "What do you call them—the ones without knots?"

"Clear."

"Clear pine, vertical like paneling, painted bright white. We're not going to get much sun in here, so the brighter the better. And we'll do the same in the bedrooms this winter, when we have nothing else to do." The interior bedroom walls were rough planks from which some of the bark hadn't even been removed, and with gaps so wide that she could slip her fingers between many of the boards. "We can tear down those hideous planks and burn them."

"So you have this all worked out."

"And we're going to need a small wood stove for back there"—she pointed toward the rear of the long room, opposite the bedroom door—"because the heat from the cooker will never reach that far and I'm not about to sleep in the kitchen just to keep my toes from turning to icicles. We'll put the armchairs and rocker there, too, in front of the new stove, and the wind can howl all it wants to because we can sit together in the evening and be safe and comfortable."

Will, after a long pause, and without much enthusiasm, said, "Why not."

So on Thursday Will and Tom Gorman had set off for Gallup. Their first stop would be the lumber yard, where they planned to pick up not only pine boards and paint and other items to help in fixing up the trading post, but also a variety of essentials for stocking the store. With the advice of both Gormans, Julia and Will had also put together lists of trade goods that would be mailed off to suppliers. A number of Navajos had already stopped by to scrutinize the new owners, though without the presence of Carmelita Gorman—she was to start work in two weeks, when they hoped to have *something* to sell—communication was usually limited to the minimal "Trader Navajo" Julia had picked up in Ganado.

Soon after Will and Tom headed south in the Gorman's wagon—Tom would help Will choose another for the trading post—Julia began ripping lath, both bare and plaster-coated, from the long wall's studs with a claw-tooth hammer. An armful at a time, she carried the detritus out back; it would provide kindling for the foreseeable future. By late Thursday she'd completed that task despite aching back and arm muscles, and on Friday she began the day by scrubbing the floor down to remove all powdery traces of the plaster, which had floated everywhere, coating even the cook stove and the sills.

But now it was Saturday morning, the sun dazzling, and she didn't know what to do with herself. She'd go for a walk. Up the canyon, toward the forest, where she'd not yet been. Then she thought better of it. She'd have to pass the Yazzie place, and this might be a very foolish thing to do, given what Rodrigo Peña had told Will about Clement Yazzie. She hadn't seen any of the Yazzies except the boys, who'd continued to pass by at a distance, curious but too shy to approach—not Clement Yazzie himself nor the boys' grandmother nor Yazzie's mute sister, Johanna. Given the grandmother's condition, she would certainly be at home, even if the boys and Johanna weren't, so how likely was it that Mr. Yazzie would do something untoward, or worse, in his mother's presence? And if she encountered him she could ask about that milk cow.

Still, she hemmed and hawed. (As the new arrival, it should be her role to *receive* welcoming neighbors, but this wasn't Pittsfield, was it? No, she told herself for the hundredth time, this was definitely not Pittsfield.) She'd bake something. She'd managed her first decent loaf of yeast bread several days before but wasn't going to count on repeating her success. She could make in her cast iron skillet a cornbread, the batter spiced with the last of the chile seeds Carmelita had gathered, and with honey drizzled on top. That would do. Yes, she'd make cornbread. Which, if she changed her mind again and didn't go for her walk, she'd have for Will's return.

But she didn't change her mind. Despite many sighs and reconsiderations, in the early afternoon she wrapped the still-warm cornbread in muslin and set off, up the canyon.

Though less than a quarter-mile wide at the trading post, Many Springs Canyon quickly opened out to the west, its floor rising in a steady but gradual ascent, without twists and with only one turn, toward the Yazzie place, half a mile farther in. The Yazzie hogan was nestled beneath the northern sandstone wall, which, here, rose only fifty feet above the peak of the log and mud roof. The doorway faced east, permitting the sun's rays to enter at sunrise; also, in its south-leaning winter arc, the sun would warm the walls and roof until blocked by the mountains in the afternoon. A corral and adjacent shelter—really, no more than three horse stalls (two open gates and one closed) with a slanting roof—stood nearby. Well to her left, she noticed an even cruder lean-to of roughly trimmed irregular pine poles and a roof of lopped pinyon and spruce branches. Julia didn't see any activity; even the two horses in the corral stood still, sideways, eying her with one eye each and flicking their ears and tails at flies.

She knew something of Navajo etiquette, that one never knocked on the door of a hogan but instead stood off at a distance, waiting to be seen and invited to approach. This she did.

"Hoo-hoo!" a voice startled her. Standing at the corner post of the ramshackle pine enclosure was a boy, the older one she'd seen passing by the trading post. He waved her over. A smaller boy, a forefinger in his mouth, his unkempt hair concealing his brow, appeared beside him.

"*Yá'át'ééh,*" she said as she drew near.

"Aoo', yá'át'ééh," the elder said. He was a handsome boy, fine-featured, his skin a light walnut, and with black, black hair. His small companion was similarly complected but scruffy from head to bare toes.

"Do you speak English?" Julia asked.

"Yes," the older boy said.

"Oh," she said, relieved, "that's wonderful because I'm afraid I haven't learned very much Navajo yet. I'm Mrs. Halley, and you must be Mr. Yazzie's boys." The younger's eyes kept traveling between her face and what she was carrying. She held the cloth-covered cornbread out. "I brought this for your family."

The older boy didn't take it from her. Instead he looked behind him, around the corner post of the shelter, and said something in Navajo. A thin voice replied. Through the gaps in the poles Julia could see someone sitting on the ground before a large loom.

The boy turned back to Julia and said, "My grandmother asked what you brought."

"Cornbread."

"*Ntsídigo'í,*" the boy said to his grandmother, who spoke again, after which the boy held out his hands and said, "My grandmother says I should thank you."

Julia gave him the cornbread. "You're welcome."

The elder boy and Julia stood looking at each other; the younger boy's wrinkling nose was drawn to the round loaf. Not knowing what else to say Julia asked, "May I greet your grandmother?"

"My grandmother doesn't speak English."

"Ah, I see."

Nevertheless, he stepped away from the corner post, permitting Julia to pass. A gray-haired Navajo woman, very thin, obviously very weak, sat on a Navajo blanket before a traditional vertical loom on which she was weaving a rug of intersecting diamonds and perpendicular lines, white, brown, and black wool against a tan background. She wore a dark red velveteen blouse, a loose-fitting brown cotton skirt, and a large squash blossom necklace of silver and turquoise.

The woman looked up at Julia and spoke. The boy said, "My grandmother says her name is Niłtsa Nineez. She's from the Bitter Water Clan, born for the Towering House Clan."

"And you?" Julia asked the boy.

"'Atsá Yazzie," he said. "And my little brother is Níyol. But he's only three and can't talk English yet."

"Well," Julia said, "please tell your grandmother that my name is Julia Halley. My husband is Will Halley. My parents are Joseph and Heloise Marshall, from Massachusetts." She hoped that that would be a sufficient introduction.

The grandmother listened to the translation and nodded. "*Kwe'é dah nídaah,*" she said, patting a place beside her, and Julia sat down.

"The Navajo word for cornbread, would you say it again for me?" Julia asked 'Atsá.

"*Ntsídigo'í.*"

"*Ntsídigo'í,*" Julia did her best to repeat. "Would you like a piece?"

The boy deferred to his grandmother, who appeared to understand what had been asked. She spoke a few words and 'Atsá ran off to the hogan. In short order he returned with a thick-handled knife and handed it to Julia. Both boys sat down, and, balancing the loaf on her lap, Julia cut four wedges.

They began to eat, and the old woman, after one small bite, said, "Good."

Julia smiled. "Your grandson said you didn't speak English."

'Atsá rolled his eyes, his mouth still full. He swallowed and said, "She doesn't, but *everybody* knows 'good.' "

Julia laughed and looked more closely at the half-finished rug on the loom. Hoping that she wasn't completely botching what she intended, she slowly and carefully said, "*Díí dahiistł'ǫ shił nizhóní.*" Then she quickly asked 'Atsá, "Did I speak correctly?"

Wiping his empty hands on his pants, the boy said, "You sort of said what she's weaving is beautiful."

The elderly woman, touching the weaving at various places, proceeded to speak extensively, explaining, Julia assumed, the task before her. Julia understood only an occasional word but followed the woman's gnarled hands as they fingered the warp cords and traced the weft patterns. When Niłtsa Nineez stopped, Julia turned to 'Atsá for an explanation, but he simply shrugged and said, "Grandmother wants you to know that this will be her last weaving. Her hands are too old and tired to do another."

"Has she been working on this long?"

"Aoo'. She only does a few rows a day now."

For the first time, Níyol, the younger brother, his gaze fixed on Julia, spoke, which evoked a sharp response from his brother. Julia caught the word "bilagáana."

"What did your brother ask?"

'Atsá, averting his eyes, didn't want to say.

"It's all right," Julia said. "Youngsters have a right to ask questions, don't you think?"

"He wanted to know what was wrong with your face," 'Atsá said.

Julia lifted a hand and brushed each cheek, thinking she'd smeared flour there when she was baking, but then she realized that the little one was referring to the color of her skin. It occurred to her then that, quite possibly, Níyol had never seen a white woman before, at least not one with such pale skin. "Come here," she said to him, gesturing with her hand and smiling. He slid a bit closer on his rump, close enough for her to reach out and take his small hand. She bent down and stroked her cheek with his fingers. To 'Atsá she said, "Tell him that skin has many different shades, but that underneath there's no difference."

When his older brother had finished speaking, Níyol seemed satisfied, and he turned his attention to his grandmother's piece of cornbread; she'd taken only a couple of small bites, and seeing the direction of his eyes, the old woman handed him what was left.

"My grandmother doesn't eat much anymore," 'Atsá said.

"I understand," Julia said. Then, "Is your father away?"

"Just for the day. He went up to Blue Hawk Lake to see Hastiinsání."

The Old Man? "An old friend?" she asked.

'Atsá was watching his brother eat the second piece of cornbread. Julia cut another wedge and handed it to 'Atsá. "He's more like my father's"—he struggled for the word and then smiled when it came to him—"godfather. His name is Tim Be'ak'idii, but we call him Hastiinsání."

"Your English is very good," Julia said. "You must go to school." Where else would he have learned the term "godfather"?

"Sometimes."

"Where?"

"Tohatchi."

"Ah. With Mrs. de Vore."

"Aoo'," spoken without enthusiasm.

"You seem to be a smart boy. Don't you like learning about things?"

He shrugged. He was sitting back on his heels; he brushed crumbs from his pants legs. "My father said I have to learn to read and write English good."

"Well."

"What?"

"You have to learn to read and write English *well*."

He scrunched his nose. "Were you a teacher?"

"No," Julia laughed. "Is your aunt visiting Mr. Be'ak'idii, too?"

The boy looked puzzled. Surely, he knew the word "aunt." "Your father's sister?" Julia said. "Johanna?"

"Oh," he said. He hit his forehead with the heel of his hand. "*Shádí.*" Older sister. "That's what we call her."

"Why's that?"

"I don't know, we just do. She likes it better."

"So she went with your father?"

"Yes. Hastiinsání lives by himself up in the mountains, and we bring him things."

"Are there many trails up there?" Julia asked. The boys' grandmother had returned to her work, slowly threading a strand of yarn in and out of the warp. "My plan was to take a good long walk for myself this afternoon, up through the forest."

He nodded. "Many trails."

"Where do they go?"

He bit his lip, as if trying not to laugh at the silly question. "Everywhere. All through the mountains."

"Do many people live up there?"

"Some. More to the north, near Washington Pass, or to the south, closer to Tohatchi."

"Do you think I'll be safe, hiking way up there?" Her wide eyes and hushed voice told him that it wasn't a serious question.

This time he couldn't conceal his mirth. "Unless you get lost."

"Or fall off a cliff?"

He laughed louder. "You're funny."

He was quite endearing, and his younger brother, too; Níyol had edged closer, and now sat almost hip-to-hip with her. Sometimes his hand would stray to hers, as if making sure the white didn't rub off; she left her palm open for him. "Maybe you should come with me and be my guide."

"I can't leave my grandmother," 'Atsá said, quite serious about the responsibility that had been entrusted to him. "It isn't good to leave her alone. She needs help standing up and walking."

"I see. I'm very sorry."

He laughed again.

"Why are you laughing now?"

"Bilagáanas don't say sorry to Navajos."

"Who told you that?" Julia said, taken aback. "Your father?"

"I don't know." Then he added, "They never do at school."

"I stayed a night with Mrs. de Vore and Mrs. Haskell. I thought they were very nice."

"Huh, you don't get hit on the knuckles by their rulers. They have these big, heavy wooden ones."

"Do you misbehave?"

He shrugged. "Sometimes."

"School is where you can learn all about the world."

He shrugged again. His grandmother was nodding off, her chin dropping to her chest.

"I bet there's something you'd like to know right now about where I come from."

"Maybe."

"Go on, you may ask."

'Atsá put his fingers to his chin in thought. "Did you come here on the train?"

"I did, as far as Gallup."

"Where does it start from and where does it turn around?"

He was only a young boy, eight or maybe nine; nothing was obvious about the world he had yet to see. "You know, there isn't just *one* train," Julia said. "There are *many* trains. They crisscross the whole country. Hundreds of them."

His expression said that he didn't know whether to believe her.

"There are many, many railroad tracks and they connect with each other, just like the trails in the mountains intersect, and there are many, many stations like Gallup, all across the country. Some are much bigger, in the bigger cities, where thousands and thousands of people live. And many, many trains are running all the time between the cities."

He took this in and then asked, "But where does the *Gallup* train start from?"

"You might say St. Louis—have you heard of St. Louis?"—he nodded—"which is where I boarded it to come out here. But before *that* I rode other trains, starting in Pittsfield, Massachusetts, and those trains took me to Chicago, Illinois, and then St. Louis, Missouri, where I lived for a time. When I got off the train in Gallup, that train continued west, all the way to the Pacific Ocean." She had no idea how much of this made any sense to him. "Have you studied geography at school?"

He nodded slowly. "I know where Washington is."

"You can find it on a map?"

"Aoo'. And Mrs. de Vore read to us about Boston, Massachusetts, where white men dressed up as Indians and threw English tea into the sea."

Of course, Julia thought. To a Navajo child who knew nothing of the British or the thirteen colonies, what could possibly be more memorable about the founding of the United States? What other lore had he heard? The Pilgrims and the first Thanksgiving? George Washington cutting down the mythical cherry tree? "Have you ever had that kind of tea?" she asked.

He shook his head.

"It's my favorite thing to drink. If you and your brother come visit me, I'll make you some. With sugar and milk."

A shy smile lit his face.

"Keep going to school. You'll learn many important things." Why wasn't he at the school now? she wondered—he would have to board there to attend regularly. Perhaps because of his grandmother?

"Are you going to have peppermint candy?" he asked.

"In the store? I suppose we might. But if you want some, you'll have to earn it. Maybe you could come sweep the floor for me when you're not away at school."

He shook his head. "My father wouldn't like that."

"Why not?"

"He didn't want me going to the trading post before."

"When Mr. Taskin was here?"

He nodded.

"Well, you're much older now, and maybe your father will have changed his mind. You can come and sweep and also help me learn Navajo."

He seemed to ponder this.

"Or you can just come and visit, if you have your father's permission. You never know, a stick of peppermint might find its way to you now and then even if you don't sweep."

Níyol, the sweet boy, had moved to Julia's lap. He was wearing just a long cotton shirt and his bare legs felt cold to her touch, but he didn't seem to mind. Julia tried to recall the last time she'd held a child in her lap. At some church social function—it seemed ages ago. "Do you think your brother's cold?" she asked 'Atsá.

"No, why would he be?"

She had asked another silly question, obviously.

The boys' grandmother started, suddenly opening her eyes and then sighing deeply. The sight of Julia sitting there surprised her, but then she seemed to recall who this white woman was, and she smiled a toothless smile. She said something to Níyol, who awkwardly climbed from Julia's lap and took the few steps to his grandmother's other side. She patted his shoulder and whispered something in his ear. He stood there, rocking heel to toe.

"Could you ask your grandmother about Mr. Taskin's cow?" Julia said.

'Atsá spoke too quickly for her to follow, but she did hear Ab Taskin's name and made out the word "*béégashii.*"

Waving a shaky hand, the boys' grandmother delivered another long reply.

"My father sold it," 'Atsá said, reducing the answer to its fundamentals.

"Oh," Julia said. She wasn't particularly surprised. Clement Yazzie had probably concluded that Will didn't want it. "Do you have your own cow?" she asked.

"No."

"You and your brother don't drink milk?"

"Sometimes. We have goats."

"Well," Julia said, rising, "I should probably be on my way. 'Atsá, it was a pleasure meeting you and Níyol. Tell your grandmother that after I've learned a little more Navajo, I'd like her to tell me all about her weaving. Please ask her if I may visit again and if there's anything I can bring her."

The boy and the old woman exchanged a series of sentences. "Grandmother says, yes, you can come again. And," he said with a wicked grin, "she'd like some peppermint candy."

A large hat with a round, flat, broad brim. That's what she noticed first, shading the dark face and darker eyes, when she opened the door in response to a firm single knock that had made her jump. It was still Saturday, dusk, and Will hadn't come home yet.

Barely taller than she, Clement Yazzie was in no way physically imposing despite his broad chest and shoulders. He was wearing a cheap but clean blue chambray shirt, buttoned at the straight collar. Smooth brow, wide nose with a prominent bump at the bridge, a deep concavity above the center of his upper lip, a straight mouth, a strong chin and jaw line—all impossible to read. She'd expected . . . in truth, she didn't know what she'd expected. But his posture, his stare, told her that she shouldn't trifle with him.

"I'm Clement Yazzie," he said. His voice was husky, as if he had to force the words from his throat. He left it at that, without the traditional identification of clans.

"Mr. Yazzie," Julia said, trying as best she could to retain her composure, "It's a pleasure. What can I do for you?"

"Is your husband here?"

"No, but he may be back at any moment."

"I saw him and Tom Gorman on the Gallup road Thursday, heading out."

So he knew that Will might not have returned yet. She extended her hand. "I'm Julia Marshall Halley. I'm from Pittsfield, Massachusetts. My father is Joseph Marshall, and my mother, before she married him, was Heloise Gaillard. Her people were French; they emigrated to Canada and then eventually to Massachusetts. My father's people were English." She'd rehearsed this, the long form.

He looked at her for a moment before replying. "I'm from the Bitter Water Clan, born for the Shaking Aspen Clan of Second Mesa." He briefly wrapped his hand around her fingers, so briefly and so lightly that the handshake was barely a touch.

Second Mesa. "You're half Hopi?" Julia said with surprise. Why hadn't anyone mentioned that before? She'd been told that the Navajo and the Hopi didn't get along, had in fact engaged in sporadic raids and other violence against each other long before the Hopi Reservation was created in 1882 right in the middle of the Navajo Reservation.

"Aoo'."

She asked for the second time, "So, what can I do for you?"

"My older boy said you asked about Taskin's cow."

She was thinking, Should I invite him in? They were neighbors. But this wasn't— "Yes, I did. My husband had mentioned it, and I thought I'd inquire."

"He didn't come to get it."

"Yes, I know, and your deciding to sell it is certainly understandable."

"You can have the money."

What a surprising thing for him to say! "I wouldn't hear of it," Julia said. "You had every right to do as you did. The money is yours."

He thought about this for a moment. "I should talk to your husband."

She bristled at the dismissal but at the same time didn't want to appear to be challenging him. His eyes, as she read them, told her he wouldn't take it kindly. Her thoughts clambered over each other. Could he harm her? But he'd done nothing to provoke the question. She told herself that he was no different from the Navajo men she'd encountered at the Hubbell Trading Post, the ones who hung back, who didn't know how to communicate with her, no more than she did them. Except that there was no trading counter, no protective barrier, between her and Clement Yazzie, who had already demonstrated—she had no reason to disbelieve the stories—that he was capable of killing someone in cold blood. (Was he ever prosecuted?) Now he'd come to her door. He hadn't even removed his hat. From disregard for the niceties of civilized behavior? From disrespect?

"You're certainly welcome to speak to him when he returns, but he and I usually think alike." Though on this matter she wasn't so sure.

"But you'll want a cow."

"Yes, I suppose we will at some point, but—"

"I'll get it back."

"Mr. Yazzie, don't trouble yourself. I'm sure we'll be able to buy one in Gallup."

"Hunh." It wasn't quite a grunt. He looked away.

Was she insulting him by refusing his offer, first of the money and now of the cow? Or would she be insulting him even more by accepting? A white woman taking money or a valuable animal offered by an Indian? Everything about it seemed a reversal of some right order.

"My son also said you wanted him to work in the store." His face held its neutral gaze, but she feared that nothing good lay behind it.

"Really, Mr. Yazzie—"

He cut her off again: "My boy is eight years old. He will not work in your store."

"Mr. Yazzie, please," Julia rushed to explain, "this is a simple misunderstanding. I would never employ any eight-year-old. And even if 'Atsá were twice his age, I wouldn't ask him to work for us"—better to say "us," she calculated, than "me"—"without first speaking to you. All I said was that if he wanted peppermint candy—it seems to be his favorite sweet, or that's what I gather—he could earn some by occasionally sweeping the floor for me—us. I also said," Julia added after catching her breath, "that even then, he'd need your permission." Was she prattling? If she had a towel at hand she'd be wringing it. "I liked your son very much, Mr. Yazzie—I liked both your boys as well as your mother—and I certainly wouldn't set out to offend you before we'd even met."

He took all this in. "So this is about peppermint candy."

"Yes."

"The striped sticks."

"He didn't specify the shape." A little humor, too awkward. "He also implied that your mother likes it, too."

"Don't believe everything he says. He's sly."

Something had changed, she could hear it in his more relaxed voice. She could feel it. Because she liked his boys? Because of her little joke about the candy? "So I gathered."

"I'll go now," Yazzie said, turning away.

She considered letting him leave, closing the door and throwing the bolt now that she was ahead, or at least even, but instead she said, "If you don't mind my asking, did you work for Ab Taskin?"

"No."

Short and succinct, Julia thought, but then he added, "Sometimes I worked for McElroy, before Taskin bought him out."

"May I ask what you did?"

"I helped him build the trading post, hauling the logs down from up above"—he tilted his chin toward the upper reaches of the canyon—"and putting up the walls and roof."

"And after the store opened?"

"This and that."

"Is there a reason why you didn't work for Mr. Taskin?"

"He never asked."

Why was she about to do this, without even consulting Will? Because Clement Yazzie, the man who stood before her on the veranda, somehow seemed unlike the man she'd been warned about. But how could she truly know? All they had really talked about was a cow and a child, his son, and even the most contemptible of men were capable of loving their children and recognizing that reflection in another's eyes, even a stranger's. Nevertheless, she felt that she'd gone too far to retreat. "Well, I'd like you to work for us when we need extra help. I can't say exactly what you'd be doing—'this and that,' probably"—she attempted a smile—"and we can't afford to pay you in cash money, but we can give you store credit. Would you be interested?"

"Why?"

Why . . . what? Why was she asking him, or why should he accept store credit, or why should he want to work for Will and her? And why did his question annoy her so? Because he'd intended to gain the upper hand again.

"Better to have the devil on your side?" he said.

"I beg your pardon?"

"If you want me to work for you, you should see what Tom Gorman has to say about it."

"I take it that the two of you don't agree about much," Julia said.

"We let each other be." He pulled from a pocket a folded square of muslin and handed it to her. The muslin smelled of cornbread and honey.

"Was there any cornbread left for you and Johanna when you got home?"

"Aoo'," he answered. "Little ones understand fairness, if their stomachs don't get in the way." He turned to leave again—but then stopped. "I hear that your husband has been saying things."

Saying what? But she didn't really need to ask, did she? Charges and allegations, rumors of deceit, tales of the imprudent or nefarious. She and Will might be fifty miles from anywhere, but it didn't matter. Word spread, like seepage through cracks. The Gormans or Rodrigo Peña or Matilda Rodriguez said something to someone who said something to someone who said . . . It was a valuable lesson: there would be no secrets; word would always reach Clement Yazzie.

"Someone did break in, if that's what you're referring to," Julia said. And of course Clement Yazzie would be the logical suspect in many eyes.

"Maybe it happened later."

"Later?"

"After everything was already gone."

Why?—

Because, obviously, whoever broke in didn't know. Contrary to what Carmelita Gorman had said, in all likelihood they *were* Navajos; maybe they were hungry, maybe they were just ordinary thieves with bad timing. She didn't doubt for a second that Clement Yazzie knew who they were, but he wouldn't tell her or anyone else.

She watched him walk up the trail until the dusk claimed him, and then she went in and sealed the door against the night.

When Will returned on Sunday morning, she told him that she'd met Clement Yazzie, but she didn't reveal everything about the conversation. Why trigger another tirade about their having been cheated? She felt guilty for keeping her own counsel, but they both needed to focus their attention on the tasks ahead, fixing the walls, finishing the ceiling, stocking the store, opening for business.

CHAPTER THREE: Safety

Owen had slept long and deeply, waking several times both before and after dawn but then comfortably slipping under again, dreaming in the later hours of Beth Burrows and her family, the dream blending the genuine and the fanciful, he in his martyrdom at the center of everyone's sympathy and concern.

At one point, chilled, he managed to don the clothes Julia had laid at the foot of the bed, and at another she'd come in and bandaged his feet. It was afternoon before he forced himself to stay awake, struggling into a sitting position, propping himself against the headboard. His feet still burned. The house was quiet. He tried to remember the day: Sunday. He could hear melted snow dripping outside the single window; bright sunlight filtered through the curtain.

He needed to make his way to the privy. He threw back the blankets and swung his legs to the side. Fluid from an open sore had seeped through the cotton cloth covering his right instep. He didn't know if he could stand. Julia had placed a pair of deerskin moccasins beside the bed. Could he get his feet into them? The moccasins were oversized, large enough to accommodate the bandages, and he could stand, but nothing felt right: the wrappings filled in his arches, he had no sensation whatsoever in two of his toes, and he stumbled painfully and had to brace himself against the mattress to keep from falling. Was this what he had to look forward to? He shuffled forward a few steps toward the open doorway, found his balance, and walked slowly and carefully into the parlor and then to the kitchen. A covered bowl sat on the stove warming, and he lifted the cloth to discover several servings of oatmeal; he had no doubt that Julia had added butter and egg whites. He dug into the bowl with a serving spoon, realizing how hungry he was only after his mouth was full. Julia had added something else, cinnamon, which made him smile. He ate half the bowl, more than he should have, then moved to the sink and drew himself a glass of cold water from the pump.

The outside door swung open; it was Pete Pietrowski, carrying a camera, a box of glass plates, and a tripod. "Well," Pete said, "back from the dead?"

"Temporarily," Owen said. Had Julia told Pete about his illness, and the prognosis?

"True for all of us," Pete said, laying down his equipment on the dining table.

"I have a favor to ask," Owen said. "I'm a little unsteady—could you help me outside?"

"Nature calls?"

"It does."

"I never like to see a man caught short." Pete walked over and took Owen by the arm. "You won't need a coat. It's downright balmy today."

Owen, through Julia, knew a bit about his companion. Blustery, effusive, and ill-kempt, Pete Pietrowski, born and raised in Cincinnati to a poor family of Polish immigrants, had escaped thanks to the Franciscans, first by attending a boys' school that they ran and then by becoming a brother—a life that he rejected after spending a terrible winter as part of a failed mission to the Navajo at Hunters Point, a few miles south of the current successful mission at St. Michaels. Somewhere along the way he'd learned photography well enough to set up his own shop in Gallup.

Patches of snow deep in shade were all that remained of the previous day's storm; the melt had turned the surface of the ground a deeper red, though where footsteps had dislodged the slippery mud Owen could see that the wetness had penetrated only an inch. As soon as he and Pete stepped off the veranda Owen saw Johanna Yazzie at a distance, sitting in her favored spot, on a flat rock at the edge of the earth and rock dam that held back a manmade pond. She was looking in his and Pete's direction as they made their way around back, but she gave no indication of any interest.

About a decade younger than her half-brother, and a full Navajo—her father had disappeared even before her birth, Julia had told Owen—Johanna, quite apart from her muteness, was decidedly odd, so much so that if she had been born in New England she might well have been declared unsound and either kept as a shut-in or institutionalized. Here in Many Springs Canyon, however, she came and went as she wanted. Everyone accepted her peculiarities, Julia had added, most notably her desire to maintain a distinct physical distance from everyone but her brother and Tóya and, eventually, Julia herself. During meals, she preferred to sit at the far end of the dining table, and when people gathered around the stove in the parlor, she sat on an old Indian rug against the wall, often with her back to the conversation but always listening.

"So she understands English?" Owen had asked Julia.

"You should decide that for yourself," she had replied. "We're of a divided opinion. I believe she knows much more than she lets on, whereas Pete Pietrowski, ever the contrarian, believes not."

"And what does her brother say?"

"He doesn't weigh in."

"Isn't that a bit odd?"

"Perhaps. You can ask him yourself, if you'd like. But I believe Mr. Yazzie thinks that Johanna should be as she is, without our judgment." Julia paused. "I will, however, say this much. She is *not* feebleminded, and it would be a mistake to assume that she is."

During his short time in Many Springs Canyon, Owen had encountered Johanna often, usually from afar, but on several occasions inside, at Julia's. Clearly, Johanna had her tasks to perform, most particularly attending to the canyon's sheep, which roamed freely in the upper and lower meadows, guarded by two herding dogs. (It wasn't at all clear to Owen which sheep were Yazzie's and which Julia's; they all seemed to have the same brand.) He'd observed Johanna using whistles and hand signals to communicate with the dogs; two high, sharply punctuated whistles drew their attention, and a circular wave sent them running after strays. Owen assumed she had other responsibilities as well—tidying the Yazzie's hogan, cooking, and the like—and she also helped out in Julia's kitchen whenever she happened to be around. Johanna was often simply *present*—he couldn't think of a better way to put it—stoking a fire, setting the table according to what must have been Julia's dictates at some earlier time, clearing the dishes after a meal and washing them in Julia's deep sink without a word from the mistress of the house.

By the time Owen had relieved himself and rejoined Pete just beyond the outhouse, Johanna had disappeared from her rock.

Owen and Pete reentered the kitchen to find that Julia had returned (from the store, Owen assumed) and was heating water for a pot of tea. She immediately directed Owen to get off his feet—to pick a chair in the parlor, sit down, and use the hassock. Owen, still walking carefully, obeyed. Pete, meanwhile, walked to the larder and then carried to the dining table bread and a block of cheese, which he proceeded to slice.

"I don't know how you stomach that gruel of yours," Pete said from the table. "Don't you ever want to grab a joint of meat and tear into it?"

Owen could only conclude that Julia, faced with questions, had told Pete about the diabetes. At this point, what did it matter?

"Oh," Owen said, "I take a little meat and cheese as well, with no ill effects, at least none that I can feel."

"And why oats but not wheat?" Pete asked.

"The doctors said it has something to do with how quickly things get digested. Oatmeal takes longer than flour."

"How would they know that?" Pete pieced his sandwich together.

"Autopsies and animal experiments I suppose."

Pete grimaced. He then said to Julia, "I'll be off." He tucked his sandwich into a jacket pocket and picked up his photographic equipment again before heading to the door. When he was gone, Owen asked Julia, who was pouring boiling water into her teapot:

"He just helps himself?"

"To food?" she said, carrying the pot and two mugs into the parlor. "He does."

"And he just comes and goes?"

"He does."

"So what is he photographing out there?"

"Whatever strikes his fancy. Some days, nothing. Today, I'd guess it's the melting snow."

"He photographs *melting snow?*"

Julia, taking a seat in her rocking chair, laughed. "He has somewhat unconventional ideas, and not just about photography. He likes people to think he's an unschooled vulgarian, but he's well educated. Better than I am."

"Why is that?"

"I left school before my mother died. My sister was just a child at the time, and she needed me at home. That's how it was." She stopped there, leaving Owen to conclude that she greatly regretted not finishing her formal education.

"I take it that Pete and Dr. Whitaker know each other," Owen said.

"Oh yes," Julia said, "quite well. So well, in fact, that they know exactly how best to annoy each other."

"They don't get along?"

"They do, which is even more remarkable given their temperaments. Pete loves to stir the pot, whereas Harry is usually the voice of reason, with a touch of Southern gentility."

"He's from—?"

"South Carolina. Charleston."

"How did he end up out here?"

"He arrived right after the Spanish-American War. A friend he met in Cuba was from Gallup."

"He served in Cuba?"

She nodded. "He volunteered. Afterward, he came out here to see a bit of the West and was urged to stay and set up a health station in Tohatchi, where plans were under way to convert the day school into the reservation's second boarding school. He agreed to do it for a year."

"He's been here all this time?"

"He has."

"Is he married?"

"Neither he nor Pete, as a matter of fact." She poured the tea and handed a cup to Owen. "I expect Pete will marry one of these days, and probably badly."

It seemed such an uncharacteristic comment that Owen asked, "Why do you say that?"

"He can be impulsive and judgmental and obstinate, qualities unlikely to lend stability to a marriage." She added, archly, after a brief pause, "I know whereof I speak. And just so you know, I'm speaking of *my* failings, not my husband's."

She'd never spoken directly of her marriage except for that one awkward instance in the midst of what he considered their first real conversation, when he'd revealed his illness. Prior to that they'd chatted, enjoyed each other's company, but never ventured into the thickets.

He found Julia Halley far from unattractive, though she did nothing to call attention to her appearance. She wore her hair braided and wound in a bun; her face was brown, her skin roughened by years of exposure to dry winds. Her dresses and skirts, uniformly brown or gray, were functional. She wasn't above throwing a few quick stitches where a nail had snagged the fabric; he'd once seen her sitting on her veranda, bending over and mending the torn hem of a skirt she was still wearing. He didn't know her age, although he knew she'd been living in Many Springs Canyon for eleven years; she had to be in her mid-thirties, to be sure, but he wouldn't venture a guess beyond that. How long had she been married before arriving here? He didn't know that either.

Reaching for his tea, he changed the subject: "Do you always feel safe here?" He'd wondered about this for some time. At Chaco Canyon more than one ranch hand, hearing that Owen intended to visit Many Springs Canyon, had warned him about Clement Yazzie. No one at Chaco actually knew Yazzie, but that didn't prevent them from spinning lurid tales of how he'd killed a man and gotten away with it. Owen had encountered Yazzie at least a dozen times in the last six weeks, most often when he passed near the Yazzie hogan on his way through the lower and high meadows to the trails that crisscrossed the Chuskas. On these occasions Owen didn't stop to talk, but he would tip his hat or wave, gestures that never drew more than a minimal response—a nod of the head—from Yazzie. Johanna might be mute but

Yazzie was, in his own way, equally reserved, even on the two occasions when Owen and he had sat opposite each other at Julia's table for a meal and, afterward, moved to her parlor. In truth, Owen didn't know what to make of him.

Julia took his question coolly. "Why shouldn't I feel safe?"

"For one reason, you're usually alone at night."

"I'm not afraid of the dark and I'm an excellent shot. I can shoot the lid off a tin can at thirty yards."

"Now you're making fun of me," Owen said.

"Just a little," Julia said, "but I do know how to shoot. Tom Gorman taught me."

"It isn't an illogical question, you know."

"About my safety? Do you care to guess how many times I've been asked that, or—more to the point—how many times I've been told that I'm *not* safe?" There was a distinct edge to her voice.

"I can imagine." He sipped his tea, black and strong.

"I was two years on my own before I even told my family back East. I thought they might send detectives to kidnap me."

"Really?" At times he was still uncertain how to take her comments.

"No, not *really*." Her expression told him he should know better, but when she spoke again her tone was more serious: "And what about you?"

He looked at her quizzically. "What do you mean?"

"Do *you* feel safe?"

"Here?"

"Yes."

"Ah. Well, our circumstances aren't exactly the same."

"Of course not. You're a man and I'm a woman."

"That wasn't—"

She cut him off: "—what you meant. I know, but I'm not referring to your illness."

He waited for her to go on.

"Imagine a woman doing what you did—saying goodbye to her prior life, packing a bag, getting on a train, and going somewhere utterly foreign, where she knew no one."

"I suppose she'd have to be a very unusual woman."

"Men do it all the time."

"Some men." He frowned. "I can't say that I ever saw myself as one of them."

"And yet, here you are. So do you feel safe?" she asked again.

He still didn't know how to answer her. "I suppose nothing's truly safe," he finally said, "and sometimes it just doesn't matter."

"Despite our differing circumstances," Julia said, "we seem to have arrived at a similar conclusion."

Later, Julia, Pete, and Johanna, who'd simply showed up in the late afternoon, dined on the mutton stew left over from the previous night, while Owen settled for a dish of broth and reheated oatmeal. He ate much more slowly than the others so as not to finish well in advance, given that he could consume so much less.

Julia sat at the head of the table, he and Pete nearby, opposite each other, and Johanna as far as possible from them, at the foot. She never used a fork or a spoon; she ate with her fingers and drank from a bowl. It took some getting used to, to not be distracted by her manners, although Julia obviously didn't mind.

Owen knew Johanna was at least as old as he, but he couldn't quite reconcile that with her appearance. She simply didn't look her age and probably never would—one of those rare, lucky, ageless women. He estimated that she was five feet tall in her bare feet, and slender—as much as he could tell given that she always wore a heavy, sleeveless blanket dress. (And not much more than that, if anything, judging by the way her body moved beneath the wool.) Her oval face—her skin was at least two shades darker than her brother's—and generous mouth, full and wide, suited her, although her hooded eyes contributed to a lack of guile in her countenance that most people, he suspected, would see as evidence that she was simple. Her personal hygiene might not meet the standards of polite white society, but there was nothing unusual about that out here: getting too near some of the white cowhands he'd encountered at Chaco could suck the breath right out of your lungs. (He himself sometimes went more than a few days without a good wash, something that never would have happened back East.) But Johanna's dresses—she seemed to have just two, both of black wool and nearly identical—were always clean, her face washed, her hair bound and cloth-tied, and he never found her presence offensive.

"So tell me about home," Pete said to Owen. "I know you're from a small town in New Hampshire and that your family has a farm, but that's about it."

"Calling Ashuelot small makes it sound bigger than it is," Owen said. "My father's people have been farmers going back generations. At some point they moved from Massachusetts to New Hampshire. My mother's people started out in Connecticut. They were farmers, too, although my maternal grandfather, the youngest in the family, owned a dry goods store at one point. I never knew him. My father's the only one left of either generation.

"What does he grow?" Pete asked.

"Mostly potatoes."

"My father worked the docks in Cincinnati," Pete said. "It made him old before his time. Later on, he and my mother both worked on a tobacco farm in Kentucky, but by then his health was already failing."

"Do you still have family in Cincinnati?" Owen asked.

"No, they're scattered about eastern Ohio and West Virginia now. They've moved from the docks to the coal mines. Downward, you might say." His mouth twisted into a sad grin.

"It's certainly a hard life," Julia said as she ladled more stew into Pete's bowl.

"What about *your* family?" Owen asked Julia. "I mean, other than your parents and sister."

"My mother's parents were French Canadian. Her father worked at the Revere Copper Company in Canton."

"Revere, as in *the* Revere?" Owen asked.

"Joseph, one of Paul's sons. And my paternal grandfather was a minister in Boston."

"So your father followed in his father's footsteps?"

"He did. They both graduated from Andover Theological Seminary, but they had a falling out. For a time, my father was an avid supporter of Theodore Parker. Have you heard of him?"

"No."

"He was a Unitarian who was drummed out of his own association for taking transcendentalist views too far. Fortunately, my father and grandfather eventually reconciled."

"Who saw the light?" Pete asked.

"My father."

"Ah, he got older and wiser."

"That's one way of looking at it."

"So you were raised as a—?" Owen asked her.

"Congregationalist."

"Lutheran, Methodist, Congregationalist—the differences are beyond me," Owen said with a shake of his head. "I figure you believe or you don't."

"Did you attend services growing up?" Julia asked.

"My mother used to take me."

"And her church was—?

"Presbyterian."

"Not so far from Congregationalist," Julia said.

"But not nearly as wishy-washy," Pete said. "The Presbyterians know their Calvin."

"On behalf of my father, I should be insulted," Julia said with a little smile.

"Any siblings?" Pete asked Owen.

"A brother. But I never met him. He died years before I was born."

"I lost a brother, too," Pete said, "but I suspect the circumstances differed. Mine ran afoul of some friends of his. Hoodlums."

"I'm sorry," Owen said. "Were you close?"

"Not at all."

"Still—"

"Exactly."

Julia began gathering the empty dishes and flatware, placing them neatly on a serving tray; Johanna added her own bowl and then accepted the tray from Julia's hands and carried everything to the kitchen, where wash water was already heating on the stove. Then she set to work. This was their routine.

Curious to know more about the Indian doctor, Harry Whitaker, Owen asked Julia.

The only son and the youngest of four children, Julia told him, Harry had trained at the University of Virginia and was working at the Army Medical College in Washington when the Spanish-American War broke out. As a member of the medical corps attached to the 1st Volunteer Cavalry—Teddy Roosevelt's "Rough Riders"—he'd been among the first to land in Cuba. The experience included a nearly fatal bout of yellow fever. "Some time after," Julia said, "his father died, leaving him a considerable fortune, I believe."

"Considerable," Pete echoed.

A wealthy doctor living a remote life on the country's largest Indian reservation, Owen thought. This would be a man worth meeting under any circumstances.

"And what about the Navajo woman, Tóya?" Owen asked with less assurance.

"You sound skeptical," Julia said.

"He should be," Pete said. "For an illiterate Indian, she has a very high opinion of herself."

"Pete and Tóya," Julia said, "rarely see eye to eye. About anything."

"Don't get me wrong," Pete said to Owen. "I give her her due. Harry Whitaker swears by her herbs and potions, but if you're an ordinary white man, she'd as soon spit in your eye as look at you."

"She's my good friend," Julia said to Pete, "and she tolerates you, so she can't be that bad."

"Huh."

"Does her name mean something in Navajo?" Owen asked.

" '*Tó*' means 'water,' but Tóya is just a nickname she lets us use," Julia said. "She took pity on us Anglos—her full name is 'Asdzáán Bítóyiszééyiztał, which means something like 'Woman Who Kicks Up Still Water.' "

"That couldn't possibly be her birth name," Owen said.

"No, it's the name she took after the Long Walk. I met her soon after I moved here. I'd see her pass by on her way to visit the Yazzies—she knew Mr. Yazzie's mother from when they were both interned—and that's how I met her."

"So you knew Mrs. Yazzie, too?"

"I did. I liked her very much. Actually, though, she was never 'Mrs. Yazzie.' 'Yazzie' was the name they gave Mr. Yazzie at the Fort Defiance Indian School. It's one way to spell a Navajo word for 'small,' but it also wasn't far, phonetically at least, from his father's last name, Katsi."

"Was having a Hopi father an issue?"

"Not for the school, but, yes, for some of the other boys."

"And the name 'Clement'—that's also from his time at the Indian school?"

"It seems he had a habit of running off and then getting punished as a consequence—so often, in fact, that a teacher told him he should ask for clemency. Some of the other boys considered that hilarious and began calling him 'Clemency.' And 'Clemency' became 'Clement.' It isn't a name he favors."

"Then it's odd that he kept it."

"Everybody just calls him 'Yazzie,'" Pete added, "except for Julia, who retains the old-fashioned notion that it's disrespectful to call anyone by his last name alone."

"I see no reason to change my thinking," Julia said to Pete.

"Hopis and Navajos aren't exactly on friendly terms, are they?" Owen said. "So how did Mr. Yazzie's parents meet?"

"By chance. After the Long Walk, in the winter of 1869, Mr. Yazzie's mother and her family were living near Crystal—it was called Cottonwood in those days. Her grandfather, Hosteen Naalnish, was a member of a hunting party that came upon Mr. Katsi and several other Hopis, who told Hosteen Naalnish that they were traveling home after meeting in Farmington with a delegation from Washington. This was back when the Hopis were trying to convince the government to give them their own reservation. Anyway, Hosteen Naalnish gave the Hopis shelter for the night—after confiscating their horses and weapons—and that's how Mr. Yazzie's parents met. Mr. Katsi returned in secret after that to see her, and one night she stole away with him. They went to Second Mesa, where Mr. Yazzie was born, but in the end things didn't work out and she came back with her son to Many Springs Canyon, to where her parents had moved."

Owen asked, "Does Mr. Yazzie ever see his father?"

"He died several years ago in Mexico, but Mr. Yazzie visits his uncles and their families now and then."

"And his mother passed away some time ago?"

"She was already very ill by the time I arrived. I'd walk up to their place and visit on Sundays. Mr. Yazzie's boys—they were only eight and three—would be playing a game of some sort with sticks or round stones, and Mr. Yazzie's mother would sit at her loom and tell me stories about her weaving. She didn't speak any English, so I couldn't always follow her, especially at first, but it didn't matter because she often forgot what she'd told me on previous visits and therefore repeated herself. It was actually very helpful to me—at each visit I understood a bit more of the language. She told me about Spider Woman, who lives at the top of Spider Rock in Canyon de Chelly and who taught the People how to weave . . . well, she told me so *many* stories. And she also showed me the proper way to spin wool—always by hand, never with a machine. Most afternoons, Johanna was also there, tending to her mother with great care."

"And Mr. Yazzie?"

"He was almost always around as well, but he kept his distance. After the weather turned, however, and he moved his mother's loom inside their hogan, I think my presence there made him uncomfortable. He would always leave as soon as I arrived. One day in the store when we weren't within earshot of anyone else, I voiced my concern that I was intruding, and, as usual in those days, before we came to know each other better—which, I might add, took a *considerable* time—he answered indirectly, saying only that his mother looked forward to my visits. I took that as permission to continue. I must say, I enjoyed those visits, too, during that first winter. I could forget about the isolation and the lack of customers. A few times Tóya was also there to visit her friend. I could tell that Tóya was suspicious of me, but eventually she warmed up. I guess she concluded that I didn't have any ulterior motives."

"If she doesn't know you," Pete said to Owen, "or doesn't like you, or simply prefers to cut you out of the conversation, she sticks to her native lingo even though she speaks English as well as I do. It can be damned annoying."

"Maybe you should learn more Navajo," Julia said.

"I know enough to get by. When an Indian comes into my studio for a portrait, I can quite handily tell him in his own language to sit down, hold still, and pay up."

"You're incorrigible," Julia said.

"What happened to the Yazzie boys?" Owen asked.

"Diphtheria," Julia said, "almost six years ago now. It took them both."

"You were very fond of them?"

She nodded and smiled—a thin smile, the corners of her mouth turning upward ever so slightly. "When I would go to visit their grandmother, I always brought along a book to read to them, something that would enthrall 'Atsá in particular, a sea adventure or the *Arabian Nights*, which he couldn't get enough of—Aladdin and Sinbad especially. I remember 'Atsá asking me why they couldn't read books like that at school. I told him that school was a much more serious endeavor, an explanation that he didn't like, not at all. And the little one, Níyol, was starting to pick up English. I had to laugh sometimes because he'd interrupt the story to ask his brother for a translation, which frustrated 'Atsá to no end because it slowed things down and 'Atsá wanted me to keep *moving*, to keep turning those pages." Julia laughed at the memory. "Sometimes 'Atsá would visit the store and do odd chores when he wasn't away at school. I had a little wooden box under the counter for him, and he took great delight in watching me drop his 'wages' into it, a coin at a time." She couldn't restrain a sigh. "I still have it," she said, "with the coins still in it."

"I'm not the sentimental type," Pete said, frowning beneath his mustache and folding his hands in front of him on the table, "but they weren't bad boys. Mischievous, that's all. I found them poking around my wagon once. I told them I'd skin them if they ever laid hands on my cameras or any other equipment, and I never had another problem with them. They were all right. Who's to say how they would've turned out, but they may well have grown up to be a credit to their race."

Johanna, having finished her kitchen chores, walked to the door.

"*Ahéhee', Jóhonaá. Yiskáago índa,*" Julia said.

The Indian woman, as was her way, left without acknowledging Julia's thanks.

"How did you say her name?" Owen asked, and Julia repeated it:

"Jóhonaá. It's the Navajo word for 'sunny.' "

"Not exactly her disposition," Pete said.

"That's rather unkind of you, isn't it?" Owen said. "Given her difficulties?"

"I didn't mean anything by it," Pete said.

"Then maybe you shouldn't have said it," Julia told him.

"My apologies." Pete bowed his head. To Owen, the gesture seemed as sarcastic as his earlier words.

"Johanna, Jóhonaá," Owen tried them both. "Do they have anything in common except that they sound so much alike?"

"Ne'er the twain do meet," Pete said. " 'Johanna' probably derives from 'Joan,' the feminine form of 'John,' or the Greek 'Ioannes,' which means 'Gracious' or 'God's Gift.' "

Owen let out a quick laugh of surprise.

"So you *did* learn something from the Franciscans," Julia commented.

"Latin and Greek—not my forte," Pete said with a shake of his head, "but you're bound to pick up something when you hear one or the other every day for years."

Pete Pietrowski retreated to the trading post storeroom, where Julia allowed him to keep various supplies and equipment for developing photographic plates, while Julia and Owen settled themselves in the parlor. Before this Owen had heard pieces of the history of the Many Springs Trading Post in passing, during casual talk with Julia while chatting on the veranda in the evening, but the pieces, out of sequence and of seemingly equal importance, hadn't cohered into a narrative. Now, however, at his urging, Julia related a fuller history:

The Many Springs Canyon Trading Post began as nothing more than a seasonal tent first raised some twenty years earlier, in 1888, by a wagon trader named Sam McElroy, who'd been making periodic bartering trips along the eastern side of the Chuska Mountains for nearly a decade, exchanging hardware and foodstuffs and cheap dyed cloth for Navajo weavings and jewelry and wool, which he would then sell in Albuquerque. McElroy, so the story went, had learned both Navajo and Mescalero Apache between 1864 and 1868, when both tribes were interred at the hell-on-earth of Bosque Redondo—in the Navajo language, Hwéeldi, the Land of Suffering— near Fort Sumner in eastern New Mexico. Some said he was an army guard there, others that he was a sutler who worked for a supply business out of Tucumcari, providing cut-rate goods to the incarcerated Indians and giving kickbacks to the less-scrupulous army supply officers. In later years he was never very forthcoming about his background since either prior livelihood might have contributed to his getting his throat slit by any of the Navajo survivors, who were permitted to return to their native country by the Treaty of 1868. McElroy obtained permission to erect a tent and then to build a store from Manuelito, the most powerful and respected headman on the eastern reservation. At the time, there were few other traders in the region, except for summer tent stores at Cottonwood, Naschitti, Manuelito Springs, Tuye.

"The only other person McElroy had to convince was Tim Be-'ak'idii," Julia said.

Owen had encountered the Old Man only once. Several weeks ago his first visit to the small, pristine Blue Hawk Lake had been cut short by the barrel of Tim Be'ak'idii's rifle. The Old Man couldn't speak English and since Owen couldn't speak Navajo, he had no way to explain that he was merely following a trail and had no evil intent. He retreated. After telling Julia of his encounter, she made sure that Clement Yazzie informed the Old Man that Owen posed no threat and shouldn't be shot on sight.

"It's a rather sad story, actually," Julia continued. "Mr. Be'ak'idii has been around here forever. He hid out in the mountains during the Long Walk. Afterward, he was devoted to Mr. Yazzie's mother, but different groups of Navajo clans are too closely related to permit intermarriage—she was Bitter Water, and Mr. Be'ak'idii is Deer Spring. Still, he decided to stay near, to look out for her and her son—he became something of a surrogate father to Mr. Yazzie."

"I take it that he didn't like the idea of an Anglo, McElroy, living so close."

"Certainly not, but Mr. Yazzie's mother saw the advantages, and he acquiesced."

McElroy's Many Springs Canyon Trading Post was initially two large rectangular rooms back to back, the public trading room in the front and the smaller living quarters behind. Within a year, however, he began adding on an indoor kitchen, two bedrooms, and the area Julia now called her parlor, all to accommodate his fiancée, a widow from Farmington, and her two children. But the marriage never came to pass, and McElroy, by nature a wanderer like many of the other early traders, was lured north by the Cripple Creek gold rush in 1892, and he sold out to Abner Taskin. In the next several years other traders built stores in Cottonwood Pass (renamed Crystal by J. B. Moore when he became sole owner in 1897), Coyote Canyon, Sanostee, and Two Grey Hills, although ownership changed frequently.

Unlike J. B. Moore, his nearest competitor, Ab Taskin was a drunk, and his venture proved far less successful than the Crystal Trading Post. Taskin could barely speak Navajo, but for a brief time he committed himself to showing his four older brothers, who operated various enterprises out of Las Cruces, that he, too, could succeed in business. He failed and took further solace in the bottle. When he couldn't find a local buyer to get himself out of debt, his brothers offered to step in if he'd sell the place and return home, where they could keep an eye on him. Through family connections they found a Gallup businessman, Alberto Rodriguez, who agreed to act as their agent and who placed advertisements in a number of newspapers, including the *St. Louis Post-Dispatch*. And that led to the only inquiry, from Wilford and Julia Halley, originally of Pittsfield, Massachusetts, and then of St. Louis.

"So you agreed to buy the business sight unseen?" Owen asked, incredulous. It seemed so rash—so unlike the Julia he'd come to know.

"We did," Julia said, "unless you count the photographs that Alberto asked Pete to take. That's one of them on the wall behind you." She pointed to a simply framed picture, a view of the trading post and canyon. Owen had noticed this and half a dozen other photographs hanging on the wall during prior visits but hadn't looked that closely at them. Now he turned in his chair, his attention drawn not only to the indicated picture but one beside it, which showed a younger Julia sitting in a wagon loaded with furniture—including, unless he was mistaken, the chair he now occupied. "Tell me about that one," he said, pointing.

"Pete took that, too," Julia said, laughing. "I coerced him into it. It was the morning I left Gallup for Many Springs. That's how he and I met, and we've been friends ever since, though we've had our differences."

Whereas most photographers, Owen assumed, would simply have positioned the camera to face the side of the wagon straight on, with Julia turning her head toward the lens, Pete had placed his camera obliquely, toward the middle of the wagon's side and angled back toward Julia, who sat sideways, her right arm draped over the back of the bench, her hand resting on this very chair, and one leg apparently drawn up beneath her skirt. She'd removed her straw sun hat, which she held in her lap. The sun caught the side of her face, framed in a soft cloud by her pinned-up hair. In the background, a blur of horses shifted in their traces. Eleven years ago. The woman in the photograph wasn't beautiful, but she had about her a comeliness that drew the eye and the mind.

"Let me ask *you* a question," Julia said. She rose and added another piece of pinyon to the fire in the box stove.

"All right."

"You know that living in your tent isn't practical anymore."

Johnny Gorman had located the tattered tent, half buried in snow, that morning.

"Because of—?"

"The weather, of course."

"I thought you might mean my—." He gestured toward his feet. The burning was fading, although ugly blistering had erupted and he still had little or no feeling in and around several toes.

"Your health and the weather aren't unrelated, are they? Besides, you've known from the first day that the nights would eventually get bitterly cold."

"I've managed to stay warm enough so far."

"In view of what happened yesterday, that isn't a serious response. The days almost always warm to above freezing, even in the middle of winter, but with very little cloud cover the nights can be perilous. And when it *does* snow—"

"Yes, I know."

The curt response led Julia to raise an eyebrow. "And I assume you've realized by now that you aren't going to find in the canyon or mountains whatever you came here looking for."

So, Owen thought—deflated by his circumstances, and feeling more than a little sorry for himself—I guess she's finally had enough of me.

"Did you intend to return to the Wetherills?"

"No," Owen said. He'd overstayed his welcome at Chaco Canyon, too. Not that Richard or Marietta had said anything, but Bill Finn, one of their hands, had begun goading him, asking if he intended to hang around until he could marry into the family; Elizabeth, the elder daughter, was nine years old. "I mean, I had no plans to go back to Chaco Canyon, except to pay my respects at some point. Beyond that . . ."

"Then to Leominster? To your friends?"

He shook his head. "Leominster's the one place I can't go." He would let her draw her own conclusions about that.

"You've mentioned the hospital where you received such fine care."

"Mary Hitchcock Memorial."

"Would you want to be nearby?"

"I've considered it, of course. But . . ."

"But what?"

"If that's what I wanted, I wouldn't be out here, would I?"

"No, I suppose you wouldn't."

He knew he sounded defensive and that she deserved a better answer. "I won't spend my life scheduled around a series of consultations and examinations and tests. I'm probably already in some obscure medical journal, Patient A or B or Z in a series of case histories."

"I take it that returning to Ashuelot is out of the question?"

"To my father's farm?" He thought, but wouldn't say, that he'd have to be at death's door. "I could, of course," but he knew that his tone gave him away.

"I understand—believe me, I do," Julia said quietly.

He couldn't leave it at that, letting her think that he had no plan whatsoever. "I've been considering New York. I'd like to see the Anasazi collections at the Museum of Natural History. I think I could spend considerable time there. Richard would provide letters of introduction to the Hyde Expedition people and others that he guided through Mesa Verde and Chaco and Grand Gulch in Utah."

"That sounds like something worth looking into," Julia said, sounding encouraging. "And you could get excellent care in New York whenever you need it."

"Yes, that also occurred to me." As did the expense, but he wasn't about to discuss his financial situation.

"But you hadn't definitely settled on New York?" Julia said.

"Well, I hadn't," Owen said, "but maybe I just did."

* * *

At bedtime, Pete accompanied Owen on a final trip to the privy. This time Owen wore a jacket; he could see his breath materializing in the much colder night air.

"So," Pete said, "I guess you've joined the Many Springs Social Club." There was alcohol on his breath; he'd been doing more than developing his plates in the storeroom. "I'm a charter member."

Owen's grip on Pete's arm was lighter than it had been earlier in the day. Apart from the occasional twinge, his left foot seemed fine, but much of the right felt like it was asleep, or half sleep, leaving him unsteady.

"Julia said you were taking pictures of the snow melt today."

Pete laughed loudly and elbowed Owen. "And that strikes you as peculiar?"

"I suppose it does."

Pete stumbled but caught himself by grabbing Owen's arm. It occurred to Owen that he was assisting Pete as much as Pete was assisting him.

"Business considerations aside," Pete said, "it would suit me just fine if I never saw another face through a camera."

They took turns in the privy.

Heading back to Julia's, Owen asked, "So who else is a member of the Many Springs Social Club?"

"Whoever shows up. Harry Whitaker. Tóya, unfortunately. Yazzie, although most evenings he's usually working on this or that at his little folding table by the bookcases, mending tack, making Navajo belts that he sells. Alberto Rodriguez, when he's on his way to or from his brother's place in Aztec. Sometimes another trader or a salesman. Used to be one of the Wetherill brothers—but never Richard—would stop by, although not since Win sold his interest in Two Grey Hills and Al went to work for the Post Office in Gallup, and John and his wife moved up to Kayenta."

"The Gormans?"

"Rarely. They'd rather head home to their kiddies. Besides, they pretty much keep their mouths shut when we get going about this or that—they don't appreciate the art of repartee. But now we have you."

"I doubt I'll be here long enough to become a regular."

Pete shrugged. "When you're here, you're here. That's all there is to it."

"No membership fee?" Owen asked.

"Nah. No secret handshake either. But we do have a loyalty oath."

"To?"

"Julia," Pete answered. "To Julia."

SHE COULDN'T FALL ASLEEP. Bouts of insomnia had been frequent companions since her mother's death, coming and going as they wished. Their arrival no longer surprised her. She rose and, wrapping herself in a blanket, returned to her parlor and sat in the dark close to the box stove, which still radiated.

She should have sent Owen in the wagon to Tohatchi. He wasn't her responsibility. Harry Whitaker would have treated him by now, probably given him a place to sleep for a day or two while waiting to see what developed from the frostbite. In the frozen predawn she'd found Owen's field journals, undamaged. Later, Johnny Gorman had gathered his surveying equipment as well as his tent and most of his clothing. She could have packed it all up for him and sent it on to Harry's, and been done. Owen wouldn't have returned.

Safety. She kept returning to their afternoon conversation, when he'd asked her if she felt safe here, being alone, without a man's protection. He'd meant, of course, a white man's protection. Didn't he realize? Maybe he hadn't been around long enough.

She herself had been oblivious for almost a year, until August 1899 and a confrontation over a pawned saddle, on a day when Will had gone to Gallup.

That August day in the trading post the argument with a customer had been going on for some time when, from the corner of her eye, she saw Clement Yazzie open the door and enter, and she couldn't deny the relief she felt. A saddle sat on the pawn counter, which separated Julia from a square-faced man with a mouthful of rotting teeth.

"I've cleared your account, Mr. Nalwood," Julia said. "Please take your saddle and go."

Nalwood leaned over the counter. "*Ani'įįhii,*" thief, he called her, and added, continuing in Navajo, "You think you can cheat the People, but we're too smart for you." He picked up the saddle, threw a contemptuous glance toward Yazzie, who was leaning against the door frame with his arms folded, and stalked out.

"If you don't mind my saying so," Julia said, brushing loose strands of damp hair back from her face, the tips of her fingers feeling the film of moisture on her cheeks, "you were supposed to be working this morning."

Yazzie, without speaking, walked over to the counter and picked up the pawn ticket that lay there. "Did you get your money back?" he asked, looking at the ticket.

"No, I didn't get my money," Julia said hotly. "We're better off without him as a customer. He's been a problem ever since he first set foot in here."

Yazzie lay down the pawn ticket and headed for the door.

"Mr. Yazzie!" Julia called after him. "Please, let it be!"

Yazzie left. Julia put her head down on her crossed arms. She heard nothing from outside. Several minutes later Yazzie, carrying the saddle, strode in. He dropped the saddle on the floor in front of the counter. Recoiling from the *thump*, Julia straightened up.

"What did you say to him?" she asked.

"It doesn't matter."

"What do you mean? How could it *not* matter?"

He dipped his head. "There's your saddle."

"It's *his* saddle."

"It *was* his saddle. Now it's yours."

"Did I ask you to do anything? The matter was settled."

"No, it wasn't. Now it is."

"It *was* settled. *I* settled it." She hit the glass counter with her palm.

"He made an agreement when he pawned the saddle. He didn't keep it."

"I settled it when I gave him his saddle back."

"You can't do that."

"I can't do what?"

He placed his hands on the edge of the counter and leaned forward. Julia instinctively took a step back.

"If you want to let people run up accounts that they can never repay, it's your business. Yours and your husband's. But this is different. When Nalwood pawned the saddle, he accepted the terms. You gave him store credit. And cash. And now he comes back and says you cheated him. He wants the saddle but won't pay what he owes. Maybe he plans to ride away from here and brag to his relatives or friends about how he got the better of you. Before too long others would try, too. He might even come back himself and try a little harder to get something else he thinks he deserves."

"You don't even know him."

"No." He placed a blunt finger on the pawn ticket. "But you gave him too much for the saddle to begin with. That's probably what gave him the idea to try his luck. Never give anyone more than he expects to get. Better to give him less."

"This is *my* business, not yours, Mr. Yazzie, and you're telling me what I can and can't do? I suppose you think I should thank you."

He removed his hands from the counter and straightened up. "Thank me or don't, it doesn't matter."

"You *threatened* him! Am I right?"

"Don't open the store unless you have a man here."

"I've been told that before. Did you forget, *you* were supposed to be here."

"I was away."

"And how can I run a business if we don't keep regular hours? It's Saturday. We're open until one o'clock." The Gormans, in addition to Will, were absent, attending a church celebration in Tohatchi.

"Don't open the store unless you have a man here," he repeated without any change of tone.

"Are you here now, or are you leaving again, just so I know?" Julia folded her arms.

"I'm here." He turned from the counter and went outside.

The next day, Sunday morning, from far down the rutted trail Julia could hear the echoing *chunk, chunk,* so she wasn't surprised when she found Clement Yazzie outside his hogan splitting pinyon. Johanna was hanging wash on a rope clothesline that ran between two forked posts, one beside the hogan and the other planted next to the horse shelter. Yazzie's horses were standing in the corral beside the water trough. In the shade of the willow that had overhung Yazzie's mother's makeshift summer hogan, now gone, were half a dozen sheep. As she approached closer, one of Yazzie's two sheep dogs rose and directed its attention to her, though it made no sound.

Johanna had stopped hanging the wash; three shirts, a dress, and a pair of pants moved with the breeze. Yazzie, however, continued to focus on the task before him.

"Yá'át'ééh," Julia said.

"Aoo', yá'át'ééh," he replied.

Chunk.

'Atsá and Níyol didn't appear to be around, which was just as well. She always enjoyed seeing them, but this was not a social call.

"You have a beautiful view here," Julia said, looking back down the trail.

Chunk.

Why was she always on the defensive with this man? She was trying to be polite, to ease her way by offering a mundane compliment, and he'd made her feel like a dolt once again. Enough, damn him. "You don't like small talk, do you?"

He kept chopping. Beads of sweat stood out on his forehead, and the exertion had stained his blue shirt, front and back. He picked up another piece of wood, a section of thick limb, and set it into the V-shaped notch he'd carved into the stump. With one arm he brought the flat end of the maul down on the round limb, steadying it for the splitter blade.

"How is that different from other talk?" he asked.

"I would appreciate it if you would stop what you are doing and look at me."

"This isn't your trading post," he said. With a compact stroke he split the limb in half. Then he turned to her and rested the iron head of the maul on the ground.

"I'm well aware of where I am. I was asking you for a little courtesy." Julia wasn't sure if Johanna could understand what they were saying, but she was certainly taking her time hanging up the wash. "I'm here on a business matter."

"Where's your husband?"

Oh, he certainly knew how to annoy her! Why did he always ask her that? "I don't need my husband's presence or his permission to discuss business with you or anyone else. You should know that by now."

Yazzie studied her, showing no emotion whatsoever. With a forefinger he wiped the sweat from his brow.

"I understand," she continued, "that in addition to working for us, you have other responsibilities that require your attention. And that's fine. We have no problem with that." Well, she thought, at least *I* don't. "But you must let us know in advance when you will be unable to work."

"This is Sunday, isn't it?"

"Yes."

"So it's not a work day."

"No. I didn't mean today." He knew very well what she meant; infuriating, he was absolutely infuriating! "I mean other days, when we're expecting you and you don't show up."

He rocked the handle of the maul back and forth.

"We need to be able to rely on you."

Yazzie turned and called, "Jóhonaá." Speaking in Navajo, he asked his sister to bring them water from the pump. She left her laundry basket, now nearly empty.

"There's shade under the tree." He turned away.

Julia hesitated but then followed him to the willow. He motioned for her to sit down on an upturned crate, and then he sat down on the ground facing her, with his legs crossed. Johanna, having filled a pitcher, brought it to the tree along with two metal cups. She filled one and handed it to Julia and then did the same for her brother, who drained his at once. Then Johanna, with Julia's thanks unacknowledged—having accommodated herself to Johanna's ways during the past months, Julia took no offense—returned to hanging the wash.

"I agree," Yazzie said.

"You agree?"

"I'll tell you when I need to be away."

"Very good," Julia said. "Then we have an understanding."

"Maybe."

Maybe? With Clement Yazzie, nothing was ever settled, not completely. *Maybe.* Something was always left dangling, needing clarification, but he never offered it.

He emptied his cup a second time and set it on the ground between them. Julia held out her empty cup and he took it and refilled it for her from the pitcher. His damp black hair gleamed in a scattering of light from between the leafed-out branches.

"Yesterday, with the saddle, what would you have done if Mr. Nalwood had resisted?" Julia asked.

"He did resist."

"I meant with violence."

"That depends."

"On what?"

"On how far he took it."

"The saddle was *nothing* to you!" She tried to contain her irritation. "It was just a beat-up saddle! How far were you prepared to go?"

"What do you think?"

Johanna and her laundry basket were no longer in sight; she must have gone back into the hogan.

"It's common knowledge that you killed someone in a dispute of some sort." She'd said it, and she regretted it immediately. Saying it transmuted her anger into . . . not quite *fear*, but something akin. Disquiet. Discomposure. She raised the cup. Her hand was shaking.

"So that's your question. You want to know if I'd kill a man over a saddle that isn't even mine."

She looked up. "Suppose it *was* yours."

"You want to know the truth." It wasn't a question. He took out a corncob pipe and a small knife from his pants pocket, and began scraping the bowl. "A good thing to know." His eyes returning to hers, "Maybe what you heard is mostly rumors."

Something different showed in his face. Something he hadn't let her see before. His impenetrability had faded, unsustainable in the August heat, after the honest labor of arms and back and sweat, with the sun near its zenith. What she saw in his face was resignation.

"Then why not deny them?" she said quietly.

He shrugged with one shoulder. "Sometimes rumors are best left alone."

"Even when they tarnish your reputation?"

"They can be useful."

"I've never found that to be so." She drained the cup, stretched out her arm, steadier now, to return it to him. He accepted it and she then rose. "You don't owe me an explanation."

"I will say this much." Yazzie tapped the bowl of his pipe against the tree. The cold ash fell to the ground and with a finger he ground it into the reddish dirt. "Not so long ago Anglos, even Indian agents, preferred leaving some Navajo matters to the Navajos. Less trouble for everybody."

"I take it you're saying that I should follow their example and mind my own business."

He fished in his pocket for a small pouch of tobacco. She'd never seen him smoke. She waited for the scratch of the match against the tree bark, and then, nothing more having been said, she left.

Do you always feel safe here? Owen had asked, so she had turned the question around, but of course nothing was safe. Not the trodden path, certainly not untrodden paths. She'd sensed, however, since shortly after the altercation over the pawned saddle, that she was under Clement Yazzie's protection. He had every right to wish her ill, with her coming out here, to his country, his land, his home, knowing nothing, thinking she was entitled to . . . to what? To do as she wished? To disregard her own ignorance? But instead he'd placed her under his protection. At the time, she didn't know what to make of it. She couldn't point to anything specific. He acted no differently. He came and went as before. Nothing was said. She didn't even mention it, this sense that she had, to Will (certainly not to Will!), nor to anyone else. But as time passed, others knew. The Gormans—maybe they knew it before she did—though they, too, said nothing. At some point, Harry Whitaker knew, certainly. Tóya, of course—nothing got by Tóya. And Pete, whose comments about it were barbed but never spoken when anyone else could overhear.

In ten years there had never been a repetition of the pawned saddle incident; in ten years, no Navajo had ever threatened her in any way.

Now, sitting in the dark in her parlor—her poor excuse for a parlor, but everyone humored her—Julia returned her thoughts to Owen Rouse. He had a limited time left, and she feared that he didn't know what to do with it. He'd talked about going to New York City, but she knew that he hadn't thought it through. She tried picturing him in New York, studying the Anasazi relics in the museum and going home in the evening to . . . to what? To a room in a boarding house or a hotel for single men. Going home to no one. Until he ran out of money, and then he'd have no choice but to retreat to New Hampshire, to his father's farm.

She could ask if he wanted to stay here. For now. Until his feet healed. (She had no idea how long that would take. Harry should be able to tell her.) For now she could offer him protection from the elements, if not safety. And weeks-old Chicago newspapers to read, courtesy of her sister Penelope. And the latest popular magazines and books, also sent regularly by Penny. She could offer him her companionship, which wasn't nothing. And time. Time to prepare for his leaving.

CHAPTER FOUR: Owen (The Past)

1. Leaving

He was their second son, a sickly boy, baptized Robert Owen Rouse the day after his birth, April 9, 1885, when no one, not even his mother, believed he could survive. His father, a New Hampshire farmer all his life, was fifty-three. His mother, forty-six, was a farm wife with her chickens and taciturn husband and sewing circle and little else. They had long ago given up any hope of conceiving a second son to replace their first, Robert Oliver Rouse, born 1855, died 1875, crushed under tons of rock during the final stages of digging the longest railroad tunnel in North America, four and three-quarter miles through the mountains of northwestern Massachusetts.

The Rouses were courting bad luck, some of the local gossips said, by naming an unexpected second son after the deceased first-born, but then, the gossips figured, it made no difference since the already doomed newborn, six weeks premature by the doctor's estimate, couldn't possibly survive.

But he did, and six weeks later his mother, as if trying to fend off the fates, insisted that they call him by his middle name, Owen, a decision with which her husband concurred since no one could replace the extinguished light of Robert Oliver, who had left the farm in order to earn the wages needed to build the Rouse & Son Dairy they had jointly envisaged. The dairy had never come to pass.

The Rouse farm, originally over 120 acres, going back three generations in the family, had been reduced by economic vagaries and prior profligacy to 50: 25 hilly acres of hardwoods—oak, maple, poplar, sycamore, hickory; 10 almost useless acres of rocky terrain suited only for chickens and goats; and 15 acres of fertile bottomland along the south bank of the Ashuelot River. The Rouses lived off those 15 productive acres—10 in potatoes, 5 in hay for the animals—and sales of maple syrup and cut timber. (Rouse, once flush with youthful ambition, had tried to cut the forest line back, had worked gnarly stumps out of the ground in a futile effort to create another tillable acre, but the land defeated him; no matter how many boulders he and his team of oxen rolled out of the ground, more migrated upward from the pit of the earth and then lay in wait to ruin the blade of the plow come the next spring.)

When fellow members of the local Grange ribbed him about being a potato farmer, Rouse would respond that he'd rather grow potatoes than be a potato head, a poorly veiled reference to his nearest neighbor, Harmon Handke, with his oddly shaped cranium and pox-scarred skin. The area's most prosperous landowner, Handke had long coveted Rouse's 15 fertile acres, owning as he did the adjoining land on both east and west. Moreover, Handke and Rouse had nearly come to blows when Rouse, following the invasion of the Colorado potato beetle into the Northeast, began applying Paris green to save his plantings. As a consequence, Handke claimed, runoff from Rouse's farm was periodically poisoning the river with arsenic, causing fish kills that turned the river bank of his downstream property into a fetid dump. Handke offered to buy Rouse out, and when Rouse refused, took him to court over the arsenic and won. To pay the settlement, Rouse had to bring in a logging company, which clear-cut ten acres of his timber. That was when Robert Oliver, called Robbie, surveying the trees as they fell to the saws, convinced his father that they should try dairying on the newly opened land—cows could graze around the stumps as the bare ground filled in with low growth—and then went to work on the Hoosac Tunnel to earn the necessary capital.

During a quarter of a century of blasting and digging and shoring, 193 men died completing the infamous railroad tunnel—the Bloody Pit, the workers called it. Robert had joined the list when a premature nitroglycerine detonation brought 50 tons of rock down on him.

Oliver Rouse irrationally blamed Harmon Handke for Robbie's death. Everyone, including Handke, knew this. Handke, for his part, offered his sincere condolences in a carefully worded sympathy note but wisely stayed away from the committal service. Six months later, again in writing, Handke made Rouse another offer for the land, stating that should Rouse ever decide to sell, he would pay double the farm's assessed value and permit Rouse, if he wished, to retain title to the acre surrounding his home and barn and sheds until both Rouse and Mrs. Rouse passed. Rouse wrote his succinct reply on the inside of a torn Paris green sack.

This had all happened well before Robert Owen Rouse's unexpected arrival—so unexpected that for several months his mother had been convinced that a cancer was growing in her womb.

During the interval between Robert Oliver's death and Robert Owen's birth, Harmon Handke had died of apoplexy, which brought no joy to Owen's father because Handke's heir, Howard Handke, was a worse son of a bitch. There were no relations between the two families beyond what transpired at the local school, where Howard's twin daughters were classmates of Owen's. Most of the time the girls were more interested in goading each other than in bothering Owen, which suited him just fine: by the time all three reached the sixth grade, the twins were identically homely, pampered, and as stupid as the stumps that still littered the Rouse farm.

Owen, always a wan child, spent half of each winter home in bed, asthmatic, layered under a mustard plaster and wool blankets. He suffered allergies to tree pollen in the spring and then to hay and ragweed in the summer; the allergies disappeared in the autumn after the first hard frost, only to be replaced by a hacking cough aggravated, in the confined common spaces of their small house, by the unavoidable haze of wood smoke. And then there were the typical childhood illnesses. Nothing readily communicable from other children passed him by; his scrawny frame played host to the measles, German measles, chicken pox, mumps, all on top of the annual colds and less-frequent influenzas. Worst of all, one year scarlatina laid him up for the better part of a winter and spring.

From a very early age Owen recognized that he was a great disappointment to his father, who saw the thin bones of a weakling's arms where robust muscles suited to hard work should have been pinned. Owen could barely swing an ax forcefully enough to cut down a middling hickory, although years of practice made him adept at splitting wood for sugaring: he learned that accuracy stood him in better stead than brute force and that the secret was to simply guide the weight of the head to the target. Of course he could haul water for his mother, but he was most useful shoveling out barn stalls or, in the spring, bending beside his mother, the two of them planting quartered seed potatoes—Early Rose, Brown Beauty, Peerless, Dakota Red—in methodical formation, row after plowed row, and then, day after day, through the height of the annual infestation, plucking potato beetles off the leaves of the rapidly growing plants, hour after hour, up and down the rows. His father wouldn't let him near the Paris green, which Rouse continued to use against the beetles, although more judiciously than before the lawsuit, or the Bordeaux mixture—copper sulfate, slaked lime, and water—which he sprayed repeatedly to ward off powdery mildew and late blight. Owen never knew if his father refused to let him handle the poisons from concern for his son's health or distrust of his abilities. Some days even the fairness of Owen's flyaway hair and the swath of freckles that burst onto his cheeks each summer seemed to annoy his father.

On top of that, Owen feared horses, beyond reason or understanding, even before, when he was seven, one of the matched pair of Belgian plow horses, spooked by a falling branch while being harnessed, knocked him to the ground and stepped square on his chest. Owen lay in the mud, his lungs frozen, watching the thick chestnut legs repeatedly miss him by inches while his father, cursing, yanked at the traces. Afterward, everyone agreed that the mud of the barnyard, dispersing the force of the hoof, had saved his chest from being crushed. The ferocious bruise took weeks to fade from black to a mottled green and blue, to a brownish yellow. After that, when forced to, Owen still rode—he'd learned, under duress, at age five despite his infantile fear—but he knew that, try as he might to contain his anxiety, the animal under him could sense it through the bit and the saddle and wanted him off. Several times in his remaining years on the farm he lost control of his mount; twice he was bucked off, and once a stallion panicked and took off at a gallop that ended at the bank of the melt-swollen river.

During one harvest Owen asked his father why they just didn't leave some of the potatoes in the ground for the next year.

"They'd freeze and then rot," his father said. "Don't you even know that?" He shook his head in disgust.

"Isn't there *something* you could grow that would just come up again?" Owen asked.

"There's rhubarb, but it grows like a weed, so there's no market. A farmer needs to make a profit. You can't survive on rhubarb, growing it or eating it."

"I like rhubarb," Owen mumbled.

Oliver Rouse was stern, uneducated, undemonstrative, but he wasn't stupid when it came to his farming. Through the Grange he kept abreast of the latest developments and planted only cultivars developed in New England, most of them by Albert Bresee over in Hubbardton, Vermont—now *there* was a man, Rouse said, who knew the climate and the soils of the region as well as anyone. Bresee's work could be relied on, and as proof Rouse grew the best potatoes in southwestern New Hampshire. (He'd have nothing to do with older varieties propagated elsewhere. He thought the Irish had to be the thickest farmers in the civilized world, relying on watery, knobby, blight-prone lumpers—the world's most vile potato, as far as he was concerned, lacking in color, shape, size, and every other conceivable marketable value. Thus the nickname, Lumpy, he bestowed on the Handkes, father and then son.) Nevertheless, it was a constant struggle to make a decent living off ten acres of potatoes, at the going price of fifty cents a bushel. In a very good year, one when the beetles and the fungus didn't threaten to wipe him out, Rouse's ten acres yielded about three thousand bushels. But when you subtracted what had to be put aside for seed stock, and when you accounted for the cost of seasonal labor and other expenses, the Rouses never seemed to have any money to spare, even with off-season earnings from maple syrup and the small number of trees Rouse cut and sold each year.

Although both Mr. and Mrs. Rouse were literate, in those days only two books could be found in their home, a Bible that had arrived with Owen's mother, and a collected works of Shakespeare. Owen never saw his father open either, while his mother limited herself to the Bible. On occasion she haltingly read passages to him from Genesis, Exodus, Deuteronomy, Ecclesiastes, Job, Matthew, Mark, Luke, John, her blunt forefinger moving from word to word across the page. Her poor skills led, however, to a remarkable development: by the age of five Owen, his eyes running just ahead of her finger, was able to recognize many words before she spoke them, and by the time he entered school, he could read better than she. He began correcting her when she stumbled, which never led to any recrimination sharper than a raised eyebrow and the sobriquet "Mr. Smarty," which was often followed by either "I do believe you're right, Owen," or, more rarely, "I do believe you're mistaken"—in which case they'd talk over the suspect word or phrase until they reached agreement. His father, from the depths of the living room's only armchair, where he read and reread newspapers and farm bulletins in the evening, never commented on these discussions except to pronounce, "I'll give you what-for if you don't show Mother some respect."

Owen preferred the Shakespeare—or at least the illustrations: the bloody dagger appearing before Macbeth's horrified eyes, Hamlet addressing Yorick's skull in the graveyard, Richard III pleading for a horse on the battlefield of Bosworth; Henry V addressing his outnumbered forces at Agincourt; Prospero taming the monstrous Caliban, with Miranda cowering behind her father; Julius Caesar dying under the knives of Brutus and the other conspirators . . .

When he first discovered the Shakespeare—he must have been seven or eight—he was troubled by the prospect that these were graven images, which the Bible warned about, but since his parents didn't take the book from him, instead warning him only that he had to be very careful so as not to rip the pages as he turned them, he soon forgot his concern. Owen asked his parents one evening where they'd acquired the Shakespeare, but neither knew; its presence on a shelf in the living room predated his father's memory of it. (Owen couldn't imagine his father ever spending good money on a book.) Where it came from therefore remained an unsolved mystery.

At school, Owen took to his lessons immediately. The biggest surprise of his first days was that not everything between hard covers was composed in Shakespearean verse or biblical prose, and when he asked his teacher about it she patted him on the head and said that while she couldn't speak for Mr. Shakespeare, it was only proper that God's Word should be exalted.

He liked the structure of the school day and even of the schoolroom itself: the neat rows of iron-legged desks, each with its inkwell and tray for pens and pencils; the blackboard in front, behind the teacher's massive desk, and the precisely swirling chalky letters of her Spenserian Script; the logical distribution of the pupils, youngest in the front, oldest in the rear. And best of all, he was quickly identified as a bright pupil, one who excelled at every subject. From then on he instinctively knew that his mother would defend him if his father ever tried to discourage him from his studies. But his father never did; he saw at least a marginal value in a utilitarian education. When his health permitted, Owen performed his daily chores, split wood, kept the sap boiling in the late winter, participated in the spring planting and the fall harvest, and undertook as best he could whatever tasks his father assigned him during school vacations, and in return his father allowed him his studies.

For Owen's eleventh birthday his mother somehow managed to lay hands on a used copy of Sir Robert Stawell Ball's hefty *The Story of the Heavens*. His father took great delight in pointing out to Owen that the book was "over his head," which mainly encouraged Owen to try even harder to understand the dense prose. Fortunately, Sir Robert had included dozens of plates and illustrations, because Owen, at first disappointed and then bored, did in fact find much of the book incomprehensible. He spent most of his time with Chapter XVIII, "The Starry Heavens," which, with its simple illustrations of the constellations and directions for locating them, gave a human structure to the previously chaotic night sky. From there, he learned the principal stars and their movements so thoroughly that, a dozen years later, he could still draw a celestial map, in any season, from memory.

The elder Rouse was a man of opaque silences. When he'd finished perusing the newspaper or the seed catalogs, which he poured over endlessly in the winter months, he'd sit in his chair without speaking for hour after hour, smoking his pipe, studying the calluses on his rough hands. What did he think about? Owen wondered. He did think—he *did* think, didn't he? You couldn't shut down your brain to the elemental level of the beasts in the barnyard, could you? Owen couldn't imagine, as he grew older, that kind of . . . emptiness. Except when he imagined his own life indefinitely tethered to this vile rectangle of farm and woods, with no prospects except tedium season after season, repeated year after year. Sometimes he'd feel a brush of compassion for his father as well as a brute sadness for his mother—brute and brutal, because he could do nothing to alter her life, bounded like stone-walled property.

In 1902, age seventeen, Owen won a scholarship to the New Hampshire College of Agriculture and the Mechanic Arts in Durham. After twenty-five years of sharing a campus with Dartmouth College in Hanover, in 1893 the Ag College had moved to Durham, near Portsmouth and the Atlantic Ocean, which Owen had never seen before. The new campus was scarcely more than a hundred miles east and a little bit north from home, but the only sensible way to get there, given the hopeless inadequacy of New Hampshire's east-west roads, was to catch the Boston & Maine's western line at Greenfield, Massachusetts, and make the necessary connections to Durham.

Time amplified the miles traveled, and the first journey east proved such a shock to his system that Owen found himself, within days of his arrival, relegated to his bed and forcing his sodden lungs to breathe. During his week of bed rest he read through all of his basic texts for the Fall Term, an opportunity that, despite his being confined by white sheets and gray wool blankets, expanded his known world so profoundly that he knew he'd never return to the godforsaken farm on the Ashuelot. He regretted his separation from his mother—not for his sake, but for hers, the diminishment he knew it meant for her life—but even at seventeen he knew he couldn't live under his father's cold yoke again.

Not that he'd inherited nothing from Oliver Rouse. He hadn't inherited stature or physical stamina or temperament, but instead a determination to master his world. His father relied on animal force; Owen, using his brain, planned to begin by learning more than his father had the capacity even to imagine, and then he intended to dig much deeper, below the top-soil and roots, all the way to the bedrock, using the core principles of science.

As soon as he was up and about again, he not only caught up with his class exercises, but also began his part-time job in the greenhouses. His Grange scholarship covered the tuition of $60 per year but not his other expenses: $20 in fees, $30 for a shared room, $3 a week for board, extra dollars for books and supplies . . . It all added up to at least an additional $130, so he considered himself fortunate to get the greenhouse job, which had the additional benefit that he wouldn't have to work outside during Winter Term. As for his schedule of mandatory Fall Term freshman courses, he suffered through Rhetoric and German; tolerated Algebra, which consti-tuted little more than a review of what he'd already learned in school; en-joyed Inorganic Chemistry; stumbled through Woodworking; and took a fancy to Mechanical and Industrial Drawing—he learned that he had a good eye for free-hand drawing as well as a brain that moved easily between iso-metric illustrations and orthographic projections.

He got along well enough with his roommate, a mousey fellow named Michael Dooley who intended to pursue electrical engineering and whose most cherished possessions were his slide rule, which Owen had to promise never to touch, and a penny whistle. Dooley, it turned out, was proficient at both instruments, and when he wasn't engrossed in calculations, spent much of his time playing jigs, reels, sea shanties, and the odd lullaby. Fortunately, when not in class or in the greenhouse, Owen preferred to work in the li-brary, surrounded for the first time in his life by books, whereas Dooley stayed shut in their room on the top floor of the three-story Schoonmaker House on Main Street. It worked out well enough. Dooley even offered Owen free lessons on the whistle, but Owen showed little interest and, after learning a handful of simple melodies, gave it up. Neither made many friends—in Dooley's case because he was inept at casual conversation. Although Owen felt most comfortable on the periphery of social gatherings, he did strike up friendships with a few of the women who also preferred the library and who were pursuing the General Course of study, intending to become teachers of standing, and even principals, in their home communities. (Most of the women, primarily for reasons financial or matrimonial, never graduated, but then, neither did the majority of men.) In pursuit of one young lady he even joined a college chorus—he was a decent but untrained tenor—during his sophomore year, but lost out to a bass.

In general, Owen didn't venture far from Durham, a pleasant enough community, except for occasional forays into Portsmouth. Each spring, however, he and various acquaintances would sometimes cross over to Kittery Point in Maine; once, they ventured down the coast to Hampton Beach for a dip in the ocean. Owen wasn't much of a swimmer—keeping afloat in a calm lake presented a challenge—and when the first frigid wave swept him off his feet, he decided to keep to the shore.

It was during the spring of his freshman year that Owen attracted the attention of the imperious Francis Burrell, professor of Mathematics and Geology. Professor Burr, as he was called behind his back, never accepted excuses for late or incompetent work, and he rarely handed out A's. In the Spring Term the college required all freshman ag majors to take Burrell's course in Surveying, which most of Owen's classmates regarded as an ordeal. Owen, however, having never been challenged by trigonometry, approached the course with a more open mind and quickly found the field work, employing transit, plane-table, compass, and level, a relief from the lecture hall.

After the second examination of the term, Burrell called Owen into his office. Having received a perfect score on the first test, Owen was confident that he'd done well on the second, so he was more curious than concerned. Professor Burrell, well over six feet tall, with a triangular face that narrowed from a wide forehead and somewhat bulging eyes to a thin mouth and dimpled, pointed chin, proceeded to lecture him about the need for precision and the demerits of sloppiness, after which he tossed Owen's exam back to him from the far side of his heavy oak desk. The grade was a 99.

"Find your error, Mr. Rouse," the professor growled.

There were no corrections marked on the several pages, and Owen spent ten uncomfortable minutes pouring over each problem and his solution before he spotted the mistake. "I believe this is it," he said, pointing to an answer on the third page. He'd carelessly used a single prime symbol instead of a double prime to indicate the arcseconds in a calculation.

"I daresay that's an error you won't make again," Burrell said, wrinkling his brow.

That forehead was a formidable thing to contemplate, given the widely acknowledged brain power that lay behind the bone. Francis Burrell had studied Mathematics at Harvard before becoming interested in Geology. He'd traveled widely across North American, initially, in the late 1860s and early 1870s, as a member of Clarence King's famous Geological Exploration of the Fortieth Parallel, from Sacramento to Cheyenne, and later at the head of smaller geological and mapping expeditions into northern Quebec, the Canadian Rockies, and Mexico's Copper Canyon. Now in his early sixties and somewhat hobbled by an arthritic hip, he'd left Dartmouth when the Durham campus opened in 1893.

He didn't appear to care what anyone thought of him, which was partly what appealed to Owen—that and his flamboyant intelligence, his ability to command the classroom, limping back and forth, rapping the blackboard with his cane to draw attention to a point or to startle the inattentive, and constructing each lecture toward a denouement that brought the key principles home, just as the best storytellers did. In personal demeanor he was more Nathaniel Hawthorne than Washington Irving (Owen's favorite American writer). In philosophy he stood with Locke and not Kant. In politics he was a Roosevelt man through and through, a firm believer in American commerce and carrying the big stick while also busting the trusts and protecting America's natural heritage from corrupt exploitation—"The only thing worse than a man who eats and defecates in the same place is a man who defecates where other people eat," he once put it to Owen. His heroes, in addition to the president, were Clarence King, Ida Tarbell, and—someone Owen had never even heard of—Ida B. Wells. Burrell favored crusaders.

No one wanted to fall into Professor Burr's disfavor. Sometimes he'd yell out a "sonny-boy" to put a self-satisfied upperclassman in his place—a position that was at least three rungs down the ladder from where the professor's well-heeled shoes rested—but his most favored epithets were "flatlander," which he applied indiscriminately in the classroom as a label for those he considered dolts or slackers, and "farmerette"—the ultimate insult—employed against both students and, somewhat more judiciously, fellow faculty members whom he regarded as having no practical experience of the world. He despised dilettantes and aesthetes, which was why, he claimed, that he'd left Dartmouth and thrown in his lot with the "hoi polloi" of the New Hampshire College of Agriculture and the Mechanic Arts.

Professor Burrell began inviting Owen to join what he called his "little talks," gatherings of half a dozen or so favored students, all of them male and all but Owen upperclassmen. More often than not, announcement of an upcoming little talk would send Owen scurrying to the library so that he wouldn't appear as ignorant as he felt. The subject under discussion could be anything—the Powell expedition down the Green and Colorado rivers in

1869, the volcanic origins and topography of the Hawaiian Islands, the unearthing of partial *Tyrannosaurus rex* skeletons in Wyoming and Montana, the discovery by the Wetherill brothers of cliff ruins in the Southwest, the prospects for having at any foreseeable time a complete geological map of North America to rival William Smith's 1815 map of England. Of course Owen had never heard of either the Wetherills or William Smith, but both subjects intrigued him. Smith, the son of a blacksmith, made his invaluable discoveries about geographic strata while working as a surveyor but didn't achieve fame for his 1815 map until recognized by the Geological Society of London more than a decade later, after he'd endured a stint in debtor's prison. The Wetherills, living in Mancos, Colorado, in 1888, chanced upon Cliff Palace, the largest and most famous of the ruins at Mesa Verde, while searching for stray cattle, and Richard Wetherill, in particular, later became a central figure in the Hyde Exploring Expeditions in Utah and New Mexico Territory, toward the end of the 1890s.

What Owen found most intriguing about the Wetherill discoveries was the bare fact that such ruins even existed. He'd never given much thought to how long Indian tribes had inhabited North America. In the East, there were virtually no artifacts predating Columbus because they'd decayed in the wet climate. Furthermore, no one he'd had regular contact with except his mother's Presbyterian minister, who contended that the Indians were a lost tribe of Israel, had ever expressed much interest regarding the origins of the native Penacook or Abenaki, most of whom had been wiped out by disease or warfare or had fled north, to Quebec. But out in the Southwest, the dry climate had helped preserve Anasazi dwellings and artifacts—clothing, hunting implements, pottery, food stores, and even mummified bodies that might date back a thousand years or more.

Owen didn't take a second course with Francis Burrell until the beginning of his senior year, when elementary Geology was required for all Agriculture majors, but by then he was so well schooled in the subject that he could have taught the class, especially after spending the preceding summer assisting Burrell with research for a new elective, Historical Geology, which brought together the principles of geology and evolutionary theory. Owen had long since given up any interest in farming. The Agricultural major required him to take Agronomy, Animal Husbandry, Dairying, and Horticulture, but he enrolled in as few of these courses as he could get away with. There were also obligatory courses in Physics, American History, and Military Science, but whenever possible he filled out his schedule with what Burrell considered useful electives, including Architectural Drawing, and Military Map-Reading and Sketching. Burrell, without being asked, proposed Owen's senior thesis, "The Application of Surveying and Geological Methodologies in the Dating of Ancient Ruins."

By then, Owen knew what he wanted to do: he wanted to work for the United States Geological Survey, which had been established in 1879 under Clarence King to survey and classify public lands and explore the country's geology and its mineral resources. It struck him as an ideal occupation, one that would combine his expertise in surveying with his knowledge of geology, and since most of the virgin land under study was in the West, he might also be able to pursue his nascent interest in the Anasazi. But Professor Burrell put a damper on his scheme: "No one should land a government job who hasn't actually worked for a living," he told Owen. "Get out there with the hoi polloi. Engage in commerce. Participate in society. Get yourself some practical experience."

"Doing what?" Owen asked. They were conversing in Burrell's office.

"It doesn't matter. Everything you know is up there," he said, pointing to Owen's skull. "You need to get it into these." He held up both hands and wiggled his fingers. "Work for a couple of years. After that . . . There's a century's worth of work to do out West, mapping down to the half-section and quarter-section and eventually the quarter-quarter section, and you might be good at it. You've got the eye and the brain and a little training. But first, go get yourself some experience. When the time comes, I'll find you a job with the USGS. I know the right people. If your circumstances haven't changed."

"My circumstances?"

"Maybe you'll decide you like making more money than a government job offers. Maybe you'll be married, with a child on the way. Maybe your wife will object to moving all over creation. These things happen. Youthful ambition surrenders to the practicalities."

"I don't know what I can say to that," Owen had mumbled.

"Take my advice or don't." Burrell was puffing on a stogie. "I never take offense where none is intended."

Owen knew very well that this was blatantly untrue, but he held his tongue.

"Are you going home for Christmas?" the professor asked.

"Yes."

"Ask your folks what they think."

Owen bridled at that. "I'm twenty."

"I'm aware of your age, Mr. Rouse. Ask them anyway."

"My parents are probably the last people I'd take career advice from. My mother still thinks I'm going back to that wretched farm after commencement."

"Well, maybe it's time to disabuse her."

"Believe me, I've tried." His mother's health was in decline, and that didn't make his situation any easier. His father, now in his seventies, was also slowing down, as his mother frequently reminded Owen in the monthly letters she wrote in an increasingly shaky hand. Owen had an obligation to provide the necessary relief, she insisted. After all, the land would be his one day, and he needed to earn his inheritance. His "inheritance." As he saw it, his inheritance was abuse, drudgery, and filth. The only obligation Owen felt was to her, and if not for that, he'd never go near Ashuelot again.

WHEN HE ARRIVED HOME on Christmas Eve, he saw immediately how she'd failed since his last visit, six months ago. She was sleeping in her rocking chair, her jaw slack, her chin almost touching her chest. He pulled up a chair but he let her be. His despondency consumed him, but he didn't weep. What he felt was impotent anger. How had her life come down to this . . . this shell? Fortune had never seen fit to give her anything of value.

Without warning, she choked on her saliva and woke with a start, coughing, turning red, struggling to clear her airway. Owen rose, took one of her hands in his, and patted her back firmly. The coughing grew less intense, and with her free hand she wiped away the tears that the fit had brought on.

"Are you all right, Mother?" Owen asked.

Tremors in her hands were now constant, and her head jerked and rolled on her thin neck, the cords under the control of a merciless puppet master. Her clothes hung on her like wash on a clothes line. He could smell the sourness trapped beneath the limp folds of skin as he bent down and wrapped his arms around her. Her thinning gray hair was turning white. Even her flaking scalp smelled fusty. She'd lost more side teeth from her bottom jaw, and her cheeks had caved into the emptiness. She looked up at him with rheumy, distant eyes.

"How're you doing, Mother?" Owen asked.

"Oh, I'm doin'." The hand he held gripped back with unexpectedly bony firmness. "It's good to see you. It's been so long." She spoke slowly, giving each word the concentration required to avoid slurring.

"It has, Mother." Six months. She barely looked like the same woman.

"Are you home for good? Are you done?"

She'd been getting a bit forgetful. "One more term."

Her grip relaxed, and he let her hand descend to her lap. "How long is that?"

"Five or six months."

He couldn't be sure that her nod was deliberate, meaningful. "That's good. Be sure to tell your father."

"I will."

The nodding continued, without control. "I've been so worried. The work is so dangerous. And they don't pay you enough. They can afford it, they just don't want to part with it."

Time no longer anchored her. She'd drifted, slipped back. He spoke gently, separating his voice from the unintended injury, which stung his eyes and tightened his throat. "I'm Owen, Mother. Not Robbie."

"That's—" she started to say but broke off. He watched her collect herself—clasping the arms of the chair to arrest the tremors, stiffening her back, squinting to see him more clearly—and the haze gave way to a clearer vision. "Of course you are," she said, indignant. "I know my own son, don't I?" She recaptured the present: "Your studies . . . they're going well?"

"I'd say so. But how are you and Father managing?"

"As well as can be expected. Your father's taken over some of my chores, and the ladies from the knitting society and the Grange help out now and again. I don't even have to ask. One'll just show up—to chat over a cup of tea, they all say, but I know better. Before you know it, the kitchen's been cleaned or the walls wiped down or the rugs beaten over the clothes line."

"They're good people," Owen said, smiling.

"They are." To punctuate her affirmation she began rocking. The braided rug beneath her chair was well worn by the runners. "Not that I'm an invalid, mind you." She was fully alert now, her strength gathered. "I can still get around when I put my mind to it, and I still do some cooking and such, although your father does help with the lifting."

Owen looked around him. Everything occupied its familiar place. A white candle in its shallow pewter holder stood in each window, waiting to be lit at dusk. Above the hearth a faded banner, printed who knew where, proclaimed, "Welcome, Baby Jesus." The top of the oak sideboard had been cleared for a paperboard crèche and crudely carved and painted wooden figures of the Holy Family, several shepherds, the wise men, sheep, cows, and a camel whose missing fourth leg had been replaced by a stripped twig. There was a covered pie dish on the kitchen counter—pumpkin, in all likelihood.

Dinner tonight would be meatless—creamed salt cod over boiled potatoes. Tomorrow would be wild turkey, assuming his father's aim was still on the mark. If not, a goose.

He heard the door open. Owen couldn't see the mud room from this angle, but he knew it had to be his father. He heard the clotted muck boots drop to the slate floor, and Owen could picture him stripping off his insulated coveralls. That's what his father always wore this time of year—nothing else to protect him from the weather except gloves and a hat, not even in the worst storm. His father loomed in the doorway. "So you're here," he said.

That evening, they opened their presents. Owen received a hand-knit scarf and a quart of maple syrup to take back with him to Durham. He gave his father a nicely boxed tailored shirt and tie—a shirt and tie that, Owen suspected, would be kept in a drawer until taken out for his mother's funeral. He gave his mother a vase encrusted with seashells of various shapes and sizes, from periwinkles to scallops.

After his mother retired for the night, Owen and his father sat at the dining table, drinking coffee. They kept their voices low. It had been a good year for potatoes, his father told him, but that kept the prices low; yield versus return, income evening out to about average. Owen had heard it all before, in every variation.

"You should've written me about Mother," Owen said.

"She wouldn't hear of it." His father held his cup in both hands. His fingers were callused, dirt embedded deeply in the cracks and under the cuticles.

"What does her doctor say?"

"Well, I'm not privy to their conversations. I bring her, and I wait outside."

"Doesn't she tell you?"

"What's to tell? I see for myself." He raised his cup to his lips but took only a sip.

"Nothing you say is reassuring."

"Reassuring? You can be sure that your mother's going to meet her Maker, and none too soon, as she sees it."

"And how do *you* see it?" Owen said with restraint. He couldn't let his anger overtake him or he'd get nothing more from his father.

The old man leaned closer, elbows on the worn tabletop. "Lord knows, I wouldn't wish what she's going through on anyone. I'm doing the best I can to ease her way. It ain't much, and I know it. You ain't here, and I am."

Owen could feel the heat in his cheeks. He tightened his thin lips, said nothing.

His father continued, "And one more thing: she still seems to think that you'll be coming back here when you finish up at that college. There's no harm in letting her think so, but me and you both know better." And with that he pushed his chair from the table and rose. "You done with that cup? Your mother likes a clean kitchen when she gets up."

"You go on," Owen said. "I'll wash out the cups and the coffee pot."

"Put the grounds in the scrap bucket under the sink. The pigs'll get them in the morning. It aids their digestion."

Owen wondered if his Animal Science 101 professor would agree.

"I'll say goodnight, then."

Owen nodded. "Goodnight."

Still, his father lingered. "Me and you are like chalk and cheese. I don't hold it against you. It's just how it is."

"I know," Owen sighed.

"Anyway," the old man said, clearing his throat, "Merry Christmas."

Owen looked up. "Merry Christmas, Father," he said.

They had goose for Christmas dinner. Owen knew it was futile to suggest to his mother that she stay in her chair and let him prepare the meal under her direction, but he tried to make himself useful, no more than a step or two away from her. She let him peel the potatoes and the squash and periodically skim the fat from the roasting pan. But she and only she could make the baked navy beans with salt pork and brown sugar, and the dried plum compote, and the powder biscuits.

The next day, his last day there, she spent in her rocker. She'd worn herself out. She could barely walk, and only with him or his father holding her arm. She slept most of the time. The last thing Owen remembered her saying to him, just before he left for Durham, was, "Come for Easter. I'll cook a ham."

In March she fell and broke a hip, and, anesthetized by morphine, her body shut down, organ by organ, so quickly that he arrived too late. She was buried in consecrated ground, in the cemetery behind the Presbyterian church, next to her loving son Robert Oliver Rouse.

2. Loving

DIPLOMA IN HAND, Owen went to work for a firm in Springfield, Massachusetts, that specialized in land development. His job sent him traveling throughout the Pioneer Valley, as far north as Deerfield. Without any personal attachments, he didn't mind being on the road. He had a knack for dealing with those newly wealthy industrialists and entrepreneurs who favored bucolic river views, instead of the ocean vistas of Long Island Sound or Cape Cod, for their "cottages," where they planned to ensconce their families from June through August, with the master of the house then visiting on long weekends, taking the train from Worcester or Hartford or Waterbury. His clients tended to know exactly what they thought they wanted but often gave little consideration to unfamiliar constraints—the exorbitant cost of trying to sink a foundation into concealed traprock, the need for cross-breezes and afternoon shading on west-facing slopes, and so forth. But Owen, who'd quickly learned to dress well for client meetings and to agree before politely disagreeing, managed to win over most of them, who were impressed by his knowledge of the region's geology and an eye that took into account the beauty of the basalt ridges and cliff faces and the sedimentary layering of Sugarloaf, Mount Tom, and the Holyoke Range, not to mention the winding Connecticut River below. Shorter, thinner, and infinitely younger than his clients, Owen presented a reassuring smile to the wives, who, when they were allowed their opinions, always supported his vision. With the siting having been agreed upon, the detailed surveying, which, at last, allowed him to roll up his sleeves, seemed to take no time at all.

Less than two years after he graduated, his firm approached him about opening an office in Leominster that would largely cater to a similar clientele, but from Boston, Lowell, and Lawrence. Leominster, Fitchburg, Shirley, Harvard, Ayer, Littleton, all lay along the Boston & Maine corridor, and there should be money to be made in country homes, even if they proved to be less ostentatious than the Connecticut Valley cottages. He'd be his own man, at least until the venture proved itself, responsible for every facet of the office. If it all worked out, who knew what might come next, maybe even a partnership? *Trask, Dubois &Rouse.*

Owen still thought about the USGS. He remembered what Francis Burrell had said: "Youthful ambition gives way to the practicalities." He supposed that the USGS could wait another year or two.

And that was how he made the acquaintance of Bethany Petunia Burrows, called by her father "Pet"—a nickname that she despised and forbade Owen from ever using, even in jest. She worked as a stenographer and typist in the Leominster offices of Patterson, Smith & Downell, specialists in real estate, civil contracts, wills, and estates. Owen's job brought him to their offices on various occasions. Beth immediately struck him as presentable and well-spoken. He thought her face rather classical—hazel eyes, straight nose, firm chin, porcelain complexion, tightly wound crown of blonde hair softened at the temples by fine strands that always managed to escape. But her smile was hesitant—her teeth were small, with a gap front and center, and she displayed them self-consciously. As they became more familiar with each other and she therefore felt no need to give him her full attention when he leaned into her desk, chatting, he couldn't help but notice how easily she could carry on a rather flirtatious conversation with him (when no one else was within hearing) while she simultaneously, expertly pounded the keyboard and, without a glance, flung the carriage return. When he finally overcame his timidity and asked her to attend their first Sunday afternoon band concert, she laughed. "It took you long enough," she said.

Her father and her married elder brother owned Burrows & Sons, a men's clothing store. Her other brother, two years her senior, was studying law. Her mother, who managed the household with martial precision, took no guff from any of her men as they sat around the spacious dining room table for Sunday dinner, joking with each other, discussing in an uninterrupted flow the price of lightweight wool pinstripe cloth, John's legal studies, the escapades of President Roosevelt's daughter Alice Longworth . . . Owen, having accepted the first of many invitations to join them, was bewildered and flustered—he'd never experienced such a family dinner, where the consumption of food, although hardly neglected, proved secondary to the free-flowing conversation. By the meal's conclusion he couldn't help noticing that Beth's mother—slight of build, like her daughter, and with the very same smile (and very same teeth)—had taken on a glow and a calm, a happiness, that, looking twenty years ahead, he could easily see gracing her daughter.

In the following months he anchored his life more deeply in Beth and her family, so unlike his own. He didn't quite know how to respond, one evening, when Beth's father, for no discernible reason other than good spirits, presented him with an elegant gray homburg, asserting that a man of business needed something more stylish than the old bowler Owen had been wearing for years. Owen didn't know whether to simply thank him or offer to pay him or both. So, embarrassed, sitting in the parlor beside Beth, with the hat box open on his lap, he said nothing until Beth, having snatched the homburg and perched it on his head at a rakish angle, kissed him on the cheek, just beyond his lips, with surprising firmness and duration.

"What will your father think?" he stammered.

"What do you think he'll think?" she said, and her father chuckled. Then he leaned over and, with a wink, straightened the hat.

When did Owen know he loved her? When did he know Beth loved *him*? He knew nothing about love and romance. Apart from a couple of brief flirtations during his days in Durham and a mortifying encounter in a back room of a Portsmouth "dance parlor" favored by drunken classmates, he'd had few memorable encounters with the fairer sex. One of his clients, when he was working out of Springfield, kept hinting that he wanted Owen to meet his daughter, but when they finally did meet, construction of the cottage was already under way and, his assignment completed, Owen never encountered her again.

Owen and Beth hadn't yet spoken directly of marriage, but they play-acted, engaging in flirtatious conversations about how newlyweds should honeymoon in Pittsburgh, Pennsylvania, the most dreadfully hellish city either could imagine, so that they'd have an excuse for not leaving their fashionable hotel room, or about how society should revive the colonial practice of bundling, of which Owen initially had to admit his complete ignorance, which in turn allowed Beth to "scandalize" him, as she put it, by explaining that courting couples, fully clothed or tightly wrapped in individual blankets and sometimes separated by a thick board, were permitted to sleep in the same bed so that they could become "better acquainted."

To a point, Owen enjoyed the silliness. After all, this was part of courting, wasn't it? But it also revealed the four-year gap in their age. He was twenty-three, and by that age many men were already married, and fathers. The same could be said, of course, for Beth; by the age of nineteen her mother had already given birth to two sons. But Beth, the baby of the family, demonstrated a sometimes grating mix of the childish and the womanly, though always well aware of what her fervent kisses and the pressure of her breasts against his chest did to him.

They began talking about arranging a surreptitious trip to Boston, just the two of them, unchaperoned. In Leominster they could never be anonymous. No matter where they went together, someone inevitably recognized Beth. Well, there were half a million people in Boston, which made it highly unlikely that they would encounter a single familiar face. They could do whatever they wanted, and no one would notice or care. Such freedom! So, Beth would go to her father and ask if she could pay an overnight visit to Cheryl Robbins, a friend from stenography school who had accommodations in a young ladies' boarding house in Somerville. Her father had met Cheryl and liked her, and Beth was confident that she could convince him to allow her this unprecedented liberty. After all, she was no longer a child who needed constant supervision. Meanwhile, Owen would book a room for himself in a nearby hotel, and they could spend all their waking hours together in the big city.

They'd both visited Boston many times before, Beth, from an early age, always in the company of one or more relatives. In contrast, Owen began visiting the city regularly only in his senior year of college, initially because he considered Boston a logical place to seek work after graduation. But his trips had continued even after being steered to his present job in Leominster. He liked the city—its pace, its history, its attractions, especially its museums, and most particularly the Peabody Museum, on the Harvard campus. He admired the excellent collection at the Museum of Fine Arts on Copley Square and looked forward to seeing the expanded galleries when the new building on Huntington Street opened, but, to tell the truth, Italian portraiture and Greek sculpture and Paul Revere's silversmithing didn't hold his interest the way the fragments of lost civilizations displayed at the Peabody did.

When they met at the train station for their Boston trip, they greeted each other with feigned surprise (in case someone who knew them might be observing), and then maintained a certain reserve as the train lumbered through a steady rain. They sat facing each other but spoke very little at first even though, it being a Saturday morning, the car wasn't crowded. They had already decided on an itinerary: a nice lunch in Boston, followed by a tour of the Peabody. Later, they would stroll around Boston Common or take a swan boat ride in the Public Garden. They would dine late, and then he would escort her to Cheryl's. He would retrieve her by midmorning, and they'd still have an additional half a day together in the city before boarding the return train.

To escape the coal soot and smoke of the train shed, they made their way as quickly as possible along the Union Station arrival platform and entered the old Lowell terminal. Carrying both their valises, Owen led Beth through the crowded western arcade—the gray light pouring through the clerestory windows was disheartening, and everyone appeared to have the common goal of moving through the dank dimness as expeditiously as possible—and into the main concourse. Once outside, under the soaring arch that, flanked by pairs of Ionic columns, dominated Union Station's façade, Owen put down their bags for a moment and unfurled a large black umbrella. Causeway Street was bustling: horse-drawn delivery wagons, two electric trolley cars disgorging and picking up passengers, a handful of hardened vendors hawking their wares from canopied carts, pedestrians dodging a scattering of automobiles, of which there seemed to be more each time he came to Boston.

They had both dressed for the March weather—hats, gloves, long coats, high shoes, all in black except for the quail feathers, dyed a luminescent blue, affixed to the crown of Beth's hat. Owen moved the umbrella closer to her, and they abandoned the shelter of the arch and, with her slender hand on his uplifted arm, walked to the nearby el station, where they boarded a car that took them to Congress Street and Faneuil Hall.

They were surprisingly hungry. Well, they admitted, not *so* surprisingly since neither had eaten any breakfast to speak of. After a lunch of hot pot roast sandwiches, a salad of sliced beets and cucumbers, and coffee and ginger snaps, Owen hired a carriage to drive them across the new Cambridge Bridge, with its steel arches and stone towers. The rain had stopped at last, though the clouds still draped low overhead.

At lunch they'd decided they would stop at Owen's hotel and check their overnight bags at the desk. They could easily retrieve Beth's valise before making their way, that evening, to the Spring Hill neighborhood of nearby Somerville.

Owen's Beacon Street hotel was an unassuming, quietly serious four-story establishment not far from Harvard Square. The desk manager, a mildly officious middle-aged gentleman, politely accepted the two pieces of luggage and asked if Mr. Rouse would like to sign the register now or later. The room would be ready within the hour. Owen glanced at Beth, who hadn't ventured far beyond the entrance and now, her back to him, stood beside a large potted schefflera, looking out at the street through a sidelight.

"Now would be fine," Owen said, turning back to the clerk. "Thank you." He quickly signed the register and returned to Beth. Without a word he held the door for her and they left the hotel, crossed Beacon Street, and headed west toward Divinity Avenue.

The Peabody was a sober six stories of red brick and dark mortar, with brown stone sills, caps, and cornices, and granite steps leading to the arched entryway. Owen steered Beth directly to the rooms displaying American artifacts in wood-framed glass cases. Along the walls the cases rose eight shelves high, while free-standing cases—storage below, horizontal displays at waist level, and shelving behind—filled much of the open floor space.

The museum was oppressively hot, the air dead. They moved from case to case and room to room holding their outer coats, which they'd shed soon after entering. The artifacts were arranged without labels, which left Beth adrift. A glaze soon settled over her eyes. As he talked about the photographs of the ancient Anasazi ruins, Beth couldn't stop yawning, though she tried to conceal her boredom behind the back of her hand. Owen did his best to stir her interest, to no avail, and he felt a sense of hopelessness descending over him.

"Owen," she said, stifling another yawn, "could we leave now? I feel a bit light-headed."

"Oh, of course!" He manufactured enthusiasm. "There's no ventilation in here. Let's get you outside, into the fresh air."

The outside air was an immediate relief.

"I thought I was going to fall asleep," she laughed. But then, acknowledging his obvious disappointment, added, "We should come back again sometime when we aren't having such a busy day."

"That's true. You must be very tired."

"To tell you the truth, I didn't sleep more than a wink or two last night, and it's catching up with me."

What to do? he wondered. Although the rain hadn't returned, the clouds still threatened, turning the afternoon light into near-dusk. They could recross the Charles River to Boston and head to the Common with the hope that the skies didn't open up again. Or maybe it would be best if they returned to Beacon Street now, collected her valise, and made their way to Somerville. Beth could rest and freshen up at Cheryl's; he'd find somewhere to occupy himself for an hour.

Beth immediately brightened up at the latter suggestion, and they retraced their steps toward the hotel.

"Ah, Mr. and Mrs. Rouse," the clerk said as they approached the desk. "Your room is ready." He turned to a rack of hooks and retrieved a key. "Third floor, to the right as you leave the staircase, second door on the left."

"Thank you," Owen said. He took Beth's arm and guided her to a leather settee near the mahogany staircase. Beth sat down and looked up at him.

He cleared his throat. "It was a logical assumption."

"Oh, I know," Beth replied. Her tone gave nothing away.

Owen positioned himself, still standing, so that the desk clerk, if he were looking, wouldn't be able to see either of their faces. "I can go to the room and retrieve your bag. You can wait here for me. I won't be a minute."

"Won't he think that very odd?"

"It doesn't matter what he thinks. He's an employee and we'll never see him again."

She frowned and her shoulders sagged. Her eyes drifted away from him, toward a modestly dressed elderly couple who were sitting across the lobby, beneath a large framed mirror.

"We'll take a carriage to Somerville," he said.

She said nothing.

"Or you can go up to the room and rest there."

Without redirecting her gaze she said, "I'm so very tired."

"Then that might be best—for you to go up and rest a bit. I can wait for you down here. I'll find a newspaper to occupy my time." Bending down and adopting a lighter tone, he said, "Don't worry, that elderly couple hasn't even noticed us."

At that she smiled slightly. "Yes, they have." Her eyes filled but didn't spill over. "I really can't go up to the room alone. I've never done that, in a hotel. I really can't."

It was a decent enough room lit by a converted gas chandelier. Clean red carpeting covered the floor, and matching drapes framed the sole window, which overlooked Beacon Street. An antique armoire—American chestnut, Owen thought, although he was no expert on wood—stood against one wall, facing fashionable twin beds, which were separated by a small night table. A paneled door, painted with a white enamel, opened into a rather nice, though small, bathroom tiled to within a foot of the ceiling with white hexagons; a vanity with a marble sink stood on the right, while on the left a claw-footed bathtub occupied most of the remaining space. A partition stood between the vanity and a flush commode.

During Owen's brief inspection, Beth stood just inside the hallway door. Their bags had been placed side by side on a luggage rack beside the window. "This'll do nicely, don't you think?" Owen said with half-feigned good cheer.

"May I sit?" she asked.

There was no chair.

"Of course!" He rushed to help her with her coat, and then he didn't know what to do with it—to place it on the far bed or to carry it to the armoire and hang it up. He lay it across one bed, and Beth, removing her hat, sat down on the other. She turned and placed the hat on the nightstand.

"Do you want to freshen up?" Owen gestured to the lavatory door.

Beth shook her head and then, giving in to her fatigue, sighed and lay down on her side at an angle, with her legs straight so that her shoes didn't contact the white spread.

"Let me," he said, circling the foot of the bed and bending to unfasten her laces. As he removed each shoe he marveled at how small and light her foot felt in his hand. It all seemed so intimate.

"Are you cold?" he asked. "Would you like a blanket?" Before she could answer, he turned to the armoire, assuming correctly that extra blankets might be stored there. He removed one and draped it over her legs.

He was still wearing his homburg and overcoat. He took them off and lay them beside her coat.

Without turning toward him Beth asked, "What about you? Are you tired too?"

"Yes, I guess I am," he said. "I didn't sleep much, either, last night."

With her free arm Beth patted the mattress behind her.

He removed his suit coat and shoes and lay down on his side, bare inches between them. Beth reached for his arm and pulled it across her, tucking his hand against her ribs. He edged closer, until his chest was against her back.

He realized that he *was* tired, extraordinarily tired—so tired that he could almost ignore the pressure of his cock against the front of his trousers. He might actually fall asleep, smelling the slight scent of some herb from her hair.

He thought she was on the edge of sleep when she began speaking:

"Did you know that my father didn't want me to go to stenography school? He didn't think it was proper for his daughter. He thought it would make me less marriageable. He wanted me to marry a doctor or a lawyer—someone with real social standing." There was a long sigh before she continued. "I love my father very much."

"I know you do."

"He's the kindest of men. But if he knew what we were doing—"

"We haven't done anything wrong."

"Would you like to explain *this* to my father?"

He had no acceptable answer.

"Nothing has felt right, not since I stepped from the platform to the train this morning."

"How can I make it right, Beth? I so want to make it right." The sound of running water distracted him—the radiator under the window: the heat had come on. "Should we leave here right now?" he asked. He raised himself on an elbow so that he could see the side of her face. "I can take you to Cheryl's. Or if you want, we can go back to Union Station and take an evening train home. Whatever you want."

"I'm not as innocent as you think," she said.

"No?"

"Carolyn has told me everything about what men expect."

Carolyn, her brother Buddy's wife, who was very free with her opinions, in Owen's view.

"Why are there two beds?" Beth asked.

"Single rooms don't come with private baths, and I thought that at some point during the day you might want to freshen up."

"I see." She closed her eyes, and for a moment he thought she *had* fallen asleep, but then she said, "We could stay right here by ourselves—we could bundle like this for the next twenty-four hours."

He kissed her cheek and then put his head down on the pillow beside her, with his face buried even deeper in her hair.

"What about Cheryl? She's expecting you."

"Yes, there's that." Moments later the rise and fall of her breathing confirmed that she'd fallen asleep.

He closed his eyes. He wanted to loosen his clothing, but he didn't want to chance disturbing her, so he just lay there beside her, and within minutes he, too, was asleep.

WHEN THE VARIOUS doctors asked him—first Arthur Endicott, who was a good friend of Mr. and Mrs. Burrows as well as their family physician, and then the slew of physicians that he saw at the Mary Hitchcock Memorial Hospital in Hanover, New Hampshire—he couldn't pinpoint when he'd begun feeling off, not himself, although he was sure it began before the bout of influenza that laid him low later in March. The blinding headache, the dry cough, the complete loss of appetite, aches in his muscles and joints, the fatigue—all could be attributed to the flu. But before that he'd had night sweats, soaking through his nightshirt and dampening the bed sheets. They were the oddest things, feverless, disconnected from any dream or nightmare he could remember, and also disconnected from the fierce thirsts and bouts of excessive urination he'd been having. He dismissed the latter as a consequence of the water he drank, glass after glass, to slake the thirst, and for that he tried to blame the saltiness of Mrs. Burrows's soups, smoked hams, and briskets, and the sweetness of her custards, crumbles, and tarts, the likes of which he'd never eaten before—certainly nothing remotely like them had ever emerged from his mother's oven!—and of which he couldn't get enough. But he'd tried to put the whole matter out of his mind, as he did the occasional brief episodes of dizziness and lassitude, because he was genuinely happy, doing survey work that he found satisfying, even in the harshest winter winds, and spending nearly every evening with Beth: encompassed by the extended arms of her family; taking advantage of her mother's open invitation to "get fattened up" at their dinner table three or four nights a week; and always attending Sunday midday dinner with the whole family, including Buddy and Carolyn and John and often various aunts, uncles, and cousins. He had indeed put on a bit of weight, enough to fill out his clothes, which had never fit particularly well on his thin frame.

On the train back from Boston, he and Beth had decided to announce their engagement at Easter, before which Owen would speak to her father. They had no doubt whatsoever what response would greet the news. But his drawn-out bout of the flu led to a postponement. Early on, Mrs. Burrows tried to convince him to relocate to John's room, since her younger son's legal studies meant he was rarely at home, but Owen absolutely refused. It was bad enough, he insisted, that her and Beth's daily visits to his bedside, always bringing food and early spring buds from the garden to replenish the vase on his nightstand, had exposed them to his illness, and he wasn't about to put the whole family at risk. In the end, however, after nearly three weeks as an invalid, he agreed to be seen by their family doctor.

Arthur Endicott, MD, his graying hair brushed straight back off his forehead, his black tie knotted impeccably at the center of the white starched collar, carried himself with imposing authority. Owen, sitting on the side of his bed, admired the cut of the charcoal gray suit and the waistcoat, which was two shades lighter than the suit and tightly buttoned across the flat stomach.

Dr. Endicott began by asking Owen to provide a complete medical history. As scrupulously as he could, Owen listed all the childhood episodes and recurrent ailments while Dr. Endicott made a series of brief notes in a leather-bound notebook. When Owen was done, the doctor capped his gold-nibbed fountain pen, laid the book and pen on Owen's nightstand, and removed a stethoscope from a well-oiled doctor's bag. He listened to Owen's chest and back, shifting the position of the stethoscope several times and tapping firmly with his strong fingers. His first comment was, "Your lungs seem to be clear, but you have a pronounced heart murmur. Did you know that?"

"No, I didn't."

"You said you had scarlatina when you were a child?"

"Yes."

"Did you see a doctor?"

"I'm sure I did, even though my father didn't believe in them. Or at least he didn't believe in paying them."

"But no one ever mentioned a murmur?"

"Our local doctor didn't graduate at the top of his class, if you get my meaning."

"If he couldn't hear *that* murmur, I'd say he must have finished at the bottom."

The doctor draped the stethoscope around his neck and began palpating glands under Owen's chin and around the neck. "Some swelling," he noted, "but nothing inconsistent with influenza." He asked Owen to open his mouth as widely as possible. "Thank you," Endicott said when he was done, and then he sat back in his chair and for more than a minute did nothing but stare, which Owen found extremely disconcerting.

"Is there something . . . ?"

"No no," Dr. Endicott said. "I've found over the years that by giving too much attention to the detailed examination of a patient, a physician can miss something in the patient's overall appearance—the color and texture of the skin, whether the eyes bulge slightly, the alignment of the jaws, and so forth—that speaks of general well-being."

"I see."

"Please lie down on your back so that I can examine your abdomen."

Again, Owen did as directed. Standing and bending over, the doctor applied the bell of the stethoscope to Owen's belly.

"Do you move your bowels regularly?"

"I haven't been eating much lately."

"Try to relax your stomach muscles. I'm going to palpate various organs—your liver and so forth—and the pressure will be uncomfortable, but less so if you don't resist."

Owen hadn't known that fingers could be pressed so far upward, under the ribcage. It felt as if he were being prepared for the spit.

"Do you take strong drink?"

"Not really. I'm not a temperance man, but I've never developed the taste."

"That's just as well. You say you sometimes experience excessive urination?"

Owen told him about the bouts of thirst and the frequent urge to relieve himself.

The doctor sat down again and folded his arms across his chest. He wore impressive gold cufflinks. "And this predates the influenza?"

"Yes."

"Any burning sensation when you urinate?"

"No."

"Please stand and lower your drawers."

The fingers again, thrusting upward into the groin; Owen expelled a sharp breath.

"You say you haven't been eating regularly."

"I have no appetite, although Mrs. Tuffy, my landlady, has tried her best to tempt me with puddings and pies."

"You may pull up your drawers." Dr. Endicott continued downward, examining Owen's legs and feet. "I'll want to take a urine specimen with me for analysis, if you have no objection."

"None at all."

"And, if you don't mind, a blood sample. Have you ever had one taken before?"

"No."

"It's quite painless. A slight pinch. Please sit with your legs over the side of the bed."

Owen complied, and then he watched the doctor prepare a glass syringe and very fine needle, both of which he wiped with denatured alcohol. Owen scarcely felt the needle enter a prominent vein just above the inner elbow. The sight of his blood flowing so cleanly into the syringe was surprisingly enthralling. "You don't bleed people anymore, do you? As a treatment, I mean."

"Personally, no." The doctor slid the needle from the vein and asked Owen to apply pressure at the insertion point. "It's a rather barbaric notion, but it's still practiced by a minority—the uninformed." He placed the vial in his bag. "Prior to the flu, did you have any unusual soreness or stiffness in your joints?" He began lifting and flexing Owen's arms, elbows, wrists, and then he moved to his knees and ankles. "Any numbness or tingling in the extremities?"

"No."

"Very well." The examination was over.

"So what can you tell me?" Owen asked.

"Right now, very little that you don't already know." Dr. Endicott returned his instruments to his medical bag. "You've had a rather severe bout of the flu, but you should gradually recover your energy. Leave your bed for short periods, and begin going outside for some fresh air. Walk about for an hour or so each day, half an hour at a time if you feel fatigued." He stood up and straightened his waistcoat—he checked his pocket watch, a handsome gold piece on a gold fob—and then added, "I'm going to leave additional specimen bottles for you. I want you to eat a normal dinner this evening—whatever Mrs. Tuffy prepares for her other boarders. And then I want you to collect a urine sample two hours afterwards and another before you retire for the night. I'll send someone by to pick them up in the morning." He took three smallish jars from his bag and placed them on the night table. "Make sure each is labeled with the date and time of collection, and also provide a list of everything you eat, including an estimate of the quantity—so many ounces of meat, so many ounces of each liquid, and so forth—between now and when you retire for the night." He left the room while Owen produced the initial urine sample. When Dr. Endicott returned, he added the jar to his bag before closing it. "So," he said, "I'll be back to see you in two days. And in the meantime, I'm going to advise Mrs. Tuffy to stop baking desserts for you, at least for now. Good day, Mr. Rouse."

They shook hands and the doctor left.

Two days later, the afternoon in its decline, Dr. Endicott returned. Owen was feeling somewhat better, and they met in the downstairs parlor, a modest but well-lit room where boarders were permitted to host visitors.

The doctor wasted no time on pleasantries: "I recall your saying that you're from New Hampshire."

"Yes."

"You still have family there?"

"My father, but we aren't close."

"I gather you've been 'adopted' by the Burrows family?"

"I suppose you could say that, although adoption isn't exactly what I had in mind."

"No, I don't suppose it is. Bethany's a lovely young lady." Endicott frowned. Having anchored an elbow on the arm of his chair, he stroked his lower jaw with thumb and forefinger. "Sometimes in my profession, circumstances require me to assess a person's character."

"I see." Owen fully understood that what he was about to hear would not be good news.

"Shall I proceed?" Dr. Endicott asked.

Was there an alternative? "By all means," Owen murmured.

"You have a condition—I hesitate to label it a disease—called diabetes. In essence, for unknown reasons, you retain too much sugar in your blood.

The body's natural inclination is to excrete the excess. When that excess reaches a certain level, it triggers extreme thirst and urination." He paused. "Do you understand?"

"I've heard about diabetes. Please, go on." Owen's hands began to shake.

"The influenza had nothing to do with your diabetes except that it constituted an insult to your system. I've seen this many times before: a patient exhibits no evidence of a chronic disorder until a challenge exposes the underlying condition. For example, an elderly patient's congestive heart failure is discovered during treatment for what everyone thought was a simple pneumonia. You see, a buildup of fluid in the lungs occurred because of the weakness of the cardiac muscles, and so forth . . ."

Dr. Endicott's pause seemed to demand a response. "I understand," Owen said.

The doctor resumed: "With diabetes, medical science hasn't solved the puzzle yet. We know that it has something to do with the pancreas, which excretes enzymes that aid digestion. And we know from experiments with animals that removal of the pancreas leads to immediate, irreversible diabetes. But that's neither here nor there." He paused and then went on. "Your case is rather unusual. In fact, you're such an unlikely candidate for this condition that I found myself questioning my own judgment this morning. I admit that I've seen no more than a handful of cases resembling yours, and one of those was a child—a pretty Polish girl, only twelve, who dwindled away rapidly and succumbed within months. For some reason, in the very young the regulatory mechanism suffers a complete collapse—as if the pancreas had in fact been removed. Your situation isn't nearly as dire—your pancreas continues to function, but at a significantly reduced level. Still, we should repeat the blood test just to be sure of the diagnosis."

"So maybe there's been a mistake?"

Dr. Endicott looked at him directly but said nothing.

"You haven't mentioned any cure."

"There is no cure. And the only treatment is to impose a strict dietary regimen."

Owen said, "I feel fine today—better than I have in weeks."

This time it was the doctor, nodding, who said, "I understand." He paused. "With diligence, you should have many fine days."

Owen, his face flushed, gathered himself and cleared his throat. "For how long?"

Dr. Endicott chose not to answer directly. "I suspect that you've had the condition for some time, but your blood sugars remained low enough that you had no obvious symptoms. Now, that's changed. Controlling what you consume will help, but eventually complications will rise to a level that . . . isn't sustainable."

"How long?" Owen asked again, his voice a whisper.

"No one can say for sure. If you adjust your life, your expectations, to what your condition demands, it's conceivable that you could live six or seven years, maybe more, but I must tell you in all candor that for individuals of your age, the average is about four years."

"Four."

"Yes, but averages can hide a wide variance."

Owen took several deep breaths to steady himself. His hands felt clammy but his mouth was dry. *There's been a mistake.* The late afternoon light shone into the room from the two windows behind the doctor, and Owen shifted in his chair to keep the sun from pouring into his eyes. "What do you suggest?" He struggled to control the tremor in his voice.

"If you were a middle-aged fat man—like our new president—I'd put you on the strictest of diets and hope that by losing the excess weight your condition would improve. Sometimes, losing weight significantly reduces the level of blood sugar, which is the key indicator of severity. But you're neither fat nor middle aged, and I doubt that reducing you as rapidly as possible to skin and bones would have more than a marginal effect.

"What I recommend instead is that I admit you to Burbank Hospital in Fitchburg. By varying what and when you eat, we may be able to determine the severity of your condition and then recommend a diet that you can best live with. It'll be trial and error, but I can guarantee you that you'll come out of the process with more knowledge than we have now."

"How long would this take?"

"At least three weeks. Maybe a month or longer."

"And if I choose not to?"

Dr. Endicott frowned; his eyebrows formed black wings. "Then, if you wish, I'll recommend a diet and you can . . . resume your life. Or I'd be happy to refer you to another physician, one with more expertise. But that would require your traveling elsewhere—to Boston, for example."

"I need time to think."

"Of course. In the meantime, I'd like to return tomorrow morning, before you've eaten anything, and collect a last blood sample, to confirm the diagnosis."

"I don't want anyone to know about this—especially not Mr. and Mrs. Burrows."

"Well, I'm bound by your wishes, Mr. Rouse, but experience tells me that you'll need help sorting this out. If not your father . . ." He waited to see if Owen contradicted him and then went on: "And if not Mr. or Mrs. Burrows . . ."

Owen shook his head.

"Is there a clergyman or a confidant—"

Owen's emotions raced through the fog, and his reply was curt. "No one."

Dr. Endicott heaved a sigh. "I'm speaking now as a good friend of the Burrows family. If you won't let me explain your condition to Mr. or Mrs. Burrows, *you* need to do so. Bethany's very young. Someone will have to prepare her." Dr. Endicott extended his hand a second time, and after a moment Owen took it. "If I've overstepped the bounds, Mr. Rouse, I hope you'll forgive me."

When the doctor left the sitting room, he closed the door quietly behind him.

The next morning, Owen agreed to a hospital stay. "But not at Burbank," he told Dr. Endicott, who had just withdrawn a needle from Owen's arm. The sun was barely up, but Owen had already dressed. He sat on the side of his bed.

"Why is that?" the doctor asked as he labeled the blood sample.

"I need to be away. I don't want people hovering. Is there another hospital where I can go?"

"I'll make a telephone call or two this afternoon. I have a friend, a former classmate, in New Hampshire who may be willing to assist you."

"I don't have money for any place fancy. I have a little savings to . . ." To start a life with Beth.

"That shouldn't be a problem. In the meantime, restrict your diet. Meat, fish, eggs, cheese, green vegetables, black tea or water. Nothing else. No potatoes, bread, sweets of any kind." The doctor sat back in his chair, and Owen realized he was once again the subject of Endicott's intense gaze. "How do you feel today, Mr. Rouse?"

Owen thought about it for a moment. "Well enough. Hungry, wouldn't you know. For the first time in weeks."

"Would you mind if I conduct a brief physical examination again? There's no need to undress."

"Of course."

The doctor withdrew his stethoscope from his leather bag and performed another auscultation, chest and back. He spent a full five minutes, listening and tapping. When he was satisfied, he returned the instrument to his bag and then began speaking:

"I believe we need to talk about complications."

"Complications?"

"From the diabetes. We don't fully understand why or how, but diabetes affects every organ system. The kidneys are often damaged, as is the circulatory system. Due to an inadequate blood supply, many patients encounter difficulties with their legs and most often their feet—ulcerations, which, in the worst cases, can lead to serious infections and even gangrene, requiring amputation. There's also the possibility of peripheral nerve damage—a numbness of the extremities or, in contrast, severe pain that's been described as like lightning. Also possible damage to the eyes, even blindness. Most distressing to some men, they can experience a loss of their ability to perform the marital act. But one of the most common consequences is a progressive enlargement and weakening of the heart."

"So what did you hear with your stethoscope?"

"Apart from the murmur, nothing unusual," Dr. Endicott said, "but an evaluation by a cardiologist would be justified."

Owen slowly rolled his sleeve down and buttoned the cuff. "Can you do anything about a weakening heart?"

"Treatment, such as it is, is typically introduced to counter obvious signs of distress—extreme fatigue, chest pain, shortness of breath, and so forth." He removed his notebook from his bag and made a quick jotting. "Have you reconsidered telling the Burrows family?"

"Obviously, I can't simply disappear for a month." Owen's mouth began to tremble, and his eyes overflowed. "I'm sorry." He covered his face with his hand and began to sob. Each broken breath opened a deeper shaft into despair.

"Think nothing of it, Mr. Rouse. Think nothing of it." The doctor adjusted the knot in his dark blue tie. He was wearing his charcoal gray suit today. "Neither the time nor the place requires stoicism. That will come later."

The next evening, Owen told Beth and her parents that because of a heart murmur Dr. Endicott was sending him for further evaluation at Mary Hitchcock Memorial Hospital, in Hanover, New Hampshire. He'd be leaving Leominster by train in two days. Yes, it was unfortunate that he wouldn't be closer, but a hospital in rural New Hampshire was far less expensive than a stay at Massachusetts General or one of the other Boston hospitals.

He never mentioned diabetes.

Later, when he and Beth were alone in the parlor, he told her that of course he'd write frequently—no, not every day because he'd run out of things to say, to which Beth had replied, what would he be like after a year or two of marriage? Dull as toast, he told her, trying with little kisses to calm her distress. He touched his lips to her lips, to forehead, eyebrows, eyelids, cheeks, chin, nose, ears, and down to her neck—always so warm there, where he could feel her pulse—and back to her lips. He wanted to trace every bit of skin he could reach, and his fingers followed his mouth everywhere and his ears absorbed every sigh because he expected that he'd never do this again.

HE HAD NOTHING TO DO each day except walk the hospital corridors and grounds. He didn't feel ill—still a bit tired, but without other complaints except periods of intense hunger. He knew, however, that he couldn't lapse into thinking that all would be well—that *he* would be well—and that he could resume fabricating a life with Beth; after a week he'd pissed into enough bottles and watched enough blood drawn from his arms to know that if Dr. Endicott had erred in his diagnosis, it certainly would have been discovered.

He had to accept the chemistry. Three or four years. Three. Four. Maybe five. He could try to think of that as a long time. He could accomplish something in that span. Something.

The staff at Mary Hitchcock Memorial Hospital gave him every courtesy, even a private room. Dr. Stamper had arranged it. Sidney Stamper, friend and classmate of Arthur Endicott, had stayed on to practice in Hanover and teach at Dartmouth Medical College. He had an interest in metabolic disorders and enthusiastically welcomed Owen to his service without fee on the condition that Owen agree, as he put it, to be poked, prodded, and awakened at abnormal hours by medical students and staff.

On sunny days Owen escaped the hospital confines to sit on the spacious front lawn. From there, Mary Hitchcock Memorial, with its pale yellow brick walls and decorative touches of terra cotta, all capped by roofs of red tile, looked more like a resort than a hospital. A circular drive led to a porte cochere and veranda and, through the entrance doors of the central building, a welcoming rotunda. Sun-filled corridors proceeded to two pavilions that housed the patient and treatment rooms. The main hospital building was only a hundred yards from the Dartmouth College campus, where spontaneous ball games would often break out in the afternoons. Owen stayed on the hospital lawn, sometimes sitting on one of the wrought-iron benches spaced along the curve of the driveway, and sometimes lying on the grass, where, too often, he wept.

He wept with the iron of a coward's fear on his tongue. He wept from hunger, which gnawed at his gut like a feral animal. He wept from anger, a primitive rage without direction except when it turned inward, toward the aberrant workings of his own physiology; he wanted to claw his way inside, to sink his fingers deep into the treachery. He wept for his distance from Beth and for the naïve sweetness of her letters, and because of the half-truths he told her twice weekly. He wept that he'd never lie beside Beth again. He wept for all the fucking he never did, would never do. He wept for his intended life and his unplanned life, both lost. He wept for his dead mother, for the dead brother he'd never met, and for his stunted father, the last of the family, who'd be accompanied into cold death only by ghosts. He wept for the absence of his mother's God, whose presence he'd never felt and to whom, therefore, he could not surrender. He wept for the mustiness of the yellowing well-remembered pages of the collected Shakespeare, with all of Macbeth's weary tomorrows and last syllables. He wept with anger (again, anger) that someone else would slip inside Beth—into her heart first— and that she, faithless in the end, would carry someone else's children. He wept because his only legacy would be as an anonymous patient, the subject of a case study in some medical journal. He wept for the blueness of the sky and for the hidden stars. He wept when he smelled the fresh greenness of the April grass and saw how the yellow daffodils were already fading to on-ionskin in the flower beds, and how the tulips, their buds still tight, would soon advance the season toward the scent of lilacs—he wept for that remem-bered scent. He wept with a drunkard's maudlinism and a martyred saint's grace and a confidence man's regrets and then with humility until finally, drained, there was nothing more for him to do but put all the weeping aside and get up off the grass and go back inside and let them drain another vial of his too-sweet blood.

In the middle of his second week, Dr. Stamper introduced a regimen of small meals every four hours, and that kept the hunger at bay. The sci-ence of nutrition had made great strides in recent years, Stamper informed him, and thanks to research by W. O. Atwater, a professor of chemistry at Wesleyan University, doctors now knew the caloric content of most com-mon foods and therefore could advise diabetic patients what they should and shouldn't eat: avoid carbohydrates—especially sugars and white starches, which digestion metabolized quickly, producing surges in blood sugar lev-els—except those containing chlorophyll and carotenoids; proteins and fats were digested much more slowly and could be consumed in moderation.

At one point Dr. Stamper, responding to the continued presence of sugar in Owen's urine, asked him how far he was willing to go. A German doctor, Carl von Noorden, had developed what was widely called the oat-meal treatment, encompassing a diet of butter and vegetal or egg albumin as well as boiled oatmeal. The diet was intended for the most extreme circum-stances, when nothing else seemed to rid the urine of sugar and acetone and when coma appeared imminent. At least in theory—many doctors were dis-missive—when consumed for a brief period the oatmeal diet would provide relief and also produce an increased tolerance for regular carbohydrates, which could gradually be reintroduced. Although Owen was not at risk for a diabetic coma—at least not here at Mary Hitchcock—trying the von Noorden diet for one or two meals a day might be advantageous. It was, however, all conjecture, Stamper cautioned, and some patients were unable to stomach the unpalatable oatmeal formula. Moreover, food was a source of pleasure as well as nourishment, and the dining experience, sharing a meal with colleagues or friends, was part of the social fabric. How much was Owen willing to give up? It was a philosophical as much as a medical question, the doctor said. Longevity wasn't, in the end, everything. Of course, millions of people lived on less—not well, but they lived. And some even chose extreme asceticism. Buddhist monks living in the mountain kingdoms of Asia. Hermits in the forests of Europe. Misanthropes galore. . . Owen would need to find his own balance.

Two weeks later, Owen left Mary Hitchcock Memorial Hospital. Nothing more could be done. As for his heart, yes, he had a murmur and the heart appeared to be slightly enlarged, but marginally helpful medications—bromide of potassium, cimicifuga, gelsemium, aconite, digitalis—were available if he began to experience weakness, shortness of breath, palpitations, angina, etcetera. Some success in relieving cardiac symptoms had also been obtained using the Schott method of mineral baths and resistance exercise.

WHEN BETH ANSWERED the door, he saw shock drain the color from her face. He knew how he looked. He'd lost all the weight he'd gained in the previous six months, and then some, partly during his bout with the flu but mostly during his nearly month-long absence. His suit hung limp, and the stiffness of his now too-large starched shirt collar made it even more apparent that nothing he wore fit properly. Beth, attempting to recover her smile, kissed him on the cheek and wrapped her arms around him. "What's happened to you?" she whispered.

Owen had written to Mr. and Mrs. Burrows before leaving Hanover. The letter had informed them that although his heart was sound enough, the underlying cause of his difficulty, diabetes, was untreatable. He left the decision in their hands as to how much to tell Beth, but he felt that she needed to know, at the very least, that his health had experienced a serious setback. He concluded by saying that he'd like to arrange an immediate visit, to be attended by both of them as well as Beth, upon his return to Leominster.

Now, holding her in his arms in the hallway, he wanted to stroke Beth's lovely hair, but he dared not. "Are your parents here?" he asked.

She led him into the parlor, where Mr. and Mrs. Burrows rose from their armchairs as soon as they saw him. Their smiles were cemented in place. Mrs. Burrows came to him, reached up to kiss him on both cheeks. "It's so good to see you," she said. "How are you feeling?"

"I'm fine, Mrs. Burrows." He extended a hand to Mr. Burrows, who took it and gripped Owen's elbow with his other hand.

"Sit down, son, sit down," Mr. Burrows said, directing Owen to the armchair he'd just vacated. He and Mrs. Burrows, one on each side, joined Beth on the couch. "I assume they treated you well in New Hampshire?"

"I had the best of care."

Beth, her voice still hushed, asked again, "What's happened to you, Owen?"

Owen looked at her father, who turned his eyes away. So, Beth hadn't been told. Mrs. Burrows held Beth's hand in her lap.

"Do you know what diabetes is?"

Beth nodded. "It's the sugar disease."

"I have it, and there's no cure."

"What are you saying, Owen?" Tears began to streak her face.

"My poor girl," Mrs. Burrows said, patting Beth's hand.

"In all likelihood, I won't see thirty. I'll be fortunate to even come close."

There, it was out. He couldn't look at Beth, not if he wanted to keep the dispassion in his voice. He focused on Mr. Burrows, who was repeatedly pursing his lips.

"Beth and I didn't have a chance to formally announce our hopes, as we'd intended to do at Easter, with your blessing," he said. "Surely, you knew we'd begun planning a life together. That's no longer possible. I've already resigned my position. I'll be leaving Leominster immediately."

"For your health?" Mrs. Burrows asked.

"Where I am makes no difference."

"Then why are you leaving?" Beth asked.

"I think it's best."

Beth folded her hands in her lap and looked straight at him. "You promised me, not so long ago, that you would never abandon me. Have you forgotten that?"

"I haven't. But these circumstances couldn't have been foreseen, and now I find that I have to break that promise."

"For my own good."

He didn't answer.

"And I have no say in this?" Her voice, stronger now, expressed both hurt and anger.

"Pet—" her father attempted to interrupt.

"No," Owen said, "you have no say."

"Because?"

He needed to speak in the harshest of terms. "You can't possibly understand what you'd have to live with, and it would be no comfort to me. In the end, you'd not only be a widow at twenty-five, you'd be an old woman at twenty-five, and I won't have it."

"You give me no credit, Owen. You give my character and my love no credit at all."

He'd expected this. "Look to your parents, Beth. They understand what I'm saying."

"Don't speak for *me*," Mrs. Burrows said.

He wasn't surprised that Mrs. Burrows would take Beth's side. For now. "I apologize. That wasn't my intention. But neither you nor Beth can make more than the most . . . sentimental argument."

"At least hear me out," Beth said, now pleading.

"No," Owen said, "it would be painful and it would change nothing."

"This is *very* unfair," Mrs. Burrows said with surprising vehemence.

"Fair or unfair, I'm afraid it's all the same."

"What if we were already husband and wife?" Beth said.

He knew what she was thinking: she was remembering the time they'd spent together, side by side, in the Cambridge hotel. "But we're not."

"But what if we were?" she persisted.

"That would be different. As husband and wife we would have had time to grow beyond a childish infatuation."

"Childish infatuation!"

"Yes."

"Is that what you felt when you were making love to me, when we were lying next to each other?"

He saw Mr. and Mrs. Burrows shoot a look of utter dismay at each other; Mrs. Burrows's mouth hung open; Mr. Burrows clenched his jaws—the muscles at each hinge bulged.

Owen hadn't expected Beth, in her anger and desperation, to risk this much. She knew what her parents would be thinking. She straightened herself, drew her shoulders back. Her chin rose. "I know you're deliberately trying to hurt me, but it won't work." Her hazel eyes defied him. "You don't mean it."

"You need to accept that everything has changed."

"No, I don't."

"You *do*, Beth." He couldn't allow himself to give her any other option.

"Where will you go?" Mr. Burrows now asked.

"Home."

"To your father's farm?" Beth was clearly incredulous. "You despise that farm."

"It has its appeal."

"As what?"

"As a place without distractions."

"Am I a *distraction?*"

Yes, you silly girl, he thought with a wave of cruelty that first startled him and then immediately receded, leaving him barren, bereft of all hope. He just as suddenly ached to call her to him, but he didn't.

Beth had heard enough. She stood up. "If you do this," she said, "I will never forgive you." And she walked out of the room.

"You're being very cruel to her, Owen," Mrs. Burrows said. "And to us." She rose, prepared to follow her daughter. "I don't know what you've . . . already done, and I don't know what I'd do if I were you. But it wouldn't be this." She turned to her husband. "You need to talk to him." Then she traced Beth's steps.

Owen and Mr. Burrows sat in silence for several minutes. Owen knew he'd never enter this room again. He loved the people who lived here, all of them. Finally he said, "I should take my leave, Mr. Burrows."

Mr. Burrows shook his head. "This is a very sad day, my boy, for all of us."

"Yes, sir."

"You're *absolutely* determined to handle it this way? Because if you're not, we'd do everything we could to—"

"I'm determined."

Mr. Burrows cleared his throat. "Look here, I have to ask—"

"Beth and I have done nothing that you need to be concerned about, Mr. Burrows, despite what she may have wanted you to think in the heat of the moment. I give you my word. And I'm sure that when Beth recovers her composure, she'll also reassure you."

"Very well." His shoulders relaxed and he leaned back against the throw pillows that lined the back of the couch. "I must say, I'm relieved. You do your best to raise your children properly, but these days, you never know . . ." He reached into the inside pocket of his coat and withdrew a cigarette case and a small box of matches. Having lit the tobacco, he inhaled deeply and then exhaled the smoke through his nostrils. He inhaled again and fiddled with the cigarette, as if it were an unfamiliar object. "I daresay, there'll be many more tears shed."

"Better now than later."

"Maybe. Maybe." Mr. Burrows tapped a bit of ash into the pedestal ashtray that stood beside the arm of the couch. "If it weren't for Pet, you wouldn't be leaving, would you?"

"Speculating is pointless. It drains you. I learned that much in my month away." Owen needed to end this. He rose. "I should be going."

"Of course." Mr. Burrows, stabbing out his cigarette, struggled to his feet.

Owen held out his hand. "It's been a privilege to know you and your family, sir."

"Likewise." Mr. Burrows smothered Owen's hand in a firm grip. "I wish . . . well, you know what I wish, my boy."

"I'll see my way out," Owen said.

Owen closed the door for the last time, descended the porch steps, and followed the walkway to the street. He knew which second-story windows, above the porch roof, were hers, but he didn't turn to see if she stood there, cloaked in the white lace curtains.

3. Living

HE DIDN'T BOTHER knocking. He opened the door to the mud room, entered, dropped his two suitcases, and looked around. The boxes he'd shipped from Leominster had been stacked in a corner. He moved through the house quietly. All the windows were shut, the sills coated with a thick layer of grime. Spring hadn't penetrated; the house smelled like damp manure, sweat, and dried mud. He circled back to the kitchen. A half-hearted effort to clean the kitchen floor had left rag mop swirls; the corners, untouched. Standing over the deep sink, he turned the tap; the pipes groaned but clean cold water flowed into his hands. A permanent rust stain marked the shallow channel to the drain. He drank and then wiped his wet hands across his forehead and down his cheeks, and then he shook them dry. He knew his father wasn't plowing down by the river; one of the plow horses, gnawing at the fence, had watched him walk up from the road.

He heard, from out back, the sound of something heavy hacking into the ground. *Thwump.* Owen left through the mud room and rounded the corner of the house. His father, maul in hand, stood with his legs spread, up on the slope beyond the tool shed. He raised the maul over his right shoulder and brought it down with full force again. *Thwump.* Hands in his pockets, Owen watched the old man attack the ground for several minutes. His father had obviously been at this project for some time. A swath of hillside ten feet wide and fifty feet long had already been cleared of brambles, bushes, and, Owen realized, his mother's rhubarb patch.

"Father," Owen called out, "what are you doing?"

His father pivoted and saw him. Then he rested the maul on its head and wiped his face with the sleeve of his coveralls.

"Taming the wilds." He resumed the assault. Owen watched for another minute and then went back into the house.

When his father came in half an hour later Owen had a fresh pot of tea brewed and encased in a cozy, as his mother had always done. He had no reason to think that his father's habits had changed, taking his meals by the sun, not the clock: breakfast at first light from April to September, a large dinner at midday, tea as the sun began tipping toward the crest of the Green Mountains, supper as the last blue light departed. Owen had fixed his father a fried egg and toast and butter along with a wedge of sharp cheese from the round he found in the icebox. For himself, he carried a bowl of plain oatmeal to the table. He'd brought a small bag of rolled oats with him after calculating that even if his father still had a sack in the larder, it would probably be infested with weevils.

The elder Rouse, looking askance at the bowl of cereal, made no comment as he sat down and poured tea for himself. He mashed the egg into the bread with a fork, sprinkled a pinch of salt on top, and lifted the food to his mouth. He smelled fierce, like the barnyard; Owen wondered when he'd last washed his coveralls, which he hadn't bothered removing. Owen's mother never would've allowed him to come to the table like this.

"You need ice," Owen said, nodding toward the wooden icebox, "but I suppose you know that."

"The iceman's due." He slowly chewed the egg and toast. Then, having finished the mouthful, he wiped his hands on the legs of his coveralls and finally asked, "So what is it?" His mouth, beneath the salt and pepper of the mustache, falling beyond a simple frown, displayed a sadness as deep as the human face could express without words or tears.

Although Owen had rehearsed this scene many times on the way up here from Leominster, he found that he couldn't begin. He hadn't visited the farm since his mother's death, and communications back and forth had been infrequent and spare.

Nothing passed between them for an unbearable interval, but still Owen couldn't speak—he could feel the heat in his face and the deathly cold in his fingers, but he couldn't speak. He watched as his father began to cut his cheese into bite-sized pieces. The old man asked, "Why the oatmeal?"

The question was concrete, specific, and Owen swallowed a knot of phlegm and then answered, "Doctor's orders." He lifted the teapot and poured, and then he wrapped his fingers around the warming cup.

His father's gaze glanced off Owen's face but wouldn't hold; his eyes focused on the knife as it divided the cheese.

Owen didn't want or expect sympathy, but his father deserved to know the clinical truth. So he began.

The old man listened without interrupting. Owen explained the diagnosis and spoke about his evaluation at Mary Hitchcock. He added that he'd resigned from his job but said nothing about Beth Burrows or her family. "I won't overstay my welcome," he finished.

His father had stopped eating. His hands, hard and creased with dirt, had moved from the table to his lap, and he sat slumped in his chair, his shoulders collapsed. He looked defenseless—that was the word, Owen thought: he'd never seen his father defenseless, not even at his mother's funeral. A face like aged plaster, darkened by exposure, cracked and scored, his features otherwise colorless except for a ruddiness where his straight razor scraped across wattles and over a prominent Adam's apple. His face, Owen thought, could have been Lincoln's, had Lincoln lived so long: the broad brow, unruly eyebrows, strong nose, the long face tapering from prominent cheek bones to chin. Or as Lincoln's might have looked if he'd known that his youngest son, Tad, would soon follow his brothers Eddie and Willie Lincoln into the ground.

The old man straightened up. "It's your home. Stay as long as you choose."

"I'll make myself useful. Have you done the plowing yet?"

He shook his head. "Soil's still a little wetter than I like. I can wait a bit. Besides, there's less to do down by the river. I've let more of it go to hay. Potatoes are too much work, and I don't need the money. There's just me and the animals." Two horses, a couple of pigs for slaughtering, the hens, two milk cows. "I don't need both cows, but Sukey's pretty old and may go dry on me and I wouldn't want to do without. When it sours, I feed the extra milk to the pigs."

"There must be something I can do."

"I suppose the inside of the barn could use a whitewashing."

Owen scraped the last bit of oatmeal from his bowl. He'd learned to eat slowly, deliberately. His father was watching him. "That's no way to live," he said.

"There was a choice to be made. This is what I chose."

"I'm not sure what I'd do if I were you—I mean, your age. At my age . . ." He shrugged, his wide shoulders lifting and holding there, as if asking a question, and then quickly falling in answer, as if to say that he'd choose to go on about his daily business, such as it was, until nature finished him off.

"I won't be a burden to you," Owen said.

His father waved a hand in dismissal. "I have no burdens. When your mother crossed over, somehow she carried mine with her for the Good Lord to dispose of."

"Have you gone back to the church?"

"Well, I wouldn't say I'm the most God-fearing of men, but now and again I pay my respects. There's a certain comfort in it. Not that I think He's listening much."

"I never got anything out of it," Owen said. "I stopped a long time ago." Then he added, "I went a few times with a family I got to know in Leominster."

"Not papists, I hope."

"No, not that it would've mattered." Owen finished his tea.

"I take it this family has a daughter," Rouse said.

"They do."

Owen twirled the teacup on the table. How many times, when he was growing up, had his mother reprimanded him for doing exactly this?

"If you have no objections," Owen said, "I'm going to give this place a good cleaning for starters."

"Suit yourself," his father said.

It only took Owen a day to give the farmhouse—mud room, kitchen, living room, two bedrooms—a thorough cleaning, including the floors and windows, and another sunny day to wash, wring, and dry all the bed linens and towels. There wasn't much he could do about his father's upholstered chair and the living room couch except drag them outside and lay into them with a rug beater. Then he started on the barn, scraping and shoveling out the stalls to bare ground; scaling the old whitewash; sweeping away the cobwebs, dried-up wasp nests, and other accumulated filth, including the detritus dangling between the floor boards of the hay loft. He tried not to disturb the nests of the barn swallows and swifts tucked above; he liked the chatter and their swooping in and out. He was about to start on the whitewashing when his father announced toward late May that he intended to plow and then immediately plant the first few acres. He always staggered the planting so that the harvest would be spread out over six weeks. So Owen offered to ready the seed potatoes, stored since last fall in the root cellar.

Owen hadn't ventured into the dank gloom of the root cellar since before leaving for college. Because the house rested where the slope of the land paused in its rise from the river, the root cellar could be entered either through a door facing east or a trap door in the floor of the mud room. When he was growing up, the root cellar's plank shelving held the jars of corn, beans, tomatoes, pickles, beets, pepper relishes, and cauliflower that his mother put up during canning season, as well as bushel baskets of carrots, onions, potatoes, swedes, and winter squashes: butternut, hubbard, acorn. Now, however, the shelves stood almost empty, except for a dozen or so pint jars that undoubtedly contained something his father didn't stomach. Most of the rest of the cellar held burlap sacks filled with seed potatoes, each sack labeled by variety. Before planting, they needed to be quartered (being sure each quarter had at least one eye) and laid out for at least three days to dry—a tedious job he and his mother had shared each spring. Owen shouldered a bag and lugged it outside, into the sunlight. He suddenly felt incredibly fatigued. He wanted to collapse where he stood, but he dropped the sack, shook off the spell, and returned to the root cellar, intending to drag out another of the many bags. Instead, the near-empty shelves and the neatly spaced row of jars caught his eye for a second time, and in the half-light he made his way through the potato sacks to the shelves.

Rhubarb jam, labeled and dated. Rhubarb, sugar, a bit of lemon juice; his mother's legacy. His mother had always said that in New Hampshire you could count on only three edibles poking up out of the ground on their own early each spring: dandelions, horseradish, and rhubarb. She liked dandelion greens sprinkled with a little salt and vinegar, and his father enjoyed grated horseradish root on cold beef sandwiches, but Owen was the one who loved rhubarb. His father never ate it. He said it gave him the shits.

Owen sat down on a sack of potatoes and unscrewed the lid from a jar. He took out his pocket knife. The light from the door guided his hand. He drove the tip of the blade into the half-inch paraffin seal. The white chunk broke into three pieces, and the grayish-pink jam oozed up from beneath. Owen used the knife to lift out the chunks of paraffin. With two fingers he scooped the rhubarb jam into his mouth.

OWEN LAY IN HIS BED. He hadn't eaten solid food in two days, but he wasn't hungry. His father had found him lying in his own mess down in the root cellar. He'd worked his way through three jars of the rhubarb jam and had started on the fourth before he began vomiting, and once he began, he couldn't stop. After a while the dry heaves took over, and at some point he passed out. His father cleaned him up, put him to bed, and went for the doctor, who, as far as Owen could remember, had little to say other than advising, when he heard Owen's diagnosis, that Owen drink plenty of water and take it easy for a day or two. Beyond that, there was nothing the doctor could do except express his sympathies to Owen's father.

Why hadn't he ignored the impulse to open that first jar? By the third he already felt ill, but he'd continued on, letting the sweet, viscous jam slide down his throat as rapidly as he could. So stupid—he should have known his stomach would revolt. He *did* know, yet he didn't stop.

That first night, after the doctor had left, his father brought in his shotgun and stood it against the wall by the side of the bed. A kerosene lantern on the chest of drawers provided a little light, but not enough for Owen to clearly see his father's face. The old man said to him, "If you're going to do the job, do it right. If it was me, I'd take that shotgun down to the river, leave my clothes folded on the bank, walk in about hip deep, and then I'd put the barrel under my chin. No fuss, no mess, let the river wash it away."

"You've thought about this," Owen said.

"Indeed I have," his father said. And then he left the room, shutting the door behind him.

The next morning, the rain pounding on the roof woke Owen up long before he heard his father's steps on the creaking floorboards. The shotgun was gone.

He heard his father leave the house and then, maybe half an hour later, return, banging around in the kitchen—starting a fire in the stove, turning on the tap to fill the kettle and what sounded like a large pot; whacking something with a heavy knife or cleaver. Owen drifted off, and the next thing he remembered—quite a bit later, judging by the light pouring into the room from the single window—his father was standing by the bed, a cup and saucer in his hand. "Weak tea," he said. "Drink it. Can you manage that?"

"Yes," Owen said. He struggled to a sitting position and accepted the tea from his father. "What's that I smell?"

"Our dinner."

Owen came to the table in his nightshirt when the food was ready. His father ate the chicken; Owen drank the broth. He had more broth at tea time and more, with a few mouthfuls of tough, stringy chicken, for supper. Afterwards, they sat in the living room. All day, with his father coming and going, they'd said little to each other. Owen, wrapped in a wool blanket, felt no awkwardness in their continuing silence. His father perused a recent newspaper and then a seed catalog. Owen rocked in his mother's chair. At one point he asked, "Where's the Shakespeare?"

"Gone," Rouse said. "Before your mother passed, she gave it to the town's new lending library."

"I wonder if anyone's borrowed it."

"I wouldn't know. I suppose you could go see for yourself. The library's open for a couple of hours in the afternoon on Tuesdays and Fridays."

"It doesn't matter," Owen said.

The next morning, still lying in bed, still not hungry, Owen told himself he should get up, but he didn't. While at Mary Hitchcock he'd read that people in the throes of starvation often reach a point in their lethargy when they no longer desire food, that in fact their bodies begin rejecting nourishment as their organs begin the process of shutting down. Was he there? Not likely. Not yet.

He thought about Beth and what she'd be doing now, readying herself for work. He thought about her parents, their house, their joyous family.

He told himself again that he should get up. He thought about the sacks of potatoes waiting to be quartered, down in the dank of the root cellar, and the remaining unopened jars on the shelf. He thought about his mother, lost, and his unknown brother, lost, and then he thought about the Hoosac Tunnel and the trains that traversed it—the contained fury, the billowing smoke and the soot blackening the arched walls, the sharp sparks of wheels on rails, the yellow beams from the headlamps cutting into the darkness and the pale lights shining from the windows of the passenger cars, the passengers going . . . somewhere, anywhere.

So why not him?

What in God's creation did he need beside clothes on his back and maybe a simple tent for shelter and a little cash for a room in a flophouse and a bath when he passed through a city? And money for food. He started to laugh. You don't need food if you know how to starve. Dry rolled oats, eggs, butter—if not butter, lard, which would do—consumables available at every country store and outpost of civilization between the Atlantic and the Pacific.

What bound him to this bed? Death was coming for him, regardless. If he left this bed, the farm, and thereby, in the end, shortened his life by a month or even a year, what did it matter? Lying here offered neither comfort nor security. Discomfort he could face—at least he thought he could— but not debilitation, losing control of body, emotions, self.

The house was quiet. His father had already left for the fields. Owen could hear birds, phoebes or wrens, singing outside. He got up. He walked into the kitchen. On the table: a new box of Quaker Oats, a half dozen brown eggs, and butter in a covered dish.

After dinner, sitting again in his mother's chair across from his father, Owen said, "I'll start work on those seed potatoes tomorrow. I'll do enough for your first planting, and then I'll be going."

"Suit yourself," his father replied, tamping tobacco into his evening's pipe.

"Did you ever see where Robbie died?" Owen asked.

The old man drew the flame to the tobacco. "Once, back before you were born, but your mother wanted no part of it."

"What's it like?"

"Tracks running into a black hole. A stone wall around the entrance, holding the hillside in place. Scrub brush and saplings growing up all around."

"Did you take the train through to North Adams?"

"I did." He relit the pipe, which had failed to catch. "The Western Gateway, that's what the railroad called it." He shook his head and blew out the match. "All those boys that died in there. People forget."

"I hear there's plans to electrify the tunnel."

"Is there now?" The old man sat, staring off.

"I've been thinking about traveling out West," Owen said. "I have a little money saved."

"Well, that could be a fine thing."

Owen sensed that his father didn't want to talk anymore, and he let him be.

In the morning, Owen set to work on the potatoes. His father headed off to town, intent on some vague errand. When he returned, just in time for dinner, he sat down and slid a thick yellow envelope across the table toward Owen, who'd fixed them tinned corned beef, mashed carrots, and also boiled potatoes for his father. "What's this?" Owen sat down. He lifted the flap of the envelope without picking it up. It was filled with new bills.

"Just take it."

"Where did this come from?"

"I got an advance."

"On what?"

"Howard and me came to an agreement."

"Howard?"

"Howard Handke. Lumpy."

"You sold him the river acreage?"

"The whole kit and caboodle, in a manner of speaking." Rouse laughed, a rumble deep in his throat. "I made him a happy man. He got what his father never managed to. So now we're on a first-name basis."

"What do you mean, 'in a manner of speaking'?"

"The purchase agreement will be executed—that's the word his lawyer used, 'executed'—in five years or upon my demise, whichever comes first. Until then, I can take advances, up to eighty percent of the sale price, and he can do what he wants on the fifteen acres down by the river."

"But if you're still here in five years, what then?"

"I can live out the rest of my days in the house, use the barn for whatever animals I still have, and tap the maples." Pushing the plate of food away, he added, "I ate in town. Howard paid." He chuckled.

Owen tucked the flap into the envelope. "Why now? Do you need money?"

His father grunted. "I'm getting too old to be farming potatoes."

"That's not the reason."

Rouse unbuttoned his shirt sleeves and began rolling them up. "You were never going to come back here to stay, even before. If I died on a Wednesday, you'd've sold the land on Thursday. But here's the thing." He leaned forward and put his hands flat on the table. "Hear me now." His eyes held Owen's. "That would've been all right. Keep it, sell it—it was to be yours to do with as you saw fit. There's nobody else left on my side of the family. With both of us gone, the land would go to your mother's second or third cousins up in Laconia, or wherever they got themselves to. They'd probably kill each other, fighting over it. So I decided to take Lumpy's money." He reached out and with a gnarled index finger inched the envelope closer to Owen. "Go back and marry that girl of yours in Leominster, if she'll still have you. Or go out West, if that's what you choose. See Niagara Falls and the Rocky Mountains. Sail to China. Whatever you want. Just get on with it. Go."

"Maybe you should go, too—someplace you've never been."

"Oh, I've seen enough of the world to know I wouldn't take any pleasure in seeing more of it."

One autumn when he was a boy, after the harvest was in, his parents had taken a trip to Gloucester, Massachusetts, to see the ocean. They'd always thought the ocean was blue, but it wasn't. It was gray, he remembered his mother saying. They couldn't tell the clouds from the sea, except for the waves. They didn't care for it, so they came home a day early. After that, Owen knew, they'd talked a few times about going to see Niagara Falls, but they never did.

"What do you think Lumpy will do with the house when it's his?" Owen asked.

The old man snorted. "Douse it with kerosene and light a match."

His father was probably right. "And that'll be that," Owen said.

"That'll be that," his father echoed.

The following day, at Owen's insistence, they went into town and set up a bank account in both their names. They deposited all the advance Rouse had received from Howard Handke so that they'd both have access. Owen wasn't about to squander the money, but the undefined horizon felt less daunting, knowing he could go where he pleased and rely on Western Union to rescue him if need be.

A plan was taking shape. He'd travel light: a pup tent, an oilskin slicker, and a large knapsack packed with a change of clothes, toiletries, a mess kit, binoculars, a tape measure, his Brunton pocket transit, a field notebook. Anything else he needed, he could pick up along the way.

He parted from his father two days later at the Ashuelot train depot. They shook hands but had difficulty speaking. The old man's Adam's apple rose and fell, rose and fell, and his lips were tight beneath his mustache until he finally cleared his throat with a gruff cough. "You come back when you're finished with your traveling."

"I'll try," Owen said. If he looked straight ahead, his eyes met his father's unshaven, stippled chin. "I will," he corrected himself for the old man's benefit.

"I'd like to have the family together."

In the graveyard, behind the Presbyterian Church. Owen had always imagined that his father's burial plot would be on the slope above the farmhouse, but now the land wouldn't be his to lie in. So they might as well all lie side by side. "That would be good," he said, again to appease his father. Let the old man take a bit of comfort in the thought. Owen's thoughts lay elsewhere. He intended to board the Boston & Maine, pass through the murderous Hoosac Tunnel, emerge from the western portal in the sharp brightness of the afternoon, and keep going as long as he could.

4. Mesa and Canyon

HE COULDN'T COUNT the cities he'd passed through on the way to Durango, Colorado, although he retained the prominent names—Albany, Buffalo, Cleveland, Chicago, St. Louis, Kansas City, and then Denver, where he boarded the Denver & Rio Grande narrow gauge. He'd taken one train after another, waiting in stations from the ornate to the rustic for the next connection, not venturing outside into the cities that he would never see, eating sparingly in depot restaurants, dislocated, sleeping sporadically and dreaming wild dreams.

He arrived in Durango in the late afternoon. The coke smoke discharged by the stacks of the American Smelting and Refining Company's silver and gold smelter hung low, smelling like rotten eggs, and in combination with the gray cover of clouds obscured the tops of the mountains to the north. He wandered the streets as a drizzle began to fall. His footfalls echoed on the wooden sidewalks, a high step up from the wide dirt streets, the horse dung, and the tracks of the electric streetcars. He took it all in: storefronts of glass and raw timber; wooden freight wagons of every size showing their age and weathered wear; horses harnessed, ridden by cowboys, or tied to hitching posts, silent or snorting, watching with protuberant, fathomless brown eyes; women whose long skirts stirred up street and sidewalk dust not yet settled by the rain; businessmen in vests and suits and ties; the refuse-strewn banks of the Rio de las Animas, the River of Souls. The sulfurous air made his head throb and he felt utterly lost, on the edge of perdition.

He stopped at the corner of Main Avenue and Seventh Street, behind him the four-story Strater Hotel, all red brick and sandstone and glass, and didn't know where to turn. He needed to sleep, but he knew, without even walking into the lobby, not that he couldn't afford the Strater, but that he would later regret the extravagance. He headed east, past Second Avenue to Third, and there he turned north, into a neighborhood of middling residences, including, not far up the block, a boarding house. The sign on the porch read

Miss Maude Stoner, Prop.
Only Gentlemen Allowed
Vacancy

Miss Stoner, who, she promptly informed him, preferred to be called Miss Maude by her boarders, was a gray-bunned, middle-aged stump of a woman with a brusque tone and a perpetual squint. Yes, he could have a room for two nights, paid in advance, breakfast included at no additional charge, although she preferred letting rooms for no less than a week at a time to discourage a transitory clientele—she directed her tightened squint toward his knapsack—and she didn't rent to Eye-talians or slant-eyes, even if they worked at the smelter, or allow lady visitors beyond the front parlor, or permit alcohol on the premises, and if he intended to frequent the "district" between the depot and the river and thereabouts, he'd best take lodging elsewhere. Owen waited a full ten seconds, to be sure she'd finished, before replying that, yes, he'd take her vacant room. With that matter settled and the cash in her hand, she added that dinner would be steak and kidney pie, fifty cents extra. This wasn't a proprietress who'd take it kindly if he asked her to fix him oatmeal instead, so he silently counted out another four bits.

Miss Maude showed him to his room on the second floor, with a view of the privy out back, and he asked her to wake him for dinner. She left and he fell onto the bed, the springs under the thin mattress rolling beneath him like waves, and he was instantly asleep.

After dinner the four other boarders—an apprentice lawyer, a bank clerk, a deskman for the Durango & Silverton, and a drummer who visited regularly—invited Owen to join them for a cigar in the parlor, but he demurred, choosing instead a bath (which gave him the surreptitious opportunity to wash his dirty laundry) and a long sleep. In the morning, over oatmeal, eggs, and coffee, he inquired about guides who led inexpensive tours of the cliff ruins at Mesa Verde, only to be told that if he didn't want to be robbed blind by a local outfit that organized two-week expeditions for well-heeled tourists, he needed to try his luck at Mancos or Cortez, a day farther west. Now that Mesa Verde had been made a national park, the government was trying to control access to the whole mesa, partly to discourage pot hunters, but he could still find a local rancher, if he asked around, who could take him up there on the quiet. He asked Miss Maude to save any leftover oatmeal for him and, if she'd be so kind, to hard-boil a half-dozen eggs, which he'd gladly pay for. She raised her wicked eyebrows and, with last night's half-eaten dinner obviously in mind, disparaged "picky eaters," but she accepted his twenty-five cents.

An hour later, with the eggs and an old bail-handle candy tin of congealed oatmeal at the bottom of his knapsack, Owen set off to buy a pair of high boots, a flannel shirt, corduroys, and a woolen jacket—his tablemates had warned him that even in midsummer the mesa could be crisp at night, and snow in June couldn't be ruled out—and to check the Rio Grande Southern schedule for tomorrow. It'd be a short ride: his destination, Mancos, was less than thirty miles west, tucked in a valley beneath Mesa Verde.

Walking about under a dome of solid blue after having slept solidly and eaten in affable company, and with the worst of the stink from the smelter lifted from the city by the day's prevailing winds, Owen felt less intimidated by his surroundings, less alien. Less Eastern.

The next morning, with Miss Maude's permission, he mixed the leftover glutinous breakfast cereal with egg whites and lard. With a look of utter disgust, she asked if he planned to take that with him on the train. He told her that he did. She grabbed the spoon from him, added additional eggs, a teaspoon of baking soda, another of nutmeg, and an additional cup of uncooked rolled oats to the bowl. She reached for her sugar canister, but he told her he didn't like sweets, which drew a long look from her before she spooned the concoction into a baking pan that she then slid into her oven. Later, after the pan cooled, she cut the loaf into wrappable portions. Owen couldn't tell if Miss Maude had taken a shine to him or if he was the object of motherly pity.

Later that morning he boarded a rusting passenger car, behind a second-hand Denver & Rio Grande locomotive that looked ready for the scrap yard. The train coughed its way across the Animas and followed the three-foot-wide track into Wildcat Canyon, in the gap south of the La Plata Mountains. He sat idly, observing through the grimy window the sharp drop-offs; the walls of red rock broken by gullied slopes where heavily rooted stumps looked ready, come the next flood, to claw their way out of the ground; the neatly cultivated plots and crude log cabins when the canyon floor widened; and always the startling blue overhead. Owen took a square of cold oatmeal loaf from his pack and nibbled at it.

The train delivered him to Mancos an hour later. To the west the harsh walls of Mesa Verde rose, by Owen's guess, at least 1,500 feet to the table top, which was tipped slightly downward toward the south. The Alamo Ranch, just outside of Mancos, had been home to the Wetherill clan when, two decades ago, first Al and then Richard and their brother-in-law, Charlie Mason, stumbled upon the Mesa Verde cliff dwellings. Owen knew that Richard was now running a trading post down in Chaco Canyon, some 150 miles south, but he hoped he could convince one of Richard's brothers to guide him into the ruins.

Owen soon learned, to his great disappointment, that the Wetherills had all moved on. According to the Mancos station clerk, they still passed through Mancos now and again, but the Alamo Ranch had been sold at public auction. Al Wetherill, the last owner, burdened by the debts he'd inherited when his father died, had ended up in Gallup, New Mexico, where he'd taken over as postmaster. John Wetherill and his wife had established their own trading post at Oljato, in southern Utah, and Clate, the last to leave Mancos, had moved up above Creede, on the other side of the Weminuche Pass, and was building a fish hatchery with his sister Anna's husband, Charlie Mason. Win, having run several trading posts on his own, including the one at Two Grey Hills in the Chuska Mountains, without notable success, appeared to be helping Richard run horses in Chaco Canyon—that was the latest the station clerk had heard, anyway.

"I'm guessing you want to see the mesa," said the clerk, an old codger with a tobacco-stained beard. "Most tours are being run out of Durango or Cortez." He jerked his thumb westward.

"I don't want a tour."

The clerk looked askance. "It's a national park now, you know. No pot hunting allowed." He paused. "Unofficially, you can do whatever you damn well please, but I'm guessing"—he leaned forward over the counter, the better to see what Owen was wearing and if he carried anything other than his knapsack—"you don't have a lot of backcountry experience."

"You're doing a lot of guessing," Owen said.

The clerk shrugged.

Owen wanted to win him over, so he added, "But you strike me as a man who knows what he's talking about. Any recommendation?"

"Find a guide, preferably one with camping equipment and a pack mule."

"You know of somebody who might be willing?"

Bruce Fielder had a small spread down on the Mancos River, a mile or so beyond what had been the Wetherill homestead, itself three miles southwest of Mancos. With a sturdy wife and two nearly-grown sons who could manage the ranch in his absence, Fielder had been guiding small groups up onto the mesa for ten years, and he didn't indicate any surprise when Owen stated that rather than taking the favored northern trail, he wanted to travel the route the Wetherills had used, crossing the Mancos River at the foot of Soda Canyon and proceeding up onto the mesa from Cliff Canyon.

"It's longer and more rugged," Fielder said. He wore his broad-brimmed hat pushed back on his head, with the sides curled upward above his jug-handle ears. "Tougher on the horses too."

"I won't need a horse," Owen said.

Fielder grinned and spat. "You plan to walk?"

"I do."

Incredulous, Fielder asked, "Why, on God's green acre?"

"I don't get along with horses. I'm better off on my own two feet."

Fielder gave Owen an appraising up-and-down. "Are you sure you're up to it? Climbing at eight thousand feet ain't easy unless you're accustomed to the altitude. It's hard on your lungs, and the thin air can make your head swim. And, pardon me for saying it, you aren't the fittest specimen I ever seen."

"My lungs are fine," Owen said. He'd given careful thought about how much he should reveal—and conceal. "I have a condition that makes it hard to keep weight on." He stretched the truth: "I'm plenty fit."

"Well, if you say so," Fielder said, despite his obvious skepticism. "Just don't go taking sick up there, if it's just you and me."

"I'll be fine."

"Huh." That appraising look again. "There's another thing you should know," Fielder said. "A hired crew, mostly fellows from Mancos, has headed up to Cliff Palace. A fellow named Fewkes from Washington is running things. He was here last summer, too, working at Spruce Tree House. They did a right good job, shoveling out the clutter and rebuilding walls and everything. Of course, I'm assuming Cliff Palace is what you came here to see. If you've heard of Mesa Verde, you've heard of Cliff Palace."

"Can we get up there ahead of them?" Owen asked. He desperately wanted to experience Cliff Palace—the crumbling walls, the collapsed roofs and ruined towers, even the mounds of rubble—as Richard Wetherill had. "Can we leave tomorrow?" Owen urged.

Fielder offered him a place to sleep for the night. Once again, so as not to offend, Owen ate sparingly of what Selma Fielder put on the table that evening, supplemented, when he crawled into a bedroll before the hearth, by one of Miss Maude's oatmeal cakes, and early in the morning he, Fielder, and a pack mule headed out, following the shallow, snaking river south, past the cultivatable fields and good grazing, drawing closer to and then paralleling the steep east wall of the mesa. They made slow progress as tumbled rocks, sloughed from the cliff face, increasingly replaced the more stable upstream footing. That night they camped beneath aspen and gamble oaks, near the juncture with Moccasin Canyon—still several miles from the entrance to Soda Canyon—one of numerous clefts between the fingers that spread south from the back of Mesa Verde's veined and tendoned hand.

At midmorning of the following day, they turned due north into Soda Canyon and, soon after veering into the offshoot called Cliff Canyon, began to scale the wall, switchbacking when possible, but more often seeking out paths discovered by the Wetherills' stray cattle twenty years before. Across the canyon, two-thirds of the way up, stunted trees, mostly evergreens, clung to the uneven ledges perched above variegated layers of sandstone and shale. At the top, above the most recent sandstone deposits and anchored in sand blown there over millions of years, a canopy of fir, spruce, and pine stretched unbroken, just back from the cliff edge.

Owen tried to conceal that his lungs felt ready to burst. His heart pounded against the front wall of his ribs. At least they'd been climbing in the shade. Fielder, who'd barely broken a sweat, stopped opposite the stunted trees and, unscrewing the cap from a canteen, sat down to rest for the final ascent. Owen collapsed beside him. "Much farther?" he wheezed.

"Nope."

Owen extracted two oatmeal cakes from his knapsack and offered one to Fielder, who bit into it, chewed, and then commented, "Could use more sugar." The slant of the cliff blocked the sun, but Fielder said, "Judging by the shadows coming off those trees"—he pointed across the canyon to the top—"if we don't dawdle, we should be able to get to the overlook while the sunlight's still deep in the alcove. It's something to see, let me tell you."

"I didn't get the impression," Owen said, his breathing having slowed enough for him to string a phrase together, "that you thought much of the ruins."

"Oh, I respect the skill and the determination. Whoever built it, all they had was stone and wood and their hands."

They sat for another ten minutes before continuing on. An hour later, having finished the climb, they proceeded along the rim of the mesa, through the pinyon, juniper, and scrub brush that had taken root.

Owen knew what to expect. At the Peabody he'd seen the photographs taken by Baron Gustaf Nordenskiöld, a Swede who showed up in Mancos in the summer of 1891 and, astounded by the ruins, asked the Wetherills to help him collect relics. The Wetherills obliged, but when Nordenskiöld tried to ship his collection east, a group of outraged Coloradans served him with a warrant at the train station in Durango, accusing him of plundering the state's heritage. The baron hired a local lawyer who quickly pointed out that neither the state nor Washington had any law that prohibited removing pottery, bones, arrowheads, tools, or anything else. So some of the first objects removed from Mesa Verde ended up in Europe.

Now Owen's heart was racing as much from anticipation as exertion. The sun, still high overhead, cast barely a shadow beneath them. They emerged from the tree cover onto a sandy ledge, and across the canyon, tucked away beneath a sandstone overhang, diagonally cut by sun and shadow, stood Cliff Palace . . . no longer abandoned.

"Shit," Fielder said.

At least a dozen men were working in the ruins, mostly filling buckets and wheelbarrows with shovelfuls of rubble from collapsed roofs and walls. Owen took out his binoculars. He could see that at the southern end they'd already cleared a ramp and walkway along a lower plaza. Near the northern end, several men appeared to be getting ready to repair a wide break in the wall of a four-story tower, which looked ready to collapse. The alcove was immense—more than 300 feet wide, he guessed, and 60 feet high, and at its deepest, 80 feet or more. The Wetherills had counted over 200 rooms.

"Can I borrow those?" Fielder asked. Owen handed him the binoculars and sat down, wrapping his arms around his pulled-up knees. His feet hurt. He wanted to take off his boots but he didn't, figuring that his blistered feet might swell and he might not get the boots back on.

He'd wanted to see the unoccupied ruins, to walk through them alone, selfishly, trying to smell the fires that had blackened the ceilings of the rooms, and imagining the chanting from deep within the ceremonial kivas under his feet. A foolish fantasy.

"I know most of those fellows," Fielder said, the glasses still held to his eyes. The high pitch of his cackle surprised Owen. "A couple of them I wouldn't trust to shovel out the barn. But I guess it don't matter. Everything of value's long since been taken out of there and shipped off."

To Denver. To Philadelphia via Chicago. To Sweden.

Owen watched someone, a kerchief over his mouth, dump a wheelbarrow load of stones over the lip of the cliff, onto the refuse mound below. A cloud of dust rose, hung like a veil in the air.

"What d'you want to do?" Fielder asked, handing the binoculars back. He removed his hat and scratched his sweating scalp. Someone, spotting them across the ravine, waved, and Fielder waved back, sweeping his hat in an arc over his head. "D'you want to go down? Fewkes'll probably let you in as long as you stay out of their way."

"I'm too late," Owen said.

"Well, that depends on what you're after, doesn't it?" Fielder donned his hat and adjusted the crown until it fit just so. "If you're set on seeing ruins that haven't been tampered with at all, you should head up to Marsh Pass, in Arizona Territory, and look up John Wetherill. By chance, that cliff ruin he just discovered was already on government-protected land. Not even the pot-hunters have gotten into it."

"Maybe I'll do that," Owen said. They continued to watch the men working across the way.

Owen, with great ambivalence, understood what Fewkes and his crew were doing. They had no alternative if they wanted to study the underlying structure and see what needed shoring up to prevent further collapse. But the end result would be less than authentic for all those who, afterward, came to study or simply walk through the ruins. Something would be lost by the preservation. Part of him wanted them to leave the fallen walls and buried walkways to time and the elements. He wondered how Richard Wetherill, with more practical experience than anyone else, first in Mesa Verde, and then in Utah's Grand Gulch, and now in Chaco Canyon, felt about these matters. "How far is it to Chaco Canyon?" he asked Fielder.

"About 150 miles from Mancos. Richard's not doing any more digging in the ruins down there, you know. He signed that part of his homestead over to the government last year, though he still has a stream of visitors passing through."

Owen frowned; he hadn't heard. "Have you been there?"

"Me?" Fielder shook his head. "Too far afield." Another wheelbarrow of debris was tipped over the side. "From what I've heard the ruin they call Pueblo Bonito is so big that you could drop this here palace in the middle of it and still have room to hold a good-sized country rodeo. But if you're thinking of heading down there," Fielder went on, "you surely don't want to walk it. Most of the way's as dry as an old woman's privates. Your best bet would be to make your way to Farmington, across the line in New Mexico Territory. Richard's hands pick up most of his supplies and trade goods in Farmington, and chances are you could hitch a ride."

"All right," Owen said, standing up, "I've seen enough. Let's go."

"Back to Mancos?" Fielder asked.

"After making that hellish climb? You must be kidding. There are other ruins to see, aren't there?"

Fielder grinned. "Well, we can make it to Spruce Tree House in an hour, if you care to see what it looks like all cleaned out and spiffed up. From there, if we hike north another six or seven miles, we can circle around Long Canyon, skirt the north rim, and come back south onto Wetherill Mesa. You can take a gander at Long House and some of the other big ruins that nobody's touched except to dig for pottery and skeletons and the like."

"How long will that take us?"

"A few days to do it up right."

"You've got the time?"

Fielder's grin widened. "If you've got the money, I've got the time."

TWO WEEKS LATER, Owen stood on the north mesa above the ruins of Pueblo Bonito in Chaco Canyon, waiting for the Southwestern summer to burn into the sky, which was still, just before sunrise, a cloudless iridescence seamlessly varying: a flattened arch of golden yellow at the eastern edge, dispersing into a pale blue above; and then gray, and grayer still. Even the gray possessed a clarity, disturbed only by the dark plume of coal smoke rising behind them, from inside the Wetherill's home. Owen dug in his pocket for his watch: 4:55. The sun was due to break the horizon.

"Keep scanning the north," Richard Wetherill said.

Beneath their feet lay the ruins of Pueblo Alto—maybe a hundred or more rooms in its heyday—which, unprotected by the canyon, had disintegrated to fragmented walls around a D-shaped plaza and, along the periphery, clusters of rubble-filled rooms and kivas. They had ascended the 200-foot canyon wall behind Pueblo Bonito, using the steps and toeholds cut by the Anasazi. At the top, guided by the barely visible profile of Pueblo Alto against the sky, they crossed the mesa in silence, making their way around the greasewood and sagebrush and then, with dawn approaching, scaling the slope of debris on the eastern side of the ruin. They found secure footing at the highest elevation of the eastern wall and waited. Beyond, below their northward line of sight, Escavada Wash separated the edge of north mesa from a long, coarse, treeless expanse of high desert. To the west: the much smaller New Alto ruins and the narrow channel called the Rincón del Camino, and, farther on, the juncture of the Escavada and the Chaco Wash.

Owen had reached the Wetherill's trading post a week earlier. At Bruce Fielder's insistent invitation, Owen had returned to Fielder's ranch after their descent from Mesa Verde, and then, having spent two days resting up, rode the narrow-gauge back to Durango, where he hitched a ride south to Farmington with a Smith & Wesson salesman who filled the journey with lurid tales of ambushes and slaughter in an unsuccessful effort to convince his passenger that he needed a firearm to protect himself from man and beast in these wilds. Owen arrived in Farmington on the same day that, fortuitously, two freight wagons were being loaded with merchandise destined for Chaco Canyon—crates of canned goods, sacks of grain and flour, three drums of kerosene, twenty bolts of cloth (plain cottons and bright sateens), and, in the larger wagon, lumber and rolls of tar paper. One of Wetherill's men, a tall sullen fellow named Bill Finn, brushed off Owen's inquiry with a scowl, but Owen had greater success with the other teamster, lanky, middle-aged, amiable Gus Thompson, who "wouldn't say no to company." A crippled foot relegated Thompson to teamster and stableman. He'd worked for Wetherill, he told Owen during the journey south, since the founding of the Hyde Exploring Expedition in 1896 by Wetherill and Fred and Talbot Hyde, heirs to the Babbo soap fortune. They opened up a string of stores and trading posts after the government, late in 1901, responding to accusations that the ruins were being despoiled, ordered a halt to all excavations. It all got out of hand, though, Thompson told Owen, partly because the younger Hyde brother, Fred, who'd remained a close friend of Richard and still, unannounced, wandered in and out of Chaco Canyon, was a dreadful businessman, buying on credit and running up unpayable debts. These days, with a wife and four youngsters to support, Richard devoted almost all his time to building the Triangle Bar Triangle Ranch. They ran about 1,500 horses, 5,000 sheep, and over 100 cattle.

"What about the trading post?" Owen asked.

"He's about ready to sell that off," Thompson replied. "Navajos owe him more money than he'll ever be able to collect."

They stopped the first night at Simpson's Store in Gallegos Canyon, twenty-five miles south of Farmington. Owen couldn't help noticing that Bill Finn said little and kept to himself. Nor could he help noticing that Finn wore a .45 revolver strapped to his thigh. Owen had seen a number of men, generally the scruffier sort well coated with dust from the trail, wearing pistols in Durango and Farmington, but they were a small minority. When Owen commented to Thompson about Finn's surliness, the teamster told him that he had best steer clear. Finn had shown up at the Triangle Bar Triangle about five years ago. None of the other hands knew anything about his past, though rumors circulated about his having robbed banks and rustled cattle and run from the law down in Texas. Finn was a top ranch hand but hated hauling goods and rarely did so, which accounted for his present ill temper.

"What about the .45?" Owen asked. "Does he ever take it off?"

"For Christmas dinner," Thompson said.

Three days later, peppered by grit from a foul wind and by Bill Finn's curses, they crossed the Escavada, just above its juncture with the Chaco Wash. The water ran low and turbid, barely reaching the wheel hubs, although the widely spaced, entrenched banks of the arroyo made it clear that flood waters could flow through here with considerable force. This year, the rainy season of frequent afternoon thunderstorms, many of them menacingly violent, was late in starting, and the vegetation—mostly reeds and canes in the channel; black greasewood, saltbush, and rabbit bush above—was so sparse that Owen asked Thompson how horses, sheep, or anything else could find enough grazing to survive.

"They go up the rincons that open into the canyon," Thompson said. "There's grasses and chokeberry, golden current, squaw bush, Mormon tea."

Owen looked up. Sitting on a bluff, a jagged fragment of ancient wall rose against the sky.

Richard Wetherill was in Albuquerque on business, but Owen was greeted in the kitchen of their home by his wife, Marietta, a short, plump woman with a round, pleasing face and vibrant brown eyes. She was much younger than Owen had expected, probably in her early thirties, which would make Richard close to twenty years her senior. Even before he told her that Bruce Fielder sent his regards, Marietta had directed Gus Thompson to show Owen to the bunkhouse, where he was welcome to stay until her husband returned. In the meantime, she'd set another place at the table. When he offered to pay, she refused, noting that she and Mr. Wetherill, as a consequence of living at such a remove, always welcomed visitors.

The Wetherill house, built with stones gathered from the collapsed walls of nearby ruins, was modest: kitchen, dining room, bedroom, nursery, and a combined den and office. Bancos for extra seating lined the walls of the large dining room, and ponderosa beams scavenged from Pueblo Bonito served as vigas, with thinner logs, aged to a deep brown, set perpendicularly. Generally, everyone—family, ranch hands, hired girls who helped in the kitchen and with the children, visitors—ate together, and at the very first meal Owen saw why adding one more to the roster presented no burden. The supper table, always laid promptly and without fanfare at six o'clock, featured such a variety of dishes—most often a stewed chicken or a cut of mutton, beef, or horse; rice and pinto beans or dumplings or potatoes; canned peas, carrots, asparagus, green beans, or, less often, fresh greens or a winter squash or turnip left over from last fall's harvest; bread or rolls; farmer's or hard cheese; and dried fruits, pie, or rice pudding for dessert—and was consumed so quickly by the collective maw that no one paid much attention to what anyone else ate. Breakfast always included oatmeal, eggs, bacon, and biscuits or hotcakes, whereas midday dinner tended to be more catch-as-catch-can since, most days, several of the ranch hands were out on the range or off to Farmington or Thoreau, the nearest railhead, although no one ever left the ranch in the morning without something for his saddlebag.

When Mrs. Wetherill inquired about Owen's absence from dinner two days running—he'd been at Chaco Canyon for almost a week and Richard Wetherill hadn't returned yet—he said he'd lost track of time during his explorations of the various ruins and was too far afield to return. She offered to have one of the girls pack him a lunch each day he expected to be absent, but he declined. He wouldn't add to anyone's chores, he said, although he'd accept any leftover oatmeal and eggs from breakfast. Mrs. Wetherill gave him the eye.

"I guess that sounds like a peculiar request," he said.

"Well, just as long as you don't go hungry—*that* I won't allow. I remember too clearly the days when the only meat on the table was some varmint that Mr. Wetherill shot."

He could have let the moment pass, but instead he explained that he had a medical condition that limited what he could eat.

"I see." She bit her lower lip and appeared to take a closer inventory of his appearance, the oversized collarless shirt, the corduroys bunched at the waist and held up by a belt long enough to wrap once around and then half way to his back again. "If I'm not prying, what foods are bad for you?"

"Sugar. Rice. Potatoes. Corn. Bread—anything made with flour."

"Heavens, that's more than half of what I put on the table!" She sounded genuinely distressed. "What *can* you eat?"

"Oatmeal. Eggs. Butter. Cheese. Meat." He added, in response to her frown, "Some vegetables, too. Green beans, onions, tomatoes—things like that. And I've really learned to like chiles, the hotter the better, and garlic. And spices. Cinnamon, nutmeg . . .

"I can't do much about spices," she said. "I've got salt, black pepper, and dried parsley and dill. I buy fresh chilies in the fall, but by the end of winter even the ones I've dried have been used up. I save cinnamon for special occasions. But garlic," she brightened a bit, "I love a roast leg of lamb with little slivers of garlic poked deep into the meat, although the crowd around my dinner table would just as soon eat mutton stew with posole, just as long as it's salty enough." She straightened out the skirt of her apron. "I promise you, before you leave here, I'll fix you that leg of lamb."

"It sounds wonderful," Owen said, smiling. "But please don't go out of your way on my account. I make do, and I don't mind."

"You aren't the first guest to find our table unpalatable."

"That's not true at all!" he protested. "And I enjoy the company."

A smile illuminated the finest features of her youthful face. "A German couple showed up here last year and thought they could order from a menu." Her eyes flashed with mischief. "I said that if they wanted schnitzel they should try McTague's in St. Louis." She gave a quick laugh. "People get peculiar notions."

"Maybe it's from those travelogues they attend—travelogues have become quite popular in salons back East."

"Salons," she huffed. "I'm still waiting for that sort to give Mr. Wetherill the respect that he's due. Some very nasty things have been written—about how he plundered Mesa Verde for his own gain, when from the very start he wanted the government to come in and protect the ruins. Does it look to you as if he's made a fortune selling antiquities? He could've sold off piece by piece what he collected from Mesa Verde and Grand Gulch and Pueblo Bonito, but instead he kept those collections together and now they're in museums. And if that's not enough to put up with, now Mr. Wetherill has to contend with politicians like that Indian superintendent up in Shiprock, William Shelton, who sends his spies down here and writes reports about how Mr. Wetherill steals from and mistreats the Navajos!" She brushed a stray lock of hair back from her forehead. "Don't get me going, Mr. Rouse." She released another pleasing, throaty laugh. "But I guess I get myself going, don't I?"

"I greatly admire what your husband has accomplished," Owen said. "I wouldn't have come all this way if I didn't."

She beamed. "That's kind of you to say. You stay as long as you see fit. I think Mr. Wetherill will enjoy having you around."

"And you're very gracious," he said.

She brushed off his compliment with a wag of a forefinger. "Just don't you go hungry."

Owen saw no point in telling her that he was hungry most of every day but had learned not to attend.

Richard Wetherill's return the next afternoon generated no fanfare except from his four children, from Richard Jr., the eldest at eleven, to toddler Marion. Introduced to Wetherill at supper as a land surveyor from New Hampshire, Owen exchanged few words with the rancher, saying as they shook hands that he hoped Mr. Wetherill would find time to chat some evening soon. He added, with true modesty, that he didn't want to overstay his welcome.

"Tonight I have some bills and correspondence that demand my attention," Wetherill said, "but perhaps tomorrow."

Owen thanked him, praised Mrs. Wetherill again for her hospitality—which drew a nod and a smile from Wetherill—and retreated to his end of the table.

The next day, Owen saw Wetherill and Bill Finn head out together first thing in the morning—Finn had his revolver strapped to his leg and also carried a rifle in a saddle scabbard; Wetherill didn't appear to be armed—riding toward the South Gap, between South and West mesas. Both had returned by late afternoon, just before the sky darkened into a roil of thunderheads that soon let loose a downpour as heavy as anything Owen had ever witnessed. In less than half an hour, though, the lightning had been swept to the east and sunlight streamed through the departing clouds in several directions at once, which, in concert with the soaking rain, made visible an unexpected range of colors—the dark mud, the deepened grays and tans of Pueblo Bonito's formidable stonework, a hint of bronze in the upper, sunlit face of Fajada Butte, the now-distinguishable greens of the grama grass and desert shrubs, the unfathomable depths of the bluest sky—and conjured from the totality a sweet, untainted, rising scent that Owen took to be the high desert itself: vegetation, water, earth, air.

After supper Owen followed a number of ranch hands as well as the Wetherill family and a Navajo servant girl, Des-glena-spah, who helped with the children, into the comfortable room that served as Wetherill's office and den. (Ordinarily, in the warm weather everyone would adjourn to the front veranda, which stretched the entire length of the house, but a wind was kicking up so much dust and sand that comfort was impossible.) In the den were two couches, several additional armchairs, a pot-bellied stove, Wetherill's roll-top desk against the wall, layers of rugs to warm the floor, bronze oil lamps hanging from the exposed beams, a gun rack with four rifles, and adorning the walls, a hodgepodge of decorations—a colorfully striped Navajo blanket, Hopi kachinas, baskets or beadwork woven by several tribes, the mounted heads of deer, antelope, a mountain lion, and other game. Shelving held hundreds of books, mostly scientific and literary, and recent issues of assorted magazines. The only natural light filtered into the room through a skylight, so the oil lamps had already been lit.

This was Richard Wetherill's domain. He seemed to ease into the room—or rather, the *room* seemed to ease *him*. His stiff carriage and shoulders relaxed, and with obvious pleasure he lowered himself into an armchair beside his desk. Elizabeth, his sprightly older daughter, all of eight or nine, came running across the room and launched herself into her father's lap, eliciting a laugh from him as he wrapped his arms around her. Owen couldn't help smiling at their mutual delight.

Richard Wetherill was not a large man, five-eight, with broad shoulders but an otherwise narrow build. Owen had anticipated a more commanding physicality, but, he realized, that supposition had been based on nothing other than the way others, Bruce Fielder and Gus Thompson in particular, had spoken of him and, even before that, a sense that such an adventurous life—homesteading in Mancos, finding and exploring Mesa Verde, delving into the layers of Grand Gulch, discovering the Keet Seel ruin in Arizona Territory, running the Hyde Exploring Expedition's operations, uprooting his family and starting over again in Chaco Canyon—could only be accomplished by someone physically imposing: someone larger than life, to use the grossest cliché. In Wetherill's presence, however, Owen settled on a simpler descriptive: solid. Far from handsome, his broad face had been deeply creased by the sun and dry climate, aging it beyond his fifty years, although his deeply set dark eyes projected a younger man's intensity. His wiry, unruly hair, gray now but still holding dark traces, was matched in color and texture by bushy eyebrows and a broad, thick mustache that concealed his upper lip. Buried in his favorite armchair, which was draped by colorful throws, and with a daughter in his arms, Wetherill appeared quite content.

Elizabeth, with a quick giggle, abandoned her father's lap and skipped across the room to her mother, and her father's gaze then turned to Owen, who'd been standing by the book shelves, a nearly empty coffee cup serving as a prop in his effort to fit into the larger group of men, whose conversation he'd been pretending to follow. In addition to Gus Thompson and Bill Finn (minus his six-shooter, Owen had noticed at the dinner table), those in attendance included "Black" Phillips, whose moniker derived from his full head of midnight hair but just as easily could've reflected his quick temper; Lee Ivy, barely more than a boy, who'd arrived from nowhere and stayed on to perform odd jobs, and whom Gus, not without affection, had described as "at least six bits short of a dollar"; and Joe Schmedding, a horse wrangler who often accompanied Gus on freight runs. Several were smoking cigars while listening to Bill Finn narrate how he and Mr. Wetherill had wasted the day trying to collect debts from various Navajos. "If I'd had my druthers," he said, "I'd've pistol-whipped the first one, tied him across a mule, and carted him around for the other deadbeats to see. Maybe then they'd start paying up."

"You'd have Stacher after you mighty quick if you tried that," Gus said. Samuel Stacher, the agent for the newly created Eastern Navajo Jurisdiction—and certainly one of the Shelton "spies" Marietta had mentioned—had been living since April in a stone and adobe house near Pueblo del Arroyo that Wetherill had built for visitors—the "hotel," the hands called it. Owen had encountered Stacher and his wife, Flossie, and their children twice at dinner. They seemed nice enough.

"Mr. Rouse," Wetherill said, summoning Owen with a quick flick of his head. Owen swallowed the last of his coffee and set the cup down on the cold stove. His host gestured for Owen to pull up the desk chair and then sat back, his hands folded across his stomach.

"So you visited with my friend Bruce Fielder," Wetherill said.

"He took me to Mesa Verde. We hiked up through Cliff Canyon."

"Did you? What's happening up there *these* days?" His voice was of a higher pitch than Owen would've expected, reaching almost a squeak when he emphasized a word.

"Well, you probably know that Spruce Tree House has been cleared out and stabilized. Now they're doing the same for Cliff Palace."

"They'd best take care." But Wetherill's tone was sanguine, reconciled to the obvious—that nothing he thought or said would be of any influence.

"Do you know a Jesse Fewkes from the American Museum of Natural History? He seems to be in charge."

"We met once at a Hopi Snake Dance. He seemed reputable enough." Wetherill stroked his mustache with a calloused forefinger. "I wanted to interest those folks in Mesa Verde in 1889. Back then, no one at the museum thought the ruins were of any import." A rueful smile crossed his face. "Their thinking has progressed."

"When I was up there, watching them clearing out the rubble, I thought that maybe everything should just be left as is."

"I suppose a case could be made. But there are things to be learned. You only get to them by digging—carefully. You use a hand trowel, not a shovel. That was the first thing Baron Nordenskiöld taught me when we began working together. The second was, photograph and document everything. You know about the baron?"

"Some."

"He was about your age," Wetherill said. "An impressive young man. A bit full of himself, but with good reason. A child of wealth and privilege, but dedicated to science and learning. And then he died before his twenty-seventh birthday from tuberculosis." Wetherill shook his head.

Owen looked away and said nothing. Twenty-six.

Wetherill's tone lightened. "My wife tells me you've come all the way from New Hampshire to see our ruins."

"I did," Owen said. "I've been interested in the ruins and the Anasazi ever since I first heard about them."

"And where was that?"

"The New Hampshire College of Agriculture and the Mechanic Arts."

"What did you study?"

"Well, my family's always been farmers, so I went there to study agriculture, but I learned that my talents, if that's what they are, lay elsewhere."

"Doing what?"

"Surveying. Geology. I thought for a time that I'd like to work for the U.S. Geological Survey."

Wetherill's nod was noncommittal.

"But professionally I'm a land surveyor. I don't have enough field experience to call myself a geologist." Owen suddenly had the feeling that he was prattling.

"There was a geologist out here for a couple of summers. He thought he could date the Anasazi settlements geologically."

"That doesn't seem likely. Geological time is too slow. An inch of sand can hold a thousand years. You need a marker that gives you a finer time line."

Wetherill nodded. "Of course you can date cultures relative to each other, the oldest at the bottom. That's what we learned up in Grand Gulch with the Basketmakers. But I take no credit for that. It was hardly a new idea. Look at the great civilizations of Europe and the Middle East, one following another, layer after layer. It shouldn't have been a revelation to anyone that the same principle would hold true here."

Across the room, Mrs. Wetherill, her knitting in her lap, began singing "Put on Your Old Gray Bonnet," and Richard Jr., Elizabeth, and Robert joined in. Des-glena-spah, sitting on the floor, was dandling Marion.

"What do you think happened to them?" Owen asked.

"The Anasazi? That depends on what you mean. They built their villages and then they left. Speculate about the wherefores all you want."

"You don't speculate?" Owen found that hard to believe.

"Less and less as time passes, Mr. Rouse. Now, my brother Clayton and Charlie Mason say invasion and warfare brought an end to it. The cliffs of Mesa Verde and elsewhere provided security for a time, but against determined invaders, escape routes could easily be cut off. And Chaco Canyon, out here in the middle of nowhere"—he raised his hands, as if to say *just look around you*—"offered no protection at all."

"But you disagree."

"When there's evidence, I look at the evidence, and I see no evidence of warfare—violence, to be sure, judging by the condition of some of the skeletons we've found, but not warfare. No evidence of looting or mass graves or cremation sites . . ."

"Then why did they leave in such a hurry?"

"Did they?" Wetherill let the corners of his thin mouth rise into a smile. "That's what just about everybody seems to think, but did they?"

"Why would they have left so much behind—all that pottery, the clothing, the stores of food—if they weren't forced to leave in a hurry?"

"Maybe because they wanted to."

"But—"

Wetherill waved him off. "We have one set of facts—the evidence in the ruins. Interpreting the evidence is another matter entirely."

Owen waited for him to go on.

"Was there a prolonged drought that caused their crops to shrivel year after year? Or a rust that wiped out their corn? Or a plague of locusts? Did they finally cut down all the trees from the rincons and run out of fuel to cook and keep their homes warm? Or maybe religious divisions or clan rivalries led to trouble. It's all just conjecture." He leaned forward. "But if I were prone to speculation, I might first try to think with an ancient's mind. I'd try to put aside our science, the way we see history, our religious convictions." Bruce Fielder had told Owen that Wetherill was from Quaker stock and, accordingly, didn't curse, drink, smoke, gamble, or dance.

"And if you could do all that—?" Owen said.

Wetherill sat back and smiled. "Well, you might wonder, for example, if the Anasazi left all that behind because they wanted to ensure that the spirits of their ancestors would feel welcome when they came back to visit."

Across the room, Black Phillips had pulled out a deck of cards, and Gus Thompson and Joe Schmedding were trying to convince Bill Finn to join them in a friendly game of poker. "Come on, we need at least four," Gus said.

"Ask Lee," the stone-faced Finn said, which produced a round of groans. Lee Ivy laughed.

"Or let me put this to you, Mr. Rouse," Wetherill said. "Why do we write books and cherish paintings and save them in libraries and museums?"

"Because they provide a record of who we were and are. And because we appreciate beauty."

"So do you think those human impulses are limited to civilizations with the written word and an understanding of how to blend linseed oil and minerals?"

"But I don't see how you could ever prove any of this."

Wetherill emitted a slow laugh. "Well, Mr. Rouse, if it's *proof* that you're looking for, you've come to the wrong place. There'll always be things that can be known and things that can't be known. And that's why"—for emphasis he slapped his knees with his large hands—"I don't choose to speculate, this conversation to the contrary."

Marietta Wetherill had moved on to other songs—"In the Good Old Summertime" and, now, with Marion in her lap, tucking her head against her mother's bosom and yawning, "Slumber My Darling."

"Mrs. Wetherill has a lovely voice," Owen said.

"She does indeed. And she can play any number of instruments—the guitar, the piano, the B-flat cornet . . . Her family are all musicians. When she was a girl, they traveled all over the West giving concerts."

"Is that how you met?"

"No. Her father brought the whole family to Mancos late one summer because he'd heard about Mesa Verde and wanted them all to see it. Thank heavens, 'Asdzání inherited her parents' adventurous spirit and fortitude." *'Asdzání*—Navajo for "Young Woman"—was how Wetherill frequently addressed his wife, who was now carrying the sleeping Marion to the nursery.

"Where do you think the Anasazi went when they disappeared?" Owen asked.

"Ah!" Wetherill said. "That, Mr. Rouse, doesn't require speculation. They didn't 'disappear.' That's twaddle, regardless of what some of those academics and ethnologists back East think. The descendants of the Anasazi are all around us." He swung an arm wide. "In the west, the Hopi. Along the Rio Grande, the Taos and the Nambe and the Tesuque and all the other pueblo tribes. Closer to hand, the Jemez. To the south, the Acoma and the Laguna and the Zuni. Ask them, ask any of them, and they'll tell you—if you're really ready to listen. But because their stories aren't written down, what they say gets dismissed by people who want all the gaps in the time line filled in. It isn't possible—it never will be—to go back step by step through forty generations."

"It seems pretty obvious when you state it," Owen said, but he wasn't completely convinced. He'd have to think about it when he wasn't so influenced by Wetherill's presence and so elated that he, Owen Rouse, was actually sitting in Wetherill's home in Chaco Canyon. Just a handful of weeks ago he was lying in a hospital bed in Hanover, New Hampshire, inert.

Bill Finn, his hands in his pockets, walked over to where Owen and Wetherill were sitting.

"What is it, Bill?" Wetherill asked.

Finn spoke with a Texas drawl. "I've been told that a couple of Navajos came to the store today complaining that you've been cheating them out of their half share for the sheep they tend. They wanted more credit."

Wetherill shook his head. "That's nothing new. Who was it?"

"A couple of the usual bunch. They say they're going to go see Shelton."

"Let them."

"I could have a talk with them, if you want."

"No. I don't want to rile anybody else up. There's always going to be bad seeds"—he turned to Owen—"usually the ones who don't feel obliged to pay their debts, as if I were at fault for extending them credit in the first place. And maybe I was."

"All right," Finn said, "if that's the way you want it." He wandered off.

Wetherill shook his head again. "Short of murder, I've been accused by somebody of just about every offence you can think of, from rustling to torture. It makes you wonder." But he quickly changed the subject. "So, Mr. Rouse, you claim to be a surveyor."

"Yes, sir."

Wetherill, nodding several times, drummed his fingers on the arms of the chair. "And are you an early riser?"

"Usually, yes."

"Good. Meet me in the kitchen tomorrow morning about an hour before sunrise. There's something I want to show you, and it's best seen with a clear eye at sunrise. Are you game for an early hike?"

"I am," Owen said.

The rim of the sun broke the horizon and the golden light flowed across the high desert toward them, turning the pale sand a faintly orangish brown, and the drab scrub various greens. Shadows, Owen's and Richard Wetherill's included, suddenly appeared, stretching west. The two men were still standing in the ruins of Pueblo Alta, on the mesa behind Pueblo Bonito.

"Tell me what you see," Wetherill said, pointing in sequence north, north-northwest, and then northwest. "Tell me what you see, there, there, and there."

CHAPTER FIVE: Healing

Owen sat in an armchair with his feet propped up on the hassock, drifting in and out of sleep, watching Julia each time she entered the room, either through the kitchen door from the outside—the weather had warmed up dramatically—or through the inside door from the trading post. He tried to read from the stack of newspapers she'd set beside him, Chicago papers that were a month old. Julia had also handed him a novel—he'd requested something about the West, which led her to pull Frank Norris's *The Octopus: A Story of California* from a shelf—but he couldn't get past the first few pages without his attention drifting.

Julia had fixed him his oatmeal and butter and egg whites (with cinnamon) in the morning, while he was still camped in the spare bedroom. Since then, she'd brought him in the parlor mutton broth, black coffee, more oatmeal, English tea, as she came and went.

The sun was still high when he heard the sound of a wagon and voices in the yard. Julia, who'd been sitting at her desk near the dining table, set aside her accounts and went outside. A minute later she reentered, followed by a white man in a tan duster and bowler hat, and an old Navajo woman wearing a shawl, a traditional dress, and ornate cowboy boots, and leaning heavily on an ivory-headed cane; in her other hand she carried a big, lumpy burlap sack. Dr. Harry Whitaker hung his hat and coat on the Shaker peg rack beside the door and immediately brought his worn leather satchel over to Owen. He set the satchel down beside the hassock and extended his hand toward Owen, who, shifting his weight and leaning forward, extended his own. Julia introduced the two men.

"My pleasure," the doctor said with an unmistakable Southern accent and with a quick, stiff nod of his head. "Now, Mr. Rouse, let's get those feet unwrapped so I can see what we're up against." After washing his hands at the kitchen sink, he sat down on a chair that Julia had carried over from the dining table, realigned his spectacles above the bridge of his nose with a middle finger, and immediately turned his attention to Owen's feet, which Julia had earlier washed, wrapped lightly in clean gauze, and covered with a wool blanket.

"I'm glad you saw yourself clear to come all the way up here, Harry," she now said. "I hope the road was in decent shape after the snow."

"The washes were muddy, but Yazzie got us through just fine. He's a good man."

Harry Whitaker was a bit taller than average, thin, and looked to be about forty. His reddish hair was thinning, revealing a tanned scalp heavily blotched with brown patches. His ears were large, with long lobes, and the bones in his triangular face were thick and prominent, as if barely covered by the combination of lean flesh and his freckled skin. His lashes and eyebrows were paler than the rest of his hair, and he was clean shaven except for a toothbrush mustache and a small triangle below his lower lip. He was not a handsome man. He wore a collarless white linen shirt, buttoned to the neck, black and gray striped pants, and a concho belt with green turquoise stones inset around the rectangular buckle.

"Why don't you tell me what happened to you," Dr. Whitaker said while unwrapping the gauze.

"I was coming down from the mountains, along one of the trails that take you north, up toward Blue Hawk Lake. It was already freezing—well, maybe not freezing yet, but the mercury had dropped—and then it started snowing. I was all right under the trees and for a time after I came out of them, though I couldn't see much, the way the snow was blowing. I've crossed the high meadow toward Mr. Yazzie's place so many times in the last six weeks that I thought I could do it blindfolded. But everything turned white—I've never seen anything like it, not even back in New Hampshire. The wind whipped the snow so hard that I couldn't keep my eyes open. I covered them with a hand and opened a crack between two fingers, but I still couldn't see, and then I slipped and went down and somehow lost my bearings. I didn't know which way was which. Have you been up there, in the high meadow?"

"Not in a blizzard," the doctor said. He lifted Owen's right foot by the heel and examined it closely, bending and spreading each toe, running a thumbnail up the sole and observing the response, pressing as hard as he could in the hollows beneath the ankle bones and simultaneously flexing the foot up and down. Owen went on:

"Everything seems more-or-less flat, but in truth the land flows in waves. Just slight downs and ups. For a time I just stood still, hunched over, hoping the squall would break, but it didn't and my face and ears were burning from the cold. I pulled my coat up as high as I could, over my nose. I jammed my hands inside my coat to keep my fingers from freezing, too. Before I knew it, I could barely feel my toes. I could walk, but I had to watch every step—make sure my foot was flat before putting my weight on it. The snow was piling up. My feet went numb. I thought it was best to keep moving as long as I could, and I guess it was, because that's how Johanna found me." The memory was vivid: Johanna, a snow-covered gray shawl protecting head and shoulders, on a saddleless pale horse dappled with gray; a slow, silent, looming movement, coming out of the white. He hadn't said anything, just gripped a handful of mane and leaned into the horse's warm, muscular shoulder, which protected him from the wind. Johanna reached down for his arm, but his legs didn't have the strength for him to mount. He told her to leave him, to go get her brother. Instead, she dismounted and wrapped one of the split reins around his hand several times. Then, gripping the horse's throat lash, she coaxed it forward. Owen stumbled after. He didn't know how long they walked—time fell away—until they reached the wooden railings of Yazzie's corral.

"Tell me how your feet feel," Dr. Whitaker said. He was now examining the left.

"They feel all right," Owen said.

"That isn't helpful."

Owen sighed. "The sores hurt if anything rubs against them. It's like salt in a wound. Other than that, there's still some burning and tingling, and every now and then I get a jolt."

"Where?"

"Mostly in my right foot. I can't feel anything in the outer toes."

"Tell me when you feel this," Dr. Whitaker said, and he proceeded to press what looked like a large sewing needle into various spots, but not the sores. Owen could feel every prick except in part of his right foot, where large blisters had formed.

"How long were you out there in the cold?"

"I don't really know."

"And your feet were wet."

"Yes, after a while. The snow got in and melted."

"All right," Dr. Whitaker said, standing up. He said something in Navajo to the old woman who'd entered with him, Tóya. She had remained standing by the dining table, conversing with Julia.

Owen guessed that Tóya was at least sixty years old. Her black hair was widely streaked with gray, and the deep facial lines in her bronze skin ran from the corners of her eyes to the edge of her upper lip. Other creases flowed below. She carried her broad chin high, almost as if she were pointing with it, and her dark eyes narrowed to slits as she crossed the room to where Owen sat.

"This is 'Asdzáán Bítóyiszééyiztał," Dr. Whitaker said. "She is of the Mud Clan, born for the One-Walks-Around Clan. She understands English but sometimes chooses to speak only in Navajo." He then added, diplomatically, "She is an honored hand-trembler and has come here tonight, at Julia's request and mine, to see if she can recommend salves or potions that will help with the frostbite and those ulcers." He turned to the woman and spoke again in Navajo. She listened and glanced at Owen's feet now and then but said nothing until Whitaker had finished. She spoke quickly and then was silent.

"Tóya wants to know how long you've had the ulcers on your feet."

"Since September, I guess, but they weren't so bad then."

"He walked from Chaco Canyon to here, and from here to Gallup," Julia said.

"That's a ways," the doctor said.

The hand-trembler spoke to him again.

"She says that she needs to taste your urine."

Owen's face turned a bright red. "Are you serious?"

"Quite. Julia told her you have diabetes."

"Jesus help me," Owen muttered, shaking his head. "No, no, that isn't going to happen."

The Navajo woman scowled.

"I suggest you do as she asks," Dr. Whitaker said.

Owen turned to Julia, his plea visible.

"This isn't Hanover, New Hampshire," she said, making no effort to appease him.

"But—"

"Don't assume." Her quick, clipped words made her meaning clear: he should not assume that this old Indian in her native dress didn't know exactly what she was doing.

"Do you think you can provide a sample?" Dr. Whitaker calmly asked, as if it were nothing out of the ordinary.

Owen wanted to disappear but he nodded.

Dr. Whitaker turned to Julia. "Get him a clean jar, will you?" Then he helped Owen up and they slowly walked to the spare bedroom.

Owen couldn't get his bladder to relax, and the doctor left him alone. When he was finally done, he opened the door and handed the glass jar to the doctor, who in turn handed it to Tóya. She took it into the kitchen.

Dr. Whitaker, leading Owen back to the parlor, whispered, "Remember that Tóya understands English. She can be temperamental, so watch what you say while she's within earshot. And if it's any consolation, not that long ago many practitioners of European medicine, given what must have been your symptoms back East, would be doing precisely what she's doing."

Having settled Owen back in his chair, the doctor turned to Julia. "Where's Pete? Yazzie said he was here."

"Oh," Julia said, "you know Pete—he's out and about. I'm just grateful that he hasn't been hanging around in here all day, making himself useless."

Tóya returned to the parlor and spoke briefly.

The doctor turned to Owen. "Tóya has informed me that your urine is a bit sweet and smells of honey." He added, "I'd be surprised if it didn't. She also says it could be much worse."

Tóya then spoke to the doctor at some length before he explained:

"She needs to gather some dried plants and prepare medicines to treat the ulcers. When they're ready, she'll be back with them. In the meantime, she wants you to start sitting with your naked feet in the direct sunshine for an hour a day, no more or we'll be dealing with sunburn as well. As far as the frostbite goes, she brought with her a jar of ointment that Julia can apply."

"I can do it myself," Owen said stiffly.

"We'll just make it part of the daily routine." Julia smiled at him, but he couldn't smile back.

"How long is this going to take, Doctor? I mean, for everything to heal?"

Harry Whitaker frowned. "You may lose those two outer toes on your right foot to the frostbite. The blistering isn't a good sign—that and the loss of feeling. It may take a couple of weeks to know for sure. Any dead tissue will turn black. Often it simply sloughs off. If it's a whole toe, it takes time—months—and you need to watch out for infection, but I may not have to intervene. The *real* problem may be the ulcers. If they get infected, you could lose the entire foot." He paused. "I can't say that the ulcers will ever heal completely, not with your diabetes." He added, "And you're going to need to stay off your feet for now. You shouldn't be walking any farther than the privy."

Owen said nothing at first.

"If you're smart you'll allow sufficient time for new skin to grow."

"Dr. Whitaker," Owen said, "I can't stay here that long."

"Well, that's not up to me"—he glanced up at Julia—"but wherever you go, the advice is the same. Stay off your feet and be patient."

"Can I speak to the doctor in private?" Owen asked.

"Of course," Julia said. She and Tóya (with a parting scowl) retreated to the kitchen.

Whitaker drew the straight chair closer. "And call me Harry."

"Mrs. Halley is *not* my nurse," Owen said. "She barely knows me."

"No, she's not your nurse," Harry said, "but she's one of those people who does what needs to be done."

"Is all this really necessary? Sitting in the sun, spreading her"—he nodded in Tóya's direction—"whatever it is, over the frostbite?"

The doctor sat back. "I can't offer you anything better. The sun and fresh air can't hurt the frostbite and may well help the ulcers—germs prefer darkness and wet. So if I were you, I'd follow her advice." Harry pulled a stethoscope from his bag. "How much weight have you lost?"

"Twenty pounds or so the last time I was checked."

"When was that?"

"Right before I left the hospital where I was being treated."

"And since?"

"I don't know. A little more."

"Well, let me check out the rest of you," and then he added with a deliberately exaggerated accent, "so Ah can tell Julia Ah did a thorough job."

"So what brought you to Many Springs Canyon?" Harry Whitaker asked Owen.

It was late in the evening. Owen, Harry, Julia, and Pete—who had returned from his day's wanderings just in time for supper—were sitting around the box stove in Julia's parlor. Nearby, Yazzie was leaning over his small folding table, positioned between the bookcases and under the window at the end of the room. He was working on a Navajo belt, stitching and adding stamped silver and turquoise-studded conchos made by a Navajo silversmith whom he knew. He worked slowly and meticulously. Owen had seen some of his belts for sale in the trading post, but Yazzie saved the best for a Gallup store that took them on consignment. At the other end of the open room, around the corner of the *L*, Johanna was busy in the kitchen, washing the supper dishes as she always did, even though Julia had tried to convince her that she should leave the clean-up for later and join the others—efforts to dissuade Johanna from her routines never succeeded. Not to Owen's knowledge, anyway. Tóya, meanwhile, taking advantage of the cleared dining table, had set to work harvesting nuts from the burlap sack of pinyon cones she'd brought with her.

"I guess there were places I wanted to see," Owen said in response to Harry's question. He assumed that by now everyone present had a clear understanding of his long-term prospects—that is, that he didn't have any.

"Well," said Pete, releasing a cloud of cigar smoke from the comfort of Julia's second armchair, "that tells us something without telling us much."

Owen considered how much he wanted to say, now that he knew that his visit to Many Springs Canyon was a fool's errand. But, he reasoned, laid up, with winter approaching, his search at its end, why not take advantage of sympathetic ears—Julia's and Harry Whitaker's anyway; Pete might scoff, and Yazzie and Tóya, he suspected, wouldn't show any interest at all.

"A road," Owen said. "An Anasazi road led me here."

He'd seen the first roads in the dawn, he told them, the morning that he and Richard Wetherill climbed to the top of the north mesa, behind the ruins of Pueblo Bonito.

"There, there, and there," Wetherill had said, pointing.

Owen had seen nothing at first, but as the rising morning spread more light across the reddish brown and ocher landscape, he noticed something odd about the vegetation, something in the mixed coloration and heights—in the patterns of growth of plants that he couldn't even name—and as this aberration became more distinct, lines appeared to form, fanning out from the mesa, lines too straight to be natural.

"You've ridden out there?" he asked Richard Wetherill.

"I have."

"And what did you find?"

"What do you think?"

"Roads."

Wetherill nodded. "Roads, twenty to thirty feet wide."

"*Thirty* feet?"

Wetherill nodded again. "They're very shallow, although some of them are marked by the remains of rock berms. Whoever made them, for whatever purpose, they scraped off the sand and soil, down to rock. Of course, there's been a lot of sand drift since then. But paying attention to the plants helps. Some plants find it easier to take root than others when the soil is very thin. So they serve as markers. These aren't the only roads, either. One heads southeast from the canyon, past Fajada Butte"—he turned and pointed toward the isolated sandstone formation, five miles from where they stood, then swung his arm directly south—"and another goes out through the gap, and yet another branches off from there and heads southwest."

"Where do they lead?"

"To outliers—smaller ruins—although the northernmost road goes straight on towards Aztec." The misnamed Aztec Ruins, though smaller than those in Chaco Canyon, were a significant Anasazi site.

"So the roads connected villages to Chaco Canyon?"

"They did, but they must have had some other use. The Anasazi didn't have the wheel. They didn't have horses or other pack animals, so why build roads so wide?"

"Why do you think?"

Wetherill, his face wrinkled up in a smile, said, "As I've said before, I don't usually care to speculate."

"Something ceremonial?"

Wetherill shrugged.

"But it's definitely a network of roads?"

"It appears so."

Owen stood silently for several minutes. As the sun rose higher, the light began to wash out the lines. "And they haven't been surveyed?"

"No," Wetherill said.

"So that's what you've been up to?" Julia said. "Surveying Anasazi roads?"

"Well, not really—not right here, anyway. I was looking for signs of outlier settlements. They should be easier to spot than the roads themselves. I thought that if I found any, I could work in reverse—take a bearing back toward Chaco Canyon and see if I'd overlooked something."

"And have you found anything nearby?" She seemed genuinely interested.

"Nothing of consequence," Owen said with a shrug. "Part of me didn't expect to, not up in the mountains, but I decided I had to be thorough. I also thought there might have been an east-west trade route, but I didn't find that, either, not here, although the remains of one road go southwest from Chaco and probably skirt around the southern end of the Chuskas."

"Toward the Hopi mesas?" Julia asked.

"In that general direction."

"All those pottery fragments you showed me, they weren't helpful?"

"In a sense they were, but only because there wasn't anything special or unusual about them."

"If the Anasazi wanted to travel east-west," Pete said, showing more inquisitiveness than Owen had expected, "wouldn't they have used Washington Pass, just like we do today?"

"You'd think so," Owen answered, "but none of the roads from Chaco head there. What's especially odd is that the larger ponderosa beams in the ruins almost certainly came from the Chuskas. There's no evidence of a forest any closer."

"I'm curious," Harry Whitaker said. "Why did you decide to make Many Springs Canyon the site of your camp, beyond the practical consideration that there's a trading post?"

"Well," Owen said, "there was the possibility that the Anasazi knew there was water here. Before they abandoned Chaco Canyon, the whole region may have experienced a prolonged drought, and they might have gone out of their way to find water."

"Do you think they knew about the springs?" Julia asked Owen.

"Probably not. I haven't found anything in the canyon that suggests they spent time here. But there's a bigger question—well, maybe more of a puzzle than a question. I found traces of a road—not the widest, but still sizable—that starts from just south of where the Chaco and Escavada washes join to form the Chaco River, and it runs west, straight as an arrow, past Lake Valley and White Rock, all the way beyond Coyote Wash. Then it just seems to end in the middle of nowhere—no ruins nearby, no nothing." And now he smiled. "But if you keep going due west for another eight and a half miles, you walk right into Many Springs Canyon."

"Ah," Julia said.

Tóya had removed all the pinyon cones from the table and was now using Julia's rolling pin to gently crack the nuts open. Johanna, the dishes done, had repaired, as she often did, to an old Navajo rug between Julia's desk and the box stove; she showed no interest in the conversation.

"But why the Anasazi?" Pete asked. "Don't you have enough of your own Indians back in New England, Squanto and King Philip?"

"Many tribes but few artifacts," Owen said. "If you try to go back before 1600, there's little to be found. They didn't build in stone, and the climate ate away at whatever they left behind."

"So," Harry said, "the Anasazi offered something you could lay your hands on."

"I guess you could put it that way. It intrigued me—a culture right here in America that we knew next to nothing about, probably going back a thousand years."

"Can't see the fascination, myself," Pete said, "but to each his own."

Tóya, her work at the table done, approached and handed Owen a shallow bowl. She said something in Navajo to Julia and then returned to fetch a straight chair. The small kernels were a pale gold. Owen looked at Julia.

"Tóya says you need to eat a handful of pinyon nuts every day, starting now." Owen put one of the nuts in his mouth and bit into it with his front teeth. It was soft and tasted piney. He wasn't sure he liked it, but he poured a few into his cupped palm. Then he held out the bowl to Julia, who, putting down her needlework, rose to take it. With her other hand she waved away the cloudy residue of Pete's cigar.

"Pete," she said, "that cigar is vile. Next time, buy something decent, if you insist on smoking."

"Yes, ma'am," he said, "for you, anything." He stubbed out the cigar and asked Owen, "Do you smoke?"

"No, I don't." He was watching Tóya, who, unable to handle both the chair and her cane, was listing heavily to one side, in obvious pain. The problem appeared to be her hip. He struggled to rise, intending to offer her his comfortable armchair, but Harry, seeing him and then Tóya, said, "Stay right there." Harry quickly rose and took the chair from Tóya, and then made room for her between his chair and Julia's rocker.

"Some say smoking improves the circulation by relaxing the nerves and easing the heart," Pete was saying.

"You might think differently if you saw the inside of a smoker's lungs," Harry said.

"No thank you," Pete said.

Julia handed Pete the bowl, and with his fingertips he dropped a few nuts into his mouth.

"Well," Harry said. Seated once again, he folded his hands behind his head and looked around with pleasure. "It's been too long since our last little gathering. Ah guess we have Mr. Rouse to thank."

"Or at least my ignorance of the weather."

"One thing you need to know about our social club," Pete said, chewing, "is that you're free to say any damn fool thing you want."

"Anything?" Owen asked.

"Anything. And no one's allowed to take offense."

"This is news to me," Harry said. The bowl came to him, and he helped himself to a few nuts.

"Julia keeps us in line," Pete said.

"I do nothing of the sort," Julia responded, "although there are times when I wish I could." She'd taken up her knitting, a front panel of a cardigan that Owen had seen her start in October.

"In the end, all is forgiven among friends," Pete said. "Just look at how civilized we are! Julia's knitting or crocheting, or whatever that is. Yazzie over there is toiling with his leather and awl while marking every word we say but showing admirable restraint. Harry is his usual gentlemanly self, helping the lady with her chair. Tóya has provided us with a nibble. Why, we're being as well-mannered as a ladies' sewing circle." He slapped his knee. "Toss me a needle and thread and I'll darn my socks."

"Tchh," Tóya grunted.

"Speaking of manners and such, how are things in Tohatchi these days, Harry?" Pete asked.

"Tolerable."

"Are you and the headmistress getting along any better?" Pete turned to Owen and offered an explanation: "Harry has objected to the pedagogy at the boarding school."

"Why is that?" Owen asked.

"The school forbids the use of the Navajo language," Harry said, "which might be understandable if it limited the prohibition to the schoolroom."

"They beat it out of the students," Pete said.

"That's a gross exaggeration," Harry objected. "Discipline, yes, but beatings, no. The school will never get the Navajo support it needs if corporal punishment goes too far."

"Maybe," Pete said, "but some Anglo parents like to drub their children into submission, and I don't see why Navajos would be any different."

"Stop being the instigator," Julia said.

Pete screwed up his nose and continued in the same vein: "And is the Rev. Mr. Brink still instilling the Lord's Word in the benighted scholars?"

"He is," said Harry, who added for Owen's benefit that Leonard Brink was the current minister of the Christian Reformed mission in Tohatchi.

"Where's the harm in religious education?" Owen asked Pete.

"There isn't any," Pete said, "although the reverend has butted heads with Harry over the latter's refusal to condemn traditional Navajo healing ceremonies." He shifted his eyes to Tóya. "And practitioners."

"The missionaries should all go to hell," Tóya said, speaking English for the first time in Owen's presence. He didn't know if this was because, in her irritation, she forgot that he was there, or because Pete wouldn't understand if she spoke Navajo.

"Oh, I don't know," Pete said, "you can't paint them all the same color. The brothers at St. Michaels respect the Navajo way."

"You're prejudiced in their favor," Harry said.

"If anything, you'd think I'd be prejudiced *against* them."

"The Jesuits kicked Pete out for trying to seduce a nun," Harry told Owen.

It was such an outrageous statement that Owen burst into laughter.

"Damn it, Harry," Pete huffed, "I didn't try to seduce a nun, which you damn well know, and it was the Franciscans, not the Jesuits, which you also know." He settled back in his chair. "You're just trying to get a rise out of me. Again."

"A task at which Ah'm invariably successful," said Harry, who winked at Owen.

"The good doctor," said Pete archly, "eschews organized religion. He worships only at the Cathedral of the Confederacy."

"Uh-oh," Harry said, anticipating what was coming.

"For devout Southerners the only true faith is the Old South, although they grant Jesus permission to cross the Mason-Dixon line if he genuflects."

Harry smiled and waved his hand in circles, which Owen interpreted as an acknowledgement that Pete was just getting started.

"Our doctor has peculiar views regarding the Civil War. You see, he believes it wasn't worth fighting, on either of the two great questions, preservation of the Union and the abolition of slavery."

"Slavery was an abomination. You know my opinion very well," Harry said, unruffled.

"But you think the South should have been allowed to secede?" Owen asked. He'd never encountered a Southerner before, at least not one willing to make this argument.

"I do, in view of the carnage that resulted—more than 600,000 dead, nearly another million wounded or missing."

"Hindsight," Pete said.

"Of course."

"How did your family see it?" Owen asked. "I mean, at the time."

"Contrary to what you might expect, my father opposed secession. He believed that if the South avoided rash actions, Lincoln would negotiate. He also thought that the South couldn't win a protracted war." Harry paused. "My father was a businessman first and foremost—"

"A slave-holding businessman," Pete cut in. "Let's not ignore that little fact."

Harry paused, but then went on: "He understood the importance of industrial capacity and recognized that the South couldn't possibly match the North. When war ultimately broke out, he thought the only chance for a Southern victory was to scare the bejesus out of the North, and to do it quickly—capture Washington and burn it to the ground, and march from there toward Philadelphia. In other words, force the North into negotiations. That's what he told me, anyway, long afterward."

"Also hindsight," Pete said.

"And what about emancipation?" Owen asked.

"My father thought that slavery was destined to become less and less profitable, especially if a negotiated settlement led to a free status for all Union territories. So in the end, the moral argument against slavery would have prevailed. As I see it, by now the Union might well be reunited."

"Forgive me," Pete said, leaning forward, "I generally prefer lightness and levity, but this can't go unchallenged."

"I'm not surprised," Harry said with a slight smile.

"What you just stated is utterly, utterly misconceived. If slavery had ended as you suggest—and let me note that you placed the economic argument before the moral—the legend and lore of the Old South as an Eden would've become myth, even more viciously than it did during Reconstruction. Combine that with a visceral hatred of the prosperous North, and by now the myth would be theology—cast in stone. No," he shook his head, "there wouldn't be reunification, not in this generation, nor the next, nor the next."

"On principle, I hate to agree with Pete," Julia said, "but I'm afraid that his view is closer to my own than yours, Harry." She turned to Owen. "You haven't given us your opinion."

"My degree is in agriculture," Owen said, "not history or ethics. I'm just a surveyor. I try to stay grounded." It was a line, not very clever, that he'd used before when he wanted to sidestep a question.

"An admirable strategy," Pete said, "but we won't let you skip out." He waved his hand. "Speak up."

Owen sighed. "I grew up surrounded by neighbors whose sons and brothers went off to fight and never returned. The war wasn't discussed much, let alone debated. But I have to believe the cause they fought for was just."

"I'm a doctor," Harry said. "My first cause must be to preserve life. So at the risk of repeating myself: one and half million casualties. Where's the justice in that?"

"The just and the unjust," Pete said. "Justice is a tricky concept. One man's justice is another man's injustice."

"Eeyah!" Tóya erupted, startling everyone. "Talk, talk, talk, you men like to hear yourselves talk, even if you don't say anything. Your Lincoln freed the *zhinii* but left the Diné rotting in Hwéeldi. To the army, we were all enemies—women, children, it didn't matter. Don't talk to me about justice."

"Whoa!" Pete said. "What brought *that* on? Have you *ever* heard me defend what the army did out here?"

Tóya swiveled to face Owen, who could read in her expression that he was now in her crosshairs.

"I've seen ones like you before—ones who couldn't care less about the People. The Anasazi mean more. We just get in your way."

"Now Tóya," Harry said, "you're being unfair to Julia's guest."

"And not to me?" Pete said.

"Oh you, you can defend yourself," Harry said. "But Owen here is new, and it puts him at a great disadvantage."

"Tchh," Tóya clicked her teeth.

"Harry's right, Owen," Julia said. "You've been put on the spot quite unfairly, I must say"—she looked pointedly at Tóya—"and you shouldn't feel compelled to respond."

Tóya, her lips pursed, still held him in her gaze.

Owen didn't know what to say. To say nothing would not stand him in good stead even though he did indeed think it grossly unfair of the Navajo woman—she didn't know him at all!—to corner him like this. He glanced at Clement Yazzie, who, bent over his table, appeared disengaged from the conversation—there'd be no support from that end of the room. Still, Tóya was Julia's friend, and Dr. Whitaker's, and she'd come all this way to help him, so out of respect he said, "I know a little history, and a little about the Anasazi, but when it comes to the Navajo, I admit my ignorance. But that doesn't mean I would place my interest in the Anasazi over the needs of any living, breathing Navajo."

"Huh," Tóya said.

He had no idea if his answer had satisfied Tóya, but Julia, at least, gave him a little smile.

"Julia mentioned that you're from Charleston, South Carolina. What's it like these days?" Owen asked Harry, attempting a less troublesome subject.

"Genteel, I suppose." Harry stroked his thin mustache. "I don't visit often."

"Genteel," Pete mocked, "just as in the old days before Fort Sumter," but Harry didn't take the bait.

"And your family?"

"My mother in her frailty continues to reign. I'm not involved. Maintaining the household and the property has fallen to my sisters and their husbands. Besides, to some former friends and neighbors, I did the unpardonable: after completing my studies, I went to work for the U.S. government."

"If you'll excuse me, I need a breath of air," Pete said, rising from his chair. Owen assumed that he was heading to the privy.

When the outside door closed behind him, Julia muttered, "I hope he stays away from his wagon."

Owen looked quizzically at Julia.

"Liquor," Harry said for Owen's benefit. "He keeps a bottle in his wagon."

"I won't let him drink in here," Julia said.

"I think he has another in your storeroom," Owen said—and then immediately wished that he hadn't. This wasn't his business, and he should stay out of it.

"That's a new trick," Julia said through tight lips.

"Do you want me to go find it?" Harry asked.

"No," Julia said. "I'll speak to him."

"He's jeopardizing your license," Harry said.

She brushed Harry's comment aside. "If the commissioner of Indian Affairs went after every trader who ever took a drink, there wouldn't be many traders."

"I'll give him a minute and then, if necessary, coax him back," Harry said.

"Do," Julia said and then added for Owen's benefit, "A little drink loosens Pete's tongue. A little more and he can get nasty."

Clement Yazzie, polishing a concho that he'd added to his belt, said, "A 'little drink' isn't something drinkers understand."

It took Harry Whitaker a good half hour to return with Pete Pietrowski, and when he did, Owen saw him roll his eyes in Julia's direction.

Julia, as she did every evening, had made a pot of tea for herself and anyone else who cared to partake, which tonight included Harry, Johanna—she always took her tea with milk and sugar—and Owen. Clement Yazzie didn't like English tea, and Tóya took the opportunity to tell Owen that for his health he should be drinking Navajo tea instead. Yazzie and Pete shared the dregs of the day's coffee.

Pete, his broad face slack, listed to one side in his chair, but he managed to balance his cup of coffee on the arm without spilling it.

The conversation resumed, but on less touchy topics. An offhanded remark by Harry about the suffrage movement—which he supported—led to an extended discussion of a woman's place in society and, more particularly, to Alice Ramsey's recent 3,800-mile automobile trek, New York City to San Francisco, mostly over unpaved roads and sometimes over no roads at all. Julia, who read out loud an account from the *Chicago Tribune*, found the public hubbub over Mrs. Ramsey's excursion quite ridiculous; praise for her tenacity in completing the first cross-country road trip by a woman was countered by condemnation for her having "abandoned" her husband and young child for two months. Harry agreed with Julia: the journey couldn't have been undertaken without Mr. Ramsey's full support, and therefore the critics had no grounds for complaint. Pete, hemming and hawing, wondered if the average woman was suited to such strenuous activities, to which Julia replied, "And is the average man?" Yazzie, as usual, made no comment; Tóya having seen her first "horseless carriage" on the streets of Gallup barely a year earlier, said it was a noisy, useless toy.

"Why would a woman want one?" she asked, continuing to speak in English.

"I would," Julia said.

"Julia the Adventurer," Pete commented with his eyes half closed. Owen couldn't tell if the strong coffee was having a sobering effect.

"And why just an automobile?" Julia said. "I fully intend to ride in an aeroplane first chance I get. Just last month Wilbur Wright flew around the Statue of Liberty and up the Hudson River. The photographs were printed everywhere. Can you imagine doing that?"

"Our Julia," Pete said. "You don't find many like her."

"Stop," Julia said.

"What about you, Rouse?" Pete said. "Would you put up with a woman so headstrong?"

Owen didn't know if Pete was referring to Mrs. Ramsey or Julia. One thing for sure, he couldn't see Beth Burrows tolerating the discomfort and inconvenience of either a cross-country automobile trip or life on an Indian reservation—a thought that seemed a betrayal, in an odd way.

"I bet you left a sweetheart back East."

Owen said nothing.

"It's none of our business," Julia said.

"You *did*, didn't you?" Pete said, leaning forward with an exaggerated laugh. This was a hook and he wasn't going to let Owen go.

"Leave it alone," Julia told him.

"I bet *you* know the story," Pete accused Julia.

"I don't."

He turned back to Owen. "Did you break her heart?"

Owen gave Pete a cold stare, and Pete, as if suddenly recalling Owen's circumstances, assumed a more somber mien, elbows on knees, mustache drooping around a frown. "But Julia's right, as usual—none of my business. My apologies."

"I had a fiancée," Owen said. "Well, almost—we were waiting to announce our engagement." He feared that he'd revealed too much. These people didn't know him; or he, them, except for Julia Halley.

"But then you left," Harry said with considerable sympathy.

"I couldn't offer her any future."

"And now you have regrets?" Julia asked.

"Part of me regrets it every time I think . . . ," he said, struggling to keep his voice under control and knowing that what he was saying in the moment was as true as anything else he might declare.

"So if you could, you'd choose differently?" Julia now asked.

Except for the ever-distant Johanna on her blanket, they were all half-watching him, their eyes cast down, even, unexpectedly, Tóya. These people were probably as close to being his friends as he would ever have again.

"I would not," he answered. "It was for the best."

" 'You're a better man than I am, Gunga Din,' " Pete said.

Owen was thrown. "What?"

"Kipling," Julia said. She held her knitting needles still in her lap; her eyes, mere slits, fixed on Pete. "A poem. A very *bad* poem."

Owen cleared his throat. "I can't say that poetry is one of my strengths."

"Nor Pete's," Harry said.

"Is that so?" Pete said. He stiffened his back, thumped his fists once on his knees, and began reciting in stentorian tones:

> By the shores of Gitche Gumee,
> By the shining Big-Sea-Water,
> Stood the wigwam of Nokomis,
> Daughter of the Moon, Nokomis.
> Dark behind it rose the forest,
> Rose the black and gloomy pine-trees,
> Rose the firs with cones upon them;
> Bright before it beat the water,
> Beat the clear and sunny water,
> Beat the shining Big-Sea-Water.

"Hah!" Pete concluded, pounding his fists on his knees a second time.

"That's supposed to be about an Indian?" Tóya said.

"Hiawatha," Julia said. "An Iroquois."

Tóya began laughing, and it was infectious. The laughter didn't stop for some time.

Tóya shook her head, tossed a "Tchh" in Pete's direction, and then announced, "These old bones are tired. I'm going to the hogan." She leaned heavily on her ivory-headed cane as she rose, and then she spoke to Yazzie, who was gathering his tools and materials: "*Béésh bii' ko'í diiłtłáád ńt'ę́ę́'?*"

"Aoo'," Yazzie said. "*Hooghangi honeezdo.*" He began folding up his small table.

"*Ahéhee', shiyáázh.*"

"Pleasant dreams, Tóya," Julia said.

"Tchh, *shik'i'oolchííł lágo,*" Tóya replied on her way out.

Julia translated for Owen: "She said she hopes she doesn't have a nightmare."

"If she does, she'll probably blame me for it," Pete grumbled.

Harry turned to Owen—they'd both risen from their chairs when Tóya did—and pointed to Owen's legs. "Put those feet up."

With a sigh, Owen sat back down and lifted his feet to the hassock. "What did Tóya say before that?" he asked Julia.

"She asked Mr. Yazzie if he started a fire in the hogan's stove, and he said yes, it would be warm in there now. Then she thanked him."

Owen shook his head. "I don't think I'll ever pick up any of the lingo. I don't have the ear for it."

"Few do," Julia said. "It requires immersion, but start with *yá'át'ééh* and *ahéhee'.* 'Hello' and 'thank you' go a long way."

"And *dibé,*" Harry added.

Julia laughed and then translated for Owen: "Sheep."

"Are your feet hurting you at all?" Harry asked Owen.

"Nothing I'm not used to."

"I'll leave some drops."

Pete stood up with the exaggerated stiffness of someone trying to disguise his unsteadiness. "I'll also bid adieu." He bowed. "My wagon awaits."

"It's going to be very cold again tonight," Julia said to him. "Maybe you should sleep in the hogan, too."

"With Tóya in there?" Pete shook his head. "She'd witch me in my sleep." Treading cautiously, he left, followed soon after by Yazzie and Johanna.

Harry moved to the vacated armchair and Julia returned to her knitting.

"What's this hand-trembling Tóya does?" Owen asked.

"First," Harry said, "you have to understand that Navajos don't separate medicine and religion. It's all one." Owen listened intently as Harry went on, explaining how, to a Navajo, illness reflects a life out of balance with nature's forces. The role of a hand-trembler is to identify both the underlying imbalance and the remedy, which most often involves a healing ceremony performed by a *hataalii*—in simplest terms, a medicine man or, the preferred translation, "singer." There were many such ceremonies: the Night Chant, Red Ant Way, Mountaintop Way, Enemy Way . . . some lasting as long as nine days.

"Have you seen Tóya do this hand-trembling?" Owen asked.

"I have. A few times."

"Who did she learn it from?"

Harry shook his head. "It can't be taught. Certain individuals simply have the ability."

"And what happens during it?"

"A hand-trembler begins by asking about symptoms, along with other questions intended to determine if the patient has violated a prohibition or might be the victim of witchcraft. Prayers and singing follow, and eventually the hand-trembler enters a trancelike state—I've seen it described as a seizure—that always includes severe shaking in one arm, which is passed over the patient, seeking the source of the ailment."

"So hand-tremblers and singers are something like faith healers."

Harry pondered this. "Many would say so."

"But you don't?"

Harry lifted his cup of tea, although by now it wasn't even warm. He took a sip. "Let's say a Navajo has been hit by lightning. He survives but has suffered a bad burn on his back. As a physician, I'd treat the burn by debriding whatever dead tissue I could and by applying a salve and bandages to protect the wound. Once the burns heal, my job is done. From the point of view of medical science, the patient is now well." He took another sip and then put his cup down.

"But the *patient* doesn't think so—far from it. Lightning is one of the most powerful forces in the Navajo universe. Something frightening and profound happened to him, and he won't be well until his sense of order and well-being is restored."

"And that falls to the singer," Owen said.

"Yes. Not that medicinals aren't also involved," Harry added. "And the practicalities aren't ignored—no ceremony will set a broken leg or suture a gash. But much of what a hataałii does involves ritual—sweat-baths, prayers, songs, the use of corn pollen, masks, and other paraphernalia. And sand paintings—mostly ground stone, in all the colors of the rainbow, and then some—displayed on the dirt floor of the ceremonial hogan. They can be incredibly intricate and time-consuming to create, and quite beautiful. Anyway, as you can imagine, singers often spend many years learning just a few ceremonies. Some are centuries old and very complicated, and they must be performed precisely."

"What happens to the sand paintings after the ceremony?"

"As soon as it's served its purpose, each is destroyed. The remnants are swept up and the sand scattered."

"It seems almost silly to ask," Owen said, "but does it all work—the hand-trembling, the ceremonies?"

"If they didn't work—if they didn't somehow help people recover—I imagine the ceremonies would have been discarded and forgotten long ago. So I give hand-tremblers and singers their due." Then Harry quickly added, "Unlike your typical faith healer, who, in my experience, is either a religious fanatic or a scoundrel."

"And do the singers accept your being here?"

"Well," Harry said, "Ah can't say Ah'm universally beloved."

* * *

Owen opened his eyes when he heard the gentle rap on the half-open bedroom door. Julia was checking on him one final time before bed, and she asked if she might come in for a moment.

"Of course."

"Are you cold?" she asked. "Do you want the window closed all the way?"

"No, it's fine," Owen said. The drab muslin curtain moved slowly, as if the room were breathing in and out.

"The air can get thick in here."

"That was an interesting conversation tonight," he said.

Julia gave a quick laugh. "We can get a bit testy with each other."

"Pete and Tóya in particular?"

"Not always, but often."

"I'll make sure I never sit between them."

"They rarely come to blows," Julia said.

"Sometimes my fiancée's—Bethany's—family would have raucous discussions across the dinner table, and I learned to play my part—I came to enjoy it—but it wasn't something that I grew up with. My father and mother could go an entire evening without exchanging a single word, and they thought nothing of it. So I grew up the same way. Even when I was at college, when some of the fellows would get tipsy, they'd go on and on, but there was no thought behind it. It was usually just blather and idle boasting."

"About their conquests?"

Owen detected the sly teasing in her tone. "Too often."

"I should let you sleep," she said. But then she asked, "Why didn't you ever tell me about the Anasazi road?"

"I can't give you a good reason," Owen said, embarrassed. "It wasn't much of a secret, was it?"

"To you it was."

"I suppose." He felt the need to explain. "I wanted to wait until I'd learned everything I could. Richard Wetherill used to rib me. He called it my 'quest.' I thought I could at least find a plausible explanation for it, and I wanted to do it alone. Does that make any sense?"

"Of course it does, Owen," Julia said. "You wanted to discover something all your own."

"I guess I did."

"And now?"

"If there was something to find, I think I would have found it by now." His answer stretched into a yawn, but he didn't want their private conversation to end. "I like Harry Whitaker," he said.

"I thought you would. There's not a mean bone in his body."

"It's obvious that he likes visiting you."

Julia beamed. "Yes, he does. Not that he doesn't get along well enough with Mr. and Mrs. Brink at the mission and with the ladies at the boarding school, despite their differences of opinion."

"Do you know the Brinks?" Owen asked.

"I met them once. I've invited them to Many Springs but they always decline."

"Why's that?"

"They don't approve of me." Owen was too surprised to reply, and Julia, seeing his reaction, went on: "They disapprove of my marital situation. Nor do they think it's proper for a Christian woman to live on her own amid Navajos."

"That must be a sore point for Harry—that they treat you so disdainfully."

"I've advised him to ignore it. Tohatchi is a very small community, and it would be miserable for everyone if they didn't all get along—or at least if they weren't cordial."

"I suppose," Owen said, "but still . . ."

"Which leads me to a related matter." She cleared her throat. "I hadn't planned to say anything tonight, but maybe it would be best if I did. When Pete told you that in our little gatherings we can say anything we please, he was exaggerating. Certain things are out of bounds."

Owen waited for Julia to go on; this was deeper than a matter of conviviality.

"May I sit?" she asked.

"Certainly."

She pulled the straight chair to the side of the bed and sat down.

"For one, Tóya's hand-trembling. She may or may not ignore you if you ask about her skills as an herbalist, but she won't discuss *anything* to do with hand-trembling. It's a gift from the Holy People, and we are not entitled."

"Except for Harry?"

"As a doctor to the Navajo people, he has a privileged position."

"Of course," Owen said.

"And we don't discuss Johanna when she or Mr. Yazzie is with us."

"You mean, her mute—"

"No, I mean *Johanna*."

"Does Mr. Yazzie object?" Owen asked, but he knew immediately, from the look Julia gave him, that it was a dim-witted question.

"*I* object," Julia said. "I will *not* have her treated with condescension—talked about as if she weren't even in the room."

"I don't believe I've done that," Owen said in his own defense.

"No," Julia said, "I didn't mean to suggest that you had. But you wouldn't have been the first."

"If I may ask, what's this business about Pete and the nun?"

Julia chuckled; the sound burbled up from her chest. "There wasn't any nun. Pete told a story once about kissing a girl in a rectory, and now we tease him about it. What annoys him more is Harry's deliberately confusing the Franciscans and the Jesuits."

"And what about the drinking?"

"I don't like it. Nor do I defend it."

"You could forbid it."

She cast a thin smile toward him, a smile in which he saw an accusation—that he was so *young*—and he couldn't help resenting it a little.

"And would that make him stop?"

"I don't suppose so." Owen sighed.

"I won't abandon him," Julia said. She shifted in her chair and straightened her shoulders.

"I shouldn't have said anything about . . ."

"The storeroom? It's all right. I'll deal with it." Then she sighed deeply.

"What is it?" he asked.

It took her a moment before she spoke: "I hope you realize this is very difficult for me, but it needs to be said: we do not call attention to Pete's affection for me."

Of course, Owen thought. Now it seemed so obvious. But for whose sake was it not mentioned, Pete's or Julia's? Probably both. And what about her husband—was Will Halley ever discussed? Should he come right out and ask her? It would be too presumptuous, so no, he wouldn't.

"I understand," Owen said. Just then he heard the outer door open.

"Julia?" Harry Whitaker called. He'd come in from the privy. And, Owen suspected, from checking on Pete, bundled in his wagon.

"In here," Julia answered, "with Owen," whom she then asked, "Should I leave your door open tonight?"

His door. "Yes, why don't you." He didn't relish waking up in the deep blackness with nothing familiar except his dislocated thoughts.

"Then I'll say goodnight." She extinguished the lamp.

Julia and Harry Whitaker sat at the far end of the dining table, where Owen, should he still be awake, couldn't possibly make out their whispering. She'd made another pot of tea. She always made tea. In the morning it focused her attention on the day's requirements. In the late afternoon, it roused her from lethargy. At night, in the absence of spirits, it served as a soporific, settling her down.

"What do you think?" Julia asked.

"He seems to be in pretty good spirits." Harry had removed his eyeglasses and had set them on the table, and now he rubbed his eyes.

"So you won't say?"

"What do you *want* me to say, Julia?" He swirled the milky tea in his cup. "Do you have any of those biscuits I like to dunk?"

She rose and walked to the pantry, happy to provide him with a little treat he would never think to buy for himself.

She'd known him for a decade now. When she first met him she was expecting someone less mannered, less meticulously dressed and groomed. She didn't know the Indian woman, introduced as Betty Roanhorse, who sat in the examining room with them; either Betty or Tóya or a female relative of the patient was present whenever he examined a woman or girl, Dr. Whitaker had explained. As a consequence, Navajo men were less reluctant for their wives and daughters to consult him.

He had asked her to describe her symptoms, their onset and duration. He took his time, asking question after question during the examination: did anything relieve her discomfort, how regular were her menstrual cycles, did she experience any pain during marital relations, had her husband remarked on any change, had she ever been pregnant, were they hoping to have children? And about the other matter, the insomnia, how long had she had it, was she experiencing undue strain, did anything seem to relieve it? When he was done with his examination, he left the room so she could dress. She thanked Mrs. Roanhorse and entered Harry's adjoining office.

First of all, he reassured her, he did not believe she had anything concerning; she did not have a tumor in her abdomen. She showed the classical symptoms of an ovarian cyst, which would vary in size and tenderness according to her monthly cycle. He would give her a prescription of potassium iodide, which often helped, and he also recommended application of a heated poultice containing various medicinal plants. In all likelihood the cyst would gradually disappear, over the course of several months. Whether the occurrence of cysts affected prospects for pregnancy was much debated in medical circles but unresolved.

She felt embarrassed to have taken up his time. Not at all, he told her. He was always delighted to provide reassurances. As for the insomnia, if it persisted he could offer her a tonic that would help, but since it contained a powerful sedative, chloral hydrate, he preferred not to unless it became unmanageable. Unmanageable? she asked. If she found herself unable to rise in the morning or unable to conduct her daily business, he explained. He then asked if she had ever taken chloral hydrate. She told him that her mother had. For? he asked. Neurasthenia. The names we attach to symptoms, he replied, can be as damaging as the symptoms. She, Julia, was by no means a neurasthenic—she should put that out of her mind. He came from Charleston, South Carolina, he told her, where half the women of a certain age were afflicted. For the first time during her visit, Julia smiled. Surely, not *half,* she said. His own closed-mouth smile, one side rising higher than the other, mixed irony and sadness, and he said, Surely, *at least* half.

They had talked for another hour. About Charleston and her hometown, Pittsfield, and about what it meant to be white and living on the Navajo Reservation, and, finally, the manifestations of nervous strain.

Time proved him right; her symptoms passed, as did the bout of insomnia, although it took a good six months.

She went to see him again a year later, to see if he had anything further he could advise regarding her apparent inability to conceive. He suggested that she might want to see a specialist. There might be a suitable doctor in Denver, but, then again, she might have to travel as far as St. Louis. She sat for some time, considering his advice. He said he would be happy to make inquiries for her. At the conclusion of the consultation she invited him to visit her and her husband at Many Springs Canyon and suggested that he bring Tóya with him; she regretted that she hadn't seen much of her after the death of Clement Yazzie's mother.

Soon after, Harry Whitaker made the first of what would become regular visits to the Many Springs Trading Post.

Julia retrieved the tin of biscuits from a shelf in the pantry and returned to the dining table. Harry pried off the lid and took out a yellow cookie flecked with nutmeg.

"As for our patient in there," Harry said, "the large blisters from the frostbite will break and drain of their own accord. Watch the color over the next couple of days. If any flesh gets darker—deep red, purple—then it won't recover. As for the ulcers, Tóya will be back in a few days with something that may help heal them. Until then, keep his bandages loose. You don't want to interfere with his circulation. And keep your nose on the alert for gangrene." He snapped the cookie in two and dunked half into the warm tea.

"And after that?"

Harry rubbed his nose with a forefinger. "I've only had a couple of patients with diabetes, and they were both well on in years. It isn't common among Indians. Has he told you much about it?"

"Some."

"It affects the blood circulation among other things, especially in the legs and feet. That's probably why those ulcers formed, that and ill-fitting shoes. Other than that . . ."

There was something in his tone that didn't feel right. "What else?"

"He has a heart murmur, a bad one. It means there's a leaky valve inside his heart." Harry tapped his chest. "Has he said anything?"

"No."

"Ordinarily, at his age I wouldn't be terribly concerned." He gave her a rueful smile.

She understood what he meant. She squeezed the back of her neck, beneath the pinned up hair, with weariness. "I'm going to bed. Help yourself to the biscuits. You'll be all right in the hogan?"

"Certainly."

She pushed herself up from the table. "Leave the cups. I'll wash them in the morning."

"Thank you, Julia," he said. He retrieved his spectacles and put them on. Then he looked up. "He may not be long for this world, you know."

"No one arrives with a guarantee," Julia said.

The next morning, Pete, Harry, and Tóya departed together—Tóya without saying another word to Owen, which led him to ask Julia if the Indian woman would actually return with her medicines.

"Of course she will," Julia said, as if no other answer was even conceivable.

Owen did as he was told while waiting. He applied the obnoxious paste that Tóya had left to treat his frostbite—the principal ingredient appeared to be some turpentine-smelling pitch, mixed with red clay and tallow. Sitting on Julia's veranda, with the fall weather at its most beneficent in a succession of beautiful skies, he exposed his bare feet to sunlight for precisely an hour on each of those quiet three days. He ate his oatmeal sprinkled with Tóya's pinyon nuts, which Julia had pan-toasted for him. And at other times he lay in bed or he sat, sometimes in one of the armchairs in Julia's parlor, or in a straight-backed chair at the dining table, keeping Julia company while she prepared meals or, between her abbreviated hours behind the counter in the trading post—abbreviated, he knew, because of his presence—canned carrots and yellow turnip and red beets and small white potatoes for the winter. She had a small root cellar that kept some vegetables fresh into the early spring, she explained, but by then most of them would be peaky and limp, and some would already be lost to a slow rot, so in the fall she preserved part of each crop as time permitted. That would last her until her new garden started yielding fresh produce. Each year she put frost-tolerant spinach, peas, cabbage, and broccoli into the ground in early May.

He was laid up, not sick, he told her, so he should help; so she gave him a paring knife and a cedar slab to use as a cutting board, and he set about peeling and cutting carrots and turnips.

In the evenings, after the trading post closed and the canyon emptied of all but its residents, they sat in the parlor, reading by lantern or talking. They discussed the news of the last month from Chicago, which led her to tell him more about her sister Penelope, who had two young children, a boy and a girl, neither of whom Julia had met although she hoped to convince Penelope to bring them out to New Mexico the following summer. She had little to say about her sister's husband; Owen concluded that she and Philip Malott did not get along. In turn, Owen told her more about his father's farm, how hard his family's life had been when he was growing up.

"My mother was forty-six when I was born. She thought I was a gift from God—"

Julia's quick, bright laugh interrupted him.

"I didn't mean it *that* way," Owen said.

"All mothers think their boys are God's gifts, don't they?" Julia teased him.

"What I *meant* was, she used to say that I came along because God wanted to bless her for having never questioned her faith, even after he took Robbie from her."

"And your father, does he have faith?"

"Well, he's never been much of a church-goer, although he told me before I left to come out here that he's started to attend services now and then. I assume it's at my mother's church, but it doesn't matter—his true denomination has always been hardscrabble farmer. I take after him more than my mother, at least when it comes to religion. I never understood faith, though I tried, but I guess if you need to *understand* it, then you don't have it." He paused. "Your father is a minister, so your upbringing must have been very different."

"I was brought up to believe, first and foremost," Julia said, "that my father ruled my world, that he should therefore be obeyed and paid fealty. But once, when I was still a child, he took us to a Quaker meeting—he'd received an invitation and didn't feel that he could decline. The meeting house wasn't at all like a church—small, more like an ordinary house, with white plaster walls and ceiling. I remember four rows of benches—two rows on each long side of the meeting room, facing the center—and at one end of the room, a Bible on a heavy lectern. My father had explained that there was no minister, that Quakers believed they needed no intercessor to commune with God. We sat on a bench for what seemed a very long time, and then a clean-shaven balding man in a dark suit and stiffly collared white shirt rose and went to the lectern, where he proceeded to read aloud a passage from the Bible, Hebrews 11:1–16—'Now faith is the substance of things hoped for, the evidence of things not seen . . .' When the man was finished—he read in a quiet, masterful voice—I expected him to comment as my father would, explaining the faith of Abel, Enoch, Noah, Abraham, and Sara, and why they were described in the Bible as strangers and pilgrims who died in faith even though they only saw God's promises from afar. But the man simply returned to his seat. No one else spoke. Not long after, everyone rose from the benches, spoke quietly to one another, or smiled and nodded collegially, and filed from the building. I thought it very odd at the time and didn't think much about it until years later, after my mother had died. By then, I was indifferent to my father's church—I regarded God as something of an absent landlord. I began reading more about the Quakers and found qualities that I admired, including their belief in the value of women's voices, and the view of the more liberal believers that the Bible was not God's delivered word, but instead the often competing words of those struggling to understand His creation."

"You became a convert?" Owen asked.

"Well, I don't know about that, but if I ever return to religious practice, I think it would be as a Quaker."

Julia resumed reading her weeks-old newspaper. Owen, staring over the top of his own yellowing sheets, watched her reading; the newspaper in front of his face allowed him to quickly divert his eyes to the text if she appeared about to look up. They'd spent much of the last two days' waking hours in sight of each other.

"I think my father's fundamentally decent enough," Owen said, straightening his newspaper and turning a page. "I didn't always think so, growing up."

"I take it he was a strict disciplinarian," Julia said, letting her newspaper fall back against her chest.

"Yes, but it was more than that, of course. He was knotted up inside himself, and it kept him from communicating through anything except demands and explosions of anger." Owen paused. He propped an elbow on the arm of the chair and rested a cheek against the backs of his folded fingers. "After I fell ill this past spring and ended up back home, he sold his best piece of farmland—the only decent piece, in fact. He knew I hated that farm with a passion. So he sold the land so that I'd have the money to leave. And then he told me, just before I left—" Owen had to catch himself, because he felt his voice beginning to seize up.

Julia let him be.

"He told me," Owen began again, "that he'd like us all, the whole family, to lie together."

Julia let the ensuing silence linger before she said, "He loves you, Owen."

"Oh, I know he does, in his peculiar way," Owen said, "and sometimes it breaks my heart to think that he'll probably live just long enough to see his second son lowered into the ground."

TÓYA, THE WOMAN WHO Kicks Up Still Water, showed up alone on the fourth day, riding a small dappled mare. Owen had half hoped that she wouldn't return, not only because he doubted her herbal remedies would do much good, but also because she unnerved him. They had nothing in common except Julia and his other recent acquaintances, and he didn't even know what language she would be talking. But here she was—old, wrinkled, gray, with chitinous hands—her ancient, stained paisley satchel tied to, surprisingly, a sidesaddle. Watching her dismount, Owen realized that her ancient hips no longer had the mobility needed for a regular western saddle. Tóya produced from a pocket a carrot that the mare took from her upturned palm. Tóya speaking quietly to the horse, reached back and withdrew from a scabbard—suited for a sword, not a rifle—her ivory-handled cane. Tóya looped the reins once around the hitching post, and only then looked up at Owen.

"Yá'át'ééh," he called to her.

She didn't return his greeting. Leaning heavily on the cane, she walked toward him, and he could see the pain etched by each step. How long had she been on that horse? The journey had to be agony. And yet she'd come.

Julia emerged from the kitchen door, and the two woman, each speaking Navajo in turn, wrapped their arms briefly around each other.

"Tóya wants to know how your feet feel today," Julia said.

Owen was momentarily tempted to reply that Tóya should ask him herself, but he held his tongue. Did he have to prove himself to her again—and what did *that* even mean—before she would speak to him directly?

"The burning from the frostbite is gone," he said.

Supported by Julia's arm, Tóya made her way to him—the three steps up to the veranda were taken slowly, one at a time—after which she stared at his feet as she and Julia engaged in an animated conversation in which he soon lost all interest since he couldn't understand anything they said. Strange objects of interest, his feet.

Julia retrieved from Tóya's horse the paisley satchel. The Navajo opened the bag and took out a large jar of brown liquid and a smaller one that appeared to contain dried, crumbled plants.

Julia said to Owen, "Once each day we need to boil a tablespoon of this"—she shook the smaller jar—"in a quart of water, and you're to expose the ulcers to the vapors for an hour. Then, after your feet have absorbed their daily dose of sunshine, we'll need to wet cotton patches with the brown solution and apply them over the ulcers, and wrap your feet for the rest of the day. No stockings, no shoes. And at night you need to keep your feet bare but warm. You may wear moccasins when you need to visit the privy, but other than that, you must stay off your feet."

"For how long?" Owen asked. He waited for Julia to translate Tóya's answer.

"Until new skin covers the sores."

That was impossible; Harry Whitaker had already made it clear that it would be a long, slow process.

"Tóya is going to lie down in my bed for a while," Julia said.

"Tell her—" he began, and then he shook his head. "I'm sorry, this language business . . . I'd like to offer you," he said, speaking directly to Tóya, "fair compensation for your services and your trouble, but I have no idea how much that would be. So I'll leave it to you. Tell Julia what you decide, and I'll see that you receive it. Cash money or trade goods—however you choose."

Julia led her to the door, where Tóya paused and, without turning around, said, "*Baa ntséskees*, Owen Rouse."

Owen held up his hands in supplication. Julia gave him her little smile and said, "She'll think about it."

Owen and Tóya sat and stared at each other. He kept a smile on his face, his hands folded in his lap, even though she'd shown no mercy at dinner, refusing to speak in English and responding only to Julia, who, obviously familiar with this game, translated selectively and behaved as if the three of them were engaged in a normal conversation. Now, however, Julia had abandoned him in favor of her kitchen chores, and he and Tóya sat across from each other in the parlor.

"Owen Rouse, how long do you want to live?" Tóya suddenly said—in English!

Her directness stunned him, but he wouldn't let her see it. "Three score and ten," he answered. "Seventy years."

"I know how much three score and ten is," she said. "And I know where it comes from."

"Ah, well then," Owen began with a hint of apology.

"You won't make it."

"No," Owen said, "I won't."

"I'm sixty years old," Tóya said, "and I won't make it either."

"So at least we have that much in common," Owen said.

Her laugh grew, until her nearly toothless mouth was wide. "Maybe you're lucky you've lived for this long, eating that pigswill of yours. It makes no sense. Butter comes from milk. If you can eat butter, you can eat milk and cheese, too. If you can eat eggs, you can eat the birds that grow inside the eggs. And if you can eat birds, you can eat mutton and beef and horse and rabbit. That's what I have to say."

He couldn't argue with her logic. "What about your pinyon nuts?" he asked.

"I'll tell you about pinyon nuts," Tóya said. She had a way of snapping her words off when she spoke, which made her seem perpetually opinionated, if not perpetually angry. "When it's a bad year, when the corn dries up in the field, the People can survive through an entire winter on pinyon nuts. Maybe pinyon nuts will keep you alive just a little longer."

"In that case, thank you for the pinyon nuts."

"We call them nuts, but they're really seeds. One of those little seeds, a tree can grow from it."

They could hear Julia in the kitchen, humming something to herself, but he couldn't tell what.

Tóya slid her chair closer to him. "Let me see your legs now," she said.

He was sitting with his feet on the hassock, covered by a throw. He pulled the throw aside, but his feet were wrapped as she'd directed. Instead of unwrapping the bandages, Tóya pushed up his pants legs.

"What are you doing?" Owen asked curtly.

"Shush," she said, studying his lower calves and shins. "You see this?" she said, poking his flesh with her forefinger.

He flinched from surprise. "What?"

"They're swollen."

"No, they're not." He turned each leg. "They look perfectly normal to me."

"They're swollen," she repeated, poking him repeatedly just above the ankles. "You need to make more water."

He wasn't having any of this. Was she obsessed with his urine? It was beyond embarrassing.

"You," she said, "*ílizh*."

"Not likely," he said.

"Tchh." She sat back and gave him her evil eye once again. "How long do you want to live, Owen Rouse?"

She'd spoken the same words just minutes before, but this was a different question; this was a question with serious intent. In a loud voice, speaking Navajo, Tóya called to Julia, who soon appeared around the corner from the kitchen carrying Tóya's paisley satchel. Julia handed it to her and then retreated to the kitchen. Tóya rummaged in the bag and withdrew several small deerskin pouches. She opened and sniffed one and then put it on the hassock next to Owen's bare feet. "You brew this like tea," she said. "It will help you make more water."

"I make enough water," Owen said.

She slapped his leg with the back of her hand. Then she poked him again, hard. Her finger left a depression. "You drink a cup of this tea every morning and every evening until *that* doesn't happen."

Harry Whitaker had told him to trust her. What harm would there be? "All right," he said, mildly contrite, "I'll drink your tea."

Tóya pursed her lips and nodded, satisfied. "And I'll tell Clement Yazzie to build you a sweat-house."

Owen sighed. "I don't think Mr. Yazzie appreciates being told to do anything."

"Ha! If I tell him to build a sweat-house, he'll build a sweat-house."

Owen suspected that Tóya was either a force of nature or an avenging angel, and he didn't know which was worse.

"Why do I need a sweat-house?"

"Because I say you need one. Once a week you take a sweat-bath." She handed him a second pouch. "Here. You put some of these dried leaves on the hot stones and you breathe deep."

"What are they?"

She flicked her wrist. "You don't need to know. This will help you sweat out the poisons."

"I don't have poisons—I have too much sugar in my blood."

"Everybody has poisons. Maybe sugar is one of your poisons. An hour before the sweat-bath, you need to take a spoonful of this with water." The third pouch: a white powdery substance.

"For?"

Tóya made a gesture that clearly indicated vomiting.

"No," Owen said, returning the pouch. "I won't do that. I hate doing that. And I don't see what any of this has to do with healing frostbite and the sores on my feet."

"Are you stubborn or stupid, Owen Rouse?" she asked.

"Maybe both," he said with defiance. But he heard in her assertions an echo of what the doctors at Mary Hitchcock Memorial Hospital had told him: nothing in his body worked or failed independently. His blood carried his life, and the same ruinous blood ran through every vessel and affected every tissue, scalp to toe.

"Are the two of you getting along?" Julia asked—she'd obviously overheard some of their conversation. Her chores done, she drew her rocking chair a bit closer to the box stove, which was radiating a familiar steady warmth, and sat down. Owen straightened the throw over his legs and feet.

"I suppose we are," he said. At least Tóya was speaking English to him. Julia's presence now gave him a bit of courage. He asked Tóya, "Why don't you treat white people. Ordinarily."

Tóya scowled. "Why should I?"

"That isn't what I'd expect a healer to say."

"Why not?"

"I'd think that since you have the knowledge and skills to heal ailments and ease suffering, doing so would be your calling, regardless of who was ill or in pain."

"Maybe they wouldn't be sick if they weren't where they shouldn't be."

He had no answer for that. Of course there was a logical fallacy, but if one didn't accept logic, what would be the benefit in attempting to argue the point? Owen glanced at Julia. He knew her look: calm, hands folded in her lap, her eyes half-shut, dusky in the half-light from the two lit lanterns—she was listening carefully but would not interfere.

"But frostbite is frostbite," Owen said, "here or there."

"And stupid is stupid."

"I'm not stupid. I'm trying to understand."

"Maybe so." A lengthy pause followed. "I will say this much but no more, Owen Rouse. Everybody knows what causes frostbite. But many ailments can't be seen on the skin or put back together like a broken bone."

Owen recalled that Harry Whitaker had used the same example.

"They hide, even when we can see what they do—make us blind or dizzy or lame. I know what makes a Navajo a Navajo, and sometimes the answer comes to me. But I don't know what makes white people, white people."

"I understand what you're saying. But your herbs and potions, they work the same way for me as they would for you, don't they?"

"Some do. Sometimes." She spoke with deliberation. "If I need to make more water, I drink the same tea that I give you to drink. But maybe I need to make water for a different reason, one that you can't see, and maybe I need something else, too, not just tea."

"A ceremony?"

She waved him off. "This is something you know nothing about."

"Maybe I also need something else."

"Maybe you do." She leaned over and tapped his leg with her cane. "But this much I can see. So I tell you to drink the tea."

Well, he had to admit that Tóya had her own logic. "May I ask you a serious question?"

Tóya gave him her scowl.

"Do you ever worry about the survival of your people?"

Tóya took a moment before speaking. "The Diné emerged from the Third World between the four sacred mountains. We'll be here until time runs out."

"You really believe that?" Owen asked. Nothing lasted forever, no civilization, not even America in all its permutations. "I mean, literally, as a fact, not as a vision of the world as it should be, in some right order."

"I don't see the difference," Tóya said.

She left the next day, having made no mention of payment for her services.

THE BLISTERS FROM the frostbite drained; the damaged skin wrinkled and peeled off. Owen still had very little feeling in part of his right foot, and none at all in his two outer toes, which had blackened. He knew they were lost and tried not to think about it.

He drank the herbal tea; the puffiness above his ankles, which he recognized more by its absence than he had by its presence, dissipated. He took a sweat-bath, which he shared with Johnny Gorman; the heat was so intense that he had to be helped out. He did everything else that Tóya had instructed him to do—wraps, vapors, sun—and the ulcerations across his insteps and elsewhere began to heal. Progress was very slow, but November turned to December and he could see the fierce redness shrinking and fading.

Many nights were now bitterly cold. One evening, just the two of them, Julia and he, in her parlor—Pete had made another visit in the interim, but neither Harry Whitaker nor Tóya—she asked him once again, now that they could both envisage the closing of his wounds, if he'd given further thought to his departure for New York.

He had finished *The Octopus*; he had also read the even bleaker *McTeague* and several other books, including a collection of essays that featured Frederick Jackson Turner's "The Significance of the Frontier in American History," which Turner had first presented to a special meeting of the American Historical Association at the World's Columbian Exposition in Chicago in 1893. He had read many back issues of several periodicals—*Atlantic Monthly*, *McClure's*, *The Saturday Evening Post*—and kept up with world events (a month after the fact) from Chicago newspapers: the crash landing of the army's only aeroplane, a Wright Flyer, in Maryland; the Cherry Coal Mine disaster in Illinois, which killed over 250 miners and rescuers; the naming of a new American governor-general for the Philippine Islands; the announcement by the astronomer William Pickering of Harvard that the earth would pass through the tail of Halley's Comet on May 18, 1910 . . .

It wasn't that he hadn't thought further about New York, but he hadn't made any preparations. Now, though, he could; he'd healed well enough. He was walking more in his moccasins, and spending time in the store, sitting off to one side, catching the morning sunlight through the east-facing windows, attending to everything that went on around him, picking up a number of Navajo expressions, becoming better acquainted with the Gormans and even Johanna Yazzie, who sometimes sat silently beside him—well, "beside him" might suggest a closer proximity than was true; "near him" might be more accurate—but always on the floor, never in a chair. He figured the journey to New York could be managed, and even if after his arrival his movement around the city remained somewhat restricted—if he did as he knew he should, and didn't provoke new ulcerations by walking too far on the hard pavement in tightly laced shoes or boots of hard leather—well, he could manage city life.

"As a matter of fact," he told Julia, trying to sound as if his heart were in it, "I've been thinking that I should write to Richard Wetherill and ask for a letter of reference to the Museum of Natural History staff."

Julia folded her newspaper and laid it on her lap. "You have sufficient funds for New York? Tell me the truth or I'll be very angry if I find out otherwise."

"I have the funds," he said. More than once he'd brought up the subject of paying Julia room and board, but she'd refused. He needed to do something about that, even after the fact, after his departure. He'd think of some way to repay her.

Her rocking chair began its comforting pace, forward and back, its gentle squeak against the rough pine floor. After quite some time she said, "Why don't you just stay here with me?"

CHAPTER SIX: Harry (The Past)

1. Father and Sons

During the night, as scheduled, the train stopped in Lamy, and short-ly thereafter the porter came to Harris Whitaker's berth with the telegram: "Your father died in his sleep this morning. Funeral will await your return. Advise. Regrets, S. Van Schultz."

Harris disembarked in Albuquerque, as did Aaron Belnap, who an-nounced that he would wait with Harris until the next train heading back East—he was on no schedule, and his parents weren't expecting him anyway.

Harris and Aaron had both been mustered out on September 15, 1898, but Aaron still wore his uniform, attracting admiring glances from the ladies and a combination of envy and patriotic appreciation from those men who didn't avoid eye contact. He was handsome in his uniform, that was for sure, and the cane he continued to lean on generated the expected aura of sympathy. In truth, he was the prettiest man Harris had ever seen. Cheek bones and a jaw line that Michelangelo might have carved into marble. A woman's mouth. Tawny hair, wavy, the color of a lion's mane but more dig-nified in its careful combing, parted down the middle (he carried his slouch hat in his free hand.) Blue eyes, of course. A god among soldiers, clothed in khaki from shoulder to foot: a tunic bearing brass eagle buttons, parade belt, loose-fitting trousers that added a dash of nonchalance, leggings with leather straps, boots. And pinned to his chest the campaign medal awarded to each and every man of the 1st US Voluntary Cavalry by Teddy Roosevelt himself. Who wouldn't be impressed?

Quite an outfit, Harris thought. He'd abandoned his own even before leaving the hospital in Montauk, and he now sat on the wooden bench outside the depot wearing gray pants, black ankle boots, and a gray sack coat over white shirt and black tie. He looked as if he were already in mourning. He knew that he wasn't a handsome man, and he couldn't compete with Aaron, nearly ten years his junior, a wild boy, a force of unnatural amorality and therefore—at least to Harris—astonishment.

Harris absorbed the morning's dry chill and watched as the rising sun threw light over the granite and sandstone of the Sandias.

His father was dead, which, Harris knew, made him a wealthy man. A man who could do anything he wanted. Or *not* do anything he *didn't* want to. Such was the power of capital. Assuming he knew what he did or didn't want.

Harris was the youngest of four surviving children, preceded in birth by three sisters, the oldest of whom, Marybeth, could vaguely remember when their father still had both arms. The left had been shot off at the Second Battle of Manassas, clipped by grapeshot that left just enough of a ragged stump for a quick-thinking private to strip off his belt and fashion a tourniquet that kept Harris's father from exsanguinating. Before the shelling of Fort Sumter, Douglas Whitaker had been, at best, a perfunctory participant in the South Carolina militia, but he was highly regarded for his temperament and prudence. His compatriots therefore elected him major, an office that, he reasoned, he could scarcely refuse. Thus, in August 1862 he'd found himself at the Second Battle of Manassas. He subsequently claimed that he didn't feel anything at the time of his injury except the ferocious tug that spun him around and dropped him to the ground. For a moment, he even wondered where his arm had gone and bemoaned both the sorry state of his newly made, meticulously pressed uniform and the instantaneous death of his mount, head and neck torn apart by the full whirling energy of the grapeshot. The pain came afterward, in the field hospital, and once it came, it never went away, not even after a series of surgeons removed the remainder of his infected arm and eventually much of his shoulder, leaving a scarred pit that took many, many months to completely heal over. (Though Major Whitaker later tried to locate his life's savior, he never saw the private again, which led him to presume that the young man with the square beard and thick black sideburns had met his fate later in the battle.)

Major Whitaker spent the remainder of the war back home in Charleston, where he fathered two more daughters, Cordelia and Isabel, and managed his business ventures as best he could. He had no great affection either for slavery or for his slaves, viewing them as an increasingly unproductive cost of business as the Union blockades made it extremely difficult to ship his cotton or anything else across the Atlantic. But he'd seen the war coming and had planned accordingly. In 1859, well before the November 1860 election, he'd sailed for England and the Continent, intent on investing in the factories that turned his cotton into clothing and textiles, and when Lincoln's election confirmed in his mind the near-inevitability of war, he immediately purchased part ownership of two mills he'd toured, one in England and one in the Netherlands. (He didn't trust the French, not with their string of revolutions and republics and Napoleons, as if they couldn't make up their minds what they wanted.) He knew that if war came, the price of cotton would soar, making it difficult for the factories to turn a profit despite raising their prices, but he also assumed that the war would be short. He calculated that the South could never overcome the industrial might of the North—you don't take cotton and tobacco to war against iron and steel unless you're insane or so entrenched in romantic fantasies of honor and tradition that you might as well *be* insane—and could win only by launching a quick, devastating campaign and forcing the North to negotiate; failing that, the North would soon achieve a victory, after which, once the South had kissed the boots of its Northern masters, commerce would return to normal, with or without slavery. He hadn't expected the North to be so unprepared, and he'd underestimated the tenacity of the South and the superiority of its generals.

After Appomattox and Lincoln's assassination, the initial depredations of Reconstruction delayed Douglas Whitaker's financial recovery, but he had no nostalgia for the antebellum South—he left that to Harris's mother, who continued to carry on as if the war had never happened. She needed the obedience of servitude, which her loyal negro household staff continued to provide; only the youngest exercised their newly bestowed freedom to set off on their own. But the North had won, and in all other matters outside his wife's domestic domain Harris's father played by *its* rules. He was a businessman, and the future lay in a New South. By 1870, when Harris was born—that's what he'd always been called: Harris, not Harry—his father was already on his way to economic recovery, and his European ventures were growing rapidly. The Franco-Prussian War helped nicely, since England and the Netherlands both stayed out of the fray and the French took a drubbing.

In 1874, at the age of sixteen, Marybeth was married off to Samuel Van Schultz, a half-German, half-Dutch manager of the (now wholly owned) Whitaker factories in Eindhoven, which had recently expanded into producing very lucrative tobacco products for the European markets. Cordelia's marriage to Arthur Sheppard followed three years later, after which husband and wife repaired to Arthur's home in Manchester, England. In 1881 Isabel and John Demarest, an accountant recruited from New York City, celebrated their nuptials. In 1882 Douglas Whitaker began rotating his sons-in-law—Eindhoven to Manchester, Manchester to Charleston, Charleston to Eindhoven—thereby ensuring that, over time, each knew the full range of the Whitaker enterprises. This also allowed Mrs. Whitaker to have at home on a regular schedule her daughters and a rapidly expanding coterie of grandchildren.

Harris, at age ten, benefited from the attention of a doting mother, when she wasn't absorbed in her various societies dedicated to assisting the war injured and preserving Charleston's history and cultural traditions. Except for practicing the violin, he had no responsibilities outside of the schoolroom, where nothing less than a superior performance was expected by his father, who in all other respects appeared rather indifferent to his only son. Most evenings Douglas Whitaker had dinner with the family, but he and Harris rarely spoke.

In Harris's eleventh year the still-birth of the last Whitaker child brought father and son together in a way that neither—certainly not a timid ten-year-old—could have foreseen. The resultant bond never weakened although they differed in every conceivable way: personality, worldview, goals, blindnesses, desires. It became the strongest and most profound and most loving relationship of Harris's life.

When the family doctor was summoned, Harris didn't really understand what was happening, for he knew that his new brother or sister wasn't expected to arrive for another two months. There was no family dinner that night; Harris ate his supper in the kitchen with the servants and wasn't permitted to kiss his mother goodnight at bedtime.

It was still dark when his father woke Harris and told him that the baby had died. His mother was resting; the doctor had given her some medicine to help her sleep. Harris knew what would happen next: the infant would be buried in the family graveyard. Harris asked his father if the baby was a boy or a girl. A boy, his father told him. Could he see the baby? Harris asked. His father didn't reply at first; he sat silently on the side of Harris's bed. But then he told Harris to follow him. Holding a lamp, he steered Harris into his mother's dressing room. A large ceramic bowl, decorated with pink climbing roses, sat on his mother's dressing table. Inside, something lay wrapped very carefully in one of his mother's hand towels, the ones with her monogram and an entwining vine. His father set down the lamp beside the bowl and lifted a corner of the towel, and Harris saw a face. It was very pale, bluish, very small—smaller than his father's palm.

"Look at him," his father said in a quiet voice, "every feature is perfect."

Harris looked more closely. The eyes were closed, but he could see the very fine eyelashes. The face was a little wrinkled. Maybe that wasn't unusual; he didn't know. Harris spoke for the first time. "Why didn't he live?"

"He arrived too early. His little lungs weren't able to breathe."

"I wanted a brother," Harris said. "A little sister would've been all right, but I really wanted a brother."

"Is that so?" his father said.

"Yes. I would've helped Mama with him."

"I believe you would have," his father said. They continued to look at the baby in the ivory bowl with the hand-painted roses.

"Is he in heaven now?" Harris asked.

"Hmm. Huh-hmm." His father had to keep clearing his throat. "You mean his soul?"

"Yes."

"Papists would assign his soul to limbo. Do you know what that is?"

Harris shook his head.

"It's neither heaven nor hell. Catholics say it's a place where innocents who haven't been baptized go. Do you know about Original Sin?"

"We get it from Adam and Eve."

"That's right, and papists say that if you haven't been freed from Original Sin by baptism, you can't enter heaven. Unbaptized infants are sent to limbo."

Harris knew his father wasn't a religious man—he attended church services on Christmas and Easter because Harris's mother insisted that they go as a family. Nevertheless, Harris said, "We can baptize him now, can't we?"

His father didn't answer right away. He was breathing heavily, in through his nostrils, out through his lips. He was still wearing the shirt, tie, and frock coat he'd worn the previous day. "There's a pitcher of water on your mother's nightstand. Go get it, Harris, but be very quiet. We don't want to wake her or Isabel, who's resting with her. Your mother's had a very hard time. And I don't know that she'd approve."

Despite being in his bare feet, Harris tiptoed into his mother's bed chamber. He stood beside her bed for a moment, holding the white pitcher with both hands, but he heard nothing. The bed curtains were closed. He reached over and pulled one aside, just a bit. His mother was very white. He watched her slow, steady breathing for a moment and then glanced toward Isabel, who, still fully dressed, lay on top of the covers on the far side of the large bed. She was looking at him. Her eyes and the tip of her nose were very red. She lifted a finger and pressed it to her lips. Harris closed the curtain.

"All right," his father said when Harris returned, "do as I tell you." He lifted the wrapped frail body easily with his one arm, cradling the baby's head in his hand. "We need a name," he said.

"We should give him your name, Papa," Harris said.

"Well, maybe. Pour some of the water over his head. Just a little."

Harris did as directed. The water trickled over the bluish skin and into the towel.

"Now make a cross on his forehead with your thumb, and say, 'I baptize thee Christian Douglas Whitaker, in the name of the Father, the Son, and the Holy Ghost.' "

"I baptize thee Christian Douglas Whitaker, in the name of the Father, the Son, and the Holy Ghost."

"Very good," his father said. "Now you can hold him for a minute if you'd like."

The baby weighed practically nothing in Harris's hands. The head was the heaviest part. A fold of the towel slipped a bit and Harris was shocked by the raw wound of the umbilicus. His father redraped the towel.

"Why did you name him Christian?"

"It can't hurt," his father said. They stood together for several minutes. Then Harris carefully laid Christian back down. The shape would be familiar: the curve of the bowl was like the curve of his mother's stomach, from the inside, as Harris imagined it.

Father and son left the room, but instead of returning to Harris's bedroom, his father led him down the wide staircase and into the study at the foot of the stairs. His father went to the sideboard and selected a decanter from the half-dozen bottles displayed there and poured two inches of his own sour mash into a glass. Then he reached high on a shelf, behind the sideboard, and took down a vial from which he added a number of bright green drops.

"Would you like something? Are you hungry?" he asked Harris, who was standing, still in his nightshirt, in the middle of the floor.

"May I have some of that?" Harris asked, pointing to the small bottle with the green liquid.

His father turned his head and looked at him over his damaged shoulder. "No, you may not. Go sit down."

Harris retreated to the leather chair beside his father's work desk. His father sat down with a heavy sigh in the oak swivel chair behind the desk. He swung around so that he could see both Harris and the view through the French doors to a spacious lawn.

"How are your violin lessons coming?"

"Fine." Harris hated the violin. His mother had insisted that no cultured man or women should grow up without an appreciation for music, and his father had offered Harris no sympathy. "I leave your education to your mother," he'd said. "The day will come when you'll thank her."

His father steadily sipped his drink.

"Is your arm hurting now?" Harris asked. The whole family referred to his father's "arm," although it was nothing but a ghost.

"A bit."

His father's stock answer. Harris knew when his father's arm was especially painful because the remaining shoulder muscles were corded with tension and he held his head very still on his stiffened neck.

"You've never seen a baby that small, have you?" his father asked.

Harris shook his head.

"Of course you haven't." Another sip from the glass. "I remember when you came into the world—very pink, and loud—my, how you wailed at the top of your lungs!—and I remember how wide open your eyes were as soon as you settled down." He sighed. "Sometimes when a baby enters the world, you can immediately see an intelligence light up his eyes—I remember seeing that in yours, Harris." His father closed his own eyes. "Would you open the doors for me?"

Harris went to the French doors. They opened inward, and a damp breeze immediately crossed the threshold. The first sunlight had reached the trees across the lawn, and in the slight breeze the Spanish moss looked like strands of dappled gold against the deeper green of the leaves. The weather would be sultry by late afternoon. His father was already sweating, but it wasn't because of the temperature. His glass was already empty.

"Would you refill this for me?"

Harris took the glass from his father's hand. He went to the sideboard and reached up for the decanter of sour mash.

"Just half," his father said.

"I can't reach the bottle with the green medicine."

"That's all right. I shouldn't take any more of that just yet."

Harris returned with the drink.

Sip. His father's injured shoulder relaxed.

Harris thought of Christian, the bare, mottled skin, and he began to cry.

"It's all right," his father said, "it's all right, Son. Come over here." He held out his arm and wrapped Harris in it, and kissed his boy on the top of his head. "It's a sad day. It's a sad, sad day."

"LET'S GET SOME BREAKFAST," Aaron Belnap said. "I'm buying."

Harris looked up. Aaron was standing in front of him, swinging his cane, which was balanced on one finger, back and forth like a pendulum.

"And not railroad rubbish," Aaron continued. "C'mon. I know a little place just up the street from here." He turned and walked away, leaving Harris little choice but to follow.

Aaron wasn't leaning so heavily on the cane anymore. He was lucky. When Aaron was brought to the aid station by stretcher, lying on his side in a pool of blood and thrashing with pain, Harris thought his injury was much worse than it turned out to be. He'd caught a piece of shrapnel from a Spanish artillery shell, and the steel fragment, several inches wide, had sliced all the way to hip bone, nicking a small artery but missing everything major.

Harris followed Aaron into a dim, grubby Mexican café. The bald man behind the counter at Mi Casa was the fattest human being Harris had ever seen. His eyes widened at the sight of Aaron, and they both extended their arms toward each other. Aaron leaned in over the counter and grabbed the fat man by the shoulders. "*Hola! mi buen amigo. Ha sido demasiado largo.*"

"Señor Belnap! Too long! *Sí,* too long!" The man's enthusiastic embrace threatened to pull Aaron off his feet. Then he pointed to the cane and frowned. "*Qué ha pasado?*"

"*No es nada. Metrallo en mi culo.*"

"Ah!" His eyes widened even further. "Cuba." He looked at Harris for the first time.

"I'd like you to meet my friend Harry Whitaker—Dr. Whitaker, I should say. Harry, this is the owner of the best café in Albuquerque, Señor Arturo Mérida."

Beaming, Mérida swallowed Harris's extended hand in his large paws and asked, "*Qué te trae a Albuquerque?*"

"I'm sorry," Harris said, shaking his head. "*No hablo español.*"

"Ah! I shouldn't assume!" Mérida apologized.

"Breakfast!" Aaron exclaimed. "*Los huevos y las salchichas—los con chiles verdes. Patatas fritas y cebollas y las naranjas—*you have fresh oranges?"

"Of course. Go, sit down. You're my first customers today. Did you just get off the train?"

"Yes," Harris said, wondering what food Aaron was going to subject him to—probably something that would burn all the way through his innards for the next day.

Mérida disappeared into the kitchen, and Aaron led Harris to a rickety table. He seemed truly pleased to be here. This was one of the things Harris had never mastered—learning how to make himself at home when he wasn't at home.

He'd paid a brief visit to Charleston shortly before embarking for Cuba from Florida. On the morning before he left for Tampa, he and his father were sitting in his father's study, discussing in measured terms why Harris had signed up to serve as an acting assistant surgeon for the 1st US Volunteer Cavalry.

"You heard the drumbeat," his father had said.

It was a bright June morning, already heating up. His father was propped erect by pillows, with a breakfast tray on his desk: biscuits, butter, honey, black coffee with chicory.

"No, that wasn't the reason. Our soldiers are going to get sick down there, in that environment."

Harris had been talked into volunteering by James Robb Church, the newly named regimental surgeon. Harris and he had become acquainted at the Army Medical School in Washington, where, after obtaining his medical degree, Harris had sought a position. His mother and sisters had vehemently objected, insisting that he should return to Charleston, open a practice, find a wife, become a pillar of the community. His father had been far more dispassionate. He accepted Harris's explanation that his interests were more scientific, and that all the best minds studying the germ theory of disease, especially transmission and prevention, had gathered in Washington.

But now, with war having been declared in April, both Robb Church and Col. Leonard Wood, commander of the 1st US Volunteer Cavalry and theretofore President McKinley's personal physician, understood that successfully invading Cuba not only meant surviving Spanish bullets, but also surviving wound infections and a rainy-season cesspool of disease: malaria, yellow fever, typhoid, dysentery. That was why Harris had been recruited.

"And if you contract malaria or yellow fever yourself?" his father said. He had yet to touch anything on the breakfast tray except his coffee.

"It could be educational," Harris replied.

"Don't you even think it."

"Is your arm bothering you this morning?" Harris asked. The skin under his father's chin hung in wattles. He was shrinking away, his shoulders stooped, his spine outwardly curved between his shoulder blades, his hair thinning and ash gray, his face gaunt.

"A bit."

"Is there anything I can do?"

His father ignored the question. "Your volunteering is honorable, Harris. I'm certainly not going to object even though you know my views on the war. But please come home in one piece." He raised what remained of his left shoulder to make his point. Then he let his muscles relax. "Go look in the sideboard. I have something for you."

On the bottom shelf of the sideboard Harris found a varnished, elegant wicker case. A small brass plate above the top latch read "Harris Whitaker, M.D." It was a field surgical pannier containing the highest-quality medical instruments—scissors, knives, scalpels, retractors, clamps, aspirator, amputation saw, trephine—as well as syringes, catgut and silk, needles for suturing, and a selection of compresses, iodiform gauze, cotton sponges, plaster of paris bandages, slings, and sealed flasks of ether, chloroform, morphine sulfate.

"I don't know what to say except thank you," Harris said.

"I'd recommend adding a few other items," Douglas Whitaker said. "Coca alkaloids. Atropia. Salicylic acid. Paracetanol . . ."

Even before leaving home to study at the University of Virginia, Harris had learned a lot about pain killers from his father and a procession of quacks, cranks, and charlatans that his father, who was otherwise discerning about people, had invited to Charleston in a futile search for relief. Harris had also learned, at the age of fifteen, when his father was temporarily without a manservant, how to use a needle and syringe.

"Pain is a vice," his father had said one night while Harris was helping him into a nightshirt. Harris, misunderstanding, envisaged a medieval device being cranked tighter and tighter. "Pain has a double grip. It can't kill you, but it has the power to destroy your life if you let it, just like any other vice—gambling, drinking . . ." His father fell silent; Harris administered the nightly injection, and his father resumed: "You can't let the pain get the better of you, but *that*"—he nodded toward the syringe, which Harris had placed on a bedside tray—"*that* is pain's other hand around your throat, and not just because a slip-up, a little too much, *will* kill you."

That night, having settled his father into bed, Harris sat and watched him drift off. *A little too much.* To end the pain forever. How could it not be a temptation?

2. Cuba

THE 1898 CUBAN ADVENTURE was a botch, a bungle, from the start. Forget the *Maine*. No one, not Hearst or Pulitzer or their tabloids, not the Washington politicians, including Teddy Roosevelt, could explain to Harris's satisfaction why in God's name the Spanish, who were totally unprepared for a war in the Caribbean and the Pacific, would deliberately aggravate the United States by blowing up one of its warships in Havana harbor. The Cuban insurgents had more of a reason to do it than Spain, to draw the United States into their fight against the cruel and brutish Spanish military, but it was at least as likely that the explosion had resulted from a careless cigarette or a manufacturing flaw in the ship itself.

But all that was largely irrelevant, wasn't it?

When the war cry went out, Roosevelt, eager to demonstrate his manhood, had resigned as undersecretary of the Navy, and together with his friend Leonard Wood set about organizing the 1st US Volunteer Cavalry, attracting cowboys, Indian fighters, Indians (though not so many), ex-miners, ex-lawmen, and fortune-hunters, many of them from Arizona, New Mexico, and the Indian territories but also with a smattering of ardent patriots and graduates from some of the most prestigious Eastern colleges. Brought together at a camp in San Antonio, Texas, they learned to march in formation (with much grumbling), got accustomed to their new mounts and military discipline (more grumbling), practiced their shooting, learned something of military tactics, sat around and complained about the food and accommodations, and waited. On a regular basis high-muck-a-mucks dropped in with due obsequiousness and rallying cries. By the time orders finally came through for the Rough Riders—oh! how the press loved that name, purloined from Buffalo Bill's Wild West and Congress of Rough Riders of the World—to board the trains for the staging area outside Tampa, everyone was fed up with drills and delays, and they scrambled aboard carrying their packs and their new bolt-action Krag-Jorgensen carbines and their Colt .45s and their Bowie knives.

Harris himself never even saw San Antonio. He and most of the expeditionary force's other medical corpsmen had gone directly to Tampa, where they waited to organize the vast quantities of medical supplies that didn't arrive. Harris was somewhat relieved when word spread that Clara Barton and her Red Cross volunteers, physicians as well as nurses, were preparing at least one hospital ship to follow the invading force, but that didn't explain why the Rough Riders, over a thousand men, were being accompanied to Cuba by only eight medical personnel, including three stewards and two untrained privates. It was almost as if no one expected casualties.

In Florida, chaos held sway. There wasn't enough rolling stock when the order to board the transport ships came through, and the Rough Riders only made it to the port by commandeering empty coal cars. As it was, four of the twelve companies were left behind, as were all the horses except the officers' mounts. Thus the 1st US Volunteer Cavalry was destined to enter the war on its feet, even though its recruits had no infantry training.

The landing, after more than a week at sea, was another fiasco. The troops scrambled into lines of small boats and were towed ashore at Daiquirí, fifteen miles east of the major port of Santiago, where the US Navy had bottled up the Spanish fleet and where the war's decisive battle was expected to be fought. At Daiquirí, which was little more than a dot on the map, the one pier was too rotted to be of any use, and so most of the men had to wade through the surf and scramble up the beach. Some of the mules and horses, pushed into the water to swim ashore, panicked, swam out to sea, and disappeared, and others, including one of Roosevelt's two personal mounts, also drowned.

Two days later, on June 24, contrary to directives from commander Maj. Gen. William Shafter—he hadn't even come ashore yet—the white-bearded Brig. Gen. Joe Wheeler, who'd led Confederate cavalry in the Civil War, ordered an assault near the village of Las Guásimas—an assault that primarily served to delay a Spanish pullback to Santiago that was already in progress. The attack found the Rough Riders cutting a path through unfamiliar jungle terrain, targeted by snipers and getting sliced up by the near-lethal spikes of bayonet bushes. When the Spanish resumed their withdrawal, Fightin' Joe Wheeler, flushed with success, reportedly shouted that his men "had the Yankees on the run!" Harris didn't personally hear the general's exclamation because he was in the hold of a ship anchored nearby at Siboney, nearly vomiting from the 130-degree heat and futilely trying to locate missing crates of bandages and syringes. Las Guásimas cost the 1st Volunteers eight lives and another thirty-one casualties.

Over the next several days, soldiers started dropping from fevers. It kept Harris busy. The other US medical corpsmen began setting up a field hospital at Sevilla, and the Rough Riders moved to a new camp farther inland, but the ground was still marshy and they found themselves fending off tarantulas and scorpions as well as clouds of mosquitoes that descended on them in the morning, after the daily afternoon cloud bursts, and in the evening, when the damnable pests settled in for an all-night feed.

When the commander of the 2nd Cavalry Brigade fell ill, Colonel Wood was named to replace him, and as a consequence Teddy Roosevelt took command of the Rough Riders. The men liked him. Oh, he strutted like a bantam rooster and his voice could cut steel, but he was both fearless and fair. When he said he thought they were the best men in the world, everybody knew that he meant it. Meanwhile, Major General Shafter continued to ponder how and when to launch a full-scale attack on the village of El Caney and the San Juan Heights, which guarded the eastern approach to Santiago.

Two days before the expected assault, Robb Church, Harris, and one of the privates assigned to the medical team, Billy Dutton, a lanky middle-aged volunteer who'd seen action on and off during the Indian wars, were sitting under a tarp and talking with raised voices to avoid being silenced by the usual afternoon downpour. During a momentary lull in the storm they were joined by Maj. Henry La Motte, a retired Navy surgeon who'd heeded the call to war and was named ranking medical officer for the Volunteers. La Motte sat down, waited for another lull, and then announced that the Rough Riders would be one of six regiments assigned to take the San Juan Heights. The advance would be all uphill, through barbed wire and tall, coarse guinea grass, while the Spanish took aim from trenches, a stone blockhouse, and rifle pits that they were still busily digging.

"I assume Shafter will launch an artillery barrage to clear the Heights and the approach before he orders our men in," Church said.

"Our artillerymen don't have smokeless powder," Billy Dutton said. "It won't take the Spanish gunners long to get the range."

"And then?" Harris asked.

"Then it's us against them," Dutton said.

"I imagine someone will set up a medical aid station this side of the San Juan River, below the Heights," La Motte said. "I think we should have somebody there to help out."

Everybody looked at Harris, which made him suspect that the decision had already been made.

"Why me?" Harris asked. La Motte was smoking a cigarette, Dutton working a chaw of tobacco and spitting into an empty can that had held tinned beef the night before. Robb Church was fanning himself with his hat.

"Robb and I have spent far more time in operating rooms than you," La Motte said, "and we'll be of far more use at the field hospital. No one can operate effectively close to the lines—up there, you operate only when necessary to stop the bleeding. Otherwise, you bandage and transport."

The weight of the rain was making the tarp sag. They moved closer to the center pole, where the tarp peaked. If the violent bursts of wind tore an edge loose, at least they wouldn't drown.

"I didn't recruit you for your skill with a scalpel," Church said to Harris. "But you *do* know how to stop somebody from bleeding to death, don't you?" He scrunched up his face, pretending to fear the answer.

"I believe I do," Harris said. "I'd better, if I want to take home a medal. There's not much glory in treating fevers and diarrhea."

"Speakin' of which," Dutton said, spitting into his can, "I've had a serious case of the shits all day."

They all laughed, even the ever-serious La Motte.

"Don't blame me, Billy," Harris said, "I told you to boil the water." He'd initially tried to convince everyone to boil all their drinking water—he didn't trust the supply, not what was being pumped from the distilling ship anchored with Admiral Sampson's flotilla, and especially not what came from local streams—but had quickly seen that, in this heat, it was a futile request.

"Take Dutton with you to help at the aid station," La Motte now said to Harris. "He's been under fire before."

That evening, moths and beetles the color of dried blood cruised in and out of the light from Harris and Church's campfire. Some of the beetles were the size of Harris's thumb, and the drone of their extended wings set his nerves on edge. Both men were smoking pungent cigars in a futile effort to clear their periphery of mosquitoes. Their dinner had been field rations: hardtack, boiled navy beans, a chunk of sowbelly thrown in with the beans, and a shared can of boiled beef—salty, gelatinous scraps of gristle, fat, and stringy flesh—that had been warehoused since 1894 after being ordered by, but never delivered to, the Japanese during their war with China. The canned meat had to be the most disgusting thing Harris had ever tried to eat.

"So what am I going to see?" Harris asked.

"At the aid station?" Church shifted his thin shoulders and pondered the question before answering. "The Spanish have Mausers. They use high-velocity, steel-jacketed ammunition that tends to leave small, neat holes, and that's to our advantage. You've seen photographs of what lead slugs used to do, shattering bones and ripping people open."

Harris nodded.

"A Mauser bullet can drill a hole right through a large bone without destroying any surrounding tissue. So most arm and leg wounds can be bandaged and put on hold, if the bullet misses a major artery. Even penetrating chest and abdominal wounds aren't necessarily fatal. But dealing with shrapnel is another matter. If someone is close to a shell when it explodes, he'll be shredded. A little farther away, he'll be peppered, and that's where you're going to have to decide what can and can't be done." Church slapped at his large ears, one and then the other—the mosquitoes were relentless. "Get us the ones we can save."

Harris could hear snippets of nearby conversations above the whine of the hovering insects and the crackling of the fire. Bats with wingspans the length of his forearm swirled and dove among the crowns of the guásima trees.

"Think about what you'll need beside your surgical pannier," Church continued. "If it isn't in the standard first-aid packet that all the troops have"—a bandage roll and gauze compresses and handkerchief sling—"assume you won't have it unless you bring it yourself. I know for a fact that the regimental medicine chests don't have enough anesthesia or morphine. So make an educated guess as to what else might help. Let me know in the morning, and I'll see what I can do, even if it's just signing requisitions."

"Robb, you're only a first lieutenant. Quartermasters won't accept a requisition from you."

"Everybody's going to be in a dither. Nobody will look that closely. I'll scribble and you can tell them the order's from La Motte—better yet, from Roosevelt." Church stood up, stretched, wiped his long, thin face with a bandana, and retired to his bedroll.

Harris sat a while longer. His head was swimming from the cigar—he wasn't much of a tobacco user—and his eyes were watering, but he threw a cup of water on the fire to thicken the cloud of smoke around him, which had little effect on the insects but sent him into a spasm of coughing.

Water. There wouldn't be enough safe drinking water. Much of the army was now bivouacked along the trail to El Pozo. Some of the troops would be forced to march up to three miles to the front—not a great distance, unless you were carrying rifles and 200 rounds of ammunition and wearing wool uniforms in hundred-degree heat. Harris suspected that emptied canteens would get shortsightedly tossed aside, and it wouldn't be long before some soldiers started to suffer dehydration and exhaustion, and some, bypassed in the confusion of the fight or hidden by the high grass between the San Juan River and the Heights, might die without a mark on them. Both the San Juan and the shallow Aguadores ran clear, but with as many as ten thousand troops wading across at the fords and roiling things up, and with God knows what falling into the water—certainly excrement from the horses and mules—the water wouldn't be clean for long. The effects might not show up for a day or two, but bad water always led to illness, and the uninjured troops who made it through and drove the Spanish back to Santiago—Harris had no doubt of their success—would still be needed to take the city. General Shafter wouldn't be pleased if half his division fell victim to dysentery and typhoid.

You'd think something as fundamental as water would have the highest priority, but Harris knew better after witnessing the fiasco in Tampa and hearing about the confusion at La Guásimas. Water was heavy—Harris guessed that the tank on each water wagon held about 750 gallons—and moving it over these godforsaken trails was difficult even under the best of conditions, without the afternoon rains and the constant traffic, which rendered the main route almost impassable.

He'd need to find extra canteens. And tincture of iodine to sterilize the water. And salt. Marching and fighting in this heat, the troopers would sweat out more than just water, and the salt their bodies lost would need to be replaced. He knew he could easily get his hands on salt, and he could probably confiscate iodine from a sick bay. The water would taste like hell, but anyone thirsty enough would gladly drink it.

Shortly after dawn, Harris and Billy Dutton set out for the ships anchored at Siboney, which they reached in midmorning. Billy Dutton immediately went in search of canteens and a pack mule, while Harris headed for the dock. The *USS Supply,* a schooner-rigged steamer that the Navy had purchased, renamed, and commissioned soon after the declaration of war, seemed like a likely target for Harris's one-man raiding party.

Once aboard, Harris found the mess, told the chief cook that he needed salt, and to his great surprise was told to help himself in the storeroom. If it was going to be this easy, he figured he should grab what he could. He supplemented a twenty-pound bag of salt with sixty pounds of sugar—they could add that to the water, too, along with the iodine and salt—

and four crates of packaged soda crackers, light-weight and easy to digest. It took him no time to haul his loot up to the deck. Then he returned below, found the laundry, and grabbed as many towels as he could carry. Harris made one more trip to the laundry and then another to the ship's infirmary, where he grabbed the iodine he wanted. The medic on duty was tending to four crewman who'd come down with fevers. Unfortunately, the chloroform and morphine were under lock and key, and Harris knew there was no point in asking.

When Harris returned to shore with his plunder, he found Billy Dutton waiting at the end of the dock. Dutton was sitting beside a water wagon, leaning back against a wheel with his legs crossed at the ankles, his hands folded behind his head, and a chaw bulging in a cheek.

"Jesus, Billy," Harris said. "I asked you to collect canteens and a pack mule, and you show up with a water wagon and a team of six."

"You said you were concerned about there not bein' enough water."

"Yes, but if we go riding up to the front with that behind us, we might as well paint targets on our heads for the Spanish sharpshooters."

"Nah," Dutton said, "we'll fill up the canteens I found and then leave the tank beside the trail near El Pozo. Anyone who's thirsty will see it, whether they're comin' or goin'. I also found a canvas tarp that we can rig for shade at the aid station."

"If you don't mind my asking, how did you manage to acquire a water wagon?"

Dutton shrugged. "There were four mule teams ready to head out for El Pozo and no one around to drive 'em. So I volunteered."

One of Billy Dutton's unheralded skills proved to be driving a team of six, but the usual afternoon downpour thoroughly swamped the sunken trail from Siboney, which was regularly blocked by mounted field artillery and overloaded pack trains and caissons, all sinking into the morass. And then late in the day the regiments that had been bivouacked beside the road were ordered to break camp and move forward. At various places the trail narrowed to where only a single column, four abreast, could pass. During one of the interminable stops, soldiers were already coming to the wagon to refill their canteens. Harris climbed to the top of the water tank, cranked the hand wheel to swing open one of the ports, and dumped the salt, sugar, and iodine in. He figured that by the time they made it to El Pozo, the water would have been churned enough to disperse the iodine and dissolve the salt and sugar.

Long after midnight they reached the vicinity of El Pozo and decided there was no point in going farther. Billy maneuvered the water wagon to the side of the trail, into a flattened patch of tall grass. Then he unhitched the team and led four of the mules uphill toward El Pozo, to a make-shift corral that had been thrown together from cut trees and rope. Harris and Dutton settled down under the wagon after laying out the folded tarp. Thousands of men slept fitfully around them. A gray mist penetrated to the skin. Everything smelled like muck, like a South Carolina swamp.

At sunrise, July 1, Harris and Billy Dutton loaded up twin mules and set out westward toward the San Juan Heights. The various regiments had already mustered, amid piles of discarded haversacks and blanket rolls. Leading the march were two cavalry brigades—one comprising the 3rd, 6th, and 9th (colored) regiments; the other comprising the 1st, 10th (colored), and 1st Volunteers—to be followed by three infantry brigades. Harris and Dutton wove their way through the slow-moving lines.

For some time now they'd been hearing distant artillery fire from the north; the separate assault on El Caney was under way. There had also been a brief period of artillery fire from the US battery at El Pozo, until the Spanish guns, guided by the rising clouds of white smoke, returned fire and found their range. The American cannons then went silent.

Sporadic Spanish shells, some of which seemed to scream right over his head—Harris instinctively ducked—began exploding behind them and a little to the north, in a forest of mixed trees. The mules had been remarkably placid up to that point, but now, disturbed by the explosions as well as by the close quarters, they had to be coaxed forward a step at a time. Harris was beginning to wonder where the aid station was supposed to be located. He kept looking for a tent or a Red Cross flag—something.

Now, in addition to the bursting artillery shells, they could hear the incessant whistling of Mauser bullets, stripping leaves and cracking branches no more than a few feet above their heads. Pieces of green foliage and brown splinters showered down. Somewhere ahead, probably at the San Juan crossing, a major bottleneck had formed and those behind were barely moving forward.

"Goddammit!" someone shouted. "Give me something to shoot at!"

Harris and Dutton rounded a bend. Ahead lay the stone and gravel ford of the shallow Aguadores River, knee deep at best. The western bank, a mere three feet high, offered the only shelter; a group of men were shoveling gravel from the stream to expand a natural strand, which was some twenty feet wide and extended only eight or nine feet from the bank to the water line. Others were beginning to spread ponchos over the gravel. Farther down the stream, on the eastern side, stood a cluster of several palms. A soldier had managed to climb one of the palms and was throwing down cut fronds.

An officer, standing beside what Harris immediately recognized as a standard regimental medicine chest, appeared to be in command. Several casualties were already sitting or lying on the ground. There was no tent, no water wagon, and none of the expeditionary force's six ambulances—distinguished from other wagons by spring suspensions and a canvas top and curtains that could be rolled down.

"Christ," Billy Dutton said, "I think we found our aid station."

The senior officer was Capt. George Newgarden, regimental surgeon of the 3rd US Cavalry, the first regiment to reach the ford. It had been Newgarden's decision to stop here, at the Aguadores, where the bank offered nominal protection. Farther forward, there was none. Newgarden, responding to Harris's inquiry, said that as far as he knew, there wasn't any other aid station, though he wasn't sure what the three infantry brigades were going to do. He and his half dozen men, including three privates who had no medical experience, had been at the ford for over an hour and had yet to see any life-threatening casualties. A contract surgeon from the 6th US Calvary named Francisco Menocal had joined up with Newgarden's men and was tending to a soldier with a shoulder wound.

"Shouldn't we put up a Red Cross flag or something so litter-carriers and the walking wounded can find us?" Harris asked.

"That," Dutton said, shifting a plug from one cheek to the other, "would've required someone to requisition a flag pole."

Newgarden gave Dutton a look that didn't need interpretation.

"We have a tarp," Harris told Newgarden. "it isn't big, maybe fifteen by ten, but it could provide some shade for us to work in." Newgarden nodded and ordered his steward to find saplings or anything else that could serve as poles.

"Not too tall," he said, "or it'll make an easy target for the Spanish snipers. We can stake it at the top of the bank and then sink support poles near the stream." The steward hurried off.

"Where are the snipers?" Harris asked.

"We've had reports that they're hiding up in the trees and targeting the wounded and litter-bearers."

"Billy, see those palms?" Harris pointed downstream. "Set up a holding area there, in whatever shade you can find." He turned to Newgarden. "We brought with us canteens filled with treated water, iodide to sterilize creek water if we run out, crackers if the men need something to hold them over, and towels we can soak to treat heat prostration."

Newgarden nodded again. "You've thought about all this."

"Some."

Two litter-carriers were splashing through the Aguadores at the ford. The man they carried was holding his abdomen, his legs drawn up.

"Do you have any particular surgical expertise?" Newgarden asked.

"No," Harris answered. "Actually, I'm an epidemiologist."

Newgarden didn't even glance at him. After a long pause he said, "Then I guess I'll take this one."

Harris quickly walked downstream to where Billy Dutton was unpacking the mules. "Give me an armload of towels," he said. He almost had to shout because the Spanish artillery had begun a steady barrage, accompanied by the increasingly steady pop and whine of Mausers. He could feel his heart jumping in his chest.

With the towels in hand, Harris turned around, back in the direction of El Pozo, and his jaws clenched. Barely above tree level, and coming directly down the trail toward the ford, was an observation balloon. A basket hanging beneath it carried two men. On the ground, a crew of four struggled with guy lines. The Spanish were aiming for the balloon, and as a consequence errant rifle fire and shrapnel began raining down on the mass of men directly below and behind. The troops on the trail broke formation and scurried to the sides, but there wasn't any cover. The balloon, shining of varnish, floated forward, ethereal, dipping and swaying above the fray. One of the men in the basket appeared to be trying to use a telephone connected by wire to the ground. The balloon's attendants splashed and stumbled across the ford, and the balloon glided on.

Harris saw half a dozen men fall almost simultaneously, two of them into the Aguadores, one with his head split by shrapnel. Two more shells exploded in the vicinity of the balloon, and the double concussive thump hit Harris so deeply—he could feel it in his bones—that it overwhelmed the sound of the blasts. Billy Dutton, splay-legged and bent low, was already running toward the trail, as were stretcher-bearers from the aid station.

Harris had seen dissections and the ravages of disease, and even the consequences of individual violence, but he'd never seen bodies ripped apart like this. The sight of Newgarden and Menocal, focused on nothing but the tasks in front of them, steadied him, and he turned and opened his pannier, preparing to treat his first casualty.

By early afternoon most of the first infantry division had joined the six regiments of the cavalry division on the far side of the Aguadores and San Juan rivers. Massed in the bottom of a thickly wooded basin, five hundred yards from the Heights, they were all taking heavy casualties while waiting for the order to advance. The Rough Riders, Harris heard, were positioned farthest to the north, below what everyone was calling Kettle Hill. At some point the order finally came from General Shafter to marshal for the assault on the Heights—the infantry to advance on San Juan Hill, on the left; the dismounted cavalry units, on the right, to take Kettle Hill—but by then Harris was too busy to care who went where.

The first serious wound Harris saw: an infantryman who had taken a bullet in the top of his skull; there was no exit wound but he was comatose, his pulse rapid and his pupils unreactive. Harris told two stretcher-bearers to move him aside. Then a black cavalryman from the 10th who'd been shot in the abdomen; Harris put a compress on the wound but couldn't do anything else except inject morphine and have the man carried to a passing supply wagon that was headed in the right direction. Then a shattered ankle that Harris cleaned as best he could and splinted; Harris thought about his limited supply of morphine and decided that this kid—that's all he was, a kid, no more than eighteen—was tough. The shattered ankle would have to wait beyond the shade of the tarp, amid a growing field of wounded, for transport. As wagons became available, those with injuries serious enough to require the quickest transport were crammed against each other in the wagon beds, cushioned only with bunches of grass and palm fronds.

Newgarden, Menocal, and Harris, doing their best not to get in each other's way in the confined space, were so overwhelmed that soldiers who staggered back across the ford with heat exhaustion or minor wounds were being told to go to the holding area Billy Dutton had set up under the palms.

Another Spanish artillery shell burst directly over the ford. A courier hurrying toward El Pozo was thrown from his mortally injured horse, which fell into the Aguadores, disgorging blood and the contents of its ruptured gut as it thrashed and screamed. An infantryman quickly shot it through the brain, but it took half a dozen men, slipping and falling in the mud and stones, to pull it out of the water. They left the carcass on the east bank; there wasn't anything else they could do. A horde of flies immediately congregated.

Not far from Harris, a private was kneeling over a splayed cavalry sergeant, the private's ear pressed to the wounded man's chest.

"Can I help him?" Harris asked.

The private, tears in his eyes, looked up. "No, it'll only be a minute," he said.

Harris turned back to his current casualty, a bullet wound through the cheek and lower jaw. Out of nowhere, a Red Cross nurse—a young, thin woman wearing a white apron and the signature armband—knelt down beside Harris. She had auburn hair surrounding her white cap. The wounded man's jaw was broken; he couldn't talk. Harris flushed and cleaned the wound as best he could, and extracted several tooth fragments so that they wouldn't be swallowed. The nurse began wrapping the man's head.

Beside them, the private lifted the body of his sergeant and carried him down along the Aguadores, to the end of the line of two dozen, three dozen corpses. Heads toward the bank, feet often in the stream, they lay without regard to rank or race. Two of the walking wounded were covering the faces of the dead with whatever they could find and driving off vultures that were already inured to the dissonance of cannon, mortar, and rifle.

Harris turned to his next patient, a wound to the right hand and the ribcage. The sun was still high, the fetid, chloroformed air trapped under the tarp, and Harris began to feel light-headed. Soon he'd be of no use if he didn't get away from the smell of punctured bellies, blood, urine, vomit, sour sweat. Having directed the nurse to wrap the man's hand and side—he was fortunate, for the bone had stopped the bullet—Harris stood up and walked unsteadily to one of the poles holding up the tarp. He grabbed on with both hands, bent over, and began heaving. There was nothing in his stomach to come up. Dutton saw him and came running; he had a soaked towel wrapped around his head, which looked so ridiculous that Harris almost laughed. Harris, bare headed, realized he was standing in the sun and moved to the other side of the pole, where the corner of the tarp protected him. Dutton, panting in the heat, didn't say anything; he handed Harris a full canteen. Harris felt like an idiot: he'd spent the last day and a half thinking about how to provide enough clean water, and then he'd forgotten to drink himself. He sipped the water: too much iodine, and the sugar only made it worse; the taste was vile.

"Drink some more," Dutton said.

Harris did as he was told and then sat down, his back against the pole, breathing shallowly. He suddenly felt like he was going to vomit up the water: too fast.

A second Red Cross nurse, oblivious to the shell fragments and the bullets darting past her, stood in the middle of the ford, directing the injured who had less serious wounds toward the palms. There were so many sitting on the ground there now, unattended, that they were trying their best to bandage each other, using what little they had in their first-aid packs. Other injured soldiers, in groups of twos and threes, were struggling back toward El Pozo, some leaning on each other, some using a rifle as a crutch.

"Go back," Harris told Dutton. He nodded toward the palms. "Do what you can. If they don't have belly or chest wounds, make them drink. Dump water on them. Cool them down. Try to keep them all there until we can transport them—even the ones who want to go back up the trail to rejoin their units."

Dutton stood there in the gravel looking down at him.

"I'll be all right," Harris said. "I just need another minute. Go."

Harris tucked his forehead against his raised knees and folded arms to block out the ferocious light. After another minute he made himself stand up. Being attended to by his Red Cross nurse was a Rough Rider with a jagged piece of shrapnel embedded below his hip.

THEY SLOWED DOWN about half way through the mounds of food presented to them by Arturo Mérida. Aaron had done most of the eating. Harris was sitting back in his chair and toying with his coffee cup.

"How long do you expect to be in Charleston after your father's funeral?" Aaron asked. He dipped a piece of tortilla into the remains of the green salsa.

"I don't know. Not long. My father was a disciplined businessman. He knew what was happening. I'm sure his affairs are in order."

"Why go at all? We just came from there."

Harris stared at him. "It's called paying due respect."

"He won't care." Aaron took out a package of cigarettes and extracted one, which he lit with a wooden match. He tipped his head back and exhaled toward the ceiling. "I may be gone before you make your way back here, if you ever do." He began randomly stacking the dishes—plates, bowls, platters. "My guess is that you won't," he said with an indifferent shrug. He pushed the wobbly stack toward the edge of the table.

"Gone where?"

"I don't know. Maybe South America or China. Or the Transvaal."

"Africa?"

"Why not?"

"And do what?"

"I have marketable skills."

"Don't be ridiculous."

Aaron leaned forward but he kept his voice under control. "I like you, Harry. I consider you a friend. But I've had many friends. They come and go."

"Sounds like they come and *you* go."

"And this is why I never ask for their approval." He sat back and the silence lingered for a full minute. "I take it that your father made a lot of money from his ventures."

Harris set down his coffee cup. "Let's say he just made me a very wealthy man."

"How wealthy?"

"Probably wealthy enough to buy Gallup several times over." It was a gross exaggeration, but he didn't care.

"Well, if you do decide to buy it, do me a favor: tear it down and start over."

Mérida interrupted their conversation with fresh coffee. By now, several other tables had customers, all speaking Spanish, and he went to each in turn.

"If you dislike Gallup so much, why are you even going there?" Harris asked. He knew that Aaron didn't get along with his father, a lawyer who had expected Aaron to follow in his footsteps.

"I want to strut around in my uniform, give them all a good look." With his pinky Aaron drew loops in the grease on his plate. The sun had topped the buildings on the other side of the street and was pouring light through the café's windows. "Besides, I'm supposed to be your tour guide and Gallup's as good a place as any to start from."

On the train they'd talked about crossing the Navajo and Hopi reservations on their way to the Grand Canyon, and about meandering through southern Utah and riding up to Moab to see the sandstone arches. Now, however, Harris wasn't so sure he wanted to, not with Aaron Belnap.

THE RED CROSS NURSE quickly cut away the soldier's blood-sodden pants with a pair of shears. The patient was grinding his teeth between ragged breaths.

"Do you know how long you've been bleeding this heavily?" Harris asked while he quickly checked the soldier's smaller wounds. He'd been sprayed by bits of flying metal. All those cuts appeared superficial.

"Since one of the fellows carrying me slipped in the mud and I slid off the stretcher."

"They dropped you?"

"That's what I just said." He groaned. "Jesus."

"You need to try not to thrash around," Harris said. "The shrapnel may have nicked an artery. I'm going to have to open up the wound a little to see." The nurse was busy swabbing away as much blood as she could with a cotton sponge. "Hold his leg still," Harris told her. "Are you ready, soldier?"

The man grunted.

Harris slipped a retractor down into the wound, between the flesh and shrapnel. He flushed the wound. Fresh blood pulsed up. So it was an artery, and he wouldn't be able to get to it unless he removed the shrapnel.

"I'm going to give you something for the pain," Harris said. He reached for a syringe and a vial of morphine.

"Much appreciated," the soldier said between clenched teeth.

"Where's the pain worst?" Harris stuck the needle in, just to the outside of the hip point. The nurse was preparing a tray of surgical instruments, wiping each down with alcohol.

"Leg," he panted. "Back of my thigh. Like lightning. All the way down."

The metal was probably pressing on the sciatic nerve. Harris waited for the morphine to take effect. He'd been kneeling behind the patient, but now he moved around so that he could see his face clearly. He was stunned by the sharp blueness of the eyes, the symmetry of his face, despite the streaks of dirt, soot, and sweat. It was hard to guess his age. Somewhere in his early twenties.

Harris looked over his shoulder toward Menocal and Newgarden. Menocal was working on an abdomen, Newgarden on a chest wound. Harris was on his own. Transport—the bouncing, the jostling—was out of the question unless the shrapnel was removed. "I need to take out the shrapnel," he said to the soldier, "and in order to do that I need to extend the edges of the wound." The soldier was looking up at him. Harris saw in his eyes that the morphine was doing its job. The panting had slowed and now he was sighing, and with each sigh he relaxed more. First his shoulders, then his head and neck, his torso, his legs . . . "So I'm going to put you to sleep."

"Give me more of what's in that needle there and just pull the fucking shrapnel out."

"I can't do that," Harris said. "If the edge is ragged, I could sever an artery and you could bleed to death. Or I could cut the sciatic nerve, and if I do that, your leg may be paralyzed."

The soldier chuckled. "Well, Doc, the first thing I'm gonna do when I wake up is try to wiggle my toes, and if I can't, I'm gonna find you and cut off your dick." His speech was beginning to slur. "*Comprende?*"

"Understood."

The nurse poured chloroform onto a sponge.

"And sew me up good and tight. It's hard enough keeping one coal hole safe in the bunkhouse."

Harris knew the morphine had loosened the man's tongue, but where he came from, women weren't exposed to such vulgarities. The nurse, however, didn't react at all. She held the sponge over the soldier's nose and mouth.

"So you're a cowboy?" Harris asked.

His eyelids fluttered and he went under.

"He's a wild one," the nurse said, reaching for the instrument tray.

* * *

"Do you know him?" Harris later asked Billy Dutton, who'd returned to see how Harris was faring. The nurse had bandaged the soldier's wound, concealing the less-than-elegant stitches—fortunately, the edge of the shrapnel deep in the hip wound had been straight and tapered, and Harris hadn't needed to do much additional cutting—and was now efficiently plucking metal slivers from the trooper's back and upper legs.

"Aaron Belnap," Dutton said. "He signed up the same day I did, back in Gallup. We were shipped to San Antonio together."

Harris suddenly noticed that the Spanish artillery had ceased, and he wasn't hearing the whine of the Mauser fire overhead. Guns were still being fired in the distance, and the flow of casualties hadn't slowed, but the battle had moved away.

"He's got a mouth on him," Dutton said. "He ended up in the *Yucatan*'s brig on the way over from Tampa."

"What did he do?"

"Cussed out a lieutenant for breakin' up a card game."

"I take it he was winning?"

"I couldn't say. I don't think it mattered to him. It was more the principle of the thing."

Belnap was beginning to stir.

"Is he really a cowboy?" Harris asked.

Dutton shrugged. "I guess he's spent some time out herdin'. He can handle a horse and a rifle better than most."

In quick succession stretcher bearers rushed two more casualties under the tarp. "Get him on a wagon when you can," Harris told Dutton. Then he went to examine the new casualties.

The flow of the wounded, plus the cases of heat exhaustion and collapse, didn't let up until dusk. In the late afternoon two additional surgeons and a handful of Red Cross nurses and orderlies arrived, and Harris walked down to the palms, where he quickly assessed which soldiers could return to their units, assuming they could find them on the Heights, where a Spanish counterattack had been decimated by a well-positioned Gatling gun that swept away nearly six hundred lives in less than twenty minutes. So the American forces had prevailed despite a general disorganization that left units of the various regiments scattered everywhere. Many of the walking wounded whom Billy Dutton had helped patch up decided to spend the night by the Aguadores and find their regiments in the morning; others who needed further care decided to walk to the field hospital at Sevilla.

Harris's clothes, soaked in sweat and stained, were attracting a host of mosquitoes, and the whine of their flight past his ears nearly drove him mad. He walked downstream from the palms and dropped into the shallow water, which barely covered him when he stretched out. He lay there with only his nose and mouth above water. He was so tired he considered what it would be like to drown. But after a few minutes he rose and walked back to the aid station. Someone had managed to boil a pan of coffee. He rummaged for a tin cup among the rations confiscated from a resupply wagon headed to the front. He drank the coffee and ate a can of the boiled beef he'd previously found so disgusting. He stood at the edge of the tarp watching the new surgeons and the indefatigable Newgarden and Menocal continuing to treat patients.

A first lieutenant from the signal corps came up to him. The lieutenant was crisply dressed in full uniform despite the heat. He cut a fine figure, and Harris took an immediate dislike to him—something in his manner, in the way he looked at the disorder around him with distaste. He asked Harris who was in charge.

"Officially?" Harris said. "Your guess is as good as mine."

The lieutenant looked him over with disdain. "Whoever *you* are, you're out of uniform," he said.

"WE MEET AGAIN."

Harris Whitaker opened his eyes and looked up from his cot in one of the detention pavilions at the Montauk Point tent hospital. He recognized Aaron Belnap immediately.

"You're not supposed to be in here," Harris said.

Belnap, leaning heavily on a cane, shrugged. "You don't get anywhere following the rules."

"I assume you're not here to cut off my dick."

"No," Belnap said, "that makes you twice-blessed."

"Twice?"

"You're alive and you're intact."

Less than a week after the San Juan Heights were taken, Harris had come down with a fever, headache, chills, nausea, and vomiting. He felt better after a few days, but then the fever returned with a vengeance. The whites of his eyes turned yellow, he began vomiting blood, he became delirious. He was moved into the fever tent at Sevilla; no one with an active fever was allowed transport back to the United States.

"How long have you been here?" Harris asked. He hoisted himself on his elbows and then struggled into a sitting position. It took all his energy.

"At Montauk? Since early August. I was in the first group."

"You should sit down," Harris said. "Get your weight off that leg." There weren't any straight chairs in the tent, which held six cots; only three others were occupied at present. Harris moved his legs aside and Belnap sat at the end. The cot sagged. "How are you coming along?"

"Slowly. I'm getting some strength back."

"Much pain?"

"A bit."

Harris smiled. "I've heard that before."

Belnap looked at him quizzically. "Am I missing something?"

"No, no," Harris said, averting his eyes. "It's a family joke. Although joke isn't exactly the right word."

"I'm not getting many shocks down my leg anymore, although my instep is numb for some reason." He stuck out his slippered foot and poked the instep with the end of his cane. "What hurts the most is stretching out the muscles in my ass."

"Well, that's understandable. It'll take time."

"Those are some damned ugly stitches back there."

"I apologize," Harris said.

"Forget it," Belnap said, smiling, and Harris thought, A man shouldn't be this beautiful. The hair, the eyes, the straight nose, the prominent cheekbones, the perfect teeth, the strong chin.

"How did you get injured?"

"That fucking Roosevelt," Belnap said with a laugh. "We'd fought our way to the top of Kettle Hill, and the Spanish were pulling back. Then Roosevelt looks over and sees that the infantry is still struggling up San Juan Hill to our left, and he decides we should join in. But in the hubbub only a few of us hear him issue the order. Off we go, following him down the far side of Kettle Hill and across a swampy area to the foot of San Juan. That's when he realizes that he's only got a handful of us with him. He yells bloody hell and we turn around to go back and collect everyone else, and that's when I feel this thump and I go flying, I don't know, five or ten yards. And that finished it for me."

"And now it's all over," Harris said. Santiago had surrendered on July 17; hostilities ceased on August 12.

"So they say."

They both fell silent. Proportionally, the Rough Riders had suffered more casualties than any other unit, along with the Buffalo Soldiers in the 9th and 10th cavalries. Still, Harris knew, many more soldiers had fallen ill than had been killed or wounded.

"I should be going," Belnap said, standing up with some effort. "But I thought I should thank you in person."

Harris nodded. "Did you have any trouble tracking me down?"

"Not much. Everybody in the regiment knows who you are."

Harris was taken aback. "I doubt that."

"They know you did everything you could up at the Bloody Ford, and they know about that water tank that you left by the side of the trail."

"The water tank?"

Belnap laughed. "Everybody who made his way back down the road past El Pozo was beyond parched, and then they stumble upon this water wagon. So naturally some asked who was born with enough common sense to put it there. They knew it couldn't be one of the higher-ups. Billy Dutton said it was your doing."

"It was more Billy's than mine. Have you seen him since Cuba?"

"No. Most of the boys landed back here on the fourteenth, but I haven't seen him." Belnap turned to go but then said, "Everybody did have one question about that water tank."

"What about it?"

"They wanted to know how you managed to collect that much piss."

They laughed together. They laughed so hard and so long that tears came to their eyes and one of the men in the other cots told them to shut the hell up, he was trying to sleep.

Belnap limped away, his cane tapping on the plank floor, one hand waving a backward goodbye.

3. The Great Frontier

AARON BELNAP KEPT coming back—nearly every day until Harris was released from the tent hospital and permitted to rejoin the regiment. Robb Church had also stopped by, bearing on his first visit the dreadful news that Billy Dutton had died of typhoid on the ship back from Cuba.

Harris and Aaron took long walks together, around the camp, into Montauk, along the beaches at the tip of Long Island. Belnap needed to exercise his leg; Harris needed to build up his strength.

"You know, Harry," Belnap said one day as they were sitting on a windswept dune and looking out at the foaming Atlantic and a changeable sky of pewter and ash, "I think you should take a trip out west."

"Aaron, nobody calls me Harry. Nobody has *ever* called me Harry."

"Well then, *Harry,* don't you think it's about time? Get your head out of your coal hole. Come west. I'll take you around. You can see blue skies and wide horizons and pretty señoritas. And this is the best time of year—the days aren't hot, it rarely rains, and the nights are cool enough for working up a sweat, if you know what I mean. It may be now or never, before you settle back into the humdrum."

"My life isn't humdrum," Harris said.

"Right," Belnap scoffed. "Come or don't, your choice."

The most annoying thing about Aaron Belnap was his way of presenting these all-or-nothing ultimatums. And he didn't seem to care which option you chose. You had to vest everything in him; he, nothing in you.

They used their mustering out pay, $77, to travel in style to Charleston, where Aaron thoroughly charmed Mrs. Whitaker, Harris's sister Marybeth, and her two girls, especially Mary Anne, whose painful adoration oozed from her pubescence like a pungent fragrance. Harris had seen him do it before, to several of the nurses at Montauk. Meanwhile, Marybeth and Cordelia devoted every opportunity to berating Harris about finding a suitable wife and producing a male heir to carry on the family name.

A stroke in late June had relegated Harris's father to a wheelchair. He had round-the-clock attendants to meet his needs, which continued to include opiates, now administered several times a day. It was evident to Harris that Douglas Whitaker's body was preparing to give up the fight.

The day before leaving for the West, Harris had what proved to be his final conversation with his father. They were seated outside the study, in white wicker chairs, sipping a mixture of sour mash and lemonade.

After a long pause in their conversation, his father said, "I wouldn't like to see you get lost out there, Harris." Despite crossing the Atlantic numerous times, Douglas Whitaker had never ventured west of the Mississippi.

"Oh," said Harris, stroking his new mustache with thumb and forefinger, "getting lost isn't likely. Aaron says that these days you can't travel very far in a straight line without hitting barbed wire or railroad tracks."

"You know very well what I mean. Go have your tour of the great frontier—there's no harm in it. But keep your distance."

"From Aaron?"

His father took a sip of his drink; Harris left his on the table, where a ring of condensation was collecting around the glass; too strong for him, and it was barely noon.

"You dislike him that much?" Harris asked.

"He's charming. Glib. A sun around which others bask. I've seen him before," Whitaker said. "In the war I met dozens like him. Young men, every one of them handsome, athletic. Not one was a coward. Quite the opposite, in fact. They were all brave beyond discretion. Careless. The battlefield excited them—the thunder, the confusion, the smoke and danger. They seemed to thrive." He paused and looked out across the green lawn. "Many more died than survived."

After a while Whitaker continued, "You're the better man, Harris. By far the better man. Certainly, go ahead and bask for a while, and in the process study him—his ease, his cleverness, his ability to make people think he likes them even when he couldn't give a tinker's damn. These are useful skills, even for the resolutely serious-minded."

"Like me."

"Yes, like you." He paused again, and for a moment Harris thought his father had fallen asleep. But he hadn't. "Don't take that as a criticism. It isn't. Just don't become infatuated by what you're not."

Harris picked up his glass and sipped. "I was thinking about Christian yesterday."

"How so?"

"Did you know that Mormons baptize the dead?"

"No, I didn't."

"Aaron told me."

"He's a Mormon?"

"No." Harris laughed. "But a lot of Mormons live around Gallup."

"Do you often think about Christian?'

"He comes back to me now and then."

"He was such a little thing. So long ago." Since the stroke, his father's jaw was constantly moving, as if he were chewing, and now he said, "I'm so very glad I didn't know you were deathly ill until you were on the mend." Tears collected along the rims of his lower lids—not something that would have happened even six months earlier. Harris had seen this before, during his medical training. A stroke often left a patient more labile, the boundaries of his emotional and social inhibitions breached.

They sat in silence while Harris let his father regain his composure. Then his father cleared his throat and said, "I want you to promise me something. Go out west. See the great frontier. Have a harmless adventure or two. But I want you to come back here in three months, no longer, so that I can see for myself that you're . . . Will you grant me that?"

"TELL ME SOMETHING," Harris said. He and Aaron were still seated in the restaurant. Arturo Mérida had cleared the precarious stack of dishes, and there was nothing left on the table but coffee cups and elbows. "If someone—*your* father, say—was willing to back you, what would you choose to do?"

"My father." Aaron laughed. "There's a greater chance that we'll see the sun set in the east today."

"Hypothetically."

Aaron narrowed his gaze. "I can't be bought, Harry." But then he backed off: "And this conversation has gotten way too serious. Wasn't the idea that we'd come out here together and I'd show you a good time, you old woman?"

"Death tends to sober one up."

"That's about the last thing you need, but have it your way." He rose and reached into a pocket for his wallet, from which he pulled several bills, leaving them on the table. "Extend my *heartfelt* sympathy to your family."

"That would be impossible."

"Oh, Harry!" Aaron chuckled, and Harris felt his measure being taken. "How about you tell *me* something: If that telegram had never reached you, what would your family do?"

"Try again."

"Let's say—hypothetically—that you were out in the wilderness, beyond reach."

"They'd proceed without me."

"Then it seems to me that the question for you is, how much do you want to grieve with your loving family, and how much do you want a tour guide?"

"Oh, if life were only so simple."

Aaron straightened up, pulled his tunic down. "It doesn't seem so complicated to me. Up or down, in or out."

"East or west."

"Exactly!" Aaron grinned his beautiful grin. "What do you say, Harry?"

* * *

SAMUEL VAN SCHULTZ -------- CHARLESTON S.C.=
1898 OCT 2 AM 9 46

RELAPSE PRECLUDES MY RETURN= PROCEED WITHOUT ME=
REGRETS TO ALL=

HARRIS=

CHAPTER SEVEN: Tóya (The Past)

1. Medicine

You have to understand," she began, "we thought the Holy People
had abandoned us."

'Asdzáán Bítóyiszééyiztał, the Woman Who Kicks Up Still
Water, and Harry Whitaker sat across from each other in the surgery, and
despite the approach of sunset neither moved to light a lantern. The room
held barely enough space for the long metal table, a row of rough-hewn
shelves mounted on the wall above the sink and water pump, and three
straight-backed wooden chairs, in one of which Harry Whitaker now sat,
near the open connecting door to his examining room. Tóya occupied another, beside the only window with its wan square of light. Her bandaged
foot rested on the seat of the third chair.

Harry Whitaker had never before asked her about the Long Walk,
and she didn't know why he was asking now. Of course he knew she'd survived the 1864 march to Bosque Redondo—the place the Navajo called
Hwéeldi—and the appalling conditions there, and had walked back home in
1868, one of some 8,000 Navajos in a line that had stretched for ten miles.
This was common knowledge. But she'd told her particular story to very few
Navajos and never to a bilagáana, and even now, though she'd known Harry
Whitaker for four years—had assisted him in his clinic, initially translating
and teaching him Navajo as well as providing herbal remedies and advice
about traditional healing practices—she hesitated. She could count on the
fingers of one hand the whites whom she trusted (with at least one finger left
over for picking her nose, she took pleasure in observing). She did, however, trust Harry Whitaker. He'd come to the Southwest without a serious
intent, but he'd stayed to take care of the Diné with dedication and patience,
and without dismissing their beliefs, and not even their superstitions. Most

of the hataałiis in the Tohatchi area reluctantly acknowledged his usefulness when it came to such things as setting broken bones and delivering babies who were turned the wrong way, and he'd managed to convince many that they shouldn't stand in the way of his inoculating children against smallpox. Even when he relieved patients' symptoms, he never advised them that they didn't need a healing ceremony; in fact, she'd heard him tell many Navajos that the cure wouldn't be complete without a sing.

She didn't need a sing for her present ailment. Harry Whitaker had cut away most of an infected in-grown toenail, and the detritus lay on the table in a metal tray along with a forceps and several squares of blood-stained gauze. When she got home she would replace his bandage with a moistened poultice of herbs and grasses.

Tóya had scoffed when word first spread that a white doctor had been hired to open a government clinic in Tohatchi. Her first experiences with Anglo medicine had been at Bosque Redondo, where a doctor from Fort Sumner would sometimes agree to see sick Navajos. He rarely did any good and sometimes his advice was laughable. Keep warm in the winter, eat better food, try not to inhale the poisonous alkali dust. Her strongest recollection was of the instruments: the stethoscope (although she didn't know its name until she asked Harry Whitaker), the surgical saws and forceps and scalpels. Her only other exposure to Anglo medicine involved the patent nostrums sold to Navajos at the Tohatchi Trading Post—a trading post that, over the past thirty years, no one had managed to make profitable and which had therefore seen a succession of closures and new owners. It was boarded up again now, and the People traveled south to Mexican Springs or east to Coyote Canyon when they needed trade goods. Patent medicines were still popular—worthless, but popular because they were mostly alcohol.

What had initially impressed Tóya about Harry Whitaker was his stillness, a characteristic she didn't associate with bilagáanas. The first time she saw him he was sitting outside his empty clinic in a chair identical to the three in his surgery. His hair was short and reddish-blond in the sun. A thin mustache hugged the bow of his upper lip; a small tuft of equally fair hair under his lower lip dipped toward the shallow cleft in his chin. He sat there, his neck and back straight, his hands splayed on his knees, wearing tan trousers and dark suspenders and a white shirt with a buttoned collar. He seemed to be staring into the eastward distance, waiting for something—a patient, a shift in the breeze, an end to the day. He didn't acknowledge her presence, twenty yards away, though she stood there for several minutes before turning and leaving.

At first, very few Navajos came to the clinic. Most who did were Christians, the ones who'd completely forsaken the Navajo way under the influence of Presbyterian or Methodist or Dutch Reformed missionaries. (They were all the same to Tóya, whatever they called themselves.) A few others came because they needed to be stitched up or thought he would give them alcohol for a sham ailment. Tóya had her spy, an affable woman who had picked up a smattering of English while working as a servant at one of the missions near Gallup. Unfortunately, Betty Roanhorse's special skill was gossiping about the missionaries, and that ended up getting her fired. So now she cleaned and cooked for Harry Whitaker, which left her plenty of time to keep her friend Tóya well informed about the comings and goings at the clinic.

Harry Whitaker had arrived with a nurse, a nervous stick of a woman named Loretta Pettifrew who knew no Navajo and lasted less than a month. She couldn't take the isolation and fled back to wherever she came from. According to Betty Roanhorse, the doctor hadn't even tried to find a replacement.

Tóya finally met Harry Whitaker late in the afternoon in December 1898. She'd been away since the previous day, diagnosing a woman with failing eyesight and bad headaches. The sky hung low, threatening snow, as she trudged home—she lived off by herself, about half a mile from To-hatchi—and a vicious wind brought tears to her eyes. She could tolerate snow, which fed the springs and streams when it eventually thawed, but she saw no natural purpose in such winds beyond sheer bedevilment.

She found Harry Whitaker sitting beside her summer hogan, which, made of roughly configured saplings and tree branches, provided little shelter. Someone, probably that foolish Betty Roanhorse, must have given him directions.

She felt too tired to deal with some ignorant bilagáana, so she walked past him without acknowledgement, even though he'd scrambled to his feet and removed his hat when he saw her approaching. She went into her winter hogan and lit a lantern and started a fire in her small stove. Then she lay down on her tick mattress and wrapped a wool blanket around herself, waiting for the heat to rise. Bundled herbs and grasses hung from the ceiling beams, and their aromas mixed pleasantly with an underlying, pervading scent of pinyon from the many hundreds of fires that had burned in her stove.

The stove did its job and the temperature rose quickly, filling the small, octagonal room, but she didn't drift off as she'd expected. Too much damn curiosity, she supposed. She rose and went to the door of the hogan. Harry Whitaker was still standing in the same spot, though he'd put his hat back on and drawn the brim as low as possible. His face looked raw from the wind; his bare hands were folded under his arms. She sighed and then waved for him to approach.

Standing at her door, he obeyed the formalities, telling her in proper Navajo (which surprised her) his full name and that his parents' families, the Connors and the Whitakers, were from Charleston, South Carolina. Tóya replied in kind, naming her parents' clans, and then waited for him to explain his bothersome presence.

"I've been told that you speak English," he said.

She looked him over, top to bottom, before answering, "I do and I don't."

"Well, Ah've just about used up my knowledge of the Navajo language, except for naming various anatomical parts and the days of the week." He said it in a twangy voice, which she'd later come to recognize as an exaggerated Southern accent that he used in situations that, he felt, merited a little self-deprecation. He continued in his regular voice: "But I'll come back tomorrow with Eban Billie, if you'd prefer."

She knew Eban Billie, Harry Whitaker's translator. She regarded Billie as a worthless human being, one of those Gallup Indians who wound up in a flop house whenever he went on a bender. She figured he must have dried himself out again. How he'd come to work for Harry Whitaker was none of her concern, but she didn't want him anywhere near her hogan.

The wind was chilling her again. "Eeyah," she muttered, and waved Harry Whitaker inside. He removed his hat and ducked through the low doorway. "Don't take off your coat, you're not staying," she said in gruff Navajo. He stood there, comprehending the intent if not the words. "Tell me what you want," she said in English.

He had an Anglo patient, he told her, a pregnant woman, the wife of a missionary, who was about four months along and suffering the worst case of morning sickness he'd ever seen—she couldn't keep anything in her stomach. He'd tried various powders and tonics and had restricted her diet, but nothing had helped.

"Send her to the Gallup doctor."

"She already saw him," Harry Whitaker said, "before she came to me."

"Then send her to Albuquerque or Santa Fe."

"That might be best, but I don't think she can travel that far. She's going to lose her baby."

"These things happen," Tóya said.

"They do indeed." He paused and unbuttoned his coat. The hogan was getting hot now.

She waited to see what he would say next.

"I believe Betty Roanhorse is a friend of yours?"

"Huh."

"We've had a few friendly chats, despite the inadequacy of mah language skills"—again, the deep Southern inflection—"and she suggested, through Eban, that you might be able to help."

Tóya would have her own chat with Betty Roanhorse. "How?"

"She said that you're a hand-trembler—"

Tóya cut him off: "That's a Navajo way. It's not for Anglos."

"Yes, I understand, but she also said your grandmother and your mother and now you had learned everything there was to know about traditional medicines."

"Huh."

He perused the bundles hanging from the ceiling. "Do you know of anything that might help?"

She kept her eyes on him. She never administered any medicine without offering the proper prayer chants, which would mean nothing to this Anglo woman. "I don't like missionaries."

Harry Whitaker's pale eyes returned to her. "That may be, but . . ." He raised his hands from his sides, palms up; his fingers were long, his hands soft.

"How do you know I won't poison her?"

He didn't flinch. "Why would you do that?"

"All the missionaries should go back where they came from and leave the People alone." She took off her shawl and folded it neatly before putting it on a cluttered shelf by the entrance. "If I gave you something and then she lost the baby anyway, or even died herself, her husband would send for the sheriff."

"No one knows I've come to see you, except Betty. If anything untoward were to happen, it would be my responsibility."

"Don't be stupid," she said in Navajo, and this too he seemed to understand—the scathing tone anyway.

He had no answer for that except a frown and a wrinkled brow.

She resumed in English, "The sickness should have stopped by now. If she's as far along as you say and as bad as you say, I have nothing for you."

"Then I'll be on my way." He rebuttoned his coat as his eyes again took in the array of medicinal bundles dangling less than a foot from the top of his head. "If you don't mind my asking, where did you learn to speak English so well?"

"Hwéeldi."

Harry Whitaker nodded. "Maybe someday"—he waved a finger at the bundles—"you could teach me about some of these medicines, if you wouldn't mind."

Tóya pursed her lips but said nothing, and he left.

The next morning, when Harry Whitaker opened the door to his small house and crossed the yard to his clinic, Betty Roanhorse, wearing a wide smile that displayed her remaining five teeth, was waiting for him with a packet of herbs and clear instructions about how to brew a tea and how often it should be administered to the missionary's wife.

Several weeks later, Harry Whitaker was again waiting for Tóya when she returned to her hogan. Folded over his arm was a large wool blanket in a deep Germantown red.

"Yá'át'ééh," Harry Whitaker said, holding out the blanket to her. "I hope you'll accept this as a token of my great thanks for your help. The clerk in Gallup said it was one of the latest styles."

"I don't want your blanket," Tóya said in Navajo.

"Ah," he said, but he didn't seem surprised. It was late in the day shortly after the start of the new year, and most of the light had already left the sky. "Are you sure you won't reconsider?"

She didn't answer and he pulled his arm back and began to roll up the blanket. "Well then, you won't mind if I give it to Betty Roanhorse?"

Tóya's jaw stiffened.

"I understand you and she aren't speaking these days and I feel it may be my fault."

Tóya replied in English: "You shouldn't listen to what every silly old woman says."

"Y'all do mean *Betty*, don't you?" he said. He blinked several times, as if something had just flown into an eye.

Tóya snorted and pulled her shawl tight across her shoulders. "So how is the missionary's wife?"

"Doing well as far as I know. She and her husband decided to go back East, at least until after the baby's born. But I suppose you already know that."

Tóya gave no indication one way or the other.

"She didn't feel safe out here in the wilderness. She wanted to be in a city where she can get the best medical care if she or the baby needs it."

Tóya pursed her lips so tightly her mouth almost disappeared.

"But to tell you the truth"—his voice momentarily dropping into that sweet Southern exaggeration—"Ah get the feeling they won't be back. They've seen more than enough of the West." He tucked the rolled blanket under his arm. "So Ah guess we both got what we wanted—for me, a healthy mother and child, and for you, one less missionary."

"I count that as a good day," Tóya said in Navajo, and Harry Whitaker laughed. So, she thought, he's understanding more Navajo these days. She liked his laugh—he held nothing back. How old was he? Maybe thirty?

"Will you tell me what was in the tea?"

She narrowed her eyes.

"Ah promise not to put you out of business."

"I have a question for *you*, Dr. Harry Whitaker. How did it make you feel, to have to come to an old Navajo woman to save a bilagáana baby?"

His mouth turned up at one corner. "Moderately humble."

"Tchh," she clicked.

"But don't assume there aren't a few things I could teach you as well."

She walked toward her hogan, announcing over her shoulder, "Don't bother me again until you need me to save another patient."

"*Unless* I need you?" he called after her.

"Until," she repeated.

She heard him laugh again.

A week later a Navajo sheepherder found Eban Billie frozen to death in a ditch half way between Tohatchi and the coal mining camp at Gibson. Billie had spent the previous night carousing and, in a drunken stupor, had apparently fallen off his horse, which was found grazing beside the body.

Not long after, Harry Whitaker came to see her again, and this third time she took pity on him. Besides, she was curious. She'd heard about Eban Billie, and she also knew that the doctor had spoken with a hataałii—the only one who'd agreed to sit with him—in a mistaken effort to convince him that he was in Tohatchi to help their patients as best he could without interfering with the healing ceremonies they performed. Hataałiis apprenticed many years to learn these ceremonies, which were so complex in language and ritual that many singers learned only a handful. Tóya knew that singers were not of a mindset to accept the word of a bilagáana who, as they saw it, offered a bottle of little pink pills as a cure for an illness that, if properly diagnosed and fully understood, could be both symptom and cause of a life thrown out of balance—a loss of blessedness that encompasses man, nature, time, the supernatural, the very order of the great universe.

This time Tóya not only let him in but invited him to sit by her stove and drink a cup of Navajo tea with her. They sat on an old Navajo rug—borderless, with a primitive design featuring lightning zigzags—he with his legs crossed in front of him, she with her legs folded beneath her and her buttocks propped on the heels of the cowboy boots she always wore. She was a short woman; this pose elevated her, forced her to sit with her back straight, lending dignity, she thought. Her pleated cotton skirt formed a dark blue circle around her.

"How was your meeting with Hosteen Bisahalani?" Tóya asked.

"So you heard about that?"

"Tchh," Tóya clicked.

"I didn't get very far, but I imagine you already know that, too."

"Why are you here?" she asked.

"To talk to you."

"Not that. Why did you come to Diné Bikéyah?"

He didn't answer at first, instead stretching his neck, as if his buttoned collar were uncomfortably tight, and cocking his head from side to side, his eyes fogged with a thought, perhaps an image, that he couldn't—or wouldn't—express. "I accompanied a friend home to Gallup."

"Where did you meet someone from Gallup?"

"In Cuba."

"Cuba?" She misunderstood; the Cuba she knew of, though she'd never been there, was a Spanish farming settlement beyond Chaco Canyon, near the Jemez Pueblo. "How did you end up there?"

"The war with Spain."

"Ah-hah." She nodded without acknowledging her error. She knew a little about the war. It had been short, and the Americans had won. The Americans were always fighting somebody—the Mexicans; each other; the Navajo, the Apache, or the Sioux; most recently the Spanish. They fought a big battle on an island, although she didn't know where that was.

"He signed up in Gallup for the volunteer cavalry, and I was recruited for the hospital corps. He was wounded, and that's how we met."

"You took care of him."

"I was the first doctor to see him." Harry Whitaker picked a fragment of tea leaf from the tip of his tongue and ground it between thumb and forefinger.

"And when the war was over you came back to Gallup with him."

"Yes, but not as a doctor—as your typical Eastern tourist." He smiled wryly. "Ah wanted to see the Southwest. The Grand Canyon. The Rio Grande—which, Ah must say, isn't so *grande.* It isn't much of a river at all, by Eastern standards. Now, the Mississippi—*that's* a river."

"Why did you stay?"

"A medical colleague asked me to look up an old friend of his, Constant Williams." Tóya knew the name: he'd been the Indian agent at Fort Defiance. "He was heading to a new posting, but he and Francis Neel, the superintendent of the government boarding school, ganged up on me. They asked if I could be convinced to start up the medical station here."

"And what about your Gallup friend?"

There was a pause before Harry Whitaker smiled and said, "You might say he cast me adrift in the high desert."

"He's gone?"

"Yes, he's gone."

"And you're here in Tohatchi."

"Ah'm here." He patted the dirt floor.

"For how long?"

"A year or so."

"Tchh." Her dark brown eyes narrowed and her heavy eyebrows knit into a shallow vee. "You're wasting my time."

"Why is that?"

She spat it out: "Because a year is *nothing*. You know nothing about the People, and a year from now you'll still know nothing. Pack up your bottles of pills and your shiny medical tools and go home." She extended her arm. "Give me back my cup." She snatched the tin cup from his hand; pale tea sloshed onto the wool rug. "Go." She pointed her nose toward the door.

"Maybe two years," he said. "They'll probably hold my position in Washington that long if I can gather useful information while I'm out here."

"Useful . . . ?"

"Information about different diseases on this part of the reservation—where they show up and how often."

This roused her suspicions. Maybe, she thought, as an excuse to relocate the People again, to claim rights to "unhealthy" land that the railroad or white ranchers decided they wanted.

"Not all Anglo doctors spend all of their time treating patients. Some of us try to learn more about how and why people get sick in the first place. I study such diseases as yellow fever and malaria and typhoid—that's why I was recruited to go to Cuba. The army was smart enough to know that Spanish bullets wouldn't be the only deadly things flying around."

She thought about this before responding. "I've seen what you call typhoid."

"I'm sure you have. And diphtheria. Whooping cough. Measles. Smallpox."

"You have Anglo medicine for them now?"

"No, not yet, although I can certainly prevent smallpox with needle inoculations." He unbuttoned his left cuff, rolled up his sleeve, and pointed to the cicatrix on his upper arm. "I'll never get smallpox, no matter how many times I'm exposed to it. I can do the same for every Navajo who will let me. As for the other illnesses, I know things that can help."

Tóya said, "I've seen whole families die together, one after another, from *'adáyi' dááhodiníchaad.*"

"So have I. When diphtheria spreads through a community, it's hard to stop."

Tóya still held his cup of tea in her hand. She was peering into the cup, thinking. Harry Whitaker straightened out his legs and massaged his knees. "Do you read tea leaves?"

She looked up. The question made no sense, but he was smiling.

"People in some cultures think you can tell the future by reading the pattern of tea leaves in the bottom of a cup or by examining the entrails of chickens."

Is that what he thought a hand-trembler did? Was he that stupid after all?

Although the hogan had no windows, the draft from her door told her that the temperature was falling. The sun had set. She decided that she would hold her tongue and hear him out. "Why are you bothering me today?"

He swallowed nervously—his prominent Adam's apple bounced twice—and he rubbed his palms on his thighs. "I want to hire you as my translator. More than that—I want you to teach me Navajo so that I won't need a translator, and I want you to teach me enough about traditional herbal medicines so that I'll know when to ask for your help. I can pay you."

"You want this, you want that," she said with disdain.

"I'm sorry. I didn't say any of that very well." She listened while he told her that he'd tried to make do by using Betty Roanhorse as a translator, which was possible only because he saw so few patients, often just one or two a day. Betty's English was completely inadequate to the task, and although she managed to help him with his basic, everyday Navajo vocabulary, he had great difficulty interpreting Navajos' descriptions of what ailed them, unless they showed up with the obviously infected gash or sore throat. A common complaint was that they felt "some way," which seemed very concrete to them (and to Betty) but left him at a complete loss.

"And there's something else," he said. "If people knew you were helping me—that we were working together, I mean—maybe more of them would come to see me."

"And Betty Roanhorse?"

"I can keep her on, too. Since I've lost my nurse—she wasn't very good, to be honest—I need a woman to be in the room with me when I see female patients."

This was true. No Navajo man would bring his wife or daughter to him otherwise.

"I wouldn't expect you to do that once I no longer need your services as a translator," he continued. "I know you have other things to do, other responsibilities."

"Looking at chicken entrails."

He tried to contain a smile.

"If you want to help the People," she said, "go away, Harry Whitaker. You and all the other whites. Take your railroads and your trading posts and your repeating rifles and leave us alone."

She waited now to see how he would react, if his expression would turn black in the poor light of the one lantern, but he remained still, as she'd seen him that first day sitting outside the clinic, although now he sat in her hogan, on her mother's rug, an old weaving that she'd taken from her father's hogan the day she left Black Lake, the day she knew her family's fear made her no longer welcome.

"When I depart," Harry Whitaker, speaking barely above a whisper, said, "should I also take your Anglo stove and kerosene lantern and your Anglo cowboy boots with me? And even that tin cup you're holding?"

Well, he didn't cower. She admired that.

"What do you know about me, Harry Whitaker?"

"I know you became a hand-trembler soon after returning from Bosque Redondo and that you never married and have no children. I know there are many Navajos who fear you—some even suspect you're a witch—because of your . . . abilities. I also know that many singers respect you, although not all of them like you."

She dismissed his observations with a grunt. Then she poured what was left of his tea into her own cup, which she then, turning around, placed on the stove to warm up. Many hataałiis would disapprove if she helped him; they would probably go elsewhere when they needed a hand-trembler. Other Diné, foolish ones, would accuse her—though not to her face—of selling her knowledge just to get her hands on cash money.

"There's something else worth considering," Harry Whitaker now said to her. "I know there will always be Navajos you know whom I could help but who refuse to see me. But *you* can come to me, we can talk, and maybe I'll be able to provide something, even just advice, that wouldn't offend them or you or the singers."

When she didn't respond, he went on: "I don't claim any understanding of hand-trembling or star-gazing or however else Navajos figure out what ails someone." He paused. "I try to think of myself as a man of science, but I know that science doesn't have all the answers."

They sat in silence for several minutes before Harry Whitaker cleared his throat. "So tell me," he said, nodding toward the bundles hanging overhead, "why do you have so many plants drying? I've heard that singers prefer to use recently picked plants."

"You recognize some of these?"

"Birch and juniper bark. Sagebrush. Creosote. Some kind of mallow. Yarrow. Mint."

"Many can't be found after the hard frost. Others flower for only a short time each year, and some don't grow on this part of the reservation."

He nodded. "What would I have to do for you to teach me about them?"

She sighed and instead of answering his question said, "You've done everything wrong, Harry Whitaker. Everything wrong, except that you came to me."

TÓYA SHIFTED HER bandaged foot from the chair to the floor. Her toe was throbbing. Before removing the nail, Harry Whitaker had injected a medicine into her toe that had numbed it, but that had worn off.

"Best to keep off that foot for a day or two, until the swelling goes down," Harry Whitaker said. "And for God's sake, get rid of those damnable cowboy boots."

"Tchh," she dismissed him. "I've been wearing cowboy boots since before you were born." This was her newest pair, complete with fancy stitching and mother-of-pearl inlays.

"And look what they're doing to your feet! They're made for roping—the box is too narrow for the width of your foot. The tapered toe is designed to get a foot in and out of a stirrup quickly. The high heel's to catch the stirrup, to help keep you in the saddle. When you *walk* in these things, it distributes your weight unevenly and jams your toes together. They're all wrong for walking. That's why I just cut away an infected toenail."

"I like my boots."

"Whoever sold you your first pair did you no favor."

"I didn't buy the first pair. They were a gift."

"Some gift."

"I had no shoes. I had a long walk ahead of me," Tóya said.

2. The Long Walk

"YOU HAVE TO UNDERSTAND," she began, "we thought the Holy People had abandoned us."

How else to explain what was happening? The fall crops burned by the soldiers. Thousands of peach trees cut down in Canyon de Chelly. The reported slaughter of so many families and the rumored mass expulsion from Dinétah. No one, not the headmen nor the hataałiis, could say why the Holy People were abandoning the People. But thousands faced starvation and with it disease and death, even if the soldiers stopped what they were doing and stayed in their forts for the winter.

The Hopi and Apaches and Utes and New Mexicans had long complained about the Navajos, and many with good reason—stolen horses, pilfered flocks of sheep and herds of cattle, general thievery, the murder of isolated ranchers and travelers—but such doings were the work of a handful of the reckless and vengeful, Tóya told Harry. Attacks against Navajos by the other tribes, the capture and enslavement of Navajos by Mexicans and New Mexicans—such incidents were just as common. All were at fault. But the Navajo, the common enemy, received the blame.

"What about the attack on Fort Defiance?" Harry Whitaker asked.

Tóya laughed derisively. "You mean when those 150 brave soldiers held off 2,000 fierce Navajo warriors?"

Fort Defiance was nothing like a fort. It never had been. The site in the Black Creek Valley had long been used as a gathering place by the Navajo, who appreciated the nearby springs and a naturally sheltered meadow for grazing. The army, having selected the area for a military outpost in 1851, laid out the adobe and log buildings in a horseshoe open to the south. No effort was made to enclose it or even to establish a defensive perimeter. To the east, a sandstone wall rose forty feet to a shelf that overlooked the flat roofs and the central parade ground. To the northwest, a hillside gradually climbed several hundred feet before leveling out into a small mesa that permitted a growth of pinyon and spruce and scrub; half a mile back, it dropped precipitously into Canyon Bonito.

Against a determined enemy, Fort Defiance was indefensible. Even a modest number of Indians could control the high ground, with the only escape route being across the valley floor, which provided more than adequate cover for Navajos intent on slaughtering anyone leaving the fort.

"The great battle," Tóya said, "when 2,000 Navajos managed to kill one soldier before being driven off." She laughed again. "No one has ever *seen* 2,000 Navajo warriors in one place at one time. The army lied. It needed an excuse to wipe us out."

In 1864 perhaps there were 15,000 Navajo men, women, and children—no one knew the true count—all scattered over 20,000 square miles of territory. There were no Navajo villages, just small outfits of extended family members, and no single chief, only dozens of local headmen. "Two thousand Navajo," Tóya said again with scorn. "Let me tell you, if 2,000 Navajo *grandmothers* had attacked Fort Defiance, coyotes would have been feasting on bilagáana bones. It would've been Custer before Custer."

"Maybe," Harry Whitaker said.

"Maybe," Tóya scoffed. "You Anglos always think you're smarter than you are. You don't know the sacred mountains, the canyons, the high desert, or the seasons, but you think you have power over our world." She jerked her head toward the sink. "I'm thirsty. Get me a glass of water. My foot is throbbing."

Harry Whitaker rose and walked to the sink, where he pumped a stream of cold water into a glass and then handed it to her. She drank it down.

In early February 1864 her father, who suffered from consumption, made the decision that they would go to Fort Defiance (for a time renamed Fort Canby by the soldiers), where the People had been ordered to gather. Not even the bilagáanas would let women and children starve if they surrendered, her father said, and then when the spring came, they could all easily escape because they knew this country better than the soldiers, who would have no incentive to risk their lives chasing down stray Navajos. Her sister's husband refused to go. Tóya was fourteen, her sister, seventeen, but her sister and her husband had not been getting along. He was a handsome man, with beautiful teeth and his own stallion and fancy saddle and maybe he now thought he should have waited for a better woman. So he went north, where others planned to hide out near Beautiful Mountain. (They never saw him again; they never even learned if he lived or if he died.) Her sister was angry, but even at seventeen she was a scold, and Tóya scarcely blamed her husband for deserting.

More than a thousand Navajo had preceded them to the fort, but still there were no proper shelters, and when groups of Navajos, seeking relief from the wind, tried to move closer to the stone walls of the barracks or other buildings, they were forced away at gunpoint. There were a few tents but no hogans, nothing permanent, and many people slept with the sheep and horses and goats they'd brought with them. The soldiers handed out rations of uncooked foods that most Navajos had never seen before, including wheat flour and coffee that no one knew how to prepare. The women tried mixing the flour with water and boiling it, and they tried chewing the raw coffee beans, and soon nearly the entire encampment suffered cramps and the shits, and many died even before the Long Walk began.

Some of the soldiers tried to be helpful, to show the women how to bake wheat bread, but none of the Navajos spoke English and none of the soldiers spoke Navajo. The People couldn't even confirm where they would be going when they left the fort, except that it was several hundred miles to the east, far beyond the boundaries of the sacred mountains.

Some of the People had heard that there was a great war in the East, a war so vast that sometimes more than 10,000 men were killed or wounded in a single day of battle, and they couldn't fathom such a number or how there could be any bilagáanas left alive, and they feared that they would be marched into that war with no weapons and no understanding of where or why they were fighting.

And then the call came from the army officers that everyone should gather their possessions and be ready to leave the next day despite the cold and the ice, and that most of the wagons would be used for supplies, not to transport Indians. Some of the elderly and the youngest children and their mothers would be allowed to ride as space permitted, but any others who couldn't walk on their own were the responsibility of those who could. Those with sheep or goats or horses needed to provide for their own animals.

The first day they marched ten miles south, from Tséhootsooí, the Meadow in between the Rocks; past the two-pronged volcanic monolith Tsézhini, Black Rock; down the eastern side of Tsétł'áán Ndíshchí'í, Black Creek Valley, and beyond the Window Rock—Ni' 'Alníí'gi, Earth's Center— to the gathering place by the Spring under the Rock, Tséyaató, in the shadow of the sandstone haystacks called Tséta'cheéch'ih, Wind Going through the Rocks; and on the following day they began the trek eastward, beyond their familiar world.

There were stories of atrocities. Of pregnant women being taken behind boulders and shot, of the elderly falling by the wayside and being beaten to death with rifle butts when they couldn't rise, but Tóya never saw any of that. Not that she doubted the stories, because the Long Walk was not one walk but over fifty forced marches spread out over thirty months, some starting from the Meadow in between the Rocks, some from Old Fort Wingate, beyond Zuni and El Morro, some from other places where destitute and dispossessed Navajos came in from the mesas and canyons and valleys. Some Long Walks comprised many hundreds of the People, and on several occasions more than a thousand, while others brought only a few dozen or so to Hwéeldi. The lines of march took multiple routes—east to Albuquerque or Los Piños; north through Tijeras Canyon and on toward Santa Fe along the Camino Real wagon road, or toward Galisteo or San Antonito; east again to Fort Union and on to the southeast, through Glorieta and Hatch's Ranch and Gallinas Springs and Anton Chico to the Pecos River and, finally, Fort Sumner and the Bosque Redondo—as much as 350 miles, traversed through every kind of terrain and weather, often with short rations. On Tóya's Long Walk alone, nearly a hundred of the seven hundred who began the journey perished along the way, often during the night encampments, from a combination of illness and hunger and the freezing cold. Sometimes the soldiers tried to help the Navajos bury the dead in shallow graves; sometimes the bodies were left to the elements and marauding animals. At one point, high in the mountains—to this day Tóya couldn't say where because once the People had passed Albuquerque, not a single person among them had ever ventured so far—they lost all hope, staggering through the dark toward Nowhere. For two days their only water was melted snow, and after that even the half-rations for the soldiers were cut further. They butchered horses that fell. Her father began coughing up blood, and

Tóya and her sister took turns supporting him until a woman with a baby made way for him on a flatbed wagon. Twenty-three days, four mountain ranges. Tóya herself lost so much weight that her small breasts nearly disappeared except for their dark brown paps, and it would be summer before her monthly flow began again.

They weren't the first to arrive. Some 500 Mescalero Apaches had already been rounded up, and nearly 2,000 Navajos had also survived their Long Walks. Many more would come in the following two years, as many as 8,500 in all. Eventually, even the most influential headmen, Ganado Mucho, Barboncito, and Manuelito, would bring in their bands.

The earlier arrivers had tried to build shelters, but timber for hogans was lacking, so they had hollowed out hillsides and dug pits that they covered with branches and hides. The land was flat and the water in the Pecos River was bad—bitter, alkaline, like the soil in which, they would discover come spring, it was nearly impossible to grow anything. Bosque Redondo, Hwéeldi, was four hundred square miles of pitiless earth, with nothing beyond worth running to.

The world no longer made sense. That was when Tóya understood that they had surely been abandoned by the Holy People.

"Maybe not," Harry Whitaker said. "Your Holy People had never seen Washington or New York—the cities, the wealth, the tens of millions of whites in the East. They had no way to defend you. Your gods and Holy People are tied to the land—to Dinétah. They're your own, nobody else's. Most Christians believe our God is all-seeing, all-knowing, all-powerful, perfect. He rules the universe, not just a little bit of land on one continent."

"You don't believe this?"

"I don't know what I believe, except that when we slaughter each other, God looks down and weeps. Or maybe he laughs."

Harry Whitaker rose from his chair and began straightening up the surgery: wrapping the mangled nail in the bloody gauze and throwing both in a trash can, putting his instruments and the tray in a sink. Then he stopped and turned to look at Tóya. Her eyes were on the waste basket. "I'll burn it," he said. "There'll be nothing for any witch to find."

"Huh." Tóya nodded. If it were anyone but Harry Whitaker, she would have taken the detritus with her and disposed of it herself.

He resumed straightening up the surgery, which, as far as Tóya could see, was already very clean.

"Do you want something for pain? A touch of laudanum?"

She shook her head. She'd seen laudanum work; laudanum sent your spirit wandering and sometimes it didn't return.

It had happened to her sister.

They'd been at Bosque Redondo for nearly two years when her sister became pregnant. She wouldn't name the man responsible, and their father wouldn't speak to her. He was bitter, dried up, his skin like leather, his face pinched, his mouth a thin slash under his hooked nose. Her sister took her own anger out on Tóya, lashing her, cursing her, even when Tóya stole extra food for her. But the baby dried up anyway and came sliding out of her sister, a withered, wrinkled mouse in a pool of fluid. After that, Tóya's sister wouldn't move from her corner of their hovel, which they'd constructed along the inward curve of a hillock using mud bricks, discarded paperboard, blankets, and hides. Very few children were being born, not enough to keep up with the number of deaths. Men had lost their vitality; what dribbled from their *'acho'* was like spit. When women did get pregnant, many miscarried, like her sister, or gave birth to dead babies. The hataałiis, so far from Dinétah, could do little even though some of them continued to hold healing ceremonies.

After a week Tóya, fearing her sister wouldn't recover, walked to Fort Sumner and stood outside the infirmary. She'd picked up some English words but not enough for her to understand what the soldiers who sat outside the infirmary or passed by said to her. But she understood their laughter and their smirks.

Nevertheless, she returned the next day and again stood outside. Finally one of the soldiers motioned her over, pointing to her and curling his finger. He was thin, barely taller than she, and much older. His mustache, drooping over his upper lip, bore no gray hairs, but with his hat pushed back on his head, she could see that he had only wisps of hair above his forehead. His lean brown face was heavily wrinkled, but, out here, exposed to the sun and weather year after year, a man's skin told you little about his age. Tóya didn't like his face—his shallow chin, gray eyes, snub nose.

She told him as simply as she could that her sister had lost a baby and needed to see a doctor.

"And what do I get?" he asked.

She knew what he meant but answered, "No money."

The thin soldier's two companions laughed. One spit in her direction and then wiped a thread of tobacco juice off his chin with a stained thumb. "The doctor won't go over there," the thin soldier said. "If he's seen going over there, you people will never leave him alone. You have to bring her here, to the fort." He spoke slowly, augmenting his words with extravagant gesticulations, waving his arms, nodding and shaking his head. "But not to the infirmary. To the supply depot." He pointed. "You know what that is?"

She nodded. "Aoo'."

"Bring her this evening, just after the sun goes down." He pointed to the sun and let his hand, fluttering, drop to the horizon. "Do you understand?"

"Aoo'." And she went away.

It took Tóya all day to convince her sister to see the Anglo doctor.

When they entered the supply depot that evening, five men were sitting around a foldable table playing cards. Four of them—including the three who'd been sitting outside the infirmary that morning—started laughing and the fifth, whose back had been to the door, turned around and looked at the two Indians. The light cast by the overhead lantern filtered through tobacco smoke from cigars and a pipe.

"Your patient's here," the thin soldier said and, still laughing, ducked when the doctor cursed and threw his cards at him.

"You whoreson," the doctor said. He'd apparently been told about Tóya's afternoon visit but not that she was bringing her sister here tonight.

"She's here, so you might as well take a look," the thin soldier told him.

"Who gets first shot at the quim?" one of the others asked.

"Which is the patient and which is the quim?" said the fourth soldier, whom Tóya hadn't seen before.

"The patient is the paler one."

Laughter.

"On the left," the thin soldier said.

"The quim's the little one?"

"That's her."

"Jesus, how old is she? Ten? I've got more meat in the palm of my hand than she has between her hips." More laughter. "*Sprechen sie* English?"

"She speaks enough."

"But not too much, I hope."

Tóya felt her sister grab her hand and hold tight; her eyes were panic-stricken.

"Spanish? Know any Spanish? *Estáuna puta buena?*"

"Jesus, you know about as much Spanish as I know Greek."

Laughter.

"Clean the older one up and she wouldn't be more than half ugly. I bet she could get my little soldier to stand up and salute."

Tóya's sister dropped to the floor like a plumb.

"Oh Christ," the doctor said, pushing back his chair. "Help me get her into the back, for God's sake."

Tóya stood there, still holding her sister's flaccid hand. The thin soldier came up to her and separated their fingers. Her sister's arm fell to her side. "It's all right," he said, still holding Tóya's hand. "She'll be all right. He'll take a look at her." Two of the men lifted her sister with surprising care. The thin soldier seemed to be studying Tóya's fingers, rubbing his thumb down the length of each. She could see his scalp through his thinning brown hair. "We're really not that bad. Don't pay us no mind. It's just our way. It helps pass the time in this godforsaken hole."

Tóya pulled her hand away and followed the men carrying her unconscious sister toward the rear of the storeroom, which was filled with barrels, crates, and shelves of hard goods. In the far corner a row of wooden crates had been stacked like a wall, floor to ceiling, and a grommeted tarp hung from a ceiling beam, partitioning off an area that, Tóya saw when the doctor drew the tarp aside, contained a bare cot, a straight chair, and a lantern perched on a barrel. Her sister was beginning to stir, and the two soldiers laid her on the cot.

"Now get the hell out," the doctor said to the other men, "while I examine my patient."

"I'd like a look myself," one said, and the other laughed.

"Get the hell out." The doctor looked at Tóya and then nodded toward her sister. "Does she speak English?"

Tóya shook her head. The thin soldier had followed her, and the doctor now asked him, "How's your Navajo these days?"

"Poor as ever."

The other two men had left.

"And how much English does this one know?" the doctor asked, looking at Tóya.

"As I said before, I think she understands enough—probably more than she lets on. Enough to get the gist of our card table conversation, anyway."

"She'd have to be deaf, dumb, and blind not to get that. Now move to the head of the cot," the doctor said to the thin soldier. "Allow my patient a bit of modesty." He put his cigar down on the edge of the barrel, beside the lantern. He pushed her sister's skirt up to her hips and then lifted the front high. "Hold it up," he told Tóya, who took the hem of the skirt in both hands. The doctor spread her sister's legs. When he inserted two fingers, Tóya turned her head away. Her sister moaned. He withdrew his fingers, wiped them on his handkerchief, and felt her abdomen.

The doctor asked simple questions, gesticulating as needed—How long since she'd miscarried? How far along was she? Was there bleeding? Did she complain of pain? Where?

"Everything down there feels normal, as far as I can tell," the doctor said, "and she doesn't have a fever. She needs to drink more"—he gestured as if he were throwing back shots of whiskey—"and she needs to get some decent food into her stomach," motioning with a pretend spoon.

After successive crop failures—drought, cutworms, hail that destroyed pumpkins and squashes and beans and wheat right before harvest—the Navajo were surviving on meager rations. The few who worked as servants for officers or had found menial jobs at Fort Sumner had a little money to spend, but many of the commissioned civilian merchants took advantage of the Indians' lack of experience with money, overcharging for everything.

"Food?" Tóya asked.

The doctor laughed. "Talk to the supply sergeant here. He's your man. But my guess is, it'll cost you."

This time Tóya didn't say anything about having no money.

Her sister was wide awake now, her eyes tracking between the doctor and Tóya. "Hurt," her sister said, pointing to her abdomen.

"Fixing that will cost too," the doctor answered her.

They heard one of the other soldiers laugh from the vicinity of the card table.

"Well?" the doctor said to the thin soldier—the supply sergeant, Tóya now knew.

The two men looked at Tóya.

"Some other time," the supply sergeant said to the doctor.

"Yeah," the doctor said. "I've seen enough Indian cunt for one night." He took Tóya's sister by the arm and helped her sit up. Then he picked up his cigar and left.

The supply sergeant spoke to Tóya: "Come by in the morning. Early." Then he, too, left. None of the soldiers said anything to them when Tóya and her sister, arm in arm, walked past the card table and out the door.

At dawn the following day Tóya was waiting across from the storehouse. Soon after, the supply sergeant, carrying a small wrapped package, opened the door. He crooked his finger and Tóya approached him. "For you and your sister," he said. Tóya could smell bacon through the brown paper; a grease stain had spread along an edge.

"My father?"

He stared at her, his jaw set. "Make do," he said, "and don't come back. I can't be seen giving you things." He reached in his pocket and handed her a small vial. "From Doc. Give your sister a few drops at a time. Now go, little girl."

She took the vial and the package home. It was half-decent bacon, not like the rancid meat they usually received.

The next evening she returned. The supply sergeant was sitting outside on a chair tipped back against the log wall. When he stood up and went inside, Tóya followed him.

After that, Tóya, her sister, and her father had more food. But her sister's condition didn't get much better. Her spirit was gone. Once a week or so she went to see the doctor, who, it turned out, wasn't a doctor at all, but a medical steward. Her sister would return with her little bottle. As for their father, he ate the additional food without comment.

TÓYA TOLD ONLY SOME of this to Harry Whitaker. He was a smart man. He could figure it out. Just as she, as her English improved, was able to reimagine that first vulgar conversation, the five men sitting at the card table in the storeroom.

The surgery was dark now; only a little light from the evening sky crept in through the window.

"Did that sort of thing happen to other women?" Harry Whitaker asked.

"What do you think?"

"You were there for over four years," he said. "What did you do? I mean—*four years*! How did you spend your days? How did you not lose your mind?"

"We walked," Tóya said. "We walked to get water to drink. There were no trees, so some days we walked nine, ten miles each way just to gather mesquite roots to burn, to cook our rations and to keep warm in the winter. In the summer we tried to coax something green out of the poisoned earth—when the wind kicked up, you could taste the sour dirt. Those of us who still had sheep or goats or horses tried our best to watch over them because Comanches would raid us, and the soldiers just didn't care. They hated being there. And we had to keep our eyes on the children because Mexicans and New Mexicans sometimes stole them. The young women, too. We stayed together for safety. Sometimes we talked and told stories. We slept under the same blankets so we wouldn't freeze. We waited."

"Why didn't you just leave, walk away?" Harry asked.

"You mean like those Apaches?" One night in 1865 the Apaches, some 350 of them, disappeared. "Some Diné did, a few at a time. But most of us were too far from home, and there were many more of us. The army couldn't let us just leave. And I had my father and sister to provide for."

She went to the storehouse three or four times a month, and she always brought something back with her. Always, food. Sometimes a little tobacco for her father. An extra shirt or skirt. And she was learning English. The supply sergeant was a talker. He came from a place called Michigan, where there were lakes so big that you couldn't see across them. He didn't have a wife, or so he said. He was thirty-two. He'd been in the army for fourteen years.

One day he gave her some chocolates. It was near the end of 1867, and the crops had failed again because of drought and the poor soil. Her father was as thin as a withered corn stalk; her sister slept twenty hours a day.

She threw the box of chocolates against the wall. The candy scattered across the dirt floor. The supply sergeant sat in the chair, his drooping mustache and narrow chin and his sad eyes making him look like a chastised dog.

Something has changed, Tóya told herself, her courage rising.

"You don't bring me chocolates," she snapped at him. "My father and my sister can't live on chocolates. You bring me bacon, beans, flour, corn, lard, mutton—that's what you bring me, not candy. Do you think I come here so you can give me sweets, or maybe perfume next week?" She stood up, reached behind her, and dragged the straw-filled sacking off the cot. "Smell this. This is what my life smells like. Not sweets, not perfume." She held it up to her face and inhaled with deep disgust. "It smells like what you and all the other soldiers who bring their women here leave behind."

"The chocolates were just a Christmas gift, BeBe," he muttered. (For that's what he called her: BeBe, his nickname for her Navajo birth name, Bįįhyáázh Biinéí, Lively Fawn.)

Oh yes, she told herself, something has changed.

"Christmas?" She laughed. "The next time I meet you here," she said, dropping the mattress on the floor, "try taking a bath first."

"It's winter."

"Heat some water and wash yourself off. I live in a hole in the ground and I manage that much."

He looked up at her ferocious eyes. His jaw shifted to the side, his teeth clenched. "I could slit your throat," he said. "If I slit your throat and covered you in a foot of dirt not fifty yards from here, nobody that matters would take any notice, not even when the coyotes dug you up."

"Should I thank you for not murdering me?"

He lowered his eyes. "I'm just saying I could."

She tried to imagine him sawing through the cartilage in her throat. *No you couldn't,* she thought, *you couldn't bring yourself to do that.* And with that thought, her anger fled. He was such a pitiful creature, sitting there with his balding pate, the strands of nondescript hair plastered to his skull by his own oil and filth. "Don't you bring me chocolates. Bring me a blanket to cover myself. It's cold." She pushed the tarp aside and left.

The next time she came, she found not only *two* wool blankets and a pillow, but also a fresh mattress, ticking stuffed with clean-smelling straw. And he'd made an effort to wash away the winter stink. She wasn't stupid. She thanked him for the new mattress and the pillow and gray wool blankets, and then she took both blankets with her when she left. There were two more, identical, when she returned a week later. Those she left there.

The turn in his feelings was none of her doing. She had let him use her body and in return she took what he gave. Through it all, she'd never felt a moment's desire. She could feel him moving inside her; it didn't hurt, but she felt no pleasure.

She wasn't cruel to him again, as she'd been when he offered her chocolates, but she remained impassive as he began to speak of the future and stroke her with endearments. "BeBe" had now become "Baby." To his talk of a future she always responded that when the Diné were allowed to return to Dinétah, she'd be among the first to leave.

Once he said, "Maybe I'll follow you, Baby, when my enlistment is up."

"No," she said. "You don't want to do that."

"I haven't been so bad to you."

He was like a little boy, almost pleading. She thought, You put a badger in a cage and then you feed it and stroke its fur, but when you open the cage door, it'll chew off your leg so you can't chase it down.

"Some of the boys think you've gotten a little too uppish," the supply sergeant now said.

She smothered a laugh. It was hard to see yourself as uppish when you were lying on your back with your skirt hiked to your waist and your legs spread.

"They think you should be taken down a peg or two."

"Why do I think they would try to do it by pulling something out of their pants?"

"I'd never let them do that to you," he said. He slid off the cot and adjusted his trousers. She covered herself with a blanket.

Another time he tried a different ploy:

"There's some of your own people who don't like what we've been doing." He was lying on the cot; that day he'd given her a simple hairbrush, wood with boar bristle, and she was sitting on a chair, brushing her hair. Ever since the chocolates, his gifts—there'd been several more—were practical. "When you go back to the reservation"—it was no longer "if," because any day now a delegation of headmen would be meeting with representatives from Washington to sign a treaty, it having become evident to all but the most rabid Indian-haters that Bosque Redondo, Hwéeldi, was a stain on the earth—"what makes you think any self-respecting Navajo man would want you?"

"What makes you think that's what *I* want?"

"How will you live? Your father's too old and sick to take care of you."

She continued to brush her hair. The air was so dry that the ragged ends now flew away from each other and each stroke concluded with a crackle of static. She put the brush down in her lap and quickly tied her hair into a bun at the back of her neck. She held it in place by working a thin, oiled stick through the knot. "Thank you for the brush," she said.

"I like how you do all that," he said. "No mirror, no nothing. You just do it."

JUNE 1, 1868, SETTING THEIR hands and seals: Gen. William T. Sherman, S. F. Tappan; and Barboncito, Chiqueto, Armijo, Muerto de Hombre, Delgado, Hombre, Manuelito, Narbona, Largo, Ganado Mucho, Herrero, Narbono Segundo, Riquo, Torivio, Juan Martin, Desdendado, Serginto, Juan, Grande, Güero Inoetenito, Gugadore, Muchachos Mucho, Cabason, Chiqueto Segundo, Barbon Segundo, Cabello Amarillo, Cabares Colorados, and Francisco.

They say the line of Navajos leaving Hwéeldi, eighteen days later, stretched for ten miles. Tóya couldn't say because she walked near the front, beside her sister. Her father rode in one of the many army wagons, keeping his eye on their few possessions.

Two thousand Navajo had died at Bosque Redondo; maybe 900 had escaped; hundreds of others were never accounted for. Seven thousand three hundred walked west, accompanied by 1,500 horses, 1,000 sheep, 1,000 goats.

For the first time in her life Tóya wore on her feet a pair of cowboy boots. They were used, with worn heels, and too big for her feet, and she knew they would give her blisters, but she wore them anyway. The soles of her only pair of moccasins had worn through, and the last time she'd gone to the storeroom she'd spent part of her time cutting pieces of paperboard to insert. The supply sergeant had watched her but said nothing.

He'd often been quiet lately. Sometimes he just sat or lay on the cot while she occupied the chair. She knew he had another woman; he'd told her as much. (She had no interest in who it was.) Even so, he continued to provide Tóya with extra food. He'd told her that his enlistment was up in just a few months. He didn't plan to sign up again. He thought he'd return to Michigan. He missed the water.

The morning after the peace treaty was signed, she found outside her hovel a box with the word "Baby" scrawled on the top and the boots and a pair of army-issue socks inside.

She sensed all along the return trail that something, some transformation, was building, preparing to flow from her like lava once had from Bandera in the badlands to the south. They crossed the Continental Divide, passed through the southernmost foothills of the Zuni Mountains, rested in the shadows of El Morro, and then they turned north, arriving at the Bear Spring outpost known as New Fort Wingate thirty-five days after leaving Bosque Redondo behind.

Some of the Diné had left the westward procession even before it reached New Fort Wingate; many scattered to the north and south along the way, paying no mind to what the treaty defined as the boundaries of the new reservation. They intended to reclaim the land where their mothers and grandmothers had dwelled, and they had little regard for pieces of paper, except for where the treaty had guaranteed them provisions for the winter ahead—it was already July, too late to plant most crops—and the sheep and goats to come. Many more Navajos continued west toward the newly rebuilt and renamed Fort Defiance, which would become the site of the reservation agency, and then they scattered along the several routes that led into the numerous side branches of Canyon de Chelly, or toward Black Mesa, or north toward Cottonwood Pass and Lukachukai and Round Rock and Monument Valley. Tóya and her sister and father stayed two days at Fort Defiance because the old man was not doing well, wheezing, sweating, his skin like thin paper, but at least he wasn't coughing up blood. On the third day he insisted on going home, and they set out on foot accompanied by a small group of northern travelers who had also been delayed by illness or the exhaustion of their children.

Before leaving, though, Tóya went off by herself, down into the wash just west of the fort, not far from where the creek wound its way between the sandstone walls at the mouth of Canyon Bonito, to purge herself of everything that had happened in the last four years. She intended to return to their home clean in body and spirit, and of the many purgatives her mother had taught her about, she took the strongest. Almost immediately her gorge rose and she vomited repeatedly until nothing trickled from her mouth but a thick string of saliva and phlegm. She rinsed her mouth from the stream as it flowed over a course of smooth rocks at the bottom of the wash. She waited for the nausea to pass. By the time they reached home, just north of Black Lake, her spirit would be clean.

But the nausea kept returning, and dry heaves persisted all through the night, and by morning, having slept very little, she could feel a lightness in her head and her hands. Only her determination drove her onward, up through Black Creek Valley, past the sandstone haystacks and monoliths and the edge of the pine forests. Finally, under thickening clouds, they reached the edge of Black Lake, which was when her eyes flew out of her head and glided with wings above her, and she looked down and saw her body fall, flailing, and her mouth open in a foam of keening that no ears could hear. The fit seemed unending. Her body thrashed, the rain began to fall, she rolled half into the lake, her legs kicking, stirring up enormous waves just as a fierce wind descended on them, blowing her sister and her father off their feet.

When she woke it was still raining and she couldn't speak, but she had her eyes back and they saw the fear in her father's and sister's faces, and at first she misunderstood, tried to tell them with her thick dry tongue that she was all right, but then she realized that the fear was not *for* her but *of* her.

Later, she said to her sister, "Do you want your spirit to return?"

Her sister stared, her eyes wide.

"Go to a hataałii who knows the Ghostway. You need to free yourself from the chindi of your unborn son."

"SO YOU KNEW?" Harry Whitaker said. He adjusted the flame in the kerosene lantern.

Tóya didn't answer at first. She struggled to her feet, leaning on the surgery table and keeping as much weight as possible off the front of her right foot. "I need to find me a stout walking stick."

"You intend to walk home in the pitch dark?" Harry Whitaker asked.

"I could find my way with both eyes closed." She bent down and retrieved her right cowboy boot.

"You can stay here," he said.

"No. I need to get home and treat this toe with the proper medicine."

Harry Whitaker shook his head. "Have it your way. You always do." He held her arm while she half-hopped through the examining room and into the small waiting room. He left her, went out, but soon returned with an ornate, ivory-handled cane. "It was my father's," he said. "It should be serviceable."

Tóya took the cane from him, eyeing it suspiciously. "What is this bone?"

"Ivory. From the tusk of an African elephant. The largest animal that still walks the earth."

This intrigued her. "How large?"

"Well, Ah guess you'd just about come up to an average elephant's belly," he said, teasing. "A large tusk can weigh over a hundred pounds. I have a photograph of an elephant in one of my books, if you'd like to see it."

"It must be a very powerful animal," she said, running her hands over the ivory.

"They say that when a herd of elephants stampedes, the ground shakes."

"An elephant shakes the ground, I shake the water. It's a good match."

"Then you must keep it," Harry said.

After several steps, Tóya voiced her approval.

They stood side by side for a moment just beyond the open doorway. That was when she answered his question, *So you knew?*

"When I left my father and sister at Black Lake, I was no longer Bįįhyáázh Biinéí. *That* much I knew."

CHAPTER EIGHT: Pencil and Pen

Pete, Harry, and Tóya arrived together at Many Springs Canyon to join Julia, Owen, and the Yazzies in welcoming 1910. Owen found Tóya accommodating during her new year visit, which thankfully included only one inspection of his feet and lower legs. She pronounced herself satisfied with his progress and proposed no changes to his daily regimen, which, he assured her, he'd been following assiduously. (Harry Whitaker, concluding his own examination, had nothing more to add; he spent more time listening to Owen's heart than he did assessing the ulcerations.) Over the course of several days, however, her harsh tongue managed to skewer not only missionaries and Easterners in general, but also Mexican cowboys, mining companies, the railroads, Indian agents, bilagáanas' need for calendars and clocks, and a host of other targets, although she restrained herself on New Year's Day when Tom and Carmelita Gorman came by. In general, everyone was well fed, warm, content in each other's company. When Tóya and Harry left for Tohatchi two days later, Owen was sorry to see them go. Pete lingered for another full week before hitching up his wagon for his return to Gallup.

Julia's regular Navajo customers came less frequently during the winter months: Niłch'itsoh, when the penetrating winds arrive; Yas Niłt'ees, when the crusted layers of snow melt and refreeze; 'Atsá Biyáázh, the month when the eaglets hatch. Most of her customers resided along the eastern side of the southern Chuskas or from the area to the north known as Sheep Springs, where the trail from Washington Pass descended to meet the Gallup-Shiprock road. The number of visitors rose and fell in accord with the weather; it was easier to travel after snow and during freezes than during melt and mud.

Several times a week Owen would venture into the store and perform some menial chore—dusting and straightening the already well-organized shelves, scraping and sweeping and washing the floor—but eventually Carmelita Gorman would give him malevolent looks and he'd withdraw, sometimes to Julia's parlor to peruse the month-old newspapers but sometimes to the storeroom, which in these slow months was the frequent retreat of Tom and Johnny Gorman, who were far more affable than Carmelita and always welcomed his company, particularly if they were in the mood for a game of cards, where the betting never ventured beyond matchsticks.

But mostly, Owen didn't know what to do with himself. He always rose before dawn, when Julia did, and they would have breakfast together before she set about her chores. After she left, he would go the parlor and read until lethargy set in and he either had to get up and move or surrender and doze the day away, looking forward only to Julia's appearances throughout the day and her return when the trading post closed. He continued to follow Tóya's schedule for her various remedies, including sitting with his feet exposed on sunny days when the temperature didn't risk further frostbite—and why not? Under her regime he was feeling better, and by early February fresh skin had sealed the smaller ulcers, and the lingering redness of the larger, deeper ones was giving way to a grayish pink as scar tissue gradually closed the wounds. He tried to ignore the two black toes that had succumbed to the November frostbite; he'd asked Harry Whitaker to cut them off, but the doctor told him to leave them alone and not ask for trouble—they'd fall off when they were good and ready.

Sometimes when Julia was elsewhere, Owen would enter her room through the door the two bedrooms shared. (There was a bolt on Julia's side, though he'd never seen it thrown; she had no lock on her other door, the one to the parlor.) Here were the things of her most private life: her bed, a quilt rack at the foot and a valise and two pasteboard boxes beneath (empty or not, he couldn't say), a straight chair, a nightstand with lamp, her wardrobe, her bureau with the oval mirror above it. Sitting on the bureau, a jewelry box and five framed photographs, each in a pewter frame and lined up on a needlepoint runner of morning glories against a green field. Julia appeared in only one photograph, with her sister Penelope, both looking at the camera soberly, without a hint of a smile. Penny appeared to be no older than ten, but there could be no doubt that she would be the beauty, which was confirmed in the four other photographs—a portrait when Penny must have been fifteen or sixteen; another of her standing with her husband in their wedding attire; the third with a baby in her lap, the christening gown draping to the floor; and the most recent with two children, the older barely more than a toddler, the other a babe in arms. (Owen wondered if a sixth picture, of Julia and Will Halley on their wedding day, lay hidden in the bottom bureau drawer or one of the pasteboard boxes beneath her bed.) Once he lifted the top of the inlaid jewelry box. He found nothing of appreciable value except, perhaps, a large Navajo squash blossom necklace that he'd never seen Julia wear.

On another occasion he found that Julia had left her wardrobe doors wide. Her shoes were neatly lined up on the bottom, and her clothes were hung just as neatly. A hat box and another unlabeled pasteboard box occupied the high shelf. He touched nothing in the wardrobe but the skirt of a lavender dress.

That day—the day he found the wardrobe open—he sat down on the edge of her neatly made bed. What he saw distributed around him in her bedroom were in all likelihood her only personal possessions, apart from her other photographs, the ones mounted on the wall in the parlor, behind the armchair that they both now thought of as his, and maybe a few books that she wouldn't part with. Nothing that couldn't easily and quickly be packed in her valise and the pasteboard boxes. Of course he himself had even fewer things, which was how he preferred to live, under the circumstances. But the thought that everything precious to Julia—at least everything tangible—could be contained in the confines of this one small room left him deeply saddened. No, it wasn't a measure of her *worth*, but still . . .

He considered everything *he* owned to be disposable except his field notebooks. In his three months with the Wetherills he'd traced half a dozen Anasazi roads as far as twenty miles from Chaco Canyon, and he'd explored the full length of the inexplicable western road. He'd made very precise notations, and it occurred to him now that he could write an article based on the contents of his field books and submit it to one of the ethnographic journals back East. He could include drawings, showing how the roads fanned out from Chaco Canyon and how they could be detected by vegetation and berm. Better yet, he might ask Pete Pietrowski to photograph what he'd found. Maybe the two of them could visit the mesa behind Pueblo Bonito. Pete could try to photograph the long, straight roads that Richard Wetherill had pointed out at dawn, but Owen suspected that there wouldn't be sufficient contrast for the camera lens. Of most use would be a photograph from an aeroplane. He'd read in a Chicago newspaper that fliers were reaching altitudes approaching two thousand feet now; a mile would soon be common. But to his knowledge, no flights had yet taken place over New Mexico or Arizona. It would happen eventually, but his article couldn't wait. He'd have to make do.

Two weeks later, during a visit at the end of February, Owen asked Pete if he'd be willing to take photographs of the western road, and Pete, in jovial spirits after a pleasant dinner, a visit to his wagon, and a cigar, readily agreed. He was less enthusiastic the following morning but nevertheless hitched his horse Saddle Boy to his wagon and they set off, amid reassurances from Owen that they'd be back to Many Springs before dark (and supper). The Chuska Valley excursion, accompanied by a low-hanging sun visible only through thin high clouds, was uneventful except for Pete's litany of complaints about the wind and the cold, and his need for reassurances that, yes, Owen knew precisely where they were headed. Fortunately, the most recent snow had melted off several days earlier and the ground had refrozen, so the wagon proceeded without impediment, and within three hours of their departure they arrived.

"This is it?" asked Pete, his square face a raw red from the wind.

"It is," Owen said, carefully climbing down from the wagon seat. (He was wearing two pairs of socks under his moccasins.)

Pete, with his hands on his hips, turned around several times, taking in the austere landscape. "Rouse, this had better not be some kind of prank."

"It isn't," Owen said.

"Then kindly point out what in hell I'm supposed to be looking at."

Owen practically had to lead him by the nose before Pete could see the signs—the remainder of the berms, the disturbed terrain underfoot, the patterns in the dried vegetation. Under Owen's direction, Pete took the photographs, even, in a scene that Owen couldn't help laughing about when relating the tale to Julia that evening, going so far as to lie flat on the ground, his chin in the dirt, taking pictures of a two-inch berm against which Owen, crouching, held a ruler.

Not long after, Owen and Julia were sitting alone one evening, she at her desk pouring over her accounts. The terms of her license required quarterly reports to the Indian agent, and she was deep into it. Every transaction had to be recorded. Wary that its Indian dependents might be taken advantage of by the unscrupulous, Washington had set maximum profit rates for everything the trading post carried: 20 percent on flour and other groceries, including canned goods; 20 percent on farming implements and wagon parts; 25 percent on furniture and dry goods, including cotton and woolen blankets, shawls, quilts, and yarns, and such leather items as saddles and harnesses; 30 percent on readymade clothes, boots, and shoes, and on paint; 35 percent—the maximum—on notions, including gloves and beads. Invoices and bills of lading for every item of stock had to be submitted to the superintendent of the Fort Defiance agency. In addition, Julia was required to maintain a carefully itemized ledger describing every item sold, to whom, the price, any cash payment, and every credit granted for pawn or labor as well as, in the latter case, the rate of compensation and the character of the work. Debits, accruals—it all drove Julia mad. Furthermore, the winter quarter was the worst, because the ledgers always showed a steep deficit.

This evening Owen knew she spoke at least partly from frustration when she muttered, "I don't know how much longer I can do this."

He knew nothing specific about her finances. She continued to refuse any payment for room and board, which admittedly amounted to a pittance when compared to a trading post's expenses; the last time he'd broached the subject she threatened to kick him out in the snow if he mentioned it again. But could she be in desperate straits? He could offer something more substantial. He'd spent nothing of what he and his father had deposited in the bank back in June 1909. And considerably more could be obtained from Howard Handke, under the terms of the Rouse farm's sale. But he didn't know how he could even bring the matter up.

"Is there anything I can do?" he asked.

She looked up. "Do?"

"About whatever it is that's aggravating you."

"Oh," she said, her eyes shifting back to paper and ink, "it's nothing. Will was always better at this than I, thank God—I still do exactly what he used to, and so far I've kept myself out of trouble."

Owen wasn't convinced. Last fall there hadn't been much of a second churro shearing.

Julia turned in her chair to face him full on. "You needn't concern yourself."

"You're struggling," he said.

"It's the nature of the business. If we get a good twelve pounds of wool per sheep come the spring shearing, everything will balance out." She gave him her slight smile. "Spring is almost here."

"I have some money. It's yours for the asking."

"Owen," she said, shaking her head.

"When my father and I are gone, it'll just . . . disappear." He wiggled his fingers above his head. "Into the aether. Better that you should put some of it to use."

"I wouldn't hear of it. I appreciate the spirit of your offer, but I couldn't possibly accept. Besides, it isn't necessary."

And if it *were* necessary, she still wouldn't accept it. He pretended to resume reading his book.

A few evenings later—Julia knitting, Owen turning the pages of a newspaper—he asked her, "Where does the wool go when you sell it?"

"To a dealer in Denver who then markets it back East."

"Why don't you spin and dye it here?"

She laughed lightly. "Do you have any idea what that would involve?"

"You already figured out that you could make more money by cleaning some of the wool yourself."

"Yes, but—"

"Hear me out," he cut her off. "Back in Leominster Mr. Burrows, Bethany's father, ran a clothing store. He said that to generate sales you needed an inventory that brought customers through the door or else you had to offer an exceptional service that they couldn't find elsewhere. Ideally, you combined both. Selling shirts and collars kept him in business, but where he made his easiest profit was in hand-tailored suits. He said it was a good day if he sold a hand-tailored suit. He'd take a deposit and use that to order the cloth—with a substantial markup, of course. And he employed an Italian tailor who was the best in the area, a marvel of efficiency with his chalk and shears and sewing machine, so it was easy to calculate up front the cost of the labor for fittings, cutting, and sewing. Mr. Burrows said that with a hand-tailored suit, he couldn't lose. When the buyer paid the balance, at least half of it went into the bank as profit."

"Navajos don't buy tailored suits," Julia teased him. "At least not at trading posts."

"My *point,*" he gave back to her, "is that his profit came from selling something finely made and with no middleman."

"And so?—"

"Navajo rugs. You already know some of the best weavers. Provide them with wool—wool that you've washed, carded, spun, and dyed right here. You tell them what style of rug you want and what size and how much you'll pay them for it. And then you sell it directly."

"To whom? Have you forgotten?—we're in the middle of nowhere."

"You market your rugs by catalog."

"How—"

He held up his hand. "You distribute the catalog in a selected market. Not New York or Boston. In a city that isn't awash with the best of everything. A city that's growing, that's creating wealth, where for the first time in their lives people have money to spend on the niceties. Your sister Penelope lives in Chicago. Chicago might be perfect. It's far enough east—Navajo weavings should be something of a novelty. You could start by having your sister distribute the catalog among her friends and acquaintances. Send her a couple of your best rugs to display in her parlor. If you want, give her a commission. With luck, word of mouth will take over."

"Philip would never hear of it—his wife, working?" Julia scrunched her face in mock disdain. "And I don't know anything about putting together a catalog."

"Where's the mystery? You and I can write it together. Ask Pete to take a few photographs. You keep the cost down by using line drawings to illustrate whatever you want—warp and woof, or basic designs. I'm a decent draftsman. I should be able to do that. Tell people what they need to know in order to appreciate what they'll be buying. Get the catalog printed and bound with a nice cover featuring one of the very best rugs in full color."

"But the money to do it—"

"Pete would do the photographs for nothing. I'm just as cheap, if you don't count room and board. The printing and binding couldn't be *that* much." And he'd pay it, but he didn't say this.

"I don't know." Julia had stopped knitting. Her brow was furrowed. "I only have a few really fine rugs."

"Julia, you take *orders.* Like for a hand-tailored suit. Let the customer pick out a design. And the size. You provide made-to-order rugs, with half the money up front."

"Weavers won't stick to a precise pattern."

"All the better! You say in the catalog that each rug is a unique creation, a true work of art."

"I'd have to pay women to do the carding and spinning and dyeing."

"Wouldn't the women who help with the scouring want the additional work? How much would it cost to produce enough finished wool for, say, fifty rugs? Isn't that just a small fraction of what you already wash? Use your own wool—Yazzie's and yours. You've said it's the best. When you blend the wools you probably wouldn't even have to do that much dyeing."

"I'd have to think about it—what it would cost . . . I have no sense of the figures."

He knew he had her full—even though highly skeptical—attention, so he pressed on:

"What's the most you've ever received for a rug?"

"Twenty-five dollars. It was six-by-nine and quite fine."

"Who bought it?"

"A Santa Fe dealer."

"And what do you think he turned around and sold it for?"

"I don't know. Forty dollars?"

Owen laughed. "Santa Fe isn't the reservation. Profits are determined by the marketplace, not the government. If he gave you $25, rest assured, he sold it for at least $50. And if he took it to New York or sold it to a European, $75. Or more."

"That's preposterous."

"No, Julia, it isn't. You could sell that same rug in Chicago for . . . $60. You could pay your weavers more and still make a tidy sum."

"All rugs aren't that large."

"Still, if you could sell twenty-five a year. Or fifty . . ."

Julia fell silent.

"Maybe it'll turn out to be a pipe dream," Owen said. "But I'm ready to start working on a catalog anyway. Write to your sister. If nothing comes of it, so be it. As it is, I'm not doing anything better with my time."

"What about your article?" She knew that he'd begun writing up his field notes on the Anasazi roads.

"The days are getting longer. I can do both, and there's nothing to lose at this point. So why not give it a try?"

Owen had commandeered the quilt rack from Julia's room and positioned it near the dining table, as he now often did in the evening after supper. Several sheets of heavy paper and his drafting kit and an ink well of India ink were spread out on the table, and he was concentrating on capturing in moderate detail the pattern of diamonds and pyramidal steps woven into the rug that he'd draped across the rack. Later, he'd add the appropriate shading. He hoped a catalog reproduction wouldn't lose too much detail.

Johanna was standing behind him, watching his pen skim across the paper. For several nights now, having abandoned her old rug along the wall, she'd been watching him. Every now and then he would glance over his shoulder, as if to ask her opinion of the most recent lines he'd drawn, but she always shifted her eyes away.

Julia was sitting in her parlor reading William James's *A Pluralistic Universe*. Clement Yazzie was at his usual side table, his back to the room, working on some piece of leather that needed repair, stitching. Pete appeared to be dozing in Owen's armchair.

Owen put down his pen. He looked at the drawing. He wasn't satisfied. He crumpled up the paper and tossed it aside. Stretching, he raised his arms, cupped his hands against the back of his neck—an elbow brushed against Johanna's dress; he hadn't realized she was standing that close—and intertwined his ink-stained fingers. He turned around in the chair. Johanna had taken a step back.

He'd been the first to suggest, the day before, when only Pete and Julia were in attendance—the two had spent the morning photographing several nearby weavers with their rugs for possible inclusion in the prospective catalog—that Johanna seemed to be understanding more English.

"How can you tell?" Pete, scratching a stubbled cheek, had asked.

"She isn't opaque," Owen said, irritated at Pete's easy dismissal, "not if you pay attention. Her posture changes, her eyes . . ."

"If you're right," Julia said, "it's because you're here, Owen."

He'd drawn in his chin, doubtful. "Why do you say that?"

"Because she's been listening to you and me talk in English almost every day. Before that, she mostly heard Navajo."

Owen had been thinking about this on and off ever since that conversation. If Johanna was indeed understanding more and more English, what else was she capable of?

Owen lowered his arms and, his eyes still on Johanna, patted the chair on his right. "Come and sit down," he said.

For a moment Johanna continued to look off to the side; her lower lip drooped a bit. Then she moved forward and sat down, her back straight and stiff. This in itself seemed an accomplishment. Before this, she'd never given anything he said much, if any, notice. He pushed a piece of blank white paper in front of her, extracted a sharpened pencil from his kit, and held it out to her. Her hands stayed folded in her lap.

"Do you want to try?" he asked.

Johanna looked at the pencil and then at the pen he'd laid on the table. Again at the pencil, again at the pen. The meaning seemed clear.

"All right," he said, his eyebrows raised in surprise. He picked up his pen. "Watch how I hold it." One by one, he positioned his thumb, middle finger, and forefinger properly, and then he moved the pen up and down against his thumb, demonstrating how he steadied it, controlled it. Then he lay the heel of his hand on the table and slowly dragged it back and forth while continuing to move the pen up and down. How much was she understanding? He spoke softly to avoid drawing the attention of the others in the room; if he was wrong about this, he didn't want to become the butt of Pete's jokes; nor did he want to embarrass Johanna, if such a thing were even possible.

"See? I can make the pen do whatever I want. Now you take it." He held it out to her. She didn't move. He laid the pen down in front of her and withdrew his hand. He waited to see what she decided. He nudged the pen with a finger. "Go ahead," he encouraged her.

She did nothing.

Then Owen did something he'd never dared to do before: he deliberately touched her. He reached across and lifted her right hand from her lap (was she right- or left-handed? he wondered). He half-expected her to pull away, but she didn't. He placed her hand on the pen before withdrawing his.

She left her hand there for some time, and then she rolled the pen back and forth under her fingers.

"Go ahead," he said again.

Johanna lifted the pen delicately. Owen watched her manipulate it, mimicking each finger placement exactly as he'd done and then laying the

side of her hand on the table, wiggling the pen up and down rather ferociously.

"Loosen up," he said. He lifted his hand, shook it, let it flop back and
forth from the wrist. "It's a pen for drawing, not a knife for cutting."

Again, Johanna mimicked his gestures.

"Okay," he said, "put it to the paper. Draw a line." He pretended to
draw one with a forefinger.

Johanna let the pen hover over the blank sheet for a moment and
then pressed the tip of the pen firmly into the sheet. The black ink quickly
pooled, and Johanna lifted the pen in surprise. Her eyes narrowed, her lips
tightened, and she lay the pen down on the table. Owen retrieved it.

"Try the pencil instead," he said, holding one out to her. "It's easier."

She didn't shift her eyes from the ruined paper.

"I have lots of paper. Don't worry about it. Take the pencil and hold
it the same way you held the pen. If you make a mistake with a pencil, you
can erase it." Did she understand? Was her sense of English good enough?

Julia, catching the whispering, had turned to watch.

Johanna returned her eyes to the blotted page. Owen pushed the
stained sheet aside and slid another to her. "Take the pencil," he said, which
she did. "Draw a line. You don't have to press hard."

She did as he asked and then stopped, pencil still in hand.

"All right, try to sketch the weaving." He didn't point to it. He didn't
even nod in its direction. He wanted to see if she understood what he'd said.

She drew from the bottom, a line at a time, piling one atop another,
the way a Navajo weaver would work at a loom. Her attempt seemed so peculiar—anyone else would have started by drawing a rectangle and filling it
in—that Owen sat back and watched for several minutes. After completing
the first few lines, she drew surprisingly quickly, though with such a fierce
grip on the pencil that he knew her hand would soon tire. But he let her
proceed without interruption. The most astounding thing about her method,
if it could be called that, wasn't simply the evenness of the borders that
emerged, but the gradual appearance of the rug's interior design. There was
nothing complicated about the design, and it had a simple color scheme—
natural browns, off-white, and tan—but she seemed to understand intuitively
how to vary the intensity of the line, pressing harder for dark, lighter for
light, in such small increments that the series of three diamonds that began
just above the bottom of the rug appeared on the page as if from nothing.

Yazzie and Pete as well as Julia were now observing.

"That's very good, Johanna," he said, trying to give no indication of
his absolute surprise. "Keep going. I'm just going to stretch a bit," he told
Johanna as he rose from the table. "If the point of your pencil gets too dull,

just take another sharpened one from my kit." As casually as possible, Owen walked to the parlor.

"Is she really drawing?" Julia asked.

"She is."

"Well I'll be damned," Pete said.

"Our mother tried to teach Sister to weave," Yazzie said, "but they never got beyond a few rows. Sister always lost interest."

Owen waited a couple more minutes before returning to Johanna. Her drawing had progressed, but the sides of the interior diamonds were a bit jagged and she now stopped.

"Rest your hand, Johanna," he said. "You don't need to hold the pencil as if it were going to scurry away. Relax your fingers." He demonstrated and she complied.

"Don't worry about this," he said, indicating the side of the first diamond with his finger. "It's quite good for your first effort. You'll do better with the second row of diamonds, and even better with the third. It takes practice." He didn't ask if she understood: better to assume that she did.

But Johanna didn't continue. Instead, once again, she stared at his pen.

"Not yet," he said gently. "The pen is unforgiving. That will come later."

She put the pencil down, left the table, and returned to her blanket against the wall. Owen's impulse was to try and coax her back to the table, but he thought better of it. She wouldn't respond to entreaties. She'd try again or she wouldn't; the decision would be entirely hers.

Several days later, after he'd concluded that Johanna's attempt to draw must have been nothing but a passing whim, he found her standing behind him, watching, again. Without commenting, he pulled out the chair next to him and she sat down. He placed paper and pencil in front of her. Johanna immediately set to work drawing not the rug that now lay draped over the quilt rack but, he soon realized, the earlier one, the one with the diamond pattern that she'd previously attempted. She was drawing it from memory. Once again, the triple-diamond pattern emerged, much more exactly than it had upon her first attempt.

He'd always found her odd, to say the least, although over time, with familiarity, her peculiarities had come to seem less so—closer to a variation of normal behavior. But now, with pencil in hand, Johanna struck him as a different person; mute, uneducated, impaired, but humanly complicated, an even deeper mystery.

Owen tried to turn his attention back to his own drawing. The illustration suited its purpose, he supposed, but it disappointed him. Nevertheless, he set to work (with frequent glances at his companion's progress), persevering until he realized that Johanna had stopped. She'd completed the bottom half of the rug and now sat still.

"Is something wrong?" he asked.

Julia and Yazzie were again watching from the parlor. (Pete had returned to Gallup two days before.)

Johanna pushed the piece of paper aside, clearly done with it.

Why?— Unless she'd drawn only what she remembered, just the bottom of the rug, for, with the weaving draped over the quilt rack, the top half had been hidden from her view. But surely she knew that the top of the rug was a mirror image of the bottom half. Yet she hadn't attempted to draw it. Could she only see what she could see with her eyes? How could such a person function, survive? Such a person wouldn't know if the world fell away, disappeared beyond the crest of the next hill. No, Johanna knew what was over the crest. But maybe, having drawn the bottom half of the rug, she saw no need to draw the top. In a way, that would make her even more . . . surprising.

What should he do? Should he suggest she try to draw the new rug, the one he was now working on, which was of a more complicated design? No, that would prove nothing. He looked around the room.

"Shall we try something else?" He lay aside his pen and picked up a pencil. "If you ask most people to draw a wall, this is what they'll do." He drew a quick rectangle. "And if you ask them to draw a corner where two walls meet, they'll do this." He attached another rectangle to the first, side by side, deliberately oversimplifying. "Does that really look anything like that corner over there?" He nodded toward the kitchen corner, just beyond the pantry door. "No, of course not, because most people don't *really* look. They think they do, but they don't." He paused.

She was looking toward the corner.

"I want you to draw a simple straight line, up and down."

Her eyes shifted from the corner to the sheet of paper, and then she did as he'd asked. The line was very straight.

"Good." He slowly put his hand over hers. She didn't flinch. "Let me guide you," he said, and together they drew two angled lines, a wide vee, at the top of Johanna's vertical line, and then a similarly wide inverted vee at the bottom. He lifted his hand from hers. "What do you see?" he asked.

Johanna looked from the page to the corner and back again.

He waited for her.

"Look at where the walls meet." Then he traced the upper vee with a finger. "Look at where the ceiling meets the corner." Then the lower vee. "Look at where the walls meet the floor."

Johanna's eyes moved back and forth, between the corner and the paper.

"Pretend that the lines for the ceiling and the floor are coming towards you."

Johanna's face showed nothing.

Maybe not; maybe she didn't understand. He exhaled. How many centuries had it taken for artists to understand perspective? Maybe Johanna couldn't see with such modern eyes. He'd try adding one more detail:

"Look at the floor in the corner. Look—*really* look—at just one plank. As it comes towards us, it *appears* to get wider, even though we *know* it doesn't. You see? Things that are closer to us look bigger, and things that are farther away look smaller. Think about being outside and seeing a tree in the distance. You know that it's big—thirty, forty feet tall—but when it's far away, it may look like it's very small." He held up thumb and forefinger, parallel, an inch apart. "What I'm talking about is hard to see in a smaller space—this room—where everything is closer, but it's still true. Here, hold up your pencil." He took her hand and raised it; her arm rose without resistance. "Close one eye and use the pencil to measure how wide a plank is where it meets the wall."

Was this too much, too many words for her to follow?

After a moment's hesitation, Johanna closed her left eye.

His heart skipped a beat. When she seemed to be done, he said, "Now do the same thing with a plank beneath the table."

She sat back in the chair, turned to the side, looked down, with the pencil still raised.

"Our brain"—he touched his forehead and then hers—"tricks us into not seeing that difference. You have to learn to see in a new way."

Still, Johanna's face showed nothing.

"Now we're going to draw five or six floor boards. Look at the corner. Look at each board. Okay? Now we draw." Once again he placed his hand on Johanna's so that he could guide the pencil. He slowly brought Johanna's hand across the page. Lifted it and brought the tip of the pencil back to the wall. Across the page. To the wall, across. To the wall, across. To the wall, across. Then he stopped. He removed his hand from Johanna's but didn't say anything.

Slowly, she turned, and her eyes caught his before they darted back to the drawing.

"Let's add the pantry door." And he took her hand again. Her wrist was looser now. "Two straight lines up and down, a line at the top near the edge of the ceiling, and there you have it—a closed door. Now, let's open the door a bit." Another vertical line, parallel to and near the front of the door. Two very short horizontal lines, overlapping a bit of the wall at the top and the first floor board at the bottom. Quick shading in the thin space between the now-thickened door and the wall. "The door's open just a bit, but it's open." He raised his hand from Johanna's and sat back. That's enough, he thought. Maybe too much. He'd have to wait and see. He placed a finger on the drawing.

"This is very rough. Two hands can't draw well together." He put his on top of hers again, briefly. "You can do it better on your own. Maybe not the first time," he cautioned. "If you have to, do it over until you like what you see."

Julia and Yazzie were now standing behind them, watching. Julia's eyes, looking down at Owen, were wide.

Johanna stared at the drawing paper, looking up occasionally to the corner of the kitchen and the pantry door, covering a line of the drawing with her fingers, and then another, as if trying to see into the nature of it, how it worked. Then she turned the sheet of paper over and put the pencil to work, and in less than a minute she'd reproduced the drawing line for line, not as Owen had helped her sketch it, but from the floor boards up. She put down the pencil.

"Hunh," Yazzie grunted.

Later, after Yazzie and Johanna left for home, Julia, her eyes shining, said to Owen, "Do you realize what an extraordinary thing you've done?"

"Not me," he said, but with a touch of pride. "Not *me*."

The following day, Julia showed him a letter she'd received from Chicago:

My Dearest Julia,

I feel that I must reply immediately to your latest letter, which came at just the right time. I've been feeling so removed from life lately—not, of course, the life of my little family! By "life" I mean the greater world, or at least the world beyond our pleasant home (which you still haven't come to see!) or the too-rare occasions when the four of us are gadding about, down to the lakeshore or to a park for a picnic. When Philip—who works so hard!—is at the office or traveling to see about the opening of new rail lines, life in our abode is, I must admit, sometimes a wee bit boring, despite the infinite daily pleasures of being a mother to delightful children. They grow so fast! But, still being honest with you (for whom else can I be so open with?), we have Bertha to do all the cooking, and Marie to help with the children, and now, at Philip's insistence, we have a laundress, a wonderful negro woman from, of all places, New Orleans (!), who comes in twice a week to do our laundry and ironing and even the darning, and as a consequence I too often find myself quite useless.

Thus your proposal that I involve myself in your new "enterprise," if that isn't too grand a term, struck me immediately as a marvelous idea. I see absolutely no reason not to jump in! I am quite prepared to see to the printing of your catalog and its distribution to a select clientele. Despite my moaning about my dull life, I <u>do</u> have friends, and we get together quite regularly to lunch and play cards and attend art exhibitions and donate our time to various seasonal causes. These are precisely the people—most of whom have somewhat greater financial resources than Philip and I do (never believe that society doesn't talk about its money; at least the wives do, not to the dollar and cent, of course, but to the trips abroad, and the finery in their closets and jewelry boxes, and the price of exquisite French draperies)—who might be convinced to purchase something a little more "primitive" as the "new" fashion. When I say "primitive," I do not mean to denigrate the weavings you propose to sell, as I am sure they will be of the finest quality of their kind, but to contrast them to the necessarily more refined art of Persia.

My enthusiasm for the project is tempered only by the difficulty I anticipate in convincing Philip to let me proceed. You have met him, if only briefly, so I am sure you know what I mean. (Again, you must visit—no less than a month will do!) He can be a bit "proper," if you "get" my meaning. He is a wonderful husband and even better father, I say with considerable pride—what a wonderful choice I made in selecting him as my spouse, ha ha!—but he has a sense of propriety that must sometimes be overcome if I am to have any freedom at all. (The first time he saw me in a stylish bathing dress at the shore, you—especially you, my so-unconventional sister—would have laughed to see the colors his face turned!)

But I will prepare the ground. Write back as soon as you receive this, to confirm that you are indeed moving forward with your Navajo Catalog, and I will begin the campaign! He may be the general in our household but that does not mean that my strategies are without effect. In the end, even if he doesn't know how I've conquered, he will surrender to my will!

Your loving sister,
Penny

"She likes exclamations," Owen said, folding the letter and returning it to Julia with a smile.

"That she does," Julia said.

"So have we committed ourselves to this venture?" Owen asked.

"If we take orders and can't fill them—"

"Decide how many good weavers you can rely on."

"And then?"

He smiled and shrugged. "Find more."

Johanna's continuing lessons: a rectangular box placed at the far end of the table, a lit lamp to one side, throwing wide shadows, dim to the front, dark to the opposite side; a ball of yarn and a large round cabbage; a flower, a bunch of flowers; the guest hogan, and then the hogan positioned against the mountains.

She drew the same things over and over—corner, door, box, yarn, cabbage—executing them with ever greater precision, down to the hinges holding the door and the desiccated edges of the outer cabbage leaves. Before this Johanna had never so much as picked up a sharpened stick and doodled on the floor of the hogan, Clement Yazzie told Julia and Owen, although now she did so regularly next to her sleeping pallet. And what did she draw? Julia asked. Often nothing he could make out, he said. When she was done, she always rubbed out the markings.

One day Owen noticed Johanna standing for a long time by Julia's corral. She appeared to be watching the horses. An hour later, she was still there. Owen walked over to her and they watched together.

After a while Owen said, "I can't help you. I'm just a draftsman. I mean, I can draw maps and rugs and buildings and an easy landscape, but animals are beyond my ability. I'm even worse with people, faces." He paused. "That certainly doesn't mean that they're beyond *your* ability, just that there isn't much more *I* can show you."

Johanna seemed to take this in. He let her be, and the next time he checked, she had left. That evening he was working on the final illustration for the catalog, but Johanna, instead of joining him at the table, sat down on her old rug. When he was done, Owen walked over and squatted down beside her, his back against the wall.

The black hair framing her face. The doe eyes. The slightly parted lips. She could sit there like that, barely moving, for an hour, longer. He'd seen her do it.

"I'm sorry if I've disappointed you. But I can teach you to use the pen now," he said to her. "Whenever you want."

AS IT TURNED OUT, WRITING her part of the text for the Many Springs Navajo Catalog, though far easier than convincing her best weavers to abandon the way they'd always done business—they tended to finish a rug when they needed cash or credit for provisions or to meet a family emergency—proved a challenge for Julia. She and Owen had divided the job. Julia would describe the shearing, scouring, hand carding, hand spinning, and dyeing and would also write a brief history of the Many Springs Trading Post (omitting any mention of Will Halley). It also fell to her to calculate the rates to be charged for various rug sizes, with premiums for those larger than fifty square feet. That left Owen to describe the traditional loom and such basic terms as warp and woof and selvage as well as the various designs being offered.

Julia rejected her own first draft as too florid; the second, as too utilitarian. Underlying all was the matter of establishing an appropriate tone throughout. Should the writing be light and breezy? Rustic or sophisticated? Knowledgeable but unpretentious? Confessional or reserved? Unfortunately, their natural writing styles, Owen's and hers, bore little resemblance. When asked his opinion during a March visit, Pete Pietrowski refused to get involved:

"It's a catalog," he said, "not literature or philosophy. Start each sentence with a capital letter. End it with a period."

Harry Whitaker, in contrast, took an editor's pen to the whole thing and made such a hash of it that, after thanking him for his Herculean efforts, Julia and Owen started all over again, working together, sighing their way through, sentence by sentence. In the end, they estimated that the entire catalog, including appropriately sized halftones, would run twenty-four pages. In mid-April Julia shipped it off to Penelope (who, as predicted, had prevailed over her husband's objections), advising her to seek quotations from at least two printers. Penny had offered to pay for the printing, but Julia rejected the offer—she could only imagine Philip's response to *that* idea.

The *Chicago Tribune* of March 28, 1910 (read by Julia on April 20), had devoted an entire page to photographs from Chicago's Easter Parade, including, prominently, one of the very photogenic Mrs. Philip Malott and three-year-old daughter Katherine, looking darling, a miniature of her mother; they both wore shoulder-wide hats featuring an enormous bow in front. Several weeks of the *Tribune* had arrived in a box also bearing two birthday gifts for Julia, namely, a pair of the finest, buttery kid gloves and an exquisite scarf of Japanese silk "for motoring"—further inducements, Penny wrote in her impish voice, for Julia to visit Chicago, for she was sure there couldn't *possibly* be an appropriate occasion to wear either in New Mexico.

Apart from her sister's package, Julia's fortieth birthday went unremarked, which is how she preferred it, though it did indeed "mark" something: it pushed her into a new decade, her fifth, one in which most women would witness another kind of parade, their youngest children setting forth, one by one, advancing into their own adulthoods. Julia didn't have this to anticipate, this emotional jumble of pride and fear and sorrow. Would her life soon be in decline? Was it already?

Meanwhile, wagonloads of bagged wool were being brought into the trading post. Tom Gorman was in charge of weighing and dickering—there was always somebody trying to sneak past him a bag half-full of useless scraps and well-distributed barnyard filth, but Tom had the proper temperament for handling the situation: "Well, you know," he'd say in his laconic drawl, accented with a frown and a shake of his head, "this just isn't right, trying to take advantage . . ."—but Julia supervised the sorting herself and made sure that the three women she'd hired to do the cleaning were kept busy in the wash shed. She was kept running, for this was also the most active season behind the store counter. Johnny Gorman was on the road to and from Gallup regularly, leaving her and Carmelita to answer questions, complete sales, reconcile individual accounts. In the spring Navajo women could spend hours in the store, examining every item they might desire, weighing its worth, calculating, and some days the floor was crowded with customers. Owen Rouse lent a hand, but Clement Yazzie, aided by Johanna, was preoccupied with their own sheep, shearing and keeping a watchful eye over the lambing.

Julia was pleased that Owen had come through the winter healed as well as could be expected, according to Harry Whitaker, and he'd begun returning to the trails above the high meadow, not going far, but still . . . progressing. There were still moments when she regretted agreeing to the catalog, more his than hers, in her eyes. Putting aside even a fraction of her best wool would reduce her income, and she'd have to cover the cost of carding and spinning and dyeing, but she'd gone too far to withdraw from the venture now, not without at least a perfunctory effort. Owen's enthusiasm had enlivened the whole process.

But there was something else, and it troubled her whenever she settled into herself, when the day calmed down enough for her to work quietly in the garden, or when she lay in bed unable to sleep, or when she was sitting alone at her desk, as she was now, the account ledger open before her (but ignored). She'd seen. The way Owen sometimes looked at her. She didn't know what she would do when he finally declared himself. As long as it remained unspoken, they could continue on. Once spoken, however, he certainly couldn't continue occupying the room on the other side of the connecting door, bolted or not. She genuinely cared—part of her already mourned his loss, the loss she knew would come one way or another. But she couldn't accept what he was preparing to offer.

She sighed. April was never her favored month. Her mother had died in April, which was when Julia relinquished the last bit of hope that whatever remained of her girlhood might yet blossom into an ordinary life of hyacinths and frills and giggling with girlfriends; instead, she'd donned her mourning clothes. And she'd met Will Halley in another April, which was also the month, six years ago, when he vanished. (Where was he now? Was he even alive? Was he happy? Happy, certainly, to be rid of her.) And of course her birth month, which she hadn't celebrated for a decade, and also, coincidentally, the birth month of both the Yazzie boys—and remembering *that* brought back their deaths in the room that Owen now occupied. (How old would they be now? 'Atsá, twenty; Níyol, still a boy pretending to filch peppermint sticks.) Add to the list April 1909, the month of Owen's diagnosis—another reason to belittle April.

May, in contrast, she loved. Her favorite month. Tulips, lilacs, irises—not that any of them grew in Many Springs Canyon, which nevertheless offered its own rewards. Spring melt still pouring through the wash. Green appearing around Yazzie's pond. The shearing done, the lambing season completed, the first garden shoots breaking through, the days at their most comfortable, the nights still cool enough to demand a shawl or a blanket. Life seemed momentarily content with itself in May, which this year would include the appearance of Halley's Comet and a grand gathering to mark the occasion—something to look forward to, to raise her spirits.

If only Owen would . . . not.

She sighed again. She should write a thank you to Penny for the gloves and scarf. She closed the ledger. She retrieved a sheet of stationery from the desk drawer and dipped her pen in ink.

CHAPTER NINE: Julia (The Past, continued)

5. Diphtheria

The two boys died quietly within an hour of each other, lying in the bed on either side of their father, whose breath rasped from his swollen throat. First 'Atsá, and then his younger brother Níyol. Their ragged breathing had grown ever more labored, and the foul-smelling bloody discharges from their noses more pronounced, even as their barking coughs lost ferocity; every gasp rattled in their throats. Their fevers, contained until then, spiked before dawn and Julia tried to cool them down with cold sheets that she'd left on the veranda and with wet compresses on their foreheads. She knew there was no use but she did it anyway, brushing their wild, thick, long black hair back from their exhausted faces, from their half-open, widely vacant dark eyes, from their blue lips.

Johanna sat on the floor in a corner of the room, observing everything, listening. Now and then Will would come to the door and stand there, leaning against the frame but not entering. Clement Yazzie lay in the middle of the bed, turning from one side to the other, wrapping an arm around one boy and then the other, nearly choking on his own sputum.

Finally, that most instinctive of life-forces, to keep air flowing into their inflamed lungs, yielded.

When 'Atsá died she wrapped him in a clean white sheet and tried to lift him, his limp frame so heavy with death—too heavy—and she had to call for Will.

"Where do you want me to put him?" His gruff voice revealed his anger, that she would risk both their lives this way, for Navajos.

"In the hogan." If they laid his body in the storeroom and word got out, most of their customers would never set foot in the trading post again. The hogan . . . well, if they had to, they could burn it down at no great loss.

They'd closed the trading post more than two weeks ago, when word reached them from Tohatchi that diphtheria was now spreading along the eastern expanse of the reservation. The less traveling people did, the less contact they would have with others, and the more likely the epidemic could be contained. Julia had no idea if other stores, at Two Grey Hills and Toadlena and Crystal, had done likewise, because the normal routes of communication—teamsters, traveling salesmen, the odd passing horseman or Navajo family on the move—had been broken by fear. Tom and Carmelita Gorman had hunkered down in Naschitti, keeping their children close to home, and Julia and Will unlocked the Many Springs Trading Post only when a Navajo came in need of some basic commodity—flour, sugar, coffee, lard . . .

When Níyol—younger, lighter, missing his top two front teeth, the ridges of the new bottom ones just emerging—also gave up his last rough breath, she took him from Clement Yazzie's arms and wrapped him in another clean sheet. She carried him to the hogan herself and laid him beside his brother.

Such joyful, handsome children, unmarked by life's miseries during their boyish comings and goings, constantly in and out of the store, a playground to which no one objected except Will, of course, and Carmelita, who on those rare occasions when she was angry at Tom for some unvoiced reason or was just in a sour mood, preferred a strict sense of business etiquette. They gave life to the place, Julia felt, especially on those days when few customers arrived, although lately she'd seen a change in 'Atsá, always the more introspective of the two. Sometimes from the corner of her eye she saw him observing her—he always quickly looked away if she made known by her own glance that *she* was observing *him*—his mouth turned down, his gaze narrowed, and she suspected he was beginning to understand that she somehow ranked above him in the larger world, though had he known her true standing, that she fell near the bottom of the Great Chain of Being in the Anglo world, he might have spent less energy on trying to fathom the hierarchy. But he didn't know (hadn't known) the larger world, having been as far as Gallup only a handful of times, to her knowledge, most recently as a companion to Tom Gorman on a trip to gather supplies. She remembered 'Atsá's sitting beside Tom on the high seat of the big wagon, grinning broadly, ready to assume a manly position on this adventure, to see the railroad locomotives and the stone buildings with glass windows ten feet high.

And little Níyol. What had he known of the world beyond his family's land and the forested mountains, and the canyon, and the Chuska Valley beyond, dry and unending to the eye? He knew he had no mother, that mysterious being whose role somehow was filled by his father and his paternal aunt, *shimá* (the same word also meant "mother"), Johanna, whose peculiarities probably seemed only natural—and normal—to him. Julia remembered boosting him—he was (had been) so small for his age—just last week, to a perch beside the candy jar and letting him select a peppermint stick, his heels kicking with delight against the case beneath him.

She hadn't even known the boys were sick until two days ago, when Johanna appeared at her door unusually early in the morning, the frost still heavy on the land and her breath condensing in clouds. "Johanna," she said, surprised, "is anything wrong?" Johanna looked away, discomfited by the direct eye contact, but then, when Julia stood aside so she could enter the warm kitchen, Johanna instead turned and looked up the trail, toward home. "Johanna, is someone ill?" Julia asked in Navajo. Johanna gave her a quick glance. Julia said, " *'Adáyi' dááhodiníchaad*?" Diphtheria. A second, longer glance. Julia grabbed the shawl hanging on a hook inside the door, draped it over her head, and, already in full stride, having followed Johanna down the veranda steps, threw the fringed ends across her shoulders. She could hear Will banging around in the stable and, half-running, she called to him, shouting that something was wrong at Mr. Yazzie's.

She heard the thick coughing even before Johanna led her into the hogan. Not both, she thought, let it not be both. Yazzie sat next to where they lay, and one look at his face told her.

"Why are you," he said before his own cough stole his breath, "here?"

Julia reeled. The air was fetid, hazy with pinyon smoke, oppressive. She refused to let his stare intimidate her. "Mr. Yazzie, Johanna can't take care of the three of you by herself."

"We will. Manage," he said when his hacking stopped.

"No," Julia said, "you won't." She turned to Johanna and spoke to her quietly in Navajo. Johanna looked at her brother for a moment but didn't wait for his advice. She left the hogan. "Johanna's going to hitch your wagon."

"No," Yazzie said. "Tohatchi. Too far."

"I know."

"Where?" Before she could even answer he said, "No," insistent.

Julia began gathering as many rugs and blankets as she could hold to line the bed of the wagon and cover the boys. "We'll send for Harry Whitaker."

"Your husband. Won't like this."

"That's not your concern. Your concern is your boys. Let me get them ready." She could see when she approached that they were beyond consciously caring. What did a boy so sick dream of? For 'Atsá, his mother? And for Níyol, who'd never known his mother, his grandmother?

"No. Here."

"I can't insist, Mr. Yazzie, but I'm asking you." Coughs wracked the boys. Their eyes, when they opened, drifted toward something unseen. Their lips were parched, cracked, their necks severely swollen.

Yazzie slouched with weakness. "Better. To face it." He'd already given up, that was what he meant.

She looked down at him. "Not yet, Mr. Yazzie. I hold out hope."

Will, standing in the kitchen drinking a cup of coffee, said nothing when she carried Níyol in. "Are you going to help?" she asked without stopping.

"What are you doing? We need to stay away from them."

"Too late," she said.

She settled Níyol into the bed, Will's bed, in the spare room. Yazzie, coughing violently, came through the doorway sideways, his older boy in his arms. He laid 'Atsá down and then bent over, his elbows on his knees, trying to recover his breath. Johanna appeared behind him and grabbed his arm when he staggered. "Him, too," Julia said to her. "Will, get more pillows," she called to the kitchen.

The boys were so naturally thin, they tucked easily against their father's wider frame. Julia piled pillows under their heads and necks and behind their shoulders in an effort to ease their wheezing. Johanna retreated to a corner.

Out in the kitchen Will, still dressed in his filthy barn overalls and manure-covered boots, refused to ride the twenty-five miles to Tohatchi. Shouting ensued, but despite the violence of the quarrel he didn't raise a hand to her. He never had. They fell back into silence, broken by the coughing from the room where the Yazzies lay. In the end, as a peace offering, Will agreed to go the eight miles to Naschitti; he'd ask Tom Gorman to head out for Tohatchi and the doctor. Julia thought of asking for Tóya as well, but she knew that none of the Navajo woman's potions would alter the course of *'adáyi' dááhodiníchaad.*

Julia spent the afternoon and evening fetching warmed cloths to wrap around the boys' necks and pouring kettles of hot water into basins to increase the humidity in the room, hoping that that might calm the coughing. Should she stoke the fire or would their breathing be helped by the chill? Should she sit by the bed? Would holding tightly to the boys' hands pull them back into this world?

Will didn't return until long after dusk. The Gormans were safe, so far. Tom had set out immediately for Tohatchi.

No one slept that night, unless she regarded the boys' torpor or their father's fretful tossing as rest. Whenever Julia left the room, Johanna assumed her chair, only to abandon it again when Julia returned, though the place beside the boys and her brother was rightfully Johanna's. When Julia asked her if she wanted a chair, Johanna, having tucked herself back into the corner, a blanket wrapped around her shoulders and drawn-up knees, gave no indication that she did.

In the morning, after the boys died, Clement Yazzie lay alone in the bed, unwilling or unable to talk. She had to forget about the boys; they were beyond her help. She dried her tears and washed her face with cold water. Maybe Yazzie was beyond help, too, but she couldn't allow that to stop her, not until all was lost.

She spoke in Navajo: "Johanna, help me move your brother."

They managed to sit him upright and swing his legs over the side of the bed.

"Where are you taking him?" Will asked. He was standing in the doorway, leaning against the frame.

"I'm putting him in my room."

Will walked over and grabbed her arm, pulling her aside. Through clenched teeth he half-whispered, "One sick room isn't enough? As it is, it'll be a miracle if you don't catch it yourself."

"He can't stay here. His boys died in here."

He drew in his chin and narrowed his eyes. "Because their chindis might haunt him? You must be joking."

"Let go." She yanked her arm from his grip.

Yazzie, hunched, sat on the side of the bed. The cough tore through him again. Johanna took one arm, Julia the other, and they helped him stand.

"*Hooghan*," Yazzie said. Home.

"You'd best be quiet," Julia told him. He didn't fight.

When they had Yazzie in her bed, Julia reentered the spare room and closed the door behind her. Will was still standing there, his arms folded. She said, "I need you to take everything out of here. Strip it—bedding, blankets, curtains . . . everything. Pile it outside. We'll burn it later. Everything else that can't be washed in boiling water needs to be wiped down with carbolic soap."

"Do you think you're actually helping anyone?" Will asked.

"Why don't you just move to town?" she lashed out. Why wouldn't he just get out of her way? "Get yourself a room in a boarding house until the epidemic has passed."

"What would be the point? If we haven't already caught the damn disease . . . My clothes are in the wardrobe. Should I burn them too?"

"If you'd like."

"Jesus, Julia."

"And I want you to smash the window."

"Smash—?" He was incredulous.

"As loudly as you can."

"Jesus!" he repeated. "So their chindis will have a way to leave? You've really gone Indian, haven't you?"

Julia threw up her hands and then let them fall to her sides, open in supplication. "What's important now is what Mr. Yazzie believes."

"And I suppose you're now an expert in that?"

"I don't understand *anything* about him! But he's Navajo—"

"Half-Navajo," he corrected her.

"—and his two sons just died in this room, and I don't know what else to do. We need him, Will."

He scowled. "Speak for yourself. I don't like him and I certainly don't need him."

"Please do what I'm asking. Or, never mind, I'll do it myself." Her eyes scanned the room. She could use the chair.

"He's not going to survive the night, so all of this is pointless."

"Then maybe we should just drag him out to the hogan now. Why wait?"

"Suits me."

"Why *don't* you move to town," she repeated.

"Maybe we should burn the whole goddamn building down. That's what they do with their hogans when someone dies inside, isn't it? Then we can both move to town and be done."

Julia didn't reply. She retreated, sat down at the dining table, her head on her arms. Will came and sat across from her, picking at a hangnail; she wished he would cut his nails shorter, keep them cleaner. (Back East, he'd been so fastidious.) Exhausted, she asked herself how much longer it would take for Harry Whitaker to arrive. If he arrived at all. He couldn't simply abandon Tohatchi to the epidemic.

"How did we come to this?" Will asked. He, too, appeared weary of the fighting.

"Through one catastrophic decision after another."

"Why don't we just pack up and get the hell out of here, Julia? And I don't mean moving into Gallup. Hell, I don't even like Indians. They're as ignorant as niggers, and nothing's going to change that. And the Mexicans, they're just as bad. Unless they get their hands on a little money, like your friend Rodriguez, and then they think they can lord it over us. Come on, Julia," he pleaded, "this has never been what we expected, and it never will be."

"I didn't expect anything," Julia said. "All the expectations were yours."

"But you won't leave, will you?"

"No."

"Why the hell not? Because we sank all our money into this?"

Our money? she thought. "No."

"We have what counts," he said, tapping both middle fingers to his temples. "Up here. We can still make a go of it somewhere else. Somewhere civilized. San Francisco. Denver."

"No."

"Why?"

"I can't say."

"Can't or won't?"

"I don't have an answer."

"Ah, Julia," he said, shaking his head and reaching out to take her hand. She let him. "I remember a night, not long after we came out here, when we were lying bare-ass naked, soaking the bed, and my fingers were twiddling in your bush and you started laughing. Do you remember?"

"No."

"And I was thinking, if the Reverend Daddy Marshall could see his little jewel now, splayed out like a whore and enjoying it, he'd sure as hell drop dead on the spot."

"A whore isn't necessarily what most men look for in a wife."

"I don't remember your ever turning me away in those days, except when you had your monthlies, and not always then."

"It all washed off in the morning."

"If we had a kid you'd see things differently."

"If that were going to happen, it would have by now."

"I don't blame you, Julia. That'd be like blaming God because the sun doesn't come up in the west. I assign no blame."

"That's good of you," she said.

He released her hand. "You've had your say," he told her. "I'll do what you want. I'll let that Indian die in our bed. I'll burn the mattress and the blankets and the curtains. I'll knock out the window. Hell, I'll even tear down the room, right to the studs if you want." He stood up and leaned across the table, a forefinger pointed at her breastbone; she drew back instinctively. "But you're going to wake up some morning and find yourself alone. Maybe that's what you think you want. Well, keep this up and you'll have a chance to find out."

He slammed the outside door behind him, and Julia set more water to boil before returning to Yazzie's bedside. She wished she had something she could force him to drink besides water and black tea; something astringent—a squeezed lemon, crushed cranberries (so long since she'd bitten into one back in Massachusetts!), even whiskey—that might help clear the phlegm from Yazzie's throat and ease the coughing. She had salt for a gargle, and not much else. Tóya would have something. Why hadn't she sent for Tóya? An astringent herb. Or cliff rose—didn't Tóya use its leaves for a cough medicine?

The shattering glass startled her, and Yazzie's eyes opened wide. Several additional blows followed, metal against wood. Will was attacking the jamb with ferocity. Julia folded her hands in her lap and closed her eyes until the noise stopped. The last sound from the spare room, causing Julia to start again, was that of the thrown hammer hitting the connecting door and falling to the floor. She opened her eyes and looked at Yazzie. His eyes looked into hers. She offered no explanation.

Only then she realized that Johanna had left.

"Ah should've gotten here sooner. Ah'm so sorry." Harry Whitaker looked like he hadn't slept in days, and exhaustion released his drawl as certainly as alcohol released slurred speech in the afflicted. "Both boys?"

"Yes, one after the other," Julia said.

"And Yazzie?"

"He's here. He came down with it after they did, but I'm afraid he's catching up."

"Ah thought the worst was over, and maybe it is. It's hard to know. Patients who recover can still be contagious for some time, so Ah shouldn't be surprised when there's a flare-up. That's what delayed me." His lips were nearly the color of his skin, dreadfully pale, and he hadn't shaved in several days, his reddish whiskers less blond than either his mustache or his hair.

"Harry, you don't need to explain. Please, sit down," she said, taking his hat and helping him remove his heavy coat.

"No, first I'll see Yazzie."

Julia led him into her bedroom, carrying his bag for him. Johanna, who had returned and was now sitting by the bed, moved aside.

"Yazzie," he said, "Ah'm going to look you over, if that's all right."

Yazzie opened his eyes but didn't speak. The pillow was streaked with bloody mucus; it also caked the edges of his nostrils.

Harry opened his leather bag and withdrew a white cloth, a surgical mask, that he deftly tied in place. He took out another for Julia and handed it to her.

"It's a little late, don't you think?" Julia asked.

"You never know," he said. "If Ah were you, Ah would wear a mask every time Ah come in here." He glanced at Johanna sitting in the corner and turned again to Julia. "Has Johanna shown any symptoms?"

"No."

"Well, that's something, Ah s'pose." He took out another surgical mask and, speaking in Navajo, asked Johanna to tie it over her mouth and nose. Johanna didn't move.

"I don't think she'll do it," Julia said. She took the third mask from him and placed it on the nightstand. "Maybe I can convince her later."

Harry leaned over the bed. He placed a palm on Yazzie's forehead and then the backs of his fingers on a cheek. He lifted Yazzie's chin and gently palpated his grossly swollen neck. "Please open your mouth." He asked Julia, "Would you hold a lamp for me?"

Julia picked up the table lamp and stepped closer, directing the light toward Yazzie. Harry took a metal tongue depressor and a laryngeal mirror from his bag so that he could see the upper reaches of Yazzie's throat. "Ah'm assuming you know why you're sick."

Yazzie coughed harshly.

Leaning over, Dr. Whitaker spent a full minute manipulating the instruments and then withdrew them. He straightened his back. "You know that there's no medicine Ah can give you for this?"

Yazzie looked at him through slit eyes.

"Not mine nor Navajo. Ah respect the wisdom of the hataałii, but not even the most powerful singer can set you right. Diphtheria always runs its course. People who survive do so because their bodies are strong enough to fight off the infection and its poisons." He took his stethoscope from his bag. "Can you sit up?"

Yazzie pushed himself to his elbows and the doctor grabbed an arm and helped him up the rest of the way. "This will help me hear your breathing and your heart." He placed the bell inside Yazzie's damp, rancid shirt and listened for a protracted time before moving the stethoscope several inches to the right and then the left. Next, he lifted Yazzie's shirt and applied the stethoscope to his back, left and right.

Julia turned her eyes away. Yazzie had a terrible scar, ragged and grayish purple, running down the right side of his rib cage. She'd never seen it before.

"How'd you get that scar?" Dr. Whitaker asked when he was done listening to Yazzie's lungs.

"Doesn't matter," Yazzie said hoarsely.

The doctor sat down in the straight chair. "Your throat is sore?"

"Aoo'," the voice rasped before another spate of coughing. Yazzie collapsed to the pillows.

The doctor reached for Yazzie's hand. He pinched the skin on the back of it, beside the prominent veins. "He's very dry. Dehydrated." To Julia he said, "We're going to have to get some fluids into him, and soon. Water, Navajo tea—at this point, it doesn't matter what." He returned his stethoscope to his bag. Leaning forward, elbows on knees, he sighed.

"Ah don't wish to burden you, Mr. Yazzie, any more than these terrible days have already done, but Ah'd like you to understand what's happening inside. Here." He spread a hand at the base of his own neck. "Diphtheria kills some of the lining in the throat and windpipe, which swell up. What's more, the dead tissue forms a very tough membrane—something like a thick layer of skin—and together the swelling and the membrane can cut off a person's breathing. The patient suffocates.

"Ah'm telling you all this, both of you"—he looked up at Julia and then back to Yazzie—"because Ah won't mislead you. Ah'd be much more diplomatic with most Navajos, talking about these things, but Ah'm too tired." He smiled weakly. "Besides, you already know the worst of it. You've seen it right here. But Ah also want you to understand that many people who are strong and healthy beforehand can fight it off. There's no way to predict."

Whitaker removed a small leather case from his bag and turned again to Yazzie, whose eyes had never left the doctor. "This is what Ah can try to do. You have a membrane forming up above your throat, in what we call the posterior nares, behind your nose."

"Can you remove it?" Julia asked.

"No. It sticks snug to the living tissue, and even if Ah could get at it and tear it away, the bleeding could be dangerous."

"There must be something—"

Dr. Whitaker held up his hand to hush her. "That membrane doesn't really worry me that much. Even if it closes off your nose, you can still breathe through your mouth. What worries me more is that there's something going on that Ah can't see, down in your windpipe. Ah can hear it with my stethoscope when you breathe. It may be another membrane. Do ya'll understand?"

There was nothing Julia could say; Yazzie just stared straight ahead.

"This is what Ah can do," the doctor said. "Ah can insert a breathing tube in your windpipe. Maybe it'll help, maybe it won't." He opened the small case, removed a small metal cylinder, and held it up between thumb and forefinger: about three inches long, gold-colored, slightly wider at the middle but no more than half an inch in diameter except at a broader lip. "It'll take me a minute to position it. Maybe a bit longer. It won't be pleasant. It'll cause you to cough repeatedly, and gag as well, and until Ah get it placed properly you won't be able to breathe. But it may keep the passage into your lungs open."

"May?" Julia asked.

"*May*," the doctor repeated. "If something obstructs the passageway farther down toward the lungs or if phlegm—*chátłish*," he added for Yazzie's benefit—"plugs the tube, or if you develop pneumonia, it won't help."

"That tube is so narrow," Julia said, but with a flicker of hope in her voice. "Can he actually get enough air through it?"

"You'd be surprised." He addressed Yazzie: "After five or six days Ah should be able to remove it. You should be on the mend by then. Or . . . not."

Yazzie neither spoke nor nodded, but he closed his eyes.

Dr. Whitaker said, "There you have it." He sat back in the chair. "So, do you want me to try? Ah'm leaving it up to you."

Yazzie slowly shook his head.

"You want me to let you be?"

Yazzie nodded once.

"And what about Johanna?" Julia immediately asked Yazzie. She would *not* let this happen. Everything needed to be tried.

Yazzie opened his eyes and looked up at her. He knew what she meant. "*Bizeedí*," he muttered.

"Her cousin? Your mother's niece? You think so? When was the last time they saw each other? Do you really think anyone in Crystal would feel obligated, except to get their hands on the land? Isn't that what you've told me yourself?"

Yazzie closed his eyes. His chest rose and fell heavily. "You," he said.

"*Me*?" Julia said.

"Ha! Wouldn't that just beat the band," Will said from the doorway. He'd been in the store doing something—taking inventory or sweeping the floor, Julia didn't know what—when Harry arrived and only now made an appearance.

"Will," she said coldly, "please see to Dr. Whitaker's horse." He walked away without answering. It suddenly occurred to her that he'd been drinking. She tried to put the thought aside.

Johanna, impassive, was looking at Julia, who wondered if Johanna understood that they were talking about what might happen to her if her brother died. "Mr. Yazzie"—Julia leaned in, lowering her voice—"you must have a sense of how close to the edge I am here. If we were to lose the trading post, what would become of Johanna then? *I* couldn't protect her—I couldn't do anything."

Harry sat with his head in his hands, drifting with exhaustion. Julia wouldn't have been surprised if he fell off the chair.

No one appeared to have anything more to say.

Yazzie was overcome by a prolonged fit of coughing, brutal efforts to clear the way to his lungs.

Johanna pulled her blanket tighter around her shoulders.

Dr. Whitaker's chin hit his chest.

"Clement," Julia pleaded.

Yazzie's eyes roamed from one side of the room to the other and then came to rest on the closed door to the room where his sons had died. And then on Johanna.

Yazzie stretched out his hand and tapped Dr. Whitaker once on the knee. "Do it," he whispered.

They helped him to the straight-backed chair. Julia steadied the back of his head against her bosom, one hand cupping his chin. Harry, mumbling beneath his breath, was having difficulty knotting a loop of heavy black thread through a small round hole in the lip of the breathing tube; the thread would allow the tube to be pulled out if it slipped down the windpipe toward the lungs, or when it was no longer needed.

Julia stared ahead, not daring to look down at Clement Yazzie's black, black hair and clammy forehead, coated with sickeningly sweet sweat, and the eyes bloodshot from the grim coughing. What she was doing felt fiercely intimate, more intimate than she'd ever been with any man except her husband.

The doctor tied the other end of the black surgical thread around his own wrist. He was ready. "Open your mouth as wide as you can," he told Yazzie. He inserted an instrument—he called it a gag—that looked like warped tongs. It would hold down Yazzie's tongue and also prevent him from closing his mouth. When the instrument was positioned, Julia did as Dr. Whitaker instructed, taking the handle from him. He'd need both hands free for the intubation. Yazzie was breathing heavily, taking as much air into his lungs as possible. "Are you ready?" the doctor asked him. Julia, now with both hands occupied, felt Yazzie's chin press into her palm. She glanced down. Yazzie's eyes— mahogany irises, the void at the center—were focused on her masked face, which, if not previously flushed, surely was now.

"All right," Harry Whitaker said. He took a deep breath, glanced at Julia—she needed to hold Yazzie's head and the gag steady, no matter how much Yazzie might struggle—and drew the patient's right cheek aside with his left forefinger. Using his right hand he quickly inserted the tube, which was attached to the end of a pincer-like introducer. Yazzie began simultaneously coughing and gagging. *Oh God,* Julia thought. She could feel his tongue and the muscles under his chin repeatedly contracting and his jaws fighting to close. The doctor had told them both to expect this, that there was nothing Yazzie could do to control the body's reflexes. With all the strength in her left hand Julia gripped the handle of the gag.

Harry moved his forefinger farther into Yazzie's mouth and down his throat, guiding the breathing tube past the epiglottis, which separated the passages to stomach and lungs, and into the windpipe.

Quickly! Quickly! Julia thought. She looked down again at Yazzie, stiffened against the chair, his tears, forced from his eyes by the gagging and coughing, streaming into his hair. She glanced at Johanna, whose mouth hung open, her eyes wide.

With a turn of his wrist the doctor released the gold tube from the slender introducer, which he swiftly withdrew and let clatter to the floor. Now he'd have to press the wide lip of the tube into place with his finger, anchoring it in the laryngeal bands above the vocal cords. "Almost," he said, "almost." She could feel the fingers of his right hand, thrust as far as possible into Yazzie's mouth, pushing against the gag, which she held so tightly that her hand was shaking. She didn't know how much longer she could maintain her grip.

Harry pulled his hands away. "It's there," he said. He took the handle of the gag from Julia and released it. Yazzie's chin pulled from Julia's hand and he bent forward, still coughing, but between explosions he appeared better able to pull air into his lungs.

"The coughing should ease up in a minute or two," Harry said, one hand on the Navajo's shoulder. The black thread, still attached to the inhalation tube, dangled from Yazzie's mouth.

Julia straightened up and, flexing her fingers, wiped the back of her cramped hand across her forehead. She looked down. Yazzie's sweat and snot had soaked the bodice of her dress; the mingled putrid and sweet odors threatened to turn her stomach.

Having grabbed a clean dress from her wardrobe, and having fled to the spare bedroom, Julia stripped off her soiled clothing and left it in a heap. The room's tattered curtain waved at her, driven by the cold air from the broken window—Will had done a proficient job, shattering glass, smashing sill and sash, gouging the framing—and she hurried to step into and button another dress, even as the chill erupted on her skin. The coughing from the other room had stopped. At least for now.

"And how are *you?*" Harry Whitaker, seated at the dining table, asked Julia. She'd been striding from one end of the kitchen to the other, brewing a fresh pot of coffee and spreading before him dishes of anything she could find in the larder that he might want to eat.

"In good health," she replied. They were alone; Will had disappeared again.

"How many times have you done that?" Julia now asked.

"Used an O'Dwyer tube? Twice, in children."

"And?"

"Both died anyway."

She stood still, holding a small bowl of hard-boiled eggs still in their brown shells. "What are Mr. Yazzie's chances?"

"One in three, they say."

"Even with the tube?"

"Maybe a hair better."

"I see." Julia set the bowl down on the table.

"Diphtheria can kill a body in all sorts of ways. Asphyxiation. Pneumonia. Or blood poisoning—the poison spreads into the blood stream from where the infection starts. It can mortally weaken the heart and other organs. And I've even seen children and the elderly die from sheer exhaustion. They reach a point where they can't even cough anymore."

"And if the breathing tube doesn't help?"

Harry Whitaker shook his head.

"You could perform a tracheotomy." She sat down across from him.

"Julia," he said, shaking his head again. "I need to get back to Tohatchi. I can't sit and wait to see if his condition worsens. Besides, cutting directly into his windpipe . . . it's surgery, and not very successful in diphtheria patients, even if I was equipped to try. You run the very real risk of another infection through the incision."

Selfishly, she wanted to keep Harry here as long as possible. Anyway, he needed to sleep, she could see that. She couldn't let him go back out onto the road until he'd slept for at least a few hours. After he'd filled his stomach, maybe he would realize how dangerous it would be to fall asleep traveling at night—the sun had already dipped behind the mountains—in February, with the temperature dropping below freezing. "How much longer is the epidemic going to last?" she asked.

"Probably into the spring."

"How many more breathing tubes do you have?" If he'd arrived in time, could he have saved the boys? No, probably not; she'd put her ear to their chests and had heard the rales.

"Four." He was filling a plate with cheese, bread-and-butter pickles, potted beef, bread. "I ordered more when I purchased the kit, but they haven't arrived. Some tubes are a little longer, for adults."

"And Mr. Yazzie's—?"

"The largest I had, intended for a typical eleven- or twelve-year-old. That's one of the reasons why I left the surgical thread attached. I have no way of knowing if the tube will dislodge because of his larger windpipe. I've read that patients typically cough it out when that happens, but if it were to drop into a lung . . ." He waved off the possibility but Julia understood that such a mishap would be fatal. "Anyway, someone should stay near him, just in case he suddenly starts strangling and can't pull the tube out himself." He yawned. "And he shouldn't try to talk. The tube passes right through the vocal folds, and he could permanently damage his voice. The last thing we need is *two* Yazzies who can't talk." He tried to stifle another yawn.

Good, Julia thought. He won't be able to stay awake much longer.

"How did Yazzie take it?" Harry asked. "His boys."

Julia's eyes clouded. That was yesterday. Only yesterday. "He didn't say anything when we took 'Atsá from him. He lay there with his arms around the little one, Níyol, until it was over. He let me take Níyol away, too, and then he pulled a pillow over his face to muffle his weeping."

"Where are the boys now?"

Julia wiped her eyes with her hands. "I don't know. Gone. Johanna knew what to do. She went for Tim Be'ak'idii, up at Blue Hawk Lake. Tim knew Mr. Yazzie's mother going all the way back to the end of the Long Walk. So Johanna found him and he came down and took care of the bodies the Navajo way. I suppose they're buried out there somewhere. No marker, nothing to show that they were ever in this world." Julia reached for a nearby napkin and blew her nose.

"What about Johanna?"

"I don't know." Julia took an egg from the bowl and began peeling away the shell. "She slept on the floor beside the bed last night, if she slept at all. I gave her a bedroll from the store. I suspect she'll do the same tonight."

The fatigue again filled the doctor's voice: "Ah should examine her before Ah leave. And you and Will as well."

"I doubt she'll let you touch her. And Will and I are fine."

"Julia, you've been breathing the same air as Yazzie. The closer you get to him, the greater the risk."

"Even with your elegant surgical mask?"

"Yes, even with the mask." Smiling thinly, elbows propped on the table, he was holding up his head with his hands. "Honestly, Ah don't know if the mask does any good at all." He'd stopped eating. He could barely keep his eyes open.

"Harry," Julia said, "I can't possibly let you leave here like this. There's a pallet already prepared over there by the box stove." Where she'd slept fitfully last night. "It's not the most comfortable bed, but I doubt you'll notice when your head hits the pillow. Sleep for a few hours. Even if you could make it back to Tohatchi tonight, you wouldn't be of any use."

He didn't argue.

"No one will disturb you." Where was Will? she wondered. "Make yourself comfortable. I'll wake you in three hours."

While he settled himself in the parlor, she cleared the table. Then she went to the outside door and opened it. Will had attended to Harry's horse; the traces lay empty. Maybe Will was still in the stable. She didn't care.

She returned to the bedroom carrying a bowl of water and a teaspoon. Earlier, when the breathing tube was first in, Clement Yazzie had attempted to drink a glass of water, a sip at a time, but he kept choking on it; some of the water would enter the tube in his windpipe and he'd cough uncontrollably. The last thing Yazzie needed, Harry Whitaker had said, was to aspirate. So he showed Julia what to do.

Now, she set the bowl and spoon down on the nightstand and sat on the edge of the bed. Harry had said she needed to do this every hour, a full cup of water at the very least, until Mr. Yazzie started urinating on a regular basis—that would be a sign that he was getting enough fluids. He could live for many days without food, but not without water.

Yazzie's eyes were closed, but he wasn't asleep. She touched his shoulder and he groaned. "I know," she said, "I know, but we have to do this. We've come this far." Julia, doing her best to ignore the miasma, the overwhelming stench of disease, repositioned the pillows behind his shoulders so that his head was tipped sharply backward. She lifted the spoon and let the trickle of water flow into the corner of his mouth. Johanna watched from her corner. He swallowed it cleanly, the water seeping down the back of his throat, away from his windpipe. She dipped the spoon in the bowl again. "It must hurt to swallow. I'm so sorry."

He couldn't speak; he didn't acknowledge what she said.

Teaspoon by teaspoon, he took the water, interrupted frequently by the barking diphtherial cough.

Harry Whitaker slept, oblivious. Nothing moved except his chest, rising and falling so evenly. Julia eased into the armchair beside the pallet, lifted her legs to the hassock, draped a throw over her chest and arms. It'd taken nearly half an hour for Clement Yazzie to swallow a cup of water. In another hour, they'd do it over again. Until then, she'd try to nap. Where was Will? Drinking? Not even her anger could hold her eyelids up. Where had he hidden it. In the cow shed? . . .

* * *

She woke with a start. What had disturbed her? She heard Clement Yazzie's cough. What time was it? She looked at the mantel clock she kept on a bookshelf. Three hours had passed. She needed to slap herself awake, pull herself from the chair, attend to Mr. Yazzie. Harry Whitaker—she should wake him soon. After she dealt with Mr. Yazzie.

She rose and walked unsteadily toward the kitchen. She was so tired. She looked through the doorway of the bedroom. Johanna was sitting cross-legged on the bed, her brother's head in her lap, feeding him water as Julia had done, spoon by spoon.

Julia returned to her parlor, stirred up the coals in the box stove, added two pieces of pinyon to the fire, returned to her chair. She would let Harry Whitaker sleep another hour.

"If anything changes, if you show even the slightest symptom, you need to get word to me right away. You mind me, now," Harry Whitaker said. He was diving into another meal: bacon, fried eggs, fried potatoes, bread and butter. Five hours of sleep had revived him. Even though the night was still young, he was determined to head back to his patients in Tohatchi. He sopped up the yolk and bacon grease with the bread. Then he pushed back his empty plate.

"I should check on our patient," Harry said.

"What can I give him if he wants to eat?" Julia asked.

"Broth, strained soup, custard. Things that will slide easily down his throat. In very small bites."

"The thread won't cause a problem?" Harry had tied the surgical thread in a loose loop around Clement Yazzie's neck.

"If it moves around too much, it could cause an ulceration at the top of the windpipe, but he should be able to swallow soft foods. "

When they entered the bedroom, Clement Yazzie appeared to be sleeping. Harry decided that waking him would be pointless. He was leaving a bottle of codeine syrup for Julia to administer, a teaspoon every four hours; it would reduce the coughing and also help Yazzie sleep.

Julia helped Harry harness his horse. He'd arrived well equipped for a night journey, with a heavy Navajo blanket to cover his lap and legs as well as a wool coat trimmed at collar and cuff in beaver. She'd wrapped a meal of sliced mutton, cheese, bread, and dried fruits for him.

He told her he would return in four or, at most, five days, unless he heard otherwise from her. She understood. *Otherwise.*

Harry Whitaker's rig disappeared down the trail to the canyon mouth. The sky gave enough light for him to travel without a lit lantern. Carrying her own lantern, Julia immediately turned and walked to the guest hogan. Smoke poured from the stove chimney. She lifted the latch and pushed the door open. Even with the light from her lantern she didn't see Will at first. He lay in the darkness on one of the two pallets along the rear wall.

"Don't come in here," he said, his words slurred.

"You're drunk," she said.

Then he coughed. She knew that cough. Blood drained from her head and she leaned back against the wall to keep from falling. "Will," she said, "what have you done?"

"Done?"

"Harry just left. Why didn't you *say* something?"

"I don't want him anywhere near me. If he was any good, he wouldn't be out here doctoring to Indians."

"Let's get you up and back to the house." Several quick steps brought her beside him. He smelled of spilled alcohol and cloying sweat.

"No. I'll stay right here. You put a Navajo in our *bed,* so I'll just stay here in a *hogan,* if you don't mind. All you have to do is keep the fire going if I can't tend it myself. And if you'd be so kind, empty the piss-pot now and then. 'Cause I'm gonna lay right here and sweat this out."

"Will, you can't do that."

"Can't I? I've got four bottles of whiskey, and I'm going to sweat it out. Just see if I don't."

"You're not thinking straight."

His arms waved wildly, keeping her at bay. "I know how this *works.* You think I don't? I grew up in a filthy godforsaken orphanage, remember? This isn't the first time I've seen it. Or had it. I survived chicken pox and measles and mumps and whooping cough and a hundred bouts of the shits, *and* diphtheria. I missed the typhoid. At least I think I did. Ha!" His laugh dissolved into barks.

"Will, you know we could lose our license if anyone reports that we have any kind of spirits—"

"What are you, some sort of Carrie Nation now? No one on the god-blessed planet knows except me, you, and the fellow who supplied the samples. So, you leave me be, Julia. Step back now, or you'll get sprayed," waving her off. He coughed another half dozen times before catching his breath. "Somebody was always getting sick and dying, but I made it out of that orphanage, didn't I? They used to say that if you catch something a second time, it won't be as bad as the first. I don't know what Harry Whitaker would say about that. S'pose it depends."

Julia stood there, paralyzed. She couldn't drag him to the house. She tried again to reason with him, but he wouldn't listen. If the coughing progressed, she could give him the codeine syrup Harry had left for Yazzie. There should be enough to last several days if the two shared it. What else could she do? She could try to keep him comfortable. And clean, which, judging by his present state, would be a mean task. He'd fight his way through this. Or he wouldn't.

This wasn't how it should be, between Will and her. She'd given up on him, and he knew it. Now he'd show her what he was made of.

Had she ever loved him? Oh, she remembered very well the times they'd laughed together and enjoyed each other and worked together. There had been times, all too brief, approaching something that she imagined might be love, heart drawn to him, his touch, her touch on his arm or shoulder, her fingers in his hair, in moments of peace and tranquility, a summer evening, quiet all around, the sky deepening as night slid west and the evening star or crescent moon came up over a sandstone wall. But she'd learned that you can't make the heart feel what it doesn't. She'd come no closer to love, not that kind, so insubstantial in the end, chaff threshed into the air.

True to his word, Harry Whitaker drove up in his buggy five days later. Securing the reins, he asked Julia, who'd come out to greet him, "So how's our patient?" Harry looked much better than when she'd last seen him, clean-shaven now, possibly even rested, and the color restored to his face.

"I believe he's recovering," she answered, tight lipped, "although I'm afraid you traveled all this way for nothing. He's gone."

"Gone?"

"I'm sorry I couldn't get word to you. He and Johanna must have left before dawn—it looks like he pulled out your breathing tube and just left, without so much as a thank-you-very-much."

"I wouldn't take it personally," Harry said. "It's just their way, Navajos. I've gotten used to it—I don't expect anything."

"I know, but to just up and leave . . ." Julia said. How could she not take it personally? She'd held him in her arms, fed him—maybe even kept him alive—teaspoon by teaspoon.

Harry followed her onto the veranda and through the door into her kitchen. "He's lost his wife and now his boys. He's probably not in a thanking mood."

Julia pointed out where the O'Dwyer tube lay on the dining table. "I'm assuming you can use it again." She'd found it on the nightstand, the black thread hanging half way to the floor. She'd had to walk away to keep her gorge from rising. She didn't know why. A while later she returned to her room, picked up the tube with gloved fingers, carried it into the kitchen, and dropped it, thread and all, into a pan of boiling water. When the water cooled, she'd cut the thread away and placed the tube on a towel on the table.

"I could," Harry said, "but I doubt I will, at least not for diphtheria. In the end, I'm not convinced it's that helpful." He picked the tube up between thumb and forefinger and examined it. "It looks like solid gold," he said, "but in truth it's gold-plated brass." The right side of his mouth turned slyly upward and his Southern accent emerged: "As are many things."

"Speaking of which," she said with a sigh, "you should examine Will."

Julia led him to the hogan. Will had been living in his own stink— soiled clothes, spilled whiskey, farts, foul breath, sweat—for five days but appeared to be on the mend. At his request, she'd brought him solid food— eggs, potatoes, and onions fried in bacon grease—that morning, and though she didn't stay to watch him eat, she assumed he'd managed to swallow at least some of it.

"What do you think, Doc," Will said, "will I survive?" He'd worked his way through two of the four bottles of whiskey. He balanced the half-empty third on his belly.

Harry Whitaker, kneeling beside him, was listening to his lungs with the stethoscope. "Don't talk."

"The cough still comes on, especially in the evening," Julia said.

"That's to be expected for a while," Harry said, leaning back and re-moving the ear tips. "You'll survive," he said to Will, "but keep in mind that you're still contagious. You can pass it on, and the next person may not be so lucky."

"Lucky?" he snorted. "I wasn't lucky. I knew how to beat it. Whiskey and sweat. I didn't need an Indian doctor telling me what to do."

"Be that as it may," Harry said, "take what I say to heart. You're still contagious and will be for some time."

"Don't worry," Will said. "I'll keep away from your Indian nurse there."

Julia stiffened. "Let's go," she said to Harry.

"Do I *embarrass* you?" Will said.

"Do you *care* if you embarrass me?"

Julia and Harry left the hogan.

"I'm sorry," Julia said.

"He's letting the whiskey do his talking," Harry said. "He'll see things differently when he sobers up."

"I'd like to think so, but I don't." Will wasn't nearly as liquored-up as he pretended.

Later, after she'd convinced Harry to accept her hospitality, such as it was—a rudimentary meal and the pallet by the stove for another night—they sat in her parlor drinking tea.

He told her that the worst of the epidemic had clearly passed.

"I don't know why I didn't come down with it," she said, weighing the hours spent breathing the same air as Clement Yazzie and his boys.

"Who gets taken, who recovers—" Harry broke off, shaking his head. "They say the Black Death may have wiped out a third of Europe's population in the 1300s. Rats carried the plague germ, and it's likely that flea bites transferred it to people. But why did only a third die? Others got sick and recovered, but most people never fell ill even though many of them must have been bitten, too."

Julia recalled the stories of the eastern Indian tribes who were decimated by smallpox brought to the New World by sailors and the first settlers.

Harry smiled. "Ah suppose it wasn't to the germs' advantage to kill *everybody* off."

She liked him so very much. He calmed her. He didn't put on airs the way so many knowledgeable, successful men did, relegating women, at best, to helpmeets. "Surely, germs don't choose whom to infect."

"No, but nature has its balances. When enough rats died, the flea population declined, and the plague went back into hiding." He paused. "I see one or two cases of plague every year out here. Some years, more. It's always lurking in the shadows."

"Waiting?"

Harry shrugged. "Maybe someday science will explain it to everyone's satisfaction. Meanwhile, it's a mystery. One of the things I admire about the Navajo is that they don't tie themselves in knots about such things."

"You think that's a better way to live?" She was thinking of Will, still in the hogan, probably tallying some score that would leave her on the losing side.

"No, not better, though I think Navajos are more accepting of life's vagaries." He smiled. "You and Ah, we're not so constituted."

"You think not?" Julia said with an amused laugh.

"And maybe the Navajo won't be for much longer."

"Why not?"

"We've exposed them."

"To?"

"Why—to us!"

6. Commerce

FROM THE DETAILS provided by the society page, Julia expected that readers of the Albany *Evening Journal* on a certain day in April 1904 would have correctly concluded that the wedding of Penelope Marshall and Philip Malott turned out to be a delightful affair. Penelope was radiant and her groom was tall, handsome, patrician, and distant—at least to Julia, who'd arrived in Albany without her husband. (The word was passed that their precarious "business," some western outpost beyond the edge of civilization, couldn't spare both of them.) There were few Marshalls in attendance, but the Malotts turned out in full force: brothers and wives, sisters and husbands, staid uncles and prissy aunts, nieces and nephews, cousins—so many that the introductions alone overwhelmed Julia, who ended up remembering hardly anyone's name except for James, Philip's elder brother and best man, with whom she, in her role as matron of honor, was uncomfortably paired at the rehearsal dinner until he managed to escape to his stiff-nosed wife. The wedding took place on a Saturday in the Episcopalian Cathedral of All Saints on Swan Street, grandiose in its stony, buttressed Gothicness. How different from their father's modest, unornamented churches! The immensity of the nave and crossing and choir, the seventy-foot walls, dwarfed the wedding party, and not even the sunlight through the stained glass of the Great East Window, behind the altar, managed to warm Julia.

"Oh, Philip and I don't give a whit for all that!" Penelope had whispered to her the evening before as the rehearsal dinner at the Hampton Hotel on State Street was reaching its conclusion. Maybe, Julia thought, concealing a smile, but Penny was certainly basking in the light. "It's what his family expects, all the trappings."

"And who's paying for this?" Julia asked. She'd eaten less than half the food that had been placed so carefully before her, dish after dish, and had accepted only the first glass of the several wines poured by the white-gloved sommelier.

"Well," said Penelope, beautifully flushed by the wine and the occasion and—probably fearing her sister's disapproval—a hint of embarrassment, "the Malotts are paying for this lovely dinner, as is customary, but the wedding, that's all Edna, of course."

"And Father?"

"He let her make the arrangements."

Her father wouldn't wish to know the financial details, Julia concluded. He'd slowed considerably in the six years since she'd last seen him. Angina was the latest infirmity, Penelope, frowning, had informed her, but under

Edna's care he wanted for nothing. (He'd worn to the rehearsal a fashionably cut gray wool suit far finer than she'd ever seen him wear in his clerical days.)

"It's so good that you could come!" Penny gushed.

"How could I not?" Julia smiled.

"Oh, I don't mean for my wedding!" Penny said but then immediately corrected herself: "Of course I *do* mean for the wedding, but what I really mean is for Father, to see *him.*"

Julia put an arm around her sister's shoulders—how had Penny grown so tall?—and kissed her cheek. Behind Julia's façade, however, lay concern about the money she'd spent on the train fare and the formal dress and accoutrements.

Throughout the weekend Julia attempted to engage Philip in polite conversation, but that's all it amounted to—polite conversation. He worked for the New York Central, something to do with contracts although he was neither a lawyer nor an accountant. He asked her nothing about the West or the trading post or Will. He obviously had no interest, or perhaps he thought it best not to delve further into the standing of his soon-to-be in-laws: a father who was a former Congregational minister and therefore, ostensibly, a Christian (at least he hadn't been defrocked); a divorced step-mother whose tainted money came to her as a consequence of her first husband's scandalous behavior; and an older sister who'd virtually run off with a store clerk and now lived amid some savage Indian tribe in New Mexico Territory. Fortunately, the Malotts could safely ignore Edna's children and unruly grandchildren since they were hardly members of Penelope's "real" family.

Edna appeared to pay no heed to the Malotts' sense of superiority. She'd guided her step-daughter to Mount Holyoke College, where in Penelope's very first semester she met Philip, a senior at nearby Amherst College. An engagement quickly followed Philip's graduation. Julia had to admit that Edna had performed her duties well, at least as Edna herself saw them, and it was also easy to see that she was very fond of Penelope, who could charm anyone—even the Malotts, apparently—with her rose-petal complexion, blue eyes, dimpled smile, and exemplary manners.

On the afternoon of Julia's arrival in Albany, she and Edna had sat conversing in Edna's tea room. Her father attended them but contributed little to the conversation. Julia couldn't be sure of the reason—estrangement or a bewildering lack of engagement? He was pleasant, not displeased to see her, smiling, and sampling the various tea sandwiches—cucumber, cream cheese with bits of olive, raspberry jam—and smacking his lips. (When had he started doing *that*?) They didn't discuss money, Edna's or the Malotts', or the trading post, although Edna did ask after Will, who, Julia told her,

had quickly recovered from his bout of diphtheria. According to their friend
Dr. Whitaker, Will's childhood exposure to the disease, even all these years
later, had conferred a degree of immunity, enough, at least, to prevent the
worse consequences. She also told her step-mother about the death of Clement Yazzie's boys, without, however, mentioning anything about Yazzie's
own medical ordeal. Edna, who'd lived long enough to witness nearly every
imaginable disease pass through one generation or another of her own family—she herself had lost a child to a brain fever—commiserated: "Suffer the
little children. One can only hope that God took them into his bosom."

It seemed to Julia a curious statement. *"Our* God, or . . . ?"

"Oh, *I* wouldn't know," Edna said, sipping her tea. "Your Indians
must have *some* deity who's responsible for such things."

"Not really," Julia said, and left it at that.

After the wedding they returned to Edna's house—her father and
Edna's house—for the reception because Penelope had insisted on it, perhaps fearful of Edna's having to rent a ballroom and pay for another extrav-
agantly catered meal. People came and went, parading up the stone steps
and through the brownstone's double doors into the front hallway, which
led to the parlor and the sitting room and thence, through French doors,
into the dining room—so many unknown faces that Julia spent fifteen
minutes virtually crammed in a corner, by a bay window and a potted palm
as tall as she, making small talk with an elegantly dressed, balding gentleman,
a Mr. Higgins—in the hubbub, she didn't catch his first name—an acquaintance of the groom's father whom she only later realized was the Republican
lieutenant governor of New York, Frank W. Higgins.

In the evening Penelope and Philip left by train for their honeymoon
in New York and Philadelphia. A European tour would await another day.
First, however, Penny assured Julia, they fully intended to visit her out west,
perhaps continuing on to San Francisco. Julia, who was genuinely happy for
Penny, nevertheless hated to see her leave, which left Julia alone with her
father and step-mother for three more days, until her own departure. The
threesome had already exhausted all safe topics of conversation, ranging
from the weather to President Roosevelt to the riff-raff that had taken to
frequenting nearby Washington Park.

THE RETURN TRAIN, approaching Gallup, gradually slowed, permitting
Julia a welcome view of the red sandstone cliffs, crowned by the towers of
Church Rock, to the north. The East had felt so claustrophobic, with the
trees leafing out in their various greens. All of Albany seemed to crowd her:

the horizon lay obstructed in every direction, the roads beyond the city curved into hidden esses, and even the damp air weighed her down. She hadn't realized how deeply she'd absorbed the pleasure of endless distances out here, which not even the soot and fumes coughed out by the locomotive could diminish.

She did, and yet didn't, know what awaited her at Many Springs. She and Will hadn't parted on good terms. They'd been continually at odds ever since the winter, and especially since the epidemic. These days, when they discussed anything but the most mundane task, she found no ease, no comfort; each, in the other's view, was always in the wrong. They couldn't help picking, bleeding each other into protracted silences. Days passed without their exchanging a word, and when they did speak, the subject more often than not was the business, the precarious state of the accounts, and, pending receipt of the earnings from the spring wool shearing, the necessity of ignoring repeated payment requests from a host of vendors. Wholesale wool prices were up, largely due to a shortage of cotton, enough to compensate for a slight drop in the quantity of wool brought to the trading post. They'd missed the last price crash, in the 1890s, but no one could predict when the next would come. She did know, however, that they would never survive it, not unless they found another way to do business.

Her thoughts on the matter kept drifting to Clement Yazzie.

Two weeks after Harry Whitaker's return visit to Many Springs, with the diphtheria epidemic on the wane, she'd reopened the trading post. The Gormans came back to work, bringing with them their elder son, Johnny, sixteen, who'd attended the Fort Defiance Indian School but now wanted to work. He could read and write and was good with his sums and could spare his father on the long trips to pick up freight from Gallup. Will had said no at first, insisting that they couldn't afford to pay another employee, but Julia had ultimately agreed if Johnny would accept half pay until they received their earnings from the spring shearing.

She hadn't seen either Yazzie or Johanna for over three weeks, after their silent departure in the middle of the night. The day before the store reopened, she'd walked up the canyon to the Yazzie place, only to find Tim Be'ak'idii looking after the animals. The old man, dour as ever, wouldn't tell her anything of consequence. How were Mr. Yazzie and Johanna? Good. Where were they? He didn't know. Had they gone to see a singer? He couldn't say. When would they be back? Soon.

And then one day Clement Yazzie simply showed up at the trading post. Julia found him standing, as he often did, near the bullpen, leaning back with his elbows on the counter, listening to the four Navajo men who were smoking and talking. He was thinner, his face more angular beneath the flat-brimmed hat. He observed her entrance but then turned back to the conversation. His indifferent response, though no more phlegmatic than ever, sent Julia into a temper that she barely contained. Straight on, she crossed the floor to him.

"Mr. Yazzie," she said, "I thought we had an agreement."

He turned to her. He was smoking a cigarette, which he rarely did. He said nothing.

"That you would inform me whenever you intended to be absent." She folded her arms across her chest.

He let the smoke trail from his nostrils. "The store was closed," he said. His voice was very raspy—had his vocal cords been damaged? "I didn't think it mattered."

Didn't matter. He gave her nothing, no acknowledgement of his illness, her care, his boys—

Of course not his boys. Navajos didn't speak of the dead. Which was just as well, because she might not have been able to contain her tears if he did.

Tom Gorman, who'd been working behind the counter, began whistling to himself and moved farther away. The conversation in the bullpen had ceased, which meant that at least one of the four men understood English; he'd do the translating later for the others, who'd undoubtedly be highly amused.

She said, "We've taken on Johnny Gorman, so I'm afraid there may be less for you to do." She hadn't intended to say any of this.

"If you say so."

Now she felt that *she* was the one who had to make amends:

"Is Johanna well?"

"Yes."

"When I didn't see her around, I worried."

"No reason to." He released a plume of smoke. "She left something for you."

"She did? When?"

"Yesterday, while you were here in the store."

What could Johanna possibly have left for her? "I didn't notice anything. What did she leave?"

"There's that wooden box on your dresser. Look in there."

A rosewood box with mother-of-pearl inlays: dahlias, twined stems, leaves. She'd shown it to Johanna once, more than a year ago, that and the pewter-framed photographs taken of her and Penelope, and of Penny alone when she was still a girl of fifteen. Julia had seen Johanna glancing through the doorway on a day when the sunshine, entering through the bedroom's window, happened to fall on the dresser top and reflect off the glass that protected the photographs. She brought Johanna into the room, showed her the portraits, named her sister, and, noticing that Johanna's eyes had drifted to the rosewood box, opened it for her. Inside were personal items: letters she'd kept, her birth and marriage certificates, jewelry. How odd that Johanna would put something in there!

"There's something I want to talk to you and your husband about," Yazzie said.

"Regarding?"

"Business."

"Business?"

He took a last pull on the cigarette and crushed the ember with the toe of his boot. "Aoo'."

He had nothing more to say to her?

"Then come by after dinner," she said and walked away, her face aflame.

That evening they sat at the dining table, Clement Yazzie on one side, Julia on the other, Will at the end, between them.

She'd calmed herself since the morning by going about her business, which included selling sundries—sewing needles, several yards of calico and velveteen, a can of baking powder, a carving knife—to a woman from up Washington Pass, one of the few Navajos who somehow managed to keep a surplus in her store account. In the afternoon, with activity in the store having slowed down, she'd turned her attention to a corner of the storeroom, sorting the various woven blankets and rugs that had piled up. She needed to sell more of these, not by the pound to wholesalers, but individually. Maybe she could partition off a real rug room like the one at the Hubbell Trading Post, and display the better rugs to advantage for when the odd traveler happened by.

At dinner Will had reluctantly agreed to hear Yazzie out, if only to placate Julia. Now, with the three of them sitting at the table, Will got directly to the point. "So let's have it," he said.

Yazzie folded his leathery hands on the table. "You're never going to make money selling sacks of flour."

"What's that supposed to mean?" Will said. Julia could see that he aimed to pick a fight. "We're merchants. That *is* how we make our money. A nickel here, a dime there."

Julia understood what Yazzie meant, but he, too, had started off as if he wanted a battle. Of course both she and Will knew that no small trader could possibly scratch out more than the meanest existence selling everyday supplies to the Navajo.

"Will," Julia said, "give him a chance. Go ahead, Mr. Yazzie."

"This is what I think: there are ways for Anglo traders to make money on the reservation. You can sell more wool."

"And how do we do that?" Will asked.

"The People ask around before they take their wool to a trader. They'll go where the price is best."

"Are you suggesting that we pay more than the others traders in the area?" Julia asked.

"You could," Yazzie said.

"No, we can't do that," Julia said. "No trader would come out ahead." She remembered her and Will's first conversation, more than five years ago, with the Gormans. "We all depend on wool earnings, and we can't start trying to outbid each other." Yazzie certainly already knew this.

"Or you can own your own sheep."

"What the hell," Will scoffed.

Julia jumped in before Will could say more: "I know other traders, like Mr. Hubbell in Ganado, raise sheep and cattle and horses," Julia said, "but they have homestead claims off the reservation or have purchased title to railroad sections. We don't own any land here or anywhere else, and trading licenses don't include any right to herd or run stock. We'd need permission from the tribe and the Indian agent at Fort Defiance before we could even rent an allotment."

"There's another way. Half-shares."

"Now this begins to make sense," Will said, scowling. "We buy sheep, you let them graze on your land, and then you keep half the lambs and half the earnings. So who is it that makes the money on this deal?"

Julia said, "I know you have good land by reservation standards—"

"Not exactly a lush meadow," Will cut her off.

"—but how many more sheep can it support?"

"I'd sell you some of my churro. They give the best wool on the reservation."

Yazzie had managed to keep his herd entirely churro, culling, as his mother before him, the cross-breed lambs that inevitably occurred on an open range. His sheep also showed the broadest array of colors, from white to apricot to pitch black. Spun properly, the wool could be blended into any natural shade: white, off-white, tans, browns, grays, blacks.

"Tell me this," Will said, "whose sheep are we talking about here? For you Navajos, the women own the sheep, don't they? So are these your sheep or your sister's? Or are you giving us your sister's and keeping your own? Just how would this work?" Julia brushed stray strands of hair back behind her ears and sighed. Will wasn't helping. She wanted to get this over with before it became more rancorous. "If you need money, Mr. Yazzie, why don't you—"

"I don't need cash money," Yazzie answered.

"Besides, the words "churro" and "best" don't belong in the same sentence," Will continued, "not if you're talking about value." He straightened his shoulders, leaned over the table. Julia let him talk. He knew the wool market—the sort of thing that interested him, the ups and downs of the wholesale prices for the different grades of wool. "Now, take the merino that the government gave by the thousands to you Navajo a generation ago, most of which ended up in people's bellies. Merino produce top quality wool that sells for more than triple what churro does."

"They weren't what the Diné knew."

"They're *sheep*. They eat grass. Merino wool is much the finer. That's why merino goes for seventy-eight cents a pound back East."

"Scoured," Julia said.

"Yes, scoured," Will said, giving her a nasty glance.

"You get many more pounds of wool from a churro," Yazzie said.

"No, you don't," Will insisted, his voice rising. "Not when you take away the stained skirting and the top coat. They're worthless."

"You can let churro go off and they'll take care of themselves. Their wool grows much faster. And you can't weave blankets and rugs with merino."

Not easily, Julia knew. The merino staple was too short and twisted, and greasier, making it harder to clean as well as requiring tedious carding before spinning.

"You want to make fine clothes—suits and trousers and sweaters—you can't use churro," Will said. Julia could see a vein pulsing in his temple.

Yazzie's hands now gripped the edge of the table, though his face remained calm.

She needed to stop this. She knew the predetermined outcome if they ever came to blows. Will, several inches taller and a good twenty pounds heavier, would land more than his share of punches, but Yazzie would go for the throat and groin and knees. What he'd do when he had Will down, incapacitated—that wouldn't take long—she didn't care to guess.

"Boys," she said sharply. Their eyes shifted to her and held. She kept them waiting, letting the silence speak for her. Finally, in a measured tone, she said, "This argument is pointless. Mr. Yazzie, we don't have the money to buy enough sheep to make a difference."

Will sat back and crossed his arms.

He was her husband, and she needed to support him. But she also needed to know what Clement Yazzie wanted from them. That still wasn't apparent. She said:

"Is that what you wanted to discuss—half-shares?"

"There's something else. You can make more money if the wool you sell is worth more," Yazzie said.

"Isn't that what I've been saying?" Will slapped the table. "*Merino.*"

Yazzie ignored him. "This canyon has one thing that most of the reservation doesn't. Water. So use it. Wash the wool before you sell it. Scour it right here."

"How?" Julia asked.

"You put up a windmill to pump water. You build a dam up in the arroyo, where it can hold the spring runoff and the water you pump. You build a wash shed. You pipe the water down to the wash shed."

"Where exactly would you build a dam?" Julia asked, trying to forestall a resumption of their bickering.

"Right where it used to be."

"When was there a dam here?" Will interjected.

"Long ago. A natural dam."

"How do you know?"

"The boulders in the arroyo, and the silt up above."

"What silt? I've only seen the mud that the spring runoff leaves behind."

Yazzie, tired of being challenged at every turn, shifted in his seat. "Dig down less than the width of your hand. You'll find it."

"Who pays for the windmill and the dam and for building and fitting out the wash shed?" Will asked.

"You do."

"I've heard enough." Will pushed his chair back, rose, and walked away, into the kitchen. "Your idea isn't worth a paper dollar."

"Mr. Yazzie, I don't see it," Julia said, shaking her head. "The dealers we sell to, they have contracts with factories that clean the wool. They'll always be able to beat our price."

"What do they pay their workers?"

"I have no idea."

"More or less than you'd have to pay Navajos?" When she didn't reply—the answer was obvious—he went on, "And what do they pay for the coal or wood they use to heat the water? Up there"—he tilted his head toward the west, toward the woodland above his hogan—"there's miles of forest. You cut the trees and drag them down to the wash shed and split them and burn them to heat the water. The Old Man will help. You won't have to pay him. He already gets everything he needs from the trading post."

Will, drinking cold coffee in the kitchen, piped in, "And for free."

"We're not going to begrudge an old man a sack of flour and a bit of tobacco," Julia said. Besides, Clement Yazzie put on his own account anything more substantial that Tim Be'ak'idii might need.

"How much more would you make for scoured wool?" Yazzie asked her.

"I don't know." But she could guess: per pound, at least double the twenty-two cents they expected to get this spring.

"You find out. Then see."

"What do *you* get out of this, Yazzie?" Will asked. He returned to the table and stood beside Julia. "Of course!" he said, as if the explanation had just occurred to him. "The dam and pond would be on your land. And the windmill, right?"

"There would be more water than we would need for scouring," Julia said.

"Aoo'."

"What would you do with it?" Julia asked.

"Grow hay."

She had no reason to question that. With irrigation, he could certainly grow hay, enough to feed a larger flock. If that was truly what he wanted. Which she doubted. Better put, she doubted that was *all* he wanted.

"He's crazy," Will said. "Forget it." He followed her into the bedroom. They hadn't replaced the bedding in the spare room, his room, yet. (Nor had he repaired the broken window and sash.) He'd simply showed up at the bedroom door one night when she was preparing to retire. "No more hogan," he'd said. "I figure I have a right to sleep in a decent bed for a change. If you object, *you* can go out to the hogan." He'd kept to his side of the bed that night and every night thereafter.

"Maybe he isn't so crazy," Julia said, unpinning her hair and letting it fall to her shoulders. She didn't say what she was really thinking: Yazzie was planning something, something more than hay.

"We'll have nothing to do with this," Will said. "What are we supposed to do, sign some sort of contract with Yazzie? With *Yazzie*?" He laughed at the absurdity of it.

Julia set the hairpins on her dresser and only then recalled what Clement Yazzie had told her that morning—that Johanna had left something for her in the rosewood box. Now she lifted the lid.

"Oh my," she said, bewildered. "Oh my," half under her breath.

"What?" Will asked. He'd sat himself down on the edge of the bed to remove his shoes.

Julia recognized the squash blossom necklace immediately, even before she lifted it from the box and displayed its fullest arc, silver and turquoise, wider than her spread hand, two naja crescents at the bottom. She turned to show it to Will.

"How'd you come by that?" he asked. "Give it here."

Julia had seen it several times before, when visiting the Yazzies' mother in the weeks before her death.

"Johanna left it for me," she said. "It was her mother's."

Will held it in his hands, fingering the turquoise stones. "It's old, the silverwork is pretty crude—not as good as what silversmiths are making today. But it's still worth something." He handed it back.

"I can't keep this," Julia said. What was Johanna thinking?—as if anyone, except perhaps her brother, ever knew the answer to that question. Julia had no doubt, however, that Johanna possessed nothing else nearly as valuable. Why hadn't Clement Yazzie objected?

"Do what you want," Will said, dropping his second shoe on the floor. "Give it back to her. It's nothing to me."

The next morning, not long after sunrise, Julia headed up the canyon along the edge of the arroyo. She wanted to see it with Yazzie's eyes. A considerable runoff still cascaded over the deepest rocks, raising a white foam that clung along the margins of finely crumbled sandstone and flecked gray rock. She could see where the natural dam must have been, and, displaced below, the water-worn boulders of a consistency harder than sandstone. Eons ago, something, an ice sheet, had carried them down from high in the Chuskas. At its narrowest, the gorge was perhaps thirty feet across, with no more than an eight-foot perpendicular drop from the midpoint to the base of the irregularly sloped vee. She knew nothing about dams, couldn't begin to calculate how much rock and gravel and sand and cement would be needed to fill such a gap. How thick would it have to be? That depended on how much water it would have to retain, not on average, but in a heavy runoff. But of course it would be built with a sluice that could be opened in the spring to relieve the pressure. The land immediately above ascended gently, creating a natural bowl where the water would collect, maybe no more than six feet deep at the dam, gradually shallower as the floor of Many Springs Canyon rose toward the west. Again, she couldn't guess how much water the pond might accommodate, but looking at the arroyo this way, the task of creating dam and pond didn't seem that onerous.

She found Clement Yazzie splitting wood outside his hogan: one unfailing swing of the maul into each upright piece of pinyon, two pieces falling away; the ease and economy of his movements suggested that he could do this blindfolded. She knew he'd seen her coming up the trail from the trading post, but he didn't stop until she reached him. Yazzie drew a red handkerchief from a rear pocket of his tan trousers and wiped his hands and forehead.

"Yá'át'ééh, Mr. Yazzie," Julia said.

"Aoo', yá'át'ééh," he answered, and then waited for her to state why she'd come.

She retrieved the necklace from the pocket of her canvas field coat (in truth, one of Will's, but she'd appropriated it several years before as far more practical than anything available by catalog for women). "I found this last night, after you left."

"Hunh," Yazzie said.

"I really can't accept it." She held it out to him. "Why did you let her leave it?"

"It's hers to do with as she wants."

"But it must be very precious to both of you." She needn't mention his mother directly, which might give offense.

"Not that much."

She knew he wouldn't admit any deeper attachment. Two horses were kicking up dust in the corral; the third was missing. "Where's Johanna now?" she asked.

"In the meadow."

The "meadow." She'd never heard him call his rough grazing land a meadow, but Yazzie didn't let anything get by him, did he?—and certainly not Will's slights from the night before. She turned to face back the way she'd come, shading her eyes with her palm.

"Well, I didn't see her on my way up here, so you must mean the "high" meadow, not the "lower" meadow."

"Coyotes have taken two lambs this week, and she doesn't like that. She's hunting them."

Johanna? Hunting? She had never seen Johanna handle any kind of weapon. "Isn't that a bit dangerous?"

"Only for the coyotes."

Why am I always showing him how little I know? Julia thought. "You know, Mr. Yazzie, every conversation doesn't have to be a contest."

His gaze swept across the tree line, which Julia saw as an excuse for not looking at her.

"You make it hard to know what to say," he said.

"*I* make it hard?" She punctuated her response with a sharp laugh.

"From that first day you walked up here all fierce."

Fierce? Was that really what he thought? She remembered the encounter very vividly. He'd been chopping wood that day, too. She'd felt so nervous that she nearly threw up. At the time, it hadn't occurred to her that she was as foreign to him as he to her.

"We need to be forthright with each other, Mr. Yazzie."

Only now did he turn to face her, to challenge her: "Then why did you really come up here?"

The squash blossom necklace, which she still held in her hand, weighed upon her as an excuse, at best a partial truth. Although both embarrassed and intimidated, she persisted: "I want to know what you think I should do with this."

She knew he saw through her; his whole demeanor told her so—his cold stare, the way he stiffened and leaned ever so slightly away from her. "This is what I think: for now, keep it. Give it back when you leave Many Springs for good."

"So that's what you suppose we'll do?"

Just then they heard the echo of a rifle shot rolling down from the edge of the forest.

"Sooner or later all bilagáanas leave."

Now she could do nothing except defend herself: "Then what about the wash shed and the windmill and the dam? Why would we even consider doing what you proposed last night?"

"Maybe you'll stay here just long enough to get rich."

This was too much. "You're doing your best to annoy me, and I don't appreciate it. Are you going to say what you're after? And don't tell me it's hay."

There was always a hesitation before he spoke to her, as if even the simplest response had to be carefully considered. This time his pause was longer, several breaths. "So that's why you really came to see me," he said.

"I had more than one reason." She returned the necklace to her pocket and started off down the trail.

"Wait," he said. "I'll walk with you."

They walked side by side. The unfiltered sunlight warmed them; the air, too dry for any rising mist, barely stirred.

"I hear," Yazzie said, "that buyers are on the lookout for wild horses and ponies, like the ones in the Chuska Valley. Most get sold to *zhinii* sharecroppers in the South."

"I see. Do they fetch a good price from the buyers?"

"Good enough. They're sturdy and don't need pampering. They've been running out there since the Spanish first came."

Of course she'd seen the horses, scruffy, small, skittish, intuitively wary of people, as if they retained over the centuries an ancestral memory of ill-treatment by Coronado's and Oñate's soldiers. Sometimes the horses wandered into the lower canyon, grazing, below the trading post.

"How would you go about it?" Julia asked.

"Hire a couple of hands. Drive the horses up into the canyon and corral them. Fatten them, and take them a string at a time to Gallup for shipment east."

And to fatten them he'd need a sure supply of water.

"You've been thinking about this for quite some time, haven't you?"

"The horses won't be there forever."

No, Julia thought, if a market existed, others besides Clement Yazzie would be scouting the valley. Not much could be stripped from the reservation, but whatever *could* be, *would* be, given time—of that she had no doubt. Horses and ponies. Coal. Or some as-yet-undiscovered deposit, silver or lead.

"Mr. Yazzie," Julia said, "you could do all this without us. The dam and pond and windmill—for what they'd cost, you'd only have to sell the smallest fraction of your herd. And you don't really think this business about scouring the wool here will work out, do you?"

"I don't know," he said, and she felt the reawakened chill behind his words. Something had pushed him away again. "Ask your husband. He's the one who's good with numbers."

Every mention of Will came at the point of a knife. Julia, her own irritation sharpened, said, "And why would you care? It's nothing to you, is it, what happens to the wool after you get your money?"

"No."

She stopped in the middle of the trail and pushed her hands to the bottom of the coat's generous pockets. She felt again the necklace, the uneven stones, the silver settings and flutes and beads. "Then why involve us?"

He turned to face her again. "To keep the trading post open."

She remembered how she'd told him during his illness that the trading post was on the edge. It couldn't have been a surprise. They'd been scraping along for five years. She didn't doubt that he saw some benefit in having a trading post nearby, even though if he had his druthers, he'd see every last Anglo escorted from the reservation, including her.

"So you don't have to ride twenty-four miles to Two Grey Hills just to buy *your* sack of flour?"

He returned her sarcasm. "Maybe I like the company."

"You mean the men who sit in the bullpen and gossip like old women? Well, you needn't worry. If we decide to leave, we'll sell the trading post to some other foolish bilagáana."

"No one would buy it," Yazzie said.

"You're so sure."

"Because there would be nothing left for them to buy. Except ashes."

She was stunned. He couldn't have been clearer.

"You'd make us paupers."

"You could do what the Taskin brothers did. Sell off everything you can. Before."

"Suppose Tom and Carmelita wanted to take it on? What would you do then?"

"They're Diné."

So that would be different.

"Or maybe *I'd* buy it," he said. He picked up a stone and bounced it in his hand. "For a paper dollar." He let the stone fall and brushed any lingering dirt from his hands.

She saw the cruelty in his face, hard as the stone he'd released. The furrows above the bridge of his nose, separating the severe eyebrows; the weathered skin and the even deeper furrows between the flare of his nostrils and his heavy cheeks; the deepest furrows, descending from the corners of his mouth to meet the hard line of his set jaw. And his eyes, shaded by the circular brim of his hat, pitiless.

"Oh, Mr. Yazzie," Julia said, "you make me very sad." Another rifle shot startled her, echoed.

"You don't have a right to be sad," he said. He stood firmly now. "Not about this. This isn't your land or your home."

"But it's my life," she said, "even if you see it as foolhardy or without merit."

"Other Anglos have moved on. Why not you?"

All the previous questions on their little walk had been hers, and now his turn had come. But did he really want to know? Did she want to tell him? They'd turned their walk into yet another contest, hackle to hackle, hadn't they? Had either of them intended it? So why had they let it happen once again? It was too tiring; *she* was too tired. She sighed and said, "Because if I did, I'd find myself back under my father's roof—in truth, my stepmother's roof." When he said nothing, she added, "Do you have any idea what that would mean, for a woman of my age, in my society?"

"No."

"Why don't you just do whatever it is you'd like to do and get it over with." She spoke in anger now. "Do us all a favor, Mr. Yazzie." He could be the kerosene, consuming her livelihood, her marriage—oh yes, that too—and accelerating her ruin.

"I don't understand what you're doing here."

Here. It wasn't a question. They would never understand each other, soul to bared soul. The chasms of race, birth, culture could be bridged but never leveled. This was his geography: red mesa, stark butte, black volcanic neck and dike, carved canyon, desert varnish, valley of caked mudflows, dunes, dust, mustangs with wild knotted manes. The land was *inescapably* his. She hadn't always understood that, not really, not as she did now. But she wouldn't allow herself to be so simply dismissed by him or anyone else, so she spoke:

"I came out here because I felt as if I were being strangled by circumstances I couldn't control. Or maybe it was no more than a whim. Or maybe we did want to get rich—at least one of us did." Saying it that way felt like a betrayal.

"Find out what it would cost," he now said. "For the windmill and a dam. I'll give you some of my churro. That will be my share."

Suddenly she asked, "Where did you and Johanna *go?*"

He understood what she meant: after the diphtheria. "A place where no one would bother us."

It felt like another slap in the face; her cheeks burned as if it had been.

"Not you," he quickly said. "I didn't mean you."

At that, her cheeks flushed even hotter. "Leaving like that could've been very dangerous. You were still very sick."

"It didn't matter."

No, why would it? His wife had died; his boys had died. Certainly, he was young enough to have others, a new Navajo wife, a new family. But at that moment, ill in body and soul, how could any such possibility comfort him?

"I suppose I understand that much," Julia said, brushing a bothersome fly away from her cheek. Still, her resentment lingered. *None of this made any sense!* she wanted to shout at him. Why wasn't he doing everything he could to make Will and her leave? Then he could do as he wanted; Many Springs would be his from canyon mouth to mountain. She shouldn't have revealed anything about her own . . . circumstances.

She swung around and continued down the trail. She walked faster now and didn't look back, but she knew Yazzie was following, keeping his distance.

When she arrived at the lower edge of what she, now, would always identify as the lower meadow—how had it suddenly become something so recognizably defined despite its lack of green, its barrenness?—he called her name and she turned and saw him standing across the arroyo on an outcropping, a shelf of dark rock, and he called out, "This is where we'll build the dam."

WHILE IN ALBANY, she'd looked into it, discretely. She'd had no opportunity at Many Springs. Not only was spring the busiest time of year, but she also didn't want to raise Will's suspicions that she hadn't dismissed

Clement Yazzie's plan (if it could be called something so suggestive of actual strategy and design). She now knew that you could purchase a Sears & Roebuck back-geared galvanized steel pumping windmill (with red-painted tips on vanes and tail) for twenty-five dollars plus shipping. Portland cement cost three dollars for a fifty-gallon drum. (They'd need that, wouldn't they?—there was too much sand in the soil to compact and adhere into impermeability.) Galvanized corrugated steel roofing from the Chicago House Wrecking Company went for three dollars and twenty-five cents per one hundred square feet—for the wash shed she envisaged a structure large enough to accommodate drying racks as well as multiple wash tubs, with at least two sides of canvas tarpaulin that could be rolled up to take full advantage of the dry wind, but released and tied down if the weather turned.

She had her own money, part of what had been set aside by her father in the Albany Savings Bank with the implication that she would use it only to escape an untenable situation, by which he meant, of course, her marriage. Would she break that promise again, as she had when she and Will arrived to an empty store? And how would she handle Will, who, thanks to her adept lying, still knew nothing about the money held in reserve. He would certainly oppose any such expense. She'd have to speak to Clement Yazzie again, with a clear mind, without simply assuming that he must know how to do these things: build a dam, find the proper location for a well and windmill. And after that, if convinced, she would face Will.

When the train pulled into Gallup, Tom Gorman was waiting for her on the station platform. She smiled to see him standing there, his wide-brimmed hat flat, his thumbs anchored in his belt. She didn't want to stay in Gallup a minute longer than necessary.

He immediately told her that Mr. Halley was gone.

"Gone?" Her throat tightened, closed. At first she thought Tom meant that Will had died. "How—"

"It looks like he left for a long trip," Tom said.

The negro porter set her bags down by Julia's side, but she scarcely noticed. "When?"

"Four days ago. When we got to the store in the morning, there was no sign of him. We didn't think anything of it until late in the day, though we did notice that the dead pawn case was pretty empty—not broken into, just cleaned out of everything except some junk. When the missus finally went looking for him, she took the liberty of going into your private rooms. Most of his clothes appear to be gone, as well as his shaving gear and such. We had no idea he was planning a trip. We thought about sending you a telegram, to ask, but we knew that by the time I got myself into Gallup, you'd already be on your way back."

Tom had been as diplomatic as he could. A trip, indeed. "Did he leave a note?"

"None that I saw, Missus."

Everything on the periphery of her vision faded to black, leaving an ill-defined oval, a framed tintype of depot, train, platform, Tom, all poorly focused. "I need to sit down," she said, moving unsteadily toward a bench.

"Do you want me to put your bags in the wagon?" Tom asked.

"Yes, please."

"Should I wait for you there or come back?"

"Wait. Thank you, Tom."

So. Gone. She sat for several minutes, her eyes closed, visionless except for the flashing of brief flecks, ruby and platinum. He must have been planning for some time. How much money was in the business account? Will had always written the checks, kept the books. He didn't hide them from her. Where had he gone? He took the dead pawn. Had he drained the bank account as surely as he'd emptied the glass case? They had nothing else of value. The money from the spring shearing. Had he taken it? Her hands shook, and she could feel the muscles in her thighs jump. Her lower jaw trembled, her teeth clicking. She needed to calm herself. To think this through. What should she do? She opened her eyes. She was in Gallup. She shut them again. Red and silver. Tom would've picked up the mail already. She should look for bills. Would she even miss Will? The bank. She should find out what remained in the trading post account. What would she do when the trading license needed to be renewed? He had let her leave for Albany without saying anything. He'd been standing on the veranda with his arms folded. She'd looked away, ahead, down the canyon, and then back again; he'd gone inside. Her last sight. He knew. She felt the tears leaking from the pinched lids. How could he do that to her? Just leave. How much money did she have with her? He'd offered protection, husband to wife. That meant something. Dear God, she couldn't manage. He'd return. From his trip. He'd—

I'm truly on my own, she thought. She didn't think she'd ever see her father again. And Penny, married, would soon be starting her own family. She'd never been alone before. Not this way. If she'd known, she might have said something to Edna. Edna would allow her a space. A room, three meals a day, a reputation for the gossipmongers to feast upon, and perhaps drops from a vial to let her slip out of her misery each night. She could work. What was she suited for? Nothing. A governess. Not likely. A counter girl or a waitress. A seamstress in the Cluett and Peabody shirt and collar factory in Troy. Who would bother to train a thirty-four-year-old woman? The escape money her father had given her, most of it, safe. How long would it last? There'd be obligations. Vendors who needed to be paid. She could walk away. Let them try and find Will to collect. Was there enough to buy a property? Somewhere. She could let rooms.

She opened her eyes a second time and looked up. Pete Pietrowski had turned the corner of the station and was walking along the platform toward her. She turned her head and wiped her cheeks.

"You're back," Pete said.

"I am."

"How was the wedding? And your family?"

"The wedding was quite nice. Everyone is well."

He chewed on the fringe of his mustache, shaggier than usual. "May I join you?" He nodded toward the bench. She slid aside a bit and he sat down. He removed his hat and ran his blunt fingers back through his hair. "This platform is where I got my start. Photographing travelers. Have I told you that?"

"You have."

"I thought so." He turned his hat in his hands.

"So why are you here today?"

"Oh, well, I was just passing by and saw Tom sitting out front in your wagon. He said you were back here."

"What else did he say?"

"That you've had a shock." He cleared his throat. "Of course, those weren't his exact words."

Julia looked away.

"You shouldn't expect to see your way just now. Besides, what you're thinking may not even be true."

"It is."

"Well, I don't want to say anything against him, but you deserved better."

Better than Will? Better than his desertion? "Please," was all she could say.

He stood up, hat still in hand, and looked down at her. "I can see that you don't want to talk. But you have friends, Julia."

Few friends, many acquaintances. "I know." She was being too hard on Pete, his well-intentioned blunt-headedness. Still, she wanted him to leave.

"If you find yourself short," he said, "I have a little money. You're welcome to it."

She reached out to take his hand and ended up clutching three fingers and, awkwardly, the brim of his homburg. "You *are* a friend, Pete, and I appreciate your offer, but right now I have no idea what my true situation is." She needed to find out. All else could be put aside.

Pete withdrew his hat but not his fingers. He twisted his hand to bury hers in his broad grip. He didn't seem able to speak.

She regretted her gesture. She slowly extracted her hand. "I need to collect myself."

Pete restored his hat to its perch. He folded his hands behind his back. The contractions of his cheeks, roughly stubbled and mottled with inner heat, made him look like he was chewing gristle. "I'll go chat with Tom for a minute, then."

"That might be best." Julia attempted a smile but then, fearing further misinterpretation, stiffened her lips.

He turned and took several steps before stopping and looking back at her. "You have friends," he repeated, and then continued on.

Walter Martin, manager of the Commercial Bank of Gallup, looked over the top of his glasses and smiled with his thin gray lips. Julia stared down at the part in his unnaturally black hair; the part ran in a straight line, like a stripe, dividing his skull in halves. He rose from his chair and gestured toward the chair on Julia's side of his heavy desk. They stood eye to eye. "What can we do for you today, Mrs. Halley?" he asked.

Julia sat down. He remained standing for a moment, as if to make clear who would be in charge of this conversation.

"Mr. Martin," Julia said, "I'd like to know how much money is in the Many Springs Trading Post account at the moment."

"I believe that account belongs to your husband?"

"Yes, it does."

"May I ask, is your name on the account?"

"No, but—"

He held up a hand. "Then I'm afraid I can't grant your request."

"Mr. Martin," Julia said, being as patient as she could, "my husband has taken a lengthy trip and may have neglected to pay certain bills that are coming due. I'm sure you understand that I simply need to know our present balance." She needed to spin a tale for this little man. "I don't have our books here with me, but a number of checks and possibly even recent deposits may not have been entered. I'm sure you understand that I've often signed for deposits on behalf of my husband—"

"Well, that was somewhat irregular, don't you see, but regardless, I'm afraid I can't provide access to that account without your husband's presence or his written consent."

"Mr. Martin, I'm sure you can see my plight—"

"I can indeed." That thin-lipped excuse for a smile again. "But the bank guarantees its customers a certain degree of confidentiality, not to say privacy. I believe you'll continue to receive regular statements at the listed postal address, unless, of course, Mr. Halley has changed that address. I'll be happy to check our records to see if he has done so, although if he has, I'm not at liberty to disclose any new address."

Did he know already that Will had left? Was that it? How could he know? Had Will said something before leaving?

"Of course, Mrs. Halley, you could apply to the courts for access to this account, but even then, I suspect that a judge will require some evidence regarding your husband's . . . position, don't you see, in this matter."

"So you're telling me that I won't know the balance of the account until the bank mails out a statement."

"My hands are tied."

"But I can continue to make deposits."

"Your husband's signature is not required for a cash deposit, but should you wish to deposit checks that are in his name or for the trading post . . ." He lifted his eyebrows, the supercilious twit. "I can't look the other way, can I, now that you've called attention to your previous practice? We try to oblige, but this situation does raise something of a concern."

"And if I write checks against the account?"

"We can't honor them. You could sign your husband's name, but even if there were sufficient funds in the account, you might find yourself in a bit of difficulty. And if there weren't sufficient funds . . . forgery and such, you understand."

"Then I'd like to open my own account."

"This is the *Commercial* Bank of Gallup. We do not have personal accounts."

"I'm aware of that."

"You wish to open a business account?"

"Yes."

He sat back and sucked on his upper lip. Julia assumed he was running through the bylaws of the bank, seeing if he could justify denying her request. "Under the circumstances—"

"What circumstances?" Julia asked, smiling.

"Under the circumstances, I'm afraid we could oblige you only if you have your husband's approval and guarantee of responsibility. If you were unmarried, your father could do so."

"What if I were a widow and decided to open a boarding house?"

"As a courtesy we have accommodated one or two widows when there were no issues before the court regarding wills, inheritance, probate, and the like. But as a rule, local boarding houses operate on a cash basis, apart from whatever arrangements have been made with various merchants. I needn't remind you, howsomever, that a trading post is a very different business from a boarding house."

She studied his high white winged collar, his slim black tie, the lapels of his cheap black suit; this was how he'd look, bloodless, if she lopped off his head.

"Let me be clear," Julia said. "I wish to open a new account. I will immediately transfer $750 from my personal account with the Albany Savings Bank in Albany, New York, into that account. Do you want my business or don't you?"

"My hands are tied," he insisted, "unless, perhaps, you can find someone who will guarantee the continued solvency of such an account."

Half an hour later, Alberto Rodriguez swung open the gate and held it for her as she reentered Mr. Martin's office enclosure.

In less than another hour, she'd concluded her business with the banker and, since her name in fact appeared on the trading license, had opened a new account, Many Springs Trading Post, J. M. Halley, Prop., into which would be deposited $750 from the Albany Savings Bank. She had also received assurances from Mr. Martin that should his bank receive any outstanding claims on the Many Springs Trading Post account of Wilford Halley, Prop., and should such claims exceed that account's meager balance of $5.24—Mr. Halley having withdrawn all but that amount before his departure—she would be notified. In turn, she assured Mr. Martin that sufficient funds would be transferred into that account as long as the claims were dated prior to Mr. Halley's leaving on his trip. On the off chance funds were required before the transfer could be completed, such checks would be held by the bank in anticipation of the transfer—as a courtesy. Should Mr. Halley close his account, she would be notified.

When they left the bank, Alberto Rodriguez insisted that he escort Julia to the livery stable at the corner of Coal Avenue and First Street, where Tom Gorman had brought the horses to be fed and watered.

Alberto was wearing an elegantly cut light brown suit and white shirt with a straight stiff collar ornamented by a narrow blue four-in-hand. His felt bowler had been recently brushed; his oxblood shoes, polished to a shine. There were other Mexican businessmen in Gallup—a grocer, a barber, a cigar seller, several saloon-keepers—but he'd managed to rise higher in the social order, as if the durable goods he sold, tables and chairs and bedroom suites, lent strength, stability to his name. In short, he was a solid citizen—a bank director, a leading proponent of public education, and an advocate for extension of municipal services, especially water and electricity, to the poorer neighborhoods. He was universally recognized as a true gentleman, against the backdrop of Gallup's self-promoters, itinerant confidence men, get-rich-quickers, inebriate Indians, shiftless mestizos, rootless Mexican and Anglo cowboys, Japanese and similarly transplanted coal miners, railroad hobos.

Julia's hand was resting lightly on Alberto's arm. She wasn't surprised when he adopted a patrician tone:

"I'm not convinced that this is the wisest course, Julia."

They'd always been on a first-name basis, ever since she first showed up on his doorstep in 1898. They didn't see each other often enough: Alberto had no reason to be traveling north through Tohatchi and Naschitti, unless he was visiting his brother in Aztec, and she came into Gallup so infrequently.

"What would you have me do?" Julia asked.

"You seem convinced that he isn't coming back."

"He'll come back before he starves. Short of that, no, I don't believe he'll return."

"And you have no idea where he went?"

"None."

"Would you like me to make inquiries?"

"No. At least not yet."

"Your husband has certain responsibilities to you, and he should be forced to honor them."

Responsibilities. She had her own responsibilities. Return to Many Springs. Find the account ledgers. Reassure Tom and Carmelita. Pretend that Will's departure had changed nothing. How long would $750 sustain her folly? (The accumulated interest would remain in Albany's safekeeping. That should be more than sufficient for her to reach, say, Kansas City, or some other place where no one would ever think to look for her.)

"I'd like to know," she said, deliberately changing the subject, "why you'd let a creature like Walter Martin manage the bank. He's out of a Dickens novel—a Uriah Heep but without the devious cleverness."

Alberto laughed. "Julia, that's why Mr. Martin is a perfect bank manager. He's an excellent accountant, too cowardly to embezzle, enough of a cheapskate not to recommend risky loans to the board, and a toady to all those above."

"This has been so demeaning—everything, including having to come pleading to you."

"You didn't plead. You asked."

"I value your friendship, Alberto. I just hope you haven't put your reputation at risk by vouching for me."

"Not at all." He seemed surprised by her statement. "Unless you intend to write checks that you can't cover. Then the board may have something to say."

They turned the corner from Railroad Avenue and proceeded up First Street.

"My point," she said, "is that this will all come out."

"You mean, Mr. Martin will make it known."

Or someone else. She wondered how much Alberto would tell Matilda. And how much Matilda, in strictest confidence, of course, would relay to her social circle.

"It's possible that certain businessmen may be less than willing to extend you credit," Alberto said.

"Then they'll appreciate my not putting them in that position."

"You can't run your business on a cash basis."

"I know."

They crossed the street in the middle of the block, dodging the horse droppings.

"Take the time to consider other options," Alberto advised.

"You think I should sell."

"I think you need to look carefully at your situation. You're a white woman. You'll be living alone on the reservation. The Gormans will do their best for you, but who else do you have? Who else can you rely on for support and protection? Trading posts come and go. There have already been dozens of them, and not a single one run by a woman on her own. You're putting yourself at tremendous risk, and I, for one, would prefer that you didn't."

She found the letter where she suspected it would be, tucked into the account ledger. She already knew from the bank statement what he'd done, depositing the wool money, paying the outstanding bills, withdrawing what was left—which wasn't much, but it would have been enough to pay the Gormans, including Johnny, and keep the vendors at bay until the next shearing. She unfolded the single sheet of paper:

> Julia,
>
> I have taken less than my fair share but I make no further claim. I want done with it. Do as you wish—stay or leave. You are able for it.
>
> I will not trouble you again. I expect you not to trouble me either.
>
> I am sorry enough for both of us.
>
> Will

I am sorry enough for both of us. That was the only surprising thing, almost an apology. Later that night she opened her jewelry box and saw that Johanna's squash blossom necklace was gone.

The next morning, Julia went about her business as if it were an ordinary day of commerce. Neither Tom nor Carmelita had anything to say to her about Will. Their son Johnny likewise said nothing, but he wasn't so schooled as to keep hidden his embarrassment at her situation; she caught him looking her way and immediately turning away when her eyes met his. She didn't see Clement Yazzie at all, and she didn't know what to make of that—if he was avoiding her or simply had other tasks to occupy himself. She needed to talk to him again about the dam and the windmill, but that could wait until she reviewed the trading post's ledgers thoroughly, and that she wouldn't do until she was in a stable frame of mind, able to concentrate without emotional eruptions.

The business day had concluded and she was in her kitchen when she heard the familiar sound of Pete Pietrowski's wagon pull up. She hadn't given him a thought since leaving Gallup.

Pete knocked once and, hearing her response, opened the door and entered, hat in hand.

"What are you doing here?" Julia said, putting down the knife she'd been using to slice carrots. She couldn't look at him. She thought about picking up the knife again and throwing it at him.

"I just want you to know," he began, nerves on full display, "that I'm here for just one reason, to keep you company. Friend to friend. If you prefer that I make myself scarce, I'll understand. I'll head right back to Gallup. If that's what you prefer. You don't have to say a thing except 'go.' Just that one word."

She wanted to cry, for his pathetic state as much as her own. She didn't want to deal with him! "I don't want to talk about it," she said.

"I didn't think you would. I'd be surprised if you wanted to talk about much of anything. Silence suits me just fine. Or if silence is the wrong thing, you can pick out one of your favorite books and we can take turns reading aloud. Or we could read one of your newspapers and learn what's been happening in the world."

"I just came back from the world."

"So you did." He paused. "A book, then?"

She turned and looked at him standing there, still holding his hat. "You shouldn't have come."

"I suppose not." He didn't move. "On the way, I started to turn around more than once."

"You shouldn't have come. How do you think this will look? Did you consider that?"

He looked surprised. "No, I didn't. I surely didn't."

She had a simple choice: cruelty or forbearance.

"You can stay the night, Pete," she said. "But then you have to leave. I have a lot of thinking to do, and a lot of chores, and I can't have you hovering."

"Fair enough."

"Hang up your hat," she said.

CHAPTER TEN: Pete (The Past)

1. Brothers

His clearest early memory of his father, a short, stocky, muscular man with a square face and eyebrows that arched like unfurled wings: his coming home on a stifling summer day in the late afternoon, reeking of sweat, black from loading and unloading bituminous down at the wharves, and climbing fully dressed, minus his work boots, into the rain barrel that stood beside the porch steps, behind their shack of a house in Cincinnati. His father crouched down in the barrel, splashing water over the sides, until only his neck and head were visible above the copper rim. Every few minutes he'd disappear entirely, holding his breath underwater for what seemed to Władysław an unbearably long time, and then bursting above the water line, splashing out waves of overflow, opening his mouth wide beneath the broad mustache, gasping in the rank air and heat and humidity.

It looked like fun but he knew otherwise because his father didn't say a word, not even a hello. He seemed to be staring at something unseen, as if Vaddy weren't even there. When Vaddy's mother, equally stout and equally squat, appeared at the screen door, all his father said was, "Get me the soap," which his mother did, and then she too stood watching him lather it in his red, cracked hands and then rub the coarse homemade foam of saponified fat and lye into his face and hair. He did that three times, ducking under between latherings, and now the water that splashed over the sides was laced with scum. Standing upright in the rain barrel, he began removing his clothes, shirt first, undershirt second, then pants, and then socks, leaving only his underwear on. He rang out each article of clothing as he removed it, tossing it onto the porch, where it landed with a splat near his wife's bare feet.

"I won't be able to use that water now to do the laundry," his mother said in Polish. She took in laundry to help pay the bills.

His father just looked at her. "Ask me if I give a good goddamn about your laundry," he said, which Vaddy didn't understand at all; he'd never heard his father speak so harshly to his mother.

"Don't blaspheme in front of your children," she said. She turned around and went back into the little house—three rooms for seven people, including Vaddy's two younger sisters and two older brothers.

His father saw Vaddy's stricken face. "Pay me no mind, son," he said, his voice softening. "Hand me a towel from the clothesline." In order to reach the line, the boy, five years old, had to climb the three steps to the porch and stretch. He handed a clean towel to his father, who dried his face and hair and then draped the towel over the side of the barrel and, using his powerful tanned forearms, boosted himself up on the rim until his elbows were straight, his hairy chest and white belly and the waistband of his drawers above the barrel. With a great grunt, he swung his muscular legs up and out. His arms hung at his sides, and his sopping under drawers drooped so low that Vaddy could see the dense hair below his belly button.

"I'm going to tell you something, son," his father said in Polish, placing a heavy hand on his boy's shoulder and bending down so that they stood almost eye to eye. "You're my youngest son and I love you dearly. You'll be starting school with the Sisters in the fall. You stay in school as long as you can, because if you ever ask my permission to leave and get a job on the wharves or in the mines, I'll cut off your left hand with my own axe. Do you hear me?"

"Yes, Papa," he said, barely audible.

"Do you understand why?"

Tears rolled down Vaddy's cheeks. He loved his father so very much.

"You're a smart boy, you'll do good in school, better than your brothers." He picked up the wet towel, wiped off Władysław's streaked face, and draped the towel around his own waist. It hung half way between his knees and ankles. "You mind the Sisters, even when they're hard on you and even if there are days when you wonder if God is paying any attention." Then, holding the towel closed with one hand, he wrapped an arm around his boy's shoulders and drew him to his side, and they went into the house together, letting the screen door slap shut behind them.

"ANYONE CAN understand arithmetic," Brother Archibald said. "Two plus two equals four—do it on your toes if you have to. That's why I wear sandals, so I can get to them in a pinch." He was always making jokes, and all the boys liked him; they called him Archie or Friar Tuck behind his back. "Any dolt can understand arithmetic. *Mathematics*, however, is a different creature. Mathematics is the clearest distillation we have of the mysteries of the universe."

"What mysteries?" Władysław, thirteen years old, asked. After six years with the Sisters, he'd been accepted by St. Thomas Academy, a school founded by the Province of St. John the Baptist, of the Order of Friars Minor. And now, in only his second year with the Brothers, he'd emerged as a star pupil, one who merited extra lessons from Brother Archibald.

"Well, let's start with a seemingly simple mystery. Pi."

"Apple pie?" Władysław smiled at his own joke. Brother Archibald himself never missed on opportunity to deliver a terrible pun.

"Are you being dense?" The brother leaned over and pretended to cuff him on the side of the head. "Not that a perfect apple pie doesn't possess its own mysteries. You should ask Brother Matthew about that." Brother Matthew, another favorite and in fact Brother Archibald's real brother, taught the material sciences, chemistry and physics as well as biology. "But, as you well know, I'm talking about the *mathematical* pi, the constant 3.14. Here," he said, picking up a piece of chalk and writing on the blackboard the familiar equation $C = \pi d$. "Elucidate." That was one of his favorite words.

"The circumference of a circle equals pi times the circle's diameter."

"Excellent, now express pi in terms of the circumference and the diameter."

Władysław looked perplexed. "A hint?" he asked.

Archie tapped him on the top of the head with one knuckle. "Simple algebra, simple algebra. Divide both sides of the equation by 'd.' On your chalkboard, please."

With Brother Archibald looking over his shoulder, Władysław picked up his stubby piece of white chalk and wrote each step, concluding with $C/d = \pi$.

"Correct. Now read me the new equation."

" 'C'—"

This time Brother Archibald's knuckle knocked hard enough to hurt. "Begin with pi."

Władysław, rubbing his head, said, "Pi equals 'C' divided by 'd.' "

"Which means?"

"Pi equals the circumference of the circle divided by its diameter."

"Correct. Now think about that." Brother Archibald returned to the blackboard and drew a circle and its diameter. To the side, he drew two horizontal lines, the bottom one shorter. "The top line equals the circumference, broken and extended into a straight line. The bottom line is the same length as 'd' "—he tapped his chalk along the length of the diameter.

"What can you say about these lines—and don't say something insipid, such as"—he pursed his lips, rocked his round head from side to side, and adopted a mincing tone—'The top line is longer than the bottom line.' "

Władysław thought for a full minute while Brother Archibald paced back and forth before the blackboard, his hands behind his back. Finally the boy said, "The top line is 3.14 times as long as the bottom one."

"Precisely! Now, if I draw another circle"—and he did, extending his arm so that the new circle was as large as the height of the blackboard would allow—"what is the relationship between this 'C' and 'd'?"

" 'C' divided by 'd' equals pi."

"Yes! And if my arm were long enough and I could draw a circle so big that its diameter was twice the distance between the sun and earth, what would express the ratio of the circumference—the orbit—to the diameter?" He quickly added, "Putting aside, of course, that the earth's orbit is actually an ellipse, not a circle."

"The orbit is 3.14 times longer than the diameter."

"So this is true for every circle?"

"Yes."

"In the entire universe?"

"Yes."

"There you have it." Brother Archibald paused, tapping a chalky forefinger against his lips. "I only have one more thing for you to ponder today, my boy, and it's really a philosophical question. Here it is: What if the relationship between a circle's circumference and its diameter were, let's say, 8.2 instead of 3.14?"

Władysław studied the smaller circle on the blackboard. He tried to imagine it with a much a bigger circumference but the same diameter. "A circle's impossible. Maybe you'd have an ellipse?"

"I see what you're thinking, but an ellipse doesn't have a diameter, does it? It has . . ." He waited for Władysław to provide the answer.

"A major axis and a minor axis."

"Indeed. But let's return to the theoretical circle with a circumference 8.2 times its diameter. You correctly say it's impossible. But just suppose you *could* change the value of pi to 8.2. What then?"

Władysław was stumped. "I don't know, Brother."

"And neither do I!" He slapped his open palm on the desk. "Geometry as we know it *could not exist.* And if not geometry, then not physics or chemistry or astronomy, nor anything else visible or measurable—not animal, vegetable, or mineral. The cosmos would be utterly different—in fact, inconceivable, except to God." Brother Archibald folded his hands. "Just think, what a mysterious, miraculous thing He has done for us, setting in motion this perfectly ordered universe where pi is 3.14 and 3.14 is pi."

At that moment it *did* seem miraculous to Władysław. But that night, lying on his back in the dark and trying to think about his lesson instead of his stiff dick, Vaddy considered something else. What if there were no God? Wouldn't there still be . . . pi . . . and . . . physics . . .

. . . as taught in Władysław's junior year by Brother Matthew, as thin and reserved as his brother was fleshy and voluble. Inclined planes, screws, pulleys, waterwheels, steam engines—their operation and principles came easily to the sixteen-year-old, but what he found most fascinating was *optics*: prisms and rainbows, convex and concave lenses, the movement of light through vacuum and air, reflection, refraction, diffraction. That year, following Władysław's classroom demonstration of the camera obscura and the effects of differing pinhole sizes as well as lenses and mirrors (Brother Archibald, a guest of the physics class, termed the presentation "enlightening"), the Brother brothers decided that to reward him, and to encourage a renewed commitment to academic success—though he achieved top marks when he applied himself, he couldn't attend to what failed to arouse his interest, including rhetoric, Greek, theology, composition—they would present him with one of the new Kodak box cameras, which cost an ungodly $25, a fact that they didn't reveal to the boy. Władysław, though surprised and delighted, politely tried to refuse the gift, but Archibald and Matthew wouldn't hear of it. Furthermore—and here they thought they had him in their clutches—each quarter, assuming he achieved grades commensurate with their standards, they would pay to have the film developed, a set of silver gelatin prints made, and a fresh 100-exposure roll installed. The camera had to be returned to the Eastman Company for that, at a cost of $10.50.

He loved the camera, which he immediately recognized as by far the most expensive thing he'd ever possessed, as did his mendacious middle brother Romuald, known around the wharves as Ron P. By then the first-born Pietrowski son, Stanisław, had found work in the coal mines near Carbondale and had married a local girl, Hanna, who delivered a baby six months later. Their father, meanwhile, breathing with destroyed lungs, could no longer work the coal barges. He and their mother had arranged to ship Vaddy's younger sisters, Ireneusz and Gabriela, to Carbondale, where Stan, stoic with responsibility, had agreed to take them in. At his mother's instigation, in the hope that country air might help her husband, the elder Pietrowskis intended to move to Cynthiana, Kentucky, where they'd heard they could find work on the burley farms, which were expanding their fields to meet rising demand for manufactured cigarettes. That would leave Ron and Vaddy in Cincinnati, a prospect that neither brother relished.

The weekend before Irene and Gabby left with Stan for Carbondale, Vaddy gathered his family outside their house to take a photograph with his new camera. He didn't have a tripod, so he stacked three wooden crates and placed the box camera on top, doing his best to compose the shot, being careful to follow the directions for light, distance, and focus given in the Kodak Manual. With its fixed lens and a simple crank for advancing the roll of film, the camera couldn't have been simpler to operate, but Vaddy tried everyone's patience, especially Ron's, taking half a dozen shots. Several neighbors gathered to watch, and one of them agreed to press the exposure button on the side of the camera while Vaddy joined the standing row for a final photograph. That was when another neighbor asked if Vaddy would take *his* family's photograph—he would pay for it, of course, if it wasn't too much. It immediately occurred to Vaddy that if he could offer his services to others in the neighborhood, charging two bits for each exposure and four bits for a good print . . . Well, that way, he could pay for developing and printing and reloading on his own.

He quickly found customers, but when he reached the end of that first roll he still didn't have enough money to ship it off. He needed another five dollars. He went to Ron for a loan. Ron had turned into a hoodlum, plain and simple, running numbers (and probably worse) for one of the gangs of low-lifes that hung out around the waterfront. Vaddy disliked Ron, with his slicked-back hair, pencil mustache, tilted black homburg, striped shirt with the sleeves rolled up and gartered like a card sharp. Ron had his own money, which Vaddy never asked about, though he knew Ron stashed it under a floorboard beneath his bed.

"You need a loan?" Ron said, smiling his devious grin. He pulled a handful of carefully folded bills from his pocket and peeled off a fiver. "When do I get it back?"

"Maybe two weeks?" Vaddy replied.

"Two weeks, that's fine." Ron held out the bill. "But I expect another fiver to come with it."

"But that'll leave me with nothing!"

Ron shrugged. "That's the cost of doing business. Drum up some more customers."

"I can't. I've already finished the roll."

"Doing what? Taking pictures of flowers and clouds? That wasn't too smart, was it?"

"You're a shit."

"I suppose I am." Then Ron punched him in the middle of the chest. Vaddy took the money but vowed to himself that he'd never do it again. He'd find other ways to put cash in his pocket.

Help came indirectly from a wholly unexpected source: Fr. Wilson Dubuffet, one of the provincial definers and the principal of the boy's school. No student dared cross Father Dubuffet, who remained aloof until punishment needed to be meted out to a malefactor. Władysław had endured more than one encounter with the good father's switch, and when he saw the principal's eyes on him one morning, he immediately began to run down his list of probable infractions. But Father Dubuffet wanted him for another reason: he'd heard about the Brother brothers' gift, which violated the rules. Nevertheless, he would allow Władysław to keep the camera if he made his services available to the school and the provincial offices as needed for those occasions that didn't merit hiring a professional photographer, such as visits by well-to-do parents of students. The province would pay to get the film rolls developed as long as Władysław didn't abuse his privilege.

As early as his second roll of film, he'd begun experimenting, doing things the Kodak Manual warned him not to—moving the camera during exposures, deliberately creating double images on a single negative, testing the camera's many annoying limitations, not the least of which was its inability to focus at any distance shorter than three and a half feet—and adding tricks of his own: using pieces of colored glass as filters, focusing lamplight directly on the camera's aperture. Quite apart from his deliberate trial-and-error efforts, operating the camera always involved considerable guesswork. Indoor exposures had to be timed, based on the amount and quality of available light as well as the color and reflexivity of the background. On a sunny day, in a white room with light pouring through multiple windows, a couple of seconds proved to be a sufficient exposure, but on a thickly clouded day, in a room with dark walls or drapery, even a minute and a half might not do. The most frustrating limitation, however, was that the camera shrank the world to stunted two-and-a-half-inch black, gray, and white circles.

Naturally, nearly all of his experiments disappointed him. In most cases he had to judge success or failure by peering at the negatives; the workers at the Kodak company who developed his film were trained to see all challenges to convention as errors. ("When there are failures we finish enough duplicates from the good negatives to make up the full number." Thank you, Kodak.) Fortunately, the factory returned all of the rejected negatives, which, when held up to the light, allowed Vaddy to see the reverse effects of his experiments. Most were indeed worthless, but his initial efforts taught him two valuable lessons: first, to keep a careful log of every exposure and its circumstances; and second, to abstain from games when it came to photographing school events and provincial personnel or risk the wrath of Father Dubuffet, who'd assumed a rather proprietary attitude toward the camera.

Kodak was already selling a much better model, with bigger, rectangular negatives and a collapsible bellows and rack and pinion gearing to adjust the focus—a camera that, Vaddy calculated, would make it worthwhile to develop the negatives and make prints himself, if he could set up a dark room. After the initial investment, that would be much cheaper, and more profitable, than sending the camera back and forth to Kodak. Toward that end, he saved all the money he could, hiding it behind a loose baseboard next to the confessional in the school chapel. (He certainly didn't trust Ron not to find any hideaway at home.) In the middle of winter, however, he received word through Stan that his parents were moving farther south so his father, who was failing, could escape the cold; Vaddy mailed his mother all the money he'd saved.

Shortly after, he came home from school one afternoon to find his camera and most of the furniture smashed and Ron trussed like a turkey, bent backward and bound hand to foot, his throat slit. Two roaches struggled to free themselves from the congealing blood on the floor, and a third tasted the raw edge of the gash. A blur of other insects hovered above or crawled where Ron's bowels had emptied in his pants. Vaddy needed to get out of there but had trouble turning his eyes away and controlling the jerking muscles in his legs. He didn't have to look in the bedroom to know that Ron's money was gone.

Without hesitation, the Franciscan Brothers took him in, giving him a spare cell in the monastery, just down the hall from Brother Archibald, instead of a bed in the small dormitory for boarding students. It was a wise move. Sickening nightmares rose up from the depths, and Vaddy's screams woke everyone within earshot.

He had nothing to turn his mind to, not even his camera now, except his class work—for the first time in years, a relief instead of a chore. He wrote his papers carefully, producing essays that surprised his teachers. He earned the best marks of his life in those last five months, even after he learned, the news broken to him by Brother Archy, that his father had died in Georgia. His mother would move to Carbondale, where Stan would build an extra room in his crowded home. The overburdened brother never raised the prospect of Vaddy's joining them. It was just as well, because in Carbondale he would have little choice except to join his brother down in the mines, and that, honoring his father's admonition of a dozen years ago, he swore he would never do.

He'd already reached his full height, a blunt five-ten despite sloping shoulders. His thick neck supported wide features: prominent brow, deep blue-gray eyes, large ears, thick bridge and spread nostrils, straight mouth, clean-shaven square jaw. He brushed his brown hair straight back from his forehead, making his widow's peak more prominent than it otherwise might have been. To all appearances, a tough Polack who could handle himself just fine in a back-alley skirmish. But, unlike Ron, he'd had little experience of *that* world except as an infrequent observer outside smoky pool halls and half-lit saloons.

WHEN HE SOUGHT ACCEPTANCE as a postulant, the provincial and definers of the Province of St. John the Baptist asked if he felt he had a vocation. Fortunately, he'd been well schooled by Brothers Archibald and Matthew, who encouraged his postulancy. He wanted to serve toward some good end, he told them, maybe in far-off missions (convincing himself as well as the chapter leaders as his heart gathered strength by the mere saying of it), supporting his superiors' pastoral duties in whatever practical ways he could: cooking, cleaning, driving them hither and yon, gardening . . .

With a certain reluctance, offset, no doubt, by the grim facts of his biography, the provincial leaders accepted his application, but in the following eighteen months an oft-cited indiscipline and a lack of attention to formal religious studies didn't sit well with the province, which threatened him with dismissal. In the end, however, he performed just well enough to become a novice and then to take his simple vows of poverty, chastity, and obedience in the Order of Friars Minor, at which time he adopted (at the suggestion of Brother Matthew) the name Casimir, for the Polish saint often pictured with three hands and known for his great generosity. Brother Casimir would be required to give himself to the province, serving where and how his superiors dictated for at least the next three years, after which he might be permitted to take his solemn, permanent vows. Before then, he could be dismissed for any infraction, or he could choose to withdraw from the order.

After an additional year of studies in the monastery, he found himself first in Lafayette, Indiana, performing menial pastoral tasks that repeatedly brought him to the edge of despair. After another year, the province reassigned him to the parish of St. Benno of Meissen in Over-the-Rhine, a community settled by German immigrants north of Cincinnati's Miami and Erie Canal. He spoke fluent Polish but knew no German, which made him an odd fit, he thought, but he quickly realized that he wouldn't be there long. Now dwarfed by other nearby Catholic parishes—St. Mary's, St. Paul's, St. Francis Seraph's, with their impressive Romanesque and Greek or Gothic Revival churches—St. Benno remained open only because its parishioners, many of them among Over-the-Rhine's first wave of immigrants at mid-century, demanded it. The wood-framed church, with a short wooden steeple in need of scraping and painting, had yet to be wired for electricity, and the stone foundation desperately needed repairs. Casimir could see that the building's days were numbered, as were those of the sole parish priest, Father Ewald Bergmann, who, well into his seventies, could barely perform his pastoral duties let alone look after the church property.

When Father Ewald was absent or occupied, Casimir relied on Ewald's niece, Agata, their cook and housekeeper, to translate for him whenever elderly non-English-speaking parishioners came to the rectory. Before long, Casimir found himself enjoying Agata's company far more than that of the doddering Ewald, who spent more time in private prayer and contemplation than in conversation. Father Ewald insisted on silence at meals and silence in the hours before he retired. But he didn't object when Brother Casimir, citing supposed benefits to the parish, asked to buy a used camera and convert a small space in the basement of the rectory into a dark room.

Casimir tapped into what he'd saved from his small personal allowance, but he also pilfered money from the parish accounts, which was easy to do after he volunteered to oversee needed repairs to the church. He was easily able to add an odd amount here and there to the resultant lists of expenditures for mortar, lumber, paint, and the like. Besides, he told himself, he could justify every cent he spent on his photography, even the $60 for the camera—new, not used—plus the $7.28 for the developing outfit, $1.30 for the ferro-prussiate paper (which he discarded after making the first few positives, despite the ease, because he detested the unnatural blue tint of the prints), $5.83 for the kit needed to make the more complicated silver prints on albumen paper, $2.10 for a flash apparatus and flash powders, and $2.75 for a serviceable tripod. After that, he spent as much time as he could in his dark room, working in the feeble light of the orange candle lamp.

He made good use of his camera for the benefit of the parish in addition to photographing whatever else he wanted (including, often surreptitiously, Agata). For parishioners who couldn't afford to pay professional photographers to record their weddings, christenings, and first communions, Casimir provided his services free of charge, as he did for such parish functions as the traditional Palm Sunday processional and Christmas pageant.

His frequent absences from the rectory attracted Agata's interest. As a cook Agata made a good housekeeper, and as a housekeeper she left much to be desired. She had come to Over-the-Rhine to help her uncle after the death of his longtime daily woman, but she intended to join the Sisters of the Blessed Sacrament following completion of renovations to the motherhouse in Bensalem, Pennsylvania. Casimir didn't know anything about the Sisters' order except that its founder, Mother Katharine Drexel, had approached the Province of St. John the Baptist about opening a mission to the Navajo in Arizona Territory. He'd heard about the proposal from

Brother Matthew, who'd recently been elected a provincial definer and with whom Casimir now regularly corresponded. Brother Archibald had recently suffered a stroke and had only partially recovered the use of his right hand, making letter-writing impossible.

Casimir found it difficult to imagine Agata—a handsome girl, with wide brown eyes, pouting lips, and flirtatious shoulders that set her arms and hands in motion even when the rest of her remained stayed and still—confined by a wimple, veil, and black habit, her arms reverently folded within the wide sleeves. When she saucily (or so it seemed to him) inquired one morning about what he did down there in the locked room in the basement all by himself, he asked if she would like to see his dark room. That afternoon, while Father Ewald napped, they went down. Once there, he searched through his negatives until he found the one he wanted and then proceeded to clamp it and a sheet of the olive-green albumen paper into the five-by-seven printing frame. Leaving Agata to look through collections of finished prints, he hurried back up the basement stairs so that the day's pale sunlight, filtered through high clouds, could impress the image on the sensitized paper. Twice he impatiently opened half the hinged back of the frame to check the sunlight's progress. Finally satisfied with the image, he ran back down to the dark room, where he lit the orange candle lamp and extinguished the lantern dangling from the ceiling. In a rubber tray he washed the sheet of albumen paper in water several times, and though he knew he shouldn't be rushing the process, he prepared his toning bath—a solution of chloride of gold and sodium plus alkaline phosphate and acetate—and a fixing bath of hyposulphite of soda. With tongs he extracted the print from the water and submerged it in the toning bath. Standing shoulder to shoulder, he and Agata watched the tone of the photograph—a picture of her outside the kitchen door, holding a basket of summer vegetables in one hand and brushing a stray lock back from her forehead with the other—deepen. In the close quarters the sweetness of the chemicals and her soap-scented proximity staggered him. After washing the print in a fresh tray of water, he slipped it into the fixing solution. He handed Agata the tongs and told her that to prevent streaks or spots, she should gently pass the print back and forth, back and forth, through the bath.

He stood behind her, took half a step closer, his chest a bare inch from her shoulder blades.

"Is this right?" she asked, her eyes on the submerged photograph.

"Yes." He raised his right hand to her right shoulder. His thumb found the hollow behind her clavicle. She didn't react. He pressed closer, and she said, "I have a vocation."

"Of course you do."

She put the tongs down and turned to him. Their lips met briefly.

"I can't call you Brother Casimir now, can I?" she said in a hushed voice.

"I suppose not."

"What was your name before?"

"Władysław. Władysław Pietrowski."

"No," she said, giggling and shaking her head in the muted light. "No no. You must have had a nickname."

"Vaddy."

She laughed harder. "It just won't do. I'll call you Pete. Is that all right, Pete?"

"You can call me whatever you want." He tried to kiss her again but she bit her lower lip and turned her face away.

"Am I terrible?" she asked.

"You're wonderful."

"I don't think Uncle Ewald would think so."

"I don't care what he thinks. Please, let me kiss you again."

She licked her lips and he thrust his against them and she flicked her tongue. Heat surged into this face. "Aggie," he said.

"Well," she sighed, as if she'd sampled a new confection and found it wanting. She placed her hands on his chest and with a little push moved him away. "My uncle will be up from his nap. He'll expect his tea. I have to go."

"Not yet," he pleaded.

"Can I have that picture?" she asked, looking back over her shoulder.

"Of course." He reached around her and removed the print from the water bath. "Let me dry it for you." She moved aside. He placed it face down on a thin towel and patted the back dry with another.

When Agata told Father Ewald what had happened in the dark room, Casimir wasn't even surprised.

He didn't wait for a summons from the provincial. He went to see Brothers Archibald and Matthew. They joined him in the sacristy, where, at that time of day, they wouldn't be interrupted. He was shocked to see Archy, who entered the room leaning heavily on a cane, guided by Matthew's strong hand under his weak arm. Archy couldn't be much more than fifty, but he'd lost weight, his hair had turned white, and the stroke-numbed right side of his face drooped, eyelid, cheek, mouth. Matthew hadn't changed, except that his hairline continued to recede, withdrawing toward a natural tonsure. Dressed in his habit, crowned by his remaining wreath of hair, Matthew looked like a Roman philosopher in toga and laurel garland.

"I suppose you know why I'm here," Casimir said. He sat facing the two brothers.

"It's the era of the telephone," Brother Matthew replied. "So yes, we do."

Then Archibald spoke slowly, speech slurred: "You haf' los' your call-in'?"

"I suppose I have."

"And your faith?" Matthew asked.

"I don't know." Casimir frowned and half out of bitterness added, "Faith in what?"

"Faith is only one thing."

Casimir looked around him. The lead-green walls needed to be painted. From wooden hangers draped half a dozen white albs as well as chasubles in several colors: white, gold, green, black. A long shelf held stoles, the various ritual cloths for the Mass, and undersized towels with which the priest dried his cleansed hands. A cabinet with glass doors protected gold ciboria, chalices, patens, and thuribles; cruets for wine and water; vessels of sacred oils for consecrations, baptism, confirmation, unction. Near the sole window, with its stained glass panel of St. Francis feeding the animals, a small bookcase held sacramentary, lectionary, Book of Gospels.

"What did you see in me?" Brother Casimir asked. "Back when you took me under your wings."

"Smar'," Archibald struggled to pronounce.

"Smart but . . . unformed," Matthew added.

"And now?"

Brother Archibald, his words pronounced with deliberation, spoke again: "Doub' is no im-ped-i-men' to faith. Doub' is nec-e'-sary."

"But don't there have to be limits to doubt?"

"You might benefit from a change of scenery," Matthew said. "If you choose to remain with the Order."

"I still have a choice?"

"I can see to it that you do."

At the urging of the Bureau of Catholic Indian Missions, the Province of St. John the Baptist had agreed to assume responsibility for the Navajo mission proposed by the Sisters of the Blessed Sacrament, which Mother Drexel, heiress of the Philadelphia banker Francis Drexel, had founded in 1891 to aid Indians and the underprivileged colored. Even before taking her vows Katharine Drexel had built an Indian school in Santa Fe that her order now ran, and on one of her visits west the formidable nun had personally helped select a tract of land for the Navajo mission, just south of the current reservation boundary and less than three miles due west of the Arizona-New Mexico territorial line. Mother Drexel wanted to forge ahead even though much of the parcel, located at Cienega Amarilla (Tsohotso, Big Meadow, to the Navajo), had an unclear title not only because of traditional settlement by Navajos and Mexicans, but also because of checkerboarding. When the railroads were granted rights of way after passage of the Homestead Act, they also received alternating square-mile blocks along the route, to a depth of ten, and later twenty, miles on both sides of the planned tracks, thereby creating a gigantic checkerboard. The railroad could then sell blocks to ranchers or miners or anyone else, or use the land as loan collateral. To further complicate matters, advocates for the Navajo had begun exerting pressure in Washington to expand the reservation beyond the Atchison, Topeka, and Santa Fe tracks—roughly twenty miles south of Cienega Amarilla.

The Catholic Indian Bureau proposed that while the land issues were being resolved, a temporary mission should be located some eight miles south of Cienega Amarilla, on a much smaller parcel whose title wasn't in doubt and that the Sisters had already purchased from the previous owner, a Mexican rancher named Julio Escobar. The Hunters Point tract formed a cul de sac shadowed on the north by a great curving wall of multihued sandstone, at its ridge eight hundred feet above where the formation folded into the valley floor, which was watered year-round by Black Creek. The land east and west of the creek could easily be farmed for the benefit of the mission.

The provincial leaders had decided that Father Dubuffet, who'd retired from his posts as school principal and definer, should head the Hunters Point mission. He would be accompanied by a former student of his, the multilingual Brother Absalom Cordry, whose principal tasks would be to identify cooperative translators and to attempt to introduce Christian terminology to the illiterate Indians. One additional Franciscan would be sent, one who could handle the practical tasks: keeping food on the table, gathering and chopping wood, cleaning the mission house—an existing one-floor stone ranch house, big enough for a chapel, a common room, and two bedrooms—preparing the ground for a garden next spring, tending to the horses and whatever additional animals (perhaps a few hens and a cow) they procured, traveling as needed to Ft. Defiance or the closest off-reservation town, Gallup, New Mexico, for supplies, or to Navajo Springs, the nearest freight stop, fifteen miles south.

Brother Matthew suggested to the Franciscan Order's Council, comprising the provincial and the four definers, that Brother Casimir be the third member of the mission—a proposal that Father Dubuffet immediately rejected. He had valid objections. Brother Casimir had not yet taken his final vows—assuming, given present circumstances, that he would ever be permitted to—and he should hardly be rewarded (*Rewarded*? Casimir thought when Matthew recounted the discussion) for his recent indiscretion. Only the most upright individuals, capable of model (and modest) behavior, should be dispatched to missions. Father Dubuffet went on at some length, but the Council concluded that Brother Casimir, given his youth and vigor, would be sent for six months, at which time the status of the mission—and of his vocation—would be reexamined. And perhaps by then the situation regarding Cienega Amarilla (to be renamed St. Michaels if all went well) would be clarified.

The following day, Father Dubuffet, Brother Absalom, and Brother Casimir, accompanied by Brother Matthew, met to discuss the planned venture. Absalom, a pale, wispy man with a broad forehead that seemed to suit his scholarly reputation, said very little, deferring to his mentor, Dubuffet.

"You should know," Dubuffet said to Casimir, "that I strongly objected to your selection. So make a case for yourself."

Casimir gritted his teeth. "I can cook passably well"—a lie, unless "cooking" meant boiling and frying, the two skills he'd mastered while living those last months with Ron. "I helped tend a garden in Lafayette, and during my time in Over-the-Rhine I learned a bit about masonry and carpentry, as well as about electrical wiring."

"Electrical wiring?" Dubuffet scoffed. "Do you have any idea where this outpost is located? Our only conveniences will be an outhouse and a serviceable well."

"I'm sure Brother Casimir was speaking theoretically," Brother Matthew said.

"Let him speak for himself," Dubuffet said.

Matthew ignored him. "And of course he has the necessary photographic skills to supplement your written reports, as the province and the Sisters of the Blessed Sacrament have requested."

"I notice," Dubuffet said, "that you have left out any mention of faith and devotion to Our Lord and Savior Jesus Christ."

Why bother responding? Casimir thought. "I have a practical question, if I may," he said. "It's already late September. Wouldn't it be wiser to wait until spring?"

Brother Absalom laughed, a sound like tin scraping rough stone. "Arizona is a desert. Better to arrive in the fall than in the heat of summer, wouldn't you say?" Absalom had returned to Cincinnati from Brooklyn, New York, where for over a decade he'd been teaching French, German, and Spanish at St. Francis College. He apparently relished the challenge of mastering "a primitive language." But had he ever looked at a map? Casimir wondered.

"Hunters Point is more than six thousand feet above sea level. We'll soon see freezing temperatures and snow."

Absalom discounted this with another tinny laugh. "Oh, maybe a bit."

"We're all from hearty stock," Dubuffet said. "If *Mexicans* can handle the winter there, such as it is, I'm sure *we* can. And how is it that you know so much about Arizona? Correct me if I'm wrong, but you've never been west of the Mississippi, have you?"

"No, Father."

"Enough said." Dubuffet changed the subject: "You understand that you'll be expected to do what I tell you to do, without complaint."

"Yes."

"And when I say you should jump?"

Casimir stiffly smiled. "I'll respectfully ask you, on one foot or two."

"This is what I mean about his attitude," Dubuffet said, turning to Matthew.

"It would be a courtesy if everyone present would give everyone else the benefit of the doubt," Matthew said.

Casimir wondered if he really wanted to put his well-being in the hands of these two—one an arrogant old man, the other apparently a well-schooled idiot—for the next six months. But maybe that was what he deserved. At least it would give him time to plan, because he knew that he wouldn't be returning to Cincinnati or anywhere else within the Province of St. John the Baptist. He felt guilty deceiving Brother Matthew, but he'd do his best to fulfill his responsibilities in Arizona. Work aside, it would be six months without distraction. (As for Agata, she'd already been dispatched back to her parents in Germantown, Pennsylvania; in her absence, several grandmotherly parishioners had volunteered their cooking and cleaning services to Father Ewald.)

"I'll do my best, without complaint," Casimir said.

"Then let us pray," Father Dubuffet said.

Casimir went to see Brother Archibald before leaving for Arizona. The old man was resting in his room, lying on his bed with his hands folded. There was a hole in one wool sock; a horny nail poked through. Casimir pulled up the bare room's one straight chair and sat beside the bed.

"How are you feeling today?" he asked.

"In God's han's."

They remained silent for several minutes before Casimir spoke again: "I realize what a disappointment I must be to you."

Brother Archibald dismissed this with a shake of his head.

"Do you remember our first tutoring session?"

"Re-fres' my mem'ry."

"You asked me to think about the nature of circles and pi."

"Ah, 8.2." The left side of his mouth turned slyly upward.

"I'm assuming you've put many other students through the same torment."

"One mus' not let a goo' lesson go t' waste."

"You said, change pi and this universe is impossible. But later I wondered, what if God turned his back on us? How would we even know? Because pi would still be pi. The planets would still follow their orbits. We'd continue living our little lives." He paused. "It's a silly argument, I know."

"*Deus abscondidus.*"

"Well, yes, I suppose so, in a way, but I was just a kid. I thought it was the devil's work, to think such thoughts. I had no idea that they weren't exactly original."

"You thin' God has aba'don'd us?"

Casimir avoided answering directly. "All those books I read, the Greeks and the great Christian thinkers, I'd come away thinking that I followed the reasoning, but a week after putting a book down, the arguments were already mush. Even when I went back and reread, and reread again, they didn't stay." He tapped the side of his head with the heel of his hand. "It was beyond me. I knew I'd never really understand." He paused and looked at the old man's rheumy eyes.

"We mus' re-ly on fai'h."

"But faith doesn't answer questions. It allows us to put the questions aside and move on. But if those questions nag at you . . ."

"You haf' to sur-rend'r your-self to the Lor'." Saliva had collected at the drooping corner of Brother Archibald's mouth.

"You do." Casimir said. But he couldn't. He was too thick and too obstinate. It was a bad combination.

"May-be you will fine-d your way in Ari-zona."

"It's a desert." He smiled and shrugged.

"Our Lor' wen' in-to the des-er'."

"Which is where Satan chose to tempt him."

"Wi'-out suc-cess."

The old man reached out his good hand and gripped Casimir's. They sat like that for some time.

"I should be going," Casimir said.

"God be wi' you, son," Brother Archibald said, releasing Casimir's hand.

2. The Fold

THEY LIVED BENEATH half a rainbow—but of multilayered sandstone, not of fractured light—that plunged into the ground behind them. The first sight of the eastward-arcing wall of reds and tans—a geological fold, someone had told them—with its green scattering of pinyon and scrub, brought a smile of wonder to Brother Casimir's face, but Brother Absalom frowned and Father Dubuffet saw first and foremost the threat of being crushed by falling debris from the cliff face. Sandstone slabs lay near the would-be mission house, but how frequently or infrequently did weather-worn fragments slough away? Every year? Every ten? Casimir figured that they stood a far better chance of freezing. The house wasn't livable, not once winter descended. He could wriggle three fingers through chinks in the adobe that more-or-less held the stone walls together. It would be better to tear the walls down and reuse the stones to build something proper, but there wasn't time to do that. Fortunately, greater care had been taken with the tightly laid log roof, which sagged a bit toward one end but appeared to be intact, and with the fireplace, where a proper mortar had been used. (There was no stove.) At first he didn't even recognize another major problem: the pipe from the wellhead to the kitchen pump, some thirty yards long, was covered by only an inch of dirt, which he discovered by tripping over an exposed joint.

That evening at dinner—their third day, canned food once again dumped into a frying pan and heated in the hearth—Casimir informed Dubuffet and Absalom of the latest piece of bad news. "The water pipe's going to freeze," he said.

"I doubt that, Brother," Absalom said. "It isn't going to get that cold. If it did, the Escobar family couldn't have lived here."

"They didn't," Casimir said. "Not through the winter. I'd guess that when the weather turned, Escobar herded his sheep south and stayed there until spring."

"Don't you think the Sisters would have known that before they bought the property?"

"They most likely never asked." From what he'd heard, the Sisters had given all their attention to Cienega Amarilla. Hunters Point was an afterthought.

"What do you propose?" Father Dubuffet asked. Thus far he'd surprised Casimir by remaining calm, almost disinterested, in the physical difficulties of their situation.

"I'll take the buckboard into Gallup tomorrow. It'll take me most of a day to get there, another to find what we need and return. I'll buy a stove—with your permission, of course, Father—and I'll see if I can locate a plumber who's willing to show me how to solder lead joints."

"And then?"

"I'll dig a trench to below the frost line, run the pipe under the foundation and up through the floor, and reconnect it."

"How deep a trench?"

"I don't know, maybe a foot and a half. I can ask Ricardo Medina." The Medinas lived year-round on a comfortable spread about a mile south of Hunters Point. Medina, their principal contact, spoke Navajo as well as Spanish and English, as did both his sons. Eduardo, the elder, had agreed to serve as translator for the mission. Medina, raised a Catholic, had assured Father Dubuffet that the whole family, including four daughters as well as his wife and sons, would come to the mission this Sunday for Mass. (Casimir hoped that Mrs. Medina would bring something resembling real food as an offering.)

"Brother Absalom and I need to be about our business," Father Dubuffet said, pushing Van Camp's pork and beans around his plate with his spoon. Thus far, Dubuffet and Absalom had contacted only one Navajo family, which lived about half a mile away, east of Black Creek. The Navajos had been very friendly, but trying to explain Christ's resurrection to them proved an impossible task.

"When I get back from Gallup, I can do what needs to be done here." Casimir couldn't picture either Absalom or Dubuffet digging a trench.

"Very well. In your absence, I think we'll ask Eduardo to take us up to Cienega Amarilla so we can have a better look around. We should introduce ourselves to the Day family." Samuel E. Day, his wife Anna, and their three boys—Charlie, Sam Jr., and Willie—had been living in the area for a decade. Sam worked as a freighter, clerk, and surveyor for the Navajo Agency in Ft. Defiance and knew as much about the Navajo as any white man in the area. Sam had agreed to sell all but forty acres of his homestead to the Sisters for their mission and Indian school.

They finished their meal, and Dubuffet and Absalom went off to their separate bedrooms to pray while Casimir cleaned up. Then he stoked the fire, stepped outside to scan the host of stars, visited the privy, and prepared his folding cot in the chapel while his companions completed their nighttime rituals.

Casimir didn't sleep at all well, anticipating the long road, some thirty miles through the alien landscape into Gallup, where they'd arrived only four days ago by train. Casimir told himself that he needed to do this. Not for the mission, but for himself. It was a test. Of fortitude. Of character. Of . . . abiding. He'd never ventured anywhere on his own, not really; he'd always had his family, and when that fell apart and then regathered in Carbondale without him, he'd had the Brother brothers, and with them, offering a wider cloak of safety, the Province of St. John the Baptist. He still had the cloak, or perhaps he should say the habit, but out *there*, between Hunters Point and Gallup, anything could happen. A lame horse. A broken axle. A confrontation with hostile Indians. A sudden violent storm. All he'd have for protection would be his resolve. And maybe God.

Even though they experienced increasingly frequent freezing nights almost from their arrival, the winter didn't hit solidly until late December. By then, Brother Casimir had installed the stove, which heated the common room nicely, and had dug the trench and buried the water line. He knew he hadn't managed to stockpile enough split wood, given the rate at which they were burning through it—Father Dubuffet constantly complained about the cold—which meant that he spent hours each day on that task. Fortunately, the temperature typically rose into the forties or fifties by early afternoon and held there for an hour or two, until the sun slipped behind the sandstone scarp.

For five hours every day the chapel served as a schoolroom. The older Medina children learned proper English grammar and punctuation from Brother Absalom for two hours and the catechism from Father Dubuffet for another, after which the tables were turned and Eduardo Medina taught the missionaries, including Casimir when he wasn't otherwise occupied, how to speak Navajo. Despite his reputed ear for languages, Absalom, in his effort to compile a Navajo dictionary, continually expressed his frustration because certain Navajo pronunciations, even ignoring breath stops and tonal changes, couldn't be rendered phonetically in English. At one point, weary of Absalom's whining, Casimir suggested, "Brother, you're the first person to try and write down Navajo. So use whatever system you want. Invent one."

Absalom's face registered absolute scorn. "That isn't how linguists and phoneticians proceed."

"Have it your way. Or rather, have it their way." Casimir said nothing more on the matter.

Mid-January brought the worst cold down on them, subzero nights and some days when the temperature barely broke freezing. Casimir had gotten used to sleeping in his clothes, supplemented by a second pair of socks, but one night, with the wind roaring, shaking the frosted-over window glass and skirling down the chimney, a draft infiltrated the chapel and drove him to the common room. He wasn't in the habit of adding wood to the stove during the night, but if he felt this cold, he guessed that his companions, behind their closed doors, must also be having difficulty sleeping. Dawn was still hours away. So he shook the ashes down, stirred up the coals, and stuffed as much wood as he dared into the firebox. He decided to open the bedroom doors as quietly as possible and let at least a flush of heat flow in.

Absalom's bed was empty.

Casimir opened the other door. Brother Absalom and Father Dubuffet lay together, chest to back, under a mound of covers. Casimir closed the door and listened. Someone stirred; Absalom, he assumed. He walked to the sink and retrieved a five-quart kettle that he pumped full of water every evening before retiring, just in case the water pipe froze despite his efforts with pick and shovel. He set the kettle on the stove.

Some time passed before Dubuffet's bedroom door opened and Absalom emerged. "Good morning, Brother," he squeaked. "I see you already have the kettle started. Good man, good man." He rubbed his hands together and then opened his palms toward the stove. "Brutal weather, brutal night." He coughed into a closed fist.

"Indeed."

"I heard Father praying aloud—only that thin wall separates our beds— and it seemed to me that he couldn't get settled, so I went in to ask if I could do anything to ease his discomfort. He said he was very cold."

"I'm sure."

"If the weather doesn't break, perhaps you should keep the fire going through the night."

"That's a thought."

"And if Father and I leave our doors open . . . although, personally, I'm not in distress. I mean, because of the cold." He turned and looked back toward Dubuffet's open door, listening. "He seems to be sleeping soundly now. At last."

The water was coming to a boil on the stove. "Coffee or tea?"

"We should leave him be."

"Coffee or tea?" Casimir repeated.

"Coffee, if you're going to the trouble of making it for yourself."

"It's no trouble." Casimir scooped a few tablespoons of beans into a mortar and began pulverizing them.

"He was the school principal during your day, wasn't he?"

"He was."

"A good one, I'm sure."

"He cracked the whip."

"In my day, he taught Greek and Latin. He saw my affinity for languages right away and set me on my path. I owe everything to him. And of course to Jesus Christ." Absalom blessed himself with the sign of the cross. "I'm sure you understand. You have your benefactors, Brothers Archibald and Matthew. You must have the same high regard for them."

"Maybe not quite the same."

"They taught me as well, you know," Absalom hurried on, speaking to fill what otherwise would have been silence. "But mathematics and science were never my forte. I've forgotten it all." He tittered. "Except that you can't square a circle."

"This is true." Casimir tapped the ground coffee into the filter coffee pot and added a quart of water from the kettle, and dropped in an egg.

"I'd appreciate it if this"—he gestured toward Father Dubuffet's bedroom—"remained a . . . private matter. I wouldn't want to cause Father any embarrassment. He prides himself on his personal strength."

"Does he? Well then . . ."

"I see no need to speak of this again."

"As you wish, Brother."

At breakfast—porridge and a fried egg each, the latter from the Medinas' hens—with the wind still howling between cabin and cliff, Brother Absalom suggested that Father Dubuffet might consider returning to Cincinnati, at least until spring. He feared that the Father's health was beginning to suffer.

"Absolutely not," Dubuffet said. "I'm not going to desert a post I assumed voluntarily."

Casimir didn't weigh in, but in truth Dubuffet appeared quite frail, the gray of his Van Dyke now heavy with white. He hadn't left the mission house in over two weeks and had begun taking lengthy afternoon naps. Most of the rest of his time he spent in prayer or reading or preparing his lengthy weekly reports to Cincinnati. And he'd stopped issuing directives to Casimir.

The last dispute they'd had, following a Christmas service and reception attended by the Medinas, three other Mexican families in the vicinity, and the half dozen Navajos who showed up, involved his camera, or, more precisely, the smell of the chemical baths needed for developing and printing. Casimir had devoted a whole roll of film to the gathering, as Father Dubuffet requested, in order to document that, yes, the mission was successfully reaching out to the Navajo, but when Casimir laid out his supplies and equipment at the far end of the chapel, on the table that also served as their altar, Dubuffet announced that he couldn't tolerate the stench and that Casimir should ship the film off and have it developed professionally.

"If you insist on developing the photographs yourself, do it outside," Dubuffet said.

"You must know how ridiculous that idea is."

"I know nothing of the kind. It's certainly dark enough at night, and you should be able to make allowances for the temperature."

As a consequence, the roll of film still sat in the camera.

Snow came and went, blowing through in brief storms and then disappearing from the ground almost as quickly, sublimating into thin air as much as it melted at midday. It clung only to the high ridge line above them and erratically along the seams in the sandstone fold, as if painted with an unevenly worn brush.

They waited for spring, but just as it approached, all three came down with colds within days of each other. Casimir and Absalom weathered the scratchy throat, sneezing, leaky nose, and rheumy eyes, followed by the thick cough, but Father Dubuffet, older by several decades, took to his bed with a fever, and the illness settled into his chest, obstructing his lungs with yellowish phlegm that he struggled to cough out. During a particularly difficult night, Casimir considered bundling him into the back of the wagon and taking him to the nearest doctor, several hours away in Ft. Defiance, but he couldn't guess how Dubuffet's lungs would respond to the cold air. Instead, he and Absalom agreed that the doctor should be fetched. They told Dubuffet that Casimir would ride to Ft. Defiance in the morning. Dubuffet whispered between rasping breaths, "From the moment I saw . . . that deformity of the earth . . . hanging over me . . . I knew it pointed . . . to my grave."

Casimir left on horseback at first light and returned with the doctor early in the afternoon. Father Dubuffet had pneumonia, the doctor announced after a quick examination, and nothing could be done. Dubuffet still might be able to marshal his own resources and fight off the infection, and to that end he should be kept comfortable. He should drink broth and water and tea, and a little wine or spirits wouldn't hurt. In fact, alcohol might help him clear the phlegm. The doctor recommended whiskey, hot water, and sugar, but they didn't have any whiskey, just wine, and Absalom tried substituting that. Dubuffet said he couldn't stomach it.

That night, Absalom and Casimir took turns beside the patient's bed. Sitting upright, pillows propped behind him, holding a silver crucifix in one hand and his rosary in the other, Dubuffet was drowning, his chest heaving as he struggled to draw air into his lungs.

Not long before dawn, Casimir assumed the chair. Dubuffet's face was drawn, waxy, his eyes wide and panicked, his lips and the beds of his fingernails purpling.

"What can I do for you, Father?" Casimir asked.

"This will be you . . . someday," Dubuffet said. "Do you intend . . . to spend your life . . . in service to *this*"—he lifted a fist and struck himself in the gut—"or to this." He placed his hand, the one holding the crucifix, over his heart.

Casimir didn't reply.

"I see . . . your soul," Dubuffet said. "It's black with sin."

"God be with you, Father," Casimir said and left the room. He didn't wake Absalom until the rasping from the other room had stopped.

A tearful Absalom asked, "Did he say anything at the end?"

"A Confiteor," Casimir replied.

The Medina family came for the funeral service, as did the Days from Cienega Amarilla, even though they were Protestants. The night before, Casimir and Absalom had covered two sawhorses with a white cloth that draped to the floor, and had laid the coffin, hammered together by Ricardo and Eduardo Medina, across them. Casimir would lead the opening and concluding prayers, and Absalom would say Mass—though as a Brother he couldn't consecrate the Eucharist, he could distribute the Body of Christ that had already been sanctified by Father Dubuffet—and provide a eulogy.

Casimir was glad to see the Day wagon pull up. He'd taken to dropping in on them whenever he could. He liked them immensely. Midwesterners by birth, they had no pretensions. Anna had been a schoolteacher in Illinois, and Sam Sr. hailed from Ohio but was widely traveled, to college in New Jersey, into West Virginia with the Ohio Volunteer Infantry during the Civil War, and then to the gold fields of South Dakota and the farmlands of Iowa and Colorado before settling in Arizona. Taught by their mother and fluent in Navajo language and lore, the Day boys had no formal schooling, but they were whip-smart. Casimir especially liked Charlie, at fifteen the eldest of the three and the most gregarious.

Brother Absalom, standing at the head of the closed coffin, had just begun his eulogy when everyone else in the room simultaneously took a deep breath. A snake had edged out from under the draped white cloth, inches from Absalom's foot. Absalom looked puzzled until he followed the direction of their eyes. His face froze into a horrified mask. The first person to move was Charlie Day—the nearest one to the door—who dashed outside and quickly returned, a belted holster in one hand and a cocked revolver in the other. He pulled the trigger and the snake's head disintegrated, spraying an arc of gore across the bottom of the altar cloth and Absalom's cassock; the bullet left a neat angled hole in the wooden floor. In such a small enclosed space the explosion had concussed Casimir's eardrums; he could hardly hear anything now, except a loud ringing in his ears.

Willie, eleven, the youngest Day son, let out a whoop and ran to pick up the snake. When he pulled the rest of its thick body out from under the table and gleefully held it up head-high, the rattle at the end of the tail grazed the floor. Absalom retreated to a chair.

"Take that out of here," Sam Sr. said, and Willie, with another whoop, complied.

Charlie, trying unsuccessfully to contain a broad grin, reholstered the gun.

"That, too," Sam Sr. said, pointing to the gun, and then, turning to Absalom, he added, "My apologies."

"Well," Anna Day said, "The serpent won't be tempting anyone today, will it?"

When Absalom recovered his color, they concluded the service outside, at the gravesite, beneath the sandstone arc. (Absalom had proposed that the grave be located under the cottonwoods near Black Creek, but Casimir had convinced him that a site below the rock wall would be more fitting for a man of Father Dubuffet's character.) A few final prayers were spoken, and the pine coffin was lowered into its resting place.

Afterward, following a thorough inspection of the mission premises by the Day boys, Absalom retreated to his room while Eduardo and Casimir filled in the grave. When they were finished, Brother Absalom pushed a simple wooden cross into the ground, his final act as a missionary to the Navajo. Before the day was out, he was already packing to leave.

"What are you planning to do?" Casimir asked him that evening.

"I'm returning to St. Francis College. I'll stop in Cincinnati on the way and submit a report." He added a leather-bound book to a half-filled crate. "What will you do?" he asked Casimir.

"Wait for instructions from the province, I suppose," Casimir said.

They parted for the last time the following morning at Navajo Springs, which was little more than the railroad depot, a telegraph office, and a café.

On his own, with his brown robe thrown aside, Casimir soon found that he had nothing to do. So he decided to tour the reservation. He recruited Charlie Day as a guide, paying him in advance with money he'd found in Father Dubuffet's cash box—which he'd had to force open because he couldn't find the key. Charlie, affable as always, mentioned, when they were on the road up to Canyon de Chelly, that he found addressing his companion as "Brother Casimir" a little awkward, given that they weren't brothers, not even in religious leanings, and that Casimir seemed a peculiar, foreign-sounding name.

"You can call me Pete," Casimir said.

Charlie laughed. "Where'd that come from?"

"My last name. Pietrowski. It's Polish."

" 'Pete' sounds fine by me," the boy said.

Charlie led Pete through both main branches of the canyon, pointing out the rock art and the small Anasazi ruins and the massive Fortress, a formation at the juncture of Canyon del Muerto and Black Rock Canyon where scores of Navajo had fled to escape the ravages of Kit Carson's campaign to burn and starve them out in 1864. They wandered all the way up the main canyon, passing Face Rock and towering Spider Rock, the home of Spider Woman, who'd taught the Navajo how to weave, to where tributary creeks formed the Chinle Wash. From there, since Pete wasn't in any hurry to return to Hunters Point, nor to read whatever directive might have arrived by now from Cincinnati, they rode over to Ganado, stopping overnight at the Hubbell Trading Post, and continued on to the Hopi mesas. From the vantage point afforded by the ancient village of Walpi, perched on a finger of rock, they could easily see the San Francisco Peaks, still capped by snow, seventy-five miles to the southwest, with little but bare brown land between. They rode southeast, through the Painted Desert, with its multihued layers and deposits of petrified wood, before circling back through Navajo Springs, where Pete picked up his anticipated telegram:

BRO CASIMIR PIETROWSKI OFM-------- NAVAJO SPRINGS AZ=
1895 APR 24 PM 3 15
CLOSE HUNTERS POINT= REPORT WITH ALL MISSION
RECORDS TO ABP CHAPELLE IN SANTA FE BEFORE RETURN
TO CINCINNATI=
BRO ARCHIBALD MUCH IMPROVED PRAISE GOD=

BRO MATTHEW ALLEN OFM=

Praise God indeed, Pete thought, smiling broadly when he'd finished reading the telegram. He'd never expected to see Brother Archibald again, not in this world. Pete's momentary elation faded, though. If he returned to Cincinnati, it would only be to renounce his vocation, which would injure both brothers more than he already had. And what was this about reporting to Archbishop Chapelle? Casimir knew little about him, except that he'd been high up in the Bureau of Indian Catholic Missions before assuming ecclesiastical authority over the Santa Fe archdiocese, which stretched into northern Arizona.

When they reached Hunters Point, Charlie Day continued on toward home, leaving Pete—he no longer thought of himself as Brother Casimir—to his own devices. He needed to think. He opened up a tin of sardines and sat at the table eating. He had enough chemicals to develop and print two of the five rolls of film from his trip with Charlie, which is what he wanted to do before anything else, but the summons to Santa Fe continued to trouble him. Even though the Hunters Point Mission was being run from the province of St. John the Baptist in Cincinnati and funded by the Sisters of the Blessed Sacrament in Philadelphia, everything within the geographical territory of the archdiocese also fell within the purview of Archbishop Chapelle. The reason for the side trip to Santa Fe might be as benign as the archbishop's wanting to hear a firsthand assessment of the Navajo as possible converts. But Pete smelled a rat.

For that matter, why had the telegram come from Brother Matthew instead of from the provincial office? As a definer, an adviser, Matthew had something of an official position in the provincial leadership, but still . . . Maybe someone in authority figured he would be less likely to question instructions from Matthew.

Pete wiped his oily fingers on his pants and walked into Dubuffet's room, to the father's small desk. Dubuffet's personal correspondence lay neatly stacked off to the side, beside the now-empty cash box, but Pete couldn't find the mission ledger, copies of bills, receipts, or anything of the like. Dubuffet had been assiduous about such matters, up to and probably including his last few weeks. So where were the records Pete was supposed to bring to Santa Fe?

In the paws of the rat, Brother Absalom.

Pete laughed. Records. He had none, except his negatives and prints, and he was about to be hung out to dry alongside them.

Ricardo Medina agreed to care for the mission's two horses and to look after a box of Pete's personal items until he sent for them. Pete also left in Ricardo's hands Father Dubuffet's chalice as well as the gold paten, ciborium, and thurible, none of which could be safely left in the abandoned mission house. Ricardo then dropped him at the Navajo Springs depot.

Pete never even saw Archbishop Chapelle when he reached Santa Fe. (And why was it, he wondered, that the first three archbishops of Santa Fe—Jean-Baptiste Lamy, Jean-Baptiste Salpointe, and now Placide Louis Chapelle—where every second person you met spoke Spanish, had all been born in France?) Instead, wearing street clothes, Pete was directed to an underling, a monsignor (also French) whose name Pete quickly forgot, and a nun, a representative of the Sisters of the Blessed Sacrament whose name he also quickly forgot.

He had no idea where the mission records were, he told them. Was he accusing Brother Absalom Cordry of taking them? they asked. No, he wasn't accusing anyone of anything. Could he account for any missing sums? What missing sums? They couldn't be specific in the absence of documentation. Could he provide a record of all the purchases he had made with mission funds? No, he could not. He could, however, if they wished, provide a list of merchants with whom he'd dealt in Gallup. And elsewhere? they asked. He asked, Did they have *any* idea where Hunters Point was located, because there was no *elsewhere*, unless they meant Ricardo Medina's ranch, where he sometimes purchased eggs and milk and hay. At that point the monsignor accused him of being disrespectful and noted that the Province of St. John the Baptist had asked parishes in Lafayette, Indiana, and Over-the-Rhine to examine closely their financial records during the time of Brother Casimir's residency. The sister asked what he had billed to the mission's account since the death of Father Dubuffet (may he rest in peace). The train ticket from Navajo Springs, Arizona, to Lamy, New Mexico. That was all? That was all. No incidental expenses? He'd found $13.35 in the mission's cash box. And how much of that was left? He retrieved $2.68 from a pocket and placed it on the monsignor's desk. The monsignor told him to put the money away and asked what he had used the rest for. Mostly, to pay Charlie Day, a guide who accompanied him to various locations on the Navajo Reservation. And had this trip been in furtherance of the mission's purpose? No, it had not. Was he prepared to reimburse the mission account? No, he was not. Did he consider himself a thief? No, he did not.

The inquisition continued like this for some time. When he left, he had in his pocket the $2.68 and a one-way ticket to Cincinnati via Chicago. He tore the ticket up, which he immediately regretted; he should have cashed it in.

So the former Brother Casimir found himself in Santa Fe, stranded, with the pittance in his pocket and a carpet bag containing a change of clothing, his frock, a pair of sandals, a rosary, his folding camera, three rolls of exposed film, various photographs, and a pocketknife. He sat under a massive tree in the plaza across from the Palace of Governors. To his right, two blocks away, over the tops of the adobe-clad buildings on the east side of the plaza, he could see the towers of the Cathedral of St. Francis. He tried to spit the taste of iron from his mouth.

He had his choice of saloons. He crossed Lincoln Avenue, picked the one next to a book and stationery store, ordered a whiskey and a glass of water, and placed his coins on the counter. The bartender helped himself. Pete asked if there might be a paperboard box he could have. The bartender soon returned from the back with an empty carton. Pete, taking a piece of chalk from a tray beneath the board advertising the day's sandwich specials, left the saloon and broke down the box. He walked north to Palace Avenue and turned the corner, passed the Capital Hotel, and ducked into the first passageway between buildings, where he discarded all but the largest rectangle of paperboard and put the chalk to work. He found a broken bowl and length of string among the debris in the alley and tied the string to two holes he poked through his sign. Then he hung the sign from his neck and returned to the plaza. Wearing his religious frock, he stood in front of the post office, the bowl at his feet. The sign around his neck read:

The 1st Franciscan Mission
To the Navajo Indians
At Hunters Point
Needs Your Support!
Give Your Coins—Receive God's Blessings!

He took out his black beads, made sure the silver cross dangled prominently, pretended to pray, and waited, smiling benignly and catching as many eyes as he could. The passing ladies and gentlemen proved surprisingly generous, and in less than two hours Pete had accumulated not only train fare to Albuquerque, but also sufficient money for a restaurant meal of machaca, tamales, flour tortillas, and coffee.

On the train to Albuquerque he considered another option: posing as a professional photographer in front of the San Felipe de Neri Church, the oldest building in the city and just about the only thing worth photographing. He could take pictures of visitors for a modest sum, exposing the same frame over and over again with no intention of ever delivering the nonexistent prints, but he soon rejected the plan as unlikely to succeed. He didn't have the clothes to look the part. No, he'd have to stick to his habit and beads and a new hand-lettered sign (he'd torn up the old one and sent the pieces sailing into the street), and since Albuquerque was smaller and poorer than Santa Fe, he'd best ply his confidence game at the depot: more traffic, more potential dupes, although he'd have to be careful not to overstay his welcome. If he couldn't raise the fare to Gallup, well, he'd go by train as far as he could and then repeat the scheme, deceiving his way stop by stop if necessary. After gathering the rest of his clothes and other items from Ricardo Medina, and after taking from the mission house whatever of value he might be able to pawn—Dubuffet's vestments? the wooden crucifix that hung behind the altar? the glass cruets?—he'd return to Gallup and go into business for himself. To start, all he'd need would be film, chemicals, and paper, and a room where he could sleep and, on the sly, develop photographs.

* * *

Gallup, N. Mex. Terr.

My Dear Bros. Archibald and Matthew,

I will not be returning to Cincinnati. I do not have any means to defend myself and so will not try. As you probably have realized for yourselves, Bro. Absalom Cordry should not be trusted. He will shade the truth—no, I must be direct, he will outright lie—if it is to his own benefit.

Believe what you must—some of it will certainly be true—but not the worst.

Your eternally grateful,
Wladyslaw "Pete" Pietrowski

3. Mrs. Halley

IN THE GALLUP depot he set up an easel bearing a simple sign:

PETE PIETROWSKI, PHOTOGRAPHER
Photographs $0.50
Delivered to You the Next Day; or Mailed Anywhere (10 Cents Extra)

The station master received five cents for every photograph. People getting off the train to dine at the Harvey House were his best customers: stand them up, focus, take the photograph, record name and address, pocket the money. Sometimes they were families, sometimes just a salesman on his way to somewhere else, but his best and easiest customers were the young couples.

One afternoon he was in a particularly foul mood, hung over, and the weather was stifling, the rare humid day, and a thunderstorm had just passed through, offering at least a promise of relief on a breeze from the north, and he spotted his next marks, a young couple, so out of place and tentative with each other—he, solicitous; she covering newlywed anxiety with quick smiles beneath the darting eyes—and Pete went to work: they were on their honeymoon and, yes, the man decided, a photograph to add to their wedding album would be nice. They'd been married all of two days he said, the bride blushing under her broad-brimmed hat decorated with silk flowers and bright blue ribbon. (She was quite pretty.) So Pete stood them together in the sunlight breaking through a window. He looked at them, he looked down at his camera, he looked at them again. They stood there stiff as corpses, the groom absolutely erect, his chest expanded to its full dimensions, his chin tucked in, the bride not even smiling, and Pete sighed and said, "I bet you have a very nice wedding album." Well, the groom said, of course they hadn't seen it yet, but they expected so. The bride's father had paid for a real professional, and the whole wedding party visited his studio. And Pete, folding up his tripod, said, "Then you certainly don't need another photograph that makes you look like you're attending a funeral."

The bride looked deeply offended; the groom's jaw drooped beneath the mustache that framed his mouth.

"Indulge me. Come outside," Pete said, "just outside here, into the good light." They hesitated, and he said, "I'm going to take a photograph that you'll actually want to put on your dresser, one that you'll want your children to see and that they'll keep as a treasure long after you're gone, and I'm not going to charge you anything for it. Think of it as a wedding present. All you have to do is come outside, onto the platform."

They followed him and he set up his camera at an angle and told them to sit down on the bench beneath the window through which the light had come and which now reflected their shoulders and the backs of their heads, and he told the bride to sit sideways on her husband's lap, which, blushing, she refused to do until her husband, getting into the spirit of the adventure, gently coaxed her. And then Pete told them to take their hats off because her hair would be beautiful in the sunlight, which was falling upon her thanks to a sudden parting of the clouds, and he told them to exchange hats, which they didn't understand, and he walked over, lifted the man's hat off and handed it to the woman and told her to put it in her lap, and waited for her to unpin her broad feathered hat, which he then took from her hand and set on the bench, askew, beside them, and lastly he told the groom to put his right arm tight around his bride's waist. Then he walked back to the camera and waited, and the two of them, embarrassed at the public intimacy, started laughing, containing it, though, because several passersby had stopped to watch now, behind Pete, and he told the two they had to stop laughing, which they struggled to do, and he still waited, and he could see the full blush in her cheeks, and light striking a small puddle on the platform from the shower, and still he waited, and he saw the man, grinning, take a quick glance at his wife just as she was starting to laugh again and Pete snapped the picture.

They were staying overnight in the European, and Pete told them he'd develop the photograph and deliver it to them in the morning before their train departed, and that night in his room at the Commercial he arrayed his chemicals and his paper and he brought the photograph to life. When it was done, still wet from the final bath, he looked at it carefully. This was what he'd promised them, a photograph they'd cherish for the rest of their lives, and he made three more copies, one to keep for himself.

As he'd told them he would, he brought them the photograph in the morning, and, standing there in the hotel lobby, they were so delighted that they bought the other two copies, for a dollar each, and later in the morning he tacked his copy of the photograph to his sign in the lobby of the depot.

Over the next few weeks Pete added others. An elderly couple, well endowed in girth and jewelry, leaning on parasol and cane beside the locomotive, where the grubby engineer, above and to the left, also stood looking straight at the camera through the slow steam rising from beneath the locomotive. A family of four, posed straight on, father sitting with a giggling child on each leg and with their smiling mother behind, one hand draped along the back of the bench, the other, with softly folded fingers, touching her husband's cheek. A salesman, stretched out to his full length on the bench beneath the window, propped on elbow, chin and cheek in hand, bowler perched on upright bent knee, leather sample cases for H. G. Leisenring & Co. Patent Medicines (featuring "Snyder's Celebrated Bitter Cordial") displayed beneath the bench . . .

Pete's business grew. He was soon able to rent a two-room Second Street storefront in the Caledonian Coal Company building, though he would have preferred being right on Railroad Avenue rather than around to the side. He sometimes worked through the night, developing the five-by-seven glass plates from his new Burke & James view camera. Although he still used his No. 5 Kodak on occasion, he preferred working with the Burke & James and glass plates rather than film—the plates seemed more permanent, and he stored them carefully. He kept a cot in the back for when he needed to nap or collapse or when, well after midnight, he didn't want to risk disturbing the other boarders or incurring the wrath of the landlady at the rooming house where he otherwise lived. In the evenings when he wasn't working, he frequented Gallup's saloons, in addition to paying irregular visits to a particularly favored den of whores north of the tracks.

HE DIDN'T MUCH LIKE his life, except for his photography. Not the formal portraiture that paid his bills—in the three years since he'd left the Franciscans, he'd given up trying to convince most customers that they really wanted something other than what they thought they wanted—but his *own* work, out in the air, in the canyons and on the mesas. He did, however, participate in the local businessmen's association, where, more often than not, he acted the crank and contrarian, countering the supposed civilizing influence of the bankers and lawyers and respectable entrepreneurs, Alberto Rodriguez and his ilk. Somewhat grudgingly, most of them nevertheless threw work his way since he was the only professional photographer in town. That was how he came to take the photographs of the trading post up at Many Springs Canyon that Rodriguez was trying to market for the Taskin brothers, and how he was confronted by the new owner, who pounded on his door one morning, waking him from a stupor.

When he threw open the door she immediately took a step back, apparently aghast at what she saw. He hadn't shaved in several days, his matted hair resembled a tom turkey's rising feathers, and he was wearing his usual garb for developing and printing—his old Franciscan robe, now much stained by chemicals, coffee, food, and he didn't care to guess what else. "What d'you want?" he said, his gorge rising from the alcohol he'd consumed the night before. "I'm not open for business." The severe light forced him to squint.

"Judging by appearances, that's probably a good thing," the woman said.

He shielded his bloodshot eyes and grabbed the jamb with the other hand to hold himself steady. Behind her he saw a wagon with a full load covered by a tarp, and holding the reins of the four-hitch team, Sam Bosco.

"G'morning, Pete," Bosco said. Bosco worked for Alberto Rodriguez, running freight and delivering purchases to customers of the Furniture Emporium.

"Is it?" Pete said, rubbing his temples. His gaze came back to the woman. He sighed. "What is it I can do for you, Mrs. —?"

"Mrs. Wilford Halley."

He waited for her to continue but she didn't. "Should I know you?"

"You haven't heard the name?"

"I don't believe so."

"My husband and I are the new owners of the Many Springs Canyon Trading Post."

"Ah."

"You know it?"

"I was up there once."

"To take photographs."

"Yes . . ."

"Which were then used to gull us."

"Wait a minute, I didn't—"

"The place is empty. Stripped to the rafters."

"Don't go accusing me, Mrs.—" She had him at a disadvantage, with him standing there in his filthy robe, and hung over to boot.

"Halley. Julia Halley." She stood there, arms akimbo.

"I went up there, did what Alberto Rodriguez paid me to do, and left. Go complain to Rodriguez."

"I've already spoken to Mr. Rodriguez."

Well, of course she had. Why else would Sam Bosco, Alberto's man, be sitting there, grinning at him? He ran a hand over his hair. "You know anything about this, Sam?" he asked the teamster.

Bosco shook his head. "You know me, Pete—see no evil, hear no evil."

"You're forgetting the part about speaking no evil."

Bosco launched a stream of tobacco juice into the street.

"If you get a court date," Pete said, turning back to the woman, "you have your lawyer contact my lawyer."

"And who would that be?"

"I don't have a lawyer."

"Well, my family does," she answered.

"And where would that be?"

"Albany, New York."

"I guess that's just as good as not having one." Pete scratched his whiskers. He didn't quite know what to make of this Julia Halley. Feisty, that was for sure. He hoped her husband had a strong backbone and a light touch. "I'd invite you in," he said, "but I can't even offer you a cup of coffee. What I do have, you wouldn't want, not at this time of day anyway."

Sam Bosco laughed and squirted another spurt of tobacco juice.

She looked past Pete's shoulder, into his studio. He turned sideways and took a good look himself. The room's sparse furnishings prominently included his Burke & James, mounted on a tripod in the middle of the floor and pointed toward a blank wall that he'd painted a light tan. Three matching wooden chairs in the Mexican style, one of them with arms, were positioned before the tan wall; the chairs were pale, oiled rather than stained or painted, as was a tall side table, the right height for displaying a vase of flowers or a rectangular clock or another desired prop. On the other side of the room were a small desk and a full-length mirror.

"Your photographs gulled me," Julia Halley said.

"I already told you—"

"Not the ones you took inside. The others. You painted a picture that I wanted to see."

He had to stop and think, remember. He'd arrived at the trading post not long after noon, when the sunlight was still too harsh to show anything but the stark and bare, so he'd unlocked the door with the key Rodriguez had handed him two days before. At least somebody had made an effort to clean up the living quarters, which when occupied by Ab Taskin had probably held more clutter than actual furnishings. The trading post, in contrast, was so stuffed with goods—sacked and barreled on the floor, hung from the rafters and log posts and walls, displayed on the counters and shelves, as in every other trading post he'd ever entered—that the ground-in grime on the floor and the layer of dust covering everything else made no matter. He should have brought rags to clean the filth off the windows, for better light. But it wasn't his job to spruce the place up, at least not literally.

By the time he'd finished inside, the smoke from the flash powder was making his eyes water. Outside, the sunlight had mellowed and was throwing shadows toward the southeast. He photographed the exterior from several vantages: with the northern sandstone wall behind; from the side, with the canyon running down to the east; with the tree line rising in the west and the Chuskas providing a backdrop; and, having carried, grunting and sweating, tripod and camera and several glass plates part way up the north canyon wall, the full scene from above. He took the last photograph as the sun declined behind the mountains.

Did she think he should *apologize* because she liked his photographs? Who *was* this woman? She stood before him, maybe five-five, her face freckled and freshly pinkened by exposure but not at all like the toughened, deeply tanned and lined skin of women he saw every day on the streets of Gallup; no jewelry but her wedding ring, her hands not yet roughened by hard work, which all lay ahead of her. If she stayed. She wore a straight gray skirt, no bustle for *her*, and a plain ivory-colored blouse, no frills or lace, and a blue jacket of finer quality, something, he presumed, that she'd brought with her from wherever—Albany, New York. The short jacket flared over her hips, held tight to the waist, and lay open above a row of buttons, drawing his eyes to a pleasant bosom. Julia Halley, maybe twenty-five, maybe thirty at most, was no conventional beauty despite a fine smooth neck, a mouth whose upper lip almost hid the corners where it met her full lower lip, a nose that broadened just enough to encounter, delicately, the crease of round cheek. Her gray irises, hinting of green, paired well with her light brown hair.

You painted a picture that I wanted to see. "I usually get the opposite complaint," he said.

"What's that?"

"Everyone thinks it's the photographer's fault if the bride is as ugly as sin."

Did he see a quick smile?

No, she wasn't beautiful and she knew it, but, my! she had something about her.

"Just so you know," he said, "I didn't 'paint' anything. I photographed what I saw, pure and simple, using the light which that particular afternoon gave me, that's all. So that said, what can I do for you, Missus?"

"Halley."

"*Julia* Halley. I haven't forgotten."

"I have a wagonload of new furniture, and I'd like you to photograph it."

"May I ask why?"

"You may ask and I may decline to reply."

He sighed. "Give me a minute."

"Certainly."

He walked through the studio and into the back room. He dipped a handful of water from a bucket beneath his workbench and splashed it over his hair and face. He dug the crusted sleep from the corners of his eyes with thick forefingers and then dried his face with a filthy towel that lay on the workbench. He pulled the brown robe over his head, pulled up his sagging pants, tightened the belt a notch, buttoned the top button of his collarless shirt. At least he didn't smell too bad, not as if he hadn't changed his clothes in three days—which he hadn't. He stepped back into his studio. Julia Halley no longer stood in the doorway, so he took the opportunity to glance in the standing mirror beside the desk. He ran his fingers through his wet hair a couple of times. He couldn't do anything about the three-day stubble or the circles under his eyes. He set his square jaw and gathered up his camera and tripod.

Outside, Sam Bosco had helped her remove the tarp from the wagonload of furniture: two deep-cushioned armchairs, rocking chair, dining table and matching chairs, disassembled four-poster and a mattress, wardrobe and matching dresser, small desk . . .

Pete set up his camera on the sidewalk. Unless he stood in the middle of the street, he couldn't take a full-on side view of the wagon. Instead, he set the camera at an angle, pointed toward the front corner.

"Stand beside the rump of the closest horse and look toward the camera."

She did as he ordered and he took a photograph. He removed the exposed plate and inserted another. "Climb up beside Sam," he said. She hesitated for a moment, as if expecting a hand, but then hiked her skirt well above her ankles and clambered up. "Sam, get the hell down. I don't need your ugly face mucking this up." Sam complied. Pete took another photograph and then suggested that she remove her hat, which she did.

"That should suffice," she said.

"How about one more?" Pete suggested. "Maybe of you sitting in one of your chairs in the back, surrounded by the rest of the goods."

She stared down at him. "Like a queen on her throne, appraising all that lies before her? I think not."

He couldn't help laughing.

"Just so you know, I won't pay you a dime," she said. "You've already made your money at my expense, Mr. Pietrowski."

"Hoo-whee!" Sam exclaimed. "We've got us a firecracker, Pete."

"One more photograph," Pete said. "Sam, back off. I want Mrs. Halley alone."

True words. Pete wanted to step forward and grab her hands, pull her down off the wagon and press her to him, wrap his arms around her shoulder blades.

He'd never apologize for wanting that, not ever.

PART II: HALLEY'S GATHERING

I found you and I lost you,
All on a gleaming day.
The day was filled with sunshine,
And the land was full of May.

A golden bird was singing
Its melody divine,
I found you and I loved you,
And all the world was mine.

I found you and I lost you,
All on a golden day . . .

—Paul Laurence Dunbar

CHAPTER ELEVEN: The Comet

Above a final painterly stroke of gold at the western horizon, against a deepening blue, Halley's Comet soared as if untethered, sunless, unto itself. Although Owen had expected to see something like a drawing of comets past, all fiery head and streaking tail, he saw instead a more vaporous radiance: a pure shimmering glow trailed by a gossamer veil. Oh, he knew that it was all a cheat of the eye, reflected sunlight, and that the comet, a dull cluster of rock and ice—some astronomers speculated that it was a piece of a disintegrated planet—now in retreat, was bound in its ordained orbit, but from where he sat, at the edge of a fire-lit field high in the Chuskas, the truth lay in the unimpeded brilliance, not the science.

During an early April visit to Many Springs Canyon, Pete Pietrowski had announced that he was ordering a four-and-a-half-inch refracting telescope from the John A. Brashear Company of Allegheny, Pennsylvania, complete with sturdy tripod, an equatorial mounting, four eyepieces, and a view finder. It cost the ungodly sum of $325. The arrival of the Great Comet of January 1910, which had caught the world by surprise, including the astronomers at Yerkes and Mt. Wilson, provided incentive; Pete was *not* going to miss the predictable return of Halley's Comet in May, some seventy-six years after its preceding arrival.

"We should have a viewing party," he'd said to Julia, "in honor of your namesake." Pete, Owen, Yazzie, and Julia were all sitting in her parlor. Outside, the wind howled; winter had insisted on a last tussle with spring. Johanna was seated at the dining table, drawing.

"You're deliberately misusing the term just to annoy me," Julia said. During the preceding months she'd already put up with more than a few comments tying her married name to that of the approaching comet.

"You'd be less touchy if it were called Marshall's Comet," Owen said. Needling was an essential element of Many Springs conversation, and Julia somewhat grudgingly accepted her share.

"What do you think, Rouse?" Pete asked. "Should we do it?"

"I've heard far worse excuses for a party," Owen said.

"Julia," Pete said, tapping the arm of his chair for emphasis, "like it or not, we're going to do this. Let me pick the best day. It'll be toward end of May, but I need to find out when the comet will be visible in the evening— on some days it'll rise before dawn. And we'll need the right location—to be safe, somewhere out of the canyon." He turned to Yazzie, who was seated at his little folding table, rubbing oil into a harness, yellowed newsprint spread beneath his work. "Yazzie, where would we find the best unobstructed view of the western horizon—somewhere not too difficult to get to but as high up in the mountains as practical?"

Yazzie, pausing, turned and exchanged a prolonged look with Julia before answering, "Near the top of Washington Pass. A little to the south, there's open ground."

"Then it's settled," Pete said, slapping his thighs. "We'll leave early in the day and camp under the stars. Who should we invite?"

So it had come to pass, and Pete Pietrowski now presided over the telescope on its wooden tripod, making minor adjustments to tangent screw and eyepiece as needed to track the comet. The children had lined up first. *My God, where had they all come from?* Owen wondered, chuckling to himself. Alberto and Matilda Rodriguez had brought their boy and girl, Elena and Carlos, the former dressed in the finery of a Latin princess, white taffeta and flounce and patent leather, as if she were attending a fancy party instead of a campout; followed by the Wetherills, both Al and Mary's eight-year-old daughter Martha from Gallup, and Richard and Marietta's offspring—Richard Jr., Elizabeth, Robert, and Marion Jane—from Chaco Canyon; and then Tom and Carmelita Gorman's two youngest, Annie and Jimmy, as well as Johnny Gorman with wife Sarah and baby Carmen; and a handful of other Anglo youngsters that he hadn't yet attached to particular parents. Not to mention the Navajos—at least two dozen Indian youngsters, in addition to the Gormans, ran and skittered about in such joyous disarray that even attempting a head count proved futile.

It occurred to Owen that on this singular night more Navajos might be looking through Pete's telescope than had previously set eye to eyepiece since the instrument's invention.

"Navajos don't pass up a free meal," Pete said when Owen observed that Indians held the majority. Somewhat uncharacteristically, Pete, who rarely voiced any positive sentiments about children or Navajos in general, at least not in Owen's hearing, was in fine spirits, courtesy of a concealed bottle that he'd been surreptitiously sampling.

Although Pete had to be credited with the idea for the comet-viewing, Owen doubted that he'd envisaged anything like this. How the occasion grew from a diversion into its present gathering, Owen couldn't say, except that the welcome spring warmth bred enthusiasms: for ice water replenishing the pond; for spring lambs emerging front-legs-and-head-first into the world; for short-lived mauve and white and yellow wildflowers dotting the patchy silver-green of the broader landscape; for a guest list that, in view of the once-in-a-lifetime celestial visit, soon defied restraint.

First, Julia had invited all her weavers, several of whom lived just south of the canyon, and then the other trader in the immediate area, J. B. Moore from Crystal—Moore had declined, probably because he was angry with Julia for purloining some of his best weavers—and then, at Owen's suggestion, the Richard Wetherills, whom, he was surprised to hear, immediately replied that, yes, they'd be delighted to attend. At that, Pete ventured that he might also invite the Al Wetherills and maybe a few other Gallup friends: Win Peabody, a Chicago transplant and now the local undertaker; Ashton Billings, who worked the counter at Patterson's Trading Company; and Charlie Day, who had opened Gallup's first automobile livery, among several other recent entrepreneurial ventures. Billings couldn't get the time off, but Peabody and Day came along with Pete in his wagon, and both families of Wetherills decided to meet up and come en masse. Harry Whitaker had thought it would be appropriate to add the Rev. Mr. Leonard Brink of the Tohatchi Christian Reformed mission and his wife, whom the Gormans also knew very well, and maybe even the staff and children from the Tohatchi school. Mr. Brink sent his regrets without, however, offering any explanation, while the headmistress of the school replied with her thanks but couldn't accept because of the distance and the difficulty of arranging transport for her charges. (More than likely, she feared that some of her more reluctant pupils would take the opportunity to skedaddle.) Then at some point Julia had told Tom and Carmelita to invite everyone who came into the store, and as a consequence, at least a dozen satellite Navajo campfires now dotted the clearing.

Owen had relished the coming of the southwestern spring. It had arrived without the bracing rain and the dramatic leaf-out of the East, where each variety of maple, oak, hickory, chestnut, elm, and ash displayed its particular green, but New Mexico's dry air and midday warmth and the white airy fluff from the cottonwoods along the arroyos brought their own pleasure. More importantly, he felt better than he had at any time in the preceding year, since before his diagnosis. His ulcerated feet had healed, though he had to admit to being disconcerted as he watched the frost-bitten toes of his right foot dry, shrink, and fall off: a process in miniature of life's retreat, death, and decay—a process that, in his worst moments, he saw lying in wait for the rest of him, biding its time. Still, though the toes were gone, buried beyond the reeds on the far side of the pond, he was walking just fine without them, wearing moccasins filled out with rabbit fur except when, of necessity, during his renewed explorations up the hidden trails and pathless slopes above the canyon, he resorted to sturdier footwear, oversized leather shoes high enough to support his ankles. On these excursions he took precautions, protecting the freshly pink-skinned areas where his pressure sores had healed, cushioning them with tufts of wool held in place by sleeves of fabric cut crosswise from old socks.

Moreover, his weight was holding steady; he may even have gained a few pounds since the fall. Whereas food had previously been a daily preoccupation, now he rarely gave it a thought. Though he continued to avoid breads and desserts, sweet fruits, and starchy white vegetables, he'd found, a forkful at a time, that he could safely vary his diet not only with meats and cheeses, but also with brown, red, and pinto beans; nuts of every variety; greens and watery vegetables. He'd long since trained himself to eat slowly and to stop before satiation. He understood that the diabetes would gradually have its way with him, but he couldn't measure its advance day by day or even month by month. Which meant that he could live despite the disease, his shadowy companion, for the time being.

In his prior life—which is how he thought about the life he might once have inhabited—he'd be married now, or at least the wedding day would be approaching. He still thought about Beth, but she never appeared in his dreams. Had she left so impermanent an impression that, deep within, she barely lingered, a lovely wisp, of less substance than a blonde keepsake? Surrounded by her family, she would have moved on by now; her siblings would have cajoled her out from beneath her anger and bitterness, would have revived her as only, he imagined, a close-knit family could. She was young. She'd be happy.

There were frequent nights when he thought about Beth quite differently, her skin, her hair, her lips; and inevitably accompanying such thoughts came regret. He tried to imagine her smell on his hands, the softness under his touch, the taste as his tongue darted between her teeth. For much of the past year his memories of Beth, his desire for her as she'd been, had served well enough because he'd had no future to contemplate, and therefore no expectation of desire rewarded, but lately his recollections and imaginings too often left him enervated, dissatisfied, curdled. He now desired something deeper, richer, and this carried with it a great risk, and he feared to give it a name.

Clement Yazzie and Johnny Gorman had come up to the clearing two days earlier to prepare the site. Driving wagons loaded down with gear and food, they were forced to take the long way around, north from the mouth of Many Springs Canyon and then west up the steep trail to Washington Pass. They brought with them tools for cutting back dry brush, digging pits, and chopping wood; enough heavy rope to fashion a makeshift corral for an uncertain number of horses; feed and water buckets for the horses and bales of hay; bed rolls and tarps, the latter in case the weather turned wet (an unlikely event at this time of year, when clear nights prevailed); a sack of pinto beans, a crate of canned tomatoes, half a side of bacon, a string of onions, and a pot big enough to hold them all; a doe that Yazzie had killed and cleaned several days before; two spring lambs, the ultimate extravagance; the last of the winter squash from the fall harvest, to be baked in a covered pit along with pots of Indian pudding . . . Crystal Creek, fed by small ponds and springs, would provide sufficient clean water.

Owen set out to join them a day later, partly because he was annoyed at Julia, who was on a mission and wouldn't be deterred from baking loaf after loaf of bread and turning everything she could think of into pies, sweet or savory. Rather than trace Yazzie and Johnny's route, Owen took the shorter path, up past the Yazzie place and the high meadow and into the ponderosa forest. He followed a crudely drawn map of Yazzie's that, he realized after passing Blue Hawk Lake, he didn't really need: he'd stumbled upon the clearing on one of his longer hiking expeditions into the Chuskas. There was a confluence of trails up around eight thousand feet, beneath the eastern ridge line but with no clear view of the western horizon until reaching the clearing itself, where the land rose just enough to see westward over the trees. Once at the campsite—blue and gray jays announced their objection to the human activity; a hawk, trying to circle, was being mobbed by crows—Owen tried to make himself useful, collecting stones to line both the baking pit that Johnny had already dug, and also a larger, shallower trench, over which iron grills would be laid, cuts of meat roasted, and coffee boiled by the gallon. He piled up additional rocks that could be used to encircle smaller camp fires, and then gathered dry fallen wood for burning.

The next day—the day of the comet-viewing—people began arriving in the early afternoon, and by dusk the clearing was dotted with family campfires spread over more than an acre. Pete had set up his telescope, Carmelita was supervising the cooking and carving, and Marietta and Mary Wetherill had joined Julia behind the several folding serving tables. The clearing hummed with voices and the laughter of friends, Anglo and Navajo, who saw each other too infrequently.

Sitting by himself, Owen now looked toward the comet, making its way just above the horizon, outward bound for another thirty-eight years, when gravity would again tug it back. The earth had passed through the tail yesterday, according to the astronomers, without so much as a trace left behind except in the ravings of doomsayers who'd warned of extinction. The new science of spectroscopy, using patterns in the dispersal of visible light to detect the composition of materials, had found poisonous cyanogen in the comet's fabric, leading to nonsensical speculations and precautions—the sale of anti-comet pills and protective comet umbrellas and gas masks—and even bunkum about an apocalyptic religious sect in Texas that intended to ward off the ultimate catastrophe by sacrificing a virgin. Christ, people could be so stupid. Spread across fifteen degrees of the sky's dome, the comet's tail comprised particles probably smaller than grains of sand, so ethereally bright only by reflection.

The telescope had cost Pete what a Navajo man would consider a year's wages—in a good year, a *very* good year. But the children, Anglo and Navajo, didn't care about such things. Some pressed a curious eye hard against the telescope (even though Pete, with barely contained exasperation, told them they need only look through the eyepiece, not imprint it on their sockets), saw as much as they wanted to see, and departed again for the exuberant freedom of games and the general melee. Others switched viewing eyes, cocked their heads, clearly wanted to put their hands on the instrument (strictly forbidden) to seek a better view, and sighed as if to say, *That's it*? Some stood respectfully, hands locked behind their backs and peered and peered as long as Pete allowed ("Move along now, others are waiting, and the comet isn't going to hang there all night"), and some few immediately returned to the end of the line, hoping for another opportunity before the comet disappeared. Of these curious few, what did they hope to see, what were they thinking? Owen wondered.

In groups of two or three or four, adults had joined the line. Conversations already in progress didn't stop. The viewing was an occasion, no doubt, but the talk, the gathering, mattered more. Conviviality ruled: the effusive greetings, the food—especially, for Owen, the mingled scents of roasting meat above the pinyon embers—the children's shouts, the first tentative thumpings of a Navajo drum circle that had formed at the opposite side of the clearing. Dancing would soon follow.

Some of the older Navajos and some families, Owen had noticed, held back, apparently unsure of their status and therefore reluctant to approach. He wasn't, however, the only one to notice this. It was Julia, who, leaving the company near the cook fire—Harry Whitaker, the Wetherill family, Alberto and Matilda Rodriguez, the Gormans, various others—and drawing her green shawl around her shoulders, passed through the encampment, stopping by each Indian fire, chatting in Navajo, introducing herself to those whom she'd never met, assuring them that they, too, were welcome to join the lines for the food and for the viewing; to feast as well as to observe through the telescope what the unaided human eye was too weak to see—in short, to take in whatever they wished. As it turned out, more went to the tables than the telescope, but for those whose curiosity overcame their hesitancy, Clement Yazzie was standing beside Pete, translating as needed.

The comet was close to dropping from view when Owen took his turn: the purest iridescent light, and the streaming veil.

When Owen turned around, Richard Wetherill was standing there. They'd greeted each other warmly when the Wetherill family arrived that afternoon, but one or the other had been occupied until now, their first opportunity to speak without interruption.

"It's very good to see you, Owen," Wetherill said, smiling enough to deepen the weathered creases across his cheeks.

"And you, too, Richard."

"So have you solved the mystery of your Great Western Road yet?"

Owen shook his head. "I'm afraid I have very little to report."

"Nothing notable in Many Springs Canyon or up here in the mountains?"

"Well, I haven't ventured very far north of Washington Pass, but I haven't found anything in the canyon or elsewhere, except small ruins—clusters of a few rooms—here and there."

"You should pay Chaco Canyon another visit soon, and bring those field books of yours. We can sit down and go over them some evening."

"I'll do that," Owen said, and then he added, "Mrs. Wetherill is looking well." He didn't know if it would be impolite to mention her obvious condition.

"Very. We expect we'll have one more whelp by early summer," Wetherill said with obvious pleasure.

"My congratulations."

"Not yet," Wetherill cautioned. "Let's not tempt fate." Still smiling, he looked around the encampment. "This is a fine night and a fine spot."

"It is indeed."

"I haven't seen this many people in a while." Wetherill paused, and his smile retreated. "I heard you were laid up last winter."

It didn't surprise Owen that the news of his mishap in the storm had drifted as far as Chaco Canyon. Richard might have heard it from his brother Al, who could have heard it from Pete or from Tom or Johnny Gorman on one of their trips to pick up supplies and the mail.

"I had some frostbite, mostly. Nothing serious."

Wetherill grunted. "Don't underestimate the cold. You never had a chance to meet Clayton Tompkins, my wife's uncle. He was a trapper in the Rockies. He lost both his legs from the knees down when they froze one winter. He lived his last few years at Chaco Canyon with us."

"I'm sure he was well taken care of. As I was by the people I've gotten to know here."

"By Mrs. Halley."

"Yes, and Dr. Whitaker."

"His reputation has preceded him. It's a rare man who devotes his life to serving the needs of those outside his own tribe, with little thought to his own comfort or advancement."

"All too true," Owen said, and then, wishing to be done with the topic of health and illness, "How's the ranching business these days?"

"The drought is bad," Wetherill said. "Things are drying up and blowing away." Then he added, "But we'll make do. We always have. If the politicians leave us be."

Owen remembered that Wetherill was in an ongoing tussle with William Shelton, the Navajo superintendent. "What are they on about now?" Owen asked.

"Coal."

"Coal?" Owen asked.

"The government keeps finding reasons not to grant my homestead claim. The latest is because of the coal."

"You mean the seam in the canyon wall?" Years before, Wetherill had chanced upon a thin seam in the face of the north wall, which, given the scarcity of wood, was a godsend.

"Yes, that. Someone reported that I've been illegally exploiting valuable mineral deposits."

Owen was incredulous. That seam probably didn't hold enough coal to fill a single railway car. "But you haven't been selling it, you use it for heating and cooking."

"Well, you and *I* know that," Wetherill said. "But enough about that business. I'm glad to get away from it for a couple of days. We're here to enjoy ourselves."

"Then you should take a gander through the telescope before you miss the comet."

"I believe I will," Wetherill said, removing his hat and greeting Pete with a firm handshake when Owen introduced them. "Your telescope has delighted my children, Mr. Pietrowski," he noted. "They're already insisting that we should get one ourselves."

Wetherill's turn at viewing the comet was followed by an extended conversation between him and Pete about the wonders of the Western sky. Owen listened amiably but had little to contribute.

Johanna Yazzie sat off to the side by herself. Earlier, Owen had seen her looking into the telescope. He wondered if she understood that once the comet fell below the horizon, it wouldn't be returning tonight. He thought that through and concluded that, yes, of course she understood—after all, she'd lived under the cycles of the night sky her entire life, with no city glow to detract or distract. Maybe she continued to sit near the telescope because of the land's slight rise, permitting her to observe the entire encampment with detached ease.

Pete had yet to eat, so Owen volunteered to keep watch over the telescope. Pete and Richard Wetherill, still chatting, walked toward the main circle, where most of the Anglos were gathered.

Owen had already eaten, mainly slices of venison and a chunk of lamb; they'd stimulated a hunger that he hadn't felt in many months—he could have eaten an entire joint. Although there were many other things to sample, he'd refrained. At the time, Tom Gorman was standing beside him and had asked if Owen would like to try something Navajo.

"To tell you the truth, I don't know half of what I'm looking at," Owen said, muffling his voice so that none of the other nearby Navajos, filling plates, would hear.

"Well," Tom drawled, "that there's yucca cakes." He next pointed out, in a basket, dried chokecherries and sumac. In a bowl, goat parts—lungs and intestines; Tom pronounced "intestines" with a long *i* in the last syllable, which didn't make the dish any more palatable to Owen. In another bowl, wild potatoes and white clay.

"Clay?" Owen said, incredulous.

"You can't eat wild potatoes alone. They taste bad, and too much can poison you. The clay helps. Some people like them."

"And you?"

"I wouldn't eat wild potatoes if I was starving," Tom said, but he did help himself to the yucca cakes. Clement Yazzie, who'd overheard the conversation, was still standing nearby when Tom, his plate full, moved off.

"Aren't you going to eat?" Owen asked Yazzie, who wasn't holding plate or cup.

"Later. I'll see what's left."

"It might be wild potatoes and clay," Owen said.

"Hunh," Yazzie said with a slight smile. "I'll take my chances."

"I'm surprised so many people brought so much food with them," Owen said, looking over the tables. Mostly breads—pueblo bread, cornbread, blue corn flat bread, fry bread—but also other staples, such as goat cheese. He could see that additional food, in smaller quantities intended for family or immediate friends, was being shared around the smaller campfires as well. "It's very generous."

"That's Carmelita Gorman's doing," Yazzie said with a degree of disdain that surprised Owen. "She warned people not to show up empty-handed. So most brought something." He paused. "She can be hard on her own people, especially the ones who don't listen to the missionaries."

"I guess I've noticed that," Owen said. He recalled more than one occasion when he'd heard Carmelita, speaking Navajo, giving what-for to a customer about something—their complaints about prices or the quality of the merchandise, he supposed.

"After a bad winter, this can be a hungry time," Yazzie said. "In the old days, before the trading posts, the People foraged for grasses and other plants and flowers, and they ate a lot of goat milk and goat cheese. If they had to, they'd slaughter a goat. Many still do, especially the old ones who live far from the trading posts. They'll pick out an old or weak goat and eat everything. Sometimes in bad years they'll even grind the bones and make a paste with water. You don't see any fat Navajos." He was looking at Win Peabody, the hefty undertaker, who happened to be passing by.

Owen didn't feel quite so hungry anymore.

"But they always have sheep," he said.

Yazzie shook his head. "Sheep are too valuable."

"But you slaughtered two lambs."

"They were from Mrs. Halley's flock, not mine." Yazzie obviously rejected such foolish extravagance.

When Pete returned to the telescope, holding a large piece of squash pie in one hand and a cup of coffee in the other, Owen rose and brushed off the seat of his pants. They watched Halley's Comet slide below the horizon.

"Were you planning on putting the telescope away?" Owen asked.

"I was," Pete said, "just as soon as I finish Julia's pie."

Owen glanced over at Johanna, who hadn't moved from her nearby perch. "Why don't you leave it up? I think Johanna wants to see the full moon." The comet-viewers had been lucky: although the moon had risen not long after sunset, a thick bank of low-lying clouds in the east prevented its brightness from detracting from the comet's display. Now, however, having risen above the cloud bank, the moon was obscured only by the highest ponderosa branches. It would soon be fully in view.

"What makes you think that?" Pete asked.

"Just a hunch. And I wouldn't mind taking a look myself."

"Then you'll have to spell me. I'm not going to miss out on the rest of the festivities."

"Fair enough," Owen said. He walked to the cook fire to get himself coffee. Many of the younger children had tired themselves out and were now sitting in their mothers' laps and lying on blankets. Carmelita was still carving pieces of venison—the lamb was long gone—and Owen accepted another small slice, taking it in his fingers.

"Owen, come and sit with us," Julia called to him from where she sat at the middle of an arc just beyond the fire, as if she'd drawn everyone to her.

"I will in a bit," he replied. Right now he wanted to wander, to listen to the Navajo drummers, pounding their drums and singing their chants, and to watch the Navajo dancers who, two by two, were now circling them. It occurred to him then that, apart from a quick greeting when she and Harry Whitaker arrived, he hadn't spoken to Tóya. He'd only seen her once since her visit to Many Springs for the new year, and he wondered where in the clearing she'd hidden herself.

He found her sitting alone in the dark, her legs stretched out straight and her back against a flat rock that came up to her shoulders. She was playing with a piece of string.

"New boots?" Owen asked, looking down.

"Aoo'. I get a new pair every ten years." She lifted her skirt a bit and rocked her feet side to side so he could get a better look. The inlaid mother of pearl and beaded trim caught the dim firelight. "And how are *your* feet?" she asked him.

"Fine."

"No sores?"

"No." He sat down beside her. "You're looking well."

"Me? I don't get sick. I haven't been sick a day since 1868."

"Did you take a look at the comet through the telescope?"

"No. I saw it just fine without Pete's stick. Sǫ' Bitsee' Nineezí."

He waited for her to explain.

"Star with a Long Tail."

"That's the Navajo name for a comet?"

"Tchh," she clicked her tongue. "For *that* comet. The last time it came was the year of the great Navajo victory against the Mexicans right here in Béésh Łichíʼii Bigiizh." She slapped the ground between them with an open palm. "Copper Pass. That's what the People called it in those days. In 'Atsá Biyáázh, the month when the eaglets hatch, 250 Navajos ambushed 1,000 Mexican soldiers and Jemez Indians who planned to attack Canyon de Chelly. Our warriors killed the Mexican commander and many others. They say you can still dig up old bones in this field. Later that same year, in Bini'anit'ą́ą́tsoh, the month of the big harvest, Sǫ' Bitsee' Nineezí returned to the sky."

"In 1835?"

"It was before my time. I have no need to count backward that far."

Owen had to admit, Tóya always managed to put him in his place. This was her world, not his; her world and her history, the history that mattered, that could be held in a person's memory.

"I see your point," he said.

She tapped him on the shoulder. "It's a good thing I like you, Owen Rouse, or I'd think you're just another stupid bilagáana."

"I probably am just another stupid bilagáana," Owen said, "but I wouldn't be quite so stupid if I saw you more often."

"It's these old bones," she said, thumping a fist against a hip and shaking her head. "Getting anywhere is *hard*."

"Have you asked Dr. Whitaker if he can help?"

She sniffed. "I wouldn't give him the satisfaction."

Owen, smiling to himself, knew this was bluster.

"Harry Whitaker says I should throw away my boots and stay off horses."

"But I see you're still wearing boots."

"Aoo'." She leaned in closer although no one was within earshot. "But to speak the truth, I can't mount a horse anymore without help."

"He may have something for the pain, you know."

"Oh, he's given me some little pills. He said they're made from willow bark and some plant I never heard of."

Aspirin, he guessed. "Do they help?"

"Eh, I drink willow bark tea instead."

For a while they sat and watched the Navajo dancers, young and old, across the clearing. The moon had finally ascended fully into sight. Pete had turned the telescope toward the new light and appeared to be instructing Johanna, who was bent to the eyepiece. So she *had* been waiting for the moon, Owen thought with satisfaction.

"I know some old Navajos who wouldn't dare look in Pete's stick," Tóya said. "They would think it's magic, the way it brings the sky closer."

"You mean *actually* brings the sky closer?"

"Aoo'. They would probably keep their eyes fixed on the sky to hold it in its proper place. They would see this as their duty."

And also your duty? he wondered. "I can try and explain how Pete's telescope works, if you'd like."

"No." She left no doubt about it.

"I'm glad you came to the party anyway."

"A Navajo never passes up a free meal," she said. "Haven't you heard that?"

He laughed again. "I suppose I have. Can I bring you something else to eat?"

"The lamb was good but I had enough. I hope there's a rib left for me to gnaw on in the morning."

"I'll ask Carmelita to save you one, if you'd like."

"That woman," she said with a shake of her head. She couldn't abide Carmelita's Christianity.

The chanting and drumming paused but soon continued after several alternate drummers joined the circle.

Owen leaned toward Tóya, shoulder to shoulder. "Harry and some of the others are going to be playing Anglo music later. Maybe I should teach you to dance like a bilagáana."

"Maybe you should leave an old woman alone with her thoughts."

"What are you doing with the string?" he asked.

"It's just a game. Na'atl'o'. You make the string look like the Star People." She pointed her nose toward the sky.

"The constellations?"

"Aoo'. The Sǫ' Dine'é."

She spread her hands to display a complicated web within a rectangle formed by her outstretched forefingers and pinkies. "Dilyéhi. The Planters," she said.

"And where are they?" Owen asked, looking up.

"Tchh," she said, shaking her head at his nonsense. "You can't see them this time of year. In a few weeks they'll come up again at dawn in the east and we'll know it's time to stop planting corn. She dropped her string figure and made a circle with her bony forefinger and thumb. "A little group of stars. There." She held her hand up, the little circle toward the northeast horizon. "That's where we'll see them next."

He bent over so he could see the direction of her circle. "I think that may be what we call the Pleiades, the Seven Sisters. A cluster of small stars— you can easily count six of them. With Pete's telescope, you'd see there are many, many more."

"Six, that's right. Even with these old eyes I can see six. So, you know the sky?"

"Pretty well. I learned it when I was a boy, from the first book I ever received as a present, *The Story of the Heavens.*" Now packed in a crate in his boyhood room, in his father's house.

"In one of our stories," Tóya said, "the Dilyéhi are called Béésh Ashiké, the Hard Flint Boys. But I shouldn't be telling you any of this."

"Because I'm an Anglo?"

"Because it's the wrong season. We've heard the first thunder, and the spiders have come back."

"Who put the stars up there?" Owen asked, coaxing her along. He leaned back against the smooth, rounded surface of her rock.

"Some say it was Áłtsé Hastiin, First Man, not long after the first people emerged into this world from down below. The nights were too dark, especially when the moon wasn't there, so he made a careful design using shiny stones and began placing them one by one in the sky. One of the first ones was the star in the north that doesn't move, Náhookǫs Biko', and then four others around it, like the fire in the center of the hogan, and then many others. But Coyote, Mą'ii, came by and grew impatient and threw all the other stars up there at once, which is why they're scattered everywhere near and far, and why some are bright and some are not."

"The Greeks and the Romans told stories about how their gods put the stars up there, too. And not just the Greeks and the Romans, but others before them, going back many thousands of years."

Tóya, her fingers moving fluidly, fashioned another complicated pattern with the string. "Yikáísdáhí. It Waits for Dawn. Like the corn dust we offer with our morning prayers." She thrust her nose upward one more time and swept her head in an arc.

"The Milky Way."

"Aoo'." She let the string collapse. "Of course some say it wasn't Áłtsé Hastiin, but Black God who first lit the night with the stars, some time after he set the sun on fire."

"I haven't heard of Black God," Owen said.

"Haashch'éshzhiní. He's black because he's the son of fire. He's very powerful. And he wears the Dilyéhi here." She pointed to the left side of her forehead. "His mother, they say, was a comet." Her fingers worked the string. "But I can't say more about that."

"We have string games, too, you know. Cat's Cradle. Jacob's Ladder."

Her fingers flew again and in seconds she'd made a perfect Jacob's Ladder. Just as quickly, she let it go.

Owen chuckled. "You always surprise me," he said.

For some time now, Owen had been observing a well-dressed Navajo man—leather vest, white collared shirt, bolo, brown pants, and a flat-brimmed hat—moving through the assemblage, stopping by each campfire, exchanging words with the elders. He'd moved on to the Anglos now and was talking to Julia and Richard Wetherill.

"Do you know the man over there talking to Julia?" Owen asked.

"Chee Dodge," Tóya said.

"Really?"

Tóya clearly found Owen's surprise amusing.

Everyone on the reservation had heard some version of Henry Chee Dodge's story. Born near Fort Defiance around 1860 to a Navajo-Jemez mother and a Mexican father who'd been kidnapped by the Navajos as a boy, Dodge lost both parents early on—his father during a raid to recover stolen horses, and then his mother prior to the Long Walk when small bands of Indians were trying to avoid pursuit by soldiers; one day she went foraging for food and never returned. Taken in by an aunt and then a string of other families, he survived the Long Walk and ultimately returned to Fort Defiance, where he briefly attended school and then perfected his English while clerking for his aunt's husband, an Anglo named Perry Williams. By the time he was twenty he'd become the Indian agency's principal interpreter and unofficial negotiator when trouble arose between Navajos and whites. In the following years he amassed a considerable sum as a partner in the Round Rock Trading Post and as a rancher and herder. Widely considered the wealthiest man on the reservation as well as the most influential with the United States government and its agencies, he lived in a fancy home he'd built on Sonsela Butte, just west of the Chuskas.

"I wonder if he's here for any particular reason," Owen said.

"He was probably just in the neighborhood," Tóya said. "As you Anglos say, he likes to keep his ear to the rail."

"Like a Washington politician."

"I wouldn't know. But all the great headmen, Barboncito, Manuelito, Ganado Mucho . . . they are no longer with us. I suppose we have to look elsewhere for leaders." Her tone could best be described as grudging.

Owen chatted with Tóya for a while longer, but he kept an eye on Chee Dodge and his two companions, younger Navajos whom Owen also didn't recognize. The three left the circle of Anglos behind and casually approached Clement Yazzie, who was now standing near where Johanna had been sitting. How odd, Owen thought, that Chee Dodge had sought out—for that was how it looked—Clement Yazzie, who, as far as Owen knew, kept to himself and had nothing to do with tribal politics. Chee Dodge appeared to be doing most of the talking.

Owen rose and asked Tóya, "Why don't you come over and join Julia and the rest of us?"

"No," Tóya said, "I like it here." She was manipulating her string again, and watching Johanna with the telescope. "Besides, when there's too much noise and too many voices, I have trouble hearing what's being said."

"All right," Owen said, "but I don't like to see you sitting here all alone."

"Maybe *you* don't," she said, "but *I* do. Go," she dismissed him with a nod.

But instead of joining Julia and the others at the main campfire, Owen strolled back toward the telescope—though the attraction was Chee Dodge. He was too late, however, for just as he came within earshot, Dodge and his two companions ended the conversation with Clement Yazzie and walked off toward the drum circle.

"So you know Chee Dodge," Owen said to Yazzie. He knew better than to ask what their conversation had been about.

"Everyone knows Chee Dodge," Yazzie replied. "Or claims to."

Almost in spite of himself, Owen had grown to like Clement Yazzie. He'd always admired the way Yazzie handled himself. He'd watched him working, feeding the animals, cutting down a dead tree, building a new trough to replace one that was rotting away, shearing sheep . . . Yazzie worked hard, deliberately, but he sought no thanks or praise. He simply saw a task that needed doing, and did it. Owen had also observed him with Johanna. Their communication was almost always silent or, when Yazzie spoke to her, in hushed Navajo, as if he entered her world—never completely, of course, because no one could do that—making their passage together from day to day and month to month seem effortless, without disagreement or frustration.

It had also become apparent to Owen that Yazzie truly disliked Pete Pietrowski, and that the subdued animosity was mutual, though unspoken. Sometimes peoples' temperaments were too different to permit understanding, let alone friendship. Yazzie wasn't this way with Harry Whitaker, even though Owen wouldn't say they were close. They appeared to hold a degree of mutual respect; at least Owen had never heard them challenge each other's command of their separate realms, tribal and medical. And, of course, Owen had watched Yazzie with Julia, a different matter entirely, both in kind and in degree. They interacted nearly every day, discussing the needs of the trading post or the sheep and wool business they shared with an ease that transcended mere common interests. Still, despite their obvious familiarity Owen had never heard them discuss anything personal or even exchange the endearments that accompanied close friendship between the sexes in the Anglo world. Between them it was always "Mrs. Halley" and "Mr. Yazzie."

Sometimes Owen felt that he and Yazzie might actually become friends. Given the attention Owen had recently devoted to Johanna, teaching her to draw, trying to engage her in *some* form of exchange—trying to *draw her out*, in a sense—he might have expected to detect a change in his interactions with her brother, but not so.

Pete had been joined at the telescope by his friends Charlie Day and Win Peabody, and all three were watching Johanna, who stood motionless, an eye hovering just above the eyepiece of the telescope. Alberto and Matilda's children, Elena and Carlos, stood nearby, impatient. They too wanted to see the moon.

"Why doesn't she hurry up?" Carlos asked his sister. "What's wrong with her?"

"She is as she is," Yazzie said calmly to the boy, but it wasn't an answer that could possibly satisfy a child.

"Why doesn't she say anything?" Carlos asked.

"Because she can't," Owen said, hoping that would be the end of it.

"Why not?"

"Mind your own business," Pete said gruffly.

"Pete, he's only a child," Owen said. Ill-mannered, but a child nevertheless.

"I want a turn," Carlos said with vehemence, turning to Pete.

"C'mon, Carlos," Elena said to her younger brother, grabbing his hand. Owen guessed she was fourteen or fifteen; she was old enough to feel embarrassed, particularly in front of the handsome Charlie Day. "You can look later."

Just then Matilda called out from near the main campfire, "Children! Please come over here," and they obeyed.

"Well, we know who cracks the whip in that family," Pete said.

"Mrs. Rodriguez doesn't look happy," Owen said, observing Matilda.

Charlie Day laughed. "I doubt she's having a good time, not with the car and all."

Alberto Rodriguez had purchased a car, a bright red machine, a month before and had decided, after driving around Gallup and its environs for several weeks and attracting considerable attention, to test its mettle. So that afternoon he'd driven the automobile up the trail toward Washington Pass. The trip had gone exceedingly well until, unwisely, he turned onto the much narrower, rougher side trail to the meadow and, attempting to maneuver around a low-lying boulder, broke the front axle. No one was injured despite the abrupt stop as the metal dug into the ground, but Matilda, alternately distressed and livid in the aftermath, now appeared determined not to enjoy herself.

Win Peabody, standing with his hands folded on his ample gut, was continuing to observe Johanna at the telescope.

"Johanna's been mute from birth," Owen said for Peabody's benefit.

"That *is* unfortunate." Peabody's smile was crooked, rueful. "For her, of course, but for us as well, I mean. Judging by how carefully she's studying the moon, I suspect she'd have some interesting observations to make, as it were."

Owen, feeling protective toward Johanna, wasn't entirely sure if Peabody, whom he'd never encountered before, was being genuine.

Sometimes in the evening, back at Many Springs Canyon, Owen would bring whatever book or newspaper or magazine he was reading over to the table to keep Johanna company while she drew. He'd grown comfortable talking to her as they sat together, not in the expectation that she'd ever respond, but in the belief, free of evidence, that she understood and maybe even, in her own way, appreciated his interest.

The present incongruous situation—five grown men standing around observing a mute Navajo woman watching the moon through a telescope—suddenly struck Owen as highly amusing. Maybe they were all feeling protective (Pete of his telescope), even though Peabody and Charlie Day didn't even know her.

"She was born in water," Yazzie said. 'Asdzáán Bítóyiszééyiztał broke the sac and blew life into her lungs."

Owen, surprised, didn't think he'd ever heard Yazzie speak so openly about his sister. "Tóya was there?"

"Aoo'. I was outside, in the summer hogan where my mother would weave during the day. It was a warm night. I was asleep and Tóya came out and told me I had a sister who didn't cry."

"What did you make of that?" Owen asked.

"I thought it was a *good* thing, to have a baby who wouldn't cry."

"You couldn't have known," Owen said.

Yazzie said something in Navajo to Johanna. She stepped back from the telescope, and together they began walking toward the drums.

Pete, cupping his hands at the sides of his mouth, pretended to yell after them, "You're welcome!" He shook his head. "You never get a thank-you from those people."

"Thank you, Pete," Owen said in his most mincing tone. Charlie Day and Win Peabody laughed.

Owen saw that Julia was also advancing toward the drums and dancers. Most of the other Anglos were following her lead.

Pete grumbled, "*They* should be coming to *her*. It's her party, not theirs."

"But we're holding it in *their* home, as it were," Peabody said, rocking back on his heels.

"Let's go," Charlie Day said, nodding toward the drummers. "I'm ready for a good dance."

"I don't see how shuffling around in a circle can be called dancing," Pete mumbled, but after pulling the eyepiece from the telescope and putting it in his pocket (and visiting the rear of his wagon), he joined the others as they made their way across the encampment.

Owen, feeling the observer tonight, hung back, behind the others, but soon encountered Matilda Rodriguez, who was scanning the clearing for her children, absent once again.

"I suppose this revelry will go on forever," she said, sighing with resignation.

"I couldn't say," Owen said. The Navajo voices had risen into a high keening, punctuated by the reverberant drumming. "I rather like it." He did: the fires burning high, the air crisp, the canopy punctured with stars.

"You don't have two children who will be beyond the beyond if they don't get their proper sleep," Matilda said before spotting the errant siblings, who appeared to be dashing for the woods, accompanied by several older Navajo boys. "Dear Lord, save us," she said and hurried after them.

Owen judged by the course of the moon that the drumming, the falsetto chanting, and the dancing lasted another two hours or more, and before it concluded he'd paraded arm-in-arm with Julia, Mary Wetherill (not Marietta, who begged off only because of her advanced condition), Carmelita Gorman (who apparently saw nothing sinful in dancing), and even Tóya, who'd forsaken her ivory-handled cane in favor of his arm for a few turns around the circle. Mostly, though, he'd sat and watched. The only one he really wanted by his side was Julia. With her left arm linked through his right, they'd moved together, their hips and shoulders bare inches apart, and sometimes not even that as the slightly uneven ground and an awkward step threw them, unbalanced, toward each other and they bumped. They had never danced before, he had never held her, he didn't want to let go, he wanted to defy propriety and grab her far shoulder with his free hand and swing her around toward him, and then pull her to him, breast to chest, face to face.

Owen watched Julia dancing with so many partners, Anglo and Navajo—but not Clement Yazzie, who danced only with Navajo women—that he couldn't even keep track. When the drumming concluded, Julia spoke to the drummers, and by her gestures, Owen understood that she was inviting them to come and sit at the other large campfire. He heard the words *gohwééh* and *bááh likaní*, "coffee" and "cake."

Though there were many smiles all around and the elderly Navajo man who'd led the drumming spoke at some length with Julia, most of the Navajos retreated to their own small circles. A few, mostly faces that Owen recognized as frequent visitors to the trading post, did make their way to where Carmelita, who'd left the dance circle early, already had the coffee brewing. Beside her, Mary Wetherill was slicing several large sheet cakes, with a lineup of a dozen children, way past their usual bedtimes, waiting on the other side of the table—waiting with a degree of anxious restraint that made Owen, walking toward them, laugh. Julia's apple sauce cake spiced with cinnamon and cloves. Dare he take a piece himself? Why in hell not? One little half slice of cake wouldn't kill him.

He ate his cake, and it was delicious, each crumb savored.

The intensity of the stars forecast a chilly night, but few Navajo appeared ready to leave for home; they would wait for dawn. He counted the small fires dotting the landscape—now seventeen—and he pondered the divide, Anglos and Navajos (far more Navajos) together but separate, the Anglos *here*, the Navajos for the most part *there*, and he wondered if this was how it would always be. Even *here*, eating cake and drinking coffee, two circles had formed, the Navajos mostly off to the side, speaking Navajo and laughing among themselves.

Tóya was sitting with the larger, Anglo circle, as was Clement Yazzie, but where was Johanna? Owen wondered. He didn't see her at first, but then, through the dark, he saw that she'd returned to her favored spot by the telescope and had made for herself a bed from some of the hay hauled in for the horses. She was either asleep or lying very still.

Owen turned his attention to the animated conversation around him.

"Rodriguez wants to move all the riffraff to the north side of the tracks," Pete was saying.

"Where would that leave *you*?" Harry Whitaker asked.

"Tied to the rails."

Charlie Day and some of the others laughed.

"People who work for a living, who better themselves, they'll move to better surroundings," Alberto said. "I put it to you, if you were to move to Gallup with your family, would you like to live next to a pig wallow?"

"I haven't seen any pig wallows in Gallup," Pete said.

"Look closer." Alberto released a stream of cigar smoke.

"At present, my premises are north of the tracks," Win Peabody said, "but I have my eye on a piece of property on the south side, near Sacred Heart."

"An excellent choice," Pete said. "Embalm 'em, bless 'em, and bury 'em, all within a few blocks."

"The problem is landlords who don't keep up their properties," Al Wetherill said.

"They're going to be forced to," Alberto said. "The city council intends to pass ordinances requiring them to meet basic standards. First, everyone within city limits is going to have to connect to municipal water."

"Can you make them do that?" Richard Wetherill asked. Unlike most of the other men, who were puffing on cigars provided by Rodriguez, Wetherill abstained.

"We can. And next up, municipal sewers."

"The outhouse suits me just fine," Pete said. "And who knows, before civic improvement imposes itself and sends me the bill, I just may head for greener pastures."

What did he mean by that? Owen wondered.

"I'm waiting for paved streets," Mary Wetherill interjected. "The dust this time of year is horrible. I can't keep anything clean, but you can't live with the windows shut tight."

"In your business," Al Wetherill said to Peabody, "you could use running water, couldn't you?"

"I couldn't do without it," Peabody said. "I already willingly paid for a connection."

"You saw the advantage," Alberto said, "and sooner than you think, so will everyone else. "

"Anyone in my profession will tell you that a clean, reliable water supply and a proper sewer system contribute directly to the improved health of the community at large," Harry said.

"Ah, civilization!" Pete said.

"Why the sarcasm?' Al Wetherill asked.

"Oh, he's just being Pete," Julia said, but Owen could feel the heat beneath her words. She knew Pete had been drinking.

"What do you think of all this progress, Mr. Yazzie?" Peabody asked. He and Charlie Day were already working on their second slices of cake. "Some of it's bound to benefit the reservation."

"I suppose some of these things have value," Yazzie said, but he offered no examples.

"What about electricity?" Pete asked.

"Does anyone on the reservation have it?" Yazzie said.

"Someday they will."

"Ask me then."

"The railroad?" Pete persisted.

Yazzie looked around the clearing. "I don't see any tracks."

"There's that factory in Gallup that makes ice in the summer," Tóya said. "Give us one of those and keep your railroad."

"Well," Tom Gorman said, "I can certainly see the usefulness of a telephone. I hear it's come in handy down at the Tohatchi school." He looked to Harry Whitaker for confirmation.

"There are obvious benefits," Harry said. "Being able to telephone Gallup in emergencies, for one."

"With a telephone, we could cut our trips into Gallup by half," Tom said. "And Mrs. Halley could talk to her sister in Chicago whenever she wanted to."

"You may be right, Tom," Julia said, "but I don't see anyone who'd be willing to put up another twenty-five miles of telephone poles just for our convenience."

Owen suspected that there weren't many Navajos along the route who would even see the benefit, and fewer, if any, who could afford telephone service.

"Progress has its price," Harry said, "and not solely monetary."

"So you're willing to throw out scientific advances?" Pete baited him.

"Not in the least. I didn't say the price wasn't worth paying. Your telescope, for example."

"You don't have to tell me the price of *that*. I'll be passing the hat at breakfast."

"Why the telescope?" Owen asked Harry. "You think it has a hidden cost?"

"It makes the glorious firmament a little less firm—more glorious, but less firm. To my way of thinking."

"You're talking philosophy, not progress," Pete said.

"I'm wary of neatly dividing the two."

"And religion?" Pete asked.

"You can add religion, if you'd like. Perhaps Julia's the one we should be asking," Harry said.

"Not me?" Pete pretended to be offended by the slight to his personal history.

"Definitely not you," Harry said, and then addressed Julia: "Your father was a minister. Some of his thinking on these matters must have rubbed off."

"I don't believe my father paid much attention to the sciences," she replied after thinking about the broader question for a moment. "Philosophically, he leaned toward the Transcendentalists, at least until they moved too far from traditional Christianity. Apart from that, I'd say he saw his job in very simple terms. He officiated. He offered condolences. He thought people's lives were hard enough—though he had his blindnesses, especially when it came to his own family." She drew back from further explanation. "On Sunday he preferred his parishioners to arrive fearful and repentant over their failures, but to depart uplifted, believing in God's mercy and a fresh start. He tried to provide them with hope in a sinful world." She laughed curtly. "Although he had these little truisms that drove me to distraction. At least once a year he'd preach a sermon about how 'God's love is like the ocean—it has neither a beginning nor an end.' "

"We're a long way from the ocean," Pete said.

"It depends on your perspective," Owen said, feeling at last that he could contribute something to the conversation. "At one time, most of this area was covered by an inland sea. Ask anyone who's worked coal out here and they'll tell you. They're always finding fossils of shells and sometimes even the skeletons of fish."

"Forty days and forty nights," Win Peabody said.

"Noah aside, it's more like forty million years."

"A story occurs to me," Harry said, "tangential at best, but perhaps worth relating. When I was still living in Washington"—sitting with his legs crossed, his arms braced behind him—"I had a friend, a professor of anatomy at Georgetown, and an avowed atheist, who spent considerable time at the National Zoo observing a gorilla that was housed there. They'd renamed the great beast Leopold, after the king of Belgium, because they assumed it came from the Congo, although its provenance wasn't clear. Leopold, already at a somewhat advanced age, had been rescued from some bankrupt traveling circus, where he'd been known as Beelzebub. My friend would sometimes sit for hours at a time on a folding chair, watching not only Leopold but the spectacle many people made of themselves, grunting, throwing scraps of food or garbage between the bars of the cage, trying to rile him. Unless some object struck him, causing him to bare his large teeth and pace back and forth, swinging his long arms—which, of course, always further aroused the crowd—Leopold carried himself with a certain aplomb. After a time, he got used to my friend's presence and would sit down beside him, pressing his shoulder into the bars, as my friend would also do, and they'd silently commune, shoulder to shoulder."

"A dog would do the same," Pete said.

"When Leopold finally died, the zookeepers, knowing my friend's profession as well as his great interest in the gorilla, asked if he'd like to attend the dissection. Believing that he already knew all he needed to know about Leopold, my friend declined, although he told them that he'd happily participate in a postmortem for any one of Leopold's tormenters."

"I hope you're not going to preach Darwin to me again, Harry," Pete said, "trying to make the case that the ape was our great-great-grandfather or some such rubbish."

"I'm not 'preaching' anything," Harry said. To the others he noted, "Pete and I have argued the matter of Darwin before."

"I don't know about yours, but *my* great-great-grandfathers were Polish," Pete said, "back when there was a Poland."

"Darwin would probably describe Leopold as more akin to a far, far, far distant cousin," Owen said, "not an ancestor."

"You've read him?" Pete said.

"*The Descent of Man* was required in one of my college courses."

"Oh well then," Pete said, "it must all be true, mustn't it?"

Pete was looking for an argument, any argument, and Owen wasn't going to oblige.

"I admit that I've never read Mr. Darwin's books," Julia said, "but I have to say that I'm a skeptic. We have a flock of yellow-headed blackbirds that visits the canyon in the summer, nesting and feeding around Mr. Yazzie's pond. I look at those birds, such wonderful creatures, and I find it hard to understand how or why their heads and chests are such a vibrant yellow, if it's all just a matter of chance and advantage." A laugh rippled in her throat. "My father was appalled by Mr. Darwin's ideas."

"The point of the anecdote isn't at all Darwinian," Harry said.

"Beasts can be godly, man can be beastly?" Pete said.

"We all search for meaning," Harry said, ignoring Pete's smirk, "some through God or philosophy, some through science, some through empathy with our fellow creatures—man or beast—and some, perhaps the best of us, through all that's available, and that would include, without exclusion, religion and philosophy as well as science."

"Hear, hear!" Win Peabody said.

"They cut the gorilla up?" Clement Yazzie now asked. Nothing in his tone gave anything away, but Owen suddenly and unexpectedly felt deeply ashamed.

"Yes, they did," Harry answered.

"Just to see what was beneath his skin?"

"With the greater purpose of better understanding how the human body functions. Or so they said."

"You doubt their intent?" Alberto asked.

"Not really," Harry said. "But my friend the anatomist was of a view that the workings of a civilization must be seen in their fullest, including their effects upon the least among us."

"And in this instance—?" Richard Wetherill left the question hanging. Wetherill was a Quaker, Owen recalled.

"I believe my friend would say that from a certain perspective Leopold could be considered the least among us. Darwin argued that there might be fewer distinctions between man and ape than Alfred Russel Wallace and others believe," Harry answered. "Regardless, science can inform but not answer moral questions."

"Your man Darwin would argue that the negro is not our equal," Pete said.

"My experience is that intelligence is a matter of the individual, not the race," Harry replied. "Besides, we don't have the tools to answer *that* particular question scientifically, and even if we did, a moral necessity might run counter to the conclusion."

"And what about the Oriental?" Peabody asked. "Some would say he's our superior."

"You can't speak of the Oriental, nor the negro, for that matter, as a single type. The Japanese differ markedly from the Chinese, and from the native islanders of the far Pacific. And farther south, the East Indian is as varied a people as anywhere on the globe."

"The Japanese are certainly a very industrious, disciplined people," Win Peabody said. "Look how handily they defeated the Russians, something that no one would have imagined a generation ago."

"What would you say about the Indian, Wetherill?" Pete asked. "Present company excepted." Tóya and Yazzie both sat stone-faced; Tom Gorman was stirring the coals with a stick and didn't appear to be paying much attention; Carmelita had already left the circle to join her children, daughter-in-law, and grandchild at their family campsite.

"It's still a very rude question," Julia said.

"Not in the least," Pete said. "We've just spent a fair amount of time discussing the shortcomings of the white race, haven't we? So why not the Indian? Wetherill?"

Richard Wetherill, whose frown suggested to Owen that he'd been following the discussion intently, looked up. "The New World Indian? Or should I say, Indians? Because they are of course many peoples." He gave a nod to Tóya and then to Yazzie. "I've met many smart ones and many ignorant ones, in no different proportion than I've observed among white men. But since you're speaking of race rather than the individual, keep in mind what the Anasazi managed to build without either the wheel or the horse. And where was Europe at the time? In the middle of the Dark Ages, I believe. And then there are the Aztecs and the Incas. They carved out empires before the horse and the cannon did them in."

"Not to mention the diseases the Spanish introduced," Harry added.

"So I wouldn't be too quick to reach any conclusions," Wetherill continued.

"Despite the pagan gods and human sacrifices?" Alberto said.

Clement Yazzie spoke up: "You nailed your Jesus to a cross."

"Well, I never!" Matilda mumbled, appalled at Yazzie's audacity.

Although his comment had brought the conversation to a momentary halt (as well as a smile to Tóya's face), Yazzie didn't seem in the least perturbed. He dumped the dregs of his cup of coffee on the fire, producing a brief hissing that sounded downright infernal to Owen.

"Don't conflate us with the Jews and the Romans," Alberto said, visibly irritated.

"From the perspective of the Hebrew Sadducees and the heathen Romans, it was a question of political power and social governance more than religion," Pete said.

"Argued like a former Jesuit," Harry said.

"Franciscan," Pete said.

"Mah apologies."

"Violence and atrocities are hardly unique to any race," Julia said.

"St. Isaac Jogues, among those martyred by the Mohawks," Peabody offered. He quickly added with a glance toward Yazzie and Tóya, "No offense intended."

Tóya—looking straight at Owen, as if to say, Do you see what we have to put up with?—responded, "I never heard of any Mohawks," which was such a bald-faced lie that Owen had to hide his laugh behind a cough.

"I take it Isaac Jogues was a Franciscan?" Harry said.

"A Jesuit," Pete said tersely.

"Mah *deepest* apologies," Harry said.

Owen couldn't hide his laughter any longer.

Pete eyed him crookedly. "Franciscans are permitted their fall from grace. But Jesuits . . . opting out is not permitted. The way they saw it, torture and the tomahawk guaranteed them paradise."

Matilda, her chin trembling, obviously found this all too upsetting.

"So you've totally lost your faith?" Alberto asked Pete.

"Oh," Pete said, feigning shock. "Do I sound sacrilegious?"

"God knows our souls," Matilda said.

"Does he, now? Each and every one of us—all billion and a half or so?"

"My family descends from a long line of Calvinists," Harry Whitaker said. "Everything is preordained. The Elect are the Elect and there's no escaping your fate."

"I guess," Pete said, "God's task is *so* much easier if he knows in advance how it will all turn out."

Owen, feeling a degree of sympathy for the offended Matilda and Alberto, stepped in: "My father never gave me much in the way of advice, but he did tell me to leave a man's religion alone."

"Are you from churchgoing people?" Alberto asked Owen.

"My mother attended services every Sunday and every Wednesday evening when she could. When I was a boy she would bring me with her, but I have to admit that I didn't pay much attention. I regret it now—or at least I regret my ignorance. The minister was a fire-breather—the kind that thought St. Paul's epistles came down on the soft side. He was always in a fever about earthly temptations. He preached Sodom and Gomorrah in New Hampshire."

"Fire and brimstone," Peabody said.

"There's no hell and no brimstone mentioned in the Old Testament," Pete said, but his observation didn't draw a response.

"And your father?" Alberto asked Owen.

"A churchgoer? Not regularly, at least not back then. I think he lost whatever faith he had when my brother Robbie died."

"My condolences," Rodriguez said.

"Oh, I never knew him. It happened years before I was even born. He was working on a railroad tunnel when the mountain dropped on him."

"This may explain why Mr. Rodriguez and I haven't seen you at Mass lately," Matilda, with raised eyebrows, said to Pete.

"And here I've been thinking that no parish would have him," Harry said with a chuckle.

"It isn't that no parish will have me, it's that I won't have any parish," Pete retorted. "Except perhaps the Church of the Six Deadly Sins."

"Aren't there seven?" Owen asked.

"Yes, but I'm not greedy," Pete said.

Several people laughed; Matilda Rodriguez bristled.

"Well, I guess I fell for that," Owen said.

"And I thank you for it," Pete said, with a bow.

Matilda broke in: " 'Be not deceived; God is not mocked. For what things a man shall sow, those also shall he reap.' Galatians—"

"Chapter 6, verses 7 and 8," Pete said, "and I believe you're quoting the Douay-Rheims version."

" 'God is not mocked,' " Matilda repeated.

"Nonsense. He's mocked all the time, especially by you good Christians who think you know better than anyone else what He wants."

"Pete!" Julia said.

"You go too far, Pietrowski," Alberto said. "You owe my wife an apology."

"Too far?" Pete laughed and rose unsteadily. "Not far enough. After all that coffee, I believe I'll venture even farther, to the far north. If you'll excuse me . . ." He managed only a half-bow before Harry, who'd been sitting beside him, reached out an arm and steadied him. Then Pete wandered off in the direction of the latrine.

"I feel I owe everyone an apology," Julia said.

"Not you," Alberto said, his eyes still narrowed on Pete's retreating figure.

"That man is so vulgar," Matilda said vehemently, turning to Julia, "I don't know how you abide him."

"Sometimes that's exactly what we have to do for our friends," Julia said. "Abide."

"Christian charity," Tom Gorman said.

Harry, sighing, said, "I should go after him. To make sure he doesn't fall in."

"I'll do it," Owen offered.

"Ah appreciate it," Harry said.

Owen quickly caught up to Pete. "Tell me about your friend Peabody," Owen said as they walked along; he was less concerned with Win Peabody than with keeping Pete on his feet. "He seems like an interesting fellow. Does he always go around with that smile on his face?"

"I'd say so. Except when he's working, of course. Then he's deadly serious." Pete chuckled at his own little pun.

"What's his story?"

"Grew up in Chicago. Poor family. Ended up in undertaking and somehow parlayed that into a considerable fortune. Real estate, mostly. Right place at the right time."

"Then how did he end up in Gallup, of all places?"

"Married a Zuni woman. The love of his life."

"It sounds like he has quite the tale to tell."

"He does. And he'll tell the whole bloody thing if you give him the opportunity."

"A bit long-winded?"

They'd reached the trench.

"You might say. But thoroughly pleasant. Annoyingly so. As are all happy men."

"So you and he are polar opposites."

"Exactly. Peabody is Mr. Sunshine, and I'm a goddamn *total eclipse!*" Pete, simultaneously launching a stream, yelled it out for all the world to hear. Owen wondered if any heads had turned in their direction.

"Keep it down. You'll wake the little ones," Owen said.

"Indeed."

An appropriate metaphor, nevertheless, Owen thought—a total eclipse. He was feeling a little giddy himself, though not from alcohol. Maybe from all the sugar in the cake?

"It's never a bad thing to know your place in the celestial hierarchy," Pete said, bouncing on the balls of his feet. "And to remember that there's always hell to pay."

They started back toward the gathering.

"Here," Pete said, reaching into his jacket pocket and pulling out the telescope's eyepiece. "I've had enough gab for tonight. You take it. In case anyone wants to study the stars."

They stopped and stared up into the vault, lit by too many pinpoints to count, and then their eyes drifted down toward the circles of people around the various campfires.

"How did we end up with such a motley crew?" Owen said. Julia's admirers, friends, colleagues, clientele (an odd but not wholly inappropriate word to apply to her dozens of regular Navajo customers), plus all those once-removed: spouses, children, friends of friends . . .

"Don't be a dolt, Rouse. It's *her.* Not that she sees it."

Owen thought about that. Why didn't she see it? From humility?

"She's something else altogether," Pete said, sounding sober for the moment. "She goes deep. But a word of advice, my friend." Pete veered off, toward his wagon. "Don't fall in love with her. If you do, she'll break your heart."

Too late. Because, of course, Owen already had.

Harry Whitaker had taken out his violin. Marietta Wetherill, sitting plump and comfortable on a pillow, was holding a concertina; her fingers rippled over the mother-of-pearl buttons. Richard Jr., lanky, with the long limbs of a youth on the verge of manhood, was blowing warm air into a tin whistle. Owen sat down beside Julia, whose small smile spoke of her pleasure in how well things had turned out, Pete's drunkenness notwithstanding. Marietta, who had clearly taken charge of the musical entertainment, said to her fellow musicians, "Are we ready? Dr. Whitaker? Richard?"

"Ah think somebody had better make a start of it," Harry said, his face flushed from the attention of the onlookers, and he began a simple Irish melody that Owen recognized but couldn't name.

Richard Jr. immediately picked up the tune, and a few measures later, as the melody began to repeat, Marietta added a chordal foundation. Harry, his eyes closed, left the melody to Richard and, bowing with long strokes, moved freely up and down the fingerboard, sometimes in counterpoint, sometimes doubling Richard. The three stumbled here and there, but they knew what they were about and quickly found their balance again.

After the first song—Richard Jr. blushing at the applause, tight-lipped Harry stoically fingering his strings, Marietta laughing—Matilda Rodriguez said her goodnights and walked toward where she'd settled down her children for the night. Halfway there, she turned and gave Alberto a piercing glance. He sighed, rose, nodded to all, and followed Matilda.

"Is she always so unlikable?" Owen whispered to Julia. Harry was re-tuning his violin.

"Matilda?" Julia answered. "Oh, in familiar surroundings she can be quite fine."

"Is this that foreign to her?"

"Yes and no. She was born on the prairie in Kansas, in the poorest circumstances. Eventually, her father abandoned their farm and moved everyone to Denver. He made a name for himself as a builder and within a few years was hiring out construction crews and running a building supply store. I suspect Matilda's greatest fear is to live in that Kansas kind of poverty again. So roughing it has no appeal. She doesn't understand why anyone would choose to live as we do"—she nudged him with an elbow—"divorced from the virtues of civilization."

"This seems pretty civilized to me," Owen said.

Marietta began a Viennese waltz that Harry knew, although it took her son several measures to pick up the melody and join in.

"Matilda does volunteer work and is raising money for a town library," Julia continued, "so I won't say anything against her, except that she's a notorious gossip. That in itself isn't terribly unusual. Besides, she's had her sufferings. After Elena, she lost at least two children. She was pregnant with one of them—stillborn—when I first met her, before Carlos came along several years later."

"Then I'll withhold judgment," Owen said.

After each piece Marietta would suggest something to the other players, and they'd do their best to oblige, although more than once the music stopped in midstream, eliciting good-natured comments, including that they should try practicing once in a while and refund the price of admission. Given the lateness of the hour, the trio didn't venture much beyond the sentimental or familiar, with a cohort of voices joining in when they could, although at one point Richard Jr. displayed his prowess with a hornpipe solo, after which Harry performed something of Bach's.

"Do you play an instrument?" Julia asked Owen.

"Not really." He was going to leave it at that, but then he said, "The tin whistle, just a bit. I learned about two and a half tunes when I was in college. I shared quarters with a fellow who was good but annoying." He wondered what had ever become of Dooley.

"Why annoying?" Julia asked.

"He always decided to play when I was trying to study."

"What can you play?" Julia asked, looking mischievous.

"Don't you dare," he said.

"Tell me."

"I learned a lullaby, a sea chantey, and enough of a jig to make me realize I had no facility."

"Owen's going to play us something," Julia announced.

"Julia!"

"Mr. Rouse!" Marietta said, laughing, "You have a hidden talent!"

"No, please," he pleaded, waving her off.

"Then you have to sing!" Marietta said.

"Given the choice, yes, I'd rather sing, but you won't enjoy it."

"We'll be the judge of *that*," Marietta said. "What will it be?"

Except during church services that he'd attended with Beth, he hadn't sung since his days in the chorus at college, back when we was trying to impress young sopranos and altos. What did he remember? " 'Beautiful Dreamer,' " Owen said.

"Why sure," Marietta said. "Four chords. Easy enough. You're a tenor?"

"I suppose I am."

She turned to Harry. "Are you game?"

"Ah am," he said with a quick nod.

"You're going to be sorry," Owen told Julia, whose smile turned into a girlish giggle. Oh, the firelight in her eyes!

"We'll play through the first verse, get ourselves situated, and then, Owen, you come in when we return to the beginning. All right?"

Marietta started, Harry and Richard Jr. followed, and by the time they'd finished the second line, Owen at least had some confidence that the key was within his range, that he wouldn't emit insufferably embarrassing squeaks:

> Beautiful dreamer, wake unto me,
> Starlight and dewdrops are waiting for thee;
> Sounds of the rude world heard in the day,
> Lulled by the moonlight have all passed away . . .

He didn't dare look at anyone for fear that he'd lose his place or forget the words. In the third verse he heard other voices joining him, including Marietta and Julia. It was all over quickly, and the praise that followed caused blood to rush to his cheeks. Everyone insisted that the performance be repeated, and it was easier this time since he didn't have to sing a single note alone.

"That's it," Owen said when the song came to its end. "I've run through my entire repertoire," and his audience clapped and laughed.

The music continued for some time, though the instruments grew quieter, and a number of people, including Charlie Day and Win Peabody, brought out their bedrolls and opened them right there by the cook fire, reduced now to coals. The Navajos who'd stayed nearby for the music drifted off one or two at a time, and Richard Wetherill finally insisted that his wife needed to sleep for at least a few hours before they headed back to Chaco Canyon in the morning; with pillows and bolsters and heavy blankets he'd prepared the bed of their wagon for Marietta, who these days couldn't get any rest at all unless she was propped up, half sitting, half recumbent, with her feet raised and her arms positioned just so. Their younger children had already joined their cousin under a tarp hung by Al Wetherill between the two Wetherill wagons.

The musicians, accepting thanks all around, retired their instruments, and the party softly broke apart.

"This is my last trip before I head to Albuquerque," Marietta said in parting. At the advanced age of thirty-three she did not intend to give birth in Chaco Canyon, not when more prudent accommodations could be found less than a day away by wagon and train.

Owen couldn't sleep. He sat, wrapped in a Pendleton, with his back against a front wheel of a trading post wagon, his legs stretched in front of him. He decided to take inventory: Julia was asleep above him, in the bed of the wagon; the Gormans all together; the Wetherill brothers and their families, bedded down in their own little encampment off in the direction of the tallest ponderosa, where the Rodriguez family had been invited to join them; Clement Yazzie beside Johanna, on her little knoll near the telescope, which Pete had been too obtunded to put away before crawling into the bed of his spring wagon; Harry Whitaker and Charlie Day and Win Peabody, sensible men, stretched out along one side of the cooking fire pit; Tóya, on the other side . . .

Most of the satellite fires were only glowing coals now, with their halos of light, although every so often a Navajo would stir from sleep and throw fresh wood on one of them, and Owen could see that a few men were still talking at two or three campsites. The air wasn't so cold that Owen could see his breath, but he reckoned that the temperature needed to fall only a few more degrees for that to happen. He pulled the blanket higher across his shoulders. He was always cold when he wasn't directly in the sun or positioned near a stove. He'd wrapped a scarf around his neck and ears and over his chin, and now he slid his hands inside his coat and anchored them in his armpits. The problem was his feet. He'd taken off his deerskin boots but decided to put them on again. He had to be careful when he slid his feet in, for any resultant wrinkle in his wool socks would chafe, and before he even felt anything, the skin might split or a sore open up. He changed his mind again. With his boots in one hand, and clutching the blanket across his chest with the other, he rose and walked to the cook fire and tried to settle himself down near Tóya, who stirred, rose to an elbow, murmured something in Navajo that he didn't understand.

"I'm fine," he said, which seemed to be the correct answer. Tóya rolled over, ready to toast her back, and fell back to sleep.

Seventy-six years, give or take, until Halley's Comet returned. All but the youngest among them would certainly be gone long before then. What else would be gone? He thought about Tóya, her life. What of her world, of what she'd lived through, the Long Walk, would survive? She never spoke of the Long Walk, at least not to him. She should. If she did, he'd write it down. (He was biased toward the written word. How could he not be?) And if she spoke of it, maybe other Navajos would as well. That would be something valuable, for him to record their stories. Certainly of more value than all the time he'd spent traipsing over these mountains and through the Chuska Valley looking for . . . what? The meaning of the "Great Western Road"—why it was there, where it was going seven hundred, eight hundred years ago. Built by a civilization that, for reasons both chosen and imposed, collapsed and almost disappeared before it was reborn as the Hopi, the Zuni, the Acoma, the Laguna, the Pueblo tribes along the upper Rio Grande. Against that legacy, the western road was meaningless.

Seven hundred years, eight hundred into the future, what would remain of the American West as its current inhabitants knew it? He'd read Jules Verne's *Off on a Comet* and Wells's *The War of the Worlds* and *The First Men in the Moon*, all of which failed not for their flights of scientific fancy but because they remained so grounded in the time and place of their writing. He recalled reading an article in one of Julia's newspapers or magazines not long ago, something about how the speed at which time passed was relative. At first Owen had thought the writer was referring to the common perception that time could pass too quickly or too slowly, that a pleasurable hour could seem like a few minutes, for example. But the article had turned out to be about something entirely different, namely a new scientific theory that time itself was variable. The writer had used the example of how two trains cars traveling at the same velocity on parallel tracks through a dark tunnel might be perceived as not moving at all by two travelers, each observing the other through the lighted windows of their respective train cars. And how when one train gathered speed and moved ahead, both travelers, if somehow able to see each other's pocket watches, would perceive that time was slowing down for the other but not for himself. Owen didn't understand that at all—why one wouldn't perceive that time was speeding up for the other. (He'd have to try to find that article again.) But the fundamental point wasn't that the passengers' perceptions of time had changed, but that *time itself* had changed, though by such an infinitesimal amount that it couldn't even be measured until one approached the unattainable speed of light. No, he didn't understand any of it, but something about it struck him as so *right* that his thoughts kept coming back to the idea, weeks later. He didn't know what it all meant, except that science would probably become ever more confounding and that to try and see into the future, even a mere seventy-six years, was utter folly. The course of an ordinary life was *already* impossible to predict, even without the extraordinary: the Galveston flood, the San Francisco earthquake, the burning of the General Slocum in the East River . . . thousands dead, each a victim of time and place.

The future. Ha! Forget about Halley's return. Forget even about 1920, when by all rights he should still be *on* this solid earth and not buried *in* it. Thinking ten years, even five years, did him no good. Five years, 1915. New Mexico would certainly be a state, as would Arizona. Gallup would have its municipal sewers along with its running water. Maybe Mary Wetherill would also have her paved streets. Maybe the Many Springs Canyon Trading Post would have a telephone. If so, Julia Halley, if not back in the "World," would at least be connected by wire to it. Aeroplanes might even be crossing the high desert, their pilots looking down on these mountains and canyons, jagged peaks and ragged rifts.

He felt too restive to settle down, his thoughts running off in all directions. What could he do?

Julia. He wanted to be lying beside her. She'd given him new life and he loved her. No, she wasn't beautiful—not with Beth Burrows's youthful, clean fairness of hair and face and skin (oh, he remembered Beth's skin, revealed by a night's lamplight, under his touch!). Julia's hair, wind-tossed half the time or piled into an unruly knot, was showing strands of gray; her face and skin, darkened by the sun and coarsened by the dry wind, was already wrinkled around her eyes and mouth. Her figure; well, there, Julia could outmatch Beth's promising slenderness.

Such things, hair, face, skin, figure mattered—he couldn't deny it—but what mattered more was the absence in Julia of a young woman's necessary attention to her appearance and, in its place, the presence of experience and a formed self. Julia was herself, herself alone, in everything she did. She answered to no one but herself, and part of that self, the deepest part, she kept *to* herself. Oh, he didn't doubt that she withheld insecurities from the world, thrashed them out in silent, secret hours, but she knew *how* to do this and proceed onward with her life, tending to her work and her home and those around her. That was her integrity, and he couldn't see how he could fully embrace it without loving her fully, with his body (that poor, appalling thing) as well as his soul.

His soul. (One of a billion and a half!) He'd arrived in Many Springs fearing that he had no soul anymore. His disease had robbed him of everything except the quixotic. One stumble after another. Why had he come? Some quest for meaning: the western road but more than that; his life, an insight mappable only in his befuddled head.

And now? What should he do now? Declare his love? What would be the benefit? Only a future, not the present, required a declaration, and he had no future. One month, one year, four years. All the same when time was so short. He couldn't slow it down. Nor could he still his thoughts, ever reaching forward. Mystics and holy men could do it, or so he'd heard, but he had no time to learn how. Time was beyond his reach.

* * *

He woke to find Carmelita Gorman, poker in one hand, a handful of straw in the other, stirring up the coals of the cook fire. He didn't think he could move. He couldn't feel his feet, and every bone in his back felt locked in place. He groaned and stretched and then, still under his blanket, crossed an ankle over a knee and reached down to try and massage sensation back into his right foot.

"Good morning," he said to Carmelita. There was just enough light, before true dawn, for a gray sky.

"You all need to move out of the way," she said, "if I'm going to cook everyone breakfast."

"Why so early?" Owen whined, hoping to get a smile out of her. "Have mercy."

She stopped and looked at him. When she had a mission, Carmelita brooked no interference. "There's a business to run. Somebody has to get back to the trading post at a decent hour."

"Is there anything I can do to help?"

"Just get out of my way." She waved the poker, shooing him.

He groaned one more time for effect, threw off his blanket, and sat up, reaching for his boots.

"Later on," she said, "after everybody has cleared out, you can check to be sure that all the campfires are completely out. Stir them up good. There won't be much to clean up that the coyotes and birds can't take care of, but maybe you can stay and help my Johnny fill in the latrine."

"I can certainly do that," Owen said.

Breakfast wouldn't be much to speak of: coffee, hard-boiled eggs, fry bread, corn mush; Owen wasn't hungry anyway. Tóya, nearby, was already stripping a lamb rib clean with her few remaining teeth.

Many Navajos were beginning to move about the clearing, some gathering sticks to renew their own campfires. Owen found Julia and Harry Whitaker chatting with Clement Yazzie by the trading post wagon.

"Good morning," Owen said, and Julia, her shawl wrapped tightly around her, returned his greeting with a smile.

"You're just in time," Harry said. "Will you join us?—we were just about to stroll out to the main trail and watch the sunrise. Tóya's coming, too."

"Shouldn't we ask Pete?" Owen said.

"You may if you want to," Julia said, but her tone clearly indicated that she was still unhappy about his behavior the previous night.

"Go ahead," Harry said. "God forbid he should feel left out."

Owen found Pete in his wagon, still buried under a bearskin. He groaned and told Owen to go away.

Charlie Day, sitting with his back against a wheel of Pete's wagon and drinking cold coffee, merely smiled and shrugged.

"Where's Win Peabody?" Owen asked.

"Chasing birds," Charlie answered. "He heard a couple that he said he wanted to try and identify, so off he went." Charlie gestured to the west.

Owen listened. He heard jays, and a woodpecker working, and, there, a melodious trill. "To each his own," he said.

Johanna was sitting where she'd spent the night, close to the telescope, but her eyes were closed. Owen said good morning to her and, knowing better than to expect a reply, continued on. He put his cold hands in his jacket pockets and discovered the forgotten eyepiece that Pete had handed him last night. Worried by a sudden thought, he turned around and walked back to Johanna. He reached down and touched her shoulder. Her eyes opened immediately, which led him to believe that she wasn't dozing, just waiting.

"Johanna," he said, shaking his head, "you can't look at the sun through the telescope." He extended his arms and spread his hands wide. "A telescope gathers all the light it can"—he slowly drew his hands together, as if he were catching something ephemeral, and squeezed them tight—"and brings it to you. If you point the telescope toward the sun, all that light will blind you forever." He put his fists over his eyes and held them there for several seconds. "Do you understand?"

Johanna hadn't moved or looked at him directly, but she had listened.

"Come with us," he said, extending a hand toward her. "Your brother and Julia and some of the rest of us are going to greet the morning."

Johanna sat for a moment longer, and then, without accepting his hand, she rose and they walked together to where the others were waiting at the edge of the clearing.

The six proceeded single-file along the narrow path, where a fine dew had collected on the ground plants that were sheltered by overhanging tree branches. Half way along they reached a gulley. On the far side, akilter, sat the bright red Rodriguez automobile, though it's finish had been dulled by dust from the previous day's journey.

"How is Alberto ever going to get this thing out of here?" Julia asked.

It was an impressive machine, Owen thought, but here in the wilderness, its presence demanded mischief. "I don't know, but I think we should decorate it."

"How?" Julia asked.

"Just draw or write things in the dust. With our fingers."

Their looks told him they thought he was crazy, but then Julia smiled and in wide strokes signed her name along the hood. Owen, Harry (with a flourish), and even Yazzie followed suit.

"That's bound to annoy Matilda," Owen said, stepping back and admiring their handiwork. "She'll think we're making fun of them."

"Would we do that?" Julia asked, her eyes wide with feigned innocence.

"Definitely," Harry said, "and it's mighty cruel of us."

Yazzie spoke in Navajo to Johanna, who stepped forward and slowly, carefully, using a pinky, drew Halley's comet. Her mark.

Tóya approached the car, contemplated it with a shake of her head, and gave a firm kick with a new boot to the fender, leaving a small but detectable dent. *Her* mark.

They walked on and soon came to the wider trail, which ran up from the Chuska Valley in the east, through the pass behind them, down the other side to Crystal and, beyond, the road to Ft. Defiance. The sun rose, a golden orange.

FOR A LONG TIME PETE had known that the time had come to leave, but still he lingered. A frayed rope, some strand of hope, held him. He kept thinking: one more visit to Many Springs, at just the right time, when he would say just the right words.

He was a goddamn idiot.

He'd woken up in the dark, his brain beating against the inside of his skull, his throat dry and rough. It took several minutes for his mouth to work up the spit he needed to ease the scorch. He heard Owen Rouse calling him, and he told Owen to go away. But he couldn't go back to sleep. He slid his butt toward the end of the wagon and, with his bearskin still draped over his shoulders like a cape, he managed to plant his feet on the ground and steady himself.

Charlie Day, wide awake, humming something, was stretching to his full height. His seeming good humor irritated Pete even more.

"Tone it down, Junior," he said. "Junior": a joke between the two of them, not simply because Pete was nearly a decade older but because Charlie's younger brother Sammy was the actual "Junior" in the Day family—a perversion of the proper order, Pete liked to remind Charlie.

Charlie turned, a smile already spread across his handsome face—a further reason for irritation—and said, "Wrong side of the bed?"

Pete sat down. He didn't remember climbing into his wagon last night. Or was it this morning? Whatever the time, he'd reached the point where nothing but oblivion, sleep, would suffice, not even more whiskey.

"Where's everyone?" he croaked.

Charlie, far from unobservant, knew whom he meant. "Mrs. Halley walked over to the pass, to see the sunrise."

"Anybody else go?"

"Yazzie and his sister. That Rouse fellow. Dr. Whitaker and the other Navajo woman, I think."

"Is the coffee ready over there?" He nodded toward the fire where Carmelita was ordering Johnny and Tom about.

"Doesn't look like it. Soon, I expect."

Pete threw off the skin and stumbled to his feet, which didn't help his head at all. "I could use some water," he said.

"To drink or to take a bath?"

"Just give me the water, Junior."

Charlie dipped a metal cup in a bucket and handed it to him. "Something tells me you're going to be up to your neck in water, and it's gonna be *hot*, when Mrs. Halley gets around to dealing with you."

"It won't be the first time." The cool water eased the distress, pharynx to stomach.

"Maybe you should say your prayers, Brother." "Brother": Charlie's standard retort to "Junior."

"*Dominus vobiscum*," Pete said, tossing the empty cup to Charlie. He headed for the pass, stopping on the way to relieve his bladder.

He took a good look at Rodriguez's automobile when he reached it— quite the shiny thing, under the coat of dust, but completely impractical for the terrain. What had tempted Rodriguez into the rutted rough? Pride of possession, probably: a vision of driving up to the campsite, drawing awe from the assembled multitude. Instead, the beast lay here askew, the right front wheel turned in on itself in a ditch, the left wheel six inches off the ground, the whole front end balanced on a boulder. Rodriguez was lucky his prized possession hadn't flipped over and killed somebody. Pride goeth before destruction, and an haughty spirit before a fall. Pete shook his head, added his signature to those already scrawled in the dust, and moved on. The brisk early morning air, breathed deeply, helped clear his head. After another five minutes of picking his way over the uneven ground, he felt better; he could stiffen his spine, stand erect, look presentable enough. He ran his fingers through his hair, straight back from his forehead, and then rubbed the crusted sleep from his eyes. He wished he had a mouthful or two of coffee to swish around and spit out, disguising the fug.

He heard someone laugh up ahead, around a bend. The highest elevation of the pass was a mile to the west, obscured by the ponderosa pine and the juniper—the sky directly above the trees there still held the gray of first light—but below, toward the laughter, the vista opened up to the east. He followed the trail and beyond the turn found the sun, a lovely orange rim edging into view, not so bright yet that you had to shield your eyes.

The six were standing almost in a line: Johanna off a bit to the left, maintaining her distance, and Owen and Tóya next, and then Harry Whitaker, and then Julia and Yazzie on the right. All were silent now, praying or thinking.

Pete halted, thirty yards away, held his own silence.

They'd kept it to themselves. In the nearly four years since he left them together at the Hubbell Trading Post, after their trip to Second Mesa to see the Hopi dance and visit with Yazzie's Hopi relatives—at the time, he was heading home to Gallup; they were going north, from Hubbell's to Canyon de Chelly, and from there back to Many Springs—he'd never seen their demeanor break. No sweet nothings—he couldn't even imagine such a thing, either coming from or being received by Yazzie—and he'd never seen them touch. Nothing more than the way they sometimes communicated with a look, a wordless conferring, nothing cloying, but practical, utilitarian.

But now it unraveled, the last strand that had bound him to her. Bile surged into Pete's parched throat. If he had a gun in his hand, he'd use it, swear to God; he'd put an end to that goddamn Indian, who had taken possession, putting his left arm around her waist and drawing her to him. And she, dropping her head sideways to Yazzie's shoulder. If they knew that he, Pete, was watching, they wouldn't have done it, which somehow only added to the insult.

How long did they stand there like that, not caring if the world saw them? He could only guess because he'd already turned and started back to the campsite.

"I'm packing up," Pete said. "Are you coming with me?"

Charlie Day laughed. "Nah, I told Alberto I'd get his car back to Gallup for him. He can't speak Navajo, and most of the Indians up here can't speak English. I got one to agree to hitch up a team and haul the automobile out of here at a reasonable price. I guess the family's getting a ride in the Gormans' wagon as far as Naschitti. After that, I don't know. You want to volunteer your services?"

"Save me, Jesus," Pete said. "Matilda Rodriguez is a pill in a pouch, and I don't have the temperament for their children. Give me some of that coffee."

Charlie handed his steaming, half-empty cup to Pete, who inhaled the sourness before taking a cautious sip.

"That daughter of theirs, Elena, in a few years she's gonna give them a run for their money," Charlie said, punctuating his comment with a two-note whistle.

"You good-looking devil, charming the ladies."

Charlie shook his head. "How old is she?"

"Hard to tell. Her mother dresses her like a dolly."

"You want any breakfast? It's ready."

"I couldn't stomach it." For more reasons than his hangover. "Can you do me a favor?"

"Sure," Charlie said.

"Can you collect my horse and hitch him up?"

"I suppose I can do that," Charlie said.

"It'd be much appreciated," Pete said. He could count on Charlie Day, who strode off, leaving Pete alone with the coffee. But in the end, people always disappointed him, beginning with his stupid shit of a brother, without the sense not to steal from the gangsters that hung around Cincinnati's wharves, not that Ron had deserved to get his throat slit. And even the Brother brothers, Archie and Matthew, who never replied to the letter he'd sent them after the events at Hunters Point. And worst of all, Julia Halley. Imagining her and Yazzie together sickened him. (The coffee wasn't helping.) Yazzie could behave like a civilized man in company, but beneath the surface lay something dark and primal, lurking, ready to kill a man in cold blood or drag a white woman into the muck.

Pete walked up the slight incline to where the telescope still stood on its tripod. Putting the cup down, he began disassembling it.

Though not in so many words, more than once Julia had made it clear that he would never bed her. Four years ago, after the Home Dance on Second Mesa, he should have changed his plans and gone with her and Yazzie to Canyon de Chelly. Because that was when it started between them, he was sure. If he'd been there, the moment would have passed, her weakness, her . . . appetite. She might have kept her senses. But he'd had appointments in Gallup. Which he should have ignored. He'd done so in the past. Business hadn't suffered. Everyone still wanted the wooden family portrait, for which he took their money and smiled and directed his sensibilities elsewhere, to the mesas and buttes and flumes and dikes and hoodoos and goosenecks and arches and windows and canyons, things of some permanence.

The morning light grew stronger. The hammering in his head made him squint. He rubbed his temples. Charlie Day was leading Stable Boy, his horse, to the wagon. The Navajos who'd spent the night were clearing out.

He needed to do the same. He'd almost forgotten: where was Win Peabody? He'd have to listen to Peabody's wit and wisdom all the way back to Gallup. Jesus, his head hurt, and he felt like he was going to vomit. He dumped the remainder of the coffee on the ground.

He'd shown her Halley's Comet. Hadn't that been the whole point? Look through here. See as I see. He slid the folded tripod and telescope, protected in canvas, into his wagon.

He'd tried, knowing in his heart that it wouldn't be enough. *Astra inclinant, sed non obligant.* The stars incline us, they do not bind us.

He couldn't come to her anymore.

CHAPTER TWELVE: Julia (The Past, concluded)

7. Sisters

Julia Halley, a modest valise beside her, had been waiting over an hour when the Atchison, Topeka, and Santa Fe's California Limited, in a commotion of noise and cindered smoke, pulled into the Gallup depot on a bright August afternoon in 1906. The conductor in his blue woolen uniform and cap had scarcely put a foot on the platform before a young woman, beautifully dressed but hatless—her blonde hair curled and pinned high on her head—hurried past him and, unable to contain her joyful tears, launched herself into her sister's arms.

"Oh, Julia! Oh, Julia!" was all Penelope Malott could manage to say in their first minute together.

Julia herself said nothing. She remembered the feel of this cheek against her cheek, the contours of this bejeweled ear, the texture of the sweet hair, but the fullness of the body pressed against hers, bodice and stomach, took her by surprise. (This was a different thickness than her own—vitality rather than the first decline of age.) In two years Penelope had come into her own womanhood, there was no denying it.

She saw Philip Malott walking toward them wearing a finely tailored gray suit and a homburg. At least he was smiling, though Julia couldn't be sure if he was happy to be seeing her or betraying a man's condescending admiration for his beautiful though emotionally unrestrained wife. Julia hardly knew the man; she wondered what had made her so cynical. Would this have been her attitude toward *any* man who claimed her sister's affection?

"Hello, Philip," Julia said, placing her hands on Penny's shoulders and establishing a few inches of space between them. Still speaking over Penny's shoulder, she added, "I hope your journey has been comfortable."

"Julia, what a delight," he said with a glance toward the locomotive down the track a bit. "Yes, train travel is remarkably accommodating these days. I think you'll find your sleeping compartment small but comfortable. It's quite near ours. You just have the one suitcase? Our porter will see to it while we enjoy our lunch. So this is Gallup, is it?" He took Penny's arm and looked around with widened eyes.

"It is," Julia said, "though the view from the front of the depot rather than the tracks is somewhat more civilized."

"One can only hope," Philip said, checking his pocket watch.

They took their lunch at the Harvey House. Describing her first views of the Great Plains and the Rocky Mountains and the red rock mesas and buttes east of Gallup, Penny dominated the conversation, leaving Philip, without much comment, to consume his lobster salad au mayonnaise, while the sisters, neither of whom had much of an appetite, both dined lightly on a breaded veal cutlet and minced browned potatoes. They'd have dinner on the train, before arriving in Williams, Arizona, just after 10:30 that evening. Their sleeping car would be set out on a siding, where another locomotive would take them north to the Grand Canyon, to their rooms at the recently opened El Tovar, perched right at the southern rim. The journey was being paid for in its entirety by Philip, at his insistence.

After lunch Julia quickly visited her sleeper, which included a comfortable sofa that her porter would convert to a bed in the evening, a commode, and a fold-down wash stand above the commode, permitting her to freshen up and check her hair in a small framed mirror. The train was under way by the time she repaired to Penny and Philip's more spacious accommodations, comprising a drawing room as well as their sleeping compartment. Philip had already departed for the club car for a cigar and iced coffee, thereby giving the sisters an opportunity to chatter, as he put it. The sisters settled into their chairs.

"I brought some photographs that I asked my friend Mr. Pietrowski to take last month," Julia said. "Would you like to see them?"

"I don't know," Penny said with a mock pout. "Would I? I'm a little afraid to see how you live. Your letters are never very specific about your day-to-day life." Julia handed her the first photograph. "This is where you live?" Penelope asked.

"Actually, the veranda where I'm sitting is the entrance to the trading post. My home is around to the side."

"And this is—?" She pointed to a man emerging from the door of the trading post.

"Mr. Clement Yazzie."

"Oh, of course." Penny looked a bit puzzled. "He's not wearing a side-arm."

"No." Julia smiled. "Although some of the men who visit the store do. In truth, I don't believe Mr. Yazzie even owns one. At least, I've never seen him carrying one."

"He must have a rifle." Penny added, "For the coyotes and wolves and such. To protect the sheep."

"He does. But we don't have wolves. They've been hunted nearly to extinction except far in the south. Coyotes aplenty, but no wolves."

"And who is this?" Penelope pointed to the second figure, off to the side, in the photograph. "Mr. Yazzie's wife?"

"No, that's his sister Johanna."

"I thought maybe he'd remarried." Julia had mentioned the Yazzies on and off in her letters.

"No, he hasn't."

"She's rather striking, isn't she? So dark . . . She looks as if she objects to the camera, or the photographer."

"She doesn't like being photographed."

"For heaven's sake, why not? She doesn't believe the camera will steal her soul, or some other such nonsense, does she?"

"I don't know. Most traditional Navajos don't discuss their beliefs with Anglos. Besides, as I'm sure I've mentioned, Johanna is mute. This is my kitchen," Julia noted, displaying a second picture; she was the only figure to be seen, wearing an apron.

"You have a hand pump."

"Yes."

"I haven't seen one of those in years."

"You don't get out of your Chicago neighborhood much, do you?" Julia said, teasing.

"Now, Julia," Penny chided, "don't be mean. So you don't have indoor plumbing?"

"The pump *is* indoor plumbing—but no, not like you mean. When the nights get to twenty below in the winter, we employ the most modern chamber pots."

"I don't know how you survive."

"Penny, you and I grew up with chamber pots under our beds."

She shuddered. "I know, but that seems so long ago. You know, I had a lovely shower bath this morning, right on this train."

"All the conveniences of home," Julia said. She knew the California Limited catered exclusively to first-class passengers, so she shouldn't have been surprised. She shuffled through the photographs until she found one showing the trading post's guest hogan and, beyond, the dam and windmill. "You can't see the pond at this angle, but it serves our wool scouring business quite well."

Penny took the photographs in her well-manicured hand and leafed through them, stopping at one showing Julia's "parlor," with her bookcases beyond. "This looks comfortable." Noting the lantern on a side table, she asked, "I don't suppose you'll be getting electricity anytime soon?"

"I'm afraid it'll be quite some time before the Gallup utility company is willing to run fifty miles of wire—if that's even possible—to electrify one building. But we manage."

Penelope, in a gesture Julia remembered so well, bit her lower lip, glanced back at the first photograph. "I notice you say 'we' a lot."

"Oh, I'm just being imperial."

"You haven't heard from Will?"

"No, I haven't."

Together, they looked through the other photographs, which included Harry Whitaker at his desk, his large hands clasped on his stomach and his mustache, as always, trimmed precisely to the edge of his upper lip; a young Water Gap mother, Isleta Bear, and in her lap, her toddler son, who held up a piece of Wrigley's Spearmint gum, Pete's apparent inducement for the child to sit still; Tom and Carmelita Gorman waiting on customers in the store; Alberto Rodriguez standing in front of his furniture store, arms akimbo; Julia on her pinto mare, taken beside Pete's wagon and including (deliberately, Julia thought) the shadow of the photographer and his camera spreading across the ground toward her—she doubted that Penelope even noticed that . . .

"So, you said Father is well?" Julia asked. They'd briefly touched on the subject of their father at lunch. "And Edna?"

"Quite well. It's less than a day to Albany by train, but I don't see them nearly enough, and now—" She blushed.

"And now—?" Julia asked.

"Well, I'm going to have a child." Penny giggled.

Julia leaned forward and grabbed her sister's hands. "Penny, that's so wonderful, I can't say how much it pleases me!"

"In six months you're going to be an aunt, which means you have to visit us so very often."

Julia laughed with delight. "Philip must be overjoyed."

"Oh, he is. He wants a son, of course, but my intuition tells me it's a girl."

"How are you feeling?"

"Quite well. I've had no difficulties, just a touch of morning sickness early on. Philip wanted to postpone our little trip, but I told him not to be a ninny, that there was absolutely no reason for us to change our plans."

"Have you told Father?"

"I spoke to him on the telephone. He said he wished Mother was still with us to share the news."

That produced a prolonged silence. Julia knew that Penny remembered their mother primarily as an invalid, but Julia herself could recall another time, when her mother was Blake's "fair-hair'd angel," the evening star who smiled and drew "the blue curtains of the sky" around Julia's bed when it was time for sleep. Julia hadn't thought of that poem, "To the Evening Star," her mother's favorite, in years, even though she'd heard it recited a hundred times and had repeated it herself many, many times when tucking Penny into bed.

"I'm sure he misses you greatly," Julia said.

"Not just me—you as well. He always asks after you."

"I write," Julia said. It sounded like the feeble excuse it was; a letter three or four times a year, always answered not by her father, whose hand was too unsteady, but by Edna, whose responses were newsy but never made inquiries.

"Sometimes when I see him, he isn't 'there,' if you know what I mean," Penny said.

"Yes."

"But other times, he quite enjoys himself. Edna does her best to keep him occupied. Sometimes he thinks you married John Sewell." She shook her head. "Of course he knows that you're in New Mexico, so maybe he just confuses names."

Her "great love"; Julia couldn't even recall John's face.

"You and Edna are quite alike, you know."

"Oh God!" Julia said.

"That's why you'd never get along, being in the same household. You'd go after each other with knitting needles. Aimed right for the eyes." Penelope raised both hands and extended her fore- and middle fingers.

Julia laughed. "The important thing is that *you* and she get along."

"We do. I quite like her. And admire her. You've seen how well she cares for Father. I'm convinced that she's the only reason why he's still with us. I wish you'd let your heart soften a bit toward her."

Julia, effecting an exaggerated frown, said, "I possess a rock, not a heart."

"Oh, Julia! I don't believe that for a minute!" In the confines of the car it took Penelope barely a second to stand up and, leaning forward, to wrap her sister effusively in her arms. Julia laughed again. Penny's hair was so soft against her cheek, and it smelled of chamomile and rosemary.

"I've been thinking a lot about you and Mother," Penny said, returning to her seat.

"Have you?"

"And what kind of a mother I'll be."

"I'd imagine that every expectant woman wonders about that."

"Do you wish you'd had a child?" Penny asked. "Of course you raised me until Father remarried, but I don't think you've ever said anything about wanting a child of your own."

Julia evaded the question. "You were still so very young when I left." Then she added, hoping that her sister wouldn't pursue the subject any further, "Do you plan to stay in Chicago for the birth or travel to Albany?"

"Oh, I don't know," Penny said, her blue eyes suddenly misty, "but I'd very much like you to be there."

Julia didn't doubt Penny's sincerity, but she also suspected that this was the first salvo in a campaign designed to uproot her from New Mexico.

"You could come for the holidays and then stay through my lying-in," Penny continued.

"Penny," Julia replied, "I have a business to run. I can't abandon it for two months or more."

"You wouldn't be *abandoning* anything. You've said in your letters how reliable Mr. and Mrs. Gorman are. Surely they could manage. Besides, winter is your slowest season, isn't it? I bet you spend much of your time curled up with the books I send you."

"Let me assure you that there are always things to be done, most of them all the more urgent because the days are so short." Not true, but believable.

"Still," Penny murmured, "it would be nice."

Julia studied her sister's profile: the honey locks; the peaches-and-cream skin; the sharp nose and distinct jaw line that, if physiognomy was any indication of psychology, suggested a firmness of purpose that Penny, to Julia's knowledge, had yet to demonstrate. But she was still so very young. Well, Julia thought, not *that* young. Indeed, many women Penelope's age were already mothers two or three times over. For some, motherhood would establish their personality, their lifelong dedication, if marriage hadn't already done so (for better or worse). But try as she might, she couldn't put herself in her sister's place, nor her sister in her own. Julia would never have chosen a Philip Malott (nor he, her); Penny never would have risked so much as a kiss in a darkened hallway with a Will Halley.

The countryside rolled by outside the windows, the dramatic sand-stone formations beyond the tracks gradually giving way, as they entered Arizona, to a bleaker landscape of grayish browns and stunted growth.

"You should get to know Philip better," Penny now said. "He's much more sympathetic than you seem to think."

"Sympathetic to whom? Me?"

"Yes, I believe so, but I mean in general. You know that his family is quite wealthy."

"How could I not?"

"If he so chose, he wouldn't have to work for the New York Central or any other corporation. He could spend his time doing nothing but managing his family's investments and living the high life, but he prefers to work for his living."

Yes, Julia thought, but he still falls asleep at night secure in what's stuffed in the family's mattresses. She said, "And that's to be admired."

"You know," Penny said, looking away and smoothing the contours of her skirt with her hands, "his family didn't want him to marry me."

Because they saw no advantage, Julia thought but couldn't bring herself to say.

"He threatened to defy them, regardless of the consequences."

"But you won them over."

"Not at first. It upset me terribly. But Edna advised patience and, especially, no bowing and groveling. She said they'd just think less of me."

"Ah, you confided in Edna." Julia couldn't help but feel hurt. Penelope should have come to her. But, of course, she couldn't have. She'd needed more than carefully chosen words of advice written in a letter; she'd needed the immediacy of conversation and commiseration—she'd needed someone to dry her tears and hold her hand and tell her directly how people of money thought and behaved.

"I did, and she was wonderful. And so was Philip. He stood by me at every turn."

"His family seemed pleased enough at the wedding."

"They came around, just as Edna said they would."

"Do you see much of them?"

"Oh yes, and we get along quite well."

Julia smiled slyly. "They've recognized your finer qualities."

"I should hope so." Head raised, jaw firm. Then she continued, with resolve, "You should think better of Philip, Julia. He'd do anything for me."

Perhaps, Julia thought. With a baby on the way, the more likely. But then, once the baby arrived, with his lovely wife's attention now directed toward milk and diapers and spit-up and a proper night's sleep—then would come the first true test.

8. Grand Canyons

THE CONCIERGE at the El Tovar recommended that, should they want to stroll along the rim, the best time to do so would be at first light, when the temperature was agreeable and the shadows were strong, permitting a truer sense of the canyon's vastness than when the fierce overhead sun tended to wash out the colors and reduce the dramatic effect. Thus the morning after their arrival they arose well before dawn and, fortified only by strong coffee and a brioche, proceeded eastward, following the clearly marked, leveled trail that at places brought them within feet of the canyon's edge: below, a straight drop, often of a thousand feet or more; across, an extraordinary expanse, mile after mile of the earth stripped bare by time and the forces of water and wind, to elemental reds, browns, tans, streaked purple, and ivory as the golden light broke the horizon.

Julia forged ahead, leaving Penny and Philip to follow at their leisure. She had dual purposes: first, to see the abyss on her own, without a need for commentary, hers or anyone else's; and second, to observe her companions more subtly than if she'd lingered behind them. She stopped frequently, casting her view in an arc that took in both the natural world and, through strategic glances, the married couple. Even at this hour, before the summer sun could heat the air, surprisingly strong currents rose from below, over the lip of the canyon, and threatened to carry off her broad-brimmed hat, so she removed it. She closed her eyes and listened; little broke the silence except the cawing of ravens and, also carried to her by the wind, her sister's laughter. Julia had no idea what Philip was saying to his wife as they strode, arm in arm, paying at least as much attention to each other as to the wonders before them.

They seemed happy in their relative solitude, Penny and Philip, without her inhibitory presence. (There were only a few other guests of the El Tovar strolling along the trail; two men, speaking German and wearing short leather pants and thick boots and carrying walking sticks and multiple canteens, passed at such a pace that Julia could only conclude that they intended to hike as far as the trail would take them.) Then why was she skeptical? The fault was hers, not theirs. Maybe she was jealous. She and Will had never been further than one step from financial ruin, and that had certainly taken its toll. Penury was something her sister would never face; after her younger, thankfully oblivious years, Penny had been protected by money, first Edna's and now Philip's. Did she, Julia, resent it? No, she didn't think so. She felt a touch of jealousy, perhaps, but no more than that. Jealousy, not because her sister had so clearly won Philip, and certainly not for Penny's pleasure in the particulars of the man (heaven forbid!), but because money had preceded an expansive happiness that Julia, alone now for more than two years, couldn't envisage attaining for herself with any man, or under any circumstance that didn't bear some contradictory, deadening precondition. She would never travel among the elect or the elite. With the sun now full on her face, she restored her hat to her head, holding it in place with one hand, welcoming the shade of the straw brim.

The married couple caught up with her, and the three stood together at Yavapai Point, the outer turn of a long inward curve, looking back to their hotel, across a gap of half a mile or more by raven's flight. The sun behind them had advanced two hands'-width above the horizon, and the light on the canyon formations changed continuously; across the way, the shadows on the red wall where the El Tovar perched (its facing windows mirror-blindingly-bright) were descending as the sun climbed, and suddenly, laughing with astonishment, Julia realized that their own puny forms—hers, Penny's, Philip's; hats, heads, shoulders, arms, torsos—were unmistakably outlined on the ageless rock below the hotel.

"Penny," Julia said, "quick—look over there!" and she raised her arm and saw her shadow wave back.

That afternoon, Julia crossed the gently angled balcony that overlooked the lobby, proceeded down the wide staircase, turned left at the bottom, and precisely at four-thirty swept into the dining room of the El Tovar, where most of the tables, draped with white linens, were unoccupied. Philip had chosen a table at the far end, in front of one of the picture windows that bracketed the large fieldstone fireplace. Penelope's absence didn't surprise her.

Julia had spent an hour preparing herself for tea: bathing, toweling her hair dry to bring out the natural luster and curl, stepping into a silk dress in a subtle lilac that she hadn't worn in the two years since Penny's wedding. The pale color suited her sun-browned complexion. Fortunately, the high neckline and long, scalloped sleeves hid the white skin that covered her shoulders and upper arms; she had no desire to look like a striped clown. She'd considered pinning up her hair but decided not to. Instead, she drew it back above her ears and held it in place with two thin side braids and a turquoise and silver clip—a touch youngish, perhaps, but justifiable, given the conservative cut of her dress. Rouge (but no powder: attempting to lighten her skin would have been ludicrous) and a deep red lip crème completed the picture in the three-quarter-length mirror. As for her hands, she'd done the best she could, filing her nails to a respectable roundness and applying a clear lacquer. Her shoes matched the dress; her ivory gloves complemented her clutch.

Philip, who'd risen upon her approach, made no comment about her appearance. (None had been expected, but Julia was nevertheless slightly disappointed and at the same time annoyed by her disappointment; all that work should have produced some sort of reaction.) A hostess, dressed in the typical Harvey Girl uniform of black skirt and blouse and starched white apron, settled her into a chair, after which Philip sat down again. He'd already ordered tea, scones, and finger sandwiches for them, and while they waited for their refreshments to arrive he made his excuse for Penelope's absence: a severe headache, brought on, he thought, by too much light. She was in their room, lying down, with a cool compress across her eyes.

"The light out here is very intense," Philip said.

"The air is also thinner than she's used to. That alone can induce dizziness and headaches." All true enough, but Julia had no doubt that Penelope's absence provided Philip with his first opportunity to speak candidly.

The previous night, after dinner, the three were sitting on the veranda sipping brandy and enjoying a lovely breeze as Julia revealed her plans for the rest of her excursion. She'd take the train with them back to Williams, where they would part company. Philip and Penelope were heading to Los Angeles, the last leg on their westward itinerary, which had been altered as a consequence of the April earthquake and fire in San Francisco; Julia would take the train east, but only to Winslow. Her friend Mr. Pietrowski, the photographer, would meet her there at the end of his photographic expedition to the Painted Desert. The two of them would then head north, to Second Mesa on the Hopi Reservation, where they planned to attend a ceremonial dance. Her employee and friend Clement Yazzie, who was half Hopi and whose father's family lived on Second Mesa, would join them there. The day after the dance, she and her companions would travel to Ganado, where she'd visit with her friends the Hubbells at their trading post. Mr. Pietrowski would then be returning to Gallup, while Mr. Yazzie would guide her north to Chinle and then through Canyon de Chelly, toward home. The trip had all been carefully mapped out.

The Harvey waitress, a young girl whose red eyes and red nose suggested that she was in the throes of either an emotional crisis or a severe cold, carefully positioned a silver teapot, a small pitcher, and two serving plates on the table. The scones were accompanied by a dish of clotted cream, and the crustless sandwiches, of varying thicknesses and shapes, some bearing a fluted edge, looked elegant.

"I'll pour," Philip said. The waitress curtsied and departed. "I hope you like Earl Grey."

"I do," Julia said. "I haven't had it in years."

"I'll make sure Penelope sends you some. I know you do like your tea." Steam rose from the cups as he poured. "Cream and sugar?"

"Thank you, I'll help myself."

Philip took a scone from the tray and then added a large spoonful of the clotted cream to his plate. He busied himself with splitting the scone and applying the cream to half. "I have a rather serious matter to discuss, I'm afraid," he said.

"And that is?" As if she didn't know.

The dining room was beginning to fill up with other well-dressed visitors, and there was a background murmuring of discrete conversations and laughter amid the occasional clink of silver on china.

"It greatly concerns Penelope and me," Philip said, "that you're not going directly to Gallup by train and then home."

"Why is that?" Julia asked.

"As your sister's husband, and your host for this trip, I assume a certain responsibility for you."

"You're Penny's husband, not mine." They'd been dodging the issue of Will for two days now, and she thought it was time to get it over with.

Philip didn't hesitate: "And where *is* your husband, I might ask?"

"You 'might ask' anything, but don't assume that you're entitled to an answer."

Philip, already sitting stiffly erect in his chair, drew himself up another inch; even seated, he was a head taller than she. "I *assume*," he countered, "only that you have no answer."

Having anticipated the unpleasantness, she was neither embarrassed nor intimidated. "Tuck your feathers in, Philip," she said. "I'm not Lily Bart, and this isn't *The House of Mirth*." She removed her gloves and reached for a three-layer sandwich of cream cheese, water cress, and cucumber.

The choler spread across Philip's cheeks, and when he pressed his hands onto the tabletop and pushed his chair back, she thought he was about to leave. Instead, collecting himself, he reached down and retrieved his napkin, which had slid from his lap. "Ah yes, Mrs. Wharton's novel. It's quite a success."

"Have you read it?"

"Me? No, I don't read fiction intended for ladies, even when it's written by men." He paused, as if contemplating how far to let the conversation drift from his purpose. "Henry James, for example—I can't abide him, although *The Turn of the Screw* wasn't a bad yarn. Personally, I prefer reading history. At the moment, I'm nearing the end of the first volume of the *Personal Memoirs of Ulysses S. Grant*. He writes very directly, without show."

"I did find Mr. James's recent novels a bit . . . leisurely."

"*Very* leisurely, I've heard, and too cultured, in the worst sense. In my experience, people don't really think or behave in the convoluted ways his characters do. He takes a thousand words to say what a better writer would accomplish by typing a period."

Julia laughed. Well, she thought, at least Philip has a bit of wit, which she wouldn't have expected, and wit required a certain temper as well as intelligence. "But maybe they do behave like that in the high society of New York and Boston and London."

"I prefer to think of it as the *idle* society, which bears no resemblance to the society I keep. Nor, I would think, to the society *you* keep these days."

"I thoroughly enjoy my little social circle, limited though it may be in your eyes. I enjoy it far more than the society I knew in the East. It has fewer pretensions." Julia added a bit more cream to her tea and swirled her teaspoon once around the cup. Her sandwich remained untouched on her plate. "That said, I must thank you for all the books and newspapers that Penelope sends me. I know it's not an insignificant expense, but I do read every one of them."

"Really, Julia, it's nothing. It's my pleasure. More to the point, it gives *Penelope* pleasure. I think it's a way for her to keep in touch with you, apart from your correspondence, of course—perhaps in return for all the books you read to her when she was growing up."

And there were many of them. "She loved Louisa May Alcott and Lucretia Hale."

"I liked Dickens myself, *A Tale of Two Cities* in particular. Now, I'm afraid I'd find him overly sentimental." Philip raised his cup to his lips.

"Sentimentality has its place, in literature as in life." It was such a lame comment that Julia instantly regretted it. She took a bite of her sandwich and waited for Philip to respond.

There was nothing flamboyant about her brother-in-law. Nothing in his appearance or in his manners displayed either neglect or ostentation. His summer-weight suit was well tailored, the collar of his shirt perfectly white and starched stiff, his mustache neat, his dark hair perfectly parted on the left. She suspected that he was an able worker, probably even a superior one, not that she understood precisely what he did for the New York Central and Hudson River Railroad. She didn't follow the business news closely, but she knew that the myriad rail firms across the country were constantly merging, splitting off, seeking the best rates and routes they could acquire while keeping the competition at bay. The Atlantic and Pacific Railroad, the first line through Gallup—indeed, the line that had created Gallup in 1881— had fallen victim to the panic of 1893 and been transformed into the Santa Fe Pacific and then to a branch of the Atchison, Topeka, and Santa Fe. The latter also owned the Grand Canyon Railway branch line from Williams.

"So," Philip said at last, "to return to the matter of your itinerary—"

"You needn't worry. I'll be well taken care of. Mr. Pietrowski has a quite elegant spring wagon. The seat has leather upholstery and a canopy for shade. In the event of a violent thunderstorm, there are canvas sides that he can roll down to protect his cameras and other equipment. The bed of the wagon even has a mattress for my use when we stop for the night. It'll be very comfortable. As for my tour of Canyon de Chelly, I'll be on horseback. I may even wear trousers for that—much more practical for backcountry riding, don't you think?"

"Is baiting me that much fun?" Philip asked.

Julia raised her eyebrows and smiled.

"Your mode of transport and what you choose to wear, no matter how eccentric, don't concern me, but your companions do. No respectable woman would take an excursion through the wilderness accompanied by two men, neither of whom is her husband."

Julia had thought about telling him that Pete was a former Franciscan lay brother, but she'd decided that doing so would certainly not reassure her brother-in-law; he'd undoubtedly ask why Pete had left the order, and she wasn't prepared to venture into that morass. And as for Clement Yazzie, a heathen Indian—

"And what does Penelope say?" she asked.

"We see eye-to-eye on this, of course."

"Of course."

"You say that with such scorn."

"If she didn't agree with you, there'd be hell to pay."

"Now you're the one doing the assuming. You assume you understand our marriage."

"For the purposes of this discussion, I think I understand it adequately. For example—correct me if I'm wrong, won't you?—Penelope is allowed to have her enthusiasms, for women's suffrage and the like, just as long as nothing challenges your authority."

"You're mistaken if you think this is a matter of authority. It's a matter of propriety, of proper behavior."

"Authority and 'proper behavior' are the same thing."

"Like it or not, there are standards."

"Standards are relative. I'm sure it's quite proper to go out for a Sunday stroll in Chicago dressed in your morning coat and your silk cravat and your Italian dress shoes, but here, it's rather foolish to dress like that for a hike down the Bright Angel Trail into the Grand Canyon, and on top of that, to ask the waitress at lunch for a carafe of water—with ice—to carry with you."

Just as she'd anticipated his earlier comment about her marriage to Will, Philip had prepared himself for this. Without so much as a blink, he spooned an extra dollop of clotted cream onto the last bite of his scone and said, "Well, Penelope warned me that you would take no prisoners." He added, "I admit that my sudden enthusiasm for a challenging hike momentarily overcame my judgment. But in defense of my footwear, I must say that I find your western boots to be extremely uncomfortable."

She had to laugh a second time, which elicited a slight smile from him. Julia chided, "If you want to sample extreme discomfort, try seeing how your feet feel after walking downhill for two hours in thin shoes, by which time the skin on the balls of your feet will have sloughed off and the broken blisters on your toes will be oozing."

He selected a sandwich from the plate.

She asked, "And how are the scones?"

"Quite good. Would you like to try one?"

"No, thank you. They're a little heavy for me. I prefer a light tea. Then at dinner I can gnaw at as many roasted mutton ribs as I want."

"Is that your typical fare?"

"On special occasions only. The rest of the time, it's rice, beans, and sowbelly."

Philip peeled back an edge of his triangular finger sandwich and examined the contents: cream cheese, and olive stuffed with pimento. "I'll stick with this," he said, pressing the white bread slices together again. He took a modest bite.

Julia was beginning to think that he might not be quite the prig she'd feared.

"And just so you know," he said, "I happen to support giving women the franchise. I admired Susan B. Anthony, although some of her more strident associates are a little too radical for my tastes."

"To be honest, I can't say that I'm terribly engaged by most political issues. They all seem to be happening so far away. Maybe I'll feel differently when New Mexico becomes a state."

"So you think it will?"

"Just look at a map. It's inevitable. And it won't be yoked to Arizona in a State of Montezuma, despite what a majority of the idiotic politicians in Congress apparently prefer. Montezuma! My God, don't they know the Aztecs didn't settle the Rio Grande?"

"Apparently not."

"Anyway," she continued, "people back East may argue about the tariff implications of statehood, and worry about all these Mexican Catholics and Indians, and question their loyalty, but the railroad has it all mapped out, as I'm sure you know. So statehood will come."

Without even the slightest hint of irony that Julia could detect, Philip replied, "The advance of civilization depends on the railroad."

"The advance of *commerce* depends on the railroad."

"The advance of civilization depends on the advance of commerce."

"The advance of civilization depends on the advance of indoor plumbing."

In spite of himself, Philip laughed.

"I realized the importance of plumbing," Julia explained, "after a conversation I had with Penelope on the train, while you were in the club car. It occurred to me that New Mexico will remain a sparsely populated wilderness until it can offer more people, such as our Penny, certain modern comforts."

"Such as indoor facilities."

"And in *second* place, electricity."

Philip laughed again.

"I've never heard you laugh," Julia said. "It's really quite nice."

One of the Harvey girls was preparing the dining room fireplace for the evening's blaze, which would add to the rustic ambiance. For now, the August light pouring through the windows remained intensely white, although the darkly lacquered logs and fir posts of the ceiling and walls helped maintain a comfortable temperature.

"I shouldn't be enjoying this conversation quite so much," Philip said, solemn once again. "You've convinced me that nothing I say will alter your plans for your return trip, but I still strongly disapprove. In most things there's a right way and a wrong way. If you'd wanted to, you could have made other arrangements for seeing the Hopi Reservation and Canyon de Chelly. But you apparently decided to flout convention, and for no good reason that I can see."

"Sometimes the right way and the wrong way aren't so easily defined. Sometimes you first have to acknowledge a middle ground of . . . murkiness."

"I believe that you and I would emerge from the murk in different locations."

She paused to consider how much she'd grant him. "If I were living in Chicago and my husband were a rising young New York Central executive who was away on a business trip, I wouldn't jeopardize our standing in the community by undertaking an overnight excursion with another man. But what pertains there does not necessarily apply here. Don't be fooled into thinking so by these linens and silver and china and this lovely tea."

"So you've become a relativist. I'm going to make sure that Penelope stops sending you books on modern philosophy."

"And you, I'm afraid, are an absolutist."

"I'm sorry, but I don't see why the fundamental rules of American civilization shouldn't apply even in this wilderness."

"Really?" Julia turned up her nose, as if avoiding a noxious smell. "You say you enjoy reading history. Didn't President Grant oppose the Mexican War and annexation as unjust, even though he fought in the campaign? But as a nation we Americans take what we want and always have. Isn't that our 'fundamental rule'?"

Philip looked bemused. "Are you a pacifist?"

"In personal relations, absolutely. In other domains, not particularly."

"What is your opinion on the Indian question?"

"Which Indian question? There are many."

"Assimilation."

"Do you mean, should we force them to behave as we do?"

"That's a rather superficial response to the issue, wouldn't you say?"

Julia felt herself growing more heated. "Alternatively, we could become more like them."

"Please," Philip said, dismissing her rhetoric. "I support assimilation. It's the Indians' only path to survival. Without it, they'll be overwhelmed."

"I think we'd better stop," Julia said. "You speak in the abstract, whereas I see the personal every day."

"Very well. Perhaps we can continue this discussion when you visit us in Chicago. In the meantime, I'll reexamine the issue. Maybe you could provide a list of readings for me."

Neither spoke for some time. Julia took several bites of her sandwich and finished her tea, which was now unpleasantly lukewarm.

Philip broke the silence: "Julia, why don't you come back East with us? Our house is quite large, and we can easily accommodate you. You can have as much privacy and independence as you wish."

This was basically the same case her father had made for her moving with him to Albany. But she no more believed Philip than she had her father. Privacy and independence would be permitted only to the bounds of conformity.

Julia said, "Penelope put you up to this."

"Of course she did. You're her sister. She loves you. She wants you nearby. And that'll be even more true when she's a mother. Come to Chicago. Wouldn't you prefer to live someplace where you can go to the ballet? Hear a symphony? Attend the theatre? Forgive me if I'm too candid, but your being out here is such a waste. Running a trading post on an Indian reservation! For God's sake!" He threw his napkin down on the table. "What is it that keeps you here? Do you have some misplaced sense of responsibility toward the Navajo?"

"No, I'm under no illusion. Many are just as venal and vile as any other race."

"If you stay out here you'll be old before your time. You'll grow coarse—"

"You mean, coarser than I already am."

Philip paused before replying. "Oh, I don't know. You caught the eye of more than one gentleman when you entered the dining room."

"But you weren't referring to my appearance, were you?"

The young Harvey girl who'd served them approached their table again. "May I refresh your tea?" she asked, her voice betraying an immigrant's accent that Julia couldn't place. She was pretty but thin, with straw-colored hair and a field of reddish-brown freckles across her cheeks that spoke of many hours in the sun. Julia noticed a handkerchief tucked in her left sleeve. Her irises were a coppery brown with darker striations—her eyes would be quite striking, Julia thought, on a happier day, when an observer's gaze was not so conscious of her brimful lids.

"Yes, thank you," Julia said. She watched the girl refill both cups. Philip said nothing.

"Will that be all?" the girl asked Philip.

"Yes," he said.

The girl curtsied, turned, and hurried away.

"She's very young," Julia said, "and very upset about something."

"I suppose."

"You mean, you didn't notice?"

"How could I not notice? But I don't engage."

"You don't 'engage.' "

"Julia, I take lunch out every workday. I do business at lunch. In fact, sometimes I accomplish more at lunch than in the office. I see new waiters and waitresses all the time. They do their job; I do mine. So no, I don't engage. As for that young girl, there's nothing we can do for her, whatever her difficulty. Maybe she was taken advantage of by some cad. Or maybe her supervisor criticized her shoes for being scuffed."

"You equate the two?"

Philip sighed. He was obviously growing very tired of her challenges; most likely, of the whole conversation. "I was speaking rhetorically. As you noted, she's very young, and it's probably nothing. Besides, I understand the Harvey Company is very protective of its girls, even though most of them come west looking for husbands."

"So I understand."

"I detect disapproval. Isn't finding a decent husband a worthy pursuit anymore?"

" 'Decent' is another of those relative words. Besides, if a girl has the gumption to leave her family and friends behind and travel more than halfway across the country, as many of them do, it's unfortunate that she doesn't have better opportunities."

"To do what?"

"Educate herself. Seek a profession."

" 'Doctor, lawyer, beggarwoman, thief'—to what end, if not marriage and a family?"

"This is becoming a very disagreeable conversation," Julia said.

"Don't you think women should be entitled to the protection and security offered by a good marriage?"

"Many married women find neither."

"They would if they married wisely, if they looked for the proper qualities in their prospective suitors."

"I could say the same for men and their prospective brides."

"Most respectable men look for something fundamentally different from themselves. They want someone who offers a refuge from . . . all that."

" 'All that'? You mean the world of 'business'? Or of masculinity itself?"

"Perhaps you should ask Wilford Halley."

"I don't have to. He was utterly transparent."

"How so?"

"He wanted success and wealth, preferably without having to work too hard."

"And why did you marry him?"

"It seemed the right thing to do at the time."

"That is no answer, and you know it."

"Actually, I prefer the Navajo view of marriage. Women control the land and the home, which are passed down from mother to daughter. Basically, men own their jewelry, the clothes on their backs, and their saddles."

"No self-respecting white man would find that acceptable."

"And you see no irony in that?"

"How so?"

"A white women who leaves her husband may end up with less."

Philip shifted in his seat. "Your . . . disappointment has produced a very jaundiced view of marriage. Most women have their children to think of, and they have moral authority, if they choose to exercise it."

"Well, I obviously have neither, but you can proceed to Los Angeles with a good conscience, knowing that you tried your best to counsel me, and I'll proceed with Mr. Pietrowski to the Hopi Reservation."

"Penelope would never even think of doing such a thing."

"You might be surprised."

"I sincerely hope not."

"She's not a fool, Philip—younger than her years, but no fool."

"And neither am I."

"I never perceived you to be a fool."

"Despite my Italian dress shoes and carafe of ice water."

This time, Julia couldn't help noticing, there was no self-deprecation, no sense of self-irony in his tone; it had been replaced by an unpleasantness that scarcely concealed his underlying contempt. This was a man, she realized, who had no sense of humor when it came to his pride. Previous efforts had been pretense, a gentlemanly performance. She stirred cream into her second cup of tea. "May I tell you a little story?"

Philip, holding his own cup and saucer in one hand, stirring in sugar with the other, sat back in his chair.

"The first person Will and I met when we arrived in Gallup was Alberto Rodriguez. His family has lived out here for generations."

"He's Mexican, I take it."

"American," she corrected him. "From Albuquerque. From a family of entrepreneurs who early on saw the advantages of becoming part of the United States. They helped supply General Taylor during the Mexican War, which earned them the wrath of many people but put them in a very favorable position when the war ended and annexation followed. Like his father, Mr. Rodriguez is an astute businessman. He watched the railroad expand westward and recognized that the incorporation of Gallup would open up a whole new territory to commerce. He was one of the first entrepreneurs to come out here, and now he owns the largest furniture store between Albuquerque and Flagstaff. A devout Roman Catholic, by the way.

"He met his wife in Denver. She's the youngest daughter of a good, Catholic family, and the last to marry. Mr. Rodriguez courted her and eventually won her father's permission to marry, despite initial misgivings about, I gather, his racial heritage. Her family, you see, is of English descent, through and through.

"So he brought her back to Gallup, and now they have two children, and on occasion they both come to visit me. We have these simple gatherings, now and then. We talk. The local doctor, my photographer friend . . . sometimes other traders stop by as well. We have delightful conversations about everything imaginable. And Mrs. Rodriguez will sit and listen and smile and occasionally interject a comment. But I recognize that she doesn't approve of me. More to the point, however, she's a fundamentally self-involved, shallow little woman."

"That seems rather harsh."

"She's a good wife, a good mother—"

"All things to be valued."

"Indeed, but if she knows anything about the world outside of her social sphere, she has cleverly disguised it."

"Your point?"

"Don't turn my sister into a shallow little woman."

"You *are* harsh, Julia."

"I love my sister, Philip."

"Then accept that she is no Julia. Do you mind if I smoke?"

Julia shook her head and then watched Philip slip a silver case from the inside pocket of his suit coat. He withdrew a cigar, removed the ring, and snipped the end. Philip lit a match and rotated the cigar, burning the outer wrapper slightly before drawing the flame into the center. The hostess who'd led Julia to the table appeared suddenly at his side with an ash tray.

"Our waitress—" Julia started to ask.

"Oh, I must apologize for Miss Alicia," the hostess interrupted. "She's one of our newest girls and hasn't much experience yet." Addressing Philip, she added, "We're a bit short-handed this afternoon."

"She seemed very upset," Julia commented.

"I certainly hope that hasn't detracted from your tea." She frowned and stepped closer to Julia. In a lowered voice she said, "The poor girl received something of a tongue-lashing from a matron this afternoon." She again deferred to Philip: "Would you like anything else, sir? An afternoon cordial, perhaps."

"Nothing, thank you," Philip answered, and the hostess retreated.

Julia was still thinking about their waitress, Alicia, when Philip raised a decidedly different subject: "Your husband deserted you. You have grounds for divorce." He tapped cigar ash into the tray. "Not that I'm in favor of divorce, in general. Do you know your husband's whereabouts?"

Julia didn't reply.

"If he's no longer in the territory, divorce papers can be served by publication. A judge would decide the case. There are no jury trials for divorce."

"You looked into this?"

"Or after seven years—I believe that's the standard interval—you could have him declared legally dead."

When Julia didn't respond he said, "You can continue to sit there looking aghast, or you can face the reality of your situation."

"I prefer to leave well enough alone. Wherever he may be at the moment, if he chose to he could probably return and claim the trading post."

"That might be best. It would force you to reconsider your options."

"I don't wish to reconsider them."

"Obviously."

"And as for a divorce, it's irrelevant because I will certainly never marry again."

"Now you're just being obstinate and disagreeable, Julia. You would have much to offer."

"Perhaps to one of those gentlemen—all of them of a certain age, I'm sure—who, you so kindly noted, flattered me with their eyes when I entered the dining room." She noticed for the first time that the two German gentlemen whom she'd seen hiking the rim trail that morning had taken a table. "But I fear they'd not like what lies beneath the wrappings. They'd accuse me of deceptive advertising."

"My observation was intended to be complimentary, not vulgar. But since I apparently can't talk any sense into you, I'd like to leave it like this: the offer to welcome you into our household will remain open indefinitely."

"Thank you."

"Should you ever change your mind, I believe I might even come to enjoy our conversations."

"I'd wear thin very quickly," Julia said.

"There's just one more thing," Philip said, leaning forward. "You said something a while ago that I found very offensive and that I've decided I can't ignore." He lowered his voice. "Do you really think I want the mother of my children to be a 'shallow little woman'? If so, you not only insult me, you insult your sister, which is far worse. If that is your true opinion of our marriage, please say nothing further."

She stared across the table at the handsome face of her brother-in-law, a decade younger than she. Why had she felt such a need to confront him, and had that led her to judge him *too* harshly? Had she been rash? Probably more rash than he in judging her. He appeared to treat Penelope well. So why did she distrust him? He offered her sister intelligence, financial security, propriety, love. Weren't these qualities precisely what she wanted for Penny?

"Please accept my sincere apology," Julia said. "I spoke hastily and unwisely."

Philip sat back in his chair. "Your apology is accepted," he said, extinguishing his cigar in the ash tray. "There's no need to say any more about it."

They left the dining room together a few minutes later. They were starting up the stairs to their rooms when Julia, turning on the first landing, spotted Alicia, who was sitting quietly by herself on a straight chair, in a corner adjacent to the reception desk. For a moment Julia considered turning around and walking over to the young girl, who appeared to be much more composed now. Alicia looked up and, at a distance, their eyes met.

And what does *she* see? Julia wondered. A woman approaching middle age, if not already there, and probably old enough to be her mother. A woman married (Alicia would assume from the wedding ring) to that rather handsome (but younger!) gentleman. A woman dressed in a modest but reasonably fashionable gown and wealthy enough to vacation at the grandest hotel between Santa Fe and California, and therefore far above her socially.

Dear Alicia, Julia wanted to tell her, it is all a charade.

9. The Vanishing Race

THE PITILESS LANDSCAPE, devoid of all but the sparsest vegetation—scattered mesquite, sagebrush, saltbush, low-growing cactus—stretched west, north, and east, and the dust stirred up by the horse's hooves and the iron-rimmed wheels of the spring wagon often forced Pete and Julia to ride with kerchiefs stretched across their noses and mouths and tied at the nape of their necks. The canopy protected them from the sun—Julia more than Pete, since she sat to his right—but nothing could dispatch the mouse-brown dust that covered everything they wore, sifted into their ears, collected in their eyebrows and along their cheekbones, and mixed with sweat to form streaks down their cheeks. When they stopped to rest the horse and stretch their legs, the sand cascaded from the folds of Julia's skirt as soon as she stood up. Now she understood why Pete kept his cameras covered in linen cloths and shut away in a cedar box that he'd made himself. The joints and lid of the box fit so tightly that not even the finest dust penetrated; sand and dust would destroy his lenses, some of which he'd ground himself, and bind up the mechanical parts unmercifully.

He'd met her train at the Winslow station. She'd never doubted that he would be there, and on time at that, even though he was notoriously lackadaisical about keeping studio hours and appointments. He didn't seem to worry about irritating his customers, maybe because he was Gallup's only photographer.

"Did you enjoy the Painted Desert?" Julia asked. She'd already described her visit with her sister and brother-in-law, leaving out the conflicts and concentrating on how happy she'd been to spend time with Penelope.

"Not that much." Pete's straight-brimmed hat was pulled down to his thick eyebrows, and he hadn't shaved in several days. If she didn't know him so well, this was not a man she'd want to be sitting next to, practically hip-to-hip, on a journey through the wilderness. He went on, "Everything in the landscape ultimately dissolves into shades of gray. Red is gray, rose is lighter gray. Umber and tan are somewhere in between. There are no trees, no shade, and the midday sun tends to wash everything out. I didn't see anything new, really—nothing that I haven't seen on the reservation."

"I'm sorry it was so disappointing."

He snapped the reins, and Stable Boy obliged by picking up the pace a bit. "I ran into a party of tourists, four of them. They'd come in a fancy automobile. They asked me to take their picture using their Brownie."

"Did you?"

"They were loud and obnoxious."

"But did you?"

"I did." He went silent for a moment. "I cut off the tops of their heads, just below the eyes."

"You *didn't!*" Julia said.

"They'll see four smiles"—he flashed an exaggerated grin to illustrate— "right at the top of the photograph."

Julia didn't find this at all amusing. "Why would you do that? They were just having fun, enjoying each other's company."

"They were too full of themselves." Pete adjusted his hat brim and reached for the canteen that lay between their feet. He took a drink, wiped off the rim, and passed the canteen to Julia. Then he said, "Twenty years from now, maybe less, who knows, automobiles will be driving willy-nilly through there by the hundreds, and probably everybody will own a cheap camera and there'll be a million photographs of people posing in front of rock art and petrified logs, and there'll probably be a hundred books documenting every square inch of everything."

"Will it be such a bad thing," she said, "if taking photographs really becomes so everyday? Why shouldn't people show others where they've been and what they've done? What's wrong with that? There'll still be room for formal photographs—for professional photographers, won't there?"

He scowled without replying.

"I'm not sure exactly what bothers you about this, all the photographs or all the people."

"The way I look at it, it's all one and the same. Ignorant people using cheap cameras to take shoddy pictures."

"Some of those ignorant people pay your bills."

"I provide a service, and people pay me for it, and I do the best job I can, but their ceremonies and celebrations don't interest me."

She already knew his opinion of wedding photography, the unnaturalness of it.

"So you prefer to photograph . . . what? Petrified wood?"

"Yes," he said with a vehemence that caught her by surprise. "Actually, up close, petrified wood can be interesting."

"And the rock art?"

"There's that—lots of spirals and other geometric designs, zigzagging snakes, long-horned antelopes, frogs, that sort of thing. And primitive human figures. Some were probably supposed to be gods." He gave the reins another quick snap and once again the horse picked up the pace, but only briefly before settling back into his own loping sense of rhythm and task.

"I'd like to see the ones you photographed."

"Oh, I didn't photograph any of the rock art."

"Why not? Don't tell me you ran out of plates." She knew better.

"I saw no need."

No need? "Sometimes I think you're contrary just for the sake of contrariness."

"Am I contrary?"

"If I asked you to stop this wagon and take a photograph of me against that black butte over there"—she pointed to the north, where several small formations rose up out of the scrubland—"would you do it?"

"Of course I would. If having a photograph of yourself posed in this wilderness would please you, of course I'd take it."

"But you'd prefer to take a photograph of the butte without me in front of it."

"That depends on how long you might be willing to wait."

"For what?"

"For me to take your picture."

"You mean, for inspiration to strike?"

"For your presence to make sense."

From his point of view, she thought, her presence against the butte would make sense only when her bones turned to dust.

His lips drawn tight, Pete didn't say anything for a long while. The horse loped along, pulling them through the desert silence, closer to the butte. "It's called Pyramid Butte," Pete said.

"It's misnamed," Julia said; Pete wasn't the only one who could be contrary.

"Maybe it shouldn't have any name."

"What brought all this on?" Julia asked.

"Brought what on?"

Enough. She'd let it go. They had a long drive ahead of them and she had no desire to spend it exchanging barbs, inciting each other's ill temper.

"You still intend to go into Canyon de Chelly with Yazzie?" Pete asked.

"I do. Is there any reason why I shouldn't?"

"Beyond the obvious?"

A white woman alone in the wilderness with a Navajo man; more of her brother-in-law's propriety. "If I understand your logic, I shouldn't be here with you, either." A sharp laugh erupted from the back of his throat, which caused her irritation to rise further.

"I trust Mr. Yazzie with my life," she said.

"That's exactly what you'll be doing. I nearly got myself killed there last month."

"In Canyon de Chelly?" She was genuinely shocked. "What happened?"

"Some foolishness involving a medicine man."

She waited for him to continue, but when he didn't she said, "Are you going to tell me or not?"

PETE HAD FIRST HEARD about Edward S. Curtis from Charlie Day two years earlier, in 1904. A photographer and photoengraver based in Seattle, Washington, Curtis had concocted a grand scheme to document by word and picture all the extant western North American Indian tribes, with the results to be published in twenty volumes and accompanying portfolios. It all sounded rather grandiose to Pete, even though, according to Charlie, Curtis had won an early endorsement from Teddy Roosevelt and, later, financial backing from one of the richest men in America, J. Pierpont Morgan. In 1904 Curtis had presented a letter of introduction to Charlie's father, Sam Day, and then spent a good month at St. Michaels—Cienega Amarilla, recently renamed for the Franciscan mission and school—during his first extended visit to the reservation. With the Navajos as well as the Apaches and Jicarillas to be included in the first volume, scheduled for publication in 1907, Curtis now, in the summer of 1906, needed to visit the reservation again to finish his Navajo field work, for which he'd enlisted Charlie Day as guide, translator, and intermediary. Charlie, with Curtis's permission, had invited Pete along.

In the decade after Pete left the Franciscans, he and Charlie had frequently run into each other in Gallup. Never at a loss for energy, Charlie had ambitiously extended his family's trading operations up and down the Arizona border—at Honeymoon Springs, on the high trail between Canyon de Chelly and Fort Defiance; for a brief time at Chinle, where he'd also finagled an appointment as postmaster; near St. Michaels, where in 1905 he'd bought the last private parcel of land; and in early 1906 at Navajo Springs, where he and a friend named Daniel Mitchell formed the Malpais Ranch and Trading Company, with a branch at Adamana, south of the Petrified Forest. Moreover, in 1903 the secretary of the Department of the Interior in Washington, in an effort to discourage the looting of Anasazi and Navajo ruins, had named Charlie custodian of Canyon de Chelly despite the objections of the Navajo agent, Reuben Perry, who just last fall, 1905, had tried to sue Charlie for promoting "heathen rituals"—specifically, a Night Chant ceremony at St. Michaels that Edward Curtis had intended to photograph. Curtis, however, had been forced to cancel his plans, although the ceremony proceeded as scheduled (and was photographed in part by a Franciscan brother and an acquaintance of Pete's, Simeon Schwemberger).

To save Charlie a trip into town from St. Michaels, Pete had volunteered to meet Curtis, accompanied by his family, in Gallup. Curtis and his son, eleven-year-old Hal, as well as a field assistant and a cook were coming directly from a weeks-long visit to the Jicarilla Reservation. Curtis's wife Clara, nine-year-old Beth, and seven-year-old Florence had journeyed by train from their home in Seattle.

"It's the first trip into Indian country for my wife and girls," Curtis informed Pete while they waited at the station. "We're hoping for a glorious holiday together." Charlie had described Curtis as something of a dandy, and Pete could see it in his mannerisms, but his current appearance gave the lie, dressed as he was in trail clothes and scuffed shoes, and with a heavy, uneven growth of brown beard.

The Curtises boarded two canopied wagons stuffed with two canvas-floored tents, each large enough for a grown man to stand erect; bedding, cooking gear, folding chairs and tables, food, and a chest of books; and for Edward's make-shift studio, a typewriter, equipment for making wax cylinder sound recordings, a film camera, and all the necessary photographic paraphernalia. The trail cook, a fellow named Justo, also turned out to be an experienced wrangler who handled the lead four-horse team expertly, while the second was driven by Bill Phillips, Curtis's most versatile associate and a cousin by marriage. With Pete following in his own spring wagon, the party made its way to St. Michaels, where Charlie awaited its arrival. The next day the caravan headed north to Chinle, where they stayed overnight at the former Day trading post, now run by a friend of Charlie's, Charles Cousins, and then ventured into Canyon de Chelly, following Chinle Wash beyond its junction with Tsaile Creek and Canyon del Muerto. The height of the red sandstone walls gradually increased as they ventured farther into the canyon, and by the time they reached the Anasazi ruins known as White House, the cliffs rose five hundred feet above them.

They picked for their camp a grove of cottonwoods between the wash and the ruins. The children weren't allowed into the better-preserved upper ruins—a difficult climb up the rock wall even for an adult—but ran freely through the lower ruins on the canyon floor. Despite the daytime heat, which approached one hundred degrees, the children had a fine time: amusing themselves with crudely fashioned bows, chasing each other in and out of the wash, playing hide-and-seek, riding a burro offered by one of the many Navajos, both men and women, who frequented the camp, coming and going throughout the day and often staying for meals.

Curtis was intent on supplementing the photographs he'd taken during his 1904 visit, much of which he'd also spent in and around Canyon de Chelly, and also recording as many Navajo tales as possible on his wax cylinders. He further intended, he told Pete, to film a Yeibichei dance led by Charlie's brother Sammy, the only white man who'd ever been fully initiated into the nine-day Night Chant ceremony and whose dance team performed at ceremonies across the eastern and central reservation.

The first evening at the camp, while Clara tried to keep the children within sight and earshot, Curtis, who'd spent the previous hours arranging his work space, breaking only for a rambunctious dinner with his family, asked Pete and Charlie if they'd like to see the work he'd already completed. He had a set of the 1904 proofs with him.

"Certainly," Pete answered. He and Charlie followed Curtis into the studio tent.

Curtis undid the ties to a large, heavy leather-bound portfolio. Each photograph, held in its own paper sleeve, was further protected by a sheet of tissue. Curtis handled each with exceeding care.

Many of the photographs—some to be distributed throughout the volume, others intended for the accompanying, large-format portfolio—were magnificent, and Pete suspected that no expense would be spared in their reproduction: portraits of Navajo men and women facing the camera, landscapes with silent riders, moments captured from the everyday life of weavers and herders, and most surprising of all, photographs of a number of god impersonators, costumed and masked, all posed against neutral backgrounds—rock walls and what may have been cloth drapings, as if in a studio. How had Curtis convinced the impersonators to let him photograph them at all? Though Pete hadn't seen any of Schwemberger's pictures from last fall's Night Chant at St. Michaels, Charlie had told him that a few captured fully costumed impersonators performing their ceremonial roles, but Pete's impression was that none had willingly *posed* for the camera. Still, the costuming in Curtis's photographs looked authentic: Talking God, grandfather of the yei; the hero brothers Monster Slayer, with his black, lightning-streaked face, and Born-for-Water; Humpedback God; Black God . . .

"This will be the first print in the portfolio," Curtis said. He laid before them a large photograph, more than a foot high and half again as wide. " 'The Vanishing Race,' " he added. The photograph pictured Navajos mounted on their horses, riding away from the camera, along a dusty trail at the bottom of a canyon, shadows to the right and a cliff line ahead, beneath a dim sky.

Pete took half a step back. During dinner he'd listened while Curtis presented a conceptual framework for his project. While far from denying the artistic aspect of his work and, indeed, the inherent aesthetic aspects of the landscape and aboriginal life, Curtis intended to photograph "directly from Nature." (There could be no doubt about the capital *N*.) He wanted to show life as it really exists, or existed until very recently, not only through his photographs but through summarizing direct accounts by Indians themselves of their creation myths and folklore, supplemented by his own written observations of primitive life. He thereby hoped to present, in miniature, insight into the life and thought of his subjects. All well and good, Pete had thought while listening to Curtis expound, but also egotistic—to think a few weeks spent in the vicinity of any tribe would provide deep insight into their traditions, habits, and state of mind. Ah well, Pete had thought, who was he to judge another man's folly? Especially when he was helping himself to that man's freely offered campfire-grilled lamb, squaw bread, and roasted corn-on-the-cob.

But now, standing over "The Vanishing Race," Pete felt considerably less charitable toward Edward Curtis. "Well," he said, "it's a fine photograph, but why that title?"

"You object to it?"

"The Navajo—they are Navajos, correct?—are hardly 'vanishing.' They're increasing like rabbits."

"This isn't a matter of absolute numbers," Curtis said calmly, "though I'd argue that the population of most tribes is in fact declining. I'm speaking about cultures, the native way of life. 'The Vanishing Race' is a metaphor for the darkness of an uncertain future."

"Metaphors work best when they're also literal, in my opinion," Pete said.

" 'My love is like a red, red rose'?" Curtis said, smiling. "You find the simile unacceptable?"

"Not at all. But photographs are not words, and we're speaking of photography."

"Then you *do* object to the photograph as well as the title?" Curtis raised a hand and stroked the bearded chin beneath his wry smile.

Pete paused to gather his thoughts. "Would you say it's 'from Nature'?"

"I would."

"Let me ask you this. Did you ask the riders to halt while you positioned your camera? Or until the light was just so, casting shadows just so? Perhaps you already had the title, or at least the concept, in mind?"

Curtis had lost his smile. "Are you suggesting a degree of duplicity?"

"I haven't used any such word," Pete said.

Charlie Day coughed and shuffled his feet.

"Navajos have ridden along that trail, in that canyon, at that time of day and season, for five hundred years."

"I grant you that," Pete said, though it struck him as irrelevant to his argument. He pointed to "The Vanishing Race" as Curtis was preparing to slip it into its protective sleeve. "Why not title it 'Leaving the Camp'? Or 'Homeward Bound'? Or even 'On the Warpath'?—in which case, there they are, the Navajo, riding off in the morning, perhaps to raid a Mexican farm. It could be the morning, couldn't it? Which would mean they're riding southward in the eastern sunlight instead of northward in the evening, which is what your title implies. You *could* call it 'On the Warpath,' you know. No one would know the difference."

"Anyone looking at my photograph and reading what I've written in my foreword will understand the title as symbolic. 'On the Warpath,' indeed!" Curtis said with unalloyed irritation. "That would constitute a lie of the first order. Is that what you really think of these?" He swept his hand in an arc above the table.

"Pete here can be sort of bull-headed," Charlie interjected.

"Too true," Pete said. "And no," tempering his tone and again addressing Curtis, "of course that isn't what I think of your photographs. Many of them are magnificent, probably the finest work of their kind that I've ever seen."

"I accept your compliment," Curtis, also more pliant, said, "because I don't believe you'd say it if you didn't mean it." He looked down at "The Vanishing Race," which he still held in his hand. "Jests aside, what title would you suggest, Mr. Pietrowski?"

"None at all," Pete said.

"I must say, you have an interesting viewpoint." Curtis returned the remaining photographs to the portfolio. "If I may ask, where are you from?"

"Cincinnati. I grew up not far from the docks."

"But you're an educated man."

"My teachers did their best, without notable success."

"You're too modest," Curtis said. "The quality of a man's education reveals itself quickly in the course of any conversation." His eyes suddenly shifted to Charlie Day. "No offense intended."

Charlie's handsome face responded with the widest possible display of white teeth. "No offense taken."

Charlie was truly an extraordinary fellow, Pete thought. He wasn't of a disposition to anger easily or hold grudges; he didn't seem to care what others thought of him, just as long as they didn't stand in the way of his numerous ventures. The only people he held in contempt were Indian agents who claimed to have the best interest of the particular tribe in mind but, when you got right down to, were woefully ignorant. He never apologized for or tried to hide his spotty education, and why should he?—he might not know Greek, but he knew Navajo, and he knew the Navajo Reservation, especially Canyon de Chelly, as well as any white man ever had, or probably ever would.

"I myself am an autodidact, born on a farm in Wisconsin and educated in a one-room schoolhouse," Curtis said. "A lack of formal schooling indicates very little about a man's intelligence or capacity." And then, turning back to Pete, he laughed. "You know, I've had similar discussions before about my work, in the comfort of drawing rooms. Having them out here in the wilderness, in the natural environment, they take on a different character. I'm very glad you decided to join us. Speak your mind. Hold nothing back."

"Then I won't," Pete said, though he knew that nothing he might say would alter Curtis's trajectory. Curtis had made his choices, and too much depended on his proceeding on course and apace.

The three men spent the following morning exploring side canyons. Pete left his own equipment back at the camp. Curtis brought with him only a 6½ x 8½-inch camera, a mounting stand, and a box of glass plates. They stopped frequently. Pete watched Curtis carefully—the way he framed the views, always seeking the natural contrasts of light and varying degrees of shade. For this the canyons proved ideal: the lighter tones of sandy floor washed by sun and shadows; the groves of trees, and the summer corn stunted but erect; the nearly vertical walls, some coated with streaks of black desert varnish; and then the light-filled blue sky spread above. At one point they encountered three Navajo women on horseback, and Charlie, slipping them a couple of coins each, convinced them to pause while Curtis set up his camera. Later, the three men passed a vacant mud-covered hogan that became the subject of another photograph. In the afternoon, back at the camp, Curtis recorded on wax cylinders several elderly Navajos telling stories and legends.

At dinner, much of the conversation centered on the technical aspects of the photographic trade—the merits of various cameras, lenses, exposures, developers; Curtis's practice of making cyanotypes in the field; the difficulties involved in the photogravure process, which required the production of glass transparencies and their transfer to etched copper plates for printing, and which Curtis intended to use for all twenty volumes of his Indian series. Pete and Curtis, much to Charlie's amusement, traded stories about studio disasters and midnight darkroom manipulations in frequently unsuccessful efforts to rescue, as Curtis said, "the silk purse from the pig's ear." The conversation, much more temperate than the previous night's, concluded with a discussion of what the inevitable introduction of full-color photography would mean for the art. Pete, ever the contrarian, argued the merits of monochromism, the inherent ability of black, white, and grays to capture the essential nature of the subject. Curtis, seeing an opening, accused Pete of a fundamental contradiction in his thinking: how could he reject color and still argue for a need to capture Nature in its truest forms? The good-natured argument went on for a solid hour.

The next morning Curtis busied himself making cyanotypes of the previous day's plates while awaiting the arrival of a Navajo named Billy Jones, an acquaintance of Charlie's who had agreed to produce a series of sand paintings that could be photographed and included in the first volume. Few sand paintings had ever been reproduced outside of a ceremony, during which a patient would come into direct contact with images of the Holy People and thereby permit their spirits to enter his body and help in the healing. Sand paintings were created anew for each ceremony and obliterated afterward, with the colored sands, ground from mineral rocks, then being scattered. Curtis felt that his portrait of the Navajo would be incomplete without several of these healing works of art. But for some reason Billy Jones never showed up.

Charlie's brother Sammy arrived in the early afternoon with ten members of his dance team. Pete saw immediately that Sammy, shorter and scrawnier than his older brother, wasn't at all pleased to be there.

With Edward Curtis out of earshot, Sammy, shaking his head, said, "I don't know about this, Charlie. I never should've let you talk me into it. Some of the boys aren't happy."

"Do they need time to rehearse?" Charlie asked. Pete knew that a Night Chant could only be held in the fall and winter, after the last thunder and while the snakes were in hibernation, so it was many months since the team had last gathered for a Yeibichei performance, which occurred on the final night of the ceremony.

"That isn't it," Sammy drawled, "and you gall-darn know it. We're out here in the middle of the day, in the middle of summer, dancing when we shouldn't be, and letting a bilagáana film us in full costume. It was bad enough two years ago, when you and me posed for those photographs. Now we're really asking for trouble. If word gets out . . ."

Word always gets out on the Navajo Reservation, Pete thought, but he stayed out of the argument.

"Sammy," Charlie said, "let Curtis get his ten minutes of film. No harm done."

"Says you." Sammy looked around the campsite. "Where are we going to do it? Not out here in the open, that's for sure."

"Up a little side canyon I spotted. Your team can don their outfits back in the brush while Edward sets up his film camera. It'll all be over before you know it."

"If we were doing this properly, Charlie, there'd be a singer to offer his blessing."

"You don't bother with that when you practice, do you? So think of this as practice."

"We don't practice in head and face masks and body paint, and dressed with all the other paraphernalia." Sammy sighed. "I said we'd do it, so let's get it over with. But I'll tell you this, Curtis had better be sure he's got that camera working properly because we're only going to do it once."

"Oh, come on, Sammy," Charlie said, trying to lighten the mood. "What happens if your boys trip all over themselves?"

Sammy gave his brother a piercing look. "If that happens, you should assume they *intended* to trip all over themselves."

Pete had never gone out of his way to attend a Navajo sing, although Anglos regularly attended the final night of the Night Chant. He had, however, encountered a trio of god impersonators one winter afternoon when he was visiting Julia at Many Springs. On the sixth and seventh days of the Night Chant, several impersonators go out into the wider community seeking gifts of food, tobacco, and other sundries. On that particular day, which followed a night of heavy snowfall, the clouds broke in the early morning but the temperature stayed well below freezing, and when Pete, intent on retrieving something or other from his wagon, opened the door from Julia's kitchen and saw the three masked and costumed figures standing in a row in front of the steps, his jaw dropped. The trading post, Julia had told him, was a prime destination for Night Chant "beggars." None, by ritual, was allowed to speak beyond uttering a wordless, eerie chant or song; however, their mission was well understood, and to deny them a gift risked an assault by their yucca whips. Julia always provided as much as the costumed figures could carry away.

When Pete recovered from his surprise, his first thought was to wonder why the visitors weren't freezing to death. All three daunting figures wore deerskin boots high enough to protect their legs from the foot of snow that had fallen, but there were few other concessions to the weather. Only Talking God—Pete recognized him from the distinctive white buckskin head mask, above a green wreath of spruce and beneath a wig of dark horse mane and a fan of eagle feathers—was fully, if not warmly, clothed. The other two, both in blue masks, wore nothing but kilts over thin cotton union suits, although one also sported several fox pelts draped around his neck and waist and was further decorated by a generous use of spruce branches wrapped around legs and torso and also attached to his dark wig. This, Pete suspected, was Water Sprinkler, the clown of the Night Chant, while the other, a blue-masked female yei (though impersonated by a man, as were all yei), bore few accoutrements other than a wig, a fringed neck drapery, and the yucca whip. The three masks featured small eye- and mouth-holes but offered no view of the faces beneath. Knowing their purpose but not if they understood English, Pete, with broad gestures, led the trio toward the trading post door. They stood outside while he went to find Julia.

Pete now watched Sammy Day's troupe perform for Curtis, and the first thing that came to mind was how ludicrous they looked, chanting and dancing in the broad daylight while Curtis cranked his camera with one hand and tried to hold it steady on its tripod with the other. Sammy had donned his white Talking God mask, identifying himself as the leader of the blue-masked yei impersonators, and they'd all painted themselves with white clay. Pete and Charlie were the only observers. Nothing about the surreptitious performance seemed right and proper to Pete, skeptic though he was. He tried to imagine the dead of a winter night, with hundreds of Navajos—men, women, and children—gathered, and bonfires sending smoke and embers into the starlight, and with teams of Yeibichei impersonators dancing almost continuously, taking turns and concluding only at dawn, when final songs and prayers were offered outside the ceremonial hogan. He tried to imagine the power and mystery the Night Chant must hold for the assembled onlookers, just as he'd seen—even felt, at times—the supremacy of the Catholic Mass, performed in the holy sanctuary of the church, for those who truly believed. Here, however, his imagination failed: in the heat and brightness of the Arizona afternoon, the dancers seemed powerless and pathetic. It left him ill at ease, and he walked away after just a few minutes.

Talk at dinner that night was sparse when the conversation moved away from the children's delight in their burro rides and their visit to a summer hogan, where they watched a native silversmith fashioning turquoise and silver jewelry, and where they were treated to fry bread and honey fresh from the comb, which, they asserted, was much better than toast and jam except, Florence added, for the "waxy bits."

The adult discussion was rather subdued, in part because Mrs. Curtis had complained within earshot of all that Edward, having invited them on his expedition, should devote more attention to his family and less to his camera and tent studio. The ensuing exchange indicated, to Pete at least, that Curtis's enterprise, and particularly the consequent months spent far from Seattle, did not sit well with Clara. Pete wanted to bring up that afternoon's filming, but under the circumstances he refrained.

After breakfast, Pete, Charlie, and Curtis made their way on horseback up Canyon del Muerto, which intersected Canyon de Chelly proper just west of the Curtis campsite. Cut through the red rock by Tsaile Creek, and itself split into numerous side canyons, Canyon del Muerto derived its name from Indian burial grounds found by a Smithsonian expedition a generation earlier.

They stopped once so that Curtis could set up his camera and photograph a cornfield against a backdrop of sunlight and shadow on the rugged sandstone wall. The canyon appeared particularly peaceful, quiet except for their own conversation, the nickering of the horses, bird songs. Their destination was Antelope House, an Anasazi ruin not far up the canyon, which they reached before noon. Named for a nearby Navajo wall painting, the ruin was thought to have comprised upwards of ninety rooms in its heyday.

As Pete and Charlie watched Curtis positioning his camera, Charlie, uncharacteristically somber, said that something felt wrong. He mounted and rode farther up the canyon, hoping to find an explanation for the absence of Navajos. None had appeared for breakfast; nor had they encountered any during their ride to Antelope House. Within the hour he was back, grim faced. Without dismounting, he rode up to Curtis and said, "We have to go. Now."

"What's wrong?" Pete asked.

"There's a woman in labor who's in a bad way. The baby won't come. The hataałii who's tending her blames our being here in the canyon. He's got her family riled up."

"Is it that serious?" Curtis asked. "I've never had difficulties with the Navajo."

"I don't know the singer or anything about the family, except that they live a ways up Tsaile Creek, near the head of the canyon. I won't have any sway over what they do should the mother or baby die."

"Still—"

Charlie cut him off. "Edward, if they come looking for blood, no power on earth will save you and your family."

The three men rode as fast as they could down Canyon del Muerto to the junction with the main canyon, and turned east, toward the White House campsite. The children were playing in the wash, building sandcastles, it looked like. Curtis headed to the family's tent to tell Clara. Charlie spoke to Justo, who immediately began hitching the two teams of horses to the Curtis wagons. Pete heard Clara calmly calling the children. He himself had little to pack. He threw his bedroll into the back of his wagon, secured his equipment, hitched Stable Boy, and then he entered the studio tent, where Bill Phillips, clearly distressed, had already packed up the recording equipment and books. Curtis was giving his full attention to his glass plates and cameras. Charlie appeared in the tent opening.

"Fifteen minutes, Edward. If you can't get it onto the wagon in fifteen minutes, leave it."

"I understand," Curtis said.

They broke down the camp quickly. It was impossible to know if they were being observed from somewhere on the cliffs or along the ancient trail that wound down to near White House ruins. Anything spoken was short and hushed. Clara told the children to sit in the first wagon, out of sight.

When he had the chance, Pete asked Charlie, "Do you think the medicine man heard that Curtis filmed the Yeibichei dance?"

"I don't know, Pete. He may just be looking to save face if the woman or her baby dies. It doesn't matter. The Curtises are my responsibility. They wouldn't be here without my say. My only concern right now is to get Mrs. Curtis and her children to safety."

They agreed that the two of them would bring up the rear in the camping party's run to Chinle. Charlie passed his Colt revolver and a box of cartridges to Pete, who traveled only with a short single-shot carbine and a handful of bullets in case he encountered a rattlesnake or an unusually aggressive coyote. Like Charlie, Justo and Phillips had rifles, but neither was a marksman (nor was Edward Curtis). Besides, they couldn't simultaneously handle a lathered team and a rifle, and if it came to that, first and foremost they had to keep the wagons moving. Charlie spurred his horse ahead and spoke briefly to Justo, making sure he knew where to crisscross the shallow Chinle Wash, and where to swing wide to avoid potential pools of quicksand. If an afternoon thunderstorm didn't slow them, they could all be out of the canyon by dusk.

The favorable weather held despite the midsummer heat, and though the horses worked up a foam as they strained to pull the wagons through pockets of deep sand, nothing impeded the flight. Hours later, with the setting sun in their faces and the canyon walls dropping away, Charlie came abreast of Pete. "I think we're safe now," he said.

Pete pulled up on the reins and Charlie, after hitching his horse to the rear of the wagon, climbed up beside him.

"This is something they'll talk about for a long time," Pete said.

"The Curtises? I imagine so." Charlie drank deeply from a canteen and wiped the sweat from his face with a sleeve.

"I was thinking about something," Pete said.

"You mean, when you weren't scanning the cliffs for Navajos with rifles?" Charlie said with a thin smile that barely creased his face.

"Yeah."

"So what's on your mind?"

"I was thinking about your brother Sammy in his get-up yesterday. Did he pose like that for Curtis two years ago?"

"We both posed," Charlie said.

Pete accepted the canteen from Charlie and took long, slow gulps. "Then those photographs he showed us that first night when we were in his tent—the god impersonators weren't Navajo?"

"Most were, some weren't."

"And where did you get the costumes and masks?"

"We made some of them ourselves."

"Sammy and you?"

Charlie looked at Pete.

"So they weren't authentic," Pete pressed him.

"Of course they were authentic," Charlie said, more than a little exasperated. "Sammy knows what he's doing. All the materials, the way the Navajo collect them and put them together, Sammy does it to the letter."

"And that's enough?"

"Look, Pete, those masks we made, in the fall they were blessed by singers, and they've been used over and over again in ceremonies the past two years. You can't get more authentic than that, can you?"

Pete let it rest.

At twilight the exhausted party reached Charles Cousins's trading post, just beyond the mouth of the canyon. Cousins greeted their unexpected arrival with concern and immediately set about preparing accommodations for the night ahead. After a quick meal Clara Curtis bundled her enervated children into an adjoining room, intent on settling them down. Cousins and Justo left to see to the horses, which, though unharnessed and watered, still needed to be fed and rubbed down. Curtis, wary of the speed with which they'd packed up camp, asked Phillips to unpack all the photographic and recording gear, as well as the boxes of glass plates and wax cylinders, and check for damage. That left Pete, Charlie Day, and Edward Curtis alone at the rectangular table in Cousins's kitchen.

"Empty your cups," Pete said gruffly. He reached down beside him and withdrew from a canvas bag a half-full bottle of Old Forester. He poured a generous inch for each of them.

They sat silently for some time, sipping the whiskey, before Charlie, clearing his throat with a cough, asked, "How's Mrs. Curtis?"

Edward looked up. "Still to be faced." Her worry, her wrath.

Pete didn't envy him. He imagined that from Mrs. Curtis's perspective, her husband had committed a cardinal sin, putting her babies at risk. But sitting here now, letting the liquor seep into his blood, and suspecting that he'd not have another opportunity, he said, "That film you took yesterday, are you going to pedal that as authentic?"

Curtis sat back and sighed with weariness, "Well, Pete, I've been waiting for you to ask something like this. I must say, you haven't chosen the best moment to do it, but let's hear it." He gestured with his right hand, as if signaling for an approach—an approach to the throne, Pete thought, which only irritated him more.

"That was no Yeibichei dance. It was a burlesque."

"And you're an expert?"

"Hardly. But I don't pretend to be. How many months have you spent with Navajos? Or should I say, how many weeks? Days?"

"The performance was by an authentic dance team, wasn't it—a team that's performed at dozens of ceremonies?"

"In the fall or winter—the proper season—and in the dead of night, as part of an actual sing, not as an exercise for your motion picture camera."

"I couldn't film outdoors at night under any realistic circumstances. Anyone who sees the film will know that."

"You give people too much credit. You're assuming they know something about the Navajo."

"They'll know something about it because I'll *tell* them." Curtis finished his whiskey. "Many Navajo ceremonies have already been lost. Do you think the Night Chant will be anything but a distant memory a hundred years from now?'

"That's for the Navajo to determine."

"And that's a rather naïve response. Assimilation can't be stopped. Would you prefer that there's no filmed record, as slight as it is?"

"Why does there have to be a record? Some cultures disappear completely. Hasn't history taught us that? So be it."

"Maybe I should burn all the photographs and smash all the plates, too."

"Maybe you should." Pete refreshed his drink and held the bottle out to the others. Charlie put his hand over his cup and shook his head. Curtis did nothing, and Pete leaned across the table and poured him another two fingers.

"You must have a rather jaded view of our profession," Curtis said.

"I don't have pretensions."

"Oh, come now!" Curtis said, stirring. "We *all* have pretensions."

"When I first started out," Pete said, "I tried to convince my customers that I should give them photographs that might capture an actual moment of happiness or surprise, but they almost always rejected any such idea. They knew what they wanted. The Family Photograph. The Madonna and Child. The Wedding Portrait. In other words, what they'd seen on other people's mantels, aping the oil portraits of the nobility. Something with the artificial aura of permanence, to preserve at the bottom of a bureau drawer, beneath the sachet of rose petals and the fine undergarments. So I give my customers what they want, what they expect. As do you, I'm sure, even with your Indian portraits."

"And I thought *I* was the idealist," Curtis said. "I'd like to see your work, the photographs you take when you aren't compromised by the realities of our profession."

"I don't have white men dressing up as Navajo gods."

Reaching into the pocket of his trail coat, which he'd draped over the back of his chair, Curtis extracted a well-used pipe, a pouch of tobacco, and matches. He prepared the pipe carefully, scraping the bowl, emptying the debris onto a saucer, tamping down the shredded tobacco, lighting it. He extinguished the matchstick with a flick of his wrist and added it to the saucer. Then he said, "You may not have noticed the other night, when I showed you my portfolio, but it included several photographs of the Navajos' Humpbacked God."

"I recall," Pete said.

"The photographs are of two different impersonators. If you looked closely, you'd see that the costuming and body paint differ slightly. One was Sammy Day. The other was a Navajo. If I put the photographs side by side, would you be able to tell which is which?"

"I doubt it," Pete said.

"So what matters, the impersonator or the accuracy of the impersonation?"

"Both."

"You're making too much of nothing, Pete," Charlie Day said, speaking for the first time. He played with the whiskey in his cup, swirling it, but he wasn't drinking. It annoyed Pete that Charlie was taking Curtis's side.

Curtis spoke again: "If you can't see the difference, is there a difference?"

"Yes," Pete said, but he knew he couldn't defend his position. A photograph was nothing but a moment of light caught in the flux, absent sound, smell, taste, touch. Of course human agency played its role—in the mechanics of the camera itself; in the composition of subject, light, and shadow; in the manipulations within the darkroom. But in recording that moment of light, the image opened the mind to what it otherwise couldn't perceive in the continuous flux of fraction after fraction after fraction. It had its own truth, and the less he intervened, the truer the image to nature. Yes, he could employ trickery for the purposes of art or more mundane deceit. And yes, a viewer could misread any image, attach his own meanings, but such notions, filtered through the mind's lens, not the camera's, were not the image itself. But Pete couldn't say any of this. Certainly not to Curtis. He knew how he'd sound. Like a fool. Like a goddamn romantic, that's how he'd sound, worse than Curtis, though what he desired was to let *nature*, not Curtis's Nature, be seen as clearly as it could be. If you can't see the difference, is there a difference? Curtis had asked. He'd answered yes, but in truth he meant no. *No*, if Curtis was asking what the light revealed, but that wasn't at all what Curtis was asking.

"I'd have thought," Curtis said, "that you'd have greater sympathy for what I'm about. I want to capture the aboriginal life as it is, before it vanishes, in fact and from memory. I intend to show it in its richness, its variety."

"Then you should add photographs from a back alley in Gallup—the Indian drunks and whores."

"I don't need to show a culture in decay, physically and spiritually. That isn't my project. I'll leave that to you."

The door to the side room opened and Mrs. Curtis appeared. "Edward, please come now," she said sharply.

"Yes," he answered, and the door closed. He placed his pipe on the saucer and stood up. "I'll be saying goodnight to you gentlemen."

"Goodnight," Pete said. Charlie nodded.

Half way to the door, Curtis turned around. "I want to preserve something," he said to Pete. "Give me credit for my intentions. I want to preserve *something*."

When the door closed behind Curtis, Pete addressed his friend: "You've been very quiet, Charlie."

"Oh," Charlie said, "I was wondering about the Navajo woman and her baby."

"DID THEY LIVE?" Julia asked.

"They did," Pete said. "Charlie heard the next day."

"And the Curtis family?" Julia asked. "What of them?"

"As I understand it, Mrs. Curtis and the children left for Seattle as soon as they could. As for Edward Curtis, I suppose he moved on to his next tribe."

Julia had refrained from interrupting Pete during his tale, but throughout, her sympathy lay with Clara Curtis. "Do you think you were ever in any real danger?" she asked.

"I couldn't say. Charlie certainly thought so at the time."

"Well, I'm sure I'll be perfectly safe in Canyon de Chelly with Mr. Yazzie."

"I imagine so," Pete said, but there was vinegar in his words. "He wouldn't let anyone harm a hair on your head, not while he still had breath."

"And you would?" she tried to tease him.

He gave her a sideways glance. "No. And neither would Harry Whitaker. Or Tom Gorman. Or Johnny Gorman. The difference is, it'd take us a few seconds to decide if the threat was real, but Yazzie, he'd strike quick and think about it later."

"Can we change the subject?" Julia said. "Your attitude is making me very uncomfortable."

"Your wish is my command," Pete said.

Julia focused on several vultures circling high overhead. "Are you going to photograph the Hopi dance?"

"Not unless some tourist agrees to pay me a considerable sum." When Julia didn't respond, he continued, in a more conciliatory tone, "Besides, some of the Hopi are trying to stop all photography, and I don't want to end up in a hornets' nest. That's not why I came, anyway."

"No?"

"Why are *you* making this trip?"

"I wanted to see my sister."

"Well, I know that," he said, dissatisfied with her answer.

"And I wanted to get away. I've been out here for nearly eight years and I've hardly seen anything except Many Springs, Gallup, and the road between."

"Why did you ask me to meet you in Winslow?"

"I couldn't hire a coach-and-four."

"It's a serious question."

"You told me you were planning a trip to the Painted Desert. The timing was right."

"That's all?"

Julia sighed. "I'm not high on the social register since Will left. I'm a married woman without a husband, living fifty miles out on the Navajo Reservation. I get an annual invitation to Matilda Rodriguez's Christmas party—which I always politely refuse—and that's probably because Alberto takes pity on me. Whom should I rely on, if not my friends?"

"So I'm your friend."

"You are."

"And if I say that isn't enough?"

"I can't offer more. You very well know that."

"Circumstances change."

"Oh, God," Julia said.

"Yazzie has designs on you," Pete said.

"Don't be ridiculous. And hurtful."

"You mean you don't see it?"

"There's nothing to see. Mr. Yazzie and I have a very simple, practical business relationship. And, I admit, a friendship. Of an odd sort."

Pete's laughter held a sharp edge. "Will you listen to yourself? What in Sweet Jesus are you talking about?" He snapped the reins, startling Stable Boy from his lethargy. "You're delusional."

"Nobody's perfect."

"*You're* perfect," Pete murmured. "At least you are to me."

It was so mistaken, so maudlin, that Julia wanted to slap him. "The heat's made you lose *your* senses."

They sat in silence for a good mile.

"Sometimes my temper gets the best of me," Julia said.

"All right," Pete said. "I guess neither of us is so perfect."

They had offered their apologies. They rode on.

After a while Pete said, "You see, this is why."

She didn't need to ask what he meant.

They camped that night along Jeddito Wash, near a small butte that stood out in the moonlight, but by that time Julia was too tired to see clearly. Her head swam from fatigue and within minutes of falling onto the pallet in Pete's wagon and pulling a Pendleton up to her cheekbones, letting her breath take the night's desert chill off her weariness, she was asleep.

She woke in the false dawn, which crept into the spring wagon through the gaps in the lowered canvas awnings. She could barely stretch out her back and shoulders, and the effort produced a heartfelt groan. At least she was warm enough under the blanket, and she eased her limbs of their stiffness, flexing one at a time until she felt human again. She stopped and listened but the silence was so profound around her, apart from her own breathing and rustling, that she could only describe it as absolute. During the night her eyes had bathed themselves clean, pushing the grit into the pink of the corners and forming there nuggets of sand and salt that she had to scrape away with her forefingers before she could fully open her eyes. The edge of the lids felt like they'd been abraded. And her hair, which she raked now with her fingers—well, better to leave that alone, it was so dry and crusted with sand that shaking her head would probably be of more benefit than trying to comb the snarls out. And there was no point in thinking about changing her clothes until they were at Second Mesa. As grubby as she felt, her present attire would have to do. She drew back a canvas flap and silently slipped to the ground. Beneath the wagon, Pete seemed to still be asleep.

They were surrounded by scattered outcrops—buttes and ridges—as far as she could see across the pale brown expanse. Her sense of distance had improved over the years, but here, with no familiar landmarks, she was at a loss. Everywhere, except for the minor eruptions, she could see a panorama, with the cloudless sky growing paler, now, to the south and east. To the far north she spied a larger formation, irregular against the cerulean backdrop and still low to the horizon, but clearly distinguishable from anything else in sight. It had to be Second Mesa.

She should try to relieve herself even though she felt no need to: she wasn't drinking enough, and the dryness of the air was wicking moisture from her even as she stood there. She walked to the wash, being careful of where she placed her stockinged feet. The wash was shallow, dry; what had once been mud, had dried to cracks and gullies.

She returned to the wagon. Pete's horse, hobbled, was standing off, eyeing her and tossing its head. She walked to the side of the wagon where the horse's feed and water bags hung.

"I'll tend to him," Pete said.

So he was awake after all. "So, how far to Second Mesa?"

"Twenty-odd miles. We'll be there before noon."

"You're sure? I wouldn't want to be late."

He threw back his bear skin and rolled clear of the wagon before pulling on his boots. "I can read a map. I know exactly how far we've come."

The horse launched a mammoth stream of urine into the sand.

Julia bit her lower lip to keep from laughing.

"That's coincidence, not commentary," Pete said, heading toward the wash.

When he returned, she pointed to the nearest butte, the one she'd noticed last night. "Does that one have a name?"

"I suppose they all have names in one language or another."

"And this one is . . . ?" She continued to point.

"'Abe' Bílátahá."

The Nipple. Julia tilted her head to the side. Looked at from that angle, with the flat horizon imagined as a woman's chest and stomach, the contours did indeed resemble a young woman's breast; a bit lumpy on the underside, but she kept the thought to herself. Better to look elsewhere. She pointed to another nearby formation. "And that?" There was something beyond desolate about it, as if it had spilled from some monstrous maw—flat and burned black at the top, where the sun's rays were just now curving around it, its steep sides deeply stripped and scarred, and at its base, flows that had puddled thickly on the desert plain. "It's rather unsettling."

"It isn't labeled on the map, but it's like all the rest," Pete said as he knelt to roll up his bedding, "sandstone and volcanic rock that's eroding away." He stood up and threw his bedding into the back of the wagon. "If it's all right with you, I'll feed and harness the horse so we can start right out." He didn't wait for an answer.

As far as she was concerned, the sooner they arrived, the better. Had he been chewing his cud all night? She wished she were home now, out of the sun, which had yet to regain its ferocity, in her kitchen, toasting on the grate a piece of bread that she'd eat with tomato preserves and a cup of English tea (bless Penny!), not the flour tortilla and the hard-boiled egg she, sitting on the hard ground, was now peeling. He sat down beside her and did likewise.

Just as she was beginning to think that getting a solicitous word from him today would be like excavating a boulder with a spoon, he asked, "Did you sleep all right?"

"I did."

"That's good." He paused and scraped a final piece of shell from his egg. "I was lying there for a while waiting for the sun, thinking about the Hopi dance. We Christians tend to think you achieve grace one by one, quietly, through prayer and contemplation or divine providence. When I was with the Brothers, I thought I saw it once or twice in others. But it never lasted, as far as I could tell. Maybe the Hopis achieve it together, in these dances and such. It's something to think about."

This was the Pete she cared for—the man of thought and consideration, and true feeling—whom she saw too rarely. Part of the reason was the drink, it hid so much of him; at least as much as it hid the world from him. And part was his contrariness, whether from nature or from so many disappointments.

"Will you let me take your picture before we leave?" Julia asked.

"What?"

"I bet you don't have any photographs of yourself, do you?"

He thought for a moment. "No, I guess I don't."

10. Home Dance

THE TRAIL HAD RUN STRAIGHT to the mesa for many miles now, and Julia, shaded from the brutal light by her straw hat and a bright fuchsia parasol that had been a gift from Penelope, watched puffs of white float across the higher terrain of Black Mesa, to the north. To the northwest, wider pockets of gray released sporadic vertical veils of rain that evaporated, never reaching the ground. The Hopi mesas, each a gnarled finger extending from the massive Black Mesa, came into sharper relief. They had little in common with the red rock formations farther east on the Navajo Reservation, on the westward side of the Chuskas. Second Mesa, its southern expanse rising dead ahead, seemed to comprise a bleaker, coarser brownish gray. As they drew close, Julia could make out shattered boulders and talus, and a few adobe buildings spread along the base, close to the trail.

They stopped so that Stable Boy could drink before the ascent. Two very young children—both had shaggy black hair that hung to their shoulders and wore simple shifts that made it impossible to tell if they were girls or boys—stood in the shade of a doorway, staring at Julia. She twirled her parasol, which set the lace trim dancing in the sun, and the two broke into broad, giggling grins before they shyly ducked into the house.

The trail climbed steeply up the side of the mesa and then cut to the right, passing a large sandstone column and a small burial ground that was marked only by shallow mounds of sand and rock and a sign in English warning visitors not to intrude. The trail looped back like a snake and Julia could see all the way to the distant San Francisco Peaks, with the sun, now at its zenith, bleaching out everything between, including the road they'd taken from Winslow, which wavered in the heat and disappeared.

Near the top of the mesa, just past the first attached, boxlike adobe houses, a number of buckboards and carriages, and even an automobile with extra cans of gasoline mounted on its boot, had been pulled into a flat, open area. A Hopi man signaled Pete to pull off the trail there. Several boys were tending to an assortment of horses near wooden troughs that had clearly been stationed there for the benefit of visitors. A steep, dusty path, followed by a set of equally steep, well-worn stone steps, led up to the pueblo. The outermost ring of residences clung to the edge of the mesa, and there, where the steps ended, with his arms folded across his chest and his hat brim pulled low to shade his face, sat Clement Yazzie and, beside him, another man.

Wellesley Katsi, Clement Yazzie's elder uncle, was short but broad in the shoulders, narrower at the hips. He was wearing new denim pants, a red and purple striped shirt buttoned to the neck, a silver bolo, a leather vest, and a ring with a turquoise stone the size of a quail's egg. His graying hair fell to his shoulders, and a wispy mustache perched over his thin mouth. He greeted Julia with a small smile and gave a nod to Pete, but without extending his hand. Yazzie took Julia's overnight satchel from her, and the four made their way along the path into the village plaza, taking them down a narrow passageway between the connected adobe and stone houses. Log beams supported the roofs, which offered protective overhangs for anyone sitting on the stone benches beneath. Dozens of people, including a handful of Anglo men, sat on the flat roofs—some with their legs dangling over the side—which they had apparently reached by rather rickety wooden ladders. The plaza itself, no more than twenty yards wide and forty yards long, was an uneven floor of dirt and rock. Toward one side, a handmade drum sat on a wooden chair. An uneven row of additional chairs, most of them unoccupied, lined the perimeter, and many colorful blankets were spread out in front of them. Beneath a number of the chairs, protected from the sun, lay scruffy black-and-white dogs of unidentifiable ancestry. Hopi children played and ran in all directions.

"The kachina dancers are resting in a kiva," Yazzie's uncle said in carefully studied English. "Many people are home having lunch, but they'll be back soon." He led them across the plaza and through a maze of short corridors barely wide enough for two people to walk abreast.

Beyond a perfunctory greeting and brief introduction, Yazzie had yet to say anything to Julia, which she found both disappointing and annoying. At Many Springs Canyon he'd appeared to be quite willing to serve as her guide from here to Canyon de Chelly and home, but now he seemed discomfited by her presence. What was it with these damned men, first Philip and then Pete and now Yazzie, too? It was if they all, each in his own peculiar way, expected her to adhere to some vague code of which they were the sole guardians. But perhaps she was being too severe. This was probably somewhat disconcerting for Yazzie, too, to be introducing a white woman, his employer no less, to an uncle whom, Julia gathered, he didn't see that often. Maybe Yazzie was feeling that he shouldn't have imposed on his uncle's family to entertain Julia for the night. But she had no sense from Mr. Katsi that he had any objection, and when they turned the final corner and he led Julia into his modest home and introduced Julia to his wife, who greeted Julia with a large smile and a welcoming arm despite speaking no English, Julia couldn't help feeling relieved. Mrs. Katsi immediately led Julia into a side room—obviously the home's one bedroom, given the corn husk mattresses on the floor and a chest of drawers that had been assembled with considerable care—where a washstand and a large pitcher of water was awaiting her arrival.

After washing up as best she could and changing her clothes, Julia returned to the main room, where a table had been set with loaves of shepherd's bread, bowls of a posole stew spiced with chiles, sliced watermelon, and a steaming pot of coffee strong enough to peel bark off a tree. Two other young women, the wives of Katsi sons, joined them. The conversation was less than fluid since Yazzie and Wellesley alone spoke both English and Hopi, which meant that most of the lunchtime discourse comprised self-conscious smiles and nods. Julia did learn, however, the origin of Mr. Katsi's somewhat unusual English name, Wellesley, as well as that of his brother, Gladstone Katsi, whose absence from the table went without explanation. It seemed that when Wellesley Katsi first began dealing as a clan leader with the Americans who had settled near Moenkopi, on the western edge of the Hopi lands, a voluble trader they came to like, an English blueblood (before a precipitous decline in his family's fortunes led to his emigration), never tired of peppering his conversation with quotations from famous Englishmen. When the Katsi brothers first made acquaintance with him, neither understood English, so much of what he said was lost on them, although they were so impressed by the powerful names of those oft-quoted Englishmen, the trader's heroes, Arthur Wellesley, the first duke of Wellington, and William Gladstone, a later prime minister, that they adopted the luminaries' names for their dealings with the Anglo world.

At one point Wellesley Katsi directed his attention to Pete, who'd been uncharacteristically silent, if not sullen, since arriving. "Yazzie tells me you're a photographer."

"I am."

"Did you bring it with you?"

"My camera? Yes, I did. I always travel with at least one. It's what I do." He carefully laid his spoon down by the side of his bowl of stew. "I've been told that many Hopi object to having their ceremonies photographed and that some refuse to have their pictures taken at all."

"This is true."

"I'll respect their wishes," Pete said. "I've locked my camera away in my wagon, and it'll stay there until I leave Second Mesa tomorrow."

Wellesley Katsi looked at him and nodded. "This is the honorable thing to do." He said nothing more on the subject.

Julia looked at Pete, who resumed eating without so much as a glance at her. He'd handled himself very well. She shouldn't have been surprised—and wouldn't have been, if he hadn't been so petulant on the trail to Second Mesa.

With lunch having concluded (and after a visit to the privy, precariously perched on the edge of the mesa), Julia followed Mr. Katsi, Pete, and Yazzie back to the plaza. It seemed that the entire village was in the process of returning. Some of the Hopi women carried umbrellas to shield themselves and their babies from the unmerciful August afternoon sun, and Julia was glad to have her furled parasol in hand in case she needed it, although, at least for the moment, her broad-brimmed straw hat would suffice. Wellesley pointed to a stone bench at the corner of the plaza where there was enough room for one person at the end. A Pendleton blanket had been neatly folded and left there.

"I saved that seat for you," he told Julia. "Sit on the blanket. The stone gets harder as the sun gets hotter." He chuckled.

"I'm sure it does. But are you sure I'm not taking a seat that should belong to someone from Second Mesa?"

"You needn't worry. It's fine."

"In that case, I'm very grateful."

"I need to talk to Yazzie about a family matter. Will you be all right if we leave the two of you for a while?"

"Of course."

"Certainly," Pete added. "May I stand here in the shade?"

"Wherever you want," Wellesley said. "Each year we seem to have more and more guests for Niman. Villagers may not say much to you, but you're welcome here. Niman is for the world, not just for Hopis."

"Well, in that case," Pete said, "I'm doubly honored to be here on this beautiful afternoon."

It *is* beautiful, Julia thought. Stray clouds like handfuls of cotton were sailing above them, bearing no threat of anything but a momentary shower, and the humidity was so low that even the sun's heat wasn't terribly bothersome. She was still stiff from so many hours in the spring wagon, and she wanted to sit down and discretely stretch out her legs.

As if reading her mind, Pete said, "Go and take your seat. You look tired, Julia." His tone—his entire demeanor—had softened. She didn't know why; maybe he was tired, too, but she didn't pursue it. Better to leave well enough alone.

Julia took the last seat on the stone bench at the northwest corner of the plaza. She found herself sitting beside a young Hopi woman with a toddler in tow.

She hadn't been sitting long, observing the Hopi men and women, the children dashing about, the twenty or so other Anglos, mostly men, in attendance, when she began to hear the approach of tinkling bells and the clacking of rattles. In single file, kachina dancers, led by a casually dressed clan elder, paraded into the plaza. Their pale brown masks completely covered their heads and looked almost ceramic, but some of the dancers passed so close that Julia could see hand-sewn cross-stitches holding pieces of what may have been pigskin together. Each mask featured an elongated, piglike snout and was topped by a modest fan of feathers. Garlands of spruce formed collars around the dancers' necks. Their torsos were bare, although most of the fifty or so men seemed to have applied an uneven coating of nut-brown paint to their bodies, and some a dusting of corn powder. They wore capes of varied hue—blue, purple, green, red: a rainbow of bright colors—draped over their shoulders. Each also wore a kilt, a distinctive woven sash, and moccasins. Sets of bells and rattles made from hollow turtle shells had been strapped to their legs, and each dancer clutched a gourd rattle and a small branch of spruce. Most also carried sacks, baskets, and paperboard boxes overflowing with food—breads, pies, melons, squash, peaches, stacks of roasted corn in charred husks, cans of sardines and Heinz beans and Hormel meats, sacks of flour, and packages of licorice and horehound candy—which they set down in the center of the plaza. Instead of food, some dancers carried coiled Hopi baskets, woven plaques, and for the children small bows and arrows or hand-carved kachina dolls fastened to bound cornstalks and reeds.

When all the items had been piled up, the dancers formed a long arc, roughly three-fourths of a circle. Then, in response to an exhortation from the clan elder, they began the dance—stomping, shaking their rattles and bells, and chanting wordlessly through their head masks to the syncopated beat of the single drum. Every so often they changed direction, pivoting in sequence so that their turning flowed in a wave. Even when the syncopation abruptly altered, no one missed a beat.

For Julia, the dance quickly became hypnotic. She wasn't sure how many iterations she'd heard, how much time had passed, when the dancing suddenly stopped. Without uttering a word, the dancers broke their arc and began distributing the gifts they'd carried into the plaza. They tossed loaves of bread and small round watermelons up to Hopis sitting on the rooftops, and signaled with a pointed finger and a wave of the hand for others to come forward. One dancer handed Clement Yazzie—who'd returned to the plaza and now stood beside Pete—a piki, a paper-thin, rolled blue corn bread.

When everything had been distributed, the kachina dancers reformed their arc, which they left open in a different direction, and began the dance again, repeating the singing, rhythms, and steps they'd executed earlier. This time, however, there was an added element to the performance: the appearance of the *koshares*, the sacred clowns, the children of incest in the prior world from which the Hopi had emerged. Julia had already been warned about the koshares—that they went beyond the irreverent to the outrageous, acting without restraint, defying every conceivable social more. In sum, they held nothing sacred; they would mock the dancers, the audience, each other, the gods themselves.

Three of the koshares, carrying the shoddiest excuse for a ladder she'd ever seen, entered from the far corner of the plaza. They were all painted with horizontal stripes of white and black paint and wore only moccasins, breechcloths, and a pair of painted horns on their heads. Suddenly, a fourth koshare appeared on a rooftop above the other three, and, holding a liquor bottle at his groin, proceeded to shake it up and down, spraying what Julia hoped was water over his compatriots and the nearby crowd. It was truly the most startling display of near indecency she'd ever witnessed. Her cheeks were on fire, and not from the sun. The woman beside her, who had also averted her eyes, was giggling. Julia glanced toward Pete. He'd discretely turned away from her but she could tell he was attempting to suppress outright laughter, which was how most of the Hopi men responded. The kachina dancers, however, kept right on with their chanting and their dance, as if the clowns weren't even there.

What followed was a clearly choreographed series of acrobatic maneuvers as the koshares in the plaza attempted to position their pole ladder and climb to the roof while the clown on the roof attempted to descend. How they managed to do it, using everything at their disposal, including the shoulders of seated spectators as well as each other's arms, legs, heads, and chests, was actually quite entertaining, as was their subsequent fumble-footed efforts when they joined the line of dancers.

Julia soon lost track of time. Each repetition of the kachina dance seemed to last between thirty and forty minutes. After the second, the dancers paused only briefly, moved their arc another quarter turn to a third direction, and commenced again. After this third segment, they filed out of the plaza; their bodies were covered with sweat, and, as they passed by her, she could hear some of them panting inside their masks.

Though drifting clouds had occasionally given Julia some respite from the sun, she was sweating, too, rivulets running down her sides from beneath her arms (she'd been smart enough to wear a loose-fitting blouse and thin cotton skirt with minimal undergarments), her hair matted under her straw hat. Clement Yazzie had brought with him a large jar of fresh water, and when Pete and he approached and asked if she was thirsty, she quickly drank swallow after swallow. He also handed her a folded Chinese fan that, he told her, Gladstone Katsi's wife had offered.

Julia immediately snapped it open and put it to use. "Will I be able to thank her?" she asked Yazzie. "Will I meet her and your uncle Gladstone later?"

"At dinner. The whole family will be there."

"I'm looking forward to it. This is turning into a most extraordinary day."

She looked to Pete for confirmation, but he only looked away and said, "I think I should go check on my wagon—make sure those kids aren't getting too curious." He crossed the plaza and left the way they'd first entered.

Two of the other Anglo visitors, a middle-aged rancher and his barrel-shaped wife, came over and chatted with Julia. Archer Pippin had a logging operation down near Show Low, and his main topic of conversation was the price he could get for his timber in Tucson, although Mrs. Pippin, herself something of a pioneer, had greater interest in how Julia managed to keep sane in Many Springs Canyon, where (in her words), "Darlin', you've got to feel like the last white woman on earth." They seemed like nice enough people, and Julia responded to their conversation with smiles and non-committal comments, but she really wanted them to go away and leave her in peace. She wasn't here to blather on about herself or to listen to others blather on about themselves.

None too soon, the Pippins lost interest and moved on. Yazzie had drifted away and now was nowhere to be seen, so Julia sat in silence and awaited the return of the kachina dancers. The young woman beside her was nursing her toddler, whose eyes had glazed over from the combination of warm milk and afternoon heat; it wasn't long before the child's eyelids fluttered into sleep and his mother's nipple slipped from his lips. Julia and the Hopi woman exchanged smiles.

The next cycle of the ceremony seemed—to Julia, anyway—a precise repetition of the first cycle, complete with the passing out of gifts between the first and second dances. Once again, the koshares made a series of deliberately intrusive appearances, during one of which they proceeded to mock the Anglo visitors. They came into the plaza wearing out-sized cowboy hats, boots and spurs, and bandoliers crisscrossed across their bare chests. In place of bullets were unshelled beans, and they wore toy pistols. One carried a blunderbuss and another led a boar by a lasso. The four proceeded to put on their version of a Wild West Show, which, among other activities, included pig-bucking.

Julia, who couldn't help breaking into laughter several times, took time to note the reactions of the other Anglos scattered around the plaza. Some stood stone-faced, while others laughed as hard as many of the Hopis did. Through it all, the dancers continued to perform with unflagging concentration.

Then in the third dance of this second cycle, Julia's fears were realized. (She'd noted that Mr. and Mrs. Pippin had quietly departed.) The koshare who had announced his presence early in the afternoon by spraying water from a rooftop, and who had been looking in her direction repeatedly, approached her. She saw him coming and she looked to Yazzie and Pete; Yazzie was standing with his arms folded across his chest, but he gave no evidence of concern; Pete was frowning and appeared quite red in the face, but he didn't budge from his post beside Yazzie. She was on her own.

The koshare, a tall gaunt man with a hook nose, stopped in front of her for a moment. She couldn't bring her eyes up to his. Then he quickly took two side steps and pretended to sit down next to her. But there was no spare room on the bench. With nothing but air beneath him, and with his back pressed against the adobe wall, he mimicked as best he could her sitting posture. She couldn't help looking: the muscles of his thighs bulged and strained.

She stiffened her back; he stiffened his.

She brushed an eyebrow with one finger; he did likewise.

She cleared her throat, as did he. She was vaguely aware of a gentle laughter in the background. She stared straight ahead. She didn't know what to do; she could feel her heart thumping in her chest, and there was a sudden ringing in her ears. She could get up and leave, but he—and louder laughter—would follow her. She knew that the eyes of every spectator were on her. All right, she thought, two can play this game.

She lifted the hem of her skirt and crossed her ankles; there was no way the koshare could imitate her without completely losing his balance. More laughter. The koshare cast a narrow, sly, sidelong glance at her. Then he twisted his neck and looked over his shoulder, up at the sun, brushed sweat from his brow, and waited. She imitated him as precisely as she could. The laughter grew. He turned his head toward her and drew his face closer to hers . . . and suddenly began panting like a dog. The laughter exploded.

No, she was *not* going to pant like a dog. What could she do? Fan him with Mrs. Katsi's fan? And then she remembered the furled fuchsia parasol behind her feet. She bent over, picked it up, opened it wide, and held it out. He grabbed it from her hand, effortlessly bounced up to a standing position, preened, and, spinning the parasol, waddled off. She could almost see the bustle he was pretending to wear.

There must have been additional laughter, but the ringing in her head and the continuing chant of the kachina dancers prevented her hearing it clearly. Her immediate thought was to look again toward Pete and Yazzie.

Pete looked like a bee had flown up his nose; she realized he was embarrassed for her, and for a moment she felt close to tears.

But Clement Yazzie was laughing. She'd never seen him laugh so openly, with such unguarded surprise, and there was something else, too, in how he was looking at her. She didn't know what it was, but she forgot about Pete's red face. She sighed and let her shoulders relax. The Hopi woman next to her was chuckling, and she reached out her rough brown hand and briefly patted Julia's forearm. Well, Julia thought, her eyes returning to Yazzie's, if this was a test, maybe I passed.

The sun was already sliding down the curve of the western sky when the kachina dancers, with empty arms this time, trooped into the plaza for what would be the final dance. It began like all the others, but after just a few minutes the drumming stopped and the clan elder led the dancers into the passageway through which Julia, Pete, Clement Yazzie, and his uncle Wellesley had first entered the plaza. Everyone followed, some of the children and a number of the more spry adults clambering over the flat rooftops. The kachina dancers reassembled near a kiva entrance—a square hole in the floor of this smaller plaza, from which protruded the upper reaches of a rough ladder; the plaza itself overlooked the high desert hundreds of feet below. Behind her, Julia could see the San Francisco peaks once again, hazy bumps on the southwest horizon. Five male attendants in ordinary dress began circling the dancers. One lifted a ceremonial pipe to his lips and blew aromatic smoke toward the kachinas while his companions sprinkled corn pollen over them. Then the attendants took the spruce boughs from the dancers' hands and carefully tied feathers to their wrists, to help on the journey home. The elder began a lengthy prayer of farewell.

Julia noticed a beautiful young woman standing apart, silently watching. She wore a white Hopi gown, white deerskin leggings, and a long white shawl with black and red borders at the top and bottom; her skin had been dusted with powder, and her hair was bound in the butterfly whorls that Julia had seen in photographs of Hopi maidens. Julia suspected she was a bride-to-be.

The shadows slid eastward toward First Mesa, above which a full moon rose in the now cloudless sky. Pinyon smoke drifted lazily in the quiet air. Then the elder, having completed his prayer, led the kachinas away. In this season of relative plenty, with the first of the harvest in and their work done, the kachinas would travel homeward to rest, not to return to Hopiland until December, when the world turned its darkest and fiercest.

Julia, Pete, and Yazzie stood at the edge of the mesa while the quiet crowd slowly dispersed. The moon glowed large and pale in a field of blue, beneath which the lengthening shadow of the mesa turned the sweep of land before them to a dark orange.

"This is a place where the sky and the earth talk," Yazzie said.

By the time the three of them returned to the open area in front of Wellesley Katsi's house, the women of the extended family were already laying out dish after dish of food on two improvised tables constructed from sawhorses and worn planks. No formal introductions were made, but Yazzie circulated with Julia and Pete until, by Julia's reckoning, they'd met everyone. Only some of the children spoke more than a smattering of English, which they'd picked up at school, so conversations were very brief, with Yazzie doing the necessary translating. Julia did have the opportunity, however, to meet Gladstone Katsi's wife, a short, pleasant-faced woman with several gold teeth, and to thank her for the use of her fan. Gladstone himself remained among the missing, which Julia found curious.

Faced with the language barrier, Julia and Pete stuck close to each other. Pete was convivial enough, though reserved, and most of their talk focused on their early-morning departure for the Hubbell Trading Post at Ganado, where they were expected to arrive tomorrow night, well after dark. Julia hadn't seen J. L. and Lina since she'd stayed with them in 1898 to learn the basics of the trading business, but she'd been in sporadic contact with them by letter. She planned to spend a full day with Lina, while Pete drove on to Gallup and Clement Yazzie visited people he knew in the Ganado area. On the following day, she and Yazzie would head north to Chinle and Canyon de Chelly.

The tables were spread with roasted rabbit and mutton ribs, mutton stew, ears of corn, corn and wheat bread, fry bread, corn pudding, a dish of purslane and spinach and a bitter green that Julia couldn't identify, striped green squash, melon, and chile con carne spiced with cumin and coriander. Colored lanterns were being lit and someone had brought out a Spanish guitar and a fiddle, but before long Julia had eaten her fill and, exhausted by the eventful day, could barely keep her eyes open. The skin over her cheekbones felt stretched tight, and she knew she'd been burned by the sun despite her efforts to take advantage of the shade. She leaned against an exterior window sill and closed her eyes for a moment.

Someone said, "Hello."

Yazzie and a tall man were standing before her. Yazzie said, "Julia Halley, this is my uncle, Gladstone Katsi."

Gladstone was smiling and nodding. "It's a pleasure to meet you," he said in a very whispery voice.

Julia stood up straight and replied, "The pleasure is mine. You have a very lovely family." In the lantern light he towered over her. He was wearing a red velveteen shirt and soft trousers, and a headband that held his long black hair back off his face. He had a disarmingly boyish smile, deep-set eyes, a hooked nose—

Julia shot a glance at Yazzie, her sunburned face even hotter.

"I hope our Niman ceremony didn't disappoint you this afternoon," Gladstone said.

"No, no," Julia said. "It was quite . . . extraordinary." She wondered how long it had taken him to scrub away the black and white paint. "I feel very privileged to have seen it."

"Most Hopi welcome Anglo visitors. As do the kachinas. Of course they cannot speak to you."

"To be sure," Julia said.

"Perhaps we'll meet again someday."

"Perhaps we will."

He nodded a goodbye and gracefully moved toward the tables.

As soon as Gladstone Katsi was beyond hearing range, Julia swung around and snapped at Clement, "Why didn't you tell me your uncle was a koshare?"

"Ah, well," Clement said, rocking back on his heels and scratching his cheek, "I suppose they look a lot alike, but you must be mistaken."

"Mis—" Julia started to say, but she cut herself off.

Pete, brandishing a half-eaten rabbit leg, hurried up to them. "Do you know who I just saw grabbing a plate? I've a mind to—"

"Pete," Julia said quietly.

"What?"

When Julia was shown to her pallet that night, her parasol, neatly furled, lay on her pillow. Beside it was a bracelet made from blue string and kernels of dried Indian corn.

The gods were merciful in the morning, bestowing an unusually heavy layer of gray across the sky but holding back the rain, which could have made the road impassable. Julia, Pete, and Clement Yazzie stopped for a meal at Keams Canyon, site of the Hopi Agency and a trading post built by Tom and Bill Keams that, rumor had it, J. L. Hubbell was trying to buy. An overheard conversation made it clear that the sale was a matter of contention, but Julia didn't press for details.

Back on the road, Pete, his voice heavy with sarcasm, asked her if Hubbell intended to buy out all the traders on the reservation and parcel out the businesses to his sons.

"I'm hardly privy," Julia said. "Trading posts are changing hands all the time. He's apparently made a lot of offers over the years. So have the Days and the Wetherill brothers."

"To you?" Pete asked.

"Once."

Pete was genuinely surprised. "Really?"

"Not long after Will left. Mr. Hubbell wrote and asked if I wanted to get out—to go back East. I'm sure he asked out of friendship, not because he saw Many Springs Canyon as a lucrative investment. I think he probably would have shut it down."

They stopped again at Steamboat for water and to eat a meal that Yazzie's aunts had packed for them, but the trading post was closed up tight. From there, with the sun declining, it was straight on to Ganado. Only Yazzie, astride his big brown most of the way, seemed less than exhausted when they arrived. They were greeted by the Hubbells, fed a light dinner, and shown their beds, which Julia welcomed after minimal ablutions.

When she rose in the morning, well after dawn, a tub had been drawn for her and she enjoyed a warm soak that eased the stiffness from her muscles and allowed her to clean the sand from her thick hair. It was a pleasure to don clean clothes and to turn the rest of her traveling wardrobe over to one of the Hubbell's Navajo servants for a good washing. She ate breakfast in her room, not because she was unsociable but because everyone else had dined long before and had set about their daily business, this being a Monday and the start of a full week.

By the time she emerged it was midmorning, and Pete was harnessing his horse to continue on alone to the Franciscan mission at St. Michaels, where a Brother he knew from Cincinnati had been assigned. From there, it was home to Gallup.

Julia walked over to him. Mumbled morning greetings preceded feeble comments about what a fine day it appeared to be. Pete puttered around the spring wagon. Julia waited patiently, her arms folded, her still-damp hair hanging loose. She knew something was coming. They both saw Yazzie walking from the trading post toward them, which triggered Pete to say what was on his mind:

"I'd be better for you than Will Halley ever was."

"Don't, Pete. You don't know anything about that. And you're not going to wear me down."

"I'm truly sorry to hear that," Pete said. "At some point, you're going to wear me *out*. This will just be too damned painful."

"I don't know what to say to that."

He kissed his fingers and blew the kiss away.

"That decision will always be yours," she said.

"You're a hard woman, Julia."

"You're not the first to find that out."

"Then I have nothing more to say." He climbed up, released the wagon brake, nodded a goodbye in Yazzie's direction, and flicked the reins.

Yazzie came up to her and they watched the wagon pull away toward the main road. The horse, driver, and wagon cast shortening shadows across the arroyo amid the dust kicked up by hooves and wheels.

"Well, that's that," Julia muttered to herself.

"He's a man who's been greatly disappointed," Clement Yazzie said.

"I wasn't asking your opinion, Mr. Yazzie."

He stood with his face turned away from the sun, his brown hands in the back pockets of his denims. "He's not done yet."

"Oh, really? And why are you so sure?"

"He needs to convince himself," Yazzie said.

"And how does he do that? "

"Not with a bottle."

"We all have our frailties." Watching Pete drive off alone, she hated to see him so forlorn, but she wasn't sorry that he was gone. What could she have done? She had no choice but to discourage him.

"Drink is more than a frailty. It's stronger than family or honor."

She didn't need to ask him if he had any personal experience. Every Navajo did. A member of the family. A close friend. Someone who did grievous harm to someone he cared about. "You judge him too harshly. Pete's been a good friend to me and I won't have that disparaged."

"If you left Many Springs, me and him wouldn't give each other a second thought."

Why did she keep finding herself in the middle of these unpleasant conversations? She'd come on this trip to enjoy herself, not to be confronted by a priggish Philip, a lovelorn Pete, and now an obstinate Clement Yazzie. "Have you ever sincerely apologized for *anything*?"

His face remained impassive. "Have you?"

"As a matter of fact, I have. Quite recently." She walked away from him, to the small plank bridge that crossed the wash. The Pueblo Colorado was about the only wash in the area that ran with water throughout the summer, but the nearby vegetation was nevertheless sparse: sagebrush, salt bush, greasewood, Indian rice grass, and a few stunted junipers. Hubbell had focused his energies on making the place more livable—he'd constructed a new house since Julia's first visit, added outdoor bread ovens, corrals, sheep pens, a double post and rail fence, a plank boardwalk to the privy—as well as more financially sound, beginning with two miles of ditches from the wash to a dam and reservoir so that he could irrigate 150 acres planted with alfalfa, barley, oats, rye, sorghum, wheat, fruit trees, and a vineyard. But the immediate vicinity of the wash remained mostly as she remembered it, except for the addition of the bridge, which was partially shaded by a cottonwood. Julia sat down, dangling her legs over the side. From the corner of her eye she could see that Yazzie was still standing where she'd left him, his hands still in his pockets. And then he began walking toward her.

The planks creaked under his heavy steps. He stood above her for a moment, and when she didn't look up he said, "Once or twice."

"What?"

"Apologized. Can I sit?"

She glanced toward the trading post; half a dozen workers were tending to their chores at the corral or the two-story barn, but no one seemed to be paying them any mind. "Sit if you must."

Who were Clement Yazzie's friends? she wondered. Did he even have any? To whom was he close, other than his sister Johanna and, maybe, his Katsi uncles and their families?

"I don't think I've ever met any of your friends," she said.

"That's not so."

"Well, if I have, you've never identified them as friends."

"There are people who come to the trading post, but if I told you they were friends, you might think I expected you to give them special treatment."

"I might well have extended them some additional courtesy. There's nothing wrong with that."

He took off his hat and scratched his forehead. "No, not unless you feel obligated."

She thought she understood certain things about him—his sense of privacy and responsibility and honor—but at times she still found him frustratingly impenetrable. Now they were sitting together on a bridge, their legs dangling over the shallow flow of water and the red mud, just a few feet below. Pete's spring wagon had long since rolled out of sight; the last of the trailing dust, cast gold by the rays of sunlight, settled back to earth beneath the spacious silver-green of the drooping cottonwood.

They sat for a few minutes longer, and the longer they sat, the more uncomfortable their mutual silence became for her. He didn't seem at all troubled, sitting there, rolling the brim of his hat through his hands, enjoying the shade of the cottonwood.

"I should join Lina," Julia said.

Yazzie rose in one smooth motion, and then he held out a hand for her. She took it; she brought her knees up, swung her legs to the side and set her feet on the worn planks; and facing her, with his other hand under her elbow, he lifted her to her feet.

11. Spider Rock

JULIA ENJOYED HER visit with the Hubbells, not least because of the relative comforts of their home, though she was somewhat surprised to learn that Lina was now away most of the time, living in Albuquerque or St. Johns except in the summers. She'd had enough of the rigorous frontier life (not that St. Johns was more than half a step up from Gallup) and couldn't help expressing her own surprise that Julia continued to manage the Many Springs Canyon Trading Post on her own.

The following morning Julia and Clement Yazzie left early, riding north, past Kinlichee and into Beautiful Valley. Amid the latter's parched dunes she picked up several small pieces of petrified wood—beautiful purples and reds and greens against the various buffs and browns and milky quartz. They spent that night at the Cousins Trading Post at the entrance to Canyon de Chelly.

Having risen once again before the sun, they rode along the Chinle Wash at first light, steering the horses around the wider shallows, where, Clement had cautioned, they were most likely to encounter quicksand; he'd never seen anything bigger than a sheep swallowed up, he assured her, but horses sometimes had to be shot because their panic made it impossible to pull them out.

Thick, dark ribbons had formed from summer storm runoff, but closer to the cliffs the canyon bottom was very sandy, making it hard for the horses to get a firm footing; here, centuries of dissolving sandstone from the cliff faces and floods that poured through the frequent narrows made it difficult for foliage to take root. But where the canyon opened out, the soil held and was rich; peach and apple and pear trees grew once again, nearly half a century since the depredations of the army at the beginning of the Long Walk, and in this season the corn was tasseling, head-high, and grass was plentiful for the sheep and cattle. In these wider expanses hogans had been built, no more than two or three in a cluster; some were seasonal dwellings and would be vacated after the harvests and before winter set in.

"What do you think about when you come here?" Julia asked as they remounted after resting the horses opposite the White House ruins. She knew Yazzie wouldn't want to enter them and so gave him no indication that she might like to explore. Nor did she mention Pete's tale of camping here with Charlie Day and the Curtis family.

"It depends on the day. The time of year. The weather." Yazzie was letting his brown take its own course now. "On a day like this, I look up and check the clouds." The canyon was relatively narrow here, and they could only see a fraction of the sky; a small cumulus swelled against the blue. "I want to be ready if they start building. We don't want to get caught in a downpour or flash flood." He swung around in his saddle. "And this time of year I check the peach trees. Some years the fruit's stunted from too little rain or sparse because a late frost killed the blossoms. This should be a good year."

"It's so beautiful here. Don't you think about that?"

"I do."

"And its history?"

He dipped his head to the right, signaling her to follow, and eased the brown around a bed of nut-brown, saturated sand. Her horse followed his, tracing the brown's hoof prints. The turn brought them into the shade of the canyon's southern wall, where the air felt twenty degrees cooler. Yazzie slowed a bit and she caught up to him so that they were once again riding abreast.

"I think about the history some," Yazzie said. "The Spanish killing everyone in Massacre Cave. And your Kit Carson starving the People out. But I don't dwell on it."

"Do you have any friends living here?"

"Just what you'd call clan relatives."

For some reason—maybe the sense of history around her, the sense of time passing, the fact that she'd now been absent from Many Springs Canyon for several days—it occurred to her to ask, "If I were to give up the trading post, would you really burn it down?"

He looked at her with knitted brows.

"You as much as threatened to, not so long ago."

After a bit he asked, "Are you thinking about leaving?"

"Not really. But now and then, yes." She shook her head. "I don't know why I brought it up."

The horses loped along.

"I could put your little box stove in my hogan, " Yazzie said.

"The cook stove would be more useful."

"It wouldn't fit."

"You could always build a bigger hogan."

"Hunh."

It didn't go unnoticed that he hadn't answered her question.

They set up camp where Monument Canyon branched off, just east of the eight-hundred-foot monolith called Spider Rock, home to Spider Woman. When the moon rose, Spider Rock gathered the light.

"Tell me more about your Hopi uncles," Julia said. She and Yazzie had eaten and were now sitting by the campfire. They'd laid out their bedrolls on opposite sides.

"They follow tradition."

"They certainly treated me very well."

"Hopi ceremonies have always been open to Anglos, but that may change if too many outsiders start showing up."

"What else?" Julia asked.

"About my uncles?"

"Yes."

"They're very smart. I'll tell you this story. For many years the Indian Agency had been trying to force the Hopis to farm in a certain way and to wear Anglo clothes and give up their ceremonies and send Hopi children away to white schools, but some Hopis didn't want any part of it. They didn't even want to send their children to the school in Keams Canyon. Back in 1894 the Indian agent told the army to arrest nineteen Hopi leaders from Oraibi, over on Third Mesa. They were sent to Alcatraz prison. You know about this?"

"Some," Julia said.

"They were locked up there for eight months, until they said they would do what the government wanted. But that wasn't enough. The Indian

Agency had its sights trained on Oraibi. Oraibi would be made an example. Before long, family was pitted against family."

Julia remembered well this part of the story: Eventually, the Hopis who were willing to do what the government wanted were labeled "Friendlies," and the traditional people, "Hostiles." In September 1906 Oraibi was so severely split that the Hostiles were forced from the village and left to establish Hotevilla, over near Tuba City.

"My uncles have had run-ins with the Indian Agency, too, but they find ways to avoid fights they know they can't win. They tell the Indian agents what the agents want to hear and sign the papers the agents want them to sign, and then they go about their business as they see fit."

"You admire them," she said.

"There's much to admire, but we don't see eye-to-eye about everything."

"Such as?"

"Oh, that's another story." Yazzie rose and fussed about the campsite.

When he sat down again, his legs crossed in front of him and his hands on his knees, Julia said, "You never mention your wife or sons." She knew she had no right to ask and so had never done so before, but now, here, she no longer felt as constrained as she did at Many Springs, where too many losses and awkwardnesses marked their common history.

"I don't talk about them with people who didn't know them. And most people who knew my wife still follow the old ways, so I don't talk with them either."

"I see." She could have let the subject drop but felt the need to say something further, to somehow explain that her curiosity wasn't idle. "I'm not really asking about them," she said, "I'm asking about you." This drew nothing from him, so she tried, "How did you meet your wife?"

He remained silent for so long that she truly thought she'd offended him. Then he said:

"I once spent some months on Second Mesa, and sometimes I went with my uncles to Moenkopi, and that's where I met her."

"But you didn't go to live with her family afterwards."

"No. She had older married sisters, and the family's land had already been divided three times. And she understood that there was only me to look after my mother and sister."

"Her family didn't object?"

"They figured that the grazing rights to Many Springs Canyon would pass to her daughters. That would have been a good thing for them."

"Your wife and mother got along?"

"Well enough." He smiled crookedly. "Would you have gotten along, living in the same house as your husband's mother?"

"Well, since my husband was—is—an orphan, the possibility never arose." She stretched her palms closer to the fire to warm them. "I guess I've fallen into the habit of referring to Will in the past tense. 'Was.' "

"Hunh."

"Why haven't you taken another wife?"

"I had offers."

"Did you, now?" Julia said.

"How did you meet your husband?" Yazzie asked her.

"He joined my father's congregation."

"So he was religious?"

Julia laughed. "No, he thought it was a way to enter polite society. To get ahead."

"And you knew this about him?"

"I did."

"I thought you would move back East."

"After he left? No, I was too stubborn. Too prideful." After a while she added, "It was a bad time. For both of us, you and me." Worse for him: his boys.

Yazzie said, "I was lucky."

"Because you survived the diphtheria?"

"Aoo'." Then he said, "When I was going to the boarding school in Fort Defiance, I knew more than one Navajo who died from one sickness or another. But I learned that it wasn't just Navajos who died like that. It was Mexicans and Hopis and Anglos, too. I saw that sickness doesn't care who or what you are. It just comes and makes its claim."

He paused and she waited for him to go on.

"Why did you break the window?" Yazzie asked.

She brushed a loose strand of her hair back behind an ear. "I didn't know what else to do. Your boys—" she broke off. "I had no idea what you did or didn't believe. I told Will to smash the window and to do it as loudly as he could so you could hear. It was . . . an acknowledgement."

The crackling of the fire punctuated their silence.

"I don't understand how people can go on sometimes," Julia said.

"Sometimes you need to let life decide for you. This is how I see it now."

"And afterward you and Johanna went to a singer?"

"Aoo'."

"And did you find anything like"—she hesitated before using the only Navajo word that might express what she meant—"*hózhǫ*?"

He shook his head. "This isn't something that's meant to be talked about with Anglos."

"I know," she sighed.

"But I'll talk with you because we're here in this sacred place together. But I won't talk about it with your friends."

She wanted to say that they were his friends as well, but instead she simply said, "All right."

"Some Anglos seem to think they understand, but they don't. They say *hózhǫ* means balance, but it doesn't. Balance puts you at the center of things. That isn't *hózhǫ*. Neither is harmony. That's another wrong word Anglos like to use. Harmony is a soft word. It ignores how everything is always moving between and into and around dangers." He paused and stirred up the coals with a stick. "We've been born into Dinétah. There's no place to stand apart. Even if we move beyond the sacred mountains, we're still part of everything Dinétah means, even the bad." He looked up at her. "When I tell you this, I speak only for myself."

"I understand," she said.

"We try to move toward understanding, and if we get there in old age, in our last moments, that's all there is to achieve in life and we can be grateful. This is what *są'ah naagháí bik'eh hózhǫ* means."

"But you still have to live, day to day," Julia said. "You can't think about these matters all the time. There has to be room for something else. To just keep going."

"When Harry Whitaker was putting in his tube, I saw you."

"Oh. Well." Julia laughed with embarrassment. "I had you by the throat. You didn't have much choice." She knew that wasn't what he meant. She remembered so clearly.

"Your chin and lips and your nose."

"Oh God," she said. "My nose." She spread a hand across the bottom half of her face.

"*'Áchįįh.*" Nose. "*'Áchįįshtah ch'íish.*" Septum. "*'Áchįįshła.*" Tip of nose. His finger tapped his own.

"All that?"

"And fear."

"Of course fear! I thought you were going to *die*, Clement."

"Fear of more than that."

"You saw all that in a minute?"

"It felt longer."

She laughed sharply. "It certainly did."

"And what did *you* see?"

She wasn't sure what she could say. Dark brown irises surrounding deep blackness. "That you're pitiless."

"Hunh."

"I'm not going to make a fool of myself by sitting here and listing your better qualities."

"It's good to know you think I have some."

"When we were at the Home Dance on Second Mesa and your Uncle Gladstone was enjoying himself at my expense, I think that's the first time I ever saw you laugh out loud."

He shrugged with one shoulder. "You foxed him at his own game. It was very funny."

"Yes, I suppose it was." She straightened the skirt over her knees.

"I enjoyed that moment very much."

Caught by a momentary shift in the breeze, the smoke from the fire floated toward her, and she used that as an excuse to wipe her eyes.

"Do you really think that I'm pitiless?" Yazzie asked. He stirred the coals again and sparks sprayed into the air and died away.

"I don't know. You can certainly *seem* pitiless. And you keep too many secrets. Much of the time, I have no idea what you're thinking."

"I have only three secrets that matter."

"To you," Julia said.

"To me."

Her face was hot from the fire, but the rest of her was chilled. She didn't know what she felt or thought, heart or brain. "Does *anyone* know your secrets?" she asked. "Your uncles? Tim Be'ak'idii?"

"The Old Man knows everything."

She took off her boots and lay down on her bed roll, covering herself with her single blanket. "I'm cold."

He watched her from across the fire.

"Come lie down with me, Clement."

"What then?"

"I don't know." She hadn't the slightest doubt that he wanted her.

"After my wife . . . I've been with other women."

"Should I act surprised?" Julia said.

"With a couple of them, their husbands were away. That's just how it was."

"I see." And she too was still a married woman; a married white woman, here in the heart of the reservation, with a Navajo.

"There are already rumors," he said.

This stopped her short, but then she said: "You have to promise me that no matter what gets said or who says it, you won't defend me. By word or action. You don't have to lie—just don't say anything. I don't care who it is, whether it's a hateful Anglo who can't stomach the thought, or a Navajo stumbling out of a bar in Gallup. I couldn't bear it if you ended up in serious trouble because of me. You have to give me your word."

He hadn't moved. "Are you still cold?" he asked.

She shook her head. "That's not good enough."

"I give you my word," he said.

Late the next day, having broken camp at sunrise, they were approaching Blue Hawk Lake from the west, but they stopped and set up camp before reaching it. They'd come a very long way, and Julia was tired. More than that, they wanted to be alone for one more night and didn't want to encounter Tim Be'ak'idii.

"Have you ever thought about leaving here?" Julia asked as they lay together.

"Once, years ago, when I was staying at Hopi that time."

"Aren't there other places or things you'd like to see?"

He thought about this. "An ocean. And one of those big ships, the ones with many sails."

"A clipper ship?"

"Aoo'."

"There aren't that many left," Julia said. "Anything else?"

"A big city. I'd like to see how that many people live together."

"Largely by ignoring each other as much as possible," she said.

"What about you?"

"I suppose I'd like to see Paris, France, and the canals of Venice in Italy." She laughed. "I'm being very unoriginal, even for a bilagáana."

They lingered in the morning, but well before noon the lake came into view through the trees.

"There's something I have to do," Yazzie said. "Will you be all right going the rest of the way alone?"

"Of course. But you can't tell me where you're going?"

He shook his head. "It has nothing to do with you."

Julia smiled. "Are you sure? There isn't a woman that you have to explain yourself to?"

"I won't be speaking to any woman."

"Then you have my permission," she said with feigned hauteur. "How long will you be gone?"

"No longer than usual."

"Ah. Of course." She'd forgotten the calendar. It was August. One of his three secrets.

He turned his brown and sidled closer, and she took off her broad-brimmed hat and they kissed. He put one hand behind her head, entwining his fingers in her hair, and pulled her mouth tighter against his. And then he said, "I shouldn't be doing this."

"Perhaps not. But then again, perhaps you should." She kissed him again. "Who's to say, except us?" She watched him ride around the rim of the lake, to the north, and when he was out of sight in the trees, she turned her horse eastward.

THEY WENT ON ABOUT their business, trying to behave in the presence of Carmelita and Tom Gorman—especially Carmelita and Tom—as if nothing had changed. Julia knew the artifice was self-defeating, but Carmelita said nothing. Tom didn't appear to notice.

Pete, in his usual fashion, came and went; Harry and Tóya visited one weekend while Pete was there, and the conversation among the friends was as robust as ever even though Tóya, for some reason, was in a foul mood and refused to speak anything but Navajo. No one paid her any mind, and Harry and Julia took turns translating, as needed, for Pete's benefit. Johanna Yazzie, her usual placid self, occupied her favored place. Clement Yazzie, seemingly absorbed by repairing a harness, sat at his table but didn't participate in the chatter.

Julia demanded nothing else of the Navajo. She didn't demand that he be faithful to her, and she didn't promise that she would always welcome him into her room.

Yazzie had been there only twice since their return from Canyon de Chelly, once before her monthly flow began and once soon after it stopped. He hadn't stayed through the night on either occasion. And then he didn't return.

A month passed. It was a Saturday. Carmelita and Tom, having finished their dinner, had left for home. Julia was standing at the sink, scrubbing the last pot, when the kitchen door opened and Yazzie came in. He asked if there was any coffee left. Julia glanced in his direction but immediately turned her eyes, if not her attention, back to the pot. She told him she thought there might be a cup left but that it was sure to be cold and that he'd have to move it to a cook lid to warm it up.

Half a minute went by before she turned and looked at him more steadily. He still stood by the door. He hadn't taken off his hat or his coat. "What do you want, Clement?"

"I want to give you this." He was holding a beaded deerskin pouch.

She hadn't seen it before. Julia dried her hands on her apron and walked over to him. "It's very nice." She didn't take it from his outstretched hand. "Why are you giving me a present?" She held her voice steady.

They'd scarcely exchanged a personal word in weeks, and the distress she'd felt had hardened her heart against him. She'd done nothing wrong; she wasn't ashamed. She'd never expected expressions of love. But he'd rejected her without explanation. She could have asked why, she could have demonstrated her hurt and anger and disappointment, but she'd kept silent. Now she didn't know how to talk to him.

"Take it."

The pouch was heavy. As soon as she touched it, felt the hidden weight, she knew what it concealed. "How did you get this?" she asked. She opened the pouch: his mother's squash blossom necklace, the one Johanna had given her, the one Will had taken when he left her.

"I went after him," Yazzie said.

"You didn't."

"I did."

"Why did you do that?"

"I wanted to know if he was gone for good."

"And what happened when you caught up with him?"

"It was night and he was drunk, too drunk to even start a fire. From the last of his whiskey—the rotgut he sold on the edge of the reservation."

It hit her hard. How could she not have known? "Will was selling alcohol?" she whispered.

"When you went back East. Just before he left."

To help finance his escape, Julia thought. She'd brought him that low.

"Who else knows?"

"Not many."

"Tom and Carmelita?"

"Yes. But he was clever. He brought along a Gallup Navajo to do the selling."

"And what about this?" She ran her fingers over the turquoise settings.

"I knew he took it."

"How?" She looked up at him.

"He cleaned out the pawn case. He wouldn't have left something valuable behind."

"Did you threaten him?"

"I lit a fire and made some coffee. Then I searched his bags."

"He let you?"

"He couldn't have stopped me."

"What did you say to him?"

"I waited until he was sober. Then I told him that if he ever came within two days of Many Springs Canyon again, I'd hear about it, and I'd meet him on the road, and we'd have another talk."

Julia sighed. "Poor Will."

"Hunh." Julia read the scorn in Yazzie's eyes.

"He isn't evil. He just made bad decisions—marrying me, for one."

"You were the foolish one," Yazzie said.

She'd said the same to herself many times, but it still felt like a slap in the face. Her cheeks reddened. "And what would you have done if he'd come back?"

"I didn't think about it."

Because Yazzie knew Will wouldn't. She spread the necklace in its fullest arc, wider than her hand, two naja crescents at the bottom. How much had it been worth to Will? Not as much as to her.

Yazzie said, "I was going to hide it in your bags when you left for good."

Because sooner or later all bilagáanas left. "But I didn't leave."

"No."

She turned her back to him. "Why have you stayed away from me for so long?"

"It just seemed . . ."

"Best?" She wanted him to feel how much hurt that one word held.

"I want you to come up into the mountains with me tomorrow. It's Sunday. Sister will look after the animals. I'll have you back on Monday morning."

He leaned toward her and she felt his lips at the side of her neck, just where the fine hairs curled above the collar of her dress. She tilted her head so that he would kiss the other side.

Sunday night they camped at an overlook, above a narrow, blind canyon rimmed at one end by aspens. Yazzie called it the Place in the Mountains That the Aspens Watch Over. Down below, a small stream flowed eastward among gambrel oaks. They lay quietly in the bed roll, nothing above them but stars, and Julia decided the time had come.

"Clement," she said, "you need to tell me about that scar."

CHAPTER THIRTEEN: Yazzie (The Past)

One afternoon in 1889 Clement Yazzie's mother, returning from checking on the sheep up near the tree line, saw Joe Etsitty leaving the hogan. Etsitty saw her, too, and pointed his rifle at her. He sat looking at her from the back of his black gelding for the longest time, she told her son, but he didn't shoot.

Yazzie's mother had sold some churro sheep to Etsitty's brother Frank the previous year, and Joe Etsitty had come to help herd them back to Frank's ranch near Navajo Mountain, in the far northwest of the reservation, where Frank, a decent man, wanted to improve his herd. The Etsitty brothers spent only the one night at Many Springs, but Joe, alone, returned one other time a few months later. Etsitty had clearly been drinking. He said he was hunting and had run out of cartridges for his .44 Winchester; he was hoping to run into Sam McElroy, who sometimes raised his tent in Many Springs Canyon and traded foodstuffs and other goods to the Navajo for jewelry, wool, weavings. But since McElroy wasn't there, he thought he'd see if Yazzie had any shells he could spare. Yazzie only had ammunition for his old converted, single-shot .52 Sharp's carbine. (Yazzie remembered now that Johanna had been in the corral, riding her new horse.) Contrary to custom, he didn't invite Etsitty to share a meal, and Etsitty rode away.

Yazzie hadn't seen him again until the day they passed on the road just south of Naschitti. They didn't exchange greetings, and Yazzie continued on into Gallup to pick up supplies. Etsitty continued north. That was the day.

Two days later, Yazzie returned home and his mother told him. His sister's injuries demanded attention; this was something no singer could heal. They bundled Johanna up and took her to Ft. Defiance. The visiting Anglo doctor was short, black-bearded, wearing a crisp white coat and smoking a cigar. Yazzie carried his sister into the examining room. He told the doctor that his mother would stay in the room but that she didn't speak English. His sister didn't speak at all. Yazzie would be outside to answer his questions. A few minutes later the doctor emerged from the examining room.

"You say you're her brother," the doctor said. He stood eye-to-eye in front of Yazzie with his legs spread, his arms folded across his barrel chest.

"Aoo'."

"And she hasn't said anything since this happened?"

"Since birth."

"Uh-huh. Since birth." The doctor nodded. Yazzie had no idea what that had to do with his sister's injuries, but he had a good idea what the doctor was thinking. He'd seen that silent nod, along with that expression, before.

"I don't suppose you know who did this to her?" the doctor asked. Yazzie considered whether to answer, but before he could the doctor went on, "Is she pledged in marriage to anyone, maybe a young buck who decided he couldn't wait?"

"My sister is only ten years old," Yazzie said, struggling to keep his outrage in check. "Do you see any sign of womanhood?"

The doctor moved his hands to his hips. "Just last week I saw a twelve-year-old who was five months along. I've been treating you people for a long time in Oklahoma and before that in the Dakotas. Ever since the wars. I've seen just about everything there is to see."

An army doctor, Yazzie thought.

"When I'm done I'll have my nurse instruct you about what to do." He returned to the examining room.

It didn't take long. The doctor didn't say another word to Yazzie, just strode down the hall, his coattails flying. A minute later the nurse opened the door and invited Yazzie in. His mother was standing beside Johanna, who was curled on a table, her hair hanging over her downturned face. The nurse said, "I don't speak Navajo well enough to instruct your mother about how to care for the wounds, so I'll have to tell you what to do." Her voice was patient, kind.

"No," Yazzie said. "She's my sister. Isn't there someone here who can translate what you say for my mother?"

"Let me see if I can find someone," the nurse said.

"A woman," Yazzie said.

"Of course."

When they left Ft. Defiance, Yazzie vowed to himself that if he could help it, he would never have anything more to do with Anglo doctors.

Several weeks later, to complete the healing a hataałii performed a sing for his sister.

***

Yazzie knew the Anglo authorities would do nothing. One morning he made up his mind. His little sister was sitting on a woven rug spread on the dirt floor of the hogan. Their mother was binding Johanna's long, straight, black hair in a tsiiyéél, the figure-eight bun tied in the middle with a strip of white cotton cloth. Her face was placid, with a vacancy in her eyes that often left him wondering what she was thinking. Acid rose in his gorge again at the thought of what had been done to her.

Yazzie started in Gallup, visiting the usual haunts—the saloons north of the railroad tracks, the pawn shops, the flop houses. But no one had seen Joe Etsitty recently. He learned, however, that Etsitty had been working for a time, a couple of months back, at a Gallup lumber yard but had been fired for showing up drunk. A mutual acquaintance, Teddy Browneyes, told Yazzie that Etsitty had said he was going back to Navajo Mountain.

"He said it would be a cold day in hell before Gallup saw his face again," Browneyes told Yazzie. "So I guess you'll have to head to Navajo Mountain if you really need to see him."

"I guess I will," Yazzie said.

Browneyes frowned and scratched his cheek. "I don't know what this is about, but Joe Etsitty can be a mean son of a bitch. I saw him try to gouge out a man's eye with a spoon in a fight over a dish of mutton stew. They were both drinking at the time, but still . . ." His voice trailed off.

Yazzie thanked him for the information.

"Whatever it is, it might be better to just let it go."

"I can't do that," Yazzie said.

He didn't tell his mother he was going to Navajo Mountain until the night before he left. He knew she would try to convince him to stay, but she couldn't dissuade him and finally she gave up except to say, "Son, stop and see your father's brothers. Ask their advice."

To appease her, he said he would—maybe she thought his uncles would talk some sense into him—but passing through the Hopi Reservation would be longer than the route he planned to take around Beautiful Mountain to Lukachukai and Tsegi, and he had no intention of visiting Second Mesa. He barely knew his uncles. His father had long since moved away, and the last Yazzie had heard, was married to a mestizo and living across the border in Sonora.

The ride was long and took him farther from home than he'd ever gone, and much of it was through a deserted landscape of sand, sandstone cliffs, and scrub. He had days to reconsider what he was doing, possibly risking his life to confront Joe Etsitty. And what then? Etsitty would deny everything.

He was covered in reddish brown dust much of the time and sometimes rode with a kerchief across his mouth and nostrils. For long stretches even the mesquite and greasewood looked half dead, and in the midday sun he would see nothing moving across the landscape except an occasional scrawny coyote or, far overhead, a spectral eagle or several vultures, wings spread to catch the updraft, circling, circling.

The closer he got to Navajo Mountain, which steadily rose along the horizon, the clearer it became to him that he needed to bring Joe Etsitty before his tribal elders. If they knew Etsitty, they would know what he was capable of when drunk. Maybe they would order Etsitty to pay some form of restitution. It wouldn't be much. A bag of wool or half a dozen goats for what he had done to a mute girl from the other side of the reservation. But that would be enough. Just to know that others knew. To know that Joe Etsitty would always carry with him the reputation of a man who had beaten and raped a child.

Yazzie rode on, resolved. It took him six days.

As he neared his destination, desert grasslands cut by arroyos began to dominate the landscape. In the near distance loomed the grey lower reaches and walls of the mountain, capped by a forested dome.

Early on the last morning he stopped at an isolated outfit. There wasn't much to it: the traditional mud-plastered hogan, a small corral that held only one ancient horse, a well and trough, an outhouse, and, settled beneath the limbs of a large cottonwood, an open-air summer hogan in which an old woman, so stooped that her wrinkled face paralleled the ground, sat before her vertical loom, weaving a nondescript blanket. He introduced himself and asked where he might find Joe Etsitty. The old woman, waving her arm, told him to continue on toward the mountain until he reached a line of cottonwoods beside a wash. If he followed the wash north, he would come to the Etsitty place. She told him to help himself to their well water; she said it was hard for her to move around much these days or she would be more hospitable, and besides, she was comfortable where she was, at her loom in the shade. Yazzie emptied several ladles of well water and splashed a little on his face to wash the dust away. He couldn't miss the Etsitty place, the old woman continued, because they were fencing an area with barbed wire. She told him this with considerable disdain. Beyond, he would see a windmill and the Etsitty house—not a hogan, but an Anglo house with glass windows. He could tell she wanted to know what business he had with the Etsittys, but he didn't volunteer any information. He thanked her for her kindness.

When he reached the cottonwoods and the wash, he took out his carbine, chambered a round, put several other shells in a shirt pocket, and headed north with the gun balanced across his saddle.

Yazzie reached the barbed wire fence and turned eastward. On the other side of the fence he saw a white horse grazing on scrub grass. Near a corner fence post he saw a man bent over something on the ground, his hat pushed back from his forehead. Yazzie wasn't sure it was Joe Etsitty until the man looked up to see who was approaching.

Etsitty watched Yazzie draw closer for a minute and then returned to his task. He was wielding a fancy hunting knife, one with an elk horn handle, cutting the haunches from a sheep that, judging from its freshly torn throat, appeared to have been killed by coyotes just before they were chased off. Fencing tools and bales of wire lay nearby; bare posts continued on, northward.

"Now that you're here," Etsitty said to Yazzie, who had halted his horse at the corner post, "what do you plan to do?" When Yazzie didn't answer, Etsitty wiped a sleeve across his sweaty forehead. "Maybe you'd just better lift that carbine and pull the trigger, because whatever else you've got in mind, it ain't going to happen."

"I expect you to tell your brother and your headman what you did to my sister," Yazzie said. "After that, I'll leave it up to them."

Etsitty continued working on the dead sheep. "Frank and his family aren't here, which is a good thing for you, because if Frank saw you sitting there with a gun pointed in my direction, he'd probably take careful aim and drop you right out of that saddle." Etsitty straightened up and sighed. He turned to face Yazzie, wiping his knife on a handful of dried grass. He was solidly built, strong, but with a gaunt face—thin lips, wispy mustache, sunken cheeks, a nose that had been broken more than once. "You should know it was the liquor. Even after I stop drinking, it takes a week or two to get the poison out of my system so that I can think straight." He wiped a bloody hand on his blue jeans and pulled a pouch of chewing tobacco from a rear pocket. Yazzie watched him extract a clump and pack it between cheek and gum.

"Now you listen to me," Etsitty said. "I haven't had a drink since I got back here, close to a month ago. And I'm staying here, because there isn't a bottle within fifty miles. I won't have you stirring up trouble for me. You see that horse over there? It's a good one. Take it. It's yours. Take it and be on your way."

"I'll take it," Yazzie said, "if that's what your headman says I should do."

Etsitty spoke slowly, poking the tobacco with his tongue. "I'm asking you to take my horse and go home. Your sister's going to need you, because there isn't any man I know of who would take a dummy off your hands. That's just the way it is. Unless maybe you've got some ugly Hopi half-cousin who's desperate." Etsitty stroked his mustache with one hand. In the other, his left, he kept rotating the hunting knife with its six-inch blade, as if testing its balance. A cloud of flies buzzed around the half-butchered sheep.

"I expect your headman will believe me when I tell him what you did, even if you lie."

Etsitty held the hunting knife steady now. "I won't have to lie, because we won't be going to see him." He brought his hat brim down low to his eyebrows, cutting the sun's glare. "Before you do anything, think about this. Some men are made for the fight, Yazzie, and some aren't. The fight's got to be in your nature." He released a stream of brown spittle.

Yazzie was surveying the landscape; there didn't seem to be anyone else around.

"You know how you tell if you're made for the fight?" Etsitty said. "The fight takes over. You find yourself doing whatever you need to. You don't stop. Are you made for that, Yazzie?"

Yazzie said nothing. Etsitty wasn't wearing a sidearm.

"I'm guessing that you're not, or you probably would've done something by now. Why don't you use that carbine or put it away? Don't sit there holding it like your cock."

Yazzie still said nothing. Except for the knife in Etsitty's left hand, he didn't see any other weapons.

"Well then, if you're going to play dummy like your sister, get down off that goddamn horse and let's get this over with." Etsitty turned his back and moved away. He laid his knife flat across the top of a fence post and stripped off his sweaty shirt. The muscles in his back and upper arms rippled. He folded the sleeves inside, and then wrapped the shirt around his right arm and the back of his hand.

Clement Yazzie figured he had three options. He could turn his horse and ride away. He could point the carbine and pull the trigger. He could dismount and face Joe Etsitty.

It wouldn't be a fair fight. He and Etsitty were about the same height, but Etsitty had him by at least twenty pounds. Maybe he was faster than Etsitty, and he was at least ten years younger, but youth wasn't an advantage because it would be a short fight. He didn't have any doubts about that.

He knew how to hold a knife. Well, he thought he did. He'd taught himself back when he was in the agency school in Fort Defiance and had to learn to defend himself against older boys who baited him about being half Hopi. One time he nicked a boy with the tip of a paring knife he'd stolen from the kitchen, but he never intended to do serious harm. Back then, he'd needed to make an impression. This would be different.

Yazzie dismounted. Etsitty turned and watched him pull his trail jacket and a camping knife, still in its deerskin sheath, from his saddle pack.

Yazzie slapped his horse's flank to make him move away, and then he leaned his Sharps, butt end down, against the fence. He followed Etsitty's example and wrapped the coat around his left arm. All the while he was watching Etsitty from the corner of his eye. Etsitty was smiling, confident. And why shouldn't he be? He was going to teach Yazzie a lesson. Yazzie pulled his knife from its sheath. It wasn't nearly as handsome as Etsitty's, and the blade was shorter.

He figured Etsitty would expect him to hold back, try and defend himself by keeping his distance and swatting at Etsitty's knife hand with his protected arm. Etsitty would toy with him for a while, enjoying himself.

So, Yazzie figured, he would have to surprise him. Strike first. Aim for Etsitty's knife hand, slash him badly enough to make him drop the knife. And if Etsitty then tried to grapple him . . . He'd have to be ready to thrust his blade beneath Etsitty's ribs or under his chin or into an eye, wherever an opening appeared, because Etsitty would certainly try to kill him.

Etsitty spit out the wad of tobacco and began moving toward him, from side to side but always working his knife hand closer. "Is it sharp?" he asked, nodding toward Yazzie's knife. "It better be sharp, Yazzie."

Yazzie tried to ignore everything Etsitty said; the words were intended to distract him. He looked straight at Etsitty and began circling, but his focus was on the knife with the elk horn grip.

"Remember what I said, Yazzie. There's still time, but if we start this and the fight takes over, I'll go to the end. You'll be hurt bad or else you'll be dead. Are you ready for—"

Yazzie had been waiting for one gesture, for Etsitty to turn his left hand to the side, exposing the veins in his wrist, and when he finally did Yazzie lunged, the edge of his blade aiming toward that wrist, but Etsitty, although caught by surprise, was quick enough to twist away and deflect Yazzie's knife upward with the back of his protected hand. But he didn't come away unscathed. The tip of Yazzie's knife caught his bare inner arm at the triceps and traced an arc up to the biceps. Yazzie quickly retreated.

The gash didn't even slow Etsitty down. His jaw set, he came on, and backed Yazzie into the barbed wire fence. Then it was over.

Yazzie lay on the ground, his face to the fence. Etsitty had come in under his right arm, and the hunting knife dug into Yazzie's lowest rib. From there Etsitty could've taken the knife point down and under, deep into the liver, but he hadn't. Instead, he'd brought the knife up, bumping past rib after rib, almost to Yazzie's armpit.

Yazzie's right hand was empty. He'd dropped his knife.

There was something hard under his left cheek, uncomfortable, between his cheek and the ground. He lifted his head slightly and looked down: the stock of his carbine. He'd fallen on his gun. He wondered if Etsitty had noticed. He lay his head back down.

He was lying on his left arm, but he managed to wiggle his hand and forearm loose. He could feel steel with his fingers, and he began working at the barrel, positioning it until he could touch the breech and trigger guard. When he found the hammer, he cocked it, coughing to cover the loud click, and he slid his thumb over the trigger.

He heard Etsitty moving around, cursing to himself.

Yazzie rolled part ways onto his back, just enough so he could turn his head. He held his right arm tight to his side. Blood had already soaked through his slit shirt and sleeve. He tried to lift his right arm, but he could feel the movement opening the wound wider and he stopped. He looked up. Etsitty was pacing back and forth near the sheep carcass. He had unwrapped his shirt from his right arm and was now trying to tie it around the gash Yazzie's knife had made in his upper left arm. He wasn't holding his knife. He had stuck it into the ground, handle up.

Etsitty noticed that Yazzie was watching him. "So who do you want to see now—the headman or your mama?" Etsitty asked.

Yazzie wasn't sure how quickly he could raise, aim, and shoot. He wanted Etsitty's attention elsewhere.

"That's not good for your knife," Yazzie said. "It'll dull the blade."

Etsitty laughed. "You're not a bad fellow, Yazzie. That knife cut you up pretty good and you can still make a joke about it." He was still fumbling with the bandage.

Yazzie could feel himself getting light-headed; he could picture the blood draining from his head and emptying from the wound in his side. It didn't hurt that much. He needed to stay alert. He sank his teeth into his lower lip.

"Are you a man of your word, Yazzie? I think you probably are, so if you swear to me on your sister's bare cunt that you'll leave here and never come back, maybe I'll help you onto your horse and point you toward a hogan where you can get sewn up." He couldn't get the bandage tight, and it angered him. He cursed and threw it aside. "Or maybe I'll let you lay there and watch me finish butchering this sheep. What d'you say, Yazzie?"

"There's something wrong with your horse," Yazzie said.

Without thinking, Etsitty looked toward where his horse was grazing. Only for a second. He quickly turned back and simultaneously reached for his knife, but by then Yazzie had lifted the carbine with his left hand, pointed, and pulled the trigger with his thumb. The shot was poorly aimed, and the bullet only took a divot out of Etsitty's right shoulder. The blood spurted and Etsitty yelled in pain but didn't go down until, trying to regain his balance, he stepped backward and slipped in the sheep entrails.

Yazzie had already grabbed the fore stock with his right hand, ignoring the pain that tore the length of his ribcage. He yanked the trigger guard down with his left, lowering the breech block and exposing the empty cartridge in the chamber. Fumbling, he extracted it, tossed it aside, reached into his shirt pocket for another cartridge. From the corner of his eye he watched Joe Etsitty scramble to his knees and begin crawling to the upright knife. Yazzie clumsily seated the new cartridge and lifted the trigger guard into place, closing the chamber.

"Don't," Yazzie said, cocking the hammer.

"You're dead," Etsitty said, spittle on his lips. He'd reached the knife and was lifting one arm to throw it when Yazzie fired. The bullet caught Etsitty on the right side of his neck, just below the chin, and his arms and legs immediately collapsed beneath him.

Yazzie didn't bother reloading. He watched Etsitty's blood mingle with the sheep's, the stain spreading farther across the sand. Etsitty twitched a few times, but then he lay still and the flies began droning in.

The old bent woman's name was Dólii Tsosie. She and her husband lived alone with two mangy black and white dogs and a small herd of sheep. She didn't like the Etsittys, and especially not the one who was no longer here (she wouldn't speak his name), good riddance. He'd never passed up an opportunity to torment her about her deformity or speculate about the difficulties it had to cause old man Tsosie when he tried to perform his husbandly duties. Old Man Tsosie, his eyes so cloudy that he had to be almost blind, was more noncommittal than his wife about the Etsittys; they were his neighbors and he figured he needed to get along with them. Frank Etsitty was all right, just as long as he kept his new Gáamalii beliefs to himself. That's why Frank and his family—wife, two sons, two daughters—were away. They'd gone up to Bluff, Utah, where Frank and his wife were getting baptized at the Mormon mission.

"I don't like those Gáamalii," Dólii muttered in Navajo. (Neither of the Tsosies spoke a word of English.) "They smile and talk about their God all the time and then they try to bribe people into giving up their children."

"That's true," Old Man Tsosie agreed. "And they use their money to buy up the best land and then they dam the water so all the corn fields downstream wither away."

Yazzie heard all this over the course of many days. His fever jumbled everything in his head.

He'd left Joe Etsitty's body where it was. Somehow, holding his wound closed as best he could by wrapping his right arm along the curve of his ribs, he'd managed to mount his horse, whose right flank was a sticky, red, encrusted mess by the time he made it back to the Tsosie place. Dólii had sewed him up as best she could.

He slept and he sweated and his side burned ferociously, sending out embers that caught in his stomach and his chest and made him release his bowels where he lay. Dólii Tsosie never said an unkind word about it.

He'd left a note at the Etsitty place, stuck between a fence post and the barbed wire. He'd written it before leaving Many Springs Canyon. *My name is Clement Yazzie. I am of the Bitter Water Clan. My father is Ahote Katsi of the Shaking Aspen Clan from Second Mesa. I live in Many Springs Canyon. Tell my mother what hapened.* It had taken him a long time to write it out; he could read English well enough, but writing it had never taken hold. Even if he'd had a pencil with him, he couldn't have added anything after killing Joe Etsitty. Leaving his name was enough. Whoever wanted to, could find him.

He remembered a half-circle of men standing above where he lay in the Tsosies' hogan.

Dólii Tsosie would wash him down. He couldn't separate his own stink from that of the herbal poultices she bound to his wounded side. She made him drink Navajo tea and fed him corn mush and the thin broth and thick cream of mutton stew. Old Man Tsosie had slaughtered one of their sheep so she could make it.

When Yazzie was finally able to stand and, with Old Man Tsosie's help, walk outside and sit in the shade of their summer hogan, beneath the interlaced pinyon branches, he asked why they had taken him in.

"Everyone knows what brought you here," Old Man Tsosie said.

"How?"

"I found the note that you left on the fence. I took it to our headman, Long Tooth, and he knew someone who could read it. They decided it was written by someone who thought he might not be returning home, so they asked around. The person you did away with couldn't keep his mouth shut when he was drinking. He talked all the way from Teec Nos Pas until his liquor ran out."

"Is Frank Etsitty back?" Yazzie asked. "I should go speak to him."

"That wouldn't be smart," Tsosie said, waving off the idea with a gnarled hand. Even when he was sitting, the top of his head barely came up to Yazzie's chin. "Family is family. He heard on the way back from Bluff. It's a good thing you were so cut up, or he would have killed you outright."

"He was here?"

"Aoo'. He came with Long Tooth and an uncle and they talked about what to do with you. They knew you weren't going anywhere soon. The headman decided he would wait to see if you lived, and if you did, then he would speak with you."

Even sitting, Yazzie was devastatingly tired. He wasn't healing very well. Down low, where the knife had first gone in and scraped a rib, pus still oozed from between Dólii's awkward stitches, and he couldn't extend his arm without feeling the reknitting tissues pulling apart.

"I need to let my family know where I am."

"This is true," Tsosie said. "A mother needs to know these things."

"Do you have children?"

"Two sons. One lives in Winslow and the other near Klagetoh, where we lived before we came here to escape the soldiers. That was at the time of the Long Walk. My woman never would have survived the walk." His eyes were closed and his head nodded, as if reconfirming to himself that he had made the right decision. When he opened his eyes again he said, "And we have grandchildren and many nieces and nephews scattered around."

"None near here?"

"No."

"Why do you stay?"

"Stubbornness." He chuckled.

Yazzie lay down on his left side, cushioning his head with his arm. "When will the headman come back?"

"I don't know. When he's ready. Soon." He paused, pursing his deeply lined lips. "I wouldn't think about leaving before then. I don't think you'd get very far. Besides, they took your horse."

Old Man Tsosie sat and watched him for a while. Sunlight worked its way through the lattice of cut branches above them. Yazzie's face lay in shade; his neck and shoulder, in bright sunlight. As the angle of the sun became steeper, Tsosie rose, taking with him the blanket he'd been sitting on, which he draped over a cross pole so that Yazzie's face would remain shaded.

Yazzie drifted into sleep.

The headman came back three days later, accompanied by another headman and the Etsitty uncle. They waited in the summer hogan while Old Man Tsosie went to get Yazzie, who managed to walk to them on his own. Speaking in Navajo, they all made their formal introductions—name, "born to" clan, "born for" clan—and then sat down facing Yazzie.

The youngest of the three, Vine Growing Wild, the uncle, sat slightly apart from the headmen, Long Tooth and Hosteen Begay. He sat with his arms folded across his chest and his eyes focused unwaveringly on Yazzie, who assumed that nothing he could say would sway the man's interpretation of Joe Etsitty's death. He was a maternal uncle, which made Joe Etsitty like a son.

The oldest of the three men, Long Tooth, was wearing his hair bound in a tsiiyééł; an ornate silver and turquoise necklace hung to the middle of his chest, and he sported an equally impressive concho belt. In old age his name had become a misnomer; he appeared to be toothless. He said, "We have questions for you."

"I intended to come to you," Yazzie said.

Vine Growing Wild grunted, dismissing Yazzie's assertion.

"So we heard," Long Tooth said, pointing with his lips toward Old Man Tsosie, who was sitting some distance behind Yazzie. "Many people are angry."

"I understand."

"Tell us about your sister."

"We're not here to talk about his sister," Vine Growing Wild said. "We're here to discuss my son."

Long Tooth rocked back and forth slightly. But then he nodded to Yazzie.

"My sister is ten. She's not yet a woman. She's also mute."

The third man, Hosteen Begay, leaned forward. He too was wearing his graying hair rolled in traditional fashion, and a large mottled green turquoise pendant lay against his maroon velveteen shirt. He also wore leather leggings and moccasins trimmed with beads. His posture, as he sat with his legs crossed, was firmly erect.

"Does she have visions?" Hosteen Begay asked.

"No."

"She's simple-minded?" Long Tooth asked.

Vine Growing Wild spat.

Yazzie kept his gaze focused on Long Tooth and Hosteen Begay. "She wakes each morning before dawn and offers her prayers to the rising sun. Just as you do, but silently."

Long Tooth asked, "Did you have a sing for her?"

"We did."

"If she can't speak," Vine Growing Wild said, "how do you know what happened? Did you see any injuries?"

Yazzie turned to face Vine Growing Wild. "Your question shows great disrespect. No Navajo girl would display herself to her brother."

"Enough," Long Tooth said in a neutral tone, but it was clear to all that the comment was directed toward Vine Growing Wild.

"Where is her father?" Long Tooth asked.

"I don't know. He never knew her."

"Did your mother go on the Long Walk?" Hosteen Begay asked.

"Yes."

"She has no brothers?"

"No. She has two sisters. They still live near Cottonwood."

Long Tooth nodded. "We didn't take the Long Walk. We hid out here. The soldiers never found us. There aren't that many of us left, and we follow the old ways." He paused. "But sometimes not. Some leave and fall into bad habits." He was no more specific than that. "You should have come to us first."

Yazzie nodded. Sitting upright this long was very painful, and he could feel the beads of sweat forming on his forehead. "I thought I might be able to convince the man we speak of to come with me."

Vine Growing Wild laughed at Yazzie's explanation. "He refused, so you shot him."

"We talked. He preferred to fight."

"With knives," Long Tooth said.

"Yes."

"You must have cut him first." He pointed to his upper arm.

"Yes."

"He was very good with a knife. You were lucky."

"Yes, I was. Up to a point." There was no need to direct their attention to his ribs.

"Did you think he would kill you?"

Yazzie pondered how best to answer this question. "I didn't have much time to think, but I thought that maybe he already had."

"Are you going to let him talk his way out of this?" Vine Growing Wild said. "Why should you believe anything he says?"

"How did your father and mother meet?" Hosteen Begay, speaking for only the third time, asked.

The question set Yazzie back for a moment. He didn't know its purpose, but he saw no reason not to answer. "My father and several other men were returning from Farmington through Washington Pass. They were stopped by a winter hunting party. It was soon after the People came back from Hwéeldi. My mother's family gave them shelter for a night."

"Why was your father in Farmington?"

Vine Growing Wild threw up his hands and cursed. "What does this have to do with why we're here?"

Hosteen Begay calmly waited for Yazzie to answer his question.

"I was told that he and the other men were meeting a delegation from Washington about creating a Hopi reservation."

"And you believe that?"

"I have no reason not to."

Long Tooth looked at Hosteen Begay. "If they were in Farmington they would have returned home by going around the Chuskas, to the north, not through Washington Pass."

In frustration, Vine Growing Wild scrambled to his feet, threw a fistful of sand in Yazzie's direction, and strode from the summer hogan.

Yazzie brushed the sand from his pants, which were still stained with blood despite Dólii Tsosie's efforts to scrub them clean.

"We will think about what you've told us," Long Tooth said. "When we decide what should be done, we will let you know."

"I understand," Yazzie said. The two headmen rose and he struggled to do likewise. He felt Old Man Tsosie's hand on his elbow, helping him. Long Tooth and Hosteen Begay left the shelter of the summer hogan and, under the yellow-white sun, crossed to the corral fence, where their buckboard was waiting. Yazzie remained in the shade, his eyes focused on Vine Growing Wild, who, leading his horse, was striding back toward the summer hogan. Yazzie waited for him.

Vine Growing Wild stopped a step away from Yazzie. He stood there for a moment, slapping the reins of his horse against his leg. "Know this, Yazzie. If Frank Etsitty hadn't become a white-livered Gáamalii, with his bilagáana house and his bilagáana ways, you wouldn't be standing here now. You'd be buried out there." He tossed his head toward Navajo Mountain. "And one other thing. If the someone we've spoken of had wanted to kill you, this is where his knife would have gone." He drove two fingers of his left hand into Yazzie's belly, just under the first rib.

Yazzie flinched and his breath caught in his throat, but he didn't bend or back up.

"Go away now," Old Man Tsosie said to Vine Growing Wild. "The headmen will settle this."

Long Tooth and Hosteen Begay had been watching the exchange, but now Long Tooth flicked the reins and the buckboard moved forward. Vine Growing Wild mounted his horse and followed.

That afternoon, a thunderstorm, the first of the rainy season, rolled over Navajo Mountain. The large raindrops hit the dry soil around the Tsosie hogan like bullets, sending up fine sprays of dust until everything in sight was soaked and the ground lay covered in a coating of slick red mud. Yazzie stood just inside the doorway of the hogan, inhaling the fresh green scent given off by the scrub junipers and sage brush.

When he awoke the next morning, Old Man Tsosie was elsewhere, and Dólii Tsosie insisted on rebandaging his wound. It was still weeping a yellowish discharge, and he could still feel where Vine Running Wild's fingers had bored in yesterday. Moreover, the lower half of the wound had grown red and hot again.

Dólii, clearly concerned, clucked repeatedly. "When you get where you're going," she said, "someone is going to have to open this and clean it out again. I can't do it now."

"Where am I going?" he asked.

She didn't answer.

When she was finished, they sat and had breakfast together. She'd prepared bread and corn mush and coffee. She added goat milk to the mush, which was still thick enough to eat with their fingers.

Not long after, he heard a wagon pull up outside. It was Old Man Tsosie, and beside him Hosteen Begay. It was the same rig that had transported the headmen the day before. Tsosie's horse was tied behind the wagon, and behind Tsosie's, Yazzie's own, which he hadn't seen in the three weeks since his arrival.

Old Man Tsosie got down, but Hosteen Begay remained in the wagon. "Are you ready to go?" the old man asked.

"Go where?" Yazzie asked.

"Sunshine Springs."

"Why Sunshine Springs?"

"That's where Hosteen Begay is from. And that's where your Hopi uncles will meet us."

Yazzie walked over to the headman. "What's this about my uncles?"

"They've been asking about you."

"How did they know I was here?"

"They got word you might be."

"From who?"

"I don't know."

"Do you know my uncles?"

"We've had dealings in Tuba City." Named after a Hopi who'd converted to Mormonism, Tuba City was one of the few places where Anglos, Hopis, Navajos, and other tribesmen regularly mixed.

"Why is Old Man Tsosie coming with us?"

"Your uncles wish to thank Long Tooth for his help."

And Old Man Tsosie would be returning with whatever constituted their thanks. Yazzie wondered how Hosteen Begay himself was being thanked, but he didn't ask. "What about the Etsittys?"

Hosteen Begay held up his hand. "This matter has been settled."

Old Man Tsosie didn't want to waste any time getting on the road. They had thirty miles of rough trail to traverse. Yazzie saw that his saddle and other gear, including his carbine, were in the back of the buckboard. As they pulled away, Dólii was standing in the doorway of the hogan, bent as ever. She didn't look up as the wagon passed, but then he heard her call after him:

"Clement Yazzie, my son! Don't you ever come back here! Not ever!"

PART III: PARTING

Out of the rolling ocean the crowd came a drop gently to me,
Whispering, *I love you, before long I die,*
I have travel'd a long way merely to look on you to touch you,
For I could not die till I once look'd on you,
For I fear'd I might afterward lose you.

Now we have met, we have look'd, we are safe,
Return in peace to the ocean . . .

—Walt Whitman

CHAPTER FOURTEEN: The High Meadow

Owen wanted to put it out of mind, the arm around the waist and her head tipping to the shoulder, but he couldn't. He felt . . . he didn't know what—not simple jealousy, though jealousy couldn't be denied. A bitterness, not because Yazzie was an Indian, although he couldn't completely deny that, either. A resentment to which he knew he had no right. Yazzie's wife was long dead, and his boys, and Julia's husband, for all she knew, dead as well, or as good as. When he'd witnessed the gesture in the dawn light near Washington Pass, he wasn't even surprised; now, when he released *his* feelings, let them go, and thought about it, he could see a rightness—why shouldn't they?—a momentary rightness that, nevertheless, wouldn't hold.

The four sat as usual in the evenings, Owen, Julia, Yazzie, Johanna, all together as summer broke open. He and Julia continued to discuss the delayed news from the Chicago newspapers, and had taken to reading serialized fiction in the magazines her sister sent, from Maurice Hewlett's *Rest Harrow* in *Scribner's* or William Henry Irwin's *House of Mystery* in *The Saturday Evening Post*, discussing each part and sometimes, when neither Yazzie nor Johanna was there to hear, taking turns reading aloud, particularly when the writing struck them as so dreadful that they felt free to fashion impossibly awful dialects, which inevitably led to unrestrained laughter. But even this mocking sometimes lost its appeal. Too often Owen found himself submerged in silence—which didn't seem to bother Julia at all—brooding over that gesture at the sun's May rising in the mountain pass.

He knew what he needed to do, but he couldn't. Instead, he took himself to Gallup for the better part of a week, riding in with Johnny Gorman on a supply run and staying at a boarding house. One consequence of the comet viewing had been several offers to visit, from the Rodriguezes and the Al Wetherills and even Win Peabody, the undertaker, and he'd decided to take them up on their offers of hospitality, if not for overnight accommodations, which he viewed as too presumptive on his part (though it probably wasn't), but for dinner and an evening's entertainment. All except Peabody knew about his diabetes, so he no longer felt any embarrassed reticence about choosing foods selectively from the dinner table, and he made it clear to his hostess at the boarding house, without excuse, that for breakfast he desired the same thing each day: oatmeal, eggs, and perhaps a bit of bacon or ham, but no toast or flapjacks or biscuits. His request, presented straight-forwardly, didn't even produce a raised eyebrow.

And, he had to say, he enjoyed the visits, especially with Al and Mary Wetherill, and even with Alberto and Matilda Rodriguez, who, as Julia had said, was indeed "quite fine" in her element. He dined two nights at restaurants with Win Peabody, who was treated like royalty by the waitresses, undoubtedly for his good humor as well as for, Owen suspected—he couldn't say for sure, because Peabody insisted on paying for both meals—extremely generous gratuities. On another evening he shared a pot of tea with Peabody, who, each evening when he was resident in Gallup, took a late constitutional that always ended in the lobby of the Harvey House, in a comfortable chair where he could observe any late comings and goings through the train depot. Peabody also extended Owen an open invitation to visit him and his family—his wife Estella, her daughter Estrellita from a first marriage, and their young son Nick—in Zuni, thirty miles south, where, Peabody assured him, he'd be welcomed by one and all. The Wetherills, the Rodriguezes (yes, even Matilda), the voluble Peabody—they were all fine people, he concluded.

Visiting Pete Pietrowski, however, was another matter. Sober at a noontime meal, despite bloodshot eyes and brushed-back hair that needed a good washing, and a face that needed a close shave, by that evening, for dinner, Pete was already listing in the wind and had all he could do to keep his chin out of the soup. He'd recovered enough by the end of the meal—his first solid food that day? Owen wondered—to lead Owen to a saloon on the north side, Obie's Gentlemen's Club, where women and Indians weren't allowed and a seat at the card table cost you a dollar (one drink included). Unfamiliar with any of the other men in attendance, Owen begged off as quickly as he could.

A visit to Pete's studio had proved enlightening, however, for Owen saw, in his admittedly limited experience, unsurpassed expression of skill with the lens. Of the framed photographs hung rather haphazardly on the walls, his favorite was of a young couple—shy newlyweds, he guessed—sitting together on a bench outside the Gallup depot, but he also appreciated the unpeopled landscapes, where cloud, mountain, light, and shadow were integrated as scenes of ordinary majesty. Owen came away admiring Pete's talent, if not his alcohol-infused temperament; he'd seen Pete less than sober at Many Springs Canyon, but not nearly as obtunded as here in Gallup.

He thought his time away from Many Springs might alter his own outlook, but he soon fell back into established routine—in the evening, Julia in her rocking chair, he in his armchair, Yazzie at his work table, Johanna drawing.

Johanna. What to make of Johanna? On a preternaturally hot morning—he'd been back from Gallup for only a few days—he was sitting in the pond just above the dam, opposite the reeds, cooling off on a whim, midriff high in the freezing water, moving his arms back and forth as if floating, contemplating nothing, when he saw Johanna approach opposite him, no more than sixty feet away, and he called to her, "Johanna!" but apparently she was already aware of his presence and made no response. He was utterly naked, and when he realized that she too intended to enter the water, and so began to raise her dress to pull it over her head, he called out louder, "Johanna!" and when the dress reached her mid-thighs, he turned, belly down, legs toward her, looking away.

"Johanna, stop!" he called. "Let me get out! You can have the pond to yourself!" He waited for a full minute and then, hearing nothing, glanced back over his shoulder and she was already in the water, sitting as he had been but with her head tipped forward, her long, loosened black hair draping over face and chest and into the water, and he could see her working something into it, yucca soap. He sat up again, his back still toward her.

He tried once again: "Johanna! Turn away and let me get out!" but a second quick glance informed him that she had no regard for his state. What would anyone else think if they saw the two of them like this? He took two deep breaths and rose, his full back to her, humiliated at having to expose his thin frame and emaciated buttocks to her gaze. What would she see if she even cared to look? The shape of Death in waiting. (His cock had scarcely hardened at the glimpse of her, and his sack was so shriveled by the mountain runoff that it felt like leather between his thighs.) Dripping, he quickly pulled on his pants and gathered his other clothes and hurried to below the dam, where neither could see the other, and he said nothing about the incident to either Julia or Yazzie. That night, Johanna was again at the table as if nothing had happened. (Well, nothing *had*, had it?)

Ever since the night of the viewing in the clearing, Johanna had taken to working the same subjects over and over: the comet and the moon. She drew them as she'd seen them through Pete's telescope, without foundation or horizon, as if the earth had not been the setting for her observations, as if it didn't exist in the cosmos. Capturing Halley's Comet appeared to frustrate her, however, for she threw away sheet after sheet of paper. The moon was a different matter. Owen couldn't believe the detail she recollected, the mountains and craters, their shadowed sides, the sunlit surfaces between.

One evening shortly before his trip to Gallup, he'd been sitting in his familiar chair in the parlor when he looked over and saw her pouring ink from the bottle and spreading it with a pitch-black finger. He moved quickly to the table. She'd been unable to draw with the pen the black and deep blue sky framing the moon, and she was creating it now with ink and finger, but the flood was running into her moon and she couldn't contain it or wipe it away, and he took her wrist and said, "I understand, Johanna, be patient," and so when he returned from his stay in Gallup he brought with him an array of artist's brushes and a set of water colors. Although he knew little about painting, he knew enough to show her how to use the brush, and how mixing certain colors produced others—shades of orange, violet, tan, gray— after which she would be on her own, to proceed in her own way. He didn't know what to expect, perhaps an explosion of colors, but no, she used the ink, poured into a saucer, for black, spread wildly at first with a flat brush— each evening Julia calmly laid layers of old newspaper across the dining table to protect it—and then, with greater caution, drops of white and then yellow mixed into the black, varied in amount, until the moon in its sky appeared in its subtleties from her pen and pencil and brush. And then the comet reappeared in her drawings, but she brushed and penned in the sky first, leaving at the center a blank space, trailed afterward by fine streaks and strokes of white and gray, almost translucent. He couldn't fathom how she did it until he saw her mixing minute amounts of blue into white. Her powers of observation and recall and her natural sense of how to work the ink and paint were so unexpected that neither he nor Julia had any idea what to make of it. Clement Yazzie, with pursed lips, would also watch her working and sometimes shake his head in wonder.

One night Yazzie sat down in the parlor beside Owen and Julia, which he rarely did. Johanna continued her work at the dining table, and every so often her brother would rise from his chair and observe from over her shoulder. Then he would return to the parlor. The three had been sitting for over an hour, Julia knitting, Owen perusing newspapers, Yazzie with his unoccupied, rough hands perched on the arms of the chair, before the Navajo finally spoke:

"I need to take Sister to see 'Asdzáán Bítóyiszééyiztał, the Woman Who Kicks Up Still Water," he said.

The two of them left the following morning.

THE STORM DESCENDED, wrapping him with wind and white. He lifted his shoulders and pulled the collar of his jacket higher. Caught in the field, blinded by the stinging ice and snow, he placed his hands over his eyes and opened a crack between two fingers: he could see nothing but the wild whiteness. The nightmarish wind whipped off his hat and carried it aloft. Now the snow was over the sides of his shoes; his feet were going numb. His fingers had already lost their feeling. He closed his eyes, brushed the white crust off his bare head and his shoulders, and put his fists in his jacket pockets.

Freezing was an easier death than most, he'd heard. Why not sit down, right here, and let the snow mound up? Or should he move? To where? In the whiteness he had lost all sense of direction. But then he heard another sound, other than the wind. A huffing, almost a chant. And then something like a shadow, gray, coming toward him. He thought of the yei impersonators whom he'd heard about, who came begging before the final day of the Night Chant, but he had nothing to offer them.

He looked down at his feet again. He was wearing Tóya's cowboy boots, with the mother-of-pearl inlays and the beading.

So this was a dream.

Owen woke up, startled, to find Clement Yazzie staring down at him. The sun now leaned into the west but the light remained intense in the cloudless sky. He didn't know how long he'd been asleep. He shaded his eyes with a hand. "Did you say something?" he asked Yazzie.

"I asked if you were all right." Yazzie took one sidestep, which spread welcome shade across Owen's face.

"I'm fine." He sat up. His hat and day pack were by his side. "I was just resting a bit."

"Hunh," Yazzie grunted.

"I didn't know you were back from seeing Tóya. What're you doing up here?" They were in the high meadow, not far from where it gave way to forest.

"Stray sheep," Yazzie said. He sat down, crossing his legs. "Did you find anything today?"

Right, Owen thought, I'm supposed to be looking for something. Pottery shards and such. "No, nothing. Did you?"

"I found you." Yazzie's lips bowed into a brief smile.

"Is that what I am—a stray?" Owen reached for his pack. "I have some jerky left, and some cold tea—can I offer you anything?"

"English tea?" Yazzie asked.

"Yes."

Yazzie shook his head. "I still don't have a taste for it."

"I'm surprised Mrs. Halley hasn't forced you to develop one."

"She doesn't like my coffee—too strong—and I don't like her tea."

"Johanna does."

"If you put enough sugar in the cup, Sister will drink anything."

Owen sawed off a bite of jerky with his teeth and chewed slowly. This was one of the longer one-to-one conversations he'd ever had with Clement Yazzie. And perhaps the oddest, because they weren't really talking about anything. Anglos made small talk; Yazzie didn't. Owen lifted the bottle and let a mouthful of unsweetened tea trickle down his throat. Around them, the sparse mountain grasses and weeds had only recently greened up—cheat grass, wild buckwheat, yarrow, chamiso—with a scattering of red penstemon emerging. For the Southwest, it would do. He said to Yazzie:

"I was dreaming about when Johanna found me in the snowstorm last November. The odd thing was, I was just standing in the snow, waiting for . . ." He hesitated. "I think I was waiting for the snow to tell me where to go. I know that makes no sense."

"What did your dream think it meant?"

Owen laughed. "That's an odd way to put it." As if the dream had intent. Then again, maybe it did. "I'll have to ponder that." He laughed again.

"There's something else you need to ponder."

"What's that?"

"Mrs. Halley," Yazzie said. "Julia."

The name pulled Owen back to the present moment; he'd never heard Yazzie speak her first name. "I—what do you mean?"

Yazzie didn't repeat himself. He scratched his nose with a forefinger and looked away.

Christ, Owen thought, still logy, I need to clear my head. But he knew. He knew.

Yazzie unfolded his legs, rose, and walked away, downhill, toward home.

I should just let him go, Owen thought. Yazzie wasn't a man who often felt the need to explain himself. Owen could talk to Tom Gorman about anything—the weather, the corn crop, the poor quality of the new box of wrought iron hardware fixtures. But not Yazzie. Yazzie kept his own counsel.

Against his better judgment, Owen gathered his hat and pack and called out, "Wait up!"

Yazzie was standing with his hands on his hips, maybe twenty-five yards away, in the grasses, a mixture of short brown stalks from previous years and green shoots ankle-high. Owen caught up to him and they continued on toward home, stepping into their own long shadows.

Every few paces, in order to keep up, Owen had to take two steps to Yazzie's one. "Yazzie," he said, halting in the middle of the high meadow, "stop."

Yazzie turned to face him. Now Yazzie was the one squinting, looking back into the sun. The brim of his hat, his eyes, his lips formed straight, parallel lines.

"I'll credit you with knowing my true feelings," Owen said.

"I've seen," Yazzie said.

"Have I ever acted disrespectfully? I've said nothing—I've said nothing to anyone. I've *done* nothing."

"I took no offense," Yazzie said.

No offense? For *what*? But of course. He, Owen, was still there, in the room next to hers, separated by a thin wall and an unbolted door. Did he really think he could just stay there forever?

"When you're gone, we'll still be here," Yazzie said.

He didn't mean gone from the reservation; he didn't mean the way all bilagáanas left. "Why don't you just dig me a hole right here? I'll roll in and we can get it over with." Owen tried to swallow his bitterness; like coarse salt, it burned.

"I don't want to dig you a hole."

"No? Then how about a trade? You get Julia and I'll take Johanna. I could use a—"

Yazzie stepped forward quickly and Owen flinched, expecting the blow that followed. It caught him flush on the side of the head and dropped him flat to the ground. Pinpoint lights exploded into stars. A ringing in his left ear gradually diminished to a vague hum.

"If you don't mind," he said when his head had cleared enough to speak, "I'll just lie here a while." His tongue was heavy.

Yazzie, frowning, dropped into a squat but his eyes didn't leave Owen.

"I won't say I didn't provoke you," Owen said. The side of his head, above his ear, felt numb.

"This illness you have," Yazzie said. It was a question.

"Do you know much about it?"

"Some."

"From Julia?"

"From listening."

Owen sighed again and tried to sit up, without success. "You don't even know you have it at first. Eventually you get very thirsty. No matter how much you drink, you're still thirsty. And you piss a lot—all the time, even if you stop drinking. Sometimes you sweat rivers and get dizzy. It's all because there's too much sugar in your blood. I was lucky, I had good doctors,"

Owen continued. "They told me what I need to do. But there's no cure. Little by little, it takes its toll. Along the way, some people lose their sight. Some lose their feet or even their legs to gangrene. The end can come fast or more like the way a lake freezes over in winter—a little more ice each night, working its way toward the center."

"To the heart," Yazzie said.

Owen closed his eyes but the brightness of the high desert light shown through the scrim of his eyelids. With two fingers he tested where Yazzie's knuckles had landed.

"Did Johanna come home with you?" Owen asked.

"No."

"She's still with Tóya?"

"Aoo'."

"But she's well?"

"Aoo'."

Owen sat up, bracing himself with extended arms. "I guess that's all that matters. The two of you have never been apart for long, have you?"

"Once. I was gone for a few months. She was still a child. I think she believed I wasn't coming back. That it was her fault. When I did come back, she wouldn't let me out of her sight."

"Why would she think it was her fault? Because of . . . how she is?"

Yazzie shook his head.

Owen tried to fit Yazzie's absence into the timeline—what he knew about Yazzie's history. "Was this when you were at Second Mesa, when you met your wife?"

"So you heard about that time."

"Julia mentioned something about it once."

"What did she tell you?"

Owen wondered how much more he should say. "She said that if my curiosity got the better of me, I would have to ask you. About what people say."

"Hunh. How much do you know?"

"For a fact? Nothing."

Yazzie nodded his head. "Are you asking now?"

"No," Owen said. "Maybe someday, but not now."

"And maybe someday I'll tell you."

"Fair enough." Owen picked at a cracked thumbnail.

Yazzie eased himself down from his crouch. "You showed an interest."

"An interest?"

Yazzie made a scribbling motion with his hand.

"You mean I showed Johanna how to *draw*. It was a lark."

"Nothing is a lark for Sister."

Owen could just see the roof of Yazzie's hogan in the distance, a brown arc above a green hillock where three apricot-colored sheep were grazing.

"Now she sits and does the same sky drawing over and over."

"And you think that's different from when she was drawing the other things—the things I helped her with?"

Yazzie just looked at Owen.

"I suppose I do, too. Did Tóya have any answer?"

"She said this is not something I should talk about."

"Not even with Julia?"

"No."

After a while Owen said, "What I said earlier about your sister, I wouldn't want you to think . . ." He turned and looked toward the tree line behind them, where branches of the tallest tress were now spraying shaggy beams of copper sunlight. "Of course I've noticed her the way a man notices a woman"—immediately fearing he'd be misunderstood, he stumbled on—"but I wouldn't, I don't . . . have any intentions."

"That doesn't rule out much. For most men."

"Maybe I'd be better off if I were one of them," Owen said. Then he gave his head a quick shake. "I don't meant that."

"This is what I think." Yazzie ran a thumb over the rough knuckles of the hand that had struck Owen. "Sister has no interest in being with a man."

"Maybe *she's* better off," Owen said.

After a while Yazzie looked at him squarely and said. "You need to go back to your tent."

"I know."

"Until winter comes again."

"At least until winter," Owen said.

That evening, Owen spoke to Julia.

She tried to dissuade him: "I don't want this."

"You need your home back as it was, and I need to continue with what I was doing." Whatever that was. "There's still hundreds of square miles I can survey."

"What do you expect to find at this point?"

"Maybe not what I thought I'd find, but there are other things to see. And I assume I can still come in and sit by your stove and have a cup of tea in the evening and read the Chicago newspapers."

"I don't want you to do this." Her voice shook.

He thought that Yazzie had knocked some sense into his head. But he was wrong. He was angry and jealous and foolish. He still wanted to think that if he stayed there, in the spare room, on the other side of the door . . .

No, he'd go back to his tent. And work himself raw in the darkness, Julia's face but Bethany's body, the last bare flesh he'd touched and tasted and smelled. That night in the hotel in Cambridge, when, lying beside her, he at last kissed her breasts. She'd let him lift her nightgown, watching his face as he did. Her skin was wondrous, her nipples pursing, transforming and purpling under his lips, and when he pulled his mouth away from them her face didn't reveal if they'd tightened and wrinkled from shame or desire or simply from a slight draft brushing the wetness left by his tongue. With the utmost will, he contained himself, inhaling through his nostrils, exhaling through his mouth, his hot breath on her. He slipped his hand into her undergarment, but when he tried to move his fingers even lower she resisted, grabbing his wrist. But she'd felt the hardness pressing against her hip, and so she let him lift his nightshirt and stretch against her full length, his feet at her feet, his thighs against her thighs, his uplifted cock against the round contour of her white, smooth belly, and although she didn't look or touch, she let him rub himself there, against her, and in what seemed like only a moment he groaned and the fluid shot from him, though he managed to catch almost all of it in his hand. The rest he wiped away from her stomach with his nightshirt, and then he bent down and kissed her there and moved his face lower against the thin fabric that scarcely concealed her light thatch and, understanding now that she was indeed wet, her body ready for him to take her—he would not, he'd promised her he wouldn't—he tried to absorb her scent, like no other, of brine and burnt almond and raw citrus, before she gently pushed him away.

Or maybe he'd take Johanna after all. He could imagine her beneath that blanket dress, so easy for her to remove and completely bare herself to him in one swift gesture. She'd have been a witness—hogans were small, without privacy—even if she herself had never been touched. And what would he find under that woolen dress? How brown her skin, how long and thick the hair between her thighs, what dark obscurity? He could do with a touch of darkness. Sometimes lately he'd been unable to keep himself hard. Maybe the sugar, maybe his frustration. He wanted a touch other than his own, and it angered him that Clement Yazzie, goddamn him, could obtain it so easily while he, Owen, had only the palm of his hand and a bit of spit. Look at what Yazzie had accomplished in one brief conversation, and without offering anything: Owen was clearing out, heading back to his canvas tent, and by his own choosing. So who was the simpleton of Many Springs Canyon? Not poor Johanna, whom no Navajo man would have, and not because Yazzie's reputation had scared them all off. She wasn't ugly. She wasn't vile or cruel. She wasn't simple. Then what *was* she, besides mute? Indifferent.

"The tent's in tatters," Julia said.

Owen sighed. They both knew that wasn't true. The tent was folded up in an empty stall in the stable. After the storm last fall, Johnny Gorman had found it largely intact, a few rips, a couple of tent poles snapped. They could be replaced easily enough, and he could find suitably strong anchors among the hardware bins in the trading post.

"All right, it's not in tatters," she admitted.

"I'm not going anywhere," he said. "Fifty yards across the wash." But the distance should be measured in loss, not in yards. How do you measure loss? Along the path of the heart. Degrees of arc. Minutes. Seconds. Beats.

He had next to nothing to pack up. He could be gone in an hour. Less.

"You need your own life back," he said. A strand of brown hair had pulled loose from her bun and was hanging down across her ear, curling forward, touching her flushed neck. Owen wanted to lift the stray lock, slip it behind her ear.

"What are you talking about?" she said. "This *is* my life. No one gets to go *back.*"

"Then I'm sorry."

"For what?"

"The disruption."

She threw up her hands and walked away from him, toward the kitchen.

"Why do you have a bolt that you never throw on the door between the two bedrooms?" He had bent down to her hairbrush and breathed in her scent. He knew how many steps before he could touch the fluted lamp on her nightstand. He knew the pattern of the quilt on her bed.

She turned and stared at him. "Why is that any business of yours?"

He ignored her. "It makes no sense if you don't use it, and if you don't also have a lock on the door between the parlor and your room. You've told me yourself that you've let strangers stay in my—the second—room. Teamsters. Salesmen. People who couldn't tell north from south and found themselves lost in the middle of the night."

Now she was visibly angry, in high color. "You're saying I should feel threatened in my own home?"

"I'm saying you should be smarter."

"Locks can be broken. Wooden doors can be kicked in. All it requires is determination."

"Something I lack, apparently."

She stiffened. "Should I have seen *you* as a threat? Bolted the door against *you?*"

"What do you want me to say, Julia?" It was almost a groan. "That I never wanted to come to you?"

"But you didn't."

"Of course I didn't! How could I?" And not just because of the violation of trust. He could only pretend that he was still himself—as he'd been even a year ago—if he didn't look, and if he didn't see his physical reflection in her eyes.

"You can't move back into that tent," she said, pronouncing each word with vehemence. "If you insist, move into the hogan."

Had she and Yazzie been meeting there during the months he, Owen, had occupied the spare bedroom?

He realized now that the tent wouldn't suffice. Nor the hogan. It was time to leave Many Springs Canyon. And if so, he should first speak his piece.

"Is it the difference in our ages?"

"No, no. It's—" She shook her head with frustration. "It's not just that. If that were the only thing—"

His throat constricted.

"I'm not . . . unfeeling. Haven't you seen that? Or maybe you haven't really looked." She stopped. "How much more do I need to say?" she pleaded.

"Considerably more."

She raised a palm, fingers splayed, to her forehead and closed her eyes. "I just *know*, without so much as a touch."

"And you're never wrong?"

"I'm not wrong."

He wanted to hurt her. "I'm not your pet," he said.

Oh! he knew that look.

"Will gave me a dog once. Did you know that? As if there aren't enough sheep dogs and mongrels on the reservation. It was some breed of terrier, with short, wiry hair. Someone passing through Gallup lost it. Or left it. After two or three weeks I was beginning to get used to it, but one night it disappeared. I suspect the coyotes ate it. So I'm not one for pets."

"Is that story even true?"

"True enough."

"Do you love him?"

Julia fixed his eyes with hers. "I love my sister. *That* is unequivocal and without limit."

"Then I don't understand, if it isn't a . . . matter of the heart."

"How could it be? Look at our circumstances. Look at where we are."

Where an Indian is always defined first and foremost as an Indian. Where a white woman of a certain age, separated from her husband and choosing to live on her own, is consequently suspect. Where— He could go on.

"We give each other what we can, and we trust each other completely," Julia now said. "In every way that matters."

"And that's enough?"

"Yes."

"Then what am I to you?"

"You're my dearest companion, Owen."

"And that's all?"

"That's everything!"

"Not everything." He brushed past her and walked toward the outside door.

"Stop!" she said. "Why won't you understand?"

He rested his hand on the latch but didn't turn to look at her.

"Can't you see that what you want, even if I could give it, would be a mistake?"

"I'm going to the hogan, if that's all right with you. I'll collect my things tomorrow." He closed the door firmly behind him.

Later, still outside, he felt a calm settle over him.

He had to choose: this or that, one thing or the other; one direction or another. He needed to stay, he needed to leave—he couldn't live both lives.

If his heart stopped beating right now, it would be all right. He didn't fear it. Let winter come.

CHAPTER FIFTEEN: The Lost and the Found

Carrying little but his field notebooks, a change of clothes, a brick of cheese, boiled eggs, a pouch of oatmeal and pine nuts, and four canteens of water that slapped against his sides, Owen set off east from Many Springs Canyon on a Saturday night under a nearly full moon and an expanse of stars and planets. He gauged his progress less by the few shadowy landmarks than by sidereal time: the midnight setting of Jupiter in Virgo, the rise of Saturn not long after, the descent of the waxing moon and the appearance of Venus two hours before sunrise, by which time he'd already reached the traces of the western road. He rested from moonset to first light, the interval when crossing the uneven terrain risked turning an ankle or worse. He made good time after that and then dozed from midday in shade he found against the bank of a dry wash. There was little to see out here except ravens and small, quick lizards, and in the distance a few wild horses, which had once been plentiful, he understood, before most were rounded up and sold off. (For a couple of years Clement Yazzie had made a fair amount of money from the horses, Julia had told him, before wholesaling companies brought in their own crews. After that, the ponies became scarce.) As the sun approached the horizon and Sunday's searing heat began dissipating into the wide open sky, he set out again. Keeping up a steady pace, but treading carefully, he reached Chaco Canyon well before noon on Monday.

There had been changes at the Wetherill ranch, he soon learned. For one thing, during the previous fall Wetherill had hired Miss Eleanor Quick, a sturdy 35-year-old spinster originally from the East, as a tutor for his three older children, Richard Jr., Elizabeth, and Robert, as well as for the four children of the Indian agent for the Eastern Reservation, Samuel Stacher. Miss Quick was to live half the month with the Stachers at the three-room

Pueblo del Arroyo "hotel," which the Stachers were renting from Wetherill for a nominal sum, and half the month with the Wetherills. The arrangement didn't last long, however, because, according to Miss Quick—who, Owen immediately realized, was free and easy with her tongue, a doughy busybody—she'd discovered that Stacher was plotting against Mr. Wetherill, gathering stories from disgruntled Navajos and passing them on to Superintendent Shelton, who had a grudge against Wetherill. Shelton had already written from Shiprock to Commissioner of Indian Affairs Robert Valentine in Washington, accusing Wetherill of routinely abusing and assaulting Chaco Indians, and going so far as to incarcerate some in a windowless room in Pueblo Bonito, the largest ruin. According to Shelton, Wetherill had also allowed his employees to sell liquor to Navajos, had stolen their stock—everything from cattle to sheep to burros—had illegally fenced public grazing land on the North Mesa . . . The list went on.

Everybody had stories about Richard Wetherill, Owen knew. How could he reconcile the villainous ones with the unassuming man who, a year ago, had led him in the early morning up the ancient steps to the mesa behind Pueblo Bonito and shown him the north roads, there, there, and there. In his personal life Wetherill was a man of rectitude, a Quaker, a man who wouldn't drink alcohol or dance, not even with his wife. Would this man steal cattle from impoverished Navajos or deliberately cut off their sheep from water in the present drought, which had parched the already dry land and forced Wetherill's ranch hands to dig watering holes along the Chaco and Escavada washes? Would he lock a Navajo in a hole in the ruins, knowing that Navajos feared the chindis of the Anasazi? Owen wouldn't believe it. Could Wetherill, if pressed by responsibility or finances, be high-handed? Of that Owen had no doubt, but you could hardly condemn a man for that. So why did government men, Shelton in particular, take such a dislike to Wetherill? Because he threatened their authority, of course. Shelton and his ilk were ignorant Johnny-come-latelies, but they had at their disposal the power of the law, such as it was on the reservation, and, with it, the license to isolate and entrap anyone they deemed an adversary.

"Are the Stachers still here?" Owen asked Miss Quick. At her invitation, the two of them were having Tuesday afternoon tea in the dining room, served by a hired kitchen girl, Helga Magnusson, whose eyes as she departed didn't disguise her dislike for Miss Quick. "I haven't seen any comings or goings across the way at the hotel."

"No," Miss Quick said with pride. "Mr. Wetherill ordered them out months ago. They've moved to Crownpoint, where Stacher intends to establish his agency and start an Indian school."

So in the year since Owen's first arrival at Chaco Canyon, Eleanor Quick had arrived and the Stachers had left. And, Owen learned, Richard Wetherill had sold the trading post business to Epimenio Miera, who also owned a mercantile store up in Cuba; however, Richard continued to manage the trading post, at least in part so that he'd still have leverage to collect the debts owed him. And of course most recently, Marietta Wetherill had given birth to a fifth child, Ruth. Mother and daughter had returned from the hospital in Albuquerque just days before and, Owen gathered, Marietta remained too preoccupied with the newborn to reclaim the household responsibilities she'd apparently delegated to Miss Quick during her absence.

Something else had changed, something impossible to particularize. It was as if distraction, or desperation, had swept in like the drought. Gus Thompson was gone. Bill Finn verbally abused Lee Ivy at every opportunity, and Lee slunk away from him like a whipped dog. Helga was the only household helper apart from the Navajo Des-glena-spah, who still tended to the older children when they weren't at their lessons, but, her dark brow furrowed, she evidenced none of the pleasure Owen had seen a year ago. Only the children seemed oblivious, the happy children.

"There have been other difficulties," Miss Quick whispered, her eyebrows raised. "Living so intimately, one naturally overhears." Owen doubted the depth of any "intimacy"; Miss Quick had her quarters in the bunkhouse. "There are"—she paused for emphasis—"debts."

And what of Richard Wetherill himself? He seemed grayer, more taciturn, more restless, although at dinner on Monday he'd greeted Owen with a smile and a firm, welcoming handshake.

The next evening, after supper, the family, Miss Quick, and Owen moved to the outdoors and were comfortably occupying the shade beneath the extended roof. It was the longest day of the year, the summer solstice. Marietta Wetherill lay in a hammock rocking the baby. Miss Quick read to the older children, who sat or lay on Navajo rugs arrayed on the ground. Owen and Richard Wetherill occupied a bench near the corner of the house. Bill Finn, Lee Ivey, and several Mexican workers had headed to the barns and stables to finish up the day's work.

"So," Wetherill asked, "what have you found?

"I'm sorry to say, nothing of consequence." Owen had with him a folded map; two well-worn notebooks filled with precise dates, times, and coordinates as well as extensive field notes; and a copy of the article he intended to submit for publication to the *American Journal of Archaeology*. He unfolded his hand-drawn map. "I started here." He pointed to the center of a series of concentric circles, half way between the end of the western road and the entrance to Many Springs Canyon.

"And you walked all this territory?"

"Pretty much. Outward to about six miles." He traced the outermost circle. "But not with equal care, of course. At first I focused on the end of the road. Later, I narrowed my range to a mile north and south, but sometimes I ventured farther."

"And what about the canyon and the Chuskas?"

"I walked the canyon completely. In the mountains, I had to follow the topography."

"You didn't find anything in the canyon?"

"Nothing to suggest the Anasazi had ever built there. Higher up, you can find isolated ruins—a few rooms at most, no more than a large family would use—but they might just as easily have been built by people emigrating from Canyon de Chelly."

"Shards?"

"A mix. Nothing definitive. Mostly corrugated and black on white."

"I assume you considered the calendar?"

"I did, but nothing about the road's location or direction corresponds to where the sun rises or sets on an equinox or solstice. I suppose there are other possibilities . . ."

Wetherill continued to study the map. "So altogether you covered, what—a hundred square miles?"

"I suppose." Owen hesitated, scratching his chin. "Maybe I spent more time in the mountains and canyon than I should have." He carefully refolded the map.

"The explanation," Wetherill said, "may always lie beyond our reach."

"Doesn't that bother you?"

"No, it doesn't bother me at all. Our present vanities were not the concern of the ancient Anasazi." He rubbed his hands on his thighs and changed the subject. "How is Mrs. Halley?"

"Very well." Owen gave him a wan smile.

"We had a fine time during our visit over there last month."

"I know she was happy to have you."

"I'll never understand why she stuck it out after her husband left—why she didn't move back East to her family. It was a reckless decision."

Owen felt that he needed to defend Julia. "She seems to be making a go of it. She has determination."

"And what about you, Owen?"

"Me?"

"What do you plan to do now?"

"I honestly don't know."

"Well, stay as long as you'd like. Make yourself at home in my library if you've had your fill of Anasazi riddles."

"You're very generous," Owen said with a wealth of feeling. "I've done nothing to deserve it."

"Of course you have. You have an active mind. Such encounters are increasingly rare these days, now that I'm merely a rancher."

With that, Wetherill excused himself. He needed to ride out early the next morning to meet Tom Talle, who was driving a herd north to Chaco because other pasture land he'd rented had petered out from the drought.

"Sheriff Talle, from Gallup?" Owen asked.

"The same," Wetherill confirmed.

The next afternoon, Owen was reading in Wetherill's office when Bill Finn strode in and threw himself into an armchair.

"What's that you're reading?" Finn asked.

"Shakespeare," Owen said. "*Julius Caesar.*"

Finn sniffed and returned to his own thoughts. He was obviously unsettled; the heel of his right boot tapped out a rapid, uncontrolled drumbeat on the wooden floor, and he picked at a scab on the back of his left hand.

Not ten minutes later, Richard Wetherill entered the office. Owen had never seen him looking so perturbed, his mouth straight and tense, his eyes squinting at Finn. "A Navajo told me not half an hour ago, up on the mesa, that you'd gotten into a scrape with Nez-Begay over Elizabeth's colt. He said you were dead."

"Not likely," Finn scoffed. "Lee and me found the colt tethered behind Nez-Begay's hogan, just about dead from misuse. We brought it around front and the Indian came barreling out the door yelling that we were thieves and rustlers. I was already in a foul mood, seeing the condition of that poor animal, and told him to back off, but instead he grabbed my reins and I whacked him on the head with my pistol and he went down."

Wetherill fell silent for a moment. "How badly did you hurt him?"

"He wasn't even bleeding, and he sure wasn't dead, though he deserves to be. He must've ridden that horse into the ground and beaten him besides. If the colt doesn't die of its own accord, we're going to have to put him down. Miss Elizabeth is gonna be mighty upset."

"I may not be able to stand behind you on this, Bill," Wetherill said, shaking his head. "I sent you out there to bring a horse home, not pistol-whip the man who took it."

Finn's anger flared. "Used to be a horse thief could just be shot or strung up."

"Those days are gone, and we're better off for it. And you know as well as I do there's more involved in this than who's the rightful owner of that horse. Shelton would like nothing better than to drag me and my affairs into the courts again."

"Maybe I should ride up to Shiprock and pistol-whip Shelton," Finn muttered.

"We'll attend to this later," Wetherill said, his jaw set. "Right now we need to get Talle's drags up to the mesa."

Finn pushed his lanky frame from the armchair. "I'll get my horse," he said. He shambled out of the room.

Wetherill stood silently, his hands on his hips.

"Is there anything I can do?" Owen asked, setting the book aside.

Wetherill shook his head. "This is one of those days when I wish I were back in the Mancos Valley." On his way out he muttered something in Navajo that Owen didn't understand but that he assumed wouldn't be spoken in polite company.

Owen, his concentration broken, reshelved his book and stepped outside in time to see Wetherill and Finn mount and ride off toward Pueblo del Arroyo. It was close to six o'clock. The day still had good light left, but the dust in the riders' wake hung like a scrim beyond which their receding silhouettes were soon lost.

Owen didn't know what to do with himself. He didn't doubt that the Wetherills thought well of him (although Marietta Wetherill, attending to her newborn, had scarcely noticed his presence), but he was an interloper. He'd come here to get away from Many Springs Canyon, to apply a tincture of time, but he couldn't have come at a *worse* time for the Wetherills. His presence was certainly an intrusion, and he'd leave tomorrow, graciously.

To go where?

Julia. His thoughts always returned to her. He loved her. And what did she feel for him? Friendship. Tenderness. Protectiveness. Affinity. Empathy. Sympathy. None of which measured up.

A rifle shot echoed off the canyon wall behind him and he jumped. The sound of another shot followed quickly. Not for so much as a second did he doubt what he'd heard, not after a childhood spent on a farm in rural New Hampshire. A third shot. He couldn't be sure of the direction, but, shading his eyes, he instinctively looked west, toward where Wetherill and Finn had ridden. He waited. Across the way, Eleanor Quick had come to the door of her quarters. Her eyes caught his, but neither she nor he said anything. Then multiple shots, overlapping, from at least two rifles.

He recognized Bill Finn's horse. Finn was riding low and fast, cutting cross-country, making for the homestead through the brush in as straight a line as he could and kicking up so much dust that Owen couldn't be sure whether one or two riders were chasing him. Whoever it was, was doing all the shooting. Finn's horse seemed to burst through one fence. At the same time, Owen saw two men on foot running, angling as if to cut Finn off in his dash for the house. Marietta Wetherill had come to a window. Finn, his revolver drawn, fired several shots behind and then turned his gun on one of the running men who, swinging a club of some sort, had tried to intercept him. The man, clutching his side, fell. Finn, his revolver now empty, urged his horse on, and as one they sailed over a final fence and galloped to the front of the Wetherill house. Finn's pursuers appeared to have given up the chase.

Finn's eyes were wild. He flung his wide-brimmed hat aside. "Are all the children here?" he blurted, out of breath.

"I don't know," Owen said.

Finn pushed open the front door and hurried inside. Owen followed him.

Marietta Wetherill stood there. "Where's Mr. Wetherill?"

Finn stopped in his tracks. "By the rincon."

Her voice rose. "There's trouble and you left him down there alone?"

"They killed him dead," Finn said.

The blood drained from Marietta's face so fast that Owen thought she'd collapse.

Finn strode past her, heading for the office.

Owen grabbed his arm from behind. "You're sure?"

Finn grimaced. "Get out of my way."

Owen let go. Miss Quick came in through the front door. Her eyes flashed from Owen to Marietta, who hadn't emitted a sound or moved. Miss Quick hurried to Marietta and took her arm. "What happened?"

"The Navajos have killed my husband," Marietta answered.

Finn emerged from the office carrying a rifle and a box of shells.

"What can I do?" Owen asked him.

"There's another Winchester in the gun rack and another box of shells on a shelf above. Meet me outside."

Owen, his chest pounding, ran into the office, grabbed the rifle and cartridges and ran back through the dining room and out the door. Finn, his own rifle at the alert, stood at the corner of the house, looking up the trail toward Pueblo del Arroyo. Owen hurried over to him while awkwardly balancing the gun and loading shells.

"Can you manage that rifle?" Finn asked in a monotone. He was still breathing heavily.

"I grew up on a farm, so yes."

"Have you ever faced anything that could shoot back?"

"No, I don't have your wealth of experience."

Finn glared. "Help me drag that bench around the side."

They leaned their weapons against the stone and mortared wall and pulled the wooden bench, where Owen and Wetherill had sat the night before, around the corner of the house. Finn flung off the Navajo blanket that covered the bench, which he tipped onto its side so that it faced the wash. "If they're serious," he said, "they'll try to pin us down from the brush and send riders up out of the wash from there." He pointed toward the South Gap.

"Why?"

"Because there's no windows on this side of the house."

"Wouldn't they be smarter to wait until dark?"

"What would be smart is to hit us while we're scattered, before Talle and the others get here, so if you see horses rise out of the wash, shoot. Aim for the horses and maybe you'll hit something. The horses will be slow for a second, trying to get their footing. Once they get moving, they'll be on us fast. Use the bench for cover."

"Where will you be?"

"Right here."

"In the open?"

"I'd rather have them shooting at me than coming around to the front and sending bullets through the windows, where the women or children might get shot or cut by flying glass." His initial panic had been replaced by a ruthless energy. His hands shook and his shoulders jerked as if he had the chills, and when he wasn't talking, his teeth chattered. He looked at Owen and sneered. "Besides, those red niggers can't shoot worth shit."

"One of them just killed Richard."

"Goddamn luck. Do you know how hard it is to drop a man stone cold dead from a saddle with one distant shot when the sand and dust are flying around so much you can barely see?"

Owen disliked Finn intensely, but if Navajos attacked them now, Finn might be the only one who could fight them off. Owen had no skill with a rifle, and he knew it, and he doubted that any of the Mexican workers who might be nearby could do any better. He said to Finn, "Still, it seems rather foolhardy of you just to stand there."

"Where should I stand?" Finn growled. "Wetherill's dead. Even if the Indians turn coward and scatter, d'you think Mrs. Wetherill can hang on here with all those kids and no husband? The politicians will have her out of here, probably a pauper, and the rest of us with her."

"Getting yourself killed won't help Mrs. Wetherill."

"Just do what I told you, Nancy," Finn spat.

They stood at their post as the sun inched along its arc. Sometimes Owen could hear, inside, the sound of children weeping and baby Ruth wailing that piercing way infants do, and the scraping of furniture on the floor, perhaps for a window barricade.

Marietta Wetherill appeared at the door and spoke to Finn. "I'm going to get my husband," she said. "I won't have him lying out there."

Eleanor Quick pushed past her and turned to block her way. "Your baby needs you," she said, placing her hand once again on Marietta's arm. "I'll go. I'll take the surrey."

"You'll never be able to lift him," Finn said.

"Then I'll bring a Mexican with me, if I can shame one into it. They're probably in the bunkhouse cowering."

"Most of them are out after Talle's drags," Finn said.

"They're just itinerant cowhands," Marietta said. "They have no idea what this is about. Leave them be."

"I'll go with you," Owen said to Miss Quick in defiance of Finn. "I'm not doing any good standing here."

"All right," Miss Quick said. "Let me gather up a couple of sheets." She went back into the house.

Finn turned and focused down the road toward the rincon. Three riders were coming fast, but they weren't Navajos: Tom Talle, his man Tom O'Fallon, and Lee Ivy. Finn relaxed. "The renegades won't come now."

Talle and O'Fallon pulled up, raising new dust. Lee Ivy headed toward the bunkhouse.

"Is everyone safe?" the sheriff asked, climbing down and handing his reins to O'Fallon, whose Adam's apple bobbed as if he were trying to swallow something hard and thick. Despite the heat, Talle was wearing an ankle-length duster, and under that a vest with mother-of-pearl buttons, and a white linen shirt. Owen was surprised at how young he was—certainly under thirty.

"Did you see my husband?" Marietta asked.

"Yes," Talle said, removing his hat and brushing his long hair back with his other hand. The hat was expensive, the finest felt. "I think the ones who did it have run off, at least for now."

Eleanor Quick, the folded sheets and a cotton bonnet under her arm, returned. "I asked Des-glena-spah to move a cot onto the back porch. We'll lay Mr. Wetherill out there, if it's all right with you, Marietta."

Marietta nodded. Her jaw was trembling, her face beginning to sag into grief.

"Mrs. Wetherill," Talle said, "you should prepare your children."

Owen didn't know if he meant for the return of their father's body or for what might happen if his assassins attacked their home.

"Maybe it would be best if you helped Des-glena-spah," Miss Quick spoke softly to Marietta, who nodded again and retreated through the door.

"I think they're going on the warpath," Talle said. Then he pointed at Finn. "And you're the first one they're going to come for when they get themselves organized."

Finn spat into the dirt again.

"I don't think they had this planned," Talle said, "but with Wetherill dead, they may just decide the time has come to clear the whole lot of you out. I'm going to borrow a fresh mount and set out for Thoreau. I can get there by morning and telegraph Fort Wingate for troops. I'll leave O'Fallon here."

"Well, I don't know . . . ," O'Fallon said, shaking his head, but Talle's angry glare shut him up.

"Do you have weapons?" Talle asked.

"There's three or four more rifles inside, and enough ammunition, I guess," Finn said. His bravado had disappeared with the arrival of Talle. Owen wondered if the stories about Finn—that Bill Finn wasn't even his real name, that he'd been some sort of desperado down in Texas and was still wanted by the law—might be true. Lee Ivy, another rifle under his arm, left the bunkhouse and headed toward the rear door of the ranch house.

Miss Quick, managing to tie her bonnet under her chin while clutching the sheets, asked Owen, "Are you coming?"

"I am."

"And who are you?" Talle asked Owen.

"Owen Rouse."

"Right, right." Talle turned his full attention to Owen. "You're the fellow who's been staying at Many Springs Canyon. Have you seen any sign of trouble over your way?"

"None."

"What about from that shifty Navajo who lives up the canyon from the trading post?"

"Clement Yazzie?"

"That's the one."

"He's a friend of mine."

"Well," Talle drawled, "you might want to reconsider that."

"Seems to me this isn't the best time for a discussion of how I choose my friends." Owen glanced at Finn, who remained expressionless, and then followed Eleanor Quick toward the corral.

An elderly Mexican emerged from the stable. Miss Quick asked him, "*Cuál es su nombre?*"

"Esteban," he replied, removing his hat and dipping his head in deference.

"*Habla inglés?*"

"*Un poco.*"

"Mr. Wetherill has been shot. We're going to bring his body back. Do you understand?"

"*Sí.*"

"Will you come with us?"

"*Sí.* But I have no *pistola.*"

"You won't need one," Miss Quick said. "It seems the villains have fled. But just in case, Mr. Rouse has a rifle."

Owen saw no benefit in pointing out what little good that would do.

After Esteban had hitched a horse to the surrey, the three climbed aboard. Esteban took the reins, Miss Quick beside him; Owen rode in the back. At a trot, it didn't take them long to reach the Rincon del Camino, only a winding mile and a half down the trail. Wetherill lay sprawled among the greasewood, off to the side. A single raven stood watch in the topmost branches of a stunted tree. Esteban coaxed the reluctant horse into the brush and brought the surrey up beside the body.

"Oh my dear Lord in Heaven," Miss Quick said, turning her head away and bracing herself against the seat.

Owen hopped down, took one look, and then bent over, his elbows on his thighs, taking deep breaths through his mouth.

Esteban quickly made the sign of the cross.

"Please, cover his face," Miss Quick said in a strangled voice.

Wetherill had been shot, obviously at very close range, in the head. Most of the right side above his mangled cheek had been blown away. There were also wounds, obviously delivered from a much greater distance, to a hand and to his chest, dead center.

"What should I use?" Owen asked.

"Here." Miss Quick, without turning around, untied her bonnet and thrust it toward Owen. He took it from her, stepped forward, and dropped it, which succeeded in covering most of the gore.

The world fell silent except for the buzzing of the flies that were beginning to congregate.

The three companions didn't speak or even look at each other for what seemed like several minutes. Then Owen took the two sheets from the rear of the wagon. He draped one over the body, covering it completely, and spread the other beside it. He and Esteban tucked the cover sheet under Wetherill's right side and then rolled him a half turn in that direction; they tucked again, rolled again, folded up the top and bottom, and then tucked and rolled a third time. The two men lifted the cocoon. It was difficult for them to manage until Miss Quick climbed down and grabbed the feet, which allowed Owen and Esteban to maneuver the body into the surrey's front seat. Between them, Esteban and Miss Quick would have to balance the corpse to be sure it didn't fall out when the surrey started moving. The muslin-covered head hung forward, chin to chest.

"Your bonnet," Owen said. Dislodged when they were cloaking the body, it lay on the ground.

"Leave it," Miss Quick said. "I'll never touch it again."

Marietta Wetherill and Sheriff Talle were waiting for them when Esteban pulled up beside the rear porch of the Wetherill house. Owen and Esteban quickly transferred the wrapped body to the cot, over which the sheriff draped a gray wool blanket.

"Thank you," Marietta said in a dull voice.

"Marietta," Miss Quick said, "look if you must, but keep the children away. This should not be how they remember their father."

"Go away now," Marietta said quietly. "I need to be with my husband."

They went inside. Owen and Miss Quick stayed in the kitchen. Not long after, they heard Marietta's sobs.

Miss Quick said, "I'll go out to her in a bit. You should join the other men. I do hope they're not planning anything foolish." As much as he'd previously found her annoying, he had to admire her grit.

Owen found Bill Finn where he'd left him, outside, at the corner of the house. He sat against the wall with his knees drawn up, his Winchester in his lap. Sheriff Talle stood over him, his hands on his hips.

"Just past Pueblo del Arroyo," Finn was saying.

"How many?" Talle asked.

"Maybe ten."

"Armed?"

"Some of them."

"This Chis-chilí Biye', what about him?"

"No."

"You've had run-ins with him before?"

"Not exactly 'run-ins.' He had debts that he didn't see a need to pay. He's the kind of Navajo who asks to borrow money and then resents you for lending it to him."

"That's a trait that's hardly unique to the Navajo," Talle said.

"If you say so," Finn said flatly.

"You're sure Biye' wasn't armed?"

Finn looked up. "I'm sure. He was right there, saddle to saddle with Mr. Wetherill. He said I'd killed his brother-in-law—"

"Nez-Begay?"

"Yeah. And then Old Welo rode up waving this ancient rifle around and shouting that we were stealing their best cattle and horses to pay off debts that they didn't owe, and that we were taking their grazing land to rent out to Anglos and that his stock would starve in this drought. Mr. Wetherill didn't appreciate having a loaded gun waved in his face, so he grabbed it from Welo, unloaded the shells, and smashed the stock against a fence post. That shut them up."

"Was Richard armed?"

"No. Unless you count the bare barrel of Welo's rifle."

"And what were you doing?"

"I had my eye on some of the others, just in case they put their hands on their weapons."

"You were armed?"

"Just with my .38 Colt's pistol. I didn't even have any extra bullets with me. We were on Mr. Wetherill's homestead. No one had ever bothered us here."

"So then what?" Talle asked.

"Mr. Wetherill told Old Welo to come by the house later and he'd give him a brand-new .22, no charge, but that right now him and me had to collect the rest of your drags and herd them up on the mesa. And then we rode off to do just that."

"Where did Biye' get the rifle he used?"

"He must've hidden it in the wash. Or maybe he borrowed it from one of the others."

"Then he ambushed you?"

"Mr. Wetherill and I had split up. We were maybe 150 yards apart—I was on the road, ahead, and Mr. Wetherill had gone off into the brush—and I heard a shot. It was real dusty and the sun could blind you, but I turned in the saddle and saw Biye' between us, maybe 100 yards from me. He'd been pointing his rifle in my direction—"

"So he shot at you first?"

"I believe he did. Then I saw him swivel around and take aim at Mr. Wetherill and shoot. I think Wetherill was dead before he hit the ground because I didn't see him move at all, not even a jerk."

"But you were 150 yards away."

"That's what I said."

"So you couldn't be sure."

"No."

Owen interjected, "I think Richard was hit in the chest first. Right near the center."

"Well," Talle said, dismissing Owen with a glance, "we'll let the coroner's jury determine that." He turned back to Finn. "Then what? Did you fire back?"

"Not then," Finn said. "I told you, I only had a pistol. At that distance, there wasn't any point. Besides, that's when I realized there were others spread out ahead of me."

"How many?"

"I don't know. Two or three, I guess, and they started shooting, so I turned my horse and headed back here on the run."

"Where was Biye'?"

"By then, leaning over Mr. Wetherill. Then he fired off another round." He paused. "It didn't leave much doubt."

"So you came directly back here?"

"Two others, Hosteen Joe Yazzie and Tso-bakis, tried to cut me off. I shot Tso-bakis in the side."

"So they were in on it—the ambush?"

Finn scowled. "I didn't stop to ask."

Miss Quick appeared in the doorway. "Sheriff, do you want something to eat?"

"No, thank you," Talle said. "If you'd be so kind, just wrap something up and I'll eat it in the saddle. I'm heading out before the light's completely gone." He turned back to Finn. "Make sure you have your story straight because you're going to have to testify."

"I just told you everything I know," Finn said with considerable resentment.

Talle shook his head. "Legally, it doesn't count. Chaco Canyon isn't even in my jurisdiction. There'll be a coroner's jury, and arraignments for those charged, and trials, and you don't want to be saying different things at different times, especially since somebody's going to accuse you of starting this by clubbing Nez-Begay, not to mention your shooting Tso-bakis." He headed off to the stable.

"I swear, I'd shoot that son of a bitch, too," Finn muttered, "if it wouldn't make matters worse."

That night, all of them—Marietta Wetherill and her children, Eleanor Quick, Des-glena-spah, Helga, Bill Finn, Lee Ivy, Tom O'Fallon, and Owen—huddled sleepless in Richard Wetherill's windowless office, with Finn and O'Fallon taking turns guarding the front of the house. Esteban and the other hands kept their own watch from the bunkhouse.

Day broke quietly. No Navajos appeared. Tom O'Fallon, though, had slunk away.

The first visitor showed up in the afternoon. George Blake, who ran the Tsaya Trading Post, fifteen miles west of Pueblo Bonito, came to offer his condolences to Mrs. Wetherill and to see how she and the children were faring. How had he heard the news? Owen asked.

"Well," Blake stammered, color rising into his wattled neck, "Chischilí Biye' told me."

After a moment of dumbstruck silence, Owen started to ask, "Why—"

"He trades at the store all the time. His hogan's not far."

"He came right out and announced that he killed Richard?"

Blake nodded. "He surely did. He thought he was going to be lynched. He asked me to write down his version of what happened, and I told him to take it to Superintendent Shelton up in Farmington. He lit right out."

"You just let him go?"

"I'm a store clerk, not a lawman, what was I supposed to do?" Blake, upset by the implication, blustered. "I felt bad enough as it was. I mean, after him coming in yesterday morning all riled up and me selling him cartridges for his rifle. He was always whining, complaining about this and that. How was I supposed to know he'd actually shoot Wetherill?"

Owen's stared at him, incredulous. "He *told* you what he planned to do?"

Blake plucked at his mustache. "Sometimes you just can't tell how things are gonna play out."

Owen suddenly felt very tired. "If I were you, I'd keep this to myself, at least until the authorities get here. If Bill Finn hears any of this . . ."

"I'm not afraid of Bill Finn," Blake said, but he was gone within the hour.

True to his intention, Tom Talle had galloped through the night and made it to Thoreau, over fifty miles south, by morning. From there he telegraphed Fort Wingate with the news, requesting that soldiers be sent to Chaco Canyon. He also notified B. P. Six, Samuel Stacher's deputy, who immediately headed for Chaco with a dozen Navajo policemen. Talle then boarded a train for Gallup, where he told Al Wetherill what had happened. Word spread quickly, and late in the day James Fay, a justice of the peace up in Farmington, headed south by surrey to Gallegos Canyon, where his posse met up with the San Juan County sheriff, William Dufur. The group then continued south, arriving near daybreak at the Escavada hogan of Hosteen Joe Yazzie, where he and half a dozen of the Navajos who'd confronted Wetherill and Finn near Pueblo del Arroyo had gathered, awaiting retribution. By midday, when Fay and his companions reached the Wetherill ranch, B. P. Six and the Navajo police as well as Al Wetherill and Sheriff Talle had already arrived.

Owen stayed out of their way except when he was called to give testimony before Fay's hastily assembled coroner's jury—six men: Tom Talle; George Ransome, a friend of the Wetherill family from Gallup; the brothers John and Paul Arrington, whom the judge had sworn in as deputies before leaving Farmington; T. H. Jones, a Farmington attorney who, unaware of the murder, had arrived at Chaco Canyon for a friendly visit; and the befuddled Lee Ivy—which quickly concluded, without hearing from any Navajos, that Chis-chilí Biye' had shot and killed Richard Wetherill with the complicity of five other Indians. Apart from confirming that Richard Wetherill had been unarmed when he left his office, Owen had been able to tell them little except for what he'd seen of Bill Finn's flight: that two men had apparently tried to prevent Finn's reaching the ranch house and that, yes, he'd seen a man, presumably Tso-bakis, attempt to club Finn before Finn shot him.

Fay and Dufur intended to round up the five alleged accomplices at Joe Yazzie's hogan and immediately head back north, but B. P. Six objected, insisting that the Navajos didn't pose a threat and shouldn't be taken into custody, and, furthermore, that Bill Finn should be charged with the attempted murder of Nez-Begay. Finn sat silently, his arms folded, while Judge Fay and Sheriff Dufur conferred. When Dufur told him that he needed to surrender his weapon and accompany them and the Navajos to Farmington, Finn handed over his Colt without so much as a murmur.

It was Eleanor Quick who enlisted the aid of Fay, Dufur, and their men in one additional, unpleasant task: Richard Wetherill's body still lay on the cot behind the house, and, although it was unfortunate that no one from Gallup or Farmington had thought to recruit a man of the cloth, he needed to be buried. Now. It was June, and a very hot June at that. She didn't have to elaborate.

They dug a grave several hundred yards west of the ranch house, in a sandy slope by a round outcrop, not far from where the Anasazi steps breached the north wall of the canyon. Judge Fay quoted the Bible, the burial party sang "Nearer My God to Thee," and then they shoveled the sand back into the hole they'd dug for the rough coffin. Marietta Wetherill didn't take part.

After that, Owen returned to the bunkhouse, crawled into his bed fully dressed, and fell asleep immediately.

The next morning he stumbled from the bunkhouse into the excruciating light. Across the way from him, with his back against the shaded side of a buckboard, sat Clement Yazzie, whittling.

"Why are you here?" Owen asked, crossing to Yazzie and shielding his eyes with his hand.

"Mrs. Halley sent me to bring you home," Yazzie said.

Home, Owen thought. His nose burned with the urge to weep. He looked around him, at the rough ranch house, the bunkhouse, the trading post, the outbuildings, the corral, the red rock wall behind him, the ruin of Pueblo Bonito: the millions of ancient stones stacked so carefully that multi-story walls had stood against the elements for centuries. Hundreds, maybe thousands, had made this raw place home a thousand years ago, but forces, human or natural, had led to its abandonment, and now it would probably be abandoned once again.

"So you heard what happened?"

"Aoo'."

"It didn't take long."

"Someone told Tom Gorman."

"I need to visit the necessary," Owen said. "Then I need to get some food." He hadn't eaten a proper meal since noontime dinner three days ago, the day Wetherill was killed.

"I'm in no hurry," Yazzie said. "Better for the horses if we leave in the evening."

When Owen walked into the kitchen a few minutes later, he found Eleanor Quick drying dishes. She greeted him placidly.

"Do you think it'd be all right if I fixed myself something to eat?" he asked.

"Of course," she answered.

"I'll clean up after myself."

"That's not a man's work."

"You're a teacher, but you appear to be doing the breakfast dishes."

"Well, it's a temporary departure." She wiped her hands on an apron that was too narrow to cover the front of her ample dress.

"Where's Helga?"

"Probably home in Aztec by now. She left with Judge Fay. She decided she couldn't stay here a minute longer."

Owen, poking around in the pantry, found a covered butter dish, a bowl of eggs, and a sack of oatmeal. He carried them to the kitchen table. After pumping water into a pan and setting the pan on the stove—there was still sufficient heat in the coal box—he broke several eggs and separated the yolks and whites into two bowls.

"Well, Mr. Rouse," Miss Quick said, "you seem to know what you're about, though I don't see why you're going to the bother."

"Do you think Marietta would mind if I asked my friend Clement Yazzie to join me?"

Miss Quick's demeanor noticeably cooled. "The Navajo who's outside?"

"Yes."

"I had Des-glena-spah bring him some biscuits and coffee when he arrived."

"How long ago was that?" Owen broke several additional eggs into the bowl of yolks and scrambled them with a fork.

"A while."

"Then these eggs will sit well with him."

"As you say." She hung up the apron, smoothed her skirt, and left the kitchen.

When the food was ready, Owen called Yazzie in. They sat across from each other at the kitchen table. Yazzie ate the eggs with buttered bread; Owen ate his oatmeal concoction, but halfway through, he put down his spoon.

Yazzie looked up. "Are you well?"

"No, I can't say that I am." His elbows on the table, he propped his head up with both hands.

"It's that slop you call food."

"No, it isn't the food. Well"—Owen tried to smile—"it is and it isn't."

Yazzie pushed aside his empty plate. "Is it the sugar?"

"I don't know. Maybe. Maybe it's catching up with me. I haven't been careful enough."

"Maybe we should leave now. The horses will be all right. I don't like this place. I never have."

"Too many chindis?"

"Hunh."

"I got the impression that you didn't really believe in such . . . things." Owen had started to say "superstitions" but thought better of it.

"I don't. And I do."

"You may be the most inscrutable man I've ever known," Owen said.

"I don't know what that means," Yazzie answered.

"Hard to read."

"Is that good or bad?"

"Damned if I know."

Yazzie cupped his mug of black coffee in his large hands. "Every person and every place has its own spirit. Sometimes those spirits don't get along."

Tom Talle opened the door and entered the kitchen. He was wearing his trail coat, hat, and spurs. He stopped short when he saw Clement Yazzie but then crossed the room to the stove and poured himself the last of the morning's coffee.

"Then I'm particularly grateful that you came here to pick me up," Owen told Yazzie, ignoring Talle.

"Mrs. Halley wasn't sure that you were coming back."

"Neither was I," Owen said.

Talle, leaning back against the sink, said, "Am I interrupting?"

"No," Owen said. "Have a seat."

"I've been in the saddle for a while," Talle said. "I'd just as soon stand." He set down his cup, removed his hat, and combed back his hair with his hand.

"Suit yourself." Owen turned back to Yazzie. "I don't know as you've been introduced. Sheriff Talle, from Gallup. Sheriff, my friend Clement Yazzie."

Talle said stiffly, "I've seen you around Gallup."

Yazzie, implacable, didn't reply.

Owen said, "Where are the troops from Fort Wingate? Shouldn't they be here by now?"

It was obviously a sore point, not only because the troops hadn't arrived, but also, Owen figured, because Talle felt that his request now looked ridiculous, a pathetic overreaction.

"I suspect somebody countermanded me," Talle said.

There weren't many who'd have the authority to do that. The commanding officer at Fort Wingate. Superintendent Shelton. Maybe Samuel Stacher. Even at the possible risk of the Wetherill family's lives, politics had determined the response.

"What are you going to do now?" Owen asked Talle.

"Find a couple of reliable hands to help me bring my herd back down from the mesa. I can't leave my cattle up there with no one to keep an eye on them. A week from now, they'll have vanished. Besides, in this drought, the grazing up there isn't much better than anyplace else."

"What'll happen to Wetherill's herds?"

Talle snorted and drained his cup. "My guess is that they'll be rustled and sold off, if someone figures out a way to alter the Triangle Bar Triangle brand. If not, there'll be full cook pots over half the eastern reservation by next week. You should ask your friend Yazzie about that."

Owen turned to the Navajo. "Is he right?"

"Partly," Yazzie said.

"Which part?" Talle asked.

"The part where you said he should ask me."

Talle, his mouth tight, set down his cup in the sink. "You be sure and give Mrs. Halley my regards. Tell her I plan to swing by Many Springs Canyon someday soon. I don't get up in that direction enough."

"Why would you?" Owen said. "Isn't Many Springs in San Juan County?" Talle had no authority outside McKinley County.

"Just to be neighborly," Talle said. "I've heard things that'd make for lively conversation." He put on his hat, tipped the brim, and left.

"What's he talking about?" Owen asked. "What 'things'?"

"I don't know," Yazzie said.

A lie? Owen wondered, but he didn't pursue it. "So tell me—what do you really think'll happen to Wetherill's herds?"

"Nothing you want to hear."

"Try me."

"Most of the stock around here is let out on half-shares. Anglo ranchers turn their stock over to Navajos who have grazing rights, and the Navajos get half the newborn lambs and calves and colts and some of the profits when the stock is sold."

"I know that much," Owen said.

"Just to get by, most of the Navajos borrow at trading posts against their shares. Their debts are often greater than the value of their shares. That's why some of them owe the store so much. But now, things are tangled. Mrs. Wetherill can try to collect on the old debts, but the People have no cash money and no valuables, and if they surrender their animals, including the ones they have on half-share, they'll lose everything."

"So they won't."

"Would you? They have families to feed."

"What about the rest of the Wetherill stock—the animals that aren't out on half-shares?"

"The sheriff was probably right. Except that it won't just be Navajos doing the rustling."

"Won't the Navajo police stop it?"

"They take their orders from the government."

"Shelton."

Yazzie nodded. "It wouldn't matter anyway. The police will be gone in a day or two."

"So Mrs. Wetherill can lose everything and no one will do anything about it."

Yazzie, studying his hands, said nothing.

Richard Wetherill was dead, and everything tangible that he'd worked for in this wilderness would disappear. His only legacy to his children would be whatever History deemed worthy about his explorations at Mesa Verde and here at Chaco Canyon and in Utah. "No justice," Owen muttered.

"It's hard to come by. Ask your sheriff."

"*My* sheriff? Talle? Because I'm an Anglo? He's no more my sheriff than he is yours."

"Think that, if you want." Yazzie rose from the table. "I'll go hitch up the horses." But he stopped and considered Owen's half-full bowl. "If you're up to it."

"I suppose I am. Sitting in a buckboard doesn't take much out of you." But Owen didn't even have the energy to rise from his chair.

"We'll wait until the heat dies," Yazzie said. "Better to wait."

"If you say so."

Yazzie stood beside the table. "There's something else you want to say."

Owen looked up. "What happened here, Yazzie?"

Yazzie gave careful consideration before he spoke. "This is what I think: Even cowards can have moments when they're also something more."

It rankled Owen, who shifted in his seat and said, "Maybe you should explain what you mean."

"I mean the second shot, the one that said, 'I'm Diné and I just blew half your fucking head off. So how do you feel about that, Anasazi man?' "

"And the fact that Biye' is a Navajo justifies what he did?"

"No, but you're going to hear many versions of what happened." Yazzie stepped back and pushed his chair under the table. "Some say Bill Finn's sweet on Mrs. Wetherill."

Owen almost laughed. "Finn? That's absurd." But the implication was clear: Finn might have taken advantage of the situation to kill Wetherill himself. "No one will believe it."

"Don't be so sure," Yazzie said. "Some people will believe anything if it fits with how they see the world."

By seven o'clock Yazzie had decided that the temperature was dropping fast enough for them to leave, and Owen went looking for Marietta Wetherill to say his goodbye. He found her in the nursery, rocking Ruth, who was placidly sucking on her mother's pinky, close to nodding off.

So as not to arouse the baby, Owen spoke softly. "I guess I'll be heading back to Many Springs Canyon now, Marietta."

Visibly exhausted—her face sallow, her eyes red, lids swollen—Marietta looked up from her child. "Well, good luck to you, Owen."

"I wish there was something I could do for you."

"Is B. P. Six still around?"

Owen was taken aback. "Six? No, I don't believe so. I haven't seen him since the coroner's jury."

"Then I guess I won't have to shoot him after all." She looked around the nursery, as if for something missing, and then went on, "I told him that if I ever saw him in this house again, that's what I'd do. I don't blame the Navajos, I blame Shelton and his lackeys. They were behind it, and no one will ever convince me otherwise."

"It's your grief talking," Owen said.

"I know all about grief. I lost two babies." She looked up. "Ruth here is my seventh. So I know about grief. But this . . ." She shook her head. "Something like this turns you inside out and backwards."

Ruth had fallen asleep, milky bubbles on her lips.

"Will you be all right?" Owen asked. "I mean, with the ranch and all."

"We'll be fine," Marietta said. "Mr. Wetherill's brothers and my parents and our friends will stand by us. We'll manage, one way or another. Don't you worry yourself about us. I was a gypsy when I met Mr. Wetherill, and a gypsy I can be again, if need be."

CHAPTER SIXTEEN: The Cabin

Clement Yazzie pushed the horses on through the night and into the morning. Julia met them at the corral. Owen's muddled brain—he repeatedly yawned so intensely that his head swam and tears ran from the corners of his eyes—barely registered her greeting, her look of concern. She remained outside, talking to Yazzie as the Navajo tended to the horses. Owen went directly to the spare bedroom. His room. It was as he'd left it a week ago. The bed neatly made. The side chair next to it. The nightstand on the other side, with the book he'd been reading, Howells's *A Hazard of New Fortunes*, beside the lamp. The room was already hot despite the pallor of the light through the curtained window. He stripped off his clothes, down to his underwear, dropping shirt and pants on the floor, and lay down. The bed seemed to sway beneath him with the motion of the buckboard.

Hours later, he heard Julia knock and enter. She took no note of his dishevelment. She placed a bowl of water on his washstand. He drifted back to sleep.

When he next woke, night had already fallen. Julia was standing in the doorway, silhouetted against the light from the kitchen. "I've fixed a little meal for us," she said, barely above a whisper.

He struggled toward wakefulness. Did he feel hungry? He couldn't tell anymore.

"Just give me a minute," he said, his voice furry.

"Will you stay awake?"

"Yes."

"Then I'll leave the door ajar, so you'll have a little light."

It took him several minutes to force himself from the bed. He splashed water on his face and neck and swabbed at the sourness under his arms before donning a clean cotton shirt and trousers and emerging from the bedroom. Julia had laid the dining table: two soup bowls of mutton broth, with bits of the meat and flakes of dried parsley visible through the thin liquid, plus a small oval platter of fried eggs, liberally sprinkled with black pepper, as well as sliced cheese and a full pitcher of water. Off to the side, a pot of tea steeped. She sat waiting for him, her napkin in her lap, her hands folded on the napkin, her pale eyes studying them. He sat down across from her and she looked up.

"Does this suit you?" Julia asked. "I can fix something else, if you'd like."

"No, this is fine. Thank you." Owen poured himself a glass of water and immediately drank it down. "I'm parched." He poured another and sipped at it.

"Eat your broth before the fat congeals."

"Yes, Ma'am." Smiling took effort. He picked up his spoon.

"How are you feeling?" she asked, her brow furrowed.

"I don't really know." The broth was salty and flavorful. "Drained, I guess."

"You were limping."

"It's just a blister." He helped himself to an egg. Actually, he had several blisters, and the old sore above the bone of his right arch was threatening to open, but he didn't care to admit it.

"Maybe you should be more cautious about how far afield you walk."

She'd fried the eggs in bacon grease. "This is delicious," he said.

They ate the rest of the meal in silence. As Julia was pouring them both a cup of tea, Owen asked, "Where's Yazzie?"

"It's very late. He went home hours ago."

"I appreciated his coming all that way for me."

"He said that Sheriff Talle was there."

"He was. He'd just brought a herd up from Seven Lakes," Owen explained. Then he added, "He and Yazzie exchanged a few pointed words."

Julia folded her napkin. "Sometimes Mr. Yazzie isn't as careful as he should be. It's to nobody's benefit."

Together, Julia and Owen washed and dried the plates, utensils, and pans, and then they refreshed their tea cups and carried them to the parlor. Owen collapsed into his usual chair and raised his stockinged feet to the waiting hassock. He closed his eyes and didn't speak.

After a prolonged silence, Julia said, "What a terrible thing to die like that, with no opportunity to say goodbye to your wife and children." They hadn't spoken of Richard Wetherill before this.

"To prepare them?"

"And to prepare yourself."

"Maybe it's better this way. It's certainly easier, with no accounting to be made of affronts given and received. Like being struck by lightning."

"It was hardly an act of nature."

"Of course not, but you know what I mean." Owen wondered if she wanted to ask him if *he* felt prepared, and it released a sour taste. "You didn't think much of Richard, did you?"

"I didn't really know him." Julia went on, "I admired his accomplishments." Something unsaid hung in the thick air.

"But . . . ?"

"Maybe he was more interested in the Anasazi than in the Navajos he dealt with."

Owen jumped to Wetherill's defense: "I don't think that's at all fair of you."

Julia sighed. "You're right. Besides, now isn't the time for criticism or judgment."

"All those rumors about his mistreating Navajos—mind you, I don't dismiss them out-of-hand, but I honestly believe most are fabrications." Owen leaned forward. "He had every right to homestead in Chaco Canyon. His problem was that he ran afoul of politicians who claim to know what's best for Indians when all they really care about is their own power and influence. And on top of that, you've got arm-chair ethnographers and archaeologists back East who try to build themselves up by advancing some theory that requires attacking Richard's work." Owen eased back into the chair. "I don't know why it riles me so."

"Because Mr. Wetherill treated you well. He welcomed you when you were a stranger. He was your friend."

Owen couldn't sustain whatever anger he'd felt just moments ago, anger arising not only from Julia's rather callous criticism of Richard Wetherill, but also, he realized—it seemed so long ago—from the unpleasantness that had precipitated his decision to leave for Chaco Canyon.

"He asked after you," Owen said.

"Did he? I don't think he ever quite approved of me."

Owen didn't want to confirm or to deny—which would have been the polite thing to do, but he wasn't feeling generous.

"I'm sure he heard all sorts of snippets and innuendos, received second- and third-hand."

Owen frowned. "He's not alone in that. Tom Talle implied that he'd heard things that might lead to his paying you a visit."

Julia, settling her cup back on its saucer, seemed genuinely surprised. "Really? Well, I wouldn't worry about it. "

Owen shifted uneasily. "It seems so odd to be sitting here, talking so *normally* with you. I still see Richard lying on the ground like that . . ." And being lowered into the grave; the hasty, sad, austere burial, a travesty for a man of such worth. But maybe the Navajos had it right—unmarked sites, no hymns and psalms, no mourning attire or black crepe, and then a healing ceremony for the living. For poor Marietta Wetherill and her children. "I'm afraid it's put me in a morbid frame of mind."

"Time will make it less present."

He knew this was true, it had to be, but that didn't help in the moment. "I don't think Mrs. Wetherill will have a penny to her name when this is all over."

"She's a resourceful woman. She'll manage."

"That's exactly what she said—that they'll manage."

After a while Owen continued, "What happened to Richard makes me even more concerned about your safety. And this time I'm not talking about putting a lock on a door."

"I'm no threat to anyone, not the Navajos and not the politicians. Maybe if I were to become too prosperous . . ." Julia laughed at the prospect. "Besides, unlike the Wetherills and the Hubbells and the Days, I don't have a homestead. If Superintendent Shelton decides he wants me out of here, all it would take is the stroke of a pen."

Owen knew that trading privileges could be revoked at any time. "Is Will's name still on the license?"

"Heavens no."

"Then it's just your name?"

"J. M. Halley," she said, adding in response to his quizzical look, "Since there aren't any other women who hold trading post licenses on their own, Alberto Rodriguez suggested that I try to avoid drawing the attention of someone who might object to the very idea."

Something else occurred to him. "Is Yazzie listed as an employee?"

"No. He never has been. He works for me, not the trading post."

That subterfuge alone might be enough to get her into trouble. "That goes beyond splitting hairs, don't you think?"

"Of course it does."

Perhaps for the first time Owen saw the situation in its full clarity. Opposed by anyone with a grudge or something to gain, Julia could lose everything associated with the trading post, including the wool and rug business she'd been trying to build—everything except, ironically, what she shared with a supposedly disreputable Navajo under an agreement that they'd never committed to paper: the sheep that Clement Yazzie managed for her.

As though she'd been thinking the same thing, she said with a quick shrug, "What would you have me do?"

"I'd have you figure out a way to sell off everything you can and go back East."

"*No*, you wouldn't." Her sudden vehemence surprised him.

"Why not?"

"I'd become the person I was before."

What did *that* mean? "Are you that different? At their very center don't people remain the same?"

"Ah. You'd like to think we're like the earth, bedrock beneath the skin."

"Even sterner stuff. Some geologists think that iron and nickel lie at the earth's core, under the mantle."

"I don't go that deep."

"I can't believe that."

"Do or don't, but trust me, I'm safer here."

"*Safer*?How—"

"From myself." She impatiently tried to cut off any response: "You might best leave it at that."

"How can I?" he appealed. He folded his arms across his chest, burying his hands in the hollows.

"Are you cold?" Julia asked.

"Just my hands and feet. They're always cold when I'm not moving around."

"Let me get you a blanket," she said, quickly rising and walking to her bedroom.

"It isn't necessary," he called after her.

He heard a drawer slide open and then close. She brought him her deep green crocheted throw, which, bending over, she proceeded to drape over his feet and lower legs.

"Please, Julia, don't fuss," he said. "I'm not an invalid." But he didn't stop her. "And I won't let you change the subject."

She straightened up. "My saying anything further comes with an obligation."

"What can you possibly think I'd deny you?" He knew immediately that he'd said the wrong thing, a pitiful echo of his pleading—for that's what it had been—for her love just a week ago.

"The obligation to see me as I am and not as you imagine me to be—as you would like me to be."

"I only have one pair of eyes."

"You need to put that 'vision' away once and for all."

"How?"

"That I can't answer."

"So that's my obligation?" To surrender loving her as he did.

She'd said what she had to, and now she returned to where she'd been sitting, settled herself, and folded her hands in her lap.

Bitterly, Owen said, "And when do you need your answer?"

"What will be different tomorrow or the next day?"

Owen spread his hands on the arms of his chair. He studied her—they studied each other—as intently, as intensely, as either ever had. No teacup or knitting or book could serve as a pretense for diversion.

"Why *do* you stay here?" he asked.

"Why do you ask?"

"Don't answer my question with another question."

"I have no need to go anywhere else."

"You sound as if you've surrendered your life to . . . to . . . I don't know what." In frustration he said, "How would you feel if I left tomorrow—I mean for the East, New York?"

"I'd miss you. Profoundly."

"But?"

"I'd make do."

"You've never been lonely?"

"Of course I have. But I don't need to see myself reflected in another's eyes."

Was there anything he could say to *that*? He didn't try.

"Owen, I enjoy having you here. I enjoy our conversations, and the way we can laugh together, and the silent evenings when we're just sitting here reading. And I enjoy having other people visit or pass through, too—I *do* enjoy it. I enjoy talking to the Navajos who come to the store. I enjoy watching the women fingering the bolts of cloth and thinking so hard about every purchase. I enjoy hearing the wives snap at their husbands when they get too opinionated. There's a life to it all, for me, that I could never find elsewhere." Julia continued, "And I especially enjoy when Harry and Pete and Tóya gather here with us, which is all too rare. But even if for some reason they stopped coming, I wouldn't be desolate. It isn't in my nature."

He saw the pride she took in this, but he didn't believe her; he couldn't.

"I've learned that I'm able to live with who I am. Here."

"That's why you stay?"

"Yes."

"I don't see why you think you'd be different elsewhere."

She took a deep breath. "Before I came here I was embittered and resentful. I couldn't be pleased. I was dreadful to everyone."

"I find that hard—"

She raised a hand to stop him.

"I'm sorry, go on," he said.

"I'd always been involved in my father's congregations, at first as an ornament, a little girl in curls and proper second-hand dresses, smiling, and then standing beside my much prettier younger sister, and later still, playing the harmonium at services—it was a horrible little instrument, never in tune—and handing out glasses of punch or fruit ices at church socials. Little by little, as my mother withdrew to her bed, her responsibilities became mine—counting the proceeds from the collection plate and the poor box, copying over my father's sermons for posterity, participating in the Ladies' Auxiliary and the Ladies' Aid Society and the Church Decorating Committee—it all fell to me. I hated it. True, I was of an age, but my father never asked me what I wanted to do. He just *assumed*. Even before my mother died, I felt trapped. So you might expect that when he took up with Edna Blaine—Edna Marshall now, of course—I would have felt relieved. But I didn't. I resented him even more. And Edna I thoroughly disliked. For no good reason. As I said, I couldn't be pleased. I coerced my father into agreeing to my marriage—he saw immediately that it would be a mistake—and then I further coerced him into surrendering the money my mother had left me. Worst of all, I deserted Penelope."

"But you've said that you left her in good hands."

"As it turns out. Because I misjudged Edna. She did exactly as she said she would for Penny, and for my father. His health has gone from bad to worse almost from the day of their marriage. It can't be easy for her."

"Certainly, you can make amends?"

"In all honesty, despite recognizing Edna's better qualities, I still dislike her. I believe I always shall, and that's a very dark thing." She broke off at that point and went into the kitchen. He heard her stirring up the coals in the firebox, filling the tea kettle, placing it on the stove.

Owen followed her when she didn't return.

Her back to him, Julia said, "I can forgive my father everything except not seeing that he needed to let me go."

"If you went back now, you think it would be admitting failure."

"No, that isn't it." She turned to him. "I'd succumb."

"To what?"

"For want of a better word, the comfort."

"I don't see why that would be so bad."

"I'd be protected by my step-mother's money or, should I move to Chicago, as an aunt to my sister's children in my brother-in-law's household. In either case I'd be unapproachable, as a married woman long estranged from her husband. Oh, there'd be rumors aplenty, but people would not ask. I'd attend church, subscribe to the symphony, offer my services for some worthwhile civic project, join a knitting circle—"

"I can't see it." He shook his head slowly.

"Precisely."

"What *I* mean is, none of that need be true."

She ignored him and went on: "I'd be beholden to my step-mother or my brother-in-law. Philip has no great love for me. He would tolerate me, but only if I lived as he saw fit. And in the end I would do it—I'd succumb, and before long *this* life would be boxed and stored in an attic where I needn't ever venture again."

Someone had yet to be spoken of.

"Are you concerned about Yazzie?"

The light from the nearest lamp played along her profile. "No. If I left, he'd understand. He'd be fine."

"He's putting you in danger, Julia."

"Mr. Yazzie isn't dangerous."

"I meant your relationship."

"You'd have me give him up?"

Yes, oh yes, he thought. But then, No. No.

"I'm not asking you to deny what you feel," Julia said, reaching out and placing a hand on his chest. "I'm asking if you can put it aside. Can you do that? For my sake?"

His heart thumped once, twice, as if it had skipped intervening beats and needed to push extra blood to compensate. His losing her, no matter how grievous, would be brief—a month, a year, a twinkling: the time he had left—an exhalation lost in the aether; but when *she* lost *him*, however it came about, by volition or affliction—for lose him she must—

He felt the strength of her true feeling for him. Call it love.

Owen had nothing, nothing to offer her and no future without the hope of her. Could he let it go? He looked up. She was right there, but out of his reach. Her eyes brimmed in the lamplight. She was waiting for his answer. He knew what flesh was heir to. Clothes hung like heavy curtains from his frame. His arms dangled at the ends of his collar bones. He could easily count his ribs by sight or touch. When he sat, his abdomen lay depressed between the peaks of his hip bones. His knee caps bulged beneath his trousers. He didn't have far to go.

"Yes," he said.

She wept openly and he opened his arms to her. *This* was everything. He held her loosely, so she wouldn't feel uneasy. They stood together for several minutes before she stepped back, wiping her eyes with the heels of her hands. She said:

"We'll build you a cabin."

"You'll—" Had he heard her correctly? "Why would you do that?"

"Is there somewhere you'd rather be?"

"No," he said, "but—"

"Then you should have a cabin of your own."

"I have my tent."

She rolled her eyes. "Have you forgotten what winter in the Chuskas means?"

"I guess I didn't expect to be here for another winter." He clarified what he meant: "I mean, in Many Springs Canyon. In the West, for that matter."

"There must be places out here that you'd like to see."

"Maybe the Grand Canyon. And the California coast."

"Owen," Julia said, "you make them sound out of reach. It's the twentieth century—the hardest part of the trip is getting from here to Gallup! Then you board a westbound train, and the next morning, you're gazing over the canyon from the South Rim. Or in less than twenty-four hours, you're standing with your trouser legs rolled up and your feet in the Pacific."

She linked her arm in his and they returned to the parlor and their familiar places.

"Have you seen the Pacific?" Owen asked her.

"No, I haven't."

"We could go together." Fearing that he'd once again blundered into just the wrong thing to say, he quickly added, "And I think I'd like to visit Bosque Redondo."

"What a *horrible* idea," Julia said. "Bosque Redondo!—why would anyone want to go *there*? I'd rather visit hell. Besides, everything's gone. Even Fort Sumner. It was razed more than a decade ago."

"Still, I'd like to spend just a day there, to try and imagine what it was like for Tóya. For her generation." He fell silent. He'd run out of places that came readily to mind. "You've talked to Yazzie about this?" he asked.

"About the cabin? Yes," Julia answered. "In fact, he says he'll build it."

Overcome, Owen couldn't speak for some time. "Why would he do that?"

"You'd have to ask him." Her standard response; but then she added, "I suppose because he wants you to stay."

"For your sake?"

"Owen, you'd have to ask *him*."

But Yazzie wouldn't answer. No, for Clement Yazzie the hammer driving the nail would be answer enough.

"So I'm going to live like Thoreau." During his convalescence last winter she'd tried to interest him in *Walden*, but he never managed to get beyond page eight without nodding off. (And no, he'd told her, he had never visited Walden Pond, even though it was a mere twenty-five miles from Leominster.)

She smiled now. "Not quite so austerely. You can have a proper bedroom and a kitchen and a sitting room with a fireplace and enough room for a dining table."

"So, bigger than Thoreau's cabin."

"Much bigger. And with a nearby pond." She grew mischievous: "If not a bee-loud glade and evenings full of linnets' wings."

"Julia," he said, narrowing his eyes as if in reproach, "you're taunting me."

"How so?" All innocence. Then she laughed. "They say that Mr. Yeats was thinking about *Walden* when he wrote 'The Lake Isle of Innisfree.'"

"Do you have to keep pointing out my ignorance?"

"I do! You take it so well!" At last, she took up her knitting from the woven basket on the floor. A half-finished scarf and balls of indigo and aniline red yarn lay pooled in her lap but one of her needles was missing. She leaned over and rifled through her basket—needles of various gauges, small balls of leftover wool in a variety of colors, several unused skeins—until she found it. She adjusted her last finished row across the other needle.

"Oh, Julia," he sighed, "how many evenings will we have, to sit here like this?"

Serious once again, she said, "Even if you could know, would you want to?"

"I don't even know how I ended up here, Julia. I really don't. Not so long ago I thought I knew what I was about. And then . . . this." He spread his arms and then let them fall limp. "Some mornings I wake up and think it's all been . . ." He shook his head. For some reason, lately, Durango kept showing up in his dreams: the gray of clouds and coke smoke, the storefronts of glass and raw timber, the narrow-gauge tracks of the Denver & Rio Grande—the first place in the West where he'd stopped long enough to take it all in. And then at other times he woke up thinking that he'd conjured the western road from Chaco Canyon into existence. But no, he'd followed it to its end and beyond and walked up a canyon and found Julia sitting on her veranda stripping pole beans from their vines. "It all seems so improbable."

"Step by step, it isn't so improbable," Julia said. "It's how most of us get to where we are."

Thinking again of Richard Wetherill and how this conversation had begun, Owen said, "At least I put my affairs in order first."

"You mean, Bethany."

"I suppose. Mostly.

"You loved her."

"I did."

"And now?"

"Naturally, I still think about her." He paused. "I think I loved her family just as much. Walking into their home, being surrounded by Beth and her parents and her brothers and sister-in-law felt like arriving in a foreign country that you've day-dreamed about visiting but where you never really expected to live."

"Have you written to her?"

He shook his head. "I've thought about it, but no, I haven't."

"Would you want to see her again?"

"No. It would absolutely be the wrong thing to do. I'm surprised you'd even ask." He'd related, long before, the circumstances of their parting in her parents' parlor. But then he asked, "Do you think I should write?"

"To say . . . ?"

"Just to explain."

"And would you be honest?"

"Honest?" Why did she think he wouldn't be?

"To say that you did what you thought best for *both* of you—you as well as her."

"What was best for *me*—when I had nowhere to go except to a farm I hated and a father who—" He broke off.

"Owen," she said. Just his name; calmly in just that tone.

"Your water's boiling away," he said.

"What?"

"The kettle on the stove."

She rose and went into the kitchen and moved the kettle, but didn't prepare another pot of tea after all. She returned to her chair and resumed knitting her scarf.

He leaned forward but couldn't make out the face of the wall clock. "What time is it?" he asked.

Julia looked behind her. "It's near midnight."

He sat back.

"They're very fine people," he said after a while.

"Owen, I have no doubt that they would have tried to do their very best for you. I think it would have been the very thing for most people, to be in the embrace of a loving family."

"*Most* people?"

She didn't respond at first. "Step by step, you chose to come here."

Here. To her.

"Is there anything you still feel you need to do?" Julia asked.

To do . . . before. He thought about his father's request that he return to New Hampshire. What would be the point? (Would his mother rest any easier?) He'd soon become an annoyance to his father, who was an old man and wasn't going to change.

"I've written to my father several times. He hasn't replied, which is no surprise—I don't recall ever receiving more than a note from him."

"You still feel an obligation."

"What if he hadn't sold the acreage by the river? I'd still be there on the farm."

"Oh, I doubt it."

"Then where?"

"I don't know. Maybe even here, through some other means."

Owen considered that but had to dismiss it. "Maybe I should write to Beth's father," he said. "Just to let him know where I am and that I'm doing well."

"Be prepared if Beth writes back. Or if she doesn't."

At first thought, either struck him as equally possible, assuming that her father didn't keep the letter to himself and Mrs. Burrows. But no, Beth wouldn't write. He hadn't allowed her to have her say when it mattered, and now it was too late.

"Is this what *you* want, Julia? The cabin?"

"I do."

"You have to let me pay for it," Owen said. "You know I still have funds I can draw on. Thanks to you, I've spent very little."

"Nonsense," Julia replied. "A log cabin doesn't require much beyond purchasing windows and a sink and stove, and maybe bricks and good planks for the floor—I hate a rough floor. Tim Be'ak'idii will come down from Blue Hawk Lake to help with the logging. Mr. Yazzie says the cabin can be ready by late August."

"You and he worked all this out while I was at Chaco Canyon?"

"The idea of building a cabin has come up before, but you provided an incentive."

A cabin would always have a use, Owen thought, more so than the guest hogan that already stood beyond the corral. He withdrew his hands from under his arms and looked at them. "I know how to lay out and square corners, anyway. And I know enough about masonry to build a proper chimney." He looked up. "I've often thought about how—when—I'd leave," he said. "I haven't asked myself how I'd *stay*." He meant in the absence of the very thing, ardor, that had sustained him.

"Just stay," Julia said. "We'll build your cabin."

"Is it really that simple?"

"Yes."

He looked around him. "You do have books."

Her warbling laugh. "Many books."

"More than I could ever read." Not to mention many that he wouldn't want to; he thought again of *Walden*; but maybe he'd give it another go. "If I stay, some people won't like it. They'll think it a scandal. They probably already do."

"It's none of their business."

"It will wear on you, Julia. All of it." In the end, mortality.

"Which is one reason why we need to be so very clear with each other now."

So that they wouldn't feel compelled to revisit these decisions over and over. So that they could *live.*

Owen settled deeper into his chair. He let his head fall against the high back. He'd like to have a chair like this in his cabin.

CHAPTER SEVENTEEN: Peabody's Tale

Owen stood on the simple scaffolding that Clement Yazzie and he had erected at the side of the cabin. A dozen courses of brick to go, now that he'd reached roof level. Before the end of the week the chimney would be completed, the mortar dry enough for him to light a fire and test the damper and the draft. His hands had been toughened by the month of labor, and their roughness pleased him, as did standing with his hat tipped back and the August sun full on his face. Sweat trickled beneath his shirt, down his back and sides, but he didn't mind. He felt alive.

And hungry. A *good* hungry, because the more he labored, the stronger he felt and the more he could eat. A month ago, having resolved to build this cabin, *his* cabin, he'd also decided to live as best he could without further complaint, and that included eating in moderation everything except wheat flour; he'd grown particularly fond of the green and yellow vegetables that Julia grew in her garden—string and wax beans, peppers, lettuces, cabbage, carrots, summer squash—and that Harry Whitaker had insisted he eat if he wanted to avoid scurvy and God knows what else.

He'd carefully laid out the footprint for the cabin east of the pond and south of the wash shed but angled toward the trading post so that from his front door and windows he would be able to see Julia's veranda as well as the corral and guest hogan. From where he stood now, ten feet off the ground, he could easily step onto the roof; from that vantage he could see, to the west, the few trees near Yazzie's hogan, and a swath of the high meadow, to the dark green edge of the forest.

The work on the cabin had proceeded apace. First the stone foundation pillars to support the sills, then the v-notched and shaved pine logs for the walls, and the cross beams that would support the plank flooring, and the purlins for the roof of thinner logs, set perpendicular to the purlins and covered with ready roofing of rolled felt and asphalt hauled by Johnny Gorman and him from the lumber yard in Gallup. After completing the chimney, he would chink the outer walls with mortar and then turn his attention to the interior, which, though he'd moved his cot in a week ago, remained bare except for wall studs. He would nail in place laths and apply horsehair plaster at a more leisurely pace. (Julia had warned him that the plastering was trickier than he might think, but he was determined to have a go at it anyway.) These last jobs, the chinking and the interior work, he would do by himself, and if the season turned cold before he finished, no matter, because by then he would have his chimney and his fireplace and a stove.

Owen turned when he heard the incongruous rumble coming up the canyon trail. He shaded his eyes. The sun flashed against a red hood; it had to be Alberto Rodriguez's automobile, which Owen remembered from the comet-watching party. From this angle, the wheels of the formidable machine struck him as too flimsy for the terrain, the tires thin and, he figured, the rims easily bent by an unexpected rut or a boulder, which was just as likely to snap an axle (again) or break the wheel mounts. But here it came, nevertheless, up the canyon trail at a brisk pace, raising pale ocher billows, steered by a seemingly fearless driver, dressed in his duster and wide-brimmed flat cap and goggles. But that wasn't Alberto Rodriguez in the driver's seat, Owen suddenly realized, not unless Rodriguez had doubled in bulk since Owen had last seen him.

Spotting Owen on his scaffold, the driver waved a gloved hand and honked the horn, which set a sheep dog barking up toward Yazzie's. Two horses, tied at the hitching post in front of the store, struggled to escape, neighing, bug-eyed, their stamping hooves stirring up more dust as the automobile, its wheels locking in response to a heavy foot on the brake pedal, slid to a stop beside the veranda. The driver shut off the motor, which failed to calm the spooked animals, whose Navajo owners emerged from the trading post in response to the commotion. They were soon followed by Tom and Carmelita Gorman. The driver, grinning broadly through his beard, stood up, one hand still on the wheel for balance, and saluted with the other. "Hello!" he called out to one and all.

Inside the wash shed Julia had been discussing with Nona Ts'iini how much longer it would take for the wool she was dyeing to achieve the desired shade of yellow. Nona couldn't care less about Julia's need to get the dyed wool to the weavers who needed it for two rugs that customers in Chicago had ordered. Such things had to take their own time, Nona insisted as

she stirred the wool in its bath—Julia pictured a witch over her cauldron—
with a stick clutched in her clawlike fingers. They'd had this argument before. No matter how much time Julia allowed for Nona's vegetal dyeing, it
was never enough. It didn't matter what they used—onion skins or rabbit
brush flowers for yellows, elderberry or even indigo cakes for blues, or dock
root for gold, or a combination to produce greens—Nona had to have her
way. Not for the first time, Julia asked herself why she didn't just order ani-
line-dyed Germantown yarns and pass that out to her weavers. But she'd
promised her customers an authenticity that required doing everything right
here in Many Springs Canyon, from shearing to cleaning the wool, to carding and spinning, to natural dyeing whenever possible.

Nona was a relic, a gray-haired, broad-nosed, half-blind, arthritic
crone who still thought the proper way to obtain red yarn was to ravel cochi-
neal-dyed bayeta and spin it anew by hand. Julia had prevailed in that dispute by refusing to purchase the Spanish cloth (six dollars a pound!) and by
dying the wool herself with aniline red. Oh, Nona was a throwback all right,
but she was also an excellent teacher, showing to less-experienced Navajo
women a patience that she rarely extended to Julia. Nona had taught her
daughter Tina and her grand-daughters Wanda and Ramona, Julia's best
weavers. Wanda and Ramona, both with young children, worked at home, a
couple miles south of Many Springs Canyon, but Tina wove under the
shade of a summer hogan that Clement Yazzie had built near the wash shed,
under a tree. There were three looms set up there, two for Tina, who preferred working on two weavings at a time, switching off when the spirit
moved her, and the third for teaching. It wasn't unusual for even seasoned
weavers to bring their questions to Nona and Tina, who would use the third
loom to demonstrate solutions—how, for example, to seamlessly weave multiple colors into a single weft or produce intricate borders, which the newer
designs, in emulating Persian rugs, often required. Nona justifiably derided
what most weavers produced these days—shabbily woven rugs with incon-
sistently blended merino wool, some of which hadn't even been properly
washed and carded, leaving behind grease and streaks of excrement and
insect parts or chaff still stuck to the wool. In the last generation, the art of
weaving had nearly died, partly the fault of government allotments of merino
sheep, with their short, kinky, greasy pelts, and partly because most traders
still paid by the pound, thereby encouraging weavers to produce shoddy
work as quickly as possible. Julia provided her weavers with first-quality,
clean churro wool, and she paid them well. With a little guidance, they
could produce admirable blankets and rugs.

Drawn by the ruckus outside, drying her hands on her apron, Julia
emerged from the wash shed in time to see the driver of the automobile
whip off his goggles and hat, revealing a balding pate, creased red cheeks, a

neatly trimmed beard beneath, and a delighted grin. "Mrs. Halley!" he called out, spreading his arms wide, "what do you think?"

Julia shaded her eyes. "Mr. Peabody?"

He laughed from deep in his considerable gut. "Indeed!"

Owen was nimbly descending the cabin's scaffold. Over the last six weeks Julia had watched him gain an energy, a lightness, that surprised and very much pleased her. He was still gaunt but hadn't lost more weight and displayed in his devotion—she couldn't think of a better word—to his life at Many Springs Canyon a remarkable vigor: building the cabin but also tending the animals with her in the early morning, helping out behind the counter in the store, weeding and watering the vegetable garden beside her in the evening. (Still, there were times, too many times, when her own spirits flagged and she found herself wondering how long his renewal would last.) Now he approached the visitor, calling out, "Isn't that Alberto's automobile?"

"Not anymore!" Win Peabody replied. He tossed his hat, goggles, and gloves on the seat, stepped on the running board, and hopped to the ground, landing with a wobble.

He thrust his hand into Owen's. "Delighted to see you again," Peabody said. "Both of you!" He turned and grasped Julia's hand.

Nona had followed Julia out from the wash shed, and Tina likewise had left her looms to come and see the automobile. Julia introduced them to Peabody in proper Navajo form. Peering over the low door to the automobile's rear seats, she saw that two five-gallon cans of gasoline, two extra tires, and a tool kit occupied much of the floor. The two trading post customers, who'd finally succeeded in calming their horses, joined the conclave, as did Tom Gorman.

"How did you end up with Alberto's car?" Julia asked.

"He sold it to me for $700. That's $550 less than he paid for it, excluding the shipping cost." Peabody rocked back on his heels, clearly pleased with his transaction.

"Why would he do that?"

Peabody winked. "It seems that Mrs. Rodriguez didn't trust it after that broken axle up on the mountain, and besides, I gather she wanted something larger and more luxurious. So, calculating that it would cut my travel time to and from Zuni to two hours in good weather, I made the investment."

"And has it been worth it?" Julia asked.

"Oh yes! So far, I've made three trips to Zuni and back. And today I decided to *really* test its mettle by paying *you* a visit." He displayed an exaggerated frown. "When we met under the stars, as it were, last May, you *did* say I'd be welcome anytime."

"I did, and you are."

His frown turned to a grin. "What a night that was—truly memorable. You made me feel quite welcome. It was like the little gatherings Pete has told me so much about—with you and him and Dr. Whitaker, and Mr. Rouse here, and your Navajo friends—except writ large, so to speak. And speaking of Pete"—Peabody swung around—"he isn't here?"

"No," Julia said with some surprise. "Did he say he was coming?"

"Several days ago. When I mentioned I intended to venture up here, he said he might circle back after visiting Shiprock on one of his photographic expeditions."

"Well, he hasn't arrived yet." Nor had he stopped by on his way north.

"And I also saw Dr. Whitaker when I passed through Tohatchi. He said he might also join us but that he needed to wait for a set of twins to make their appearance. The babes were being stubborn."

"Can I take a look at the engine?" Owen asked.

"Of course!" Peabody turned and opened the hood. The men all moved closer. The heat rose in waves from the engine block. "So what we have here is the Cartercar Model H. An inline four, with an infinitely variable friction-drive transmission—it's quite marvelous, really. It eliminates all that bothersome clutching and shifting. And it delivers twenty-five horsepower."

Owen, studying the solid machinery under the hood, asked, "So it hasn't given you any difficulties?"

"None to speak of. I had to be hauled out of a ditch once, but no damage done, except to my pride. I believe that under the right conditions of weather and road, I could reach thirty miles per hour. Can you imagine that—Gallup to Zuni in little more than an hour! And to Many Springs Canyon in two! I took my time today and easily made it in well under four. I tell you, the automobile is going to revolutionize the West—forget the railroad! After all, what *is* the West but great distances, and these machines will change the calculus from days to hours, and from miles to gallons of gasoline. And on one's own schedule, not the railroad's."

Tom Gorman, looking skeptical, drawled, "Well, you can't haul coal or ship wool in an automobile."

"You're quite right," Peabody said, pausing to search his memory, "Mr. Gordon, isn't it?"

"Tom Gorman."

"My apologies, Mr. Gorman. But what about"—he cocked his head—"the many places that the railroad will never reach, such as Zuni and Many Springs Canyon?"

"There are still horses and mules," Tom said.

"Let me offer you some refreshments," Julia said to Peabody.

"Well, I'll certainly take you up on your offer," he said, wiping sweat off his brow with a forefinger. "The day's grown rather warm, hasn't it?" He slipped his arms from his travel coat. Underneath he wore a tan Norfolk jacket, a wing-collared white shirt, blue bowtie, and brown cotton trousers.

Julia led him and Owen to the shade of the side veranda, just as Carmelita Gorman, carrying a wooden tray with glasses and a pitcher of cold water, emerged from the kitchen door. "Thank you so much," Julia said.

Carmelita and Peabody exchanged greetings, and then Carmelita, having moved the pitcher and glasses to the veranda's rough-hewn table, asked, "Should I see what's in the larder?"

"That would be lovely," Julia said, smiling. Lately, Carmelita had been uncommonly solicitous. "There should be some hard-boiled eggs and cheese and the last of a joint of mutton in the icebox. And if you could put on a fresh pot of coffee? Then I insist that you come and join us." Carmelita departed, and Julia, Owen, and Peabody sat down. "I'm afraid we eat rather simply."

"Not at all, not at all." Peabody accepted the glass of water that Julia had poured for him and quickly drained it. She poured him another.

"Is your business doing well, Mr. Peabody?" Julia asked.

"Please," he said, "call me Win."

"Win, then."

He rocked his head from side to side on his thick neck. "Business is improving. I expect that in a few years my services will become as routine as they are back in the larger Eastern cities, at least among the more affluent."

The group around the automobile was breaking up. Nona and Tina had already returned to their tasks.

Owen finished off his drink and said, "It's too darned hot to climb back up on that scaffold today."

"You're doing too much," Julia said, frowning. "You're going to get heatstroke or worse."

"Yes, Ma," he said, grinning. And then he added for Peabody's benefit, "She has the worries."

The door to Julia's kitchen opened again and Carmelita appeared carrying on her tray plates, cutlery, cups, napkins, half a loaf of pueblo bread, and a platter of sliced mutton, goat cheese, peeled eggs, pickled beet root, and thin carrots plucked fresh from the garden that morning.

"May I ask how you got started in the funeral business?" Julia said to Peabody.

"That's a long story," Peabody answered. "But, in short, I accepted a job maintaining the premises for Ulrike and Klaus Holzknecht, German immigrants to Chicago who'd started their own mortuary business. Before long, I became their apprentice and eventually their partner. In more ways than one, they rescued me."

"How so?"

"I grew up on the wrong side of the tracks, so to speak, and my previous employment," Peabody said, rising at Julia's invitation and proceeding to fill a plate, "was in a rendering plant near the Chicago stockyards—a more odious job you couldn't possibly imagine. Everything went into the hopper: offal, rats, dead dogs off the street, chicken feathers, the ubiquitous heads and hooves and trimmings scraped from the floors of the packing plants. The fires burned 'round the clock—I worked the night shift—and the stink and steam engulfed everything. It was hell, incarnadine and incarnate."

"Enough to put you off your feed?" Owen said, smiling wryly and watching Peabody help himself to the spread.

"Indeed! I was a skinny kid in those days." Peabody patted his waistline and chuckled. "You wouldn't know it now, would you?" He returned to his seat. The legs of the chair creaked. "But you know what I hated most about that job? I could never get my hands clean, short of sticking them in borax and bleach." He shook his head in a shiver. "Most of us wore gloves, but by the end of a shift they were soaked through. At least they offered some protection from filthy blades and splintered bones. More than one fellow I worked with had missing fingers, and one unfortunate soul ended up dying from blood poisoning. I suffered a nick or two, but I was lucky."

Carmelita returned again with a pot of coffee, a sugar bowl, and a small pitcher of milk. Owen surrendered his seat to Carmelita and stretched out along the top step of the veranda, his back to a post.

Peabody, his napkin spread across his lap, with his plate balanced there, said, "It's a feast!" He laughed deeply. "I thank both of you ladies!"

"You're welcome," Julia replied. Carmelita, nonplussed by Peabody's effusive praise, said nothing.

Julia glanced at Owen's plate, which held only a boiled egg and a raw carrot. She herself had no appetite. She took a slice of mutton and a spoonful of pickled beets and broke off a small piece of bread from the loaf. She'd lost weight lately; she felt it in her clothing, in the ease with which she could cinch in her waist.

"My sister Penelope and her family live in Chicago," Julia said.

"Really?" Peabody replied with notable warmth. "It's a marvelous city, on the whole. You've visited them?" He wrapped a slice of mutton in a piece of bread.

"No, not yet. One of these days."

"You really must go. I return at least twice a year."

"You still have family there?" Julia asked.

"No, no, just business interests. Real estate mostly, although I'm still a partner—a financial partner—in the successor to the Holzknechts' original mortuary. If I may ask, what does your sister's husband do?"

"He's an executive with the New York Central Railroad."

"Ah! Very nice. Very stable employment."

"And in her spare time," Owen interjected, "Julia's sister is drumming up business for the trading post."

"How so?"

"Through a catalog of Navajo rugs—"

"Just a small one," Julia cut in. "Penny has been distributing it to friends and acquaintances, and in turn some of them have passed it on to others."

"Rugs? Hmm," Peabody pondered. "Just rugs?"

"And blankets," Julia said. "We've gotten a number of orders already."

"Interesting," Peabody said, nodding and pouring himself a cup of coffee. "Indian crafts sold through a catalog . . . very interesting."

"If I may ask," Julia said, "why did you leave Chicago for Gallup, of all places?"

Peabody winked. "I had a hidden motive."

A buckboard driven by a Navajo man, his wife at his side, three children of various ages in the back, came up the trail to the trading post, and Carmelita, who'd indulged in only a mug of coffee, took the opportunity to return to the store. Julia suspected she wasn't enamored of Win Peabody or his profession.

A single cloud was massing in the west, above the Chuskas. Julia had seen this happen many times before. The cloud would soon be joined by others, turning at their base dark gray. Set in motion by a rising wind and gusts stiff enough to rip bed sheets off a clothesline, the storm clouds would roll over the mountains with jagged flashes and ear-splitting concussions, and release a downpour that would veil the landscape and soon turn the washes and river beds into muddy torrents. Then the clouds would give way, just as quickly, to a freshened blue sky. The thunderstorm wouldn't be enough to lift the drought, but maybe it portended an abbreviated rainy season, more than a month tardy. She could only hope.

Owen, having also read the cloud, excused himself, saying he should cover his day's work on the chimney.

"How is our young friend doing?" Peabody asked when Owen was out of earshot.

"He's fine." Julia gave him a false smile. She could only conclude that Pete had told Peabody about Owen's condition.

"He does *seem* fine, but it's a terrible illness to see in someone so young."

They continued to chat until Peabody announced he couldn't eat another bite, and then they carried the dishes and the half-empty coffee pot inside, into the dim kitchen, and set them down on the drain board.

"You seem to have made a very cozy home for yourself here," Peabody said, strolling beyond the dining table and looking toward the parlor.

"It suits me."

"Do you mind?" Peabody asked, gesturing toward the bookcase at the far end of the room.

"Not at all. My sister keeps me supplied." Julia followed him.

Peabody bent forward to see the titles in the dim light. He straightened up, pulling a book from the shelf: Mary Roberts Rinehart, *The Circular Staircase.* "I've heard she's good. A mystery writer?"

"Yes, my sister says she's all the rage in Chicago. She does spin a good tale."

"There's something to be said for that." He returned the book to the shelf. "You alphabetize your books by author."

"I do."

"No Xenophon?" he asked without cracking a smile.

"I'm afraid not."

Then the smile came, and the laugh. "I've taken up writing myself."

"Really?"

"Oh, you know, the chronicles of a mortician. Some of my more interesting cases, you might say. Things that might attract Conan Doyle's interest. But I have no aspirations toward the literary. It's something to pass the lonely evenings in Gallup."

"Your wife chooses to live in Zuni?" she said, but what she really wanted to know was how a mortician from Chicago ended up married to a Zuni woman.

"Oh, absolutely! I wouldn't have it otherwise. Estella hates Gallup, and I can't blame her. She did live there for a time, and the experience was *not* pleasant."

A knock sounded on the door, though it was open. Tom Gorman stood in the doorway. "I'm wondering," he said, "if Mr. Peabody might be willing to give my friends a ride in his automobile before they head home?"

"Why not!" Peabody said, clapping his hands. "And you should come along, Mr. Gorman. And Julia?"

"Some other time, but Owen might be interested." Together, they returned to the veranda. Tom's friends, the two Navajo men with the skittish horses, were standing by the car.

"Get in! Get in!" Peabody called out. "Grab a seat. Where did I leave my goggles and hat?"

Owen was standing by his cabin folding a piece of canvas, cut from his old tent, so that he could more easily climb the scaffolding with it.

"Mr. Rouse!" Peabody bellowed from beside the car, his sleeves rolled up, his hands on his hips, his belly testing his shirt buttons. "Come for a drive down the canyon!" Tom Gorman and his friends began removing the spare supplies from behind the front seat. The three were talking in Navajo and laughing.

"Do you have room?" Owen called.

"For you, my friend, I'll make room!"

Peabody's run down and back up the canyon with his four passengers had barely concluded when the clouds opened up, as a result of which he quickly accepted Julia's invitation to spend the night; the prospect of driving home in the dark through a cesspool of mud, even guided by his car's excellent electric headlamps, had no appeal.

And then Pete Pietrowski finally showed up.

"Always before supper," Julia remarked from the veranda as he unharnessed Stable Boy.

"Are you chiding me," Pete said, "after I braved the elements to get here in time?"

She hadn't seen him in nearly three months, not since the night of the comet-viewing. The following morning, he'd left without so much as a goodbye. It still irritated her, but she decided not to pursue it.

They all shared a picnic supper—a laying hen that was past its prime, roasted corn, greens from her vegetable garden, freshly baked brown bread—sitting beside Yazzie's pond on coarsely woven saddle blankets. In response to an invitation delivered by Owen, Clement Yazzie had indicated that he and Johanna might join them later, after completing their evening chores.

As they finished eating, a soft breeze rose. The men were discussing territorial politics, but Julia was only half-listening. A flock of yellow-headed blackbirds several dozen strong was in residence on the marshier side of the pond, where reed grass, sedges, and cattails had sprung from seeds carried on the air. Julia had never paid much mind to birds back East, but a number of species attracted her attention here: golden and bald eagles and turkey vultures for their sheer size; various hawks, which she couldn't distinguish one from the other except for the red-tail; ravens, cliff and barn swallows, jays; and now these blackbirds, the males especially, with their canary-yellow heads and chests, black circle around the eye, white patch on the wing, and their vocal sequence of quick musical chirps and raucous screeches. She loved watching them sail aloft and swoop back into the cover, clinging to the cattails they set swaying.

"It's a terrible thing, what happened to Wetherill," Peabody was saying. He lifted his head and released a plume of smoke. All three men were enjoying cigars. Julia didn't at all mind the smoke; it helped keep the mosquitoes at bay.

"His brother Al still hasn't gotten over it," Peabody continued. "I see him down at the Post Office, and sometimes his hands are shaking like he's got the delirium tremens, though I understand he's not much of a drinker."

"He's the nervous sort," Pete added. "Always has been. I'm sure it rankles that Biye' was released into Shelton's custody until a grand jury meets in the fall."

"You're very quiet, Julia," Peabody noted.

She'd brought her knitting with her, and her hands were busy working the needles and the wool. "Oh, I'm listening to the blackbirds."

Peabody's round face spread into a broad smile. "Not to us?"

"And to you, of course. Although in my experience men smoking cigars do tend to pontificate."

"Go ahead, put us in our place," Pete said.

"Owen, would you light the lanterns?" Julia said. The sky behind the Chuskas held onto its last blue. The birds were settling in for the night.

"Yá'át'ééh," Clement Yazzie said quietly, coming up behind the picnickers, Johanna at his side.

Win Peabody scrambled awkwardly to his feet and held out a hand. "Mr. Yazzie!—and Miss Yazzie"—he nodded to Johanna—"it's indeed a pleasure to see you again."

Yazzie took the extended hand and limply shook it.

Yazzie spread a blanket off to the side for Johanna. Then he sat down facing the company, his back to the pond, legs crossed. Owen, meanwhile, had lit the first of three lanterns, each positioned on the periphery of their little circle, near enough for all to see each other's faces but far enough away to lend a softness to the reflection of light on the surface of the water. Kindling and split pinyon were piled nearby for a fire, but the August night was still warm enough without one.

"Can I offer you a parejo?" Peabody asked.

Yazzie leaned forward and accepted the cigar.

"By the way," Peabody said to Pete, "did you get the photographs you wanted?"

"I did. Ship Rock and the Hogback," he added for Yazzie's benefit.

"You must have photographed the entire reservation by now," Peabody said.

"Hardly. I'd like to get out to Navajo Mountain and take a look at Rainbow Bridge." The giant sandstone arch, located in the most remote part of the reservation, had first been seen by Anglos, including John Wetherill and his wife Louisa, just a year earlier, and President Taft had already made it a national monument. "Do you know that area?" Pete asked Yazzie.

"I've been there," Yazzie said. "To the mountain, not Tsé'naa Na'ní'áhí. If I were an Anglo, I wouldn't go alone."

"Do you think my automobile would make it?" Peabody asked.

"Maybe," Yazzie said. "But I think you'd have trouble finding enough men willing to carry it that far."

In the midst of the laughter that followed, a pebble hit Yazzie in the shoulder. Everyone immediately turned toward Johanna, whose eyes were wide.

In Navajo, Yazzie told his sister not to worry, that he wouldn't go.

Owen leaned toward Julia and whispered, "What's Johanna upset about?"

"She doesn't want her brother to go to Navajo Mountain."

"Why not?"

Julia just shook her head and Owen let the matter drop.

Her brother's reassurance had settled Johanna, and she was drawing figures—Julia couldn't see what—in the sand, wiping them out with the flat of her hand, drawing them again. Since early June Johanna had spent more time with Tóya than at home. In response to Julia's questions about his sister's absences, Clement had replied that Tóya needed her. Certainly Tóya was showing her age, and it wasn't unreasonable that she might need help going about her business, but why Johanna? Julia wondered. When she pressed him, Clement wasn't forthcoming. His reluctance told her that whatever the explanation, he wasn't settled in his own mind about it. In good time, he would tell her.

Julia returned her attention to her new guest. "If you don't mind," she said to Peabody, "I've yet to hear the story of how you ended up in Gallup and met your wife."

"Ah-ha," Peabody laughed. "How much time do you have?"

Julia held up her knitting. "I have many rows to go."

"You may wish you had fewer," Pete commented. "If Peabody gives you the long version, we may be here until dawn."

"At least your story has a happy ending," Julia said. "I think we could all use one."

"A happy ending of sorts," Peabody replied somewhat mysteriously.

"Now I'm intrigued," Owen said, stretching himself out on the ground, ankles crossed, folded hands cushioning his head.

"Well," Peabody began, folding his own hands and resting them on his belly, "first of all, my dear Julia, to set the record straight, I didn't come to Gallup and then meet my wife. I met my wife first, more than a decade earlier. Thus you could say that love at first sight brought me to Gallup."

AT SEVENTEEN, AN INDIFFERENT student, a regular ten o'clock scholar without direction or ambition, Winfield Peabody dropped out of school. He spent his afternoons cruising his Chicago neighborhood, running with a tough crowd, stealing tobacco and the latest issue of the *Police Gazette*, getting into fights over territorial disputes with rival gangs, making a general nuisance of himself, and—a new favorite activity—sneaking into the 1893 Columbian World Exposition.

Which was indeed something to behold. The White City, two hundred electrically illuminated buildings that pitched a dome against the night sky. The Midway Plaisance with its Ferris wheel, so exciting, mind you, that he and his buddies actually forked over cold, hard coins for their fifty-cent rides. The exotic Bedouin Encampment, a South Sea village, and a panorama of the Kilauea volcano. East Indian and Japanese bazaars. A diorama depicting the destruction of Pompeii. Ragtime and hula dancing, the Brazilian Music Hall, and the jaw-dropping hootchy-kootchy performed by Little Egypt. And just outside the gates of the fair, in its own arena, Buffalo Bill's Wild West Show. In addition to trying for the first time Juicy Fruit Gum and Pabst Beer and Aunt Jemima's pancakes, and every imaginable shape and size of cigar, you could step aboard replicas of Columbus's Niña, Pinta, and Santa María or a Viking ship or a U.S. battleship; ride the John Bull, America's first steam locomotive, or the Ice Railway; marvel at Krupp's artillery; tour the General Electric and Westinghouse exhibits in the Electricity Hall; or take the Moving Walkway along the Lake Michigan pier. It was a grand time to be young and at large, those summer days.

One afternoon in September 1893, caught at the fairgrounds in an unanticipated cloudburst, Peabody found himself seeking shelter under the pilastered portico of the Joint Territorial Building, built to house exhibits from Arizona, New Mexico, and the recently divided Oklahoma and Indian territories. When the rain lingered, Peabody decided to pay his two bits and step inside. Maybe he'd see cowboys and Indians or a giant saguaro cactus or a diorama of the Grand Canyon. Instead, he found agricultural displays of grains and fruits and grasses; samples of petrified wood, which, at least, were more interesting than the posted descriptions of various wheat and apple varieties; cases exhibiting turquoise mined from Las Cerrillos, and a giant block of azurite on a malachite base, green and blue, from Arizona; photographs taken at the Indian pueblos of Taos and Walpi, and portraits of noted personages (Kit Carson was the only New Mexican he recognized by name); hanging Navajo blankets and Hopi baskets, and Apache braid work; and, tucked into a corner at the rear of the first floor, a glass case containing Zuni inlay jewelry. And that was where he first saw Estella Halusewa.

The directors of the Columbian Exposition had arranged for many tribes to participate: Navajo, Apache, Iroquois, Sioux, Chippewa . . . but they were relegated to mock villages stretched along the Midway Plaisance or made the subject of exhibits in the government and anthropology buildings. In contrast, the Halusewa brothers, Connor and Roe, had been invited by the New Mexico board of commissioners to demonstrate the art of making Zuni jewelry, and they'd brought along Connor's daughter to model what they made.

In simple native dress, Estella Halusewa was the most glorious creature Peabody had ever seen, wearing silver bracelets up and down her bare arms, and rings, and three-tiered earrings of tiny turquoise beads and silver filigree, a matching tiara, and a magnificent necklace—an upward-facing quarter-moon, almost as wide as her chest, with half a dozen tear-drop pendants hanging below, all inlaid with jet and mother-of-pearl and coral and tortoise shell.

In the following days he kept returning to the exhibit hall, but she wouldn't talk to him, diverting her eyes and, when he tried asking about the jewelry, repeating that he needed to speak to her father or uncle about prices—as she'd obviously been instructed to do.

"She was all of fourteen," Peabody told his listeners. "But I didn't find that out until years later. She was so calm, just sitting on a little platform, her legs folded under her, her hands in her lap, with these enormous brown eyes and hair so black it shone like jet itself. Of course her father, looking me over, knew instantly that I didn't have the money to buy anything they were selling."

After Peabody's fifth or sixth visit, Connor Halusewa had seen enough. He was a head shorter than Peabody but ferocious in appearance when he scowled—black, black hair trimmed like a helmet at his collar, a sharp nose, pocked skin, heavy cheek bones beneath deep eyes. He pulled Peabody aside—"literally, by the collar"—and asked if he had a trade, and because Peabody couldn't bring himself to divulge his real employment, in the rendering factory, he lied and said yes, which led Halusewa to comment that in view of how much time Peabody had spent staring at his daughter, he must be very bad at whatever this trade might be. Did Peabody think he was the first Anglo to ogle his daughter? he asked. Then he said that it had been a mistake to bring her to a city where no one showed proper respect, and that if Peabody ever so much as touched her hand he, Connor Halusewa, would, as it were, emasculate him right there, on the spot.

"I must say, he was quite convincing." Peabody paused, stroking his beard. "But I wasn't ready to surrender, not yet."

"So what did you do?" Julia asked.

"I decided I needed a suit," Peabody said. "To show proper respect. I thought it might make a difference if I dressed like a gentleman." He laughed his barrel laugh. "I was eighteen! What did I know? I was a dolt!"

He'd never owned a decent suit in his entire life, and he didn't have money to buy one now. What to do? And then he remembered a wake that he'd attended not long before—in fact, for the coworker who'd died of blood poisoning. The man had lived in little more than a hovel with his wife and five children, but his friends at the rendering plant took up a collection so he'd have a decent sendoff. So, there he lay in an oak coffin—and in a fine wool suit. When Peabody remarked upon the suit to another coworker, he learned that the mortician solicited clothing donations from swells and thereby was able to clothe the dead in something that wouldn't embarrass them or their families when the deceased met their Maker.

The next afternoon, after making a number of inquiries about the identity of the mortician, Peabody found K. Holzknecht's place of business and knocked on the door. A short, rather dour woman, plainly dressed, leaning heavily on a pair of canes, her graying hair in a bun, answered.

'Have you come about the job?' she asked in a heavy German accent.

'No,' Peabody said. 'I came to buy a suit.'

'Buy a *suit*?' Her nostrils flared and her chin, a tiny pinched thing, trembled. 'Who *are* you?'

'Winfield Peabody, ma'am.'

She pointed to the sign mounted beside the door: K. Holzknecht, Esq., Mortician. 'And who do you think *we* are, mister? Do you think we strip the clothes off the dead and sell them at the door?'

Peabody bashfully explained that he knew he was making a very unusual request but that he desperately needed a suit.

Her eyes narrowed to slits. 'Are you planning your funeral?'

'I'm'—he searched for the right word—'courting.'

'*Was ist das?*'

'I have to impress an Indian girl. Actually, her father. Before they leave. They're at the fair, in one of the exhibits, and I don't know how much longer they're going to be here.'

Her jaw worked back and forth. 'You've come to a mortician to buy a suit so you can charm a wild Comanche, a Geronimo?'

Peabody saw no point in trying to explain that Zunis weren't Comanches and that Connor Halusewa was (he hoped) no Geronimo. 'Yes.'

She looked him down and back up, this scruffy fellow in a faded plaid wool shirt, corduroys so worn that the fabric over his thighs was stretched thin, and shoes that looked like they'd never seen polish. 'How about a shirt and tie as well?' she scoffed.

'Umm—'

'And shoes.'

'You have shoes?'

'Klaus!' she turned and called down the hall. 'Come to the door! You've got to hear *mit deinen eigenen ohren!*'

But the Holzknechts, husband and wife, took pity on him. They brought him in, listened to his story, discussed (in German) and laughed over his apparent plight, offered him milk and strudel, and then, in a small room that had once been a pantry but now served as their repository of donated clothing, found him a suit, a gabardine. Ulrike even did alterations, cuffing the pants to a proper length with common pins and then quick stitches, and applying a hot iron to the creases. Klaus, peering over his half-moon spectacles, red-faced, with slicked-back auburn hair, watched. 'Tell no one, young fellow,' he cautioned Peabody. 'This is no haberdashery. We can't ever do this again. *Verstehst du mich?*' He walked away, but when he returned he had over his arm a fine dress shirt and also carried a tie and real leather belt and shoes—from his own closet, Peabody later learned. Peabody would have to work off what he owed them, cleaning up six days a week—that, it turned out, was the part-time job they needed to fill—for two months.

'You don't mind working with the dead?' Ulrike Holzknecht asked him.

Peabody told them that he worked nights in a rendering plant. He doubted anything on their premises would disturb him.

'Don't be so sure, sonny boy,' Ulrike said.

And she was right. He saw some horrible things. A man who'd fallen through the ice of Lake Michigan and who wasn't found on the shore until the thaw. A woman nearly nine months along who died in a fire. But that all came later, after he'd quit his job at the rendering plant.

Peabody, pausing, now said to Clement Yazzie, "I realize, given Navajo sensibilities, that you must find my livelihood very peculiar, if not downright offensive."

"What Anglos choose to do with their dead is no business of mine," Yazzie answered flatly.

"So what happened with the suit?" Owen asked.

"Ah, the suit!" Peabody said, leaning forward and stretching his legs. "It was all for naught. I returned to the Joint Territorial Building the next day, dressed in my new finery. But I was too late. Her uncle Roe was there by himself. I didn't even ask. I knew from the look he gave me—a combination of a frown and a smirk—that she was gone. Her father had squirreled her away for the duration. I knew I couldn't find her. Well," Peabody corrected himself, "maybe I could've *located* her, but then what? And so I gave her up, my Estella. I didn't forget her—oh no, I did not—but I gave her up for lost."

Having been offered a permanent job by the Holzknechts, Peabody began learning the science of their trade, and without so much as a discussion, he became their apprentice. He devoted himself to his work, and the Holzknechts treated him like their lost son, who'd died from infantile paralysis when he was just a boy. (Ulrike, too, had contracted the disease; thus, her canes.) He easily learned the mechanics of embalming —"basically, fluids out and fluids in, as it were"—but he also discovered that he was skillful—calm, reassuring, empathetic without being overemotional—in handling grieving families. The absence of a foreign accent didn't hurt.

Klaus was an excellent mortician, but Ulrike was the miracle worker. The things she could do, her skill with the dead!—making them presentable, lifelike, for the viewing; preparing them with cosmetics and all the tools of salon and spa. When Ulrike died suddenly in 1898, Peabody did his best to replace her, and by the time Klaus died from a cancer in 1901, Peabody was already his partner. Klaus's will left Peabody the rest of the business.

Less than a year later, he took advantage of the property's location, just off Grand Boulevard in an increasingly fashionable residential community, to sell it for a considerable sum, which he invested in three properties just a bit farther south, one of which became the new mortuary. He quickly realized that a small fortune could be made in buying and reselling well-placed real estate, and he threw all his resources into it. He barely crossed the threshold of some properties before reselling them at a considerable profit.

In ten years he never took a vacation, until 1904. And that was when he came west for the first time.

"Denver, Santa Fe, Albuquerque—" Peabody said.

"Gallup," Owen added.

The closest frontier town to Zuni. Because, of course, it was the memory of Estella that drew him. He wanted to know what had become of her. He wasn't . . . unaware. Of course she would be married by now—he still didn't know how young she'd been in Chicago, but, regardless, ten years had passed and he couldn't imagine her being unwed. He had no intention of approaching her. He simply needed to confirm her continuing presence in the world and to learn, if possible, how she fared. That would be enough.

"But you didn't even know her," Owen interrupted. "Why would you—"

Peabody dismissed the objection with a flick of his wrist and a deep chuckle.

Julia thought, Oh, he's a fool, Peabody, to be sure, but maybe a Holy Fool.

It had been a moment, Peabody said, endeavoring to explain himself—the moment when he first saw Estella in the Joint Territorial Building in 1893—that had changed him forever. Why, he couldn't say, except, perhaps, because he was *ready* to change—to be *rendered* anew. (" Ha!") It had disrupted his impoverished life—dislocated him—and in so doing permitted, even if by serendipity, a previously pointless future to find direction and purpose.

"Don't you think great beauty—in art or nature or a soul—can do that, transmute your very substance?" Peabody asked, directing the question to Owen.

"I couldn't say," Owen said.

"Sorry, Peabody," Pete said. "We're all too jaded."

"You weren't always that way, my friend. I seem to recall your relating, one late night, how you were once ready to make a deal with the devil if an inamorata, if I may be so bold, would forswear joining the Sisters of the Blessed Sacrament and run off with you."

"That was the liquor talking," Pete grumbled. "Besides, it's an old story. Everybody already knows it."

"Not in grotesque detail," Owen said.

Julia, muffling a laugh, continued her knitting without saying a word.

"Grotesque? That's a bit excessive," Pete responded.

"I don't know," Owen said. "Trying to seduce a nun seems a bit grotesque to me."

"She *wasn't* a nun. She hadn't taken any vows, and I was not a seducer."

"My apologies for stirring up ancient history," Peabody said.

Julia wondered what Clement Yazzie was thinking about Peabody's story, about his infatuation with a Zuni girl. Every Navajo could tell stories of native women who'd been disgraced by white men, and Julia suspected that in this tale, Clement's fellow feeling would lie with Estella's father, Connor Halusewa.

"So what did you do, once you found yourself in Gallup?" Julia asked Peabody.

He knew a name, Halusewa; and a craft, jeweler. He started by looking in Gallup's Indian stores, and this approach quickly proved fruitful, for he found precisely what he was searching for in Patterson's Trading Company, in a locked display case. A clerk, a pleasant man named Ashton Billings

("Do you know him—tallish, balding, nasally voice, buck teeth?"—), having established that Peabody was a tourist from Chicago seeing the West for the first time, said, 'Well, if you're looking for souvenirs, little mementos, let me point you'—thrusting a thick finger forward—'to the various displays of trinkets and postal cards at the front of the store. *But'*—he paused for effect—'if you want true works of art, as I suspect you do, you've come to the right department. If you want the best basketry, Hopi'—his finger pointing dramatically again, toward shelves at his right. 'The best pottery, Acoma and Hopi'—hand sweeping wide, directly behind him. 'The best weavings, Navajo'—open hand gesturing upward, where rugs hung from the vigas. 'The best silver and turquoise jewelry, also Navajo'—finger circling nearby glass display cases. 'The best *inlay* jewelry, Zuni'—palms spread on the case between them. 'And if you want the *very* finest inlay jewelry, you're looking at it'—finger pointing straight down, nail tapping the glass—'made by the Halusewa brothers.'

'You know them?' Peabody asked, playing the innocent.

'I do.' Billings leaned over the counter and, as if imparting a secret, noted, 'Their work was featured at the 1893 Chicago World's Fair.'

'You don't say.'

'So what can I show you?'—choosing a key to the display case from among a dozen or so on a heavy brass ring hanging from a nail.

'Perhaps these earrings?' Tiered, turquoise and silver, like what he'd first seen Estella wearing.

'They're quite lovely,' Billings said, clearly disappointed that Peabody had focused on the least expensive items in the case.

The back-and-forth continued for some time, with Peabody gradually extracting from Billings various tidbits about the Halusewa family, including that they were Catholic—there were several ornate crosses in the jewelry case—and very smart in their dealings.

In the end, Peabody purchased the earrings, thanked Billings, and left.

On Sunday, for the first time in his life, Win Peabody attended a Catholic Mass for other than the dead. He'd learned that an old adobe mission, Our Lady of Guadalupe, now little more than a ruin, stood abandoned in a plaza at Zuni, but there was no proper Catholic church. Every year or so the pastor of Gallup's Sacred Heart Church, Father Juillard, traveled to Zuni and, largely unannounced—considerable anti-Catholic sentiment infested the pueblo, especially among Protestant converts—celebrated Mass in a private home. Apart from that, the more devout Zuni families had no option except to attend Sacred Heart services when they could. Maybe he'd get lucky, Peabody thought. Maybe the Halusewas would be in attendance for Sunday Mass.

Having deliberately arrived late, Peabody slid into a rear pew, far in a corner, scanning the congregation while following along in a missal as well as he could. He looked past her twice before he realized—dropping the fumbled missal to the floor, his heart leaping—that Estella sat only ten rows away, just to the right of the center aisle. Next to a child. And on the other side of the child, on the aisle, a man.

Estella wore a black mantilla that obscured her outline until she turned and looked down at the child, the top of whose head barely reached the back of the pew. The man, his thick hair cut short above a thin brown neck and white collar, leaned to the side and appeared to whisper something to the child, who, moments later, began to cry. Estella—black hair through the lace, a profile comprising temple, brow, cheekbone, nose, lips, chin, shoulder—leaning closer and stroking the child's head, tried to comfort her. The gesture didn't succeed, and soon the child was catching her breath between sobs. Estella lifted the girl into her lap and began rocking side to side, her daughter's lament—the child had to be her daughter, didn't she?—muffled by her mother's shoulder. With the wailing child attracting the disapproving attention of nearby parishioners, Estella rose, slipped past the man, and carried her daughter down the aisle.

Peabody didn't avert his eyes. She wouldn't see him, and she'd never recognize him anyway; he was heavier now, bearded, out of time and place. Then she lifted her face and he could see her clearly. Of course she had changed. The fulsomeness of youth was gone, as was the jewelry and the Indian attire. She was dressed conventionally, in a high-necked, cream-colored dress. And there was such a deep sadness in her demeanor that he wanted to weep as her little girl wept, inconsolably.

"You're probably thinking," Peabody said, looking directly at Owen, "that my telling has all been colored by what I subsequently learned."

Owen scratched his cheek. "Well . . ."

"That, for example," Peabody continued, "her husband had been fired from his job at the Talle ranch. And that he'd taken to drink."

"Tom Talle's ranch?" Owen asked with surprise.

"At the time, his father's. Do you know the sheriff?—although, of course, he wasn't sheriff yet."

"We've met."

"Well, somehow or other, Lonan Becerra—Estella's husband—was implicated in a scheme to steal cattle and run them south into Mexico. He was never even charged, but it didn't matter. No one in Gallup, where he and Estella and their daughter were living, would hire him because of the suspicions. Eventually, Estella took her little girl, Estrellita, and the two of them returned to her father's house."

"What did you do," Julia asked, "after you saw them in church?"

"Well," Peabody said, "I returned to Chicago."

He could only describe his journey east, the train rocking on the tracks, the landscape sliding by—the ragged peaks of the Rockies, the Great Bend of the Arkansas, the flatness approaching Topeka and Kansas City—as fraught with self-admonishment for his foolishness, for ever leaving the comfort and security of the Chicago life he'd earned through hard work and diligence. What had he, truly, expected to find in Gallup? Exotic innocence and purity don't survive adulthood, neither in the perceived nor the perceiver. He *knew* that—

"Unless she's a nun," Owen threw out, playing surrogate for Harry Whitaker.

"Shut up," Pete said.

—so why had he felt compelled to prove it once again? The train pulled into sooty Dearborn terminal on a close, dreary day, the open western skies far behind him. Gathering his hat and overcoat, he followed the porter carrying his two suitcases down the aisle, but before his foot hit the platform he had resolved to go back to Gallup.

Owen lifted his eyebrows. "I know you're married now and have a son—"

"And a step-daughter."

"—but you couldn't possibly foresee any of that. What did you think returning to Gallup would accomplish?"

"Nothing," Peabody replied, spreading his arms wide.

Owen looked at him askance.

Peabody smiled. His cigar, between fore and middle fingers, had gone out. "Sometimes when the spirit moves you, you have to move with it."

"The spirit?" Clement Yazzie asked.

"Certainly. You must know what I mean. Plan and prognosticate all you want, but unless something moves you, you never arrive. After all, how did any of us come to be here?—Mr. Yazzie and Miss Yazzie excepted, of course."

"But to leave a successful life in Chicago for *Gallup* . . . ," Owen said with a shake of his head.

"I know, I know," Peabody said. "It strains credulity. But something— who can say what?—told me I needed to be here."

"With no design?"

"None. "

" 'You're a better man than I am, Gunga Din,' " Pete said.

"If you quote that horrid poem one more time," Julia said, "I'll snatch you bald-headed."

"I'd pay to see that," Owen said.

Pete drew back, palms raised in surrender.

"Suppose," Peabody said to the skeptical Owen, "that I returned to Gallup intending to win Estella's affection. What could I have done? Approach her after Sunday Mass? Or on the street some afternoon while she was shopping with her pretty little girl—pretend to chance upon her in a store while she was buying lace or a bauble? Or befriend her husband in some saloon—remember, I knew nothing of his plight at the time—and thereby cozen my way into their home? Can you imagine her response to any of these pretenses? Why, she would've been appalled or frightened or both! Quite the opposite of any intention I might have had."

"You could've paid someone to dispose of her husband," Pete said.

Peabody alone laughed. (Julia saw no humor; she immediately thought of the widowed Marietta Wetherill.) "My friend, if I were that kind of man—a man of the Wild West, so to speak—you might not be speaking so freely." Then Peabody's tone turned somber. "But I shouldn't laugh, because less than a year later her husband *was* dead. And that was indeed a very bleak time." He waved a large hand. "But I get ahead of myself."

"In all those years in between, in Chicago," Julia said to Peabody, "you never gave thought to a wife and family of your own?"

"Indeed I did," Peabody said. "I developed attachments, shall we say. Once, I came very close to marriage. She was a lovely young woman. But two weeks before taking our vows, we agreed to separate. There was no blame on either part, and to this day I would be hard-pressed to explain our decision. She has since married, of course."

"And that had nothing to do with your leaving Chicago?" Julia asked.

"In a way, it freed me, I must admit. My parents were long dead and I had no siblings. And as for my business interests, the great thing about capital in the age of the telegraph and telephone is that it doesn't require your presence, just your attention."

Upon his return to Gallup (Peabody continued), he purchased a building north of the tracks that offered sufficient space for an office, viewing parlor, and a workroom on the first floor, and more than he needed in the way of living quarters on the second. He spent money wisely in the limited number of establishments that had a reputation for taste, such as Alberto Rodriguez's furniture store, and relied on his first friend, the counter man at Patterson's, Ashton Billings, for social introductions, many of which occurred at the performance and meeting hall on the second floor of Kitchen's Opera House, a hub for concerts, dramatic performances, dances, and other social events. It didn't take long to make his presence known to the town's doctors, clergymen, lawyers, and the managers of the Gibson, Weaver, and Catalpa coal mines. He joined the Merchant's Council and struck up a friendship with Sheriff Bill Smith (Tom Talle's predecessor), and the editor of the *McKinley County Republican*, and the pastor at Sacred Heart,

Father Juillard. Moreover, he found that he didn't miss Chicago that much. The New Mexico air was cleaner; the sunshine, inexhaustible; the pace of life, slower. And he rarely went more than a few days without a dinner invitation and evening frivolities.

"Did you go back to Sacred Heart?" Owen asked.

"Regularly."

"And you saw her there?"

"Not once. I saw her husband about town several times. I made inquiries, which was how I learned what had happened to him, and that Estella had returned to Zuni."

"And still you did nothing?"

"Next to nothing."

That December, Ashton Billings proposed that Peabody and another friend, a photographer named Pete Pietrowski—whom Peabody had encountered on one previous occasion—accompany him to the annual Shalako ceremony at the Zuni Pueblo. The ceremony was named after the most prominent kachinas, six of which, in spectacular costumes and accompanied by various other colorful kachinas and attendants, entered the village and danced, one in each of six honored homes, through the night before departing, the following afternoon, for the winter.

"It was colder than a witch's tit that night," Pete interjected.

Billings, Pete, and Peabody were at the fourth of the flat-roofed Shalako houses, standing at the rear of the crowd, eating pueblo bread and stew from tin plates, drinking black coffee, watching the dance—the Shalako was so tall, a trench had been dug in the dirt floor so that his headdress would clear the ceiling—when Peabody saw Connor Halusewa, Estella's father, enter with a group of other men. During a pause that allowed another Zuni man, behind a blanket curtain, to assume the Shalako costume, Halusewa and his companions moved to the drum circle, where they soon took over the rhythmic chanting. Peabody kept his hat brim low and his chin dipped to his chest, and tried to nudge his companions, the only Anglos present, toward the exit, but when he looked up, Halusewa's eyes were on him. The Zuni looked perplexed, as if trying to place the face.

"You didn't see Estella?" Julia asked.

"No. Which was something of a relief, in truth," Peabody said.

"Why was that?"

"Because there was nothing I could rightfully say to her. I had made a place for her in my life"—he tapped a temple—"but I had no place in hers."

"Then why did you go to Zuni in the first place?" Owen asked.

"Foolishly, I must say, to catch a glimpse." Peabody paused. "At some point, haven't we all acted against our best judgment, our better instincts? In this instance, I was lucky. In my experience, such lapses usually don't turn out well."

"Unless you can throw money at them," Pete said, twirling his cigar between his fingers as if it were cash.

"I'm not unaware," Peabody said.

"Unaware of what?" Owen asked.

"That I have sufficient funds to extricate myself, for example, from the complications of ill-considered actions."

"You speak from experience?" Julia asked.

"I do. For a time—fortunately a very brief time—back in Chicago I thought my business judgment infallible, and I nearly ruined myself. And, need I say, had I not remained a man of independent means, Chicago would almost certainly still be my home, and thoughts of my Estella would be nothing but that—thoughts: the fantasy of a fat, aging gent enraptured by the exotic, a pearl of great price." He cast a glance at Julia. "You see, as I said, I'm not unaware."

Maybe, Julia thought, he wasn't such a fool after all. "Perhaps we're being too cynical, Win," she said with a small smile. "We shouldn't be questioning your motives."

"And why not, my dear lady?"

"Because, of course, you're here—whatever the motivations."

"There you have it!—the bare fact beneath all the ruminations!" Peabody slammed his hand on a fat thigh for emphasis. "You and Estella would get along, I'm sure of it! She sees through me. She's better than one of Roentgen's X-ray machines—she goes to the marrow of every situation. For her, why I came to Gallup is of no consequence compared to the bare fact that I was here in her time of need."

"What happened?" Owen asked.

"Death intervened." Peabody sighed, his eyes taking in the little circle of listeners, including the ever-silent Johanna.

"Mr. Yazzie," Julia said, "would you light a fire?" She wasn't cold yet—no, the early night was still far too warm for that, though, if the sky remained cloudless, the Milky Way and its million stars an ethereal swath, the air would chill soon enough.

Owen got up to help Yazzie bring wood to the shallow fire pit around which they sat. Pine shavings, scraped free by Yazzie's knife, and dry kindling soon exploded into flame, and Julia had her fire. The light danced off everything—faces, chambray and linen and faded cotton shirts, weathered trousers and her own brown skirt, boot soles and shoes. The faces were sober all around except for Pete, who'd heard the tale before and maintained a look of bemused boredom, as Peabody resumed his tale:

Months later, he was heading out to lunch late one morning when he opened his door and found Connor Halusewa standing there. Peabody was so surprised that he emitted a gruff 'Oh!' and, his hand still on the door-knob, took a step backward. There was nothing intimidating now, more than a decade later, about the presence before him: an aging Indian, shrinking into himself, hair graying, wearing gray pants with a black stripe, a concho belt, a rough white cotton shirt, a string of irregular turquoise beads, scuffed boots. Peabody quickly collected himself. 'How can I help you?' he asked. His stomach rose against his diaphragm but he managed to keep his voice steady. 'Would you like to come in?' He stepped aside and gestured with an open hand.

The office wasn't much to speak of: a desk, a bookcase with an assortment of nondescript volumes, a Navajo rug on the floor, several straight chairs off to the side, a round parlor stove in the corner, a chandelier with four gas lights, two framed Currier and Ives prints of American farm scenes—one of an incongruously well-dressed man plowing behind a team of oxen, the other of a woman and two girls feeding chickens in a yard replete with ducks, pigs, and cows.

Halusewa, without speaking, entered and took an offered seat before Peabody's desk. Peabody sat down in his captain's chair and they stared at each other across the desk before Halusewa, unblinking, said, 'The sheriff said I might want to talk to you.'

'Sheriff Smith? Why?'

'What do you do besides sell boxes?' Halusewa asked in reply.

Peabody told him. He prepared the deceased for burial according to the wishes of the family. Some just wanted the body washed and dressed and a coffin sealed. Increasingly, people wanted embalming—preservation of the body so that it could be viewed publicly without concern for . . . giving offense. This was especially so when distant relatives wanted to attend the funeral or, in contrast, when the deceased was to be shipped elsewhere for burial. 'I try to do whatever I can to help,' Peabody concluded.

'My son-in-law was hit by a train,' Halusewa said. He sat straight, his rough hands spread on his knees.

Peabody had heard about an accident in the early morning hours, but no one had mentioned a name. Another Indian, that's all anyone had said. Peabody now knew who it was; Connor Halusewa had only one daughter and therefore one son-in-law.

Peabody offered his standard 'Please accept my sympathies.'

'My daughter wants him brought home.'

His daughter. Estella. 'To Zuni?'

Halusewa nodded.

'If you need a coffin, I have several already made that I can show you. Some have come all the way from St. Louis, but others have been made right here in Gallup. You can take one with you, if you've come by wagon.'

Halusewa shook his head.

'Then tell me what you need, sir.'

'My grand-daughter needs to see her father. So she can say goodbye.'

Peabody stared across his desk at the stony face. 'Do I understand you correctly—that you want me to—'

'Fix him.'

Peabody's jaw went slack. 'Mr. Halusewa—'

'So you know who I am.'

Peabody realized that his palms were sweaty. 'I do.'

'And I know who *you* are.'

Peabody gave his hands something to do, straightening the few objects on his desk: a humidor, a pen and inkwell, a bit of paperwork. Of course Connor Halusewa knew who he was; after Shalako, he would have made inquiries.

'Mr. Halusewa, what you ask may not be possible. Have you seen . . . ?'

A nod.

'Can you give me some idea . . .'

'He lost his legs.' With the edge of his palm Halusewa drew a straight line across the desk top.

Peabody exhaled. 'And . . . above?'

'He was dragged a ways.' The Indian pointed to his right side and then to his face.

Peabody shook his head. 'Mr. Halusewa—'

'I can pay in cash.'

Peabody waved a hand. 'Money isn't the issue.'

'I won't pay anything less than your fair price.'

'I wouldn't insult you, Mr. Halusewa, by billing you a penny less.'

Another nod.

They sat for some time. Peabody drummed his fingers on the desk. 'Mr. Halusewa, maybe it would be best if your grand-daughter remembered her father as he was.'

'People will tell her stories. She needs to see him or she'll always be troubled.'

Halusewa was clearly determined. Peabody considered his options. He could refuse and thereby bring the discussion, and other matters, to a definitive conclusion. Or he could use his skills to help, as he would for any other grieving family who came to him. He sighed. 'We'll go and see your son-in-law. I can't promise anything. If I think I can help you, I will. If not . . .'

An emphatic nod.

They were leaving the mortuary when Connor Halusewa stopped. He grabbed the door frame to steady himself.

"Sir, are you all right?" Peabody asked, reaching for an arm to support him.

'I know why you're here,' Halusewa said, 'but I do not understand it.'

They'd never mentioned Estella's name.

"So I'm sure you now begin to see why I said my little tale has a happy ending 'of sorts,' " Peabody said.

Julia had stopped her knitting. Everyone waited for Win Peabody to continue.

"A happy ending for me, but only because a man whom I didn't know and didn't regard favorably—partly, I must admit, from unpardonable resentment—paid the highest possible price. And that's without mentioning the pain felt by others along the way." He cleared his throat. "I regard myself as the most fortunate of men."

There was no more questioning. It was all too serious, death and life.

"Go on, Win," Julia said.

Before leaving Gallup that day, Connor Halusewa had selected a simple pine coffin, not because his family couldn't afford oak or walnut but because he didn't think it proper to behave as if they were better than anyone else. There would be no funeral Mass: the Catholic Church had strict rules about possible suicides (though cynics might have said that Lonan Becerra's race and disreputable personal history were more salient factors). Father Juillard, however, as a personal favor to Win Peabody, agreed, the following day, to say a few prayers over the deceased before he was brought home.

Midday, two days later. In dim lighting Lonan Becerra lay dressed in a freshly ironed shirt, buttoned at the neck, and a new pair of striped trousers and high boots. He lay not on his back but on his right side, his legs slightly bent at the knee and his arms positioned as if he might be asleep. A headband hid where six inches of scalp had been sewn back in place. Beneath the clothing, cotton packing and strips of felt filled out where muscle had been torn away and bone crushed, all held in place by concealed splints. Father Juillard, saying a rosary, sat nearby in his cassock, surplice, and stole.

When Peabody heard the door from the street open, he left the visiting parlor and entered the front office. Connor Halusewa was there, accompanied by his brother Roe and by Estella Becerra and her little girl. Estella was veiled, dressed in black, although her lovely dark-eyed daughter wore traditional ceremonial dress.

Peabody addressed Mr. Halusewa first: 'Everything has been taken care of, as you requested.' Then he turned to Estella and the girl. 'I'm very sorry this has come to pass,' he said.

'Thank you,' Estella said. "Estrellita, what do you say?"

'Thank you,' Estrellita copied her mother.

'Do you want to come through now or sit and collect your thoughts first? Would the little one like something to drink?'

'Thank you, but no,' Estella said, 'we'll see my husband now.'

Peabody held the door as they entered the long, narrow paneled parlor. Peabody had furnished the front of this room with a settee, a sideboard, and, on either side of a fireplace, two armchairs. At the far end stood a simple funeral bier, in front of which he had arranged a prie-dieu and a dozen folding wooden chairs in two rows, six to either side of a narrow aisle. The room could accommodate another eight rows, but Peabody had never required that many chairs since most families still preferred holding wakes in their homes.

Estella and Estrellita knelt at the prie-dieu together, followed by Connor and finally Roe Halusewa. Father Juillard then led the family in prayers—the Act of Contrition, the Hail Mary, the Our Father—and read several brief passages from scripture. And they were done.

Peabody watched Estella lift her veil and ask her daughter, 'Do you wish to kiss your Papa goodbye?'

Peabody strode forward and moved the prie-dieu aside so that they could reach the casket more easily. Estella lifted the little girl into her arms, and together they leaned over.

'Papa,' Estrellita said, and kissed his cheek, as if he might awaken. Mother and daughter stood for a moment longer, and for the first time Peabody's and Estella's eyes met. He saw no tears.

'Do you wish to leave something with him?' he asked. Estella shook her head at first, but then drew a black-beaded rosary with a simple silver cross from a pocket and handed it to Peabody. Their fingers didn't touch. Estella led Estrellita away.

'Is there anything else I can do?' Peabody asked Connor Halusewa. 'Or would you like me to seal the casket now?'

The old man just shook his head and stood aside.

'You're very thorough, Win,' Father Juillard said, removing his stole.

'I have to be, you see.'

When Peabody was done, the four men carried the casket out to the street and loaded it in the back of the Halusewa wagon.

* * *

The spell had been both broken and renewed. Unless Peabody gave up the remembered Estella, he couldn't approach the present Estella, though he had absolutely no idea if he would ever be permitted to do anything of the kind. He also felt that, now, he couldn't remain in Gallup if he were to be denied.

"Why was that?" Owen asked.

"I'd spoken to her and heard her voice in reply, and I assumed that she knew who I was—that her father had told her." Peabody chuckled. "It turned out that I was wrong. Her father hadn't told her a thing, and she hadn't recognized me."

"So she had no idea?"

"None whatsoever."

Peabody marked the months on his calendar, and when nearly a year had passed he wrote to Connor Halusewa. The letter stated quite simply that he wished to write to Mrs. Becerra but would not do so without permission from both of them. He further stated that if either objected, the matter would be at an end. Neither would ever hear from him again.

" 'You're a better' "—Pete began.

"Don't say it," Julia snapped.

Peabody waited a week, two weeks, and heard nothing. And then, once again unexpectedly, Connor Halusewa appeared at his door.

"We sat in the viewing parlor," Peabody said. "It was a very odd conversation, with many long pauses. We drank coffee. He asked if I'd ever been married. I said not. He asked if I owed money. I told him I was a man of modest means. He asked if I was a Christian. I said I was, but not the best. He asked if I drank. I said that, given a reason, I would never let alcohol pass my lips again. He told me his daughter would never again live in Gallup. I said I understood."

"He was negotiating with you?" Julia asked.

"No," Peabody replied, "he was setting forth, you might say, the necessary prior understandings."

" *Whose* understandings?" The very idea rankled Julia. "Because I'm assuming that Estella was in Zuni caring for her child."

Pete chortled. "Julia, you haven't met Estella Peabody. I have, and let me tell you, she makes her opinion known."

"She couldn't have come herself," Yazzie said quietly to Julia, and she knew he was right. Still, she offered no apology for her testiness.

"Did she know who you were yet?"

"Oh yes. After receiving my letter, her father finally told her that we'd met, as it were, in Chicago."

"And her response?" Julia asked.

Peabody gave a little smile and intertwined his fingers across his belly. "One might accurately characterize it as incredulity, I believe. And could you blame her? Here I was, a fat white man, a mortician no less, who'd moved to Gallup—the town she hated more than any other on the surface of the earth—because he'd been unable to forget a young Zuni girl he'd seen at a fair in 1893. A year ago he'd prepared her husband for burial and now he wanted to write to her."

"But she agreed," Owen said.

"Oh, not at first. She wanted nothing to do with me."

Peabody later learned that the widowed Estella had not been without suitors. An old man whose wife had recently died. A younger man with four children who needed someone to raise them because his own wife had run off. Another, a former suitor before her marriage to Lonan Becerra, who still had his eyes on the jewelry business even though he had no talent for it. Her father had shown a bit of sympathy to the first suitor, but the other two, he'd practically kicked through the doorway.

"Anyway, Connor Halusewa and I sat in the parlor—we were on our third cup of coffee by then—doing more sitting than conversing, and he eventually announced that Estella would receive my letter. I asked if he had any objections. There was a lengthy pause, but then he said:

" 'Two grown women in a house is not a peaceful thing. My wife and my daughter fight like cats.' "

Peabody and his future father-in-law walked outside into the full sun, which, after the dimness inside, forced them both to squint. They stood on the sidewalk.

'In Chicago,' Halusewa said, 'men offered me money for my daughter. Did you know men in Chicago who would do that?'

Peabody sighed. 'I'd have to say I did, yes.'

Connor Halusewa looked up the empty street, toward where it crossed the railroad tracks. 'I'll build my daughter a house near mine this time. But not too near.'

They were letting the fire die down. Peabody and Pete had paid a visit to the privy but had returned, and Peabody now sat in his former spot, between Pete and Clement Yazzie.

"I'm curious about why Estella let you write to her," Julia said.

"It was just a letter," Pete said. "She didn't have anything to lose."

"Don't you believe it for a second," Julia retorted.

"Win was the one risking everything."

"Sometimes," Julia said, "you're as thick as two planks. Win has his business and, safely invested back in Chicago, his money. He could pack up and leave Gallup, return to Chicago, perhaps mope about for a bit, and then still go and find a suitable woman to marry."

Pete, his jaw set, looked to Peabody and then Owen for support that wasn't forthcoming.

"Estrellita," Peabody said to Julia, his eyes shining. "That's why she allowed me to write."

The promise of a better future for her daughter. I'd like to meet this woman, Julia told herself.

So Peabody had written to Estella. It was a simple letter, asking only that she allow him to visit her. He offered no explanations because he had none that he could reduce to the written word, no matter how carefully he tried. And he did try, draft after draft, before discarding them all in favor of his simple request.

Peabody and Estella, accompanied by Estrellita and chaperoned by Estella's mother, met on a Friday afternoon. Six months later, they married, not at Sacred Heart but at the Christian Reformed Mission in Zuni; after Lonan Becerra's death, the entire Halusewa family had switched their allegiance.

"And they've lived happily ever after," Pete said.

"Yes and no," Peabody said. "After all, the imagined and the real are inevitably quite different." He winked. "My wife can be prickly. She'll have none of my nonsense. Estrellita and our son Nick—Nicklaus—always come first. And I believe she prefers having a part-time husband—my work keeps me out of her hair. Besides that, my dealings with her extended family aren't always straightforward or easy—I'm accepted, with a certain diffidence. I must say, however, that her father and I do get on very well."

"And why not?" Pete said. "You restored his peace and tranquility."

"That, and I'm a good provider, which various relatives have taken advantage of. It infuriates Estella, but I don't mind. Zuni is a very poor community." He shook his head. "Very poor. By Zuni standards Estella's father is well off, but he can't be seen as *too* well off. Jealousies and ill will abound." He slapped his thighs. "But that's neither here nor there. I'm a happy man. I choose happiness."

"Easier said than done," Pete said.

"And easier for some than others," Owen added.

"Too true, too true," Peabody said. "I think of my dear Estella when she first returned to Zuni from Gallup. She did not choose the circumstances that brought her there, nor did her choosing to return allow for anything beyond a measure of relief—certainly not happiness."

"And now?" Julia asked.

"Is she happy? I believe so. I do my best."

"I'm sure you do."

"Not that any of us are without worries," Peabody said. "Sometimes we just require a new start, don't you think? Didn't we transplants all come here, in our separate ways, seeking renewal? Isn't that the West?" His enthusiasm grew as he went on: "Take our friend Pete here. A dock man's son who ventured into the spiritual life for a time, taught himself the skills of the photographer, opened his own successful business, and now intends to try his hand in Alaska"— Julia looked up quickly; Pete, his face grim, briefly met her glance—"Alaska! as far west as you can go without ending up in the East. Ha!" Peabody's ruddy cheeks glowed above his beard. "There's all this talk about the frontier being closed. Don't you believe it! For some, the frontier will never close."

JULIA DIDN'T SLEEP VERY well, and not just because of Win Peabody's bravura snoring, punctuated by random grunts, coughs, and strangled inhalations, in the adjoining room. These days, once again, insomnia regularly disrupted her nights.

Long before the yellow edge of predawn, she gave up tossing, rose, and began her preparations for the day. Stripped to the waist, she made her morning ablutions at her washstand; her hair needed a good shampooing to wash away the residue of smoke from last night's open fire, but she'd deal with that later. She tied up her hair, dressed simply and quickly, and left her room. In the kitchen she lit the lamps, shook down the coals, started a pot of coffee, and put on a pan of water to boil eggs.

Outside, the morning sky offered enough light for her to tend to the animals. She collected eggs and threw handfuls of dried corn to the chickens; with a little more rain, they would have a better opportunity to eat their fill of bugs. She made sure that all the horses in the stable—her own plus Pete's—had sufficient water and hay. She dumped a pail of yesterday's slops for her new sow and tended to her milker. Butter was getting low; she'd leave some of the milk aside to churn. Back in her kitchen, she lowered a dozen fresh eggs into the boiling water and helped herself to the coffee. She wasn't hungry but spread a slice of bread with molasses and ate it standing by the stove as the eggs rumbled in the pan. Peabody was still sleeping. Owen would be in soon; she ladled a cup of boiling water from the egg pan and set some oatmeal to cooking, throwing in a dash of salt and a handful of pinyon nuts. Ten minutes later she removed the cereal and the eggs from the heat and poured a second cup of coffee for herself and one for Pete.

A half moon still hung in the turquoise sky. Julia had wrapped a shawl around her shoulders. Pete was leaning against the side of his wagon and, to Julia's surprise, Harry Whitaker was standing beside him, arms folded. Harry's horse, not yet unsaddled, stood nearby.

"You must be exhausted," Julia said to Harry.

"Ah'm fine," he answered. He did seem in good spirits.

"And your patients?"

"Mother and twin girls. The babes didn't want to leave the comforts of home, but all is well, I'm happy to report. You have to give thanks on such occasions, especially when the outcome was in doubt. Anyway, I slept for a few hours before setting out, and the cool air revived me." Julia handed him her cup of coffee and passed the other to Pete, who, standing there shoeless in his union suit and trousers, looked like he could use it.

"I hear that I missed a first-rate rendition of Win Peabody's courtship."

"An epic," Pete said. "And some of it was probably true."

Julia ignored him. "How is Tóya?" she asked Harry.

Harry frowned. "Her arthritis is making it harder and harder for her to get around. And her hearing is getting worse, too."

"Is there anything you can do?" Julia asked.

"Nothing. But she's planning to have a Night Chant in the fall."

Julia knew that loss of hearing was one of several ailments, including blindness and mental disturbances, that the Night Chant addressed; however, the cost of the nine-day sing, one of the most elaborate and intricate Navajo ceremonies, usually required the ready participation of an extended family in order to meet the requirements of the hataałii, his assistants, Navajos who would participate in related social events over the course of several days, and the hundreds who would gather for the final night's Yeibichei.

"Can she afford it?" Julia asked.

"She has what she needs. You needn't worry," Harry said, peering into his cup and then taking several sips of the coffee.

"You're a good man, Harry." Julia briefly touched his arm.

"Well," he said with a little shrug.

"Who's going to help her organize it?"

"Betty Roanhorse. Betty will see to it."

"Whatever I can provide, I will," Julia said. The food for the final night alone could deplete a family's resources.

"I'll let Betty know," Harry said. "So, Pete tells me he's leaving us and Gallup behind."

Throughout the exchange about Tóya, Pete had been staring off into the distance, down the canyon. Now he said, "It's a pisspot of a town anyway. It's beginning to chafe. Or maybe it's just the Indians. Or particular Indians." He looked straight at Julia.

"Excuse me?" she said. She folded her arms, gripping her elbows.

Harry, looking from one to the other, caught on quickly. He calmly said, "Christian forbearance, Pete. Christian charity."

"Oh," Pete said, "I have plenty of Christian charity. Toward your friend Tóya, for instance, who's never so much as given me the time of day. But she's an old woman, set in her ways. There's worse around. At least she's never killed anybody."

"Enough," Harry said.

"Or chased off anyone's husband." Pete's stare, cold, never left Julia.

"I should club you between the eyes," Harry said.

"It's all right, Harry," Julia said, putting her hand on his arm again, this time to make sure he didn't step forward. "Put your horse in the corral and go on in. I'll only be a minute."

Julia watched Harry walk away, open the gate, lead his horse in, un-saddle him, and proceed to the house.

Pete drank his coffee and coughed thickly. He raised his squinting eyes and looked at her from within the shade given by his wagon's canvas tarp. "You don't look well, Julia."

"I could say the same."

"You *have* said it. The difference"—he ran his free hand back through his hair, down over the back of his skull, and rubbed the back of his neck—"is that it's always true in my case. Not in yours." He lifted a forefinger and drew little circles in the air. "Those dark half-moons under your eyes are saying something." He swirled the dregs of coffee in the mug and then dumped the last out.

"When were you planning to tell me about Alaska?"

"Today."

"And when will you be leaving?"

"Soon. There's a fellow who thinks my place would make a fine bar-ber shop, if I'd let the lease go."

She remembered standing in the street in Gallup, next to the wagon loaded with her new furniture, Sam Bosco holding the team's reins while Pete set up his camera.

"I can't come to you anymore, Julia."

She wanted to grab him by his loutish ears and shake his brains loose; she felt weary enough to cry, but she wouldn't. "Will leaving make a differ-ence?"

"That's to be seen. Staying certainly won't. You've made that clear enough. First, you took a worthless husband, and now you've given away the last years of your womanhood to an Indian."

They both knew that he'd gone too far. Which, Julia understood, was his intention. "I gave away nothing," she said.

They heard a cough and turned to see Owen approaching from his cabin. They stood silently. Something, however—the stiffness of their postures, the unnaturalness of their silence—made him stop and call out, "Is everything all right?"

"Go away, little man!" Pete shouted.

"I'm fine, Owen," Julia said. "Go on in. Harry Whitaker's here, and breakfast is ready."

Owen stared at Pete, but then he turned and did as Julia had directed.

Owen's brief interruption had given her time to further collect herself, to recognize that nothing she might say would matter. "Do you need to store anything—glass negatives or anything? I've got room in the back."

"No. If I can't fit it in my wagon, I don't want it." He handed her the empty mug.

"Then I'll let you be about your business," she said and walked away.

Later, in the kitchen, Julia was washing the breakfast dishes, Harry Whitaker beside her, drying them. Win Peabody and his automobile had just left, with Owen taking a turn in the driver's seat as far as the end of the canyon.

"He probably didn't mean half of what he said," Harry told her. Pete had departed with no further words. "He'll think again when he sobers up."

"He may have had one or two to fortify himself, but he wasn't drunk," Julia said.

"Pete in all his glory," Harry said.

CHAPTER EIGHTEEN: A Cameo

They set out on a beautiful early September morning of scurrying cirrus clouds and swaying wild sunflowers that, mile after mile, had sprung up in a random scatter from the ditches lining the trail. They made only two stops, the first just south of Naschitti so that Johnny Gorman could show them the tract where he intended to build a house for his growing family—a second child was already on the way—and the second at Tohatchi so that Julia and Owen could visit with Harry Whitaker and Tóya. As Owen's cabin neared completion, Johnny had taken an increasing interest when he wasn't busy at the trading post, and now that Owen had finished the interior, Johnny announced that he intended to build a similar cabin, though a bit bigger to accommodate a second bedroom for his children. Although he'd been living in a hogan that his in-laws had erected near their own—not *too* near, given the traditional Navajo proscription against familiar contact with his mother-in-law, a proscription that they continued to honor in the fact even though, devout Christians all, they rejected all Navajo paganisms—he'd decided that a log cabin, with a real indoor kitchen and a layout that would permit a future addition if his family continued to grow, would suit him far better. He clearly was pleased when Owen approved of the site and of his ambitions.

"What else could I say?" Owen whispered to Julia before they returned to the wagon. "He thinks I know a lot more than I really do. He should be talking to Yazzie." But they both knew that wasn't likely; Johnny didn't like Yazzie's backward ways any more than his parents did.

While Johnny went off to visit with the Reverend Mr. Brink at the Tohatchi Christian Reformed Mission, Julia and Owen enjoyed a pleasant meal with Harry and Tóya. Julia had the distinct impression, however, that Tóya missed a good deal of what was being said, even though she, Harry, and Owen all made a point of facing her directly when they spoke. Julia and Owen didn't linger: they hoped to reach Gallup by nightfall.

The next day, after a night spent at the Commercial Hotel—Johnny turned down Julia's offer of a room, perhaps fearing that his presence, as a Navajo, would cause a stir or perhaps because he really did want to visit friends—Julia and Owen headed to the Rodriguez Furniture Emporium while Johnny tended to trading post business, picking up supplies and the mail. Owen, with his cabin complete, had decided to buy himself a table and side chairs, a bed and chest of drawers for his bedroom, and two armchairs for sitting by the fireplace. (The second chair would, of course, be Julia's.) While Owen perused the showroom, Julia, her ledger under her arm, entered Alberto Rodriguez's office.

She'd been in Alberto's office numerous times but never failed to be impressed. Everything was of the finest quality. A large mahogany desk dominated the room. Behind it, the finest lace curtains framed the double-hung windows. To the right, built-in mahogany bookcases held only a few books but a fine collection of Hopi baskets and pottery, which added color to the room. Opposite, two leather high-backed armchairs were separated by a small round table of inlaid woods, and a floor lamp with an exquisite stained glass shade matched that of the central ceiling fixture. The tin ceiling was embossed with delicate geometric stamping.

Julia, greeted warmly, sat down across from Alberto, who was dressed in one of his always elegant suits, and placed her ledger on his desk. In 1904, following Will's disappearance, Julia found that no surety company would provide her, a mere woman, with the $10,000 bond required by the Indian Bureau for all non-full-blooded Indian operators of trading posts. In the absence of a bond, Julia needed the support of two reputable individuals, and Alberto not only agreed to be one, but also convinced his brother in Aztec to serve as the second, his brother's only condition being that Julia submit to periodic examination of her books by Alberto. Julia had readily agreed. At best, Alberto's examination could be described as casual, and now, on this September morning, he simply drummed his fingers on the ledger and pushed the black book, unopened, back toward Julia.

"Consider my duty done," he said.

"Well," Julia said, smiling, "you mean I rode all the way into Gallup for nothing?"

Alberto smiled back and then smoothed out his mustache with two quick swipes of a forefinger. "Not for nothing. I've been meaning to visit you at Many Springs, but this saves me the trip."

"You know you're always welcome, whether you come by horse and carriage or by automobile. Or by both, as the case may be."

He laughed. "Matilda and I have complete confidence in our new Oldsmobile," he said, "so don't be surprised if I do show up one of these days."

"So tell me," Julia said, "why were you planning to come and see me?"

"Yes, my reason . . . ," he said, hesitating. "Matilda and I were in Denver visiting her parents several weeks ago, and I ran into your husband."

Julia sat back in her chair and waited for Alberto to continue.

Alberto had mentioned to a brother-in-law that he wanted to find a nice bauble for Matilda's birthday. Matilda's brother, after naming several jewelry stores, asked if Alberto might be interested in purchasing something older, more in the line of an heirloom. Given Matilda's particular fondness for cameos, Alberto replied that he might, and his brother-in-law suggested that, in that case, Alberto should visit a recently opened store owned by a fellow named George Banks, who purchased items primarily from estate sales. His merchandise was of the highest quality but not flashy.

"He was standing behind the counter," Alberto told Julia, "and as soon as he turned and looked toward me, I knew who he was. Oh, he remained very collected—didn't even blink—but he recognized me as well. I was stunned at first. He's heavier—he's grown something of a paunch—and his hair is thinning, and he has a mustache, but there couldn't be any doubt."

"What did he say?" Julia asked.

"He denied knowing any Wilford Halley. He said I had the wrong man, and when I continued to press him, he asked me to leave the premises, which I did."

"I see." Julia looked down at her folded hands.

"Julia, you should also know that in addition to a new identity he has another wife. And two children, a boy and a girl."

"And you know all this because—?"

"I made inquiries."

How quickly had Will moved on? Julia wondered. Denver, a reasonable choice, the largest city between St. Louis and the West Coast. And how soon after leaving her had he tried on his new name? And how quickly had he set his sights on the future Mrs. Banks?

"Is there anything else I should know?" she asked.

"In addition to the jewelry store, he owns two pawnshops in less savory neighborhoods, which is apparently where he got his start."

"It seems that he's done well for himself in a very short time."

"I admire your aplomb," Alberto said.

"Oh, I always thought I'd hear from him, or about him, at some point," Julia said. "The only surprise is that you're the person from whom I'm hearing it."

"I considered exposing him to the authorities but then thought better of it. I decided I should inform you first. It should be your decision."

"I appreciate it, Alberto," Julia said. "I think you did best by leaving well enough alone."

"But you're still tied to him, legally. You could certainly force his hand—get him to agree to a divorce and relinquish all claims."

"It may come to that."

"Then I should leave the matter in your hands?" Alberto asked.

"You should. Please tell no one, absolutely no one, about this."

"Of course not."

When she was leaving, Julia asked, "Did you find Matilda a cameo?"

"I did," Alberto said. "Elsewhere."

CHAPTER NINETEEN: George Banks

Clear as his view through the freshly washed window glass, complete with reflection, the then and the now.

* * *

Will Halley had held out hope for a year, two years, maybe even a touch of the third, that the railroad would build that line from Durango to Gallup and south—it made sense, goddamn it, to get the lead and copper and zinc and silver out of the Uncompahgre and to the markets as efficiently as possible, building not through the badlands but down the length of the Chuska Valley. But it wasn't going to happen. He'd have to depend indefinitely on Navajos and sheep for his livelihood. Goddamn, filthy sheep.

He was sitting, the night he finally decided, in Obie's Gentlemen's Club, on Gallup's north side. A sign on the door read:

> NO WOMEN
> NO INDIANS
> NO FIREARMS
> NO INEBRIATES

A long bar and a dozen tables filled the front room. It was the middle of the week, slow, two customers at the far end of the bar, half a dozen others scattered about, almost all of whom he knew, at least casually. On the wall above the card table, where he was sitting, another sign:

> HOUSE RULES:
> A SEAT AT THIS TABLE COSTS $1
> CASH OR FOLD—NO CHITS, NO IOUs

"Sit down and join us," Pete Pietrowski was saying to a newcomer, a fatty in a fine suit who'd just entered with Ash Billings, a clerk at Patterson's Trading Company.

"I wouldn't be intruding, as it were?" the fat man asked.

"Not at all." Obie Boino proceeded to introduce himself.

The fat man held out his hand.

"Forgive me for not making the proper introductions," Ash Billings said. "Win Peabody, this is Pete Pietrowski, proprietor of our local photography studio. And Will Halley. Will and his wife run the Many Springs Canyon Trading Post."

"Near Gallup?" Peabody asked, shaking Will's hand and pulling out a chair.

"Fifty miles north."

Peabody extracted a dollar from a pocket and slid it across the table to Obie, who nodded and said, "Your first drink is on the house. What would you like?"

"Bourbon? Do you have that?"

"If gentlemen drink it, I have it. Karl!" he called to the bartender, "one fine Kentucky bourbon." Then to Peabody: "I take it you're new to Gallup?"

"I passed through not long ago and decided to return on a more permanent basis."

"In that case, you're *doubly* welcome. Karl, make it a double! You appear to be a professional man."

"An undertaker."

"Whoa," Pete said. "Bad luck at a card table. I've been on a streak. I hope you don't break it."

"A streak," Obie scoffed. "Two hands in a row, and Will and I both folded."

"I'm not much of a player," Peabody said.

"Good," Pete said. "Ante up."

Karl, biceps like barbells, set the drink down in front of Peabody and returned to his other customers at the bar.

"Fifty miles," Peabody said with a smile. "That's a far piece. Do you get into town often?"

"Not often enough. When business demands. Or when I need to see a white face, other than my own in the shaving mirror."

"You have your lovely wife to gaze upon," Pete said.

"She's half Indian."

"Really?" Peabody raised an eyebrow.

"*Not* really," Pete said.

"She just acts like it."

"What now?" Pete asked.

"You haven't been up to see us since the diphtheria."

"No."

"The goddamn Navajos"—shaking his head and lifting his glass—"they can be inhuman."

"What happened?" Obie asked.

"You know there's a Navajo who lives up the canyon from us. Sometimes he does odd jobs that I won't dirty my hands with."

"He means Clement Yazzie," Pete said to Obie.

"Him," Obie said.

"Yes, *him.* So he and his two boys all come down with the cough, and the next thing I know, Julia's installed them in the side bedroom and sent for Harry Whitaker."

"The Indian doctor up at Tohatchi," Pete explained for Peabody's benefit.

"The boys died one after the other—"

"They were good boys," Pete said, frowning.

"They were, and I had nothing against them. Anyway, Julia wraps them up in our linens and we carry them out to the guest hogan, and then she helps Yazzie into *our* bed because, she says, he can't stay in a room where somebody has died."

At that point Will had glanced around the table; the other men were quiet, each looking with a drinking-man's frown at his glass.

"So then Julia tells me to go back into the side bedroom and bust out the window—you know, so their chindis can escape. Are you following this? So I do what she asks. I take a sledgehammer to the window and the frame, the whole thing, and I'm so goddamn angry that I really bust it up in there, which is what she wanted anyway so that Yazzie could hear it all. But here's the thing I really don't get—and you should make note of this, Peabody, because you won't be getting much undertaking business from Navajos—once those boys died, Yazzie wanted nothing to do with them. A friend of his, an old fool that lives way up in the Chuskas, came and took the bodies and that was it. Gone. Never saw them again. Never to be seen again. No headstone, no marker. As far as I know, Yazzie has no idea where his own boys—and his wife and mother before them—lay in the ground. And doesn't care. How can you deal with people like that? And then, wouldn't you know, *I* came down with the diphtheria."

"Probably from carrying those Indian boys' bodies," Obie said.

"More likely from the air," Peabody said. "The sick breathe the germs out, and we breathe them in, as it were."

"I had it before, when I was a kid, so it wasn't so bad this time. Whiskey and sweating it out did the trick."

"And your wife?" Peabody asked.

"Not so much as a sneeze. Later on I dragged the bedding outside and burned it all."

"And the boys' father survived?" Peabody asked.

"After spending the better part of a week in our bed, stinking the whole place up with his sickness."

"If I were you, Will," Obie said, "I'd say enough's enough—you need to get your woman under control. Are you married, Peabody?"

"No, I can't say that I am. You, Mr. Boino?"

"Oh yes. To a fine woman. Never gives me a moment's worry. Looks after the house, cooks, sees to the children—six of them, mind you. Another round?"

"On me," Peabody said.

"That's generous of you," Pete said.

"Not at all, not at all."

Obie signaled to Karl.

"I see you have another room," Peabody said, nodding toward a doorway beyond the bar. Behind a half-drawn curtain was a larger table surrounded by finer chairs with cushioned seats and backs. The chairs were tipped up against the table's edge.

"It costs you $5 to sit at *that* table," Pete said.

"But all your liquor is free," Obie noted.

"May I assume," Peabody ventured, "that's where the high-stakes games take place?"

"Depends on what you mean by 'high,' " Obie said.

"Who participates, as it were?"

"Anyone who can afford to."

"Except Frogs, Guineas, Japs, Chinks, and Polacks," Pete said, "and I'm a Polack."

"Your friend Alberto Rodriguez and some of his cronies were playing back there no more than a week ago," Ash Billings said to Pete. Throughout the conversation Billings—a cheapskate, tight with his dollars—had remained standing.

"He's not my friend," Pete said.

"Nor mine," said Will. "You'll never convince me that he wasn't party to the swindle that left me high and dry."

Peabody looked inquisitively at him, but it was Pete who answered:

"When Will bought the trading post, he relied on some photographs I took that showed the place fully stocked. But when he arrived, everything was gone. Rodriguez was agent for the prior owners."

"I see."

"Cleaned out except for a bucket of ten-penny nails. Which I proceeded to piss in."

"Henceforth a bucket of rusty nails," Pete said.

"Are you going to resume your card game?" Peabody asked.

"It wasn't much of a game," Pete said.

Karl brought over a tray of drinks, providing an opportunity for Will to ask: "Have you heard from Bandy Carter lately?'

"I believe he's been busy," Karl answered, giving him the nod.

"Why are you asking about *him*, Will?" Pete said.

"Oh, no reason."

"He tried to convince me that I should replace a couple of my store brands with liquor he gets from who-knows-where," Obie said. "I told him, sure, I'm going to try and pass off that rotgut as Jim Beam or Old Overholt. You gentlemen would lynch me."

"This Carter, he's a liquor salesman?" Peabody asked.

"No, a shift foreman at the Catalpa mine," Pete said. "You might say he has a side business."

Later, when they were leaving, Pete pulled Will aside. "I know what you three are up to. If I know, others know."

"It's none of your business."

"Think of Julia," Pete said.

Julia would be away for at least ten days, back East for her sister's wedding.

"Don't I always?" he replied.

* * *

Bandy supplied the goods. Karl drove the wagon north along the back trails. Will Halley set up shop just south of the reservation boundary, but a Navajo, easily bribed, did the actual selling. None of the customers so much as saw him.

* * *

He supposes it was inevitable that someone would spot him on a Denver street or in a restaurant, or would enter one of his shops and recognize him despite the mustache and the thinning hair. He'd stood there behind the counter and smiled while Alberto Rodriguez, stone faced, kept repeating the name Wilford Halley.

He isn't proud of what he did back at the end of that life, draining the Gallup bank account and departing with his share of the liquor money (and the last two unsold bottles) as well as a satchel of pawn. But it had been necessary, as simple as that.

Once in Denver, he'd rented a little storefront in a seedy district and began negotiating with the dregs of the street—thieves, whores, pimps, alcoholics, opium addicts. It took two years to parlay his earnings into enough savings to open a second shop where the rent was higher but the customers owned, maybe, one or two pieces of semivaluable jewelry or an inherited canvas by a second-rate painter. He found that he was good at judging, by the beads of sweat on a man's brow or the pallor of a woman's complexion, how much to offer for an outright purchase. He also turned out to be good at spotting people with new money but no taste—an easy proposition in a city growing as rapidly as Denver.

As a result of his successes, he has managed to purchase this little property on a bustling street. He wears finer clothes now and has his hair and mustache trimmed by a barber twice a week. He has joined a church and a civic club and has made other valuable contacts by catering to a seemingly affluent clientele that requires discretion, such as when a husband "borrows" from his wife a diamond brooch that was her mother's. Here in this store he deals in old jewelry and other antiques, including, increasingly, items from estate sales, such as a set of English Regency chairs that made its way across the Atlantic to Philadelphia and from there across the Great Plains, and has just now brought him an astounding profit. (Much to his amusement, he's discovered the importance of provenance.)

Equally satisfying, at the end of each day he returns to a loving home. He courted Marlene properly, and spoke to her father properly, and married her properly, and now they have two young children, Ellen and Jacob, born barely a year apart and named for her parents. Marlene has a slender figure and the most fragile wrists, which he can easily encircle with thumb and forefinger, and coppery irises. (He isn't even sure anymore what color Julia's eyes are—bluish gray or greenish hazel?)

When Ellen was born, he bought a cradle that gently swings on brass hinges from a solid oak frame. The cradle sits high off the floor so that Marlene doesn't even have to rise to lift Baby Jacob to her breast during the night. When their son is nearly done suckling, Marlene whispers to him, "George, time now," and he goes to the kitchen, first to stoke the woodstove so that the room will be perfectly comfortable when they rise at dawn, and then to fetch her a warm glass of milk and a wedge of cheese and a slice of bread spread with preserves to keep up her strength, for she's a little woman, barely four-foot-nine. While Marlene eats, he changes Jacob's diaper and then gently rocks the cradle for a minute or two, until his son has settled back into a deeper sleep. Then he returns to his side of the bed, which Marlene has kept warm for him, and, content, he soon falls back to sleep himself.

He would never risk this quiet, stable domesticity by engaging in foolish dalliances, which seem to be more common the higher his customers stand on the social ladder. He observes it all and even flirts mildly, as social grace requires, but he is not tempted. Nor does he ever act on what he learns about his customers' finances or other private matters. Indeed, he doesn't even acknowledge possessing such knowledge unless a client, testing him, broaches the subject, which permits him, through a placid mien and carefully chosen words, to display his prudence. Even so, their fear always reeks like stale sweat, and experience has taught him that unless they're uncommonly lucky, they'll all be found out, sooner or later.

He's certain that Rodriguez will run to Julia with his news, but like a lapdog, Rodriguez will do whatever she asks. So the question is, how will Julia react? Will she reveal any of this to anyone else? Not Pete Pietrowski, if he's still hanging around—Pete has too big of a mouth. Harry Whitaker? The soul of discretion, so no worry there, even if she does tell him. The Gormans? Never in a million years. Yazzie?

Will Halley had probably heard every variation of the story. Clement Yazzie killed a Navajo in cold-blood. In a drunken brawl. In a fair fight. Because of a slight to his honor. Because of an argument over a woman. Because of a dispute over a sheep. Or a goat. Or a saddle. Yazzie had slit the man's throat. Shot him in the back. Beat him to death with a fence post. Drilled him through the forehead from ten paces. Tied him up with barbed wire and hung him from a tree by his heels . . .

The last time he saw Yazzie was on the second night after riding away from Many Springs Canyon. Finishing off what was left of Bandy's liquor, he was sitting by his campfire, and suddenly Yazzie was sitting there as well, his legs crossed and firelight glinting off the blade he held.

"Big surprise," Will had said, tossing the empty bottle aside and nearly tipping over. It was too soon for Julia's scheduled return from Albany, but maybe she'd come back early, in which case she might already have learned that he'd drained the trading post account. "Did she send you to bring me back?"

And then Yazzie did something unexpected. He laughed. He laughed long and hard.

He knew that he should keep his mouth shut, but he couldn't:

"I see, my man. You're here to make sure I *don't* come back. So you can taste some of that sweet white meat for yourself."

Yazzie slowly moved closer.

He could do nothing except slide backward on his buttocks, pushing off with the heels of his hands and boots. It was useless, and he stopped.

Yazzie didn't raise his knife. Instead, with the point he drew a picture in the red dirt, a stick figure of a man hanging upside down from a tree limb.

"If you come within a two-day ride of Many Springs Canyon," Yazzie said, "I'll hear about it, and then we'll have another little talk."

They didn't say another word to each other. Yazzie went through the saddlebags, found the squash blossom necklace that Julia had kept in her jewelry box, and left as silently as he'd arrived.

* * *

George Banks stands behind the store window, gazing out at the street. It doesn't matter if Julia tells Yazzie. This is Denver, far from Yazzie's reach, if Yazzie even cares what became of Will Halley.

He doesn't often think about the *real* Will Halley—the one whose name he stole when the two of them parted ways, soon after leaving the orphanage together. At the time, the real Will Halley was setting out for Gloucester, intent on going to sea and living a life of adventure on some South Sea island, presumably one without cannibals; the imposter Will Halley had filched from his companion a character reference because he had none of his own, having been caught at various times smoking cigarettes, cheating on examinations, drinking sacramental wine, stealing a fountain pen from one of the nuns . . . At first, he almost regretted taking the real Will Halley's letter because the real Halley was a decent guy, even if too dreamy for his own good; these many years later he's probably baiting lobster traps in Maine, far from the South Seas, or hauling in cod off the Georges Bank.

George still thinks about Julia now and then, sometimes with manly passion, rarely with anything approaching empathy. He certainly has no desire to see her or hear from her. After more than six years, she probably feels nothing for him, either.

He recalls a brief conversation with Julia's future step-mother, Edna Blaine, just before he and Julia left for St. Louis. Edna, though far from his champion, didn't seem to have the visceral dislike for him that the Reverend Daddy Marshall did. Maybe because Edna, although she would never say so, was not displeased to see Julia go.

"You think Julia will ease your way," Edna had said. He thought she was talking about Julia's inheritance, but she wasn't.

"Julia isn't unattractive—in her own way she has a certain appeal. You think that will help you enter polite society. And it may, if all goes well. But if things don't go well, you'll both wonder what you ever saw in each other."

"I'm not sure if that's a criticism of her or of me," he'd said.

"*You* don't concern me." Edna raised her nose into the air. "If I close my eyes, you aren't even here."

"If I close *my* eyes"—he proceeded to do exactly that—"I see your late husband fondling little boys."

Wealth had bought silence, of course, but such rules didn't apply down in the muck; there, a free drink or a dollar placed in the right pocket could buy what you wanted to know.

"I retract what I said about Julia's helping you join society. You clearly have no place there," Edna had ended the conversation.

And yet here he is, within reach of securing his family's future—his daughter will marry well, his son will attend the finest college—because he's learned that respectability is perceived, not achieved, and that society's guiding principle is simple: Don't get caught. In the past six and a half years, since leaving Will Halley sitting beside a campfire, George Banks has done nothing that he couldn't answer for. Before that . . . well, that was another life, one in which Julia was as much at fault as he. Why dwell on it? The past is past, and he's a new man.

It occurs to him then, with great pleasure, that if Julia intends to continue on with her present life, she needs Will Halley's absence just as much as he, George Banks, needs her silence: Julia and George, now married by deceit, until death do them part.

Standing in the window, his hands linked behind his back, he watches two well-dressed women pause on the sidewalk to consider the jewelry on display. When they enter, he greets them with a smile and a bow.

CHAPTER TWENTY: Night Chants

Tóya's sing was being held northwest of Tohatchi, several miles up the trail that ran along Willow Wash toward Chuska Peak. The Navajos who had gathered for the final night, several hundred strong, were dressed warmly, wrapped in homemade blankets and Pendletons to ward off the November cold, except for the oblivious boys who played in their shirtsleeves, running in gangs at the edge of the firelight, tossing hoops and tackling and playing tag while their elders talked and laughed.

The visitors from Many Springs Canyon—Julia, Owen, and Johanna occupying the trading post's spring wagon; Yazzie, astride his brown—came upon the scene at the last blue length of daylight. Their departure had been delayed because Owen was visibly ill early in the day—even paler than usual and clearly in distress because of what he described as a bout of vertigo—but by noon he declared that the dizziness had passed, and they set off, at his insistence; this would be his first opportunity to see a Yeibichei, and he wasn't about to miss it. They arrived too late to see the late-afternoon blessing of Tóya by Monster Slayer, Born-for-Water, and Shooting Goddess in their phantasmal head and face masks, but the night's events all lay ahead.

The ceremonial hogan stood at one end of a narrow gathering ground newly cleared of brush and saplings. At the opposite end of a fifty-yard corridor, an arbor of vertical evergreen poles and branches had been erected for the Yeibichei dancers and god impersonators to don their masks. During the previous eight nights and days of the Night Chant, most of the healing rites had been performed inside the hogan, out of view, but tonight, the ninth and final night, alternating teams of dancers would emerge from the arbor, follow Talking God—Haashch'éélt'í, the grandfather of the yei—

through the clearing, and perform until dawn in front of the hogan, in a space defined by bonfires and rough logs intended for seating as well as fuel.

Julia didn't know anything about Tóya's singer, except that, like all Night Chant hataałiis, he'd studied and apprenticed for years; each prayer, each song, the creation of each colorfully decorated prayer stick and plumed wand and sand painting had to be executed with precision, and deviations could bode ill. That said, one extraordinary difference marked this Night Chant: for his dedication to the Diné, Harry Whitaker had been invited to witness the full ceremonial. (He'd almost missed it: he'd returned from his mother's funeral in Charleston less than a week before the first night.)

The small group from Many Springs, having found an open spot on a rise near the hogan (but not so close as to draw unwanted attention), layered blankets on the dry, hardened ground. Julia, Owen, and Johanna sat and shared a light supper that Julia had packed. Yazzie, who wasn't hungry, wandered off in search of familiar faces in the crowd.

Julia watched Owen pick at the food. Despite Tóya's invitation, Julia didn't want to be here, even before Owen's morning bout of vertigo. She didn't like his being this far from Many Springs.

Although she couldn't point to a precise moment when she'd become aware of it, as the autumn bore in, the nights dropping below freezing and the days getting shorter, Julia understood that Owen had begun to fail. Neither spoke of it. Most evenings now, whether sitting beside the box stove in her parlor or in front of his cabin's fireplace, he was having difficulty reading in the dim light, and he would often drift off. He didn't walk up into the mountains or even into the high meadow much anymore, choosing instead, when he left the surrounds of the trading post, to wander down the canyon toward the Gallup road. Even the muscles in his forearms, when he bared them to help wash the dishes in the evening, had grown slack, the skin sagging around the ever-more-prominent bones. He made no complaints. When asked if anything was the matter, he'd smile and shrug and reply, "Just a bit tired."

Each morning Julia waited for him to visit her kitchen. (He rarely used his coal cooker except to heat the cabin and to boil water.) He would come in, sit at her table, eat his oatmeal with butter and pine nuts and cinnamon, plus an egg or two when she managed to coax him into it. She would linger in the kitchen if he wanted to talk. He spoke more about his boyhood than ever before, and about college and his work life and Beth and her family, reshaping his memories into a coherent narrative. He talked about the books he'd poured over as a boy, especially a collection of Shakespeare's plays with dramatic illustrations that he could remember so clearly even now, and a book about the stars, and the handful of Bible stories that his mother had loved and that also seemed truest to his own experience of the world.

Sometimes in the evening they would discuss the success of the Many Springs Canyon Trading Post Catalog. The orders were trickling in, two or three forwarded every week from Penelope, which didn't seem like much until Julia projected how many rugs she would actually be able to ship by the end of the year, drawn from her new rug room or newly completed by her weavers. In early November she'd telegraphed Penelope, who was proving to be a very astute businesswoman, to stop accepting made-to-specification orders unless the customers were willing to wait well into 1911 for their delivery. Julia herself wrote to some customers advising that although she and her weavers would be happy to meet their demands, weaving large rugs—a number of the orders were for *exceedingly* large rugs, so much so that some of the weavers had to build larger looms—could take many months. Some buyers, with no idea of the work involved, were disgruntled to learn that their eight-by-ten parlor rugs couldn't possibly be finished and shipped by Christmas, but few canceled their orders.

Some of the Navajo women could be relied on to finish their assignments as scheduled, but others were considerably more lackadaisical, adjusting the hours spent at the loom to their need for store credit or cash. Julia understood that for most of them the idea of saving money was foreign, but what really riled her was when she learned that one of the women, despite having agreed to a price and a timetable, and despite having accepted dyed wool and a credit advance as part of the arrangement, went to the Two Grey Hills Trading Post in search of more money for the finished rug. Which she received and unwisely boasted about. (When informed of the weaver's subterfuge, Ed Davies at Two Grey Hills was more than apologetic and offered to reimburse Julia for the wool and the advance, but Julia refused since the fault was hardly his.) What could she do—prosecute the woman? A ridiculous idea. Still, she needed to make it clear to all her weavers that such behavior could not be tolerated. In the end, she added the cost of the purloined wool to the family's account, already in arrears, and cut off any further credit, something she was ordinarily loathe to do. The woman proceeded to tell anyone who would listen that Julia, that bilagáana *adiłgashii,* had cheated her, but Julia, witch or no witch, lost no other weavers.

She needed to convince more first-rate weavers to sell to her, a task that, in addition to checking on the progress of the dozen far-flung women who were already working on rugs, took her afield two or even three days a week now. Julia had begun to see a different future for herself. With the right weavers, and by expanding into Navajo turquoise and silver jewelry, and if she could produce and distribute more widely a larger catalog in the new year . . . well, who could say? Moreover, the regular wool trade had recovered from a slump in prices, and the cleaned wool business, after a slow start, was now turning a very nice profit. No longer so dependent on income from the day-to-day transactions in the store, Julia had given significant raises to Tom, Carmelita, and Johnny and was still managing to put a little money aside. She could foresee a day when her savings, if properly managed, would allow her to live modestly without fretting about month-to-month expenses.

Owen was all for expanding the catalog. He thought she could do quite nicely if she acquired an agent in another city. He suggested Boston, but Julia balked; she didn't believe she possessed the business acumen to compete successfully in an East Coast market. They agreed, however, that she would need a more colorful catalog. It was that idea—going beyond simple line drawings and descriptions, to imbue the pages with reds and grays, creams and blues, burnt orange and pale green—that had given Owen an incentive to try painting. Perhaps also inspired by having watched Johanna's eccentric efforts (an amusing turnabout, in Julia's view), on their September trip into Gallup he'd purchased himself a set of water colors, identical to the one he'd purchased earlier for Johanna, and now he spent several hours of each day at the easel, initially teaching himself how to use the thin paints and brushes properly so that colors wouldn't run or bleed. The first paintings had been laughably disastrous—he told Julia he was glad that Johanna, who was away at the time, wasn't there to see them—but he'd persisted and could now integrate lines of ink and fields of color.

Owen had made his easel himself, and when the weather permitted—that is, when it wasn't too chilly and the wind too stiff, for he couldn't tolerate the cold well anymore (another reason why Julia balked at his attending the Yeibichei)—he'd sit in the sun in front of the trading post, repositioning his chair and easel as the warmth moved westward, around the corner of the building and along her side of the veranda. When the veranda fell into shadow, which was earlier each day now, he would stop, fold up his easel, and wash out his brushes. On the colder mornings he would sit inside the trading post by one of the front windows, their exterior iron bars patterned on the floor by sunlight. Sometimes customers would gather behind him, watching but rarely commenting except in whispers to each other. Owen, unperturbed, would continue on. And sometimes, taking a break, he would sit in the bullpen, smoking a handmade cigarette—he never smoked elsewhere—and listen to the men talk, though he understood only a smattering of what they said. Seeing himself as a guest, he didn't intrude on their conversation, even when someone translated for him—typically a joke or a sly comment about his painting ("If you like Navajo rugs so much, my grand-mother will teach you to weave"), followed by general laughter, which Owen always joined.

When an illustration was done, Julia would sit with him in the evening and together they would write the accompanying text for the proposed second catalog. ("This illustration is from a weaving by Annie Bizhaahd, a master of the art. The original, 67.5 x 32 inches, was a unique design, as are all of those made by our expert weavers. You are, however, able to specify a general pattern of your choosing. The 'Ganado Red' style pictured here always incorporates a brilliant red background, accented with black, white, and grays, and includes geometric motifs, such as the illustrated 'hooks,' 'steps,' triangles, and a central diamond. The price of each rug is based on its size and the fineness of the weave, although you could expect to pay $75.00 to $100.00 for a similar Ganado Red.") These interactions were easy and filled with laughter but for Julia quietly distressing—she did her best to hide this from him—for she didn't think Owen would be there to help her write a third catalog if one ever came to pass.

With the night now upon them, Julia, Owen, and Johanna were finishing their simple meal when Julia spotted a familiar face walking toward them—the only other Anglo that she had seen among the throng gathered for the Yeibichei. Pete Pietrowski's friend Charlie Day greeted the three of them, speaking Navajo to Johanna, who made no acknowledgement except to make room for him to sit down.

"What brings you here, Charlie?" Julia asked.

"My brother Sammy's dance team is supposed to be performing," he said, "if they can get here in time. There's another Yeibichei over by Standing Rock, and they're dancing there as well."

"So they're in great demand?"

"Very much so," Charlie said, his broad smile displaying considerable filial pride. "Some singers say it's the best team on the reservation."

"And all the other members are Navajo?" Owen asked.

"They are. Sammy never has any trouble filling openings."

The friendly conversation continued, but when Owen and Charlie began discussing Charlie's numerous business ventures, Julia excused herself and said, "Jóhonaá, *yináá*—come walk with me," and the two women set off through the crowd.

Some of the earliest arrivals had pulled their wagons, often fitted with full bonnets, close to where the dance teams would perform; the extended family's youngest children, tucked into bedrolls under the hooped canvas, would be protected from the elements, but everyone else would still have a good view. Other Navajos had already claimed seats on the logs lining the performance area, which was illuminated by eight large bonfires. Farther back, amid the scatter of wagons and campsites, women were serving up mutton stew, roasted corn, dough fried in lard, coffee. Julia recognized a fair number of customers from the store, and when they greeted her she answered in Navajo. One man loudly complained to her about a rancid sack of flour, but his embarrassed wife tried to pull him away, telling Julia, in Navajo, not to listen to him, and Julia, smiling, assured her that, no, she wouldn't pay him any mind but that she stood by her merchandise and would gladly provide them with two free sacks of flour on their next visit to Many Springs. That appeared to mollify the husband, whose only response was a self-important grunt.

Julia and Johanna continued their leisurely wandering, crossing the cleared corridor near the makeshift arbor, and soon came upon Clement Yazzie. The three of them began to weave their way back toward the ceremonial hogan just as, led by the singer, five masked figures left the arbor. Of the five, the most important and impressive was Talking God, with his full head mask of buckskin painted white and decorated with a painted corn stalk, climbing from circular mouth hole to forehead, and topped by a headdress made of horse mane and eagle feathers. It was to him that the singer and then the patient would soon offer the night's long prayer.

As the costumed figures approached the hogan, Tóya emerged, followed by several of the singer's assistants and, hanging in the rear, Harry Whitaker. Julia was shocked by how frail Tóya appeared. The rigors of the Night Chant, with its sweat baths and purges and periods of fasting and prayer, had clearly taken their toll. When the ceremony concluded in the morning, she would spend most of an additional two weeks in seclusion, during which, Julia hoped, she might regain her strength. As for recovering what she had lost of her hearing, Julia had more modest expectations. Tales of near-miraculous cures were part of Navajo lore, and Julia accepted the value of firm belief in the efficacy of the Night Chant, but she considered the miraculous to be solely the domain of God and His intercessors, angels and saints, not ordinary ministers, priests, physicians, or hataałiis—although Harry Whitaker was less sure about the boundaries.

Everyone around them stood in silence now as Tóya sprinkled corn meal across and over the four blue-masked and plumed male yeis—the First Dancers, the Atsá'łei—each dressed in kilt, silver belt with dangling fox skin, and spruce wreath, and carrying spruce boughs and a gourd rattle. Throughout the blessing the yeis moved in place, tipping their heads, raising their left legs as if dancing. When Tóya returned to her place, the singer began the long prayer:

> In Tse'gíhi,
> In the house made of dawn,
> In the house made of twilight . . .

This was the Navajos' world, Julia thought: the mesas, the endless skies, the red rocks, the night's sooty pinyon smoke, the alien faces of their gods. Navajos knew better than to think that they had been created in their gods' images; the forces of belief and nature—even human nature, its worst impulses—were often so much more than the human frame could bear.

Julia spied Owen, across the way, standing next to Charlie Day, well back among the watchers. She knew she was going to lose him, and her bitterness demanded that there be blame. She'd thought they would have *time*—on average, his doctors had told him, four years. But his heart, damaged from childhood, hadn't been part of that calculation. She couldn't blame Owen. She couldn't blame the doctors. She *could* blame herself for *her* miscalculation.

Maybe, after, she would leave. Maybe she would go somewhere thoroughly new—maybe to the ocean, due east, the Outer Banks, to a place with a reckless name like Nags Head or Kill Devil Hills, where the Wright Brothers had taken flight, a mountainless place of white caps and gulls and shifting dunes and beach grass and hurricanes. She could see herself breathing sea brine instead of pinyon smoke, still selling canned goods and sacks of flour and coffee and beans, but also fishing tackle and thick coils of nautical rope and cedar shakes, to island dwellers separated by a sound from the mainland; or maybe, instead, a more genteel life in a little shoreline shop, offering shells and miniature ceramic lighthouses and amateurish seashore paintings to tourists in their white dresses and white suits and straw hats.

Tóya was now repeating the long prayer for Talking God, who, despite his name, never spoke; who emitted few sounds except whoops or birdlike callings, an announcement of arrival, a reminder to pay attention.

Julia was cold, shivering. Yazzie leaned toward her and whispered, "Are you all right?"

"It's freezing," she said. He was just being solicitous, but it annoyed her, which he obviously sensed. He returned his attention to Tóya and the masked figures.

Julia knew she was being tetchy. Maybe because her monthly period was due. But perhaps not. Lately it had been irregular, as much as two weeks late. Even as a young woman she'd never been one to give in to the cramps and the inconvenience, beyond applying a heated pad in bed at night and, now, taking Harry Whitaker's Aspirin pills as well. But her irregularity confirmed that she was nearing the end of a . . . possibility, though a remote one. Ambiguity would soon be certainty, and she couldn't help feeling diminished. Even though she'd taken great care to prevent any pregnancy with Clement. (*That* had never been even a question.) She'd asked him once, early on, if he ever gave thought to having more children.

"I can't see it," he'd said after a long silence. Which wasn't so clearly a "no."

"I didn't mean with me. You didn't think I meant that, did you?"

"No," he'd said.

At the time, he was three years out from the death of his boys, almost to the day. And more than a decade beyond the loss of his wife. Julia didn't know if he was still seeing Navajo women. She had the right to ask, but she hadn't, then or since. She couldn't expect anyone else to understand why she felt as she did about this—anyone else would think she'd lost her senses—and therefore had never discussed it, certainly not with Owen. (She saw that he was standing alone now as Tóya's prayer proceeded, Charlie Day having moved off, probably toward the arbor.) She wouldn't abuse the feelings that Owen had put aside.

Sometimes when she thought about Clement, their intimacy seemed inseparable from their losses. The Navajos said that eventually all bilagáanas left. It was a joke, and not a joke, because someday the tillers, the bricklayers, the store clerks, the school teachers, the coal miners, the bankers—the purveyors of America in the age of the telephone and automobile and aeroplane—would claim the *right* to stay. And, Julia knew, at times her very presence couldn't help but remind Clement of this, even as he embraced her.

He still came to her, but infrequently, and when he did, he hesitated, as if asking permission, even when the evening's circumstances—the way she moved when they were near each other, the way they subtly addressed each other: the stray, unobserved touch or even the simple passing of a cup and saucer—had made her answer clear. Why his hesitation? Why now? It more than annoyed her. It left her unsatisfied. It diminished her even more. It diminished *them.*

With her prayer finished, Tóya and the singer bestowed another blessing on each of the yeis with corn meal and pollen, after which patient and healer sat down in front of the hogan. The First Dancers began a choreography of repeated steps—turns to west and east, dips, swoops—and their song, mostly falsetto vocables without denotation.

Julia accepted that she would never be integrated into the press of Navajos surrounding the dance-ground. During the week, and especially tonight, some had undoubtedly eaten food that she'd donated for the ceremony, although much of it, including four sheep, would be distributed to the singer's attendants and the various dance teams as payment for their services. She had it to give, so she gave it. It was that simple. She didn't expect thanks or even acknowledgement, let alone a reciprocal gesture. Apart from her weavers, very few Navajos had ever invited her into their hogans, although a fair number had spent a snow- or sleet-filled night in her guest hogan, their horses safely sheltered in her corral. This was their way, and she, her white face among the many, many brown ones, took no offense. If they continued to trade at her store, if they respected that she did her very best to treat them fairly, that was enough.

She let the repetitions of the sacred song and dance, and the drifting smells of the food and spruce and smoke, soothe her. She let them drive away what remained of her anger and her irritability, her foolishness. She slid closer to Clement until their arms met, and she felt him link his elbow with hers. She wanted to reach out with her other hand and draw Johanna closer, too. She placed her fingers lightly on Johanna's shoulder. Johanna turned her head, those great doe eyes, and Julia smiled, and Johanna moved into Julia, whose hand dropped to the small of Johanna's back, and the three of them stood silently together.

She looked now to the small cluster of figures outside the hogan's entrance. As much as possible, Harry Whitaker seemed to be keeping to the shadows—Julia couldn't see his face very well. She looked forward to hearing about his experience, for he was a thoughtful man. Both of them, years before, had attended a Yeibichei held north of Many Springs Canyon, not far up the trail to Washington Pass, but she was sure that witnessing the full ceremony was of another order entirely.

Julia didn't expect that Tóya would have nearly as much to say as Harry. In her decades as a hand-trembler, Tóya had seen every surviving Navajo healing ritual as well as others that were no longer performed, but she never discussed them with Julia except to disparage the egotism or neglectful performances of various hataałiis with whom she had disagreements. Now, though, Tóya was the patient, committed to following every instruction from her singer, who was, Julia realized, considerably younger than Tóya (and probably younger than she herself). Tóya's wizened face, the curvature of her spine between her shoulders, the fragility of her frame, all confirmed sixty years of wear and tear. Julia didn't want to contemplate the day when Tóya would leave them, and at that thought sorrow flooded through her. Already, too few remained from the generations who had survived the Long Walk.

The small group of First Dancers concluded their performance, and Harry joined the singer's attendants in following Tóya into the ceremonial hogan. Tóya would make other appearances throughout the night, as she and the singer blessed the various dance teams, but much of her time would be spent inside, where the final healing songs would be offered.

As the First Dancers paraded down the corridor to the arbor, the Navajos surrounding Julia began moving about, conversing, all anticipating the arrival of the first full Yeibichei team, twelve dancers in all—six male yeis and six female, the latter in all likelihood youths or men of smaller stature, although it was becoming more common these days for women to participate. The team would be led from the arbor by Talking God and followed by Tónenílí, Water Sprinkler, the night's comic relief, although his antics would be far more restrained than those of the koshares, the sacred clowns, at the Hopi Home Dance that Julia had attended with Clement and Pete four years ago.

Julia scanned the faces across the way but couldn't see Owen anymore. She said to Yazzie, "We should be getting back to Owen before he thinks we deserted him."

They didn't want to cross the performance space, even though it was empty for the moment, and instead retraced their steps. As they passed the arbor they heard from inside the beat of rattles and a soft, falsetto chant and knew the first full dance team would soon make its appearance.

Approaching where they'd laid their blankets, Julia saw immediately that something wasn't right. Instead of standing and waiting for the dancers, Owen was sitting, his head bowed.

"What's wrong?" Julia asked, bending down and gripping his shoulder.

"Trouble. Breathing," Owen said.

She reached out to touch his face. Cold sweat ran in rivulets down his cheeks. His hair was pasted to his forehead.

"Are you in pain?"

"A weight. On my chest." He wiped his face with a hand. "It's all right. Leave me be," he said, and the weary defeat in his voice scared her even more.

She reached into a pocket of her coat for a handkerchief. She pressed it into Owen's hand and he wiped his face again, and then the back of his neck. *Not here, not like this,* she told herself.

"Lie down," she said, and he did, but in less than a minute he was struggling to sit up again.

"Makes it. Worse."

From the direction of the ceremonial hogan, she could hear a Yeibichei dance team beginning its performance.

"Clement," Julia said. "Go to the hogan and get Harry Whitaker."

Yazzie, watching Owen, remained where he was.

"Did you hear me?" Julia asked.

"Aoo'," Yazzie said, "but I can't do that."

Julia straightened up, her eyes flashing in the firelight. "You can't—"

"Julia," Owen said, propping himself on one stiffened arm.

"If you don't get Harry, I will," Julia said.

"You can't go into the hogan," Yazzie said.

"Then I'll stand outside," raising her voice, "and yell for him as loudly as I can."

"Julia," Owen said, "no."

She could feel the panic in her throat. "Clement," she pleaded, "please."

They were beginning to attract attention from some of the nearby Navajos, who cast wary glances toward them. The dancers' unearthly high-pitched chanting, accented by the gourd rattles, continued.

"Take me home," Owen panted. "Help me. Up."

Yazzie stepped forward and grabbed Owen's raised arm. Julia took him under the other and, off balance, he rose.

"You need a doctor," she said.

"Harry can't. Do anything."

In Navajo, Yazzie asked Johanna to go and harness the horses, which they had left hobbled, their leads tied to the rear of the wagon. Slowly, Yazzie, Julia, and Owen, his breathing increasingly labored, made their way through the crowd. Owen was so light now, Julia thought she could carry him in her arms if she had to, but Yazzie took most of his weight. Now, all the faces that glanced their way seemed unsympathetic. What would have happened if she'd tried to enter the hogan? A struggle to stop her. A fight. Clement would have tried to defend her. Someone would have gotten hurt.

Clement easily lifted Owen into the back of the wagon. Owen rolled onto his side and lay still except for his heaving chest.

"Someone needs to let Harry know," Julia said.

"I'll go find Charlie Day," Yazzie said. "When the ceremony's over, he can tell the doctor."

Something in his tone, his dispassion, set her off: "That won't be until dawn! We can't wait that long. I'll take care of this myself." She started to stride off, back in the direction of the hogan, but Yazzie grabbed her.

"Julia," he said, clenching her arm as she struggled to pull from his grasp, "you can't do that."

"Julia," Owen called from where he lay, "help me sit up."

"If he dies out here," Julia hissed so that Owen didn't hear, yanking her arm free and looking into the blackness at the center of Yazzie's eyes, "I'll never forgive you."

Yazzie turned and asked Johanna to collect their blankets and whatever else they'd left near the ceremonial grounds. Then he left to find Charlie Day.

Julia climbed into the wagon and sat down beside Owen, who, wheezing from the exertion, was trying to lift himself. "Here," she said, putting her arms around him and tipping him toward her. "When Johanna comes back, we'll make you more comfortable."

"For the ride. Home," he said.

"Yes." She didn't know if the tears in her eyes were from anger or despondency. Probably both.

When Johanna and Yazzie returned, they arranged Yazzie's saddle and the blankets in a corner at the front of the wagon bed.

"I'm cold," Owen said, shivering.

Julia put her hand inside his coat; his shirt was soaked. She spread one of the larger blankets over him and then got under it with him. She put an arm around him, and he let his head roll against her collar bone.

"Pitiful," he said. He snorted once, as close as he could come to a laugh.

Johanna climbed up beside her brother, who flicked the reins. The harnessed horses strained and the wagon jolted into motion. The brown, tied at the rear, shook his mane and followed.

The sounds of the Yeibichei carried for some distance in the clear air, and a glow from the fires remained visible even farther, until a dip and northward turn in the trail took them behind a sandstone outcropping, after which the stars alone shone.

The horses in their traces. The rumbling wheels turning, milling the packed earth, spitting stones. The creaking of the boards of the wagon bed. Owen's labored breathing. Yazzie's brown following like a shadow, a vaguely outlined darkness tethered loosely enough that it could shift from side to side, advance and retreat, barely visible except when its wall eye, having collected an ambient luminosity, appeared with unnerving clarity. She had ridden the brown, but only once. She'd found it too big, too strong for her to control.

Owen's ragged breathing—how much could his body endure? At some point the muscles that supported his lungs would be overtaxed, just as a fist clenched and released continuously would ultimately no longer obey.

Her arm, the one holding him close, had fallen asleep. She tried to ignore the discomfort, but the pins and needles gave way to a deeper pain, and she said, "Owen, I need to move my arm," and he grunted. She withdrew her arm from around him and shifted slightly so they now sat shoulder to shoulder, though before long she sensed his head again tipping toward her and she met it with her own, his hair against her temple.

"Don't let me. Sleep," he said.

"How can I do that?" she whispered. "We have so far to go." They were still several hours from home. She knew Yazzie had calculated how hard he could push the horses.

"If. Pinch me," Owen said. "Hard."

Julia thought: Words per breath, breaths per word.

"I will," she said, taking his cool hand in hers, even while she knew that her pinching him, bruising him, couldn't forestall that other sleep. She thought of Clement's boys and how she'd watched their lives expire.

The right wheels slipped into a rut in the road and her head banged against the back of the seat. Yazzie cursed.

"It's all right," she said to Yazzie. He was doing the best he could.

"If there was a moon," Yazzie said, "I could see."

"It's all right."

They continued on.

Owen would begin to drop off and then startle himself into full wakefulness. His breathing didn't improve much, but it didn't worsen either. It occurred to Julia that the drop in elevation from the site of the Yeibichei to the northward road may have helped. How many hundreds of feet would make a difference? If he were at sea level now, instead of more than a mile high on the Colorado Plateau, he might be fine. (Maybe he was the one who should leave for the Outer Banks.)

He hadn't moved in some time. If it was to be now, what better option than in his sleep? In the night she wouldn't see his fingertips and lips turn purple. Who would be waiting for him? His mother? The brother he'd never known?

She pinched his wrist. "Owen?"

"I'm here," he said. "Still here."

Apart from the turning stars, the night was still a toneless black as they neared Many Springs. By then Julia had fallen into a blankness of mind and spirit; her anxiety, the lump in her throat and the disquiet that awaited Owen's every breath, had surrendered to a numbing sense of the inevitable, and when her attention slipped away it fled elsewhere, everywhere and nowhere; to the room in Pittsfield where her mother had died, to the stained glass in the church where Penny had married; to the street outside the two grubby little rooms where she and Will had lived in St. Louis; to her first sight of clouds floating beneath the rim of the Grand Canyon; to grackles and red-winged blackbirds marking the return of a childhood spring.

The entrance to the canyon, her canyon, brought her back, and with a renewed sharpness of purpose. Yazzie had sent Johanna on ahead, riding bareback on his brown, to light fires in Owen's fireplace and stove. When Yazzie halted the wagon in front of the cabin, Owen, leaning on Julia's arm, managed to walk up the two steps to his door and then to his bedroom, where the warmth from the front room was already overcoming the chill. Julia left him there, assuring him that she would return within minutes, and hurried to her own home, where she found Johanna lighting the cooking stove. Julia stayed only long enough to take from her pantry a small jar of herbs that Tóya had given her to help with monthly difficulties. At the first opportunity Julia had asked Harry Whitaker about the safety of the concoction, and Harry had responded with a long, heartfelt laugh. "You needn't be concerned about being poisoned," he'd told her. Though he couldn't provide a list of the ingredients beyond burdock and pigweed—Tóya would reveal only so much about her herbal remedies, even to him—he could assure her that the worst effect might be vomiting (the Navajos were big on emetics) but that, yes, when brewed as a tea it might indeed relieve bloating, accompanied by a frequent need to empty her bladder. He added that Tóya used the same combination, or something very similar, to reduce the swelling Owen had experienced around his ankles and, most importantly, to help with lung congestion.

She returned to Owen's cabin and found him still awake. "I'm going to make you some of Tóya's tea," she told him and then went into his small kitchen. When the tea was ready, she propped his two pillows behind him so that he could drink. "You must be tired," she said.

"Yes and no," he said. "But my mind . . ."

"Is wandering," she finished for him.

"Something. Like that." Then he asked, "Read to me?"

"What would you like me to read?"

"Anything. Look. By my chair."

She left the room and found beside his chair in front of the fireplace a stack of reading material. She returned with a book and a magazine. "*Burning Daylight*," she said, "or the last installment of Mrs. Wharton in *Scribner's*." They'd already read the first two parts of Edith Wharton's latest story, *Ethan Frome*; Julia had given the new issue of *Scribner's* to Owen a few days before. "So, the Klondike"—the setting for Jack London's new novel— "or New England?" she asked.

"I've had enough. Of the West. For one day."

"Then *Ethan Frome* it is, " she said with false cheer. After reading the first two parts they'd debated how the novella would end. Of course tragically for the title character, an impoverished farmer whose New England scruples bound him to his shrew of a wife despite his love for Zeena's visiting cousin Mattie Silver—there could be no happy outcome for anyone. Julia sat down, found the page, and began . . .

HE DIDN'T CARE ABOUT the story. He wanted to hear her voice, that was all, her natural voice, drained of worry, and how better to do that than to force her attention to the words on a page? If it was the last thing, it was what he wanted to hear. *That* voice, lower than most women's, with the occasional scratch or squeak that he loved because it hinted at a complexity that no one else heard. Or so he wanted to believe.

She was settling into the story, and her voice eased his mind, and that in turn settled his breathing a bit. Every now and then he would lift the cup off his chest and take a swallow of the herb tea, and she would glance up from the page, a momentary pause, and he would slowly return the cup to his chest, everything slowing down, his thoughts, his heart, and sometimes what she was reading would break through and he would listen, enough so that he was able to follow the bones of the story. He didn't need to hear the end to know.

He wanted her all to himself. No trading post, no weavers, no Clement Yazzie. If he ever walked out of this room again, maybe he could play the invalid, and then she would insist that he return to the spare room beside hers. He would acquiesce and spend his days being tended to. He would allow her to go to the store, but her weavers would have to come to her because he couldn't do without her for all of a day—

Stop, he told himself.

He'd narrowed the future down from years to months, but he needed now to shrink it further, to weeks or days or just tomorrow. Nothing would extend his life, not even by one good day beyond what his body would allow. He thought of Robbie, his lost brother, in the Hoosac Tunnel, when the world collapsed. Doing a good day's hard work, and then instantly—

Julia's voice:

> . . . his eye fell on an old copy of the *Bettsbridge Eagle*. The advertising sheet was folded uppermost, and he read the seductive words: "Trips to the West: Reduced Rates."

Ethan and Mattie wouldn't make it west, but he, Owen, had. He'd taken a train through that very tunnel after his own world collapsed—Beth, her family, some other future—toward ruins and roads amid dust and sandstone, harsh and friable. He thought of Richard Wetherill, lying dead, the terrible vision that Marietta Wetherill must bear for the rest of her days. He'd seen it too, but then Yazzie had come for him, to bring him home to Many Springs Canyon—

> Ethan, rising on his elbow, watched the landscape whiten and shape itself under the sculpture of the moon. This was the night on which he was to have

taken Mattie coasting, and there hung the lamp to light them!

He startled, his legs jumped. Had he drifted off? A bit of the tea had splashed onto the blanket covering his chest. Julia's irises—he could see them, which meant that the sky was lightening outside his bedroom window. He raised the cup to his lips again. It was nearly empty. She asked if he was all right. He nodded.

Winter here was so different, without so many trees to break up the wind. Storms blew through and the sun reappeared; none of the eastern gray hung on.

Light meant the Yeibichei would be over. Charlie Day would be speaking to Harry Whitaker. What could Harry do? Very little. Nothing.

"I need. The chamber pot," Owen interrupted Julia's reading.

"All right. That's good." A note of optimism. "Can you manage?"

"Yes."

She rose and took the tea cup from him. "I'll make you more tea, shall I?"

He gave her one quick nod.

"Can I fetch you anything else?"

He shook his head.

She left the room, pulling the door half closed to afford him privacy. He threw off the blanket, swung his legs over the side, sat up, and stopped to catch his breath. Bending, reaching under the bed with a free hand, pulling the pot toward him. Stiffening his back, fiddling with buttons . . .

He finished, carefully pushed the pot back under the bed, buttoned up. Using his hands and arms, he lifted himself until he could steady his legs and stand. He felt a twinge at the base of his breastbone—a momentary panic—but it went away when he straightened up. He walked to the half-opened door; he felt an odd prickling in his feet, milder than pins and needles. Julia, her back to him, stood in front of the cooker, her arms folded, waiting for the water to boil.

He loved her so much, he felt like weeping. He felt like he couldn't breathe without her. But he wouldn't have to, would he? He'd have her for every breath to come.

He was no good at lying, never had been. Something about his face. And his father had walloped any such inclination out of him when he was a boy; he couldn't remember the lie, but he remembered the razor strop and the vow to himself that he'd never lie again. A vow that he couldn't possibly have kept—no one could—but still, he came away knowing that he wasn't able to lie convincingly about anything of consequence.

So to persuade Julia that he had made his peace, and that therefore she should do likewise, he would first have to believe it himself. That was the task. Convince himself so that he could convince Julia that he accepted what, charted by prognosis and calendar, lay straight ahead.

He said the word to himself; maybe if he said it over and over it would lose its venom, its cruelty.

"I'm feeling better," he said.

She turned quickly at the sound of his voice. The first sunlight broke through the window behind her. "Let me see you," she said, walking toward him, a small towel still twisted in her hands. "You have a little color now," she told him. "And your breathing is better?"

"I'm not quite. As winded."

"More tea," she said, turning back to the stove, where a cloud was now streaming from the mouth of the kettle. She untwisted the towel and lifted the kettle and poured the water into a small bowl.

"You're exhausted," he said. "Why don't you. Go home and sleep."

"I'm fine," Julia said. "Besides, we have to finish *Ethan Frome*. I can't leave you hanging." Such a little smile.

"There isn't much more, is there?"

"No. Shall I bring your tea to you in bed, or would you rather sit in our chairs by the fireplace?"

"Our chairs." He walked over slowly and sat. She collected the magazine from the bedroom, brought him a throw to put around his legs, strained the tea into his cup, brought it to him, sat down opposite, and resumed:

> . . . the slope stretched away below them without a sled on its length. Some erratic impulse prompted Ethan to say: "How'd you like me to take you down now?"

He'd taken Beth coasting once. Her married brother, Buddy, and his wife Carolyn had also come along. The Burrows family owned a giant wooden swan neck sled on which all four of them, packed tightly together in their heavy winter coats, were able to fit, and Buddy and Owen took turns in front, steering as well as they could straight down the slope, while off to the side the neat clapboard houses with their brick and stone chimneys swept past, and, ahead, dozens of adults and children ice-skated on a pond, beyond which Owen could see two barns and a shed, brown and red, and beyond that wet snow clinging to pines and the bare branches of the deciduous trees, and beyond the trees a plume of gray from a locomotive passing on the Fitchburg line. It was just after New Year's, a Friday, before dusk, and two neighborhood fellows were already lighting torches stuck in snow banks at the top of the slope and around the pond, and it seemed to Owen that half of Leominster (well, half of those still in their youth and health) had turned out. After a while, Buddy and Carolyn went off to skate, leaving Owen and Beth to coast alone, able now to stretch out their legs, with him behind her, his arms wrapped around and his knees clutching her tight. There were so many sledders that the morning's snow was already packed into a hard crust, and the sleds went faster and faster, the cold and their laughter taking his and Beth's breath away—

> Then the big elm shot up ahead, lying in wait for them at the bend of the road, and he said between his teeth, "We can fetch it, I know we can fetch it—"

Such a sad, sad story of thwarted people, thwarted love, but somehow true to his boyhood memory of New England winters, the stark cold, the poverty, the kindly neighbors but also those who showed complete indifference to anyone else's plight. But Ethan's plight wasn't his. He didn't feel thwarted. In the last eighteen months he'd lived a life not even remotely predictable.

Her voice, still:

> He got his face down close to hers, with his ear to her mouth, and in the darkness he heard her say his name.
>
> "Oh Matt, I thought we'd fetched it," he moaned . . .

But he wouldn't become Julia's invalid. He'd rather stand in Yazzie's pond (like his father in the Ashuelot River) and put a gun to his head. He'd "fetch it" properly—

Stop, he told himself again.

A river had flow and direction; a pond, stillness.

He remembered an old physics lesson from college, that even when an object moves at constant speed around a circle, at every moment its direction and therefore its velocity is changing. Otherwise, it would shoot off in a straight line tangent to the circle. Thus even when time and the distance yet to travel grow short, even when motion slows, direction still matters.

He thought, as he'd thought many times before, about the western road he'd found, built a thousand years ago. He'd never know why the Anasazi stopped in the middle of nowhere. Still, the road remained, if you knew where and how to look for it, and he'd traveled it, and it had brought him here. That was meaning enough.

Should he say any of this to Julia? Oh, she'd listen some evening, continuing her knitting but with a skeptical eyebrow raised, and then her laughter would tell him that she thought it all romantic claptrap. None of this suited her way of thinking, which relied on the concrete and the doing.

He wanted it to come on a bright warm day. He wanted to be sitting in the sun, reconciled, with her, without pain; thinking of her, breathing without thought, conscious one moment and slipping away the next. Being granted that, that would be grace.

He was tired now, and maybe he should piss again, Tóya's tea was doing its job, and he realized that his breathing had indeed eased, he no longer had to think about every breath even though every minute or so he had to catch up, inhale deeply and then blow everything from his lungs, and he was tired enough to sleep right where he was.

Julia read on, nearing the end . . .

A BLEARY-EYED HARRY Whitaker arrived at midday. Owen was able to reassure him that his breathing had returned to normal, although Harry's stethoscope detected a degree of congestion in one lung. Furthermore, he concluded that Owen's symptoms at the Yeibichei indicated a progressive heart failure, which was a common consequence of both a faulty heart valve and diabetes. The symptoms could recur without warning, although to strengthen Owen's heart he prescribed digitoxin, to be taken daily. He'd also leave a stoppered bottle of morphine sulfate in case the pain returned.

"No more than five drops at a time, under the tongue or in water," Harry cautioned. "Too much suppresses the breathing."

That evening, Julia, Harry, and Owen sat down to a dinner of root vegetable soup and baked beans with salt pork. In the intervening hours an unsettling wind had rolled down from the mountains, rattling everything hinged or not nailed tight.

"We should say grace," Julia said, surprising Owen. Though doing so wasn't a common occurrence at her table, the three joined hands. "Dear Lord," Julia began, "thank you for our daily bread, and for the gift of friendship, and for the mercies you see fit to bestow. Amen."

"Amen," Owen and Harry echoed. No one broke hands. They listened to the wind howl.

"Ah believe these are precious times," Harry said, his face flushed.

"I'd like to propose a toast," Owen said, and at that they dropped hands and raised their glasses (water for Owen, cider for his companions). "To true friends in precious—or perilous—times."

The three extended their arms and touched glasses, producing the slightest of tings.

The outside door opened and Clement Yazzie entered, bringing with him a gust of cold air. He returned their greetings with a nod but didn't speak.

"What's wrong, Mr. Yazzie?" Julia said.

"The Old Man," he said.

"Tim Be'ak'idii?"

"Aoo'. I hadn't seen him in a while, so I went up to Blue Hawk Lake. He's gone."

"Gone?" Owen said.

"How did it happen?" Julia asked, and then Owen understood.

"As it should," Yazzie said. "In his sleep."

"My condolences," Harry said, rising from his chair and extending his hand in sympathy to Yazzie, who accepted it.

"Is there anything we can do?" Julia asked.

"It's all finished," Yazzie said.

Owen considered what that probably meant: the body taken away, the hogan burned to the ground.

"He was my eyes and ears," Yazzie said to Julia. Owen didn't understand either the statement or the look they exchanged, but it wasn't the time to ask.

"Would you like something to eat?" Julia asked. "Please, join us."

"No, I need to help Sister with the sheep. The dogs are good, but some of the sheep have scattered. Sometimes the high wind spooks them. We'll manage. This is nothing new." And with that he turned and exited, letting in another wave of cold air.

Julia had taken to walking Owen home in the evening, and even after hours spent together in her parlor she would sit for a while with him before his fireplace. The night of Harry Whitaker's visit, with the loss of Tim Be'ak'idii still on his mind, Owen asked her, "Do you miss Pete?"

"I do."

"You haven't heard from him?"

"As you well know, we didn't part on the best of terms."

"I have to say, though I didn't *dislike* him, I never found him a very likable fellow."

"I don't think he'd disagree with you."

"Still, *you* liked him."

"Yes."

"He refused your terms for staying?"

"I never set any terms."

"Not even about his drinking?"

"He knew how I felt. He did his best." She paused. "His best hope was to leave."

A steady drumming on the roof told Owen that a hard rain had started to fall. Hope for what? Owen wondered, but he didn't ask. He could see her weighing something, something she'd kept from him.

"You look drawn," he said. "You aren't sleeping well, are you? And you aren't eating properly."

"*You* should talk."

"Proper for me isn't proper for you." Owen picked up a poker and stirred the fire; a two-foot log of pinyon buckled at its middle and, in a shower of sparks, collapsed into coals, orange, red, yellow.

"Will has another wife. And children."

Owen sat, propped an elbow on the arm of his chair, and brought his hand to his mouth. After a while he straightened himself and asked, "How long have you known?"

"Since September—that day we rode into Gallup together and you bought these lovely chairs for us to sit in." She ran her hands along the arms of her chair. "Alberto told me that he stumbled upon him during a trip to Denver."

"But how did he divorce you without your knowing?"

"He didn't bother," she said without visible emotion. "He's calling himself George Banks. Apparently, he's now in the antique business."

"Do you intend to pursue him?"

"Why would I do that?"

"To rid yourself of him once and for all. So that you can move on. Cleanly."

"Cleanly?" she commented with a slight laugh.

He knew: A divorced woman is never "clean." He said, "You do see the terrible position this leaves you in, don't you? Now that you know where he is, you can't take any action without involving him."

"I could always lie."

"Perjure yourself?"

She sighed. "It doesn't matter. I don't plan to do anything. It would ruin him and do untold damage to his children."

"That should be *his* concern, not yours. *You're* the injured party."

"Oh, Owen, everyone ends up injured," Julia said.

Owen listened to the rain pouring down—he and Yazzie had done a good job; the roof wasn't leaking.

She should talk to a lawyer, he thought, someone who could look at her situation objectively—someone who could see further down the road, toward what she might desire in the future. But that was a subject for another night, one when it wasn't so late and when he'd had a chance to prepare his arguments. For she would certainly resist.

"Would you do me a favor?" he now asked.

"That would depend, wouldn't it?" Julia said, obviously expecting that he intended to press her.

"Go to the Rodriguez Christmas party." Just last week she'd shown him this year's invitation, which she continued to receive every November even though she'd never attended. "Leave me to my own devices for a few days. Go mingle. Drink champagne. Eat hors d'oeuvres. Dance."

The abrupt change of subject had caught her by surprise. "And whom should I ask to accompany me?"

He wasn't so naïve as to suggest Clement Yazzie. A married white woman and her Navajo partner would be as welcome as the Red Death. Besides, he knew that Julia would never misuse Yazzie like that, and Yazzie would never be so foolish as to agree.

"Ask Harry. He should be respectable enough."

"Regardless, some people would be scandalized. After all, I *am* still a married woman. Of a sort."

"You'll have sufficient defenders. The scandalized will have to keep their mumbling among themselves."

"It's very late," Julia said, rising from her chair.

"Ask Harry," Owen said. "It might do you both good."

"I'll think about it," Julia said.

OWEN WAS SITTING on Julia's veranda facing the sun, which these days traveled low over the southern wall of the canyon, without intensity, although the afternoons still warmed up nicely. But winter was coming, there could be no doubt.

He was thinking about the final revisions to his article on the Anasazi roads—the *American Journal of Archaeology* had rejected it, although the editor encouraged him to resubmit it if he were willing to make significant changes, particularly in his discussion of Richard Wetherill's achievements, given that Wetherill's methods were widely questioned in academia—when he noticed a wagon, pulled by a well-matched pair, coming up the trail. Johanna held the reins, Tóya beside her. He smiled at their approach. He always welcomed an opportunity to talk to Tóya, and as for Johanna, she was often away these days. He missed her when she was traveling with Tóya. He missed her as he might miss, he imagined, a somewhat peculiar sister (but even so, a *sister*), and he missed observing as her increasingly confounding paintings emerged stroke by stroke. A month ago he'd watched her using a single bristle that she'd pulled from one of her brushes. She was painting silver-white rays of light from stars no bigger than the head of a pin; a spray of sparkling starlight fracturing the shell of night, the unreal sky. He had no idea what possessed her.

"Yá'át'ééh," he called out as Johanna brought the team to a halt. He rose to help Tóya down from her perch and up the steps to the veranda, where, leaning on her cane, she slowly lowered herself into a chair.

"And how are you, Owen Rouse?" she asked. "Not so good, I hear." It had been several weeks since the Night Chant, but her first visit since then.

"Why, as good as can be expected," he answered with a short laugh.

She peered at him with an intense squint and then nodded.

"And how have you been since your ceremony?" he asked.

"Good!" she said. "I can hear every word I need to hear."

He laughed again, longer this time. "And I'm glad to hear *that*." Of Julia's friends, and as much as he liked Harry Whitaker, he'd come to enjoy Tóya's infrequent visits the most, despite her habitual testiness. "That's a fine rig you arrived in."

"It *is*," she said. "Good springs. Easy on these old bones. It's on loan from a singer who lives near Sonesta Butte. We've known each other many years and see eye-to-eye about many things. He has sent many patients to me, and I've done the same for him." She looked over her shoulder. "And how do you like your fine cabin?"

"Very comfortable. And also on loan, you might say."

Johanna had unhitched the two stallions and was leading them to the corral, where Julia's horses were warily eyeing them.

Tóya looked off into the distance before she spoke again, this time with palpable sadness. "I can't do anything more for you, Owen Rouse."

"I suspect not," he said. "But don't let it trouble you. You healed the frostbite and the sores, and that alone kept me on my feet for a year." Then he added because he knew it would please her, "And your tea still keeps my ankles from swelling."

"Ah! I did bring more of that tea for you! I almost forgot. It's in the wagon."

"I'm very glad you did," he said. "Harry says it prevents fluid from sitting in my chest as well. It certainly helped when I had my spell."

"Good."

"Are you staying for long?" Owen asked.

"I will stay the night."

"Just tonight?"

"Aoo'."

Johanna, carrying a traveling satchel, had started up the trail to the Yazzie hogan. She moved without effort, a fringed shawl drawn up high across shoulders and neck, a narrow gap of bare leg showing between blanket dress and high deerskin boots. She was at home, she needed no other life, and he envied her that. And yet, and yet . . . He found himself close to tears. Why did he feel like this toward her, as if she should have had a different life, a better life? Most of the time, even when he was beside her at the dining table, watching her with pen and brush, she barely acknowledged his presence. Nevertheless, he'd taken to talking to her anyway, as they sat together. In a soft voice he would tell her what he was thinking about or ask her questions, and sometimes even try out answers for her: I'm going to miss sitting here with you very much, do you know that? *Shush, none of this will matter to you then.* You should draw this chair someday, the way you draw the sky, and everyone will say, That chair, it looks as if someone just left it. *A chair is only a chair.* I can see traces of bright colors, reds and sky blues and greens and yellows, on the handles of your brushes—if I asked, would you paint something for me? *I can only paint what I can paint . . .*

"Your friend, the hataałii who loaned you his wagon and team, did he do a sing for Johanna?" Owen asked.

Tóya looked at him warily.

"Maybe I shouldn't be asking," Owen said, "but it isn't from idle curiosity. I care what happens to her, you know."

"That's because you have a good spirit, Owen Rouse," Tóya said.

"No, no," he said, embarrassed.

Tóya reached out and patted his hand. "Don't worry yourself. I saw a long time ago that there's nothing wrong with Jóhonaá. We had what you would call a Blessingway, Hózhóójí, for her before we started on our travels."

He had heard of the Blessingway, the first ceremony given to the People when they emerged into this world. Unlike the other Navajo chants, it was neither a cure nor a corrective, but an expression of hope and harmony.

Just then, Julia came around the corner of the veranda from the store, and bending over she wrapped Tóya in her arms. "You're staying the night," she said. It wasn't a question.

"Aoo'," Tóya said, her wrinkled face lit by her nearly toothless smile. "Supper and a soft bed." She punched herself in the hip. "These old bones have learned to like a soft Anglo bed."

Julia sat down and Owen said, "That's Tóya's new wagon over there."

"On loan," Tóya corrected him.

"And where are you headed in this fancy wagon?" Julia teased her.

"Here and there," Tóya said.

Their travels. Here and there. For what? Gathering Tóya's herbs and other medicinal plants? Perhaps she was having Johanna paint them on site. The snows had yet to come this year, even though it was December. So that was possible, but a complete record would require a full spring and summer of gathering. Was Tóya making, in effect, a book, seeking some way to pass on her knowledge? That certainly seemed possible, even admirable. But Navajo remained solely a spoken language, so she would also need a translator to record her formulas and prescriptions. Harry, perhaps? Or Julia? But why the secrecy?

"Tóya," he decided to ask, "what are you and Johanna up to?"

"Tchh. I stopped here to see you, not to talk about that."

He looked to Julia. She would know. But she wouldn't say, not without Tóya's permission.

Then Julia did something unusual for her: ignoring him, she began speaking directly to Tóya in Navajo, knowing that he would not be able to follow the conversation. Ordinarily, Julia would pause and translate, but not now. The two women went back and forth. A smattering of words he understood, or thought he did, but he made no effort to piece together a meaning.

The dialogue ended.

Tóya appeared to carefully consider how much more to say. "Tomorrow we have to go see someone up near Sanostee. He's very old, they say close to a hundred, but his memory is still sharp."

"A singer?" Owen asked.

Tóya nodded and then sighed. "I'm an old woman, Owen Rouse. You have no idea what the People have lost. I see it. You cannot. Even Julia Halley, *shich'é'é*, my daughter, cannot see it. Many of the old ones have already left us—the ones who traveled with us on the Long Walk or hid out. Some ceremonies have passed with them. Some say that's because the People no longer need those ceremonies. But others say that the day will come in this world when we will need them all once again."

You can't retrieve a prayer, let alone an entire ceremony, Owen thought, if it's lost to memory and has never been written down. But Tóya was speaking of more than that. A way of life was at risk—in fact, soon to be overwhelmed. Assimilation was stealthily and deliberately at work, unavoidably, for all the Navajos who had already left the reservation, even if they came back to visit parents, elders, to attend ceremonies. That was a very different life, out there, with or without its potential material rewards, even if they did their very best to retain and cherish the old ways; and each following generation, the children, would inevitably find themselves at a further remove. Even for those who stayed here (and *their* children, and on . . .), there would still be, in good time—maybe in a generation, two, three—the automobile and, for all but those living at the most remote reaches, the telephone and the light bulb. Of necessity, even here, most would learn to speak and read and write English. So would they have a better life? Maybe. Quite possibly, by objective measures. But with only one certainty: it would be a different life.

There was always a price to be paid. Tóya saw this. She might well think that, absent her attention, the stars might descend from their rightful place in the sky, but her wisdom understood the predestined costs that would accrue over time for the People. So what could she save that might otherwise be lost?—what could she and Johanna, together, save that might otherwise be lost?

"The old singers that you're visiting," Owen said, "they're teaching Johanna the ceremonial sand paintings and how to decorate prayer sticks and masks."

Tóya shook her head.

"Johanna's permitted to see them, that's all," Julia said. "Apart from being a woman, she isn't a patient and she isn't initiated into any of the ceremonies, so she can't witness the sand paintings and prayer sticks being made. Afterwards, they're disposed of, as they always are. The masks are different. They're used over and over, often passed down from singer to singer. They're brought out and then put away again after she's seen them."

Owen turned to Tóya. "So they let Johanna copy them?"

Tóya scrunched up her face.

"She isn't allowed to bring her paints and brushes with her," Julia said.

"Then I don't understand."

"She commits them to memory."

"After," Tóya said. "*Then* she paints them."

He'd heard that some sand paintings were so large and so intricate, covering almost the entire floor of the ceremonial hogan, that to learn them apprentices required careful, repeated instruction during ceremony after ceremony. Could Johanna, could anyone, at one viewing, simply memorize each figure, each symbol, each line in a sand painting? It didn't seem possible. He'd heard of entertainers performing parlor tricks for the amusement of an audience. But he'd also heard of individuals who, after one reading, could recite a whole page of dense text, word for word, and of unschooled children who could hear a Beethoven sonata and reproduce it note for note. How did such otherwise ordinary individuals—some, even, whose other faculties were diminished—access such deep resources? Could anyone say? Then why not an intricate image? He'd seen Johanna draw the moon from memory in the most elaborate detail, and display every Navajo constellation in the sky and the position of many, many other stars, shifting with the season, as well. So why not this?

"So you ask her to paint from memory, afterwards?" Owen asked Tóya.

"No."

He gave Julia a look that said, What am I missing now?

"I don't ask. She does what she does," Tóya said.

"But she must understand what this is all about. Otherwise, why would she—"

"Tchh," Tóya clicked her tongue. "She understands in the way she understands. Do you and me"—she wagged a bony finger back and forth several times—"always understand things of this world in the same way?"

"What about the songs, the prayers, everything else you think is being lost—who's saving them?" he asked. "What good are the sand paintings and the prayer sticks and all the other paraphernalia without the words?"

Tóya pursed her lips. "I can only do what I can do, Owen Rouse. Who knows?—maybe the Holy People want those robes at St. Michaels to stay long enough to teach us how to put our words on paper."

Some of the Franciscan brothers at St. Michaels were attempting to compile a Navajo dictionary and grammar and to record what they could of the ceremonies, but not everyone on the reservation was pleased. Some singers, in particular, had decried efforts by such outsiders to meddle in sacred Navajo matters. It seemed likely to Owen that many of the same individuals would strongly object to what Tóya was doing. Thus the secrecy.

"I hope you're not putting Johanna at risk," Owen said.

"She is protected," Tóya replied.

By Yazzie, Owen assumed. But Yazzie was only one man, and he wasn't traveling with them. Owen recalled what he'd told Yazzie in the high meadow—that teaching Johanna the rudiments of drawing had been a lark—and Yazzie's response, that for Johanna nothing was a lark. If she was now at risk, he, Owen, who had taught her, was ultimately responsible.

He looked at Julia, and the expression she gave in response told him that she knew what he was thinking.

"Don't," she simply said. "You gave her a voice, but she's the only one who can decide how and when to use it."

Unconvinced, he turned back to Tóya. "I have great respect for you," he said, "but aren't *you* the one who's doing the deciding?"

"I take her from place to place. I let her listen to the old hataałiis. They show her things. That's all."

"But she knows what you expect."

"We all try to protect her because she's precious to us," Julia said to him, "but she isn't a child, so don't treat her like one."

All three were quiet for some time.

"Where are the paintings?" Owen asked.

"This is not your bother," Tóya said.

No, it wasn't. But he so very much would have liked to see them; the bright colors of the yeis and the totem animals and the rainbows.

"I thought that maybe you were taking her around the reservation so she could paint your medicinal plants."

"Aoo'," Tóya said. "That may happen, too."

That night, alone in his cabin, Owen kicked off his moccasins and, his feet toward the fire, closed his eyes. Too often, he couldn't sleep lying prone anymore; after just a few minutes he'd feel like he was smothering and he'd have to sit up. (He hadn't told Julia.) He reached under the chair for a blanket he kept there. He draped it over himself, up to his chin, and settled back, but his mind was a jumble.

Across the reservation, in dozens of ceremonial hogans, singers were holding ceremonies, in their proper seasons: Enemy Way, Ghost Way, Red Ant Way, Mountain Top Chant, Big Wind Way, Male Shooting Way, Big Star Way, Flint Way, Big God Way, Plume Way, Upward-Reaching Way, Water Way, Night Chant, Blessingway . . .

At least Julia had the language to speak of these things, whereas all he had, except for a scattering of Trader Navajo, was the language he'd been born into, without cognates in Dinétah. Dinétah. Where even the directional grid was askew: Blanca Peak, the easternmost of the four sacred boundary mountains, was also eight minutes higher in latitude than Hesperus, the supposedly northernmost mountain; and Mt. Taylor, the southernmost, was only six minutes south of the westernmost, Humphreys Peak. But this was his surveyor's mind speaking. (A mind that, however, easily accepted the distinction between true and magnetic north.) Dinétah wasn't his to delimit—all his science and logic wouldn't help him.

He'd given Johanna a voice, Julia had said. Had he? He'd shown her how to draw lines and a wall and a floor and a door—a simple door, the door to Julia's pantry, but Johanna had drawn it and drawn it and drawn it until it became something else, *her* door, and she had walked through it, where he couldn't follow. His eyes welled up—they were always doing that, these days.

The next morning, Owen finished the revisions to his article on the Anasazi roads and prepared it for mailing. By then, Tóya and Johanna were already on their way to Sanostee.

CHAPTER TWENTY-ONE: The Christmas Party

Julia had yet to see the Rodriguez mansion, built two years earlier for Matilda—at a staggering cost, according to Pete Pietrowski—in the heights above the city, but she'd heard about the previous Christmas gala, and now that she'd decided to attend, she was looking forward to seeing the farolitos with their cutaway angels and bells lighting the carriage path to the house, and the red and green ristras hung from the portico, and the twelve-foot Christmas tree displayed in their ballroom. She wanted to see garlands of cedar and holly strung through the balusters, and wreaths hung in the windows. She wanted to hear music played by violin and guitar and guitarrón and trumpet. She wanted to see people, dressed in all their finery, dancing by candlelight under a crystal chandelier.

She hadn't been away from the trading post for three days in a row since her trip to the Grand Canyon and the Hopi Reservation and Canyon de Chelly more than four years ago. How had she let her life become so limited, restricted? It wasn't deliberate, but the result of year after year of daily decisions. There were interesting places she had yet to visit—old Santa Fe; the Acoma pueblo, where they made the most exquisite painted pottery; Zuni, only a day's ride south of Gallup (less, if she accompanied Win Peabody in his automobile)—but somehow the reasons not to leave Many Springs Canyon always prevailed. Money, of course. The absence of an amiable companion who could accompany her. The vagaries of the weather. The work. And for much of the past year, Owen.

Not that he needed her constant presence. There was an ease about him now, after his episode at the Yeibichei. He'd spent most of the next week in his favorite armchair or, on the warmer days, sitting on the veranda, alone much of the time since Julia was sometimes gone for the entire day, checking on the progress of her weavers. At least twice a week, when she was away until dusk or later, he cooked a full evening meal for her, even if he himself sampled only one or two of the dishes. When Julia wasn't there to prevent him, he took the broom and mop to her floors and dusted her book shelves, although often stopping to skim through the pages of a volume he'd meant to read but hadn't gotten to. Some days he did his best to fill in for her behind the counter in the trading post, and even Carmelita, who had taken on greater responsibilities in return for a salary that now approached her husband's, seemed to appreciate the effort.

Julia's insomnia hadn't improved in the weeks since the Yeibichei, and when she did manage to sleep she often found herself waking during the night from upsetting dreams, usually involving her failure to complete a task required by her father or Will or a distressingly distant Penelope, and sometimes even Owen. At times, arriving somewhere in her false past, she didn't even know what the unfinished task was, leaving her to stumble through half-understood conversations. Some nights she would wake trembling, with spasms running through her chest, legs, and arms, and she would lie there thinking her heart was beating erratically when it wasn't. Once awake, she couldn't return to sleep, and by the time morning came the tension in her back would run up into her shoulders and neck. She'd experienced this before, immediately after Will left. In time, and with patience, she had righted herself, and she would do so again. And thus she had decided, as a first step, to attend Matilda Rodriguez's Christmas party.

Two nights before leaving Many Springs for her little excursion, she took from her wardrobe the one dress that might still pass for a formal occasion—the lilac gown with the high neckline and scalloped sleeves that she hadn't worn since her trip with Penelope and Philip to the Grand Canyon in 1906. When she tried it on she was disappointed but hardly surprised to find that it didn't fit very well, requiring her to spend several hours carefully ripping out seams and taking in the hips and bodice. Ah well, Gallup's fashionable society, such as it was, wouldn't be paying any attention to her anyway.

She hadn't exactly coerced Harry Whitaker into escorting her. She simply didn't give him any option. She told him that she would arrive in Tohatchi the day before the party, with the expectation that he could accommodate her for the night. They would leave for Gallup early the next morning, thereby giving her plenty of time to check in at the Harvey House and prepare herself for the gala. They could then return home the following day or, if Harry preferred, postpone their departure and spend another day in town.

Harry lived in a log cabin not far from his two-room clinic, and on the few occasions when Julia had visited it in the past, the ceiling was greased with pinyon soot from the poorly vented wood stove, but it was otherwise without apparent disorder, which she regarded as a reflection of Harry's well-ordered life. One wall of the living room accommodated rough pine shelving that was filled with medical texts and an assortment of history and science books. The only comfortable piece of furniture was a high-backed Victorian settee with maroon upholstery that could have benefited from a session in the fresh air with a wooden rug beater. A pine plank table served equally as desk and dining surface. The only other rooms were a small kitchen and, at the rear, Harry's bedroom and a second room filled with what could be called organized clutter: many storage boxes, a steamer trunk, a folding military cot, and extra dust-covered straight-backed chairs that could be brought out for the rare social occasion.

Julia half-feared Harry would be in ill humor when she arrived on the appointed day, but instead he greeted her at the door with a smile. "I didn't expect you to be so chipper," she said.

"Oh, hobnobbing is an acceptable diversion," Harry answered. "Not that I was ever good at it."

"I'm sure you had all the girls at the dances begging you to get them a lemon squash."

"Pampered Southern belles—I never saw the appeal." He took Julia's valise from her. "You brought only one?"

Julia laughed. "Isn't one enough?"

"Not if you were to ask my sisters." He led her into his bedroom and deposited her bag on the narrow platform bed. The room was spartan, the only other furnishings being a night table with lamp, a wash stand, and a wardrobe. There appeared to be freshly washed linens on his bed and a clean towel and washcloth on the wash stand. "There are wooden hangers in the wardrobe," he said. "I assume you have a gown in your valise?"

Inevitably, during their pleasant evening together, the subject of Owen's health came up. She told Harry about a brief episode of chest pain ten days ago, and he asked if Owen had suffered any further breathing difficulties or any noticeable edema. Julia replied that Owen appeared to be comfortable and was careful not to overtax himself. He continued to take Tóya's herbal tea and hadn't mentioned any swelling.

"He doesn't complain," she said. "He never has, not really. There have been moments, of course."

"We all have our moments, don't we?" He rose and walked into the kitchen, where he opened a door to a cupboard and began moving various boxes and jars around, searching for something. "Ah," he said, bringing out a small crystal bottle containing a clear liquid. He wiped a layer of dust away and asked, "Something to warm you? A little peppermint schnapps? It's been here forever. One of my sisters sent it from Belgium, as I recall. I don't know how it survived the journey."

"All right," Julia said, "for the occasion. One finger in a cup, two in a proper cordial glass."

Harry opened another cupboard and took out two wine glasses. He held them up for her inspection.

"One-and-a-half fingers," she said.

Harry rinsed out the dusty glasses, broke the wax seal on the bottle, and poured an inch of schnapps into each glass. He handed her one and sat down beside her on the settee.

The cordial burned delightfully, all the way from the back of her throat down to her stomach.

"I assume Owen gave you a little 'push,' " Harry said with a sly smile.

"What do you mean?"

"You never accepted Matilda's invitation before."

"We both know it's Alberto's invitation, not Matilda's."

"Well then, we can see which of us is the less welcome—I haven't had an invitation in years."

"An oversight, I'm sure," Julia said.

They left for Gallup by wagon before dawn, while the frost still clung, and managed to reach town in time for a late lunch at the Harvey House, where Harry also took a room. Julia didn't see him again until it was time to depart for the party. His face was still raw from a close barbershop shave, and he was wearing a finely tailored but no longer stylish single-breasted charcoal worsted sack suit and gray waist-coat, an outfit that, judging by the lingering hint of camphor, had spent considerable time stored away. All in all, the two of them were presentable, Julia decided as she took his hand to enter the carriage Harry had hired to deliver them to the party.

Although Julia thought the original Rodriguez house was quite nice, nothing had prepared her for the mansion. It dominated a hillside south of the town center and gave the appearance, lit up as it was, of a grand three-story Victorian house back East. Wood. Slate. Copper. Marble. Glass—lots of glass. There was no adobe or clay tiles in sight.

The party was already under way. Julia and Harry moved from room to room, greeting familiar faces. In the background Julia heard a string and woodwind ensemble playing traditional carols. The overall tone of the gathering was sedate, which was something of a disappointment in that she'd anticipated a more lively affair. Mary Wetherill, the postmaster's wife, greeted her with an open smile and announced that they would be seated at the same table for dinner. Julia brightened at the prospect—perhaps the conversation wouldn't be as stuffy as she'd begun to fear. Harry appeared to know just about everyone, and he whispered a series of names in her ear as they moved through the house, glasses of champagne in hand.

One name in particular drew her attention: Tom Talle, looking handsome and elegant in his formal attire.

"Delighted to meet you, Mrs. Halley," he said, smiling quite disarmingly.

"Likewise," Julia said, extending her hand.

Rather than shaking it, Talle took it in his and gave a slight bow. "It's rather surprising that we haven't run into each other before this."

"I don't come into Gallup that often, Sheriff."

"Nor do I get up to your outpost."

"Perfectly understandable," Julia said, "since Many Spring Canyon is in San Juan County, not McKinley."

"Oh, I have other business interests, you know, that sometimes bring me to Farmington. I take a more easterly road, but maybe on one of my trips north I'll make my way through Shiprock and stop by en route, if I may."

"Oh, I'm sure you'll be welcome at any time."

Talle nodded to Harry. "The good doctor and I have conferred on a few occasions, and he has said as much, but I didn't want to impose."

"Conferred about—?" Julia asked.

"Navajos in whom we've had a common interest."

"Well," Harry said with a frown, "common, but in our separate domains."

It was all very polite and indirect, which suited Julia: she didn't come to a Christmas party to hear sordid details of illness and criminality.

They parted company, with the sheriff once again extending a slight bow in Julia's direction.

"He seems decent enough," Julia said, although she couldn't put out of mind Owen's worrisome description of Talle's interaction with Clement Yazzie in Chaco Canyon.

"Yes," Harry said. "Of course, I don't know him that well, but I don't think he goes out of his way to antagonize the Indian population. Not that he doesn't have his prejudices."

Julia didn't ask for amplification.

Matilda and Alberto were holding court in the ballroom, with its ornately decorated twenty-foot ceiling. The little orchestra—ten musicians, Julia quickly counted, but no trumpets or percussion and only one guitar, another disappointment—all dressed impeccably, occupied a corner of the room. Julia suspected that the ensemble had been brought in from Albuquerque or beyond, especially since Harry didn't recognize any of the musicians. Alberto, standing somewhat stiffly at his wife's side, looked rather uncomfortable in his evening tailcoat, winged collar, white tie, and satin waistcoat. Matilda was wearing a dark red evening gown and diamonds, including a studded tiara that perched on her head like a roosting bird. She seemed in her element, smiling, gently placing her white-gloved fingers on the bare hands of her subjects. Julia and Harry approached the receiving line to await their turn.

"Oh, God," Harry muttered, suddenly pulling Julia aside.

"What is it?"

Harry's face had turned bright. He turned his back to the hosts. "The couple standing next to them," he said. Julia glanced over his shoulder. An elderly couple were glaring in her direction, the wife gripping her husband's arm firmly.

"Who are they?"

"The Belnaps. He's a lawyer. They moved away from Gallup a decade ago. I didn't know they were back."

Belnap was impeccably dressed, with a white tie and stiff collar that seemed to be holding up his prominent chin. Mrs. Belnap was rounder and softer, wearing black satin and a pearl choker. Julia returned their rude stare until the Belnaps turned their eyes away. Neither spouse looked at the other. It was clear to Julia that Harry's entering their field of vision had been as much of a shock to them as their presence was to him.

"I knew their son," Harry said.

She took note of the past tense. "The young man who accompanied you to Gallup after the war?"

"Yes. Aaron Belnap."

"What became of him?"

"He died," Harry said. "And I believe his parents hold me responsible."

This was something Julia hadn't heard before. Of course she knew about the Rough Riders who'd enlisted from Gallup. Some were cowboys or sons of ranchers, some had worked in the coal mines or for the railroad—many of them were very young. She remembered Harry's saying that he'd become friends with a Gallup volunteer while both were recuperating in a hospital on Long Island. She also knew, vaguely—Harry had never provided details—that they'd had a falling out, but she knew nothing of Aaron's death and had no idea why his parents would hold Harry responsible.

Harry was moving away from her. "Please, Julia, enjoy yourself, but I should go. No good will come if I stay."

"Harry!" she called after him. Was that all he intended to say?

He continued to make his way toward the door.

"Harry!" she called again, but he didn't stop and she hurried after him, brushing past elbows, working her way between knots of chatter. Just before Harry reached the foyer she caught up with him and grabbed his arm.

"I came with you," she said, "and I'll leave with you."

They walked arm in arm down the hill under a clear sky. Julia filled her lungs with the crisp air, but she wasn't at all cold. Drifts of smoke, mixing the scent of pinyon and the acrid taste of lignite and coal tar, rose from the chimneys below them.

"I wonder what Matilda was serving," Julia said.

"Quail with oyster stuffing," Harry answered.

"No!" Julia said in mock disappointment. She hit his folded arm. "How do you know that?"

"Ah know many things," Harry said with forced humor.

They walked on toward the shacks below and the electric halo of street lights farther ahead, from Gallup's main streets. Railroad and coal money had afforded Gallup its electric plant and several other modern facilities, such as the ice plant and a briquet factory where refuse coal and tar were crushed and molded into cheap fuel.

At one point Julia had to stop to remove a pebble from her slipper. "A good choice for waltzing, a horrible choice for walking," she commented as, holding Harry's shoulder with one hand, she slipped her foot back into the delicate shoe.

There were few full-grown trees silhouetted against the sky. The wind typically blew too steadily across the hillsides, stunting the ones that managed to take root. And as Gallup had begun to grow, many of those were cut down for firewood. All the low-growing shrubs dotting the landscape appeared black in the starlight; sprays of dead wild grasses cast gray shadows.

"I suppose I should offer you an explanation," Harry sighed.

"I'll listen if you want me to, but you owe me nothing, Harry."

They'd come to the foot of the hill. The road turned westward, between a sandstone face and hillocks of gray, and flattened out into the open amid a scattering of hovels, adobe or tar paper and wood, with flat roofs. Harry and Julia could hear through the uninsulated walls and thin windows an infant wailing and muffled talk in Spanish. Chickens were roosting in several yards, if the grassless tracts could even be called yards; in another, three pigs lay in a wallow.

"It's one of those proverbial long stories," Harry said, "a bit of the Prodigal Son, without the envious brother and the fattened calf."

She waited for him to continue.

"Aaron and his parents had been at odds for years. He refused to clerk for his father and study law. He wanted adventure. He wanted to raise hell. He socialized, if you want to call it that, with a pack of cowboys who taught him all their tricks, and along the way he picked up some of their real skills as well. And then when the word went out that we were going to war with Spain, he was one of the first in line at the recruiting station.

"Afterwards, when his parents realized how close he'd come to being killed in Cuba, they were even more adamant that he put away his childish things and don a coat and necktie—do something respectable, befitting their only progeny. He wasn't even home a day before they started in on him— they were quite overbearing—but Aaron would have none of it. The three of them argued constantly. It was like watching a barn burn, from the inside. Truth be told, Aaron's parents had my sympathy, but my intervening would have been pointless and I refused to take sides. It soon became clear that my presence was no longer welcome in their home, so I left—I went out to Fort Defiance to see Constant Williams."

Julia knew this part of the story. Hearing that Harry would be visiting Gallup, a mutual friend had asked him to visit Williams, who was the Indian agent at the time. Williams hadn't had an easy time of it—he'd arrived right in the middle of the Hopi dispute at Oraibi and he'd also had to confront frequent food shortages and problems with renegades and headmen. Although Williams, an army major, was now preparing to rejoin his infantry regiment, he set about trying to recruit Harry to open a clinic in Tohatchi. The 1868 treaty had called for the government to provide the Navajos with medical care. That promise, like most others, hadn't been kept, but Williams believed that he had finally convinced the Office of Indian Affairs of the need for clinics across the reservation. Williams felt confident that once Tohatchi was up and running, it wouldn't take more than a few months to find a permanent doctor to succeed Harry, who told Williams that he would think about it—though without any real intention of doing so.

Julia and Harry entered Gallup's downtown now, passing Aztec and Coal avenues and nearing Railroad Avenue; the streetlights pushed against the night sky and the plank sidewalk squeaked beneath their feet. Two blocks ahead, the Atchison, Topeka, and Santa Fe depot was brightly lit, and a cloud rose over the roof, exhaled from a locomotive hidden by the building. Storefronts along the way were shuttered and locked, although several saloons were open.

"Anyway," Harry said, "when I returned to Gallup from Fort Defiance—I was only gone for a few days—I found out that Aaron had taken off for parts unknown. He hadn't told his parents anything. He hadn't told me much, either, although I couldn't convince them of that. They accused me of being responsible—of driving him away, or encouraging his recklessness, or both."

"And you had no idea where he went?"

"Not really, but I had my suspicions. Three years later, I learned that he'd died in South Africa. I sent my condolences to the Belnaps—they'd left

Gallup by then—and received a scathing reply, full of accusations and invective. Why they persisted in believing that I'd had any influence over their son is beyond me."

"Why did you reconsider Williams's proposition?"

"This was right after Cuba, of course. And right after my father's death."

Julia hadn't realized that the two events were so closely associated.

"After what I'd seen in Cuba, and then my own illness, and my father . . . You might say I was feeling somewhat adrift. A few months spent basically on my own—being my own man—while taking on a worthy task . . ."

"Seemed like a good idea," Julia added.

"It did."

"You might have traveled—seen more of the West or more of the world."

"I suppose." He shrugged.

"And so a few months turned into twelve years."

"Once Williams left, Tohatchi was forgotten. I wrote to Washington and threatened to leave several times, and I received assurances that a permanent doctor was being recruited, but it never happened."

"You could have left anyway—you could have resumed your prior life."

"I could have." He shrugged again and smiled.

They arrived at the Harvey House. Harry held the door for her and they entered the lobby,

"What shall we do now?" Harry asked.

"I'm starving," she said.

The desk clerk informed them that the kitchen was still serving dinner because a train had been delayed east of Clovis and had just pulled in, hours behind schedule. In the dining room most of the tables were occupied, but a small one in a corner near the kitchen was free, and the hostess, a young woman with a broad smile and a noticeable accent, led them to it. Julia and Harry looked at the menus in silence, and when their waitress approached they both ordered Virginia ham, candied sweet potatoes, and garden peas.

Julia, whose seat enabled her to observe the crowded room, let her eyes roam. Nearest her sat a family of six, including a toddler who appeared to delight in visiting other tables, stumbling between them on plump little legs, gripping the edge of each and laughing when people peered down at her and cooed. An older brother and sister, sitting side by side, could barely keep their eyes open as they waited for their food to be delivered. The mother, her upswept hair coming undone beneath her straight-brimmed, simple hat, looked nearly as tired, while the father held in his arms a sleeping infant. Just beyond, a young couple, perhaps on their honeymoon, couldn't keep their hands away from each other: fingers intertwined, quick touches on sleeves and faces as they exchanged smiles, whispered words. Elsewhere sat businessmen, and salesmen, and older couples, the last talking with an accustomed familiarity punctuated by equally accustomed silences: they had no need to fill every gap. Despite the lateness of the train and their meal, no one seemed hurried except a table of crewman who had little to say to each other and, having already been served, ate efficiently; preparations needed to be made for the night run, and time to be made up before Winslow and Flagstaff, the train speeding through the empty landscape while the passengers slept in their berths or upright in the coaches, heads nodding, lolling, pillowed against windows and on companions' shoulders.

She and Harry would leave Gallup in the morning. Maybe she would attend church services first. It didn't matter where. Also before leaving, she would write an apology to Matilda. Although she didn't know what she would say. Best to say as little as possible. There wouldn't be a party invitation next year, of that she was sure.

She would stop at Tohatchi to rest a bit, but she wouldn't stay, if the weather held. She had no fear of traveling the road home alone, into the night.

The waitress served their food and they began to eat, still in silence. Harry had turned morose. He didn't look up from his plate.

Around the room Julia sensed a tired good humor, the notable exception being a gentleman with a walrus mustache and mutton chops who appeared to be doing his best not to be pleased by anything—the surroundings, the company, the time (he kept checking his pocket watch), the food, which he consumed with an expression of utter distaste. The three other men at his table did their best to ignore his ill humor.

The toddler from the next table had abandoned her seat once again and, this time, wobbled directly to Julia and Harry's despite her mother's insistent call for her return. Her red ringlets shook as she unsteadily splayed her little fingers on the table edge. Julia bent down and met the green eyes and smiled, and the little girl let out a spontaneous giggle. Julia extended her smile to the toddler's mother, who had risen to retrieve her wayward child and who smiled back apologetically with the half-harried look common only to mothers of small children both excited and jaded by strangers and unfamiliar surroundings, and as likely to burst into tears as laughter. The mother voiced a quick apology and steered her little girl homeward, which gave Julia another opportunity to observe the family of six. The two older children— the boy perhaps seven or eight, the girl a year or two younger—were quietly eating while giving no indication to their parents of what they were doing to each other under the table, where they were taking deliberate turns kicking each other with the sides of their shoes. The father was eating with one hand, still holding the baby with his other arm; every few minutes his wife would reach to his plate and cut a few more bites of meat for him.

The older girl gave out a sudden wail. Thoroughly versed in the sibling dynamic, and without even looking in his direction, the mother reached out and swatted her son on the back of the head, just hard enough for his jaw to drop. Julia ached for her—to *be* her—but she looked down at her knife and fork and plate and let the moment pass.

The man with the walrus mustache, just loudly enough to draw everyone's attention, called for the hostess, who immediately turned toward him. Julia started with recognition. "I know her," she said.

Harry raised his eyes from his plate. "Who?"

"The hostess."

He turned and glanced over his shoulder. "She's lovely."

"I think she was a waitress in the dining room of the El Tovar when I was there with Penny and my brother-in-law."

"Hmm," Harry mumbled, and returned to his own thoughts.

The hostess was now standing beside the complainant, giving him her full attention. Julia couldn't hear what they were saying—the woman's calm deference had led the man to lower his voice—but she saw the hostess quickly gesture for a waitress, who hurried to the table, listened to the hostess for a moment, and then headed for the kitchen. The man seemed satisfied with whatever the resolution was. The hostess stepped away but before returning to her station by the doorway took in the room at a quick glance, making sure that all appeared to be in order for the moment. Her eyes caught Julia's, passed on, then returned, as if to ask if Julia needed anything.

Julia smiled and quickly shook her head, but the hostess nevertheless made her way to their table. "Is there anything I can get for you, Madam?" she asked.

There again, the accent.

"No, thank you, but I was wondering—" Julia began again: "Have you ever worked at the El Tovar? I think you may have served me there several years ago."

The woman's smile widened. "That's certainly possible, although I was only there for a few months."

"This would have been in the summer of 1906."

"Why, that's right! It was my very first position with the Harvey Company." Her laugh was a soft trill. "I hope I didn't spill anything on you or your husband." She glanced at Harry, who had placed his napkin across his plate.

Julia saw no point in correcting her. "You were very young." Alicia. Her name was Alicia.

"It seems like *such* a long time ago."

"Have you been in Gallup long?"

"Six months. The company has been moving me around quite a bit. In fact, I'll be leaving here in the new year and returning to the El Tovar as a hostess." She spoke with obvious pride. "My fiancé is there now, working in the kitchen. We're going to be married in the spring and open our own little café in Flagstaff."

"How delightful. I wish you the very best." It was hard to believe this was the same tearful young woman she'd encountered four years ago. "It's been a pleasure seeing you again."

"I'm a bit embarrassed." The soft trill again. "I wish I could say I remembered you, but . . . so many faces . . ."

Thousands of night travelers. "Think nothing of it, dear."

The waitress who had hurried into the kitchen reemerged with a fresh basket of rolls and a butter dish. She placed them on the table of the cranky businessman, who didn't so much as acknowledge her. As soon as she was gone, he stuffed four of the rolls into his coat pockets.

The late dinner crowd was gradually thinning out. The family at the next table was busily organizing themselves for their return to the train.

"You're sure there's nothing I can get you?" Alicia asked.

"Coffee or tea? Dessert?" Harry asked Julia.

She shook her head.

"Please add the bill to my room charges," Harry said, speaking to Alicia for the first time.

Alicia left them and Harry, out of nowhere, asked, "If you could go anywhere, be anywhere you wanted, right now, where would it be?"

"A villa in Southern Italy, on the sea."

"Seriously."

"Seriously? I truly don't know, Harry. Why do you ask?"

He wiped his mouth and mustache with his napkin and then cleared his throat. "I think my time here is coming to an end."

"In Tohatchi?"

"Hmm."

"For any particular reason?"

"Ah'm getting older."

"Now *you* be serious," she chided him. She knew, of course, that he was a wealthy man and could live wherever he chose. And yet he'd spent twelve years as a doctor to the Navajo. No one had the right to ask more of him, and certainly not she.

"Will you return to Charleston?"

"No." He shook his head, "I could never live there again. When I was back there for my mother's funeral—" He rolled his eyes. "What a sad spectacle that was. Only two of my sisters were there, Marybeth and Cordelia—Isabel was in England—but I could already see them gearing up for a fight. My mother had at least five different wills, revised on the basis of momentary predilections, and with Marybeth and her husband living apart, and their adult children circling like vultures, waiting to feed on their inheritance . . . Let's just say that I'm well out of it. I made it clear that I'd sign off on whatever my sisters agreed to, that I wanted nothing."

They left the table in silence and reentered the lobby on the way to their rooms. Directly in front of them a large man was sitting in one of the four overstuffed lounge chairs clustered around a low circular table. When he saw them he immediately stood up, nearly spilling the tea cup he was holding in an ample paw.

"Good Lord," Harry said half under his breath, "it's Peabody."

Win Peabody set his cup down on the table in preparation for greeting them.

"Win," Julia said. "How nice to see you again!"

"Julia!" Peabody said, taking her extended hand and bowing as if to kiss it (though he refrained). The table was empty except for Peabody's cup and saucer and a china teapot.

"Hello, Peabody," Harry said.

"Forgive me," Julia said, "but for a moment I didn't recognize you. You've shaved off your beard since I saw you in August."

"Indeed I have," Peabody said, releasing her hand and stroking his chin. "I'm a man of habit. Each spring I grow one, and each fall I shave it off. Please, join me in a cup of tea. I'm sure they can scare up two more cups."

"We'd be delighted," Julia said.

Peabody signaled the desk clerk and pointed to the teapot. The clerk, who'd overheard their greetings, disappeared through the doorway behind his counter.

The three sat down and Peabody, settling back into his chair, said, "I have to thank you again, Julia, for allowing me to impose on your hospitality last summer."

"I did very little except offer food and a bit of conversation."

"You're too, too modest. But tell me what brings the two of you to Gallup this fine evening."

"A Christmas party," Julia said.

"Ah, the famous Rodriguez gala! I hear lobster was on the menu again this year."

"Actually, quail with oyster stuffing," Harry said. "You've attended in the past?"

Peabody cleared his throat. "Twice. Before my marriage."

Of course, Julia thought. To an Indian. "And how is your family?" she asked.

"Very well! My boy's soon turning three. He's my joy. Not that I love his sister any less—she's the spitting image of her mother."

"You didn't go to Zuni this weekend?"

"No. Pressing business. A burial this morning and another on Monday."

"Speaking of your son and daughter," Harry said.

"Yes?"

"If I were you I'd be very concerned about the current measles outbreak. You might try to convince your wife to bring them into Gallup until it passes."

"I appreciate your concern. But the fortunate thing is—if one can say there's anything fortunate about an epidemic—my children and their cousins came down with it, one-two-three, early on, and have all fully recovered."

"That's indeed fortunate."

"I hear you're seeing it on the Navajo Reservation as well?"

Harry nodded.

Alicia appeared with a silver tray bearing a fresh pot of tea as well as three cups and saucers. She smiled at Peabody and poured for the three of them.

"Thank you very much, Alicia," Peabody said.

"Certainly, Mr. Peabody," Alicia said, and then she left them, taking with her the earlier tea service.

Harry seemed amused. "You're a familiar face here?"

"Quite. I don't regularly cook for myself, and I find the staff here congenial, so this is where I usually dine when I'm in town. And often, like tonight, I stop in for tea during my evening constitutional. If you don't mind my asking, you left the gala early?"

"We did," Julia said. "I was feeling unwell and thought some fresh air might revive me, which it did."

"Ah, I see," Peabody said with a nod and then a thoughtful frown. "Actually, our fortuitous meeting may save me a trip."

"How so?"

"I've been thinking about paying you another visit."

"You're always welcome, Win."

He beamed and leaned forward. "Have you ever thought about expanding your business?"

"Taking on another trading post? God forbid!" Julia laughed.

"No, no. Have you ever considered expanding your catalog?"

"Well, it's a new venture, as you know, and it's hard to say if I'll be able to keep up with it. I didn't anticipate the number of orders I've received."

"Yes, I gather you've been doing quite well."

She raised an eyebrow and he explained:

"Everything you ship goes through the Gallup Post Office. People take note of such things—no secrets in a small town, Julia. But to the point"—he rubbed his hands together—"suppose you were to expand your catalog to include other Indian items—only of the finest quality, mind you."

"Such as?"

"Pottery from Acoma, baskets from Hopi."

"And perhaps Zuni jewelry?"

"Ah," he said, tapping the table with a finger, "precisely."

"I don't see how I could do that," she said. "I'd have to travel on a regular basis to the Hopi Reservation and Acoma, and down to Zuni as well. I already have a trading post to run and a wool business to see to." Julia glanced at Harry Whitaker, who was sitting back in his chair, stroking his mustache, but showing little interest in the discussion.

"Let Mr. and Mrs. Gorman run the trading post for you. Maintain a presence there, of course, so the government doesn't interfere, but run the catalog business from here."

"From Gallup?"

"From a small office."

"Win, I don't—" She shook her head.

"You're very highly thought of by the local business community, you know," Peabody said. "You're quite an unusual 'case.' You've been running Many Springs now for over a decade, and on your own for—what?—six years? You must know how extraordinary that is. Trading posts are notoriously unstable businesses. Even the Days and the Hubbells have had more failures than successes. But you've *held on.* Such things don't go unnoticed."

"If the catalog business is such a good idea," Harry said, "why don't you go into it yourself?"

"*Me?*" Win hooted. "My skills lie elsewhere—and my interests, too, as it were. I believe I'm quite good at my profession, which, I might add, gives me considerable satisfaction. I help people get through difficult times, as do you, Harry. What would make you give up *your* profession?"

"A villa in southern Italy, on the sea," Harry said.

Julia gave him a wicked glance.

"Nonsense! If that were what you really wanted, you could sail for Europe next week."

"I can't think clearly about this now," Julia said. "But I don't see how I could begin to take it on."

"You might need an investor," Win said, winking. He drained his cup. "There's a long winter ahead. Mull it over. And now," placing his empty cup delicately on its saucer and nodding first to Julia and then to Harry, "I must be off. I've taken up quite enough of your time."

Julia's and Harry's rooms faced each other across the second-floor hallway. They paused at their doors.

"I'm really so sorry, Julia," Harry said glumly. "I know how much you were looking forward to the party."

"Oh, Harry, I've already forgotten it." He was a dear man, with, obviously, much on his mind. "Your company was quite enough. When I was growing up, I attended so many fetes, galas, weddings, charity socials, and the like, but only because my father was a minister—we were invited when it would have been bad form to exclude us. I always felt on display, and even now, all these years later, a part of me finds it very difficult to enjoy such formal events—before very long, I tend to find myself observing from afar."

"I know *exactly* what you mean," Harry said. "I entered Matilda's foyer tonight and found myself thinking about all that I was supposed to admire, and I don't mean the holiday decorations."

"But they *were* quite lovely, the decorations."

"They were," he said with a rueful smile.

Julia kissed him on the cheek, and they said their goodnights.

HARRY WHITAKER SAT DOWN on the side of the bed and removed his shoes, dusty from the walk down the hill from the Rodriguez home, Matilda's mansion. The room was small but would do for the night. He slipped off his coat, unbuttoned his vest, loosened his tie, and lay back on the bed. Would he be able to sleep? He had trouble in strange rooms, strange beds, no matter how comfortable.

He'd never expected to see the Belnaps again. Maybe he should have faced them, but what would have been the point? Aaron had been selfish, careless, and impulsive, inflicting pain on parent and friend alike. His had been a wasted life in which he, Harry, had played no appreciable part whatsoever, a truth that he knew the Belnaps could never accept. To do so would force them to see in their son's appetites and rashness a tainted bloodline, a deficient upbringing, or both. In September 1901, when a correspondent's report of American deaths in the Anglo-Boer War finally reached Washington, it disappeared in the sea of printed tributes to William McKinley, assassinated days before by an anarchist, and in the coverage of Teddy Roosevelt's succession to the White House. Recognizing Aaron's name in the newspaper account, Harry's friend Robb Church—they still stayed in touch—had cut out the article and sent it to Tohatchi, noting in his letter that the new administration would probably have other priorities than engaging in a diplomatic spat with Britain over renegade Americans who'd died fighting for the Boers. Robb suspected that the report would be largely ignored and quickly forgotten, and he turned out to be correct. No mention made the New Mexico newspapers.

Even in his father's last days, when calendar and clock slipped away from him so often, he could foresee well enough to warn Harry off, to caution against Aaron's influence. Harry had revisited that final conversation many times—that and the most cavalier act of his life, so shortly after, lying and disregarding his obligations when his father died. It didn't matter that his family had managed quite well without him—in his sister Marybeth's case, gladly, he suspected. She was the most disapproving of his three siblings. Even at their mother's recent wake she'd plagued him, going on at length about his duty to find a suitable wife and produce a male heir to carry on the family name. His reply, that he wasn't cut out for marriage and that there were already enough other Whitakers in the world, only antagonized her further. Courting, marrying, fathering—Harry had never felt the imperative.

During dinner he'd seen Julia observing the family seated at a nearby table: mother, father, baby, toddler, two other children. Julia hadn't said anything, but her face, unguarded, unaware of his attention, had revealed all. As her doctor, he'd known of her desire to conceive, but she hadn't spoken of it in years—since well before Will's disappearance. And now . . .

What would she do in Many Springs Canyon, he wondered, when her little gatherings came to their end? Pete had already vanished into the wilderness. Owen, under her care, might survive the winter, but another year was too much to hope for. And then? To whom could she turn for companionship? The Gormans? They were fine people, but each day they went home to their families and their church. Alberto Rodriguez? Even before tonight, Julia didn't see him often, and after tonight—after the abrupt departure—who could say? Harry felt responsible, but he didn't think anything he might say or do would alter the situation. Tóya? She might still have a number of years ahead of her but wouldn't be traveling very far from home much longer. Yazzie, for all his native intelligence and wiles, his loyalty to her and his steadfastness, and despite those tender characteristics that Julia must see in him but that were beyond Harry's ken—Yazzie was not an educated man and therefore not comfortable in Julia's other world, that of culture and intellect. And Johanna; companion, sister, even in some way daughter, but always apart—though were Julia ever to leave Many Springs Canyon, Harry suspected that her greatest sorrow would be the loss not *of,* but *to,* Johanna.

As for he himself... The Rehoboth Mission of the Christian Reformed Church had opened a hospital just east of Gallup, and a telephone wire, strung across the intervening twenty-five miles, now connected the Tohatchi School and Gallup. Soon there would be automobiles traveling that route on a regular basis. Even if no replacement succeeded him, his patients would be considerably better off than before he'd come.

While he still could, he wanted to be part of something bigger. One man was a paltry thing, of no account, unless he was a Pasteur or a Koch. But many men collectively, that was another matter. The transcontinental railroad. The transatlantic cable. Even the Brooklyn Bridge. And the Panama Canal.

The hardest medical work had already been done by Walter Reed and others, convincing the naysayers that mosquitoes carry yellow fever and malaria, but the canal laborers still fell ill and needed to be cared for. Yellow fever had almost been eliminated because of sanitation measures—draining swamps, setting up public water systems instead of collecting water in rain barrels—but malaria and other diseases remained a problem, especially for the West Indian and negro workers, who lived in tent cities and shat in open trenches, whereas their white counterparts lived in screened houses and drank clean water.

It was an old story. On what remained of the Whitaker plantation, most of the negro and mulatto laborers and share-croppers still lived in the slave quarters or, where the most decrepit cabins had been torn down, in the white-washed pine plank shacks that replaced them. He didn't have to dig deep to the origins of his family's money—everything had a dark lineage. He had no control over that, past or present, and any effort to exert himself now would meet with implacable resistance and further estrangement from his family. Better that he should apply his skills and his knowledge to help those engaged in a larger task.

Not that he had any illusions about Panama, conveniently liberated from Colombia in 1903 by American money and threats, or about the purpose of the canal, secured by treaty in perpetuity, connecting the Atlantic and the Pacific; for commerce, certainly, but also for deployment of battleships and armored cruisers—the Kearsarges and the Pennsylvanias—and the rest of the Great White Fleet that had already sailed around the world in a display of America's new might. This was America the limitless, of bounding energy and righteousness, Teddy Roosevelt's America. But what Harry had seen of the new America was also often small, rapacious, pitiless.

He rose and prepared himself for bed, but when he lay down again, he was still wide awake. He reached for his oilskin kit on the nightstand and opened it. He removed the vial and tapped it with a finger nail.

His father had taught him not to anticipate happiness or even contentment; they were too fleeting and undependable. Be resolute. Without that, the world would offer little but disappointment and misery. Never allow any other need, intimate or public, to get the better of your judgment. If pain interfered with your daily intercourse, his father had told him more than once, take the drug; but if you craved the drug for itself, withstand the desire. The needle was a clever thing, it could trick you.

Harry stared at the ceiling. Getting to sleep would be hard enough. And even then he couldn't be certain that he would sleep through the night. He might go months without a nightmare but then be awakened several nights in a row; twelve years after the war, Cuba continued to insinuate itself into his dreams: the stifling, saturated heat, the raw meat of torn limbs and bellies, the taste of exploded ordinance in the air, an eviscerated horse leaking into the Aguadores . . .

The most ordinary of dreams might inexplicably be invaded. He might be sitting with his father, in his study or on the veranda and suddenly they'd both be in Cuba, amid the explosions and the whining bullets, powerless to move. Sometimes a sister or his mother, sometimes someone he knew from his childhood or college or Washington, sometimes people he knew from the reservation—a recent patient, Betty Roanhorse, Julia, Johanna Yazzie—and sometimes Aaron Belnap or Billy Dutton, would lie stretched out before him or appear among the walking wounded. He and they might be carrying on a quite unrelated conversation about the weather or a minor ailment or some bit of invective or gossip, all while chaos reigned around them. Even when no one else appeared to notice the dire circumstances, his distress would mount until it was unbearable—until he abruptly surfaced from it all and was instantly awake.

More often than not, a return to settled sleep would prove elusive. If it was nearing dawn, he wouldn't even try; he'd rise and start his day. Sometimes, though, the need for sleep weighed so heavily—

Harry returned the vial to the kit and closed it.

He hadn't said anything to Julia, but he'd already written to Washington. He should hear back any day now, and then he would tell her, if his appointment came through. He would miss her and Tóya and Betty Roanhorse and Owen and the Yazzies and many of his patients, but his time had come, as Tóya, from the very first, had known it would. He hadn't shirked his duties, not in Cuba and not in Tohatchi, not once in a dozen years, but his time had come. He saw this most clearly on nights such as this, when his body resisted sleep and craved surrender.

CHAPTER TWENTY-TWO: The Place in the Mountains That the Aspens Watch Over

They started out just after dawn. When Owen saw the saddled horses tied to the corral fence, he balked. He asked Yazzie, "Can't I go on foot?" It was a foolish question: on foot, up a mountain, through God knew what terrain, wearing moccasins because any kind of boot now pained his right foot too much.

Yazzie was tying a bedroll behind his saddle. "It's a long way. Some of it's steep."

Owen couldn't argue with him. Anything more than moderate exertion drained him, and he knew that the higher the altitude, the thinner the air. His lungs wouldn't be able to manage, and the dull aching weariness, as if his diaphragm were lifting bricks, would exhaust him.

Yazzie led Owen's horse—Julia's pinto mare—over to the veranda so that it would be easier to mount.

They rode up the canyon, Yazzie leading the way on his big brown. The light frost on the shaded ground retreated into wispy vapors as the sun met it. There was no wind, and the few feathery clouds seemed to hover, scarcely making any progress across the sky. At Yazzie's hogan, Johanna emerged. Yazzie rode over and spoke to her briefly.

"Anything wrong?" Owen asked when Yazzie rejoined him.

"No. I just reminded Sister that she should look after Mrs. Halley's animals tonight and again in the morning."

"*Yiskáągo índa,* Jóhonaá," Owen called out. "See you tomorrow!"

Despite a lingering chill in the air—vapor still formed in front of the horses' nostrils as they worked—the sun soon soaked into Owen's back, raising a thin layer of sweat beneath his union suit and flannel shirt and sheepskin coat.

They passed through the high meadow at a leisurely pace, but soon after entering the forest, the trail steepened, and the horses began breathing more heavily, their heads dropping forward with each stride. Owen had been through here on foot many times; they were heading towards Blue Hawk Lake, passing ponderosa pine, blue spruce, Douglas fir.

He still went off by himself some mornings, although never as early as he had in those first ambitious weeks more than a year ago, and not until concluding a leisurely breakfast with Julia—she'd taken a liking to oatmeal and toasted pinyon nuts and a bit of honey as the mornings began sliding toward winter. More days than not, he stayed nearby, painting pictures of rugs for her next catalog, but sometimes he'd walk down the canyon, toward the Gallup road, and back, still carrying with him a field book and pencil, more out of habit than in anticipation of seeing anything of note. He knew she worried about him, so he tried to ease her mind by keeping close. Besides, his right foot, the one missing the last two toes, was becoming a problem. To compensate for the absent toes, his weight had shifted and the second and third toes had turned outward; their joints were now frozen, unbendable, and the pad of his foot often throbbed.

On those increasingly rare days when he had energy and the will to ignore his painful foot, he might sneak away and venture into the mountains, but only as far as one of the numerous lookouts that faced east. There, he would sit watching the landscape. Sometimes he would ponder how, nearly a thousand years ago, the Anasazi had rolled and dragged ponderosa logs from these mountains to Chaco Canyon, more than 50 miles away. Over there, eastward. Sometimes he would lie down and nap until chilled by the afternoon's shadows.

Owen had agreed to this trip with Yazzie out of no particular need; he'd come because he sensed that the excursion, whatever its destination, had meaning for Yazzie, his friend. The proposal and acceptance had required no more than a couple of minutes of conversation. Last night he'd been sitting by his fireplace, inattentively reading an old newspaper—he had to hold it inches from the lamp to see the print at all clearly—when Yazzie knocked at his door.

"There's something I want you to see," Yazzie had said in his cryptic fashion.

"What's that?" Owen asked, putting down the newspaper. Earlier in the day, after many years of turning down invitations, Julia had left to attend Matilda Rodriguez's famous Christmas party in Gallup.

"It'll take a good part of the day to get there. Up in the mountains. Are you able?"

"I've been feeling okay. I guess I could manage an outing."

"I'll get everything ready. I'll come at first light and we'll head out."

That's all there was to it. A simple conversation. And now here they were on the trail. He still didn't know where they were going, but the day was pleasant and quiet, and that seemed good enough.

They stopped at Blue Hawk Lake to rest and eat, not far from where Tim Be'ak'idii's hogan had stood. Owen removed his moccasins and socks and, sitting down at the rocky shore, extended his feet into the icy water. They quickly went numb, but he didn't remove them.

On either side of him, Yazzie's brown and Julia's mare dipped their muzzles and drank.

"Does your horse have a name?" Owen asked Yazzie. "I've only heard you and Julia refer to him as 'the brown.' "

"I don't name working animals," Yazzie replied. He was unfolding a package wrapped in butcher paper. "Sister packed us boiled chicken and biscuits and apples."

"No oatmeal?"

"Hunh," Yazzie grunted.

Owen laughed.

Yazzie cut an apple in half and gave a piece to each horse.

"Just chicken for me," Owen said, but then he reconsidered and said, "Oh, what the hell, give me a biscuit, too." Wheat flour turned to sugar in the gut, but riding was work, and physical labor burned the sugar faster than it could build up in his blood. He took a bite, savoring the texture as much as the flavor.

"There aren't any sheep," Owen said. "The last time I came by here, I kept running into them." He took a drink from a cup of lake water.

"They've all been brought down for the winter," Yazzie said. "The snow could come anytime."

"Are we going much higher?" He knew that they were above eight thousand feet.

"Some. A lot of up and down. Fill your canteen, because there's no more easy water until we get there."

They relieved themselves in the bushes and remounted, Yazzie interlacing his strong fingers to give Owen a boost.

Soon, Yazzie veered off the main trail, which, climbing roughly southeast to northwest, ran on to Washington Pass—the route Owen had taken to see Halley's Comet in May. Yazzie steered the brown sharply left, to the south, along a bare slope beneath a ridge line of hundred-foot ponderosas. This trail was rocky and the mountainside steep enough that the horses had to step carefully. At one point Owen wasn't sure if they were following an actual trail or carving a new path along the side of the slope, but then, after dropping down to avoid an outcropping, they arrived at a clearly defined switchback.

The sun, arcing in the south, cast long shadows. Ravens and jays and an occasional hawk sailed above them, and now and then Owen detected the knocking of a woodpecker in the distance. The going was tedious, and he lost track of time until, eventually, they began edging their way upward toward the ridge.

Reaching it, the fall of the hooves soon softened against a cushion of pine needles, punctuated by the crushing of old dropped cones, as they moved northwestward beneath the boughs of the conifers, into and out of patches of sun. They were not climbing now and the horses' gaits grew steadier. Owen swayed slightly side to side with the mare's rhythmical movement. He timed his breathing to it and was startled when he heard Yazzie's voice say they should stop. He realized that he'd been drifting off. His knees folded as his feet met the hard ground—the soft forest floor had disappeared, replaced by rocky sandstone and scrub—and he felt Yazzie's hands on his back and left arm, steadying him. His knees throbbed; he'd committed a tenderfoot's mistake of applying too much torque against the mare's sides.

"Do we have much farther to go?" he asked.

"No."

Owen bent down to pick up a loose piece of sandstone. His head swam and the muscles in his legs twitched. He stumbled as he straightened up. He needed water. He lifted the strap of his canteen from around the gullet. The mare's reins hung to the ground and she moved off a couple of steps before stopping; the horse swished her tail, as if to dismiss him. Owen drank from his canteen, and then drank some more, and in a few minutes he felt better.

He tossed the piece of sandstone in his hand. "Some geologists think this came from giant dunes," he said to Yazzie, who was examining the mare's right rear hoof. Owen scraped sand particles off with his fingernails, leaving shallow tracks behind. "The sand may have been blown here tens of millions of years ago."

"She's going lame," Yazzie said. A stone had worked its way under a slightly loose shoe and bruised the mare's hoof. "She shouldn't carry any extra weight."

"It's all right," Owen said. "I can walk the rest of the way."

Yazzie looked up at him. "It's too much. We should go back."

"I'm fine," Owen said. "Besides, we're not just sight-seeing, are we?"

"No," Yazzie said, straightening up.

"And you said yourself, we're almost there, wherever it is you're bringing me."

"The Hopis call it the Place in the Mountains That the Aspens Watch Over."

"The *Hopis?*" Owen said with surprise.

"You ride the brown," Yazzie said. "I'll walk."

So they went on. Half an hour later, the vista opened up—the land plateaued and the Douglas fir and ponderosa pine disappeared, replaced by dispersed pinyon and gambel oak—all of the trees short, stunted—as well as low-growing juniper, whose berries had ripened into a dark purple.

When Owen drew his hat brim down to shade his eyes from the sun, he could see due west for half a mile or so, where the land appeared to stop. There was something out there that Yazzie wanted him to see, he knew it. He forgot about his discomfort. He felt a flutter in the middle of his chest, beneath the breastbone. If they were high enough, he might be able to see across the Defiance Plateau to the south of Canyon de Chelly's southern-most branch, Monument Canyon. The top of Black Mesa should be sitting at the horizon to the northwest; the Hopi Reservation would lie to the southwest. Just to the north, he should easily be able to see the trail that cut its way up the west side of the Chuskas to Crystal and Washington Pass.

They were half way to the anticipated drop-off when Yazzie, leading the way, unexpectedly turned north, toward a dark gray rock face. Owen drew in the brown's reins and stopped. "Don't we go this way?" Owen asked, pointing west.

Yazzie turned around. "It's a nice view from over there," he said, "but that isn't what we came for."

"Then what *did* we come for?"

Yazzie nodded toward the rock wall.

Owen looked again. Because of the angle of the sun, light was being reflected by fragments of something embedded in the wall. Feldspar or some other silicate. So what? That meant nothing. There was nothing over there. Except . . . low, barely above ground level, in front of the gray wall, between the scrub trees that lay in the way, he could see a yellow swath. It moved. Not all at once. Like flecks of gold caught by wind and sun. Then he knew what he was looking at. The *tops* of trees—aspens that hadn't lost their leaves yet. The Place in the Mountains That the Aspens Watch Over. "There's a canyon over there, isn't there?" he said.

Aspens dotted the slope on the north side of the box canyon, beneath the nearly vertical gray wall. On the south side, where Owen still sat astride the brown, the rim dropped away precipitously, and he couldn't see any-thing below the higher branches of the aspens, which formed a heavy golden canopy directly in front of him, at eye level.

"This way," Yazzie said, and with his hand on the bridle he urged the brown forward, eastward along the rim. A couple of hundred yards on, where the southern rim extended out, narrowing the canyon, Yazzie stopped. From here, Owen could see at the bottom, maybe three hundred feet below them, a small stream, which wound eastward and, less than a quarter of a mile farther, disappeared in a rightward turn beneath the cliff. On either side of the stream, gambel oaks, mountain sagebrush, and rabbit brush, its seed heads gone white, dominated the valley floor.

Yazzie turned to face him. "Now look back," he said.

Owen swung around. From this vantage he could see the northwest end of the canyon, where, tucked away in a magnificent alcove, almost filling the width of the cul-de-sac, beneath an enormous sandstone overhang, lay a cliff ruin, not as big as Cliff Palace at Mesa Verde, not as wide, but deeper, extending farther back into the sandstone, half in shadow in the afternoon. Owen's heart thumped. "This isn't supposed to be here," he whispered.

The ruins looked untouched. Many walls and roofs had completely or partially collapsed, leaving the expected mounds of debris, but a fair number appeared to be intact. Owen could see hallmarks of Chaco-style construction: T-shaped doorways; in the thicker walls, carefully layered courses of masonry backfilled with rubble; thinner wattle-and-daub construction elsewhere. Owen whipped off his hat and rapidly massaged the top of his skull through his sweaty hair. His voice, filled with surprise, squeaked: "Yazzie, how long have you known about this?"

Yazzie was pulling at his bottom lip with forefinger and thumb. "Since I was a young man."

Owen put his hat on again to shield his eyes from the sun. He squinted, trying to look beyond the shadows and farther into the ruins. "Who else knows?"

"Some Hopis and a few Navajos."

"No Anglos?"

"No." Yazzie thought for a moment and then corrected himself: "One." His eyes shifted to Owen's.

Julia.

Yazzie, helping Owen dismount, said, "We'll camp here." He began untying his gear from behind the brown's saddle.

The alcove faced southeast. The Anasazi always built cliff dwellings where they could catch as much of the winter sun as possible. There were multiple levels to the main ruin and, farther up, tucked into the higher recesses, long, narrow rooms with single, sealed openings—probably storage rooms for grains and other foods and seeds, located where mice and other vermin couldn't get to them. From the bottom of the canyon to the top of the alcove had to be two hundred feet.

"Is there a way to get down there?" Owen asked. "Into the ruins?"

"You have to come up from below. There are hand- and foot-holds that were cut into the sandstone long ago. Look, near where the stream starts. Some are very worn, not much left. It's sixty feet, almost straight up, and once you start the only way you can rest is by leaning into the curve of the stone. Coming down is harder. You need to feel for the foot-holds—you can't see them."

"So you've been up there."

"Many times."

"What about Julia?"

Yazzie lifted his saddle bags from the brown. "I brought her here just once. She didn't go into the ruins. She said it wasn't her place."

"Did she ask you to bring me here?"

Yazzie shook his head. "She knows nothing about this." Yazzie turned to the mare and began unstrapping Owen's bedroll and other provisions from behind the empty saddle.

"If you're worried about my being able to climb up there," Owen said, "I can do it." The tiredness in his legs wouldn't stop him, and his breathing, ever since the land had leveled, was steady. He *knew* he could do it.

Yazzie's face was largely hidden by the brim of his hat. "There's a rope up there. I can tie it to a beam and throw the other end down to you. You can wrap it around yourself, and I can keep you from falling if you slip, but you'll still have to climb."

"I can do it."

Yazzie turned to face him. "If we do this, you can't leave any signs that you've been there. If you pick anything up—a piece of pottery, a tool—put it back where you found it. And don't go beyond the doorways of any rooms. All the sand that's blown inside makes it too hard to wipe out footprints. Trying to sweep them away just makes it worse. And don't trust the ladders," Yazzie continued. "Some lead down into kivas, others to rooms up above. Keep off them."

"Understood."

"If a doorway was walled up by the Anasazi, leave it be."

Some of the sealed rooms were probably used for temporary storage. Others, if excavations elsewhere could serve as a guide, might look as if the inhabitants had planned a return: hearths prepared, cooking utensils nearby, turkey feather blankets neatly folded.

"Why is it so important that nothing gets disturbed?" Owen asked.

"Because the next time I come, others will be with me, and they can't know you were here."

"What others?"

"My Hopi uncles and other men from their clan," Yazzie said. "They come twice a year. In August during the harvest, when the kachinas leave for their home in the San Francisco Peaks. In February, when the kachinas return to the mesas."

Owen was incredulous. "Hopis cross half the Navajo Reservation, in secret, in the middle of winter, to come up here?"

Yazzie nodded.

"Why?"

"They believe this was the home of their ancestors."

And therefore Yazzie's ancestors, on his father's side. Some things that Owen had never quite fathomed about Clement Yazzie were beginning to come into focus.

"There must be an easier route up here than the one we took."

"There's one three miles south of Owl Spring, from the west. There's a shorter one from the east, too, but not if you have to ride all the way. Part of it's too steep for horses." Yazzie unbuckled a flap from a saddle bag and pulled out more provisions. "We're losing the afternoon. We should probably eat something quickly and go." He handed Owen a strip of dried venison. "I'll build a fire and cook something when we get back."

They chewed in silence for several minutes, still standing, taking in the ruins and the canyon leading toward them.

"What do the members of your father's clan do when they come here?"

"Mostly, they say prayers."

Owen tore off another bite of the dried venison. He took a drink from his canteen. The overlook where they were standing might well be the only vantage point on the south side of the canyon that afforded a clear view of the ruins, and conditions were almost certainly worse on the north side, where someone would have to be standing at the very edge of the gray rock wall, far above, to peer down into what probably looked like a nondescript canyon. No wonder so few people knew about the ruins.

"I don't see a way down to the bottom from here," Owen said.

"It's ahead a ways." Yazzie nodded to the east. "The canyon is shaped like a hook, with the ruins at the straight end. It isn't much of a trail to the bottom, and we'll have to walk the horse down the steepest part of it." He'd already hobbled Julia's injured mare. "It's crumbled sandstone and other loose rocks. It's easy to lose your footing. Once we get down, we follow the stream back to the ruins."

"All right, let's go," Owen said. He put his left foot in the stirrup, pushed off as hard as he could with his right, and used his biceps to pull himself the rest of the way into the saddle. The brown, clearly displeased, whinnied and careened to the right, but Owen was quick enough into the saddle to bring him back under control.

"You could use some practice," Yazzie said with a straight face.

They navigated the trail without incident and in an hour were standing beneath the ruins. From there, the alcove looked even more massive and the climb up considerably more daunting than it had from the overlook. The rock face wasn't quite as smooth as it had appeared at a distance, though; Owen could feel with his fingertips the transitions, the slight edge, where adjoining layers of the worn sandstone met. The Anasazi had taken advantage of these transitions to chip away at the rock for hand- and foot-holds. Owen figured he was taller than the Anasazis had been; if they could clamber from step to step, then so could he.

About twenty feet up, one of the foot-holds appeared to have been expanded, with something jammed into the rock.

"What's that, up there?" he asked Yazzie, pointing.

"A warning," Yazzie said.

They hobbled the brown and Yazzie went up first, stepping carefully but with ease, using his hands for little more than balance all the way up. Before long he returned to the edge and threw down the end of a rope. Owen tied it around himself as best he could, looping it a couple of times from groin to shoulder and around his shoulder blades and tying it at his waist. Then he started up, going slowly, not counting the steps ahead, with Yazzie, braced, keeping the rope taut. Climbing required considerable effort and attention; Owen didn't look back down. He came to the odd foot-hold. What he'd seen from below appeared to be a coyote pelt. He felt it. It had been wrapped around something. He pulled back a flap and stared into the vacant eyes of a human skull, minus the lower jaw.

He was breathing heavily when he reached out for Yazzie's hand and stepped onto the level. He needed to sit down immediately and wait for his pulse to slow. The tightness in his chest gradually subsided. He looked around.

He was sitting at the edge of a plaza, his back to the canyon. To his left, the plaza narrowed into no more than a path, rising in a shallow incline until it met the alcove wall, 50 feet away; at the outer edge the Anasazi had constructed a squat adobe wall, part of which had eroded away, while the inner side of the path was lined with perhaps a dozen rooms on the lowest level and half as many above, although all, poorly protected from the elements, were heavily damaged, so much so that only a few sticks and stones remained of some walls. To his right, however, the plaza dipped slightly downward—which afforded him a good line of sight—before leveling out and extending at least another 150 feet. He could see, half way across this stretch, at the widest point of the plaza, a square opening—the entrance, he concluded, to a large kiva—and the uprights and upper rungs of a rough ladder. There was another plaza, up a few wide stone steps still farther to the right; this plaza wasn't quite as long as the first but was deeper, its inner perimeter, where the wattle-and-daub walls of rooms rose, well protected by the sandstone overhang. Here, the roofs of three kivas had collapsed. Beyond that, a narrow street ran to what looked like several small, windowless rooms built against the northern face of the alcove. Although he couldn't see any, he assumed there were stone steps or, more probably, hand- and foot-holds going upward to a higher ledge, which was mostly filled by two long, windowless storage rooms. The ledge might well have served as a lookout, too. Behind him, when he turned toward the southeast, the canyon was no more than half a mile long until it curved.

He rose and walked slowly along the plaza. The nearest rooms had been built in three levels, almost haphazardly, overlapping each other, taking advantage of outcroppings and boulders. Some walls, especially on the first level, where they were most exposed to the weather, were eroded enough to reveal the underlying wattle, a lattice of interwoven sticks and reeds. He could see that in some of the more disheveled rooms the interior mud plaster was also gone, permitting the light to break through to the dirt floor. Most intact rooms had the familiar T-shaped doors, and a few also featured small rectangular windows. The roofs and lintels were supported by ponderosa beams of varying thicknesses; the irregular exposed ends showed the chop marks of primitive tools. Some roofs still supported ladders that had provided access to the higher levels; some ladders had fallen apart; some, though upright, had broken rungs; some looked quite serviceable despite their age.

Owen stopped half way across the alcove and took a quick inventory. He estimated that there may have been a hundred or more rooms, depending on how far back the alcove went at its deepest. He resumed his walk along the plaza of hard rock and blown reddish sand.

He and Yazzie didn't talk; the Navajo kept his distance, seemingly preoccupied with a rope burn on his left hand.

Relics were everywhere. Broken pottery—some black-and-white, some tricolor, some brown and corrugated—lay on roofs, against walls, in shards under his feet. Just past the entrance to the large kiva, at the front of the plaza, was a stone trough, separated into four side-by-side metates for grinding corn into flour. There was a mano, a simple stone pestle, lying in one of the metates, and when he brushed his moccasin back and forth lightly in the nearby sand, he uncovered several small, desiccated corn cobs, as if the site had been abandoned months ago, not ages. He turned around. Farther back in the alcove stood a three-story square tower with a column of square windows, one at each level. He walked over to the lowest window. Bending to the side and twisting his neck, he could see up the tower part way; a lower floor had collapsed, but the upper one was intact, blocking any additional light from filtering down. It was too dark to see anything except that the interior wall appeared to have been whitewashed with clay and decorated with a painted design of orangish lines and triangles that evoked a horizon and mountain peaks.

Just beyond the tower, a narrow street ran far back into the alcove, both sides lined with rooms fronted by well-sheltered patios that had probably been used for social gatherings as well as for such mundane chores as cooking. Owen noticed the remains of ancient fires—charred fragments of wood, rings of heat-cracked stones, black soot on the sandstone overhang—and also two ladders that descended into underground chambers. These roofs had partly collapsed.

Yazzie joined him. He was carrying a kerosene lantern retrieved, Owen assumed, from the same nook where the rope was kept.

"The kivas are square," Owen said, "like the ones at Hopi." At least, that was what he had read. All of the Chaco kivas were round. He didn't know of any site that had both round and square ceremonial chambers.

"Come with me," Yazzie said, and they walked, single-file, deeper into the alcove. They reached a shallow, bare pocket, beyond the last rooms. "What do you think about this?" Yazzie asked, holding up the lantern.

A narrow, thin sheet of water was running down the rear wall, pooling against it at the bottom. Moss, almost fluorescent in the poor light cast by Yazzie's uplifted lantern, grew on the wall. The air back here, in the deepest recess, was dank and dead.

"It's a seep," Owen said. "Fresh water." He could see where enough rock had been carved away to permit placement of vessels, one at a time, to collect the water.

"When I first came here, there was just a trickle. The sand was always wet, but there wasn't any standing water. Now, each year, there seems to be more."

"It's snow melt from up above."

"Last winter was dry. There wasn't much snow cover."

"That wouldn't matter," Owen said. "The snow I'm talking about fell long before your grandfather's grandfather was born. It can take hundreds of years for water to percolate down through the sandstone above us." He sat down, removed his moccasins and socks and stepped into the icy water. "Let me borrow your lantern." Yazzie handed it to him. Walking carefully, Owen crossed the ten feet to the wall.

"Somewhere beneath us there's a layer of relatively impermeable rock, probably shale, that the melt can't get through. So the water travels horizontally, maybe from miles away, until it finds a way out at a cliff face.

That's how this alcove formed. Water permeates the sandstone, dissolves the calcium carbonate that binds the particles of sand together, and the silt that results gets washed away over time. The process speeds up when the water freezes and expands in the winter, creating cracks. Whole blocks of sandstone can give way. And beneath it all, beneath the whole Defiance Plateau, there's what geologists call an uplift. Everything above it is unstable. You've seen the evidence, landslides and slumps, all over the eastern side of the Chuskas."

Owen spread his free hand against the wall, into the flow. "This is a lot of water for a seep. It may feed the stream at the bottom of the canyon, too, which would mean there's a break in the shale." Bending down, he ran a finger horizontally across the rock face. "Do you see this dark seam? It's basalt. Volcanic. Some kinds of basalt are as porous as a sponge. But some, like this, are very dense and almost as smooth as glass."

His feet were already numb, but he stayed at the wall, examining it closely. "If you drilled into this wall, I wouldn't be surprised if you eventually hit a basalt dike as well—a vertical volcanic shaft, like the gray wall out there. " Owen stepped from the pool and sat down again. For several minutes he did nothing but rub the circulation back into his frozen feet. He put on his socks and moccasins and Yazzie extended a hand to help him up.

"What does it mean?" Yazzie said.

"For the ruins?"

"Aoo'."

Owen paused. "Geologists with more training and experience might differ in the particulars, but I think they'd agree that one way or another, this whole thing"—Owen threw his arms wide—"the overhang, the alcove, all of it, is going to let go someday. Eventually, something is going to shift—maybe because of a minor earthquake deep under us, one that, up here, won't feel like more than a train rumbling through a tunnel—and there won't be enough adhesion where the basalt and sandstone or the sandstone and the underlying shale meet, and this will give way, although probably not all at once. In sections."

"When?"

"No one can say. Maybe tomorrow, maybe a hundred years from now, maybe longer."

They both turned toward the sunlight, which was now reaching only the outermost area of the alcove. Beyond, a curtain of yellow, the aspens, draped the far side of the canyon.

"I thought this might all disappear someday," Yazzie said. "I thought the water would keep coming, more and more, and"—he swept the back of his hand through the air in front of them.

"Not in quite the way you thought. You see where the aspens are growing across the canyon? Something like what I've been talking about may already have happened over there."

Yazzie sighed and looked upward, to the top of the alcove, far above them. "How long has this been here?"

"The alcove? Like this? This big?" Owen shook his head. "I couldn't say."

"So it took many years to form."

"Many many. Sometimes the numbers get so big that they don't mean anything anymore. It's hard for people to keep track of more than a few generations—parents and grandparents and great-grandparents—which is less than the blink of an eye on the geological scale." He stroked his chin. "But you shouldn't take everything I just said as gospel. I can't even say for sure why this is here—I mean, an alcove of this size. I know there are hundreds of alcoves throughout the Chuskas, but they're small, at lower elevations. You know these mountains better than I do—is there anything else like this one?"

"Nowhere," Yazzie said. "What about the trees?" He nodded toward the aspens.

"What about them?"

"How old are they?"

"Not very. Aspens live a hundred, maybe two hundred years at most. But that doesn't mean aspens haven't grown here for much longer. When conditions are right, they hold on, and they take advantage of fires and landslides and such—things that disrupt the soil and that other kinds of trees can't survive."

Yazzie unbuttoned his coat and reached inside, slipping his rough hand into a large interior pocket that had been sewn to the lining. He pulled out a book and handed it to Owen. There was a pencil tucked between the binding and the leather spine.

Owen recognized his field book, the newest one.

"I took it when you went to leave your letter."

That morning, just before they left, Owen had gone to Julia's with a note about his and Yazzie's "adventure," just in case she returned to Many Springs Canyon early.

Now Yazzie said, "We need to leave here at dusk. You have until then. And from dawn until midafternoon tomorrow. After that, we go. So write your words and do your drawings."

Owen took the field book from Yazzie but he didn't open it. "Is that why I'm here?"

Yazzie walked away, calling back over his shoulder, "I'm going to finish making camp. I'll be back for you."

"Why don't we make camp here? It would save time."

"No."

Owen could tell that this was not open to discussion. He followed Yazzie, reemerging into the pale afternoon light and retracing their steps to the first plaza. Yazzie checked to be sure the coiled rope was still tied tightly to the pine beam. "Remember. Disturb nothing."

"You don't like being here, do you?" Owen asked.

Yazzie, not bothering with the carved foot-holds, was preparing to rappel down the cliff face. "No," he said, and then he was over the edge, descending rapidly to the canyon floor.

"I don't think men from my father's clan have been coming for as long as they say," Yazzie told him that night beside their campfire, under the articulated brilliance of the stars. "I don't know how long ago they began looking, but I think they found this place after the Long Walk began, when most of the People were gone or in hiding."

They assumed, Yazzie went on, that what they were seeking was most likely located to the east. Navajos knew every inch of Canyon de Chelly and all the tributary canyons—Del Muerto, Black Rock, Monument—and the land around all the many creeks and washes that fed into the canyons, so the ruins couldn't be there. That made the Chuskas the next best choice. And they had another clue to guide their search: their name, the Shaking Aspen Clan. Aspens weren't that widespread in the Southwest. They could be found beyond the north rim of the Grand Canyon, north of Mesa Verde in Colorado, above Santa Fe in New Mexico, and to the south, in the Apache forests. And also in the Chuskas—but scattered, not everywhere.

Owen looked toward the canyon's rim. In the near-darkness, the aspens crowned the rim with a silvery iridescence. The leaves shimmered and whispered in the slightest breeze.

"The ruins had already been found by the time my father and mother met," Yazzie said. "They only met because of that." His mother, her parents, and a younger sister had returned from Hwéeldi to Many Springs Canyon in the summer of 1868, but not early enough to plant crops, and then the government failed to deliver the promised sheep and goats and cattle to help the Navajos get through the winter. So in the late autumn his mother's family moved to what was now called Crystal, to be near their clan relatives. Crystal was also closer to Fort Defiance, one of the two places to pick up winter rations.

In the middle of February 1869, Yazzie told Owen, his father, one of his uncles, and several companions were discovered near Washington Pass by a large party of Navajos who were hunting a mountain lion that had killed a number of their sheep. The Hopis claimed that they were on their way home from Farmington, where they'd met with government officials from Washington about being granted a reservation of their own, now that the Diné had returned. No one believed their explanation. Fortunately for the Hopis, the hunting party included a shrewd old man, Yazzie's great-grandfather, Hosteen Naalnish, who convinced the more belligerent Navajos that killing the Hopis would stir up unwanted trouble. Instead, he proposed, they should teach the Hopis a lesson by taking their horses and weapons. Wisely, the Hopis didn't argue. Naalnish told them that he would provide shelter for the night, and in the morning he and his sons would take them to Fort Defiance.

"Who told you about all this?" Owen asked. "Your uncles or your mother?"

"My mother a bit," Yazzie said, "my uncles the full truth, much later."

At Naalnish's compound Yazzie's mother helped pass out food, but the youngest Hopi refused it. He was taller than the others, with a square jaw, broad nose, and wispy mustache. She was startled when he whispered to her in her own tongue that she should tell her brothers that they had better take proper care of his horse, a paint, because he planned to return for it. Yazzie's mother looked him straight in the eye and said that she didn't have any brothers and that he would be crazy to come back just for a worthless horse.

In the spring her family returned to Many Springs Canyon. She was herding sheep when he appeared. He'd been watching her for two days, waiting until she was alone. She asked him if he'd gotten his horse back. He'd made a trade, he told her: he agreed not to kill the Navajo who'd been given the paint, and to let him keep the horse, if the man revealed where she could be found. Yazzie's father sneaked back again in August, and this time she ran off with him to the Hopi mesas.

"Did your mother ever say why?" Owen asked. "I mean, it must have been such a defiant thing to do."

"It was. But the Long Walk had changed everything. She was very young when she left for Hwéeldi but much older when she came back."

"Like Tóya, I imagine."

"They met there. My mother was younger and not as able, but they became friends. She told me many times how Tóya would give her extra food when she could. When the 1868 treaty was signed, everyone returned home expecting that everything would change for the better. In my mother's eyes, it didn't. She still saw illness and hunger and bad times. She watched old Naalnish die late that first winter. She saw her father beat her mother once when they ran out of corn. She thought she was going to be married off to someone she didn't like, even though that wasn't the Navajo way. So she saw a chance and left."

"Do you remember living on Second Mesa?"

"No, I was too young."

"Did you see much of your father after that?"

"He came to Many Springs Canyon a few times after my grandparents were gone, but he never stayed for long. Even so, my mother's younger sister accused him of trying to make her his second wife. She went back to Crystal, where she soon found a husband, and my father stopped coming around."

Owen saw no point in asking about Johanna's father, another man who had disappeared. "It must have been a very tough life for you and your mother."

"The Old Man helped us as much as he could."

"Ah. Tim Be'ak'idii."

"Aoo'."

"Was he the one who showed you these ruins?"

"No."

"But he knew about them?"

"He did, but he didn't come up here."

"Why was that?"

Yazzie shrugged. "He had no reason to."

"I assume your mother also knew."

"Aoo'."

"But didn't tell you?"

"No. My uncles—my father's brothers—told me."

"When was this?" Owen asked.

"For a time I was staying with them on Second Mesa. There were things they wanted me to know, and with more and more Navajos around, they wanted to be able to say they were visiting a relative if anyone saw them coming or going."

"I suppose that makes sense, but there had to be more to it than that."

Yazzie fell silent. Owen watched a rock squirrel, disturbed from his routine by their presence, hesitantly cross the campsite and disappear in the brush beyond.

"My uncles asked me to keep others away from here," Yazzie said.

"How were you supposed to do that?"

Yazzie stirred the coals and added several pieces of broken limb to the fire. "How much do you want to hear?"

"In for a dime, in for a dollar."

"Hunh. I can guess what that means."

"You're my friend, Yazzie. I won't betray your confidence."

"If that was a worry, we wouldn't be here."

Owen, acknowledging Yazzie's trust, nodded and waited for him to continue.

"Not long before the time I spent with my uncles," Yazzie said, "I had to go to Gallup. While I was gone a man I knew came to Many Springs Canyon. After, I thought that if I found him, I could force him to go before his headmen. Then they could decide what should be done. That was what I thought." Yazzie nodded, more to himself than to Owen.

"What did the man do?"

Yazzie thought a long time before answering: "He hurt a child."

No no, Owen thought, no no. He pressed his forehead into his drawn-up knees.

"He was a bad drinker and a troublemaker," Yazzie went on. "I knew his family lived near Navajo Mountain, and that's where I found him. He drew me into a knife fight. I was no match for him. Before long I was bleeding hard, but I saw in his eyes that it wasn't going to be enough. I had a gun and I used it."

Owen didn't say anything at first. "Some would say he got what he deserved."

"Maybe," Yazzie said. "I should have gone to the headmen first, but I was young, nineteen. After that, while I was at Second Mesa, I even thought about going away, starting over the way my father did, but I couldn't leave my mother and Sister."

"Why were you at Second Mesa?"

"I was in a bad way when I left Navajo Mountain. The knife wound wouldn't heal right. My uncles came and got me."

"The headmen just let you leave?"

"They were rewarded."

"By your uncles?"

"Yes. Then the Katsi family took me in and cared for me. I was there all summer, and I met my wife during a visit to Moenkopi. My uncles often went there to trade."

Owen turned his eyes to where the ruins lay partially hidden in the night. "Why would your ancestors choose to live up here? For that matter, why would anybody? It's so isolated."

"They say the canyon didn't always look like this. The ancestors cleared the land down below and farmed, and the hunting was good. And they were sheltered from the worst of the winter and could defend themselves."

"Defend themselves from whom? There weren't any Navajos or Utes here that long ago."

"So you say."

This was not an argument Owen cared to have, so he let it drop.

"There were other reasons," Yazzie went on. "My uncles say their ancestors broke many rules and were shunned for generations, but in the end the Holy Ones showed them the error of their ways and gave them the clan name Shaking Aspen, to remind them that they had grown strong in the harshest soil and were nurtured by common roots from which new trees emerged, even while the leaves of the oldest gave up their golden beauty and fell for the last time. More generations passed, and the clan began trading with other clans again and marrying with them, and finally all the clans came together as Hopis. After many more generations, the location of this place was forgotten."

This all fit within what Owen knew of the Hopi origin story: Long ago, the Hopis ascended into this, their Fourth World, from a place of emergence in the Grand Canyon. They then split up and went off in various directions on a great migration. Gradually, clans formed and most were eventually drawn to the three mesas where the tribe was still living.

"So you agreed to protect these ruins—to keep others away."

"I owed my uncles something. They healed me and made me part of their family. Some Navajos were already suspicious of me because my father was a Hopi. When I came home, I put the right words in the right ears about what had happened at Navajo Mountain. Most people enjoy hearing a good story, but even more, they enjoy spreading rumors."

"So you became a dangerous man."

"I made it known that people needed to stay away from here and keep their mouths shut."

"Or else."

"Or else."

"Have you ever had to back up the warning?"

"There was a man from Tuye Springs who sold some pottery to a trader up in Shiprock. He didn't even try to hide where he was digging around."

"What did you do?"

"I killed one of his goats and hung the carcass from a tree outside his hogan when his family was asleep."

"And he knew you were the one who did it?"

"He knew. I broke one of the pots he stole and left the pieces under the goat so that they were covered in blood when he came out in the morning."

"I assume he didn't try to sell any more pottery."

"No." Yazzie paused and looked away. "I visited a few other hogans over the years, just to remind people. And the Old Man came up here every so often. He was my eyes and ears. He knew what signs to look for."

"Still," Owen said, "to keep this place secret for so long . . ."

"But not for much longer," Yazzie said.

"No, I wouldn't think so," Owen said.

"Chee Dodge knows," Yazzie said.

Chee Dodge. The man who'd sought Yazzie out on the night of Halley's Comet.

"Does he know that your uncles and other Hopis come here?"

"He knows."

"Has he been here himself?"

"Last August. He wanted to meet with the clan leaders."

"That must have been quite a conversation."

Yazzie lifted a shoulder and let it drop again. "He told them that if they wanted to keep coming here, they had to have Navajos escort them from the time they crossed onto Navajo land until they left."

"Or else—?"

"Or else he'd see that the Indian Agency heard about this place and before long Anglos would be crawling all over the ruins. The elders told him they needed to talk about it with the rest of the clan."

"What came of that?"

"Nothing yet."

"If other Navajos start escorting Hopis, word will spread."

"I know," Yazzie said.

The snapping of wood in the fire punctuated their silence. Owen lay down on his back, his head propped on a rolled blanket. He knew his legs and back would be painfully stiff in the morning, and he didn't relish the thought of putting his buttocks to the test on the back of the brown for the trip home.

"This is what I think," Yazzie said. "It won't be long now before someone needing a few dollars leads an Anglo up here." He paused, swirling the last of the coffee in his cup. "And then the government and the people who study the Anasazi will come." He took the last swallow. "For nearly twenty years I did my best for my father's people, but this is how it will be. There's nothing I can do about it."

Owen recalled his first sight of Cliff Palace at Mesa Verde, with the crew of Anglos hard at work, taking possession, ownership, with their shovels and wheelbarrows and cement. "What do you think your uncles' clan will do?"

"I don't know," Yazzie said. Then he added, "Maybe they don't need the ruins any longer. They have the story of the ruins, and maybe that's enough."

"Yazzie, my friend," Owen said, "you brought me up here to measure and sketch and write down what I see. But what do you expect me to do then?"

Yazzie put down his empty coffee cup and stood up. "You decide."

Owen watched Yazzie going about his business: scouring with sand the frying pan in which he had cooked their dinner, filling the coffee pot with a fresh handful of grounds for the morning, moving several pieces of dry wood next to his bedroll so that he could easily toss them onto the coals during the night.

It came to Owen then that Yazzie, having done all he could for his uncles, was committing the preservation of the ruins to someone else. To him. Soon enough, they'd be pillaged by greed or by science or both. Before that happened, he wanted Owen to save them, untouched.

Owen wondered if Yazzie had ever considered bringing Pete Pietrowski and his cameras up here. Probably, but Pete couldn't always be trusted to control what came out of his mouth. And that was the other thing that Clement Yazzie wanted: silence, at least until the day when someone else brought another Anglo up here. (Or until a myth-like aeroplane flew overhead and the pilot chanced to look down at just the right moment.)

"Suppose I decide to write up an account and submit it to a newspaper or an archaeological society back East?" Owen asked. Doing so would put him in the history books; maybe just as a footnote, but his name would be there.

"It's your decision."

"You wouldn't try to stop me?"

"No."

"I suppose I could just go ahead and lie—tell you that I won't tell a soul about this place."

"And would that be what you call a 'white lie'?" Yazzie said, wrapping himself in his blanket and lying down.

"No. This matters. A white lie is a lie that someone tells for convenience when he thinks that what he says *doesn't* matter."

"Then there are no white lies—there are just lies. If the lie doesn't matter, then the truth doesn't matter."

Owen watched as Yazzie turned his back to the fire. If your back stayed warm, then all of you would stay warm. Warm enough to sleep, at least.

"What will Julia say when she finds out that you brought me up here?" Owen asked.

"As you Anglos say, she'll give me hell."

Owen chuckled. "That she will." He hadn't realized until he lay down how tired he was, how much the day had taken out of him. He felt molded to the earth beneath him. He looked up at the night sky, the myriad. He made no effort to locate any constellations, to give order to the scattering.

No virgin, scales of justice, ram, archer, goat. Just a vast expanse. It occurred to him to ask, "You must have a Hopi name."

A moment passed before Yazzie answered, "Aponivi. Where the Wind Blows Down through the Gap."

"Ah," Owen said. "It's a good name."

Yazzie shook his shoulder, and Owen was startled into consciousness. Whatever he'd been dreaming was instantly lost.

"We need to start back," Yazzie said.

"What's wrong?"

"A storm."

"Where?" Owen sat up too quickly. His head spun. He braced his palms against the frosted ground and closed his eyes again to collect himself.

"It's coming."

He opened his eyes again. At first he thought he was surrounded by predawn dimness, but then he realized that a heavy layer of clouds had moved in during the night. Yazzie knelt by the nearly extinguished coals of the previous night's fire, rolling up his sleeping bundle.

"You said I'd have most of the day." Owen wiped a hand across his eyes and forehead. His body was beginning to wake up, and it didn't like the feel of the morning. His feet felt locked to his ankles, so tightly connected that he couldn't twist or stretch them. His knees and hips ached.

"We can come back in the spring." Yazzie was on his feet now.

"And what do you think the odds are that I'll still be around?" It was an unfair question, and Owen immediately regretted it. Yazzie didn't even look in his direction. "Even if I am, I probably won't be in any condition to come back."

"We have to make it down at least to Blue Hawk Lake before the weather sets in."

"It feels warmer. It might be just rain."

"No." The wind was beginning to pick up. "A storm this time of year can drop two feet of snow in half a day. Remember last year, down below? Now get up."

"No."

Yazzie stopped what he was doing and looked at Owen.

"You're forgetting something. Our footprints are all over the ruins, including deep in the alcove, around the seep."

Yazzie took in the ruins and the clouds with a single glance. "The weather will break again before the real winter. I'll come back and take care of it."

Now Owen stood up. He tried not to wince from the tightness that extended the full length of his body. But what had been so jumbled in his brain moments ago now seemed eminently clear. "We need to move the campsite into the ruins."

Yazzie shook his head. "No one has stayed in those ruins since my uncles' clan left them long ago."

"Then we might as well be the first. At least we'll be respectful."

"The storm—"

"To hell with the storm. If we camp near the seep, we can easily ride it out. I know we have enough food—I can get by on next to nothing, I'm used to it. That way I can do what you brought me up here to do. I'll make as good a record of the site as I can—not good enough for an archaeologist, but good enough for your purposes. And when I'm done writing it all up, I'll leave my field book and the narrative in Julia's hands to keep until you see fit. And I won't speak of this to anyone else. But I need at least today and tomorrow to do it properly, without disturbing anything. And then we'll go home."

Yazzie was studying the clouds. Those overhead were a deep gray, but the ones to the west, mounting from the horizon, were almost black.

"You don't have to stay with me," Owen said. "I can do what I need to do by myself."

"Hunh."

"Yazzie, for the last year I've been stumbling around, waiting for something." He could see in Yazzie's expression that he understood. They both also knew that, short of hog-tying him and throwing him across a horse, Yazzie had no recourse.

"You can't make the climb," Yazzie said.

"I can. I know how to do it now. It isn't that hard." A white lie or a lie? Owen pushed the thought away. "Going up is the easy part."

"Carrying enough wood to keep a fire?"

"I'm not an idiot. I can gather wood, tie it in a bundle, and pull it up with your rope, which I can also use to come down safely on my own."

"So you have all the answers."

"I don't have *any* of the answers. I'm making them up as I go."

Yazzie shook his head. "This is another mistake."

"Maybe, maybe not."

Yazzie, looking into the canyon below the ruins, muttered something in Navajo. "I'll need to build a lean-to for the horses down below, up against the rock face. You go on ahead. Take my horse. I have to cut pinyon boughs to bring down for the lean-to, for covering the saplings."

"Wouldn't it be faster if you used the horse?"

"I need to get the mare down, too. She can take the first load. Then I'll use the brown."

All right then, Owen said to himself. Two days in the ruins. He felt exhilarated. He threw the saddle blanket over the brown and lifted the saddle. It took all his strength to swing it up and over the horse's back to the withers. He straightened out the blanket, which had gone crooked, and tightened the cinch. The brown didn't want to cooperate, but he was still hobbled and Owen managed to work the bit into his mouth and buckle the bridle straps. He draped the reins over the mane, removed the hobble, and mounted on his own, ignoring his weary muscles. Yazzie, brandishing a small hatchet, was already working on a nearby pinyon.

Two days in the ruins. He needed every minute he could get. He gave the brown a kick. The horse whinnied and stepped sideways. Owen tightened the reins and tried again. The horse backed up erratically but then stopped when Owen loosened the reins. "Let's go," he said in his calmest voice. He squeezed with his knees, and the brown walked forward.

Several minutes later, horse and rider reached the path down the southern slope, but this time when they came to the most treacherous part Owen didn't stop and dismount, as he had done the previous day at Yazzie's insistence. The slope wasn't *that* steep. He leaned back in the saddle as the brown tested the way, and they were almost down when the horse began to slide on the treacherously loose stones and lost his footing. Owen, still leaning backwards, was off balance and when the saddle began to shift, the brown, already panicked, turned into the upslope. His hind legs couldn't find any traction. Owen, fearing he'd be trapped under the horse if it fell, slipped his feet from the stirrups. He kept his hands on the reins, which helped break his own fall, but he still came down hard on a rotting stump, hitting just below his left ribs. He came to rest on his back, with his head pointing down the slope.

The fall had knocked the breath out of him, and his diaphragm wouldn't work. His vision was retreating, slipping toward darkness, from the periphery inward, and he fought hard to find something he could hold in focus, grasp. A moccasin. One of his moccasins had come off, and he could see it, several yards away, and he seized on it with his eyes and wouldn't let go.

He lay there for several minutes, and gradually his breathing steadied and his vision returned, but with it came the first full surge of pain. He shook it off. He could move everything: neck, arms, fingers, legs, toes, but he couldn't sit up. Not from this position. He rolled to his right side. Stretching the muscles in his left side was excruciating. He saw the brown at the bottom of the slope, bug-eyed, watching him. Owen shifted his knees toward his chest and, thrusting both hands hard against the ground, managed to slide his body perpendicular to the slope. From there, it was easier. He let his hips and legs descend farther and then, using his arms, he slowly rose into a kneeling position and sat back on his haunches.

He unbuttoned his coat, pulled it to the side, and with his right hand yanked his flannel shirt from his pants. Blood was seeping through his undergarment. He undid a few buttons, slipped his hand inside, and ran his fingers lightly along his rib cage. Nothing felt broken. Maybe he'd been lucky. He unfastened more buttons and looked down. The skin below his ribs, although badly abraded and weeping, had apparently been protected by the multiple layers of cloth. But already a purple and blue stain was spreading under the skin, and when his forefinger encountered a wall of solid pain he didn't probe any deeper. He needed to get up, but he couldn't. The slope was too steep and he didn't want to risk losing his balance and falling, causing more injury. So he began using his hands and knees to slide himself backward, down to the bottom, grabbing his moccasin on the way. When he reached level ground, he crawled to a nearby boulder and, with his arms and shoulders as much as his legs, rose, hunched over. He slowly straightened up.

He should wait here for Yazzie, he knew, but he needed to get into the ruins. The horse was standing beside the stream. Could he mount? Maybe if he did it from the wrong side, if the brown would stand still for it. That way, he could use his right leg and side muscles to lift himself toward the saddle. He collected the horse's reins, loosened the cinch, straightened the saddle, rebuckled the cinch. But when he tried to walk it back to the boulder, the horse wouldn't move. Owen looked down. A pool of blood had formed under a front leg. Owen's stomach sank. He couldn't bend without igniting the sharp pain in his side, but he didn't have to look closely to see that the brown's hoof was split. He knew he needed Yazzie. Two injured horses, one injured man. But only one thing mattered. He dropped the reins and moved forward, heading upstream.

It was all a matter of putting one foot in front of the other. He counted each step, then started again each time he reached one hundred. He didn't keep track of the hundreds or of anything else, not time nor the distance. But then he was there, at the base of the cliff. His breathing came hard now. He could see the carved steps. He'd made it up once. He could do it again. He needed to forget about the pain. He needed to do it now, before Yazzie arrived. His union suit was soaked with sweat and a patch of blood and he was shivering, but he put his left foot into the first notch. If he turned his foot slightly sideways, there was room for the ball of his foot as well as his toes. He pushed off—the pain knifed through him—and stretched with his right arm to the first hand-hold. He was almost two feet up the wall. He brought his right leg up, searching for the next carved step. He found it.

He propelled himself upward, reaching for another hand-hold, which he found, but he immediately had to flatten his chest against the stone and catch his breath until the pain beneath his ribs subsided. The sweat was running off his brow and into his eyes. Something stung his forehead. Sleet. Where was his hat? Gone.

Four feet up the wall. And again. When he reached the coyote pelt and its hidden message, he yanked it from the hole and threw it aside.

Carrying both their saddlebags over one shoulder and leading the mare, which was laden with the rest of their gear and a stack of bundled pinyon branches, Yazzie saw where the brown had lost its footing and gone down, and the pieces of rotted wood beside the splintered stump, and then he saw the horse and Owen's hat at the bottom of the slope, and the field book, and he guessed what had happened. He dropped the mare's reins and ran down the slope, maintaining his balance despite the loose scree and the falling sleet. He picked up the field book. "Owen Rouse!" he called, but he heard no reply. He couldn't ignore the brown, standing stiff and still. He took one look and knew that even if the leg wasn't fractured at the pastern, and he suspected that it was, the hoof was so damaged that the brown couldn't be saved. He returned to the mare and led it down, and then he pulled his carbine from the scabbard. He chambered a round and pulled the trigger without further thought, and the brown dropped instantly. Yazzie waited for the echo from the shot, and then he smashed the gun on a boulder—a stupid thing to do, he knew immediately. "Owen Rouse!" he called again. Then he began running and kept running, the mare trailing behind, around the curve of the canyon's hook, all the way to the cliff face below the ruins.

"Owen! Owen Rouse!" he called out.

He couldn't see him but he heard Owen answer from up in the ruins, "Here."

"Are you all right?"

Owen's head appeared above the low adobe wall at the edge of the plaza. Even at this distance and despite the sleet, Yazzie could see that Owen's face was contorted.

"There's medicine in my saddlebag. A brown vial." His head disappeared behind the wall, and he said nothing more.

The pellets of sleet slid off Yazzie's hat brim. The ice was already stripping the yellow leaves from the aspens; by evening the trees would be bare. He moved to the wall, dropped his own saddlebag to the ground, anchored a boot in the first foot-hold, and began to climb. He needed to get

Owen under the overhang. The sleet was growing in intensity, bouncing off the rock wall.

He couldn't bring an injured man down from the ruins in a sleet storm. Besides, there was no place they could get to now. He reached the top of the rock wall and peered over while slinging Owen's saddlebag to the plaza floor. Owen lay on his back ten yards away. His breathing was rapid and shallow. His head jerked from side to side as he tried to keep the sleet from his glazed eyes.

Yazzie knew they would be here for the duration.

Owen turned his head and watched Clement Yazzie poke the new fire with a stick, spraying small embers into the night air. It was dark now. "What time is it?" he mumbled.

Yazzie looked up. "Late." He moved something around in the iron skillet. It smelled like slices of fatback. They sizzled and smoked when they touched the pan's crusted, black sides. Owen lay on his back, wool blankets beneath and around him. If he took short breaths—each breath took shape, a delicate white plume—maybe he could wall in the pain for a while, keep it *there.* He didn't want more morphine. Not yet. He wanted his thinking to clear.

Julia had slipped the brown vial into his hand just before she left for Gallup. Owen had to stop and think: two days ago. "Remember, no more than five drops," she'd said, "if you start to feel chest pains." (It had only happened once, ten days ago.) And then she'd wrapped him in her arms. Strands of hair had escaped the golden pins and lay against her temple. He had turned his face and brushed her cheek with his lips.

Blood was leaking somewhere deep in his gut, filling up his left side, below the bottom rib; when he moved, it felt like a carving knife was sliding through his middle toward his spine.

He remembered how the first dose, five bitter drops in half a cup of water, had covered the pain, warming him like the blanket Yazzie wrapped around him, like the fire that Yazzie lit for him near a T-shaped doorway in the outside wall of an inner room, away from the ice storm. As his breathing settled, he had watched the wind-driven granules of sleet hit and rebound and gradually cover what he could see of the plaza . . .

He woke the first time because he was cold again, his arms and legs shaking so hard that they bounced off the dirt floor. Yazzie built up the fire and covered him in another blanket, Yazzie's own. Five more drops and then it all came back to him, the night of the Yeibichei. How he sat at the edge of the light from the bonfires, struggling for breath, trying to make his lungs work, time pressing on his chest, heavier and heavier, and how he could hear the masked yei chanting in their falsetto voices, beginning their dance. Maybe the nearby Navajos thought he was praying, sitting there silently, his head bowed. Maybe he was. Praying. To Julia, praying: *Please come back to me now, you're all I have. Come back.* And she had. And then the only thing he wanted was for her to let him lie in her arms as recompense for all the other intimacies that they would never share . . .

He woke the second time—was it the second?—to a red cleft of pain tearing open the flesh beneath his ribcage. "Yazzie," he said. His voice was so weak he needed to repeat himself. "Yazzie." Five drops and he waited, waited until the pain abated. But the ceiling of the alcove was cracking. "Yazzie," he said, "get me out! The tunnel's collapsing," and Yazzie lifted him and carried him out to the inner edge of the plaza and laid him down and swept away the ice that had drifted in . . .

He knew there was something he had to do, but it had slipped into the haze . . .

Yazzie turned the slabs of meat in the pan with his stick.

He would like an orange. He would slice it in half and, with a sharp paring knife, cut away a ring of peel, halfway down, exposing the fruit, and then sprinkle brown sugar and cinnamon on top, the way his mother had done at Christmas when he was a child, and he would sink his front teeth into first one half and then the other, suck in the juice, the grainy sugar and powdery cinnamon dissolving on his tongue.

Owen ran the fingers of his left hand through the reddish sand, its texture as fine as silt. Directly above: the highest arc of the sandstone alcove and the abrupt line where it gave way to night sky. If he closed his right eye, he saw the arc; if he closed his left eye, he saw the blackness, now studded with stars; the ice storm had passed, taking with it the clouds.

He turned his face back to the fire. He could feel it on his forehead and nose and cheeks and lips and chin.

The smell of the fatback suddenly made him nauseous.

"I don't think I'll eat now," Owen told Yazzie, his words still blurred by the lingering morphine, "but you go ahead." He fell back to sleep.

He didn't think he'd slept long this time. He could still smell the meat Yazzie had cooked. Yazzie was now sitting beside him, asleep, his arms folded inside his coat, his sleeves hanging loose, his hat pulled low, down to his eyebrows, his legs stretched toward the fire. Owen knew there was something he needed to do, but first he had a more urgent request. He said, "I have to empty my bladder."

Yazzie was instantly awake. He rose and, from behind, wrapped his arms under Owen's, trying to help him stand, but Owen couldn't bring his legs under control and the pain beneath his ribs, spreading upward, made him cry out. As gently as he could, Yazzie laid him back down on his right side, facing the fire. Yazzie moved into the shadows, and Owen heard a snap and then a crackling. Yazzie returned with something in his hand: he'd stripped a loose curve of bark from a piece of firewood. Now he kneeled down and positioned one end of the curved bark against Owen's right hip.

With his left hand Owen fumbled at the buttons of his pants. Yazzie walked away. Owen fumbled a bit more but then was able to release his urine into the bark trough. It didn't hurt to piss, but the thin stream looked dark—as black as red looks in the night—as it spread into the sand. When Owen was done Yazzie kicked sand over the wet and then helped Owen turn onto his back. "That's better," Owen said. "I feel better. I'm sorry."

Yazzie, a horse blanket draped over his shoulders, sat down beside him again.

"I know what's happening," Owen said. He had to catch his breath.

"I know you do," Yazzie said.

"Jesus, I'm scared." Owen was gulping air and he fought to control the shaking that overtook him.

After a while Yazzie said, "There's no shame."

They kept their silence for a long time after that, except for Owen's labored breathing. The night encased them in its wintry stillness.

"I remember now," Owen said. "I need to write something." He knew he would have to hurry because the pain was mounting again.

Yazzie said, "I found your field book, but I don't have a pencil."

"There should be one in my coat pocket." He freed an arm from the wrapped blankets and searched. "Here it is," he said, but then he cursed. "The point broke."

"Give it to me," Yazzie said. He shaved the end down with a knife. When he was done, he returned it to Owen.

"I need to sit up."

Yazzie lifted Owen's shoulders and back, pausing at intervals in an effort to avoid greater pain. Owen grunted but said nothing until he was upright. "I don't think I can . . ."

Yazzie slid behind Owen and sat down, positioning his shoulder blades against Owen's, and they sat like that, back-to-back, while Owen wrote very slowly, deliberately. When he was done, he carefully tore two pages from the field book, folded them, and placed them inside the front cover.

"You can read what I wrote," he said, passing the field book to Yazzie.

"I'll wait. Maybe you'll change your mind."

They continued to sit back-to-back until Owen, tipping to his side, cried out, "Yazzie, Yazzie!"

Yazzie eased Owen back down. He picked up the nearby vial of medicine and the cup of water. Owen shuddered with each breath. Yazzie dumped out all but a mouthful of water from the cup. He counted to five but before he could stopper the bottle, Owen reached out and grabbed his wrist. Yazzie looked into his eyes, and he let Owen take the vial from his hand.

Before long Owen's breathing eased and he asked, "Did you have to put the brown down?"

"Aoo'."

"I'm sorry, so very sorry." He felt the tears coming.

"It doesn't matter," Yazzie said. "There are many other horses."

"And Julia's mare?"

"Safe."

"Tell her it's a good horse."

"You can tell her yourself."

"A year and a half," beginning to slur his words now, his head lolling. "But I came to terms. I did. And then I go and fall off a horse. Can you explain that?"

"No," Yazzie said, sitting elbow to elbow with him now.

"I stole a year of Julia's life. I never meant to."

"She doesn't see it that way."

"Ah. Well. That's who she is." After a while Owen said, "I'd like a little apple cider. Isn't that funny?"

Yazzie supported Owen's head and gave him water from his canteen.

"Sweet. Try it."

Yazzie took a sip. "Good."

"Where are we? I'm a little confused," his words slipping into a soft laugh.

"Where my father's ancestors once lived. The Place in the Mountains That the Aspens Watch Over."

Owen could feel the wheels turning beneath him in time to the pulse of his blood, and the swaying, and he could see the plume rising as each breath materialized an inch from his lips. Far above, the stars, their silver-white rays. And at the horizon, a shimmering glow, a gossamer veil.

"Julia," he tried to tell her.

"You'll be home soon," a voice said.

Owen felt deep joy and at the same time an unbearable sadness, bound together. His breath slowly stilled and gravity lost its hold on his legs and arms and then even his small frame, and his only sure contact with the earth was someone's hand on his shoulder and he no longer knew if he were dreaming or thinking out loud:

Oh, Julia!—the never-ending night—your lovely light—and I—am a westbound train—

PART IV: LETTING GO

This is the Hour of Lead—
Remembered, if outlived,
As Freezing persons, recollect the Snow—
First—Chill—then Stupor—then the letting go—

—Emily Dickinson

These also are the lessons of our New World;
While how little the New after all, how much the Old, Old World!

Long and long has the grass been growing,
Long and long has the rain been falling,
Long has the globe been rolling round.

—Walt Whitman

CHAPTER TWENTY-THREE: The Hour of Lead

She was in the kitchen preparing a simple evening meal for herself when Clement Yazzie returned without him. She heard a horse whinny, which sent her to the window and then the door. The snow, falling steadily since midmorning, after the previous day's ice, covered the veranda except where Julia had swept it aside. There were two riders, three horses—Clement had her pinto mare on a lead, which didn't seem that odd. Then she realized that the second rider was Johanna, not Owen. Julia recoiled, stumbling back and grabbing the door handle. The riders stopped at the corral and dismounted; Johanna handed her reins to her brother and then crossed the yard to the veranda. She remained standing by the bottom step, clutching a dark woolen blanket she wore over her head and shoulders.

"*Yah anínááh,*" Julia said, pushing the door back farther. Johanna entered and then Julia closed the door and walked to the sink, where she'd been cleaning potatoes. She lifted her paring knife and began skinning them, dropping the brown peelings into the sink.

Clement would take care of the horses and then go to the guest hogan. When she was anticipating his winter return from the ruins, she always lit a fire in the stove and placed a large kettle of water on top. Even now, he would only come to her home after he'd thoroughly washed and changed his clothes.

Johanna had come up behind her. The younger woman reached out and took the paring knife and a half-peeled potato from Julia's hands, which were shaking. Julia wiped her hands on her apron and went and sat down at the table to wait for Clement.

At her insistence, the Gormans had left early, before the snow began falling in earnest; Navajos could read the weather, and there would be few customers. Despite her gathering anxiety about Clement and Owen's return, she'd spent most of the afternoon leafing through the Chicago newspapers from early in the month. Her mind kept drifting. Through the details of Helen Taft's debutante ball at the White House. The details of the funeral arrangements for Mary Baker Eddy, dead at 89. The details of the world's first multiple aerial fatality and, less than a week later, the first ascent above 10,000 feet by Frenchman Georges Legagneux: death and glory above the earth.

Late in the afternoon a young Navajo man had come by. She'd never seen him before. He wanted to pawn a squash-blossom necklace in return for food and a blanket for his daughter, who had a bad cough. The silver-work in the necklace was sloppy, the turquoise ill-matched and ill-fitting. This was not a winning proposition, Julia knew. She doubted the man would ever reclaim the necklace, and as dead pawn it would be worthless unless someone wanted to remove the stones and melt the silver down. But she recognized the silent desperation in the man's eyes.

"I can give you the value of the silver. Let me weigh it." Julia lifted her scales and small box of weights, each shaped like a miniature milk can, from beneath the counter. When the scales balanced, she subtracted a quarter of the weight for the turquoise and then calculated the worth of the silver. The man agreed to the sum, and Julia began making out the pawn ticket.

"If you don't return for your necklace within six months, it will become dead pawn, and I'm free to sell it to anyone who will meet my asking price." Julia was sure that this wasn't the first time the Navajo had pawned something, but she always made sure her terms were understood, even to repeat customers. They completed the transaction, and the man turned and left the store with rice, sugar, canned beans and peaches, as well as a woolen blanket. Julia followed him to the door. A woman on a sway-backed, saddle-less horse, holding a child in her arms, was waiting. The man handed the parcels up to her. She rearranged the sleeping child, lifting her to one side, and put the provisions in a sack across the horse's withers. It was already getting dark and Julia spoke again to the man:

"Where are you headed?"

"Dzilk'ihózhónii," he told her. Beautiful Mountain.

"That's a long way, especially in the snow. You can stay here." She nodded toward the hogan. "There's already a fire in the stove. You surely don't want to spend the night on the road."

The man said they had best be going.

"Wait," she said. She went into the store and returned with another blanket. "For your wife." He thanked her and then they left, the man walking at the side of the horse.

Julia pushed back her chair from the table and rose. She crossed to the larder, where she selected two more dirt-covered potatoes and an onion from a hanging basket. From the marble shelf she took what was left of a ham, covered in cheesecloth. She dropped the potatoes and the onion in the sink for Johanna to wash, peel, and slice, and placed the ham on a sideboard, where she cut off a thick slab, working her knife around the marrow bone. Johanna pumped a stream of water into the sink, while Julia retrieved a large iron skillet.

Yazzie opened the door and came in. He took off his hat and coat and hung them by the door. He didn't speak; he sat down at the table and folded his hands in front of him.

Julia took the sliced potatoes and onion from Johanna. When the skillet was hot, she dropped in a large spoonful of lard and watched it sizzle into liquid. Then she added the potatoes and onion, shifting them around in the pan with a wooden spoon until they were coated, and covered the skillet with a lid. She asked Johanna to place the ham over the potatoes when they were almost done. The meat juices and fat would seep into the potatoes and brown them.

She sat down across from Yazzie. "Tell me what happened."

She listened silently as he told her of their uneventful journey up to the ruins, Owen's insistence that they stay despite the looming storm, and then how the ice had descended on them after Owen's accident.

"Why did he climb back up there?"

"He just did." Yazzie wouldn't look into her eyes. "I had no way to get him down. Not from the ruins and not from the mountains."

Johanna quietly began setting the table as Julia had taught her to, years ago. She worked around them, placing plates, cups, and flatware carefully.

"He slept most of the day, on and off. From the morphine. He passed on during the night."

They sat in silence for several minutes.

"I thought the ice would melt this morning, but the clouds came in again and the snow started." Yazzie looked at Julia directly for the first time. "I didn't have a sound horse. The weather . . ." He removed folded papers from a trousers pocket and slid them across the table. "He wrote this."

In an uneven hand that was nevertheless unmistakably his, Owen had written:

My dearest Julia, I am very, very sorry. I did not heed Yazzie's advice and am solely to blame. I think of you always and am

Forever yours, Owen

And on the second page:

To whom it may concern: I have taken a bad fall. The fault is all mine. An ice storm has made travel impossible. Mr. Clement Yazzie, my true friend, has done all that anyone could for me.

> *Robert Owen Rouse*
>
> *December 1910*
>
> *Chuska Mountains, Navajo Reservation*
>
> *New Mexico Territory*

"Where did you leave him?" Julia asked.

He told her how in the morning light he'd washed Owen's face and hands with clean water from the seep and had then wrapped him tightly in blankets and canvas before carrying him to a small room, back where no one ever goes. Then he sealed up the doorway with stones.

"Well," Julia said, her jaw firm, "that doesn't matter because we're going to go back up there as soon as the snow stops and bring him home." She emphatically tapped the table with a forefinger.

Johanna brought the frying pan to the table, where she placed it on a folded towel. While Julia spooned some of the steaming potatoes and onion onto each plate, Johanna fetched a loaf of brown bread from a box on a shelf beside the stove. Julia cut the ham into three portions.

"He knew there would be questions," Yazzie said.

"What questions?"

"He was an Anglo. I was the only one with him."

"Don't be ridiculous. Sheriff Dufur is too busy dealing with the trial court in Aztec over Richard Wetherill's murder."

"I'm not concerned about the law." Yazzie picked up his fork and began picking at the food.

Johanna's impassive eyes moved back and forth, studying both their faces.

"Everyone knew he was very ill." Julia moved the food around on her plate and then took a small bite. "There won't be any questions."

"Don't fool yourself."

Julia's anger flashed. Her cheeks reddened, her eyes filled. "Why? Why would anyone care? He had no one except us. He was *our* responsibility."

Julia watched Johanna cut all her meat into very small pieces, which she always did before taking the first bite.

"You mean," Yazzie said, "what happened is my responsibility."

"Well, isn't it?" Julia pressed the heels of her hands into her eyes and slowly her sobs lengthened. "Why did you bring him up there? You knew how sick he was. And you didn't even tell me!"

"You wouldn't have let him go."

"Of course I wouldn't have! And now he's dead, and you left him up there!" She buried her face in her raised apron until her breathing slowed and she fell silent. Then she rose from the table and walked away. Her back to them, she blew her nose in a towel and said, "Go on, eat. Your food's getting cold." She wiped her eyes again with the hem of her apron. Then she filled the tea kettle and placed it on the stove.

What little was eaten, was eaten in silence. The remains of the meal congealed on their plates.

Johanna cleared the dishes and Julia made a pot of tea and brought it to the table. She sat down again and reread the pages torn from the field book.

"We can't just leave him up there, Clement. Someone will find him eventually, and then there *will* be questions." She spread her hand across the pages. "So we'll bring him down when the snow stops."

"No," Yazzie said. "I'm not going back up there. I'm done with it." He pushed himself up from the table, crossed the room, and retrieved his coat and hat from the pegs by the door. He turned back to Julia and said, "If you want, Sister will stay with you tonight." Then he left.

When the two women had finished cleaning the kitchen, Julia said, "I'm fine, Johanna, you should go home," but Johanna ignored her and set about preparing a sleeping place by the parlor stove. Julia knew it was useless to suggest that she sleep in the spare bed.

Later, unable to settle herself, Julia returned from her room and handed a package wrapped in plain brown paper to Johanna. "This is from Owen," she said. "It was going to be a Christmas present. I told him I'd wrap it in fancy paper and ribbon for you, but I don't think I'll be celebrating this year. So I'm giving this to you now. Open it." It was D. L. Augsburg's *Drawing, Books I* and *II* for primary school students. "There are exercises—drawing lessons—and I'll be happy to read the words to you whenever you want." She went back to her room.

CHRISTMAS FELL ON SUNDAY. The Thursday before, Johnny Gorman returned from his regular trip to Gallup with an unexpected crate addressed to Julia. At first she thought it must be from Penny.

"Mr. Rodriguez said it was a special order," Johnny said. Julia and he were standing in the trading post storeroom, looking down at the crate. "It came a while back, but he was told to hold it until now."

"Told by whom?"

"Well," Johnny said, frowning and clearing his throat, "Owen."

Julia watched as Johnny took a clawed hammer to the crate, yanking the screeching nails from the top. Inside, securely packed, was a gramophone.

"Take it back," Julia said.

Tom Gorman came in from the store. "Is something wrong?" he asked Julia.

"No."

"What's this?" He peered into the crate.

"A gramophone," Johnny said.

"Isn't that something," Tom drawled. "Where d'you want it?" he asked Julia.

"I *don't* want it."

The three of them stood there looking at each other. "All right," Julia said with a sigh, "leave it in the crate."

"Yes, ma'am," Johnny said.

Julia turned away and returned to the store.

WINTER TOOK UP RESIDENCE, hardening the ground across the Defiance Plateau, capping the ridge line of the Chuska Mountains in a glaring white, settling into Many Springs Canyon like an affliction. The sun still cut through the sky most days, as it always did in the winter, but the bitterness of the nights held sway and what snow fell, stayed.

Nothing diminished Owen's loss. But that loss, so palpable on those evenings when she found herself seated alone in her parlor, also carried with it a sense of relief because she no longer had to worry about the when and the how. Whenever abject despondency set in, she would go to his cabin. It was as he'd left it; she hadn't yet summoned the courage to organize his things or clean or do anything else with it. Sometimes she would sit there in the cold reading his first two field books. Some pages contained little but diagrams and geographical coordinates. Descriptions were objective, without personal commentary and spare on adjectives, and included details about the location, width, and direction of the ancient roads that radiated from Chaco Canyon, and then more and more precise notations about his explorations to the west, toward Many Springs Canyon and the mountains beyond, often with parenthetical references to drawings on opposite or adjacent pages. He began the second book shortly after pitching his tent on the far side of Many Springs Wash. For more than three weeks after that the same pattern of entries continued: coordinates, diagrams, illustrations of pottery shards and other artifacts he'd found, and maps of the various trial routes he'd taken. But then he began including illustrations of plants and trees. The view from various overlooks. Unlabeled drawings of the trading post and canyon. Until everything stopped in November 1909. From the beginning of his convalescence until the spring of 1910 he made few entries, and didn't begin in earnest again until his journey back to Chaco Canyon in June, during which his observations while retracing the western road were as precise as ever. These entries ended on the day of Richard Wetherill's murder.

There was, of course, the third field book, more a diary than a working journal. She knew this because he'd let her read several passages that he'd written while building his cabin—she'd teased him about it, calling him Henry David. But she didn't have the third book to read now. Clement had kept it, and she thought she knew why: because Owen had described their route and the ruins. She didn't ask Clement for it.

As the calendar drifted toward March, she thought she would go stir-crazy—especially on weekends, after the early Saturday closings and the Gormans' departures—were it not for Johanna, who continued to visit as if nothing had changed. Several times a week, and always on Saturday and Sunday, she would help Julia prepare a modest supper for the two of them. Sometimes Johanna would leave immediately after they cleaned up the kitchen, but more often she would take out her paints and inks from the bottom drawer of Julia's desk and sit at the dining table with paper and pen and brush. Every now and then Julia would retrieve the Augsburg books from her bookcase, and the two women would sit side by side, examining the illustrations, or Johanna would listen as Julia read. Never once, however, despite Julia's encouragement, did Johanna attempt any exercises suggested in the books. She was clearly more interested in the sketches from nature—animals, trees, flowering plants—than the interminable (at least to Julia) illustrations of how to draw cubes and boxes and the like, but it was as if she were disconnected from the world represented by the books, a world that she could observe but that excluded her.

Julia didn't wonder if Johanna missed Owen. She was human, so of course she missed him—in her own way, which was not a way that Julia would ever question. Johanna made known to the world what she wanted to make known, without obvious gesticulations or easily repeatable gestures. (Julia had never seen Johanna shed a tear, and she had absolutely no sense of humor, as far as Julia could tell). A quick blink or side glance or a seemingly trivial dip or tip of her head to one side or the other, or a slight move-ment of her lips, or a change in posture or the way she moved or held her hand—there was an infinite number, an impossible catalog, of possibilities for how the human body moved or held itself, and it was at this elemental level that Johanna communicated with those who cared to pay attention.

In the last two months Julia had truly come to love Johanna like a sis-ter—for her kindnesses, for her simply being *there*, and for the gifts that she had begun to leave for Julia to find: in Owen's cabin, a black and white drawing of Halley's Comet and arcing stars; on the window sill behind the kitchen sink, a painting of a boulder in the water flow from the ice-crusted dam; in her knitting and sewing basket, amid the skeins of wool and spools of thread and the assorted needles, a picture of a ball of gray yarn so precise-ly drawn that it looked as if it could be unwound.

EARLY ONE MORNING in February, Clement knocked on the kitchen door. When Julia answered, he stayed at the threshold, his hat pulled low against the cold. His breath clouded the air between them. "I'm going to be gone tomorrow. I'll be back the next day."

"Just one day?" Julia, well aware of the calendar, asked. "You always take two."

"Not this time. I'm meeting my uncles above Blue Hawk Lake, but I'm not going the rest of the way."

"I see," Julia said. Clement looked older, tired, but that may have been the brutal dawn. "And will you tell them?"

He looked past her, to where she'd set a single place for herself at the table. "I'll tell them that I can't protect the ruins anymore."

"That's all?"

His eyes came back to her, but he didn't answer.

"Do what you have to do." Julia stepped back and started to close the door. "Is there anything else?"

"No," he said. He stuffed his gloved hands in the oversized pockets of his work coat and left.

Later that same day Julia found an unexpected letter among the mail that Johnny Gorman brought from Gallup:

> *Dear Mrs. Halley,*
>
> *Forgive me for my shakey handriting. I have never been much of a one for putting words to paper. I am riting to thank you for*

your kind letter of last Dec. I have read it many times and find it a comfort to know that Owen died at peace with himself. He was always a sickly boy and more than once his mother (R.I.P.) and I thought he was gone. He wrote me a number of times about his life out there and about how you took him in after his frost bite and such. He spoke of you as a true freind. He did not have many freinds growing up because I worked him too long and hard on the farm. I look back and regret that now. I was not a good father to him unlike his mother. The Ten Commandments should have the mother first. Honor Thy Mother and then Thy Father. I asked a teacher at the local school to find a book for me about the Navaho Indians and she did but it was hard going for me but I read as much as I could. It would have been a comfort to bring Owen home and hear a few words said over him. I am partial to Matthew and Luke the early chapters allthough his mother favored Old Testament stories and such; the Book of Ecclesiastes was one. But never-you-mind. Being well past my three score and ten I do not have many years left myself and am sure that we will never meet in person so this letter will have to do.

Yours truely,

Oliver Rouse

Julia folded Oliver Rouse's letter and for the first time in several weeks remembered the shipping crate in the storeroom. That evening she and Johanna unboxed the gramophone, a Victor IV model, with a double spring motor and brass horn and tapered tone arm, and a mahogany cabinet. It had cost a considerable sum, certainly more than fifty dollars with shipping. There was a separate package inside the crate with flat ten-inch recordings. Caruso's "Vesti la Guibba" and "O Lola." Marches by Sousa. Elsie Stevenson singing "Shine on, Harvest Moon" and Elizabeth Wheeler's "Meet Me To-Night in Dreamland." Ada Crossley, "Caro Mio Ben." Best of all, three Chopin recordings, "Nocturne No. 2," "Prelude No. 20," "Waltz No. 6."

Julia and Johanna carried the gramophone into the parlor and listened to them all. Julia sat in her usual chair, Johanna on the floor near the box stove, the gramophone between them. Julia showed Johanna how to wind the spring, and then she sat back and closed her eyes and listened to the Chopin pieces several more times. She could see her hands on a keyboard, pinkish pale skin and pretty nails beyond the frilled cuffs of her dress, and the printed notes flowing without interruption as Penny turned the pages for her, a melody lifting and falling over broken chords, flowing on in common time to the end.

IT WAS TOO EARLY to call it spring, but the day that Tom Talle rode up the trail to the trading post Julia was on hands and knees in her vegetable garden planting peas. He was riding a blond-maned, light brown Arabian—not the most practical of horses, but a beauty—and wearing a tan shearling coat, nankeen trousers, tooled boots, and a Stetson, all of the finest quality.

"Mrs. Halley," he said simply, taking off his hat. His longish hair was slicked back over the crown of his head, and a neat but thick mustache touched his upper lip and extended to the creases of his tanned cheeks.

"Sheriff Talle," Julia said, wiping her hands on her dress, "It's a pleasure to see you here at long last."

"Likewise." Talle got down from the horse, which, perfectly mannered, stood quietly while he draped the reins over the railing of the veranda. Julia led the sheriff up the steps and into the kitchen, where she set about making a fresh pot of coffee.

"If I may ask," Julia said, "is this a business call or are you here for some lively conversation?"

"Well, a little of both." He sat at the dining table facing her and ran his hands through his hair.

"How so?" Julia hung an apron around her neck and tied it behind her back.

"I'm on my way up to Farmington about the Wetherill business. Chischilí Biye' 's lawyers and Superintendent Shelton are quite a bunch. We've got Bill Finn as an eyewitness and the murder weapon besides, and they're still trying to cobble together a defense. God knows when we'll actually have a trial."

"Well," Julia said. "I'm sorry to hear that. Richard wasn't a close friend, but he certainly didn't deserve what happened."

"No, not at all."

Julia left the pot of coffee to perk and sat down across from Talle. "So, you were passing by."

"I was."

"And thought you'd stop in."

"That's right."

"And?"

He scratched the back of his neck, averting his eyes. "A question has come up about this Rouse business."

" 'This Rouse business'?"

"Well, Mrs. Halley—"

"Call me Julia."

"Julia, it's come to my attention that there's some questions about the circumstances."

"Of Mr. Rouse's death?"

"Yes."

"Then shouldn't I be speaking with Sheriff Dufur?"

"That would depend," he said, smiling, "on exactly where in the Chuskas the death occurred. Anyway, I'm not here in an official capacity."

Julia rose to get cups and saucers. She also placed a tin of biscuits on the table. "Please, help yourself. Can I fix you anything more substantial?"

"No, thank you."

She sat down and waited for him to continue.

"Do you know what they were doing high up in the Chuskas in December?"

"You mean Mr. Rouse and Mr. Yazzie? Of course I do. But before I answer, Sheriff, I'd like to know who's been raising questions."

"I'm not at liberty to say, Julia."

"Then I'm not at liberty to answer."

"Then I'll have to ask Yazzie."

"Go right ahead. His outfit is less than a mile up the trail."

"He's not at the trading post today?"

"He doesn't work for the trading post."

"I see. You pay him off the books."

"On occasion he does work for me, but he has his own sheep and lands to tend to. Besides, I've turned much of the business of running the store over to Tom and Carmelita Gorman."

"Really?"

"I'm giving most of my attention to buying and selling Navajo rugs back East. Right now, I'm trying to catch up on back orders." Despite the wintry weather, word had gotten around that she was paying top dollar for high-quality rugs, and she was finding more weavers from other regions of the reservation—even Ganado—visiting her.

"Al Wetherill did mention that you've been shipping a lot of packages to Chicago."

"Did he?"

"But even so, I can't see how there's much money to be made in the rug business. What are they going for now—a dollar or a dollar twenty-five a pound?"

"I don't market my weavers' rugs by the pound. That just encourages speed and sloppiness. I price rugs based on size, the fineness of the weave, the intricacy of the design, the use of color . . ."

"It sounds like you're talking about Persian carpets." A smile failed to conceal his skepticism.

"The principles are the same."

"Well," he said, "if you can make a go of it, the more power to you." He took a biscuit from the tin.

"Are you sure I can't fix you a proper meal?"

"No, thank you, I'm fine."

She fetched the pot of coffee, poured two cups, and they took turns smiling at each other while she waited for him to come out with it.

He put down his cup. "If you don't mind my asking, what was your relationship with Mr. Rouse?"

Julia, having been expecting the question, kept her composure. "If I take you correctly, you're on the verge of abusing my hospitality."

"I'm sorry, but you didn't answer my first question about why he and Yazzie were up in the Chuskas, so now I'm asking this one."

Clement had said there would be questions, and she'd dismissed his concern. She understood now, however, that to end this would require answering Tom Talle as if he were not an adversary, but someone who could be brought over to her side. "Mr. Rouse was my guest and my friend. In fact, I have him to thank for the idea of selling Navajo rugs by catalog."

"There was nothing of—pardon me—a romantic nature between you?"

"Hardly. I'm old enough to have been his mother."

"I doubt that," the sheriff said.

Julia dropped her gaze, as if modestly acknowledging a compliment. "Is there anything else?"

"There was no possibility of, shall we say, a rivalry?"

Owen and Clement. Rivals for her affection. Two go up into the mountains. One returns. And there's no body. "I see," Julia said, nodding slowly. "Isn't it astounding, Sheriff, how much pleasure some people can take in reducing other people's lives to rubble?"

Talle cleared his throat and frowned, which buried his lower lip under his mustache.

"I've known Mr. Yazzie for many years now," Julia said. "And yes, before you ask, I've heard all the rumors about his past, but I will vouch for him. He is a man of integrity. I would put my life in his hands."

The sheriff shifted in his seat, but his expression didn't change. Julia rose and went to her desk and returned with a folded sheet of paper. She handed it to Talle. "Mr. Rouse and Mr. Yazzie were friends, *good* friends. I am speaking as forthrightly as I can."

Talle read the note silently.

"And how did you obtain this?"

"From Mr. Yazzie. He left it in my care."

"Yazzie could've written this himself."

"No, he couldn't. Mr. Yazzie can read, but he can't write in script and certainly not with correct grammar and spelling and punctuation." Logic would require Talle to ask if she herself had written it. She sensed, however, that he felt a certain sympathy for her, and she pressed her advantage: "I will vouch that this is Mr. Rouse's handwriting. I can produce other samples, if you'd like."

Talle folded the sheet and handed it back to her. "I take it that Yazzie buried him?"

"As well as he could. Mr. Yazzie had no choice. There was an ice storm and then heavy snow, as I'm sure you're aware, and he had no able horse. To do otherwise would have put his own life at risk."

"Then the matter's at an end," Talle said.

"That's all?"

"You'll not be further troubled by me or, if I have any say in it, by anyone else."

"Thank you."

"There's no need to thank me," he said. He actually sounded, Julia thought, relieved to be done with it. "All this talk . . ." He shook his head. "People are still on edge over the Wetherill business. A Navajo shoots a white man who's as famous as anyone in these parts, and there are all sorts of stories coming out about why. Because of a misunderstanding over money or because Biye' was a bad shot who was aiming for Bill Finn or because Wetherill mistreated the Navajos who worked for him—" He broke off. "You know what I mean. It gets people riled up, makes them suspicious. A lot of whites don't trust Indians, period. And I have to say there are times when I lean in that direction myself. When you deal with what I deal with—"

"I don't." She kept her tone mild. "I see things very differently."

"I suppose you do. You couldn't live out here on your own if you didn't." He lifted his hat from his knee, where he'd placed it when he sat down. Julia had noticed: most men would have put it on the table; unlike them, he had manners. "I've offended you, and I apologize. Lately I've found myself asking a lot of questions that I take no pleasure in. Who knows, maybe I'll be less mistrustful when I'm done."

"You mean with the Wetherill matter?"

"With sheriffing. When my term is up next year, I'm finished. I'm better at running cattle. The Wetherill business, and how the law and politics are being mixed up—well, it's made me see that I'm not cut out for this. Even coming here and bothering you today, it didn't sit well."

"But you did it anyway."

To that he had no reply. He stood up. "I thank you again for your hospitality."

Julia showed him to the door. The sheriff turned and put on his Stetson. "You should get into Gallup more often, Mrs. Halley," he said. "People might be . . ." He let the thought trail off.

"I'll try to do that," Julia said, and with her arms folded across her chest she watched him mount up and head down the canyon.

People might be . . . more considerate. More sympathetic. Less judgmental. *People might be . . .* less contemptible.

The anger and shame rose into her throat and she let out a rough sob. Why should she feel any shame? What mark did she bear? What hidden pestilence did she carry?

SHE'D BEEN THINKING for some time that she needed to see her father before he passed away. She hadn't seen him since Penelope's wedding. He'd had several minor strokes from which he'd made remarkable recoveries, but he was on the inevitable descent. And then on the way back from Albany she could spend a week in Chicago and meet her niece and nephew and maybe convince Penny that they should come out to visit her, perhaps in the early fall, when the high desert was at its kindest.

The day after Sheriff Talle's visit she began making plans, writing to her sister and Edna and making a list of items she'd need to go over with the Gormans. She would try to convince them to move into her residence while she was away.

A stately but accepting reply from Edna and an enthusiastic letter from Penny came almost immediately. Arranging travel was the easiest part of the planning: trains passing east and west stopped every day in Gallup, and connections through St. Louis and Chicago presented no difficulty. It was, after all, the twentieth century.

And so three weeks later she set out for Gallup with Johnny Gorman, intending to spend a night with Tóya while Johnny visited friends in Tohatchi. First, however, she stopped in for tea with Harry Whitaker, whom she hadn't seen since late December, when he'd traveled up to Many Springs after hearing of Owen's death. On that occasion their conversation had been muted at first, reflecting not only Julia's grief, but also an unexpected reserve on Harry's part, which she attributed to a lingering awkwardness about their visit to Gallup—until, that is, he told her about Panama. Ever since the night of the Christmas party she'd been anticipating such an announcement, though certainly not in these particulars. He'd just heard from Washington. The Army Corps of Engineers would arrange passage for him from New Orleans. He would be leaving in May. Time enough, he'd said. She knew what he meant: to wrap things up, to say his goodbyes.

Now, visiting his cabin, Julia could see that the process of leaving was well under way. His books were already crated, his few extra pieces of furniture, including his spare bed, gone, given away, presumably.

With evening falling, she didn't linger—she stayed just long enough for a cup of tea and to receive assurances that his schedule hadn't changed and that he would still be there when she returned from the East.

At Tóya's hogan the two women greeted each other warmly, and Tóya said, "Come, and we'll eat and talk."

They sat down on a rug near the stove and shared the meal of mutton and posole that Tóya had prepared. While they ate Tóya told Julia amusing stories about Harry Whitaker's early days on the reservation, when he couldn't do anything right.

"You taught him well," Julia said.

"Aoo'," Tóya said, apparently missing the implication in Julia's tone that *he* had also taught *her.*

"Why can't you say it?" Julia asked.

Tóya gave her a long look, her eyes narrow, her lips tight. "Say what?"

"That you're sorry he's leaving. That you'll miss him profoundly."

"Why does this need to be said?"

"Why shouldn't it be said? Would it be beneath you?"

Tóya wasn't one to take rebukes kindly. "Why are you so prickly to-night?"

"Why are you so damned stubborn!" Julia said, her voice breaking, but for the losses of winter, Owen Rouse and Clement Yazzie, as well as for Harry Whitaker.

"Shh," Tóya said, "shh. *Altso yá'at'éehdoo.*" All will be well.

Julia quickly collected herself. "You'll be coming to pick up Johanna soon?"

"When the shearing is done."

"Where will you be going?"

"West. To Black Mesa and then to Navajo Mountain."

No longer hungry, Julia set her bowl down on the dirt floor in front of her. "You've told Mr. Yazzie?"

"Aoo'."

"He didn't object?"

"He's coming with us."

"Tóya . . ." Julia shook her head.

The old woman shrugged. "What happened there is long in the past, and this is where we need to go. The old hataałiis are waiting for us."

"You and Johanna, not him."

"Tchh. This isn't your worry."

"Don't cut me off like that!" Julia's voice quavered. "You and I have known each other for far too long."

"This is true." It was as much of an apology as Tóya would give.

"I suppose you know that Mr. Yazzie and I have had a falling-out." Word traveled, even in winter.

"Over what happened up in the mountains." She wouldn't speak Owen's name.

"Do you know the place?"

Tóya chose her words carefully: "I know there is a place where I might not be welcomed."

"Well, unlike the ones who inhabit *that* place, those from Navajo Mountain—the ones who won't welcome Mr. Yazzie—are very much among the living."

Sighing, Tóya waved away Julia's challenge. "It's a long journey. Two women should not make such a journey alone."

A long journey along remote trails and through isolated outposts. There was no counterargument that Julia could make. She knew that if Johanna was going, Clement would go, too. She picked up her bowl and picked at the food in silence.

After a while she asked, "Do you think there's another world above this one?" Three times the Navajos' predecessors had climbed to a new world, from first the black and then the blue and then the yellow worlds, piercing the sky to reach this, the glittering world, where they had taken their human shape.

"This is what I think," Tóya said. "If our time in this world reaches its end, it will mean the end of all things. I think the sky will break and all its pieces will fall to earth." Tóya wiggled her fingers above her head and slowly let them descend to her lap. "This is what *sǫ' nanidéhígíí*—the falling stars— and Sǫ' Bitsee' Nineezí and the other comets try to tell us, but we don't want to be reminded."

"And the Holy People, would you finally see them again?"

Tóya slowly shook her head. "After the Holy People taught us the Blessingway, they said that they would never show themselves again. You know this. But we can still feel them in the Holy Wind, Níłch'i, which touches everything around us, all creatures and the stars and the air and even the stones." She paused and, dropping her eyes, scraped the bottom of her bowl with her wooden spoon. "Some feel their presence more than others."

But she wasn't speaking about herself. "You mean, Johanna, don't you?"

Tóya looked up and her lips curved ever so slightly. Julia could see the palpable sadness, the resignation, in the sagging lines of her old friend's face and in the stoop of her shoulders, and hear it in the scratching of wood against wood, and sense it even in the smell of pinyon smoke and the lingering taste of mutton and posole on her tongue. Everything around her spoke. Except the gods, if they were even there. Gods never explain themselves, Julia thought. They don't feel the need.

The next afternoon Johnny Gorman delivered Julia to Alberto Rodriguez's Furniture Emporium. She would walk from there to the train depot, where Johnny was to drop off her luggage.

Alberto, in a finely woven suit and a fashionable silk tie, greeted the unexpected visitor with uncharacteristic awkwardness. He rang the little bell that he kept on his desk, and within seconds a clerk entered through a side door. "*Tépor la señora,*" Alberto said. "*Con latté.*" The clerk vanished.

"Nothing for you?" Julia said, handing Alberto the trading post ledger before removing her gloves and sitting down.

"He knows what I like," Alberto said. "What brings you to town?"

"I'm leaving to visit family," Julia said. "I should be back in a few weeks. I also wanted to let you check the latest accounts."

"Very well," Alberto said, placing the ledger on his desk before taking a seat on the opposite side of the little table over which they'd chatted so many times.

Despite further pleasantries, Julia had the distinct impression that Alberto was less than comfortable, and after waiting to see if he would reveal whatever was on his mind, she ultimately spoke directly: "Alberto, don't you think it would be best if you just came right out with it?"

"With—?"

"Alberto," she said.

He puffed out his cheeks and proceeded to exhale percussive notes through tight lips. "I'm afraid that my brother and I can't provide the surety for your trading license in the future."

Somehow, this announcement didn't surprise her. "May I ask why not?"

The side door opened and the clerk brought in a tray with an ornate silver service and china cups and saucers. He poured a cup for Julia, mixing the black tea and a stream of milk from a small pitcher, and then a second cup, coffee without milk, for Alberto. He then retreated from the room.

"Matilda insists that I end all communication with you."

"I see." Julia sipped the tea.

"She threatened to see to it that the office of the Indian commissioner was flooded with letters raising questions about your fitness."

Julia put down her cup. "My 'fitness'?"

Alberto threw up his hands. "I know this is all nonsense. She wanted me to end my involvement immediately. But I told her that I would not do that to you, that our dealings were strictly above board and that the arrangement has never cost me so much as a penny."

"Well," Julia said, "I knew Matilda wasn't my friend, but I didn't know she disliked me quite so much."

"Julia," Alberto said, "I won't defend my wife to you. I can't be put in that position."

"I understand," Julia said. "I suppose that my arriving at your Christmas party with Harry Whitaker didn't help, given your friendship with the Belnaps."

"Harry told you about all that?"

She nodded.

"The Belnaps were among the first to welcome Matilda to Gallup."

"Harry had absolutely nothing to do with their son's going to Africa."

Alberto leaned forward, adjusting his cup on its saucer. "Oh, I'm sure you're right, but in the eyes of a mother whose only son met such an end . . ."

"I love this office," Julia said, glancing around. "Add a little kitchen and I could live here."

Alberto gave out a thin smile. "The house is Matilda's. This is mine. I do as I wish with it."

The tea was very good. Julia continued to sip at it.

"What are you going to do?" Alberto asked.

"About the trading post license?" Julia shook her head. "I don't know, Alberto. Maybe I've been in business long enough that a surety company will agree to provide the bond, even though I am on my own."

"If not, I'm sure you can find other sponsors. Win Peabody, for one. He always sings your praises. Or Harry."

"Harry is leaving us soon. Did you know?"

"No, I didn't," he said with surprise. "Where is he going?"

"Panama. To tend to the canal workers."

"I admire his fortitude. That won't be an easy job. Thousands have already died."

"I know."

Alberto drank some of his coffee and then returned the cup to its saucer. "Well, between now and when you renew your license there won't be any critical letters sent to the Indian commissioner."

"And afterward?"

"I have Matilda's word."

"I see," Julia said for the second time.

"You must know how much I dislike this, but she's my wife and the mother of my children, and I have to have peace in my household."

"I understand completely," Julia said. "If I may ask . . ."

"What is it?"

"You haven't told Matilda about seeing Will in Denver, have you? I know you said you'd keep the matter between us, but . . ."

"No, I haven't said anything. I know my wife very well. Even if I swore her to secrecy, at some point she'd be unable to resist telling her closest confidant. Or two. Or three."

"I won't trouble you further," Julia said, rising, "and I apologize for all the turmoil I've caused. You've been a wonderful friend to me, Alberto. As soon as I make the necessary financial arrangements, I'll let you know so that you can put this business behind you."

Alberto also rose. He retrieved her ledger from his desk. "Julia, if there's—"

"No," Julia said, taking the ledger. "Thank you, but Matilda shall have her way."

At the depot Julia learned that her train would be at least an hour late. She wanted to board the train, to let the rocking of the coach on the tracks stultify her. Instead, she would have to sit patiently in the waiting room. The benches were almost full, mainly with those who'd come to meet arriving passengers, but she managed to find a seat between two older women; one, shifting a package aside, gave her a smile, the other ignored her.

Not that long ago she'd boasted to Owen—for that's what it was, a foolish boast—that she didn't need to see herself reflected in another's eyes. She'd meant in a *man's* eyes, of course, for what else could *possibly* matter to a woman—a childless woman—except the admiration of men? But she'd too easily dismissed the gaze of other women. Matilda deserved sympathy for the loss of two babies, and admiration for her good works in Gallup, but the human trait that Julia most despised was careless self-righteousness—she had little doubt that Matilda and her circle of friends, if not the source, had spun the gossip about her into a black widow's messy web of invective, deceit, and intrigue—and for that Julia would not forgive her.

The stationmaster announced a further hour's delay, to a chorus of groans.

She had lost them all: Owen, Pete, Clement. Now, Alberto. And soon enough, Harry. And long ago, Will. And first of all, her father.

Where lay the fault, if not in her? She was the denominator in these divisions, the common factor.

But a descent into maudlin self-pity would accomplish nothing—she knew she would lose her way if she went too far into her own roiling confusions and contradictions.

Her upsetting conversation with Alberto Rodriguez still distressed her. While acknowledging all that he'd done for her and Will in their early days, when his generosity and kindness had outweighed any return he ever received, she felt that the scales had at last been balanced by Matilda's intrusion. She wouldn't criticize Alberto for his fidelity and would always regard him with admiration, but their personal relationship had reached an end. She didn't take the loss lightly—it wasn't as if she had friends to spare.

She would also always be thankful that Alberto had maintained his silence regarding Will's presence in Denver. Would she have preferred not knowing his whereabouts? In truth, with all that had happened since Alberto stumbled upon him—the loss of Owen, the loss of Clement—she didn't care anymore. She was beyond assigning blame for the collapse of their marriage; nearly seven years on, she knew that nothing would be changed by doing so. Their culpabilities, though distinguishable, were mutual and equal. She had no further interest in his present life; let him live it as he saw fit.

She could not so easily dismiss her father, however. He had treated her more as a hand maiden than as a daughter, but she didn't expect even now that he could comprehend her disappointment and animosity, which, though diminished by time and distance, lingered. She nevertheless needed to be done with it once and for all, and that required that she acknowledge her own impetuousness, her callousness, and that she ask his forgiveness. Which would also require a reconciliation with Edna. So be it. These things she could, and would, do back East.

The waiting room had quieted. Many of those irked by the train's delayed arrival had gone off, seeking refreshments or another way to pass the time. Some—no one she knew—were chatting or reading newspapers or books. A few wandered back and forth, impatient, checking posted train schedules and routes. No one disturbed her; most of the time she sat with her eyes closed, alone.

Back East, she would give way, but there were places she could not go without denying her own character; she could not follow Pete Pietrowski. Nearly seven years ago she was here, outside this train station, when Tom Gorman told her that Will was gone, and then Pete had appeared around the corner, and had followed her back to Many Springs Canyon. Should she have been more scathing, knowing very well, despite his ineffectual and mistaken effort to be supportive, what he really hoped might come of it? Was it a flaw in her own character that she had allowed him to hang on so long?

Had she enjoyed a little too much his misanthropy, an amplification of her own misgivings? It didn't matter. She'd driven him to drink. Literally, quite apart from his prior inclination. Should she have discarded him for that failing alone, refused him entry to her home? To whose benefit? He had an extraordinary eye when mediated by the camera lens, but he couldn't see his own folly—no surprise that he had no photographs in which he appeared, except for the one she'd taken on the trip north to Second Mesa and which now hung in her little gallery in her parlor, a photograph that showed a man in the desert, of his time and place, blunt faced, square headed, scruffy in his battered hat and wrinkled clothes, a photograph of which, she was sure, she possessed the only copy.

It pained her that she hadn't found a way to explain the why of it all—found a way, as she had with Owen, to leave Pete's pride intact while enabling him to release her from the obligation he sought to impose. If she'd tried harder, they might have parted on better terms. But maybe that was never to be—he wasn't like Owen in temperament. Pete's obvious disregard for her legitimate sentiments, his scorn for her uncommon bond with Clement Yazzie—his ingrained incapacity to accept an Indian as a counterpart in any capacity—once made explicit, created an unbridgeable chasm. That fault, that failure, was Pete's, not hers.

His contempt for Clement had been unreasoned—beyond reasoning. (Though she should not put aside Clement's contempt for Pete—more justified but also untempered.) Pete should have been able to see how Clement had strengthened her all along. Without Clement she would have failed too many times to recall—he had always stepped forward. Without him she wouldn't have had a livelihood, and she certainly wouldn't now be anticipating the commercial potential of the Many Springs catalogs.

Would she ever fully understand why Clement had steadied her? Not, she knew, because he'd desired her from the first—a laughable conceit. She didn't know how or even when that had come about. Before Will's departure? Clement had never said. She would never ask.

Might she have attracted another man's attention, affections, in other circumstances? To be desired was not so easily dismissed for a woman of middle age, but what might have been such a man's terms? That she offer herself as an ornament, a bauble, a mistress? That was the thing—she had never viewed herself as Clement's mistress, or Clement as her lover. *His* mistress; *her* lover—the words didn't apply, possessives or nouns. Which was not so easily explained. (Would a Philip Malott even listen?)

She should have gone to him the following morning—she should have walked with Johanna through the snow to their hogan and, if not apologized for her outburst the previous evening, then at least expressed her sorrow, not just for Owen's loss but for Clement himself. No, he should *not* have taken Owen up into the mountains—on that, her opinion hadn't changed.

But even at first, when she was overwhelmed, as the loss dropped into her heart, she understood why he had—she couldn't admit it then, but she understood. And how many opportunities had she let pass since then? And why? False pride—the pride that comes at someone else's expense, and too often at your own as well. Could Clement have come to her? Yes, of course. But *her* failure was . . . hers alone.

Who was left to stand by her now? Tom and Carmelita and Johnny. Stalwart and loyal, all three of them, but not intimate. And what of Johanna? She loved Johanna, but Johanna would always be a question that couldn't be answered. Tóya? Yes, within her boundaries, but beyond Diné Bikéyah was another world entirely, for Julia's broader associations and concerns necessarily excluded Tóya, who had no interest in that wider expanse.

And of course she couldn't forget the steadfast Harry Whitaker. She owed him her enduring friendship and, accordingly, her regular correspondence, keeping him apprised, after he left, of news about the reservation and vicinity, and always writing with the hope that he wouldn't neglect his own health and well-being in pestilential Panama. But maybe she should do something more, something before he left—why not an unexpected gesture to seal their intimacy for the years ahead, when distances might otherwise weaken ties? She would have to think of something . . .

The stationmaster announced that a minor rock fall near the Arizona border had been cleared from the tracks and that the awaited train was once again en route.

Julia thought now of Owen Rouse, who was never far away, still (and she thought also of his long-lost brother, who had died in the Hoosac Tunnel). At least she hadn't failed Owen—with whom, for whom, nothing needed to be repaired or amended. Mr. Emerson had written that of all the ways to lose a person, death was the kindest—she couldn't attest to that, not yet . . .

He'd left her with no obligations beyond penning a few letters to loved ones and acquaintances. Clothing and surveying instruments aside, his personal effects fit easily in a single paperboard box. (She should decide soon what to do with his instruments and field books, who might best use them—maybe one of the Wetherill brothers?) No one had stayed in his cabin yet, but in due course visitors would appreciate shelter, the bed, the stove, the chairs by the fireplace . . .

Oliver Rouse's letter to her had also remained on the periphery of her thoughts. Now she wondered if, back East, she might take a side trip to New Hampshire. She didn't imagine that Owen would have objected if she paid her respects. And she also thought, for the first time, that she would like to see the soil that he'd sprung from.

But what of the soil where he now lay? She could only surmise what might have been Owen's wishes, which he'd never made plain. (Though the grave and the stone were never really for the dead, were they?) Now he was beyond that, beyond caring, and no longer prey to her sorrow and concerns, but whenever she thought of him, his hasty entombment disquieted her. He would *not* lie in peace in those ruins. At some point—who could say when, but the day was coming—he would be found, and when he was, rumors would resurface, Sheriff Talle's assurances notwithstanding. Clement would be drawn in without recourse despite the lines Owen had written for him.

She opened her eyes. People around her were in motion, waking from their lethargy. She knew only this much for certain: time was utterly unforgiving, and waiting, unforgivable.

She would not have either of them made a spectacle.

She made her way on foot, up the avenue to the crossing, over the tracks to the north side, and along the dusty streets until she found Win Peabody's mortuary. She tried to peer through the window, but a heavy curtain made it impossible to see anything but her own reflection. Half expecting to find the office locked, Julia opened the door and entered.

Win Peabody was sitting behind an oversized desk reading a copy of *The San Francisco Examiner* that looked surprisingly crisp. Smiling broadly, Peabody folded the newspaper, rose, pulled down a striped vest that had ridden up over his belt, and gushed, "Julia! This is quite a surprise!"

"Are you an admirer of Mr. Hearst?" Julia asked.

"Oh, you mean the newspaper? Not really. I read whatever comes my way. I saunter through the train depot first thing each morning. It's amazing what travelers leave behind in the waiting room." He was dressed neatly in a starched white shirt buttoned at the collar, the vest, and matching black and gray striped suit.

"You've started growing your beard, I see."

"Indeed! 'Tis the season for starting anew."

Unexpectedly, the room's only interior door opened and a plump woman swept into the office.

"Ah!" Peabody said, turning to her. "Essie, let me introduce you to Mrs. Julia Halley."

So this, Julia thought, extending her hand, is the beautiful Estella: short, rather round, skin a nutmeg brown, black hair pulled tight beneath her straw flower pot hat, deep eyes above strong cheekbones, an average nose, a small chin, but a mouth that seemed perfectly designed to unify all the disparate elements into a remarkably striking—one might even say formidable—face. She was dressed quite simply, in a brown skirt and jacket, the latter displaying an exquisite brooch of various inlaid stones, cut small and tightly designed.

"My dear wife, Estella Peabody," Win Peabody said with a little bow.

"It's a pleasure, Mrs. Halley," the Indian woman said, accepting Julia's hand. "My husband is a great admirer."

"Now, Essie," Peabody said, "don't you embarrass me."

His wife gave him a sly little glance that made it clear to Julia that Mrs. Peabody was well practiced at gently embarrassing her husband and, furthermore, that he loved her all the more for it.

"He might be less admiring if he knew me better," Julia said.

Estella Peabody took an unusually long time to study Julia before replying, "I doubt that very much." She turned back to Peabody and said, "I must be going or I'll miss the train and Father will be very upset."

"Essie and Mr. Halusewa are heading to Santa Fe. A gallery there is interested in displaying her family's jewelry."

"How wonderful," Julia said. Her eyes on Mrs. Peabody's brooch, she added, "I'd love to see more of it."

"Perhaps Win can convince you to visit us in Zuni, Mrs. Halley."

"I'd like that very much."

"These days," Win said, rocking on his heels, "you aren't so very far away."

"And how *is* your automobile faring?" Julia asked him.

"Very good, very good. Scarcely a scratch on it."

Estella Peabody rolled her eyes and smiled, which indicated to Julia that at least one roading misadventure awaited the telling. "Well," she said, "I'm off." She turned and kissed her husband on the cheek, which required him to bend to her. She extended her hand to Julia again. "Until your visit, then."

"I look forward to it," Julia said, and without further ado Estella Peabody departed.

"What excellent timing," Peabody said, beaming, and extending his arm toward the chair in front of his desk.

"How is your new building on the south side coming?" Julia asked. They both sat down.

"Very well. I've already moved into the living quarters on the second floor. It has all the conveniences—a coal-burning furnace in the basement, hidden electrical wiring for every room, a water closet and bath—it's quite luxurious, really. A few final touches, and I'll complete the transition. So what brings you into Gallup this fine day?"

"I was planning to begin a trip east—probably on the same train Mrs. Peabody is taking."

"But something changed your mind?"

"Several things."

"Nothing unfortunate, I hope."

"Yes and no." She glanced around the spare office—the bookcase, the stove in the corner, the framed Currier and Ives barnyard prints hanging on opposite walls. A faintly sweet chemical smell hung in the air. "I'm here for your advice. I've decided to bury Owen Rouse in Many Springs Canyon."

Peabody's eyebrows lifted.

"And thank you for the kind bereavement note you sent."

"It was nothing."

"It was more than most did."

"Why don't you come back into my viewing parlor, where we might be more comfortable?" He rose and held the door for her, and she entered and settled herself into an armchair by the stone fireplace, which was giving off a welcome warmth. Win sat in the chair opposite hers and folded his hands on his stomach, waiting for her to continue.

"Nothing I'm about to say should be repeated," Julia said, "although there's nothing illicit or unsavory involved."

"You have my word."

"What do you know of the circumstances, Win?"

"Of Owen's death?" He shifted in his seat. "I was under the impression that he died from a fall while on an outing in the Chuskas and that his body couldn't be retrieved."

"That's correct except that recovering his body shouldn't be a problem now. At the time of the accident the weather was very bad. Mr. Yazzie had no choice but to leave him behind. But he did wrap him tightly in blankets and canvas and move him into a small room in an ancient ruin that he sealed as best he could."

Peabody blinked several times and looked up at the plaster ceiling, which was crazed with a spider web of cracks.

"The elevation is very high, over eight thousand feet," Julia added.

"We can assume that it's still very cold at night there?"

"I believe so."

"That and the dryness of the air should all be in your favor. If, as you say, the remains have been protected from the elements and depredation, it's likely that there won't be . . . physical difficulties in what you propose to do." But then Peabody frowned, as if still pondering the situation. Then he said, "You should spend more time in town, Julia."

"How interesting—I had a visit three weeks ago from Sheriff Talle, and I believe he used the same words."

"If I may ask, why did the good sheriff visit you?"

"The rumors, of course. I assume you've heard them?"

"I ply my trade on both sides of the tracks, Julia. Information seeks *me* out. All I have to do is cock an ear, so to speak." He momentarily cupped a hand to the side of his head. "As to the rumors, in my experience, facts govern science, mathematics, and the presence or absence of a pulse. Everything else . . ." Peabody held up his hands and then let them drop to the arms of his chair. "But of course I gave no credence to the gossip. In fact, I did my best to defend you whenever the opportunity presented itself. I should add that I wasn't alone in that."

"Yes, well, that's kind of you to say," Julia said, "but it might be best for you if you had nothing more to do with me. The taint may rub off, and that wouldn't be good for business."

"One must stand by one's friends, Julia. Regretfully, I haven't always done so—one doesn't make money in Chicago real estate through generosity. But that's neither here nor there." He waved the past away.

"Thank you, Win," Julia said.

"I haven't done anything of substance yet, Julia."

They picked out a rosewood casket, one of several from the St. Louis Coffin Company that Peabody kept in a shed behind the premises—a casket for which he refused to accept any payment. He would bring it to Many Springs Canyon and, if she desired, seek a minister who would be willing to make the journey.

"My father was a minister and I have a Bible," Julia said. "We don't need a visitant."

That evening she sat in her room at the Harvey House and sorted through the trading post mail that she'd retrieved from Johnny Gorman, who was greatly surprised when she informed him that she was postponing her trip and would be returning to Many Springs Canyon with him in the morning. Since visiting Win Peabody her state of mind had shifted back and forth between calm and utter despair at least half a dozen times. She'd scarcely managed to swallow any of her dinner, and she was too unsettled to sleep.

At the bottom of the pile of mail she came upon a modest-sized box that, judging by the dents and scuff marks, had traveled a considerable distance. Inside she found a carefully wrapped and framed photograph—no letter, not even a note—labeled at the bottom left "Mount McKinley/Light and Shadow," and signed at the bottom, on the right, "Władysław Pietrowski—for Julia Halley."

She studied the beautiful, stark photograph. She would hang it on her parlor wall.

* * *

The next day when Johnny and she stopped at Tohatchi to rest the horses, Julia found Harry Whitaker at work in his clinic, tending to a baby with croup. The door to his examining room was open, and she watched him with child and mother. Every question, every gesture, spoke of care and kindness.

When he was finished, the two friends stepped outside and sat in the sun, and she showed him Pete's photograph.

"So, he made it all the way," Harry said, admiring it. "I don't imagine we'll hear much more from him, do you?"

"No," Julia said. Then she told him of her changed plans:

"I'm going to bury Owen properly in Many Springs Canyon. Win Peabody is bringing a casket from Gallup and will dress him. Will you come?"

"Of course." He paused and then asked, "Shall I ask Tóya?"

"Yes, do. But make it clear that if she chooses not to come, I'll understand." Tóya was, after all, Navajo. "And one more thing."

He waited, looking over the top of his glasses.

"When you leave for New Orleans, may I accompany you?"

He laughed with surprise. "Whatever for?"

Julia felt herself flushing. "I've never been. And I'd like to see you off."

He took her hand in his. "Ah'm delighted." A beam rose across his face. "Nothing would give me greater pleasure, Julia, my dear friend, than to show you a bit of Southern hospitality." Then he paused. "You're sure you'll be back here by then?"

"By late May?" she asked with surprise. "I'm only postponing my trip by a few days. I need to be here for the shearing. It's our busiest time."

"To be sure," he said with a slight nod.

"What are you thinking, Harry?—certainly not that tired old saw that we all leave eventually."

"How many trips have you taken back East?"

"Just the one, for my sister's wedding."

"A brief trip."

"Yes."

"Going back now . . . winter's concluded, spring is coming on."

She sensed that he was speaking of more than the seasons.

"The outside world is changing rapidly, Julia. I saw that when I returned for my mother's funeral last year. Even in Charleston, which does not favor change."

"And it got you thinking."

"It did."

She patted his hand. "You needn't worry. I'll be here to accompany you."

"Of course. You'd be here then, under any circumstances."

"Harry, the Days and the Hubbells have stayed. And John Wetherill, despite what happened to Richard."

"Of course," he repeated. "They've set down deep roots."

"And I haven't?"

"It isn't for me to say. Part of me thought I had as well." He shrugged. "But I'm beginning to think another part, the dominant tendency, will always be a wanderer." He turned to face her with a thin smile. "But you? No—I don't see *that* in you. You're fully present. That's why we gathered to you—me, Pete, Owen for his short time, and now our new friend Win Peabody, I imagine." He paused, and Julia saw that he was considering how much more to say. "And Yazzie—you drew him to you as well."

"I made no effort," Julia said.

"My point, exactly."

HE SAW HER COMING, the sun behind her early in the morning so that he had to squint, but he knew it had to be her even from a quarter of a mile away. He was standing outside the hogan contemplating the day ahead and drinking a final cup of coffee. He'd seen her leaving with Johnny Gorman; something had brought her back. She came toward him at a determined pace, no hat, no coat or gloves, steadiness in her stride. He remembered how he'd seen her years ago, the morning after their altercation over the pawned saddle, her unsuspected beauty advancing toward him.

It seemed to Yazzie that he'd done so many things wrong since deciding to bring Owen Rouse into the ruins. His better judgment overcome, he'd let Owen make his drawings and take his notes, and Owen had died because of it. He'd failed Julia, too, walking away from her when he should have taken the brunt of her anger and stayed. And then in February, thinking he could rectify mistakes past and present, he gave to his uncles the field book containing the few pages of notes and drawings, and explained to them about the seep and the seams in the rock wall and how it would all collapse someday. Furious, Wellington Katsi had thrown the book into the campfire. Gladstone Katsi, with a cooler head, had retrieved it before the paper caught, but Yazzie didn't know what became of the field book after that; back at Second Mesa the clan elders might have decided to keep it in secret or they might have reduced it to ash. Either way, it would never see the light of day. Yazzie thought now that he should have given the field book to Julia to hold in trust, as Owen had intended.

He emptied his cup and let it dangle from one finger, never turning his eyes from Julia's path, and she kept coming until he could make out the highlights of the sun off her hair and the color in her cheeks, and she kept coming, didn't miss a stride, didn't stop until he could see the pale irises and the dry lips.

He'd been visiting a young Navajo woman who lived beyond Washington Pass. He'd first seen her the night they all gathered to watch the comet. She'd stayed in his mind, and in the fall he'd searched her out. He could offer her family more than they would expect. That was what he should do. She would have his children, and together they would raise them here, where he would protect them as best he could.

But in this moment Julia Halley stood before him. They had trusted each other in everything, with no need for paper and ink or the official seals of the Anglo world.

She took one step closer and placed both palms on his chest. "Clement," she said.

What had been frozen all winter broke open, even though they couldn't go back to how they had been. "You were taking the train east," he said. "Has something happened?"

"Happened? No, no, not really," she hesitated, turning her eyes away.

He placed a hand on her cheek and turned her face back to him. "Tell me," he said.

CHAPTER TWENTY-FOUR: Lessons of Our New World

Julia slept deeply for two hours on Johanna's pallet; outside, over an open fire so as not to disturb her, Johanna prepared a meal of dried venison, pinto beans, corn cakes, and coffee.

In the late afternoon, sitting in the warm sun, Julia and Clement talked by the old tree where his mother had done her weaving. Yes, he told her, he would be going to Navajo Mountain with Sister and Tóya when the lambing and shearing were done. No, it didn't trouble him to return there. Time had moved on.

Then he told her that all those months ago when he saw Johanna losing herself in her painting of the stars and brought her to see Tóya, Tóya had told him that he shouldn't interfere, that Johanna was trying to keep the stars in place. She also warned him that if too much of the Navajo way was lost, pieces of the sky would begin falling.

"Did you believe her?" Julia asked.

"Not for your world, no."

Ah, she thought. *That* world.

She'd always known Clement first and foremost as Navajo, and then as Hopi, but also irrefutably . . . as what? As a man forced to live a third way, keenly aware of the overshadowing that was also in the stars, even if he rejected most of its ways. Wasn't her very presence here further evidence of how quickly that new world was coming?

Yazzie continued: When Tóya told him that she would take Johanna to visit the old singers, the ones who knew the ceremonies that were no longer sung, he objected at first, fearing that he couldn't protect his sister, but then Tóya accused him of having lost touch with the Holy People—did he think they had given Johanna her gift for no reason? So he'd relented.

Several minutes passed before Yazzie spoke again; Julia was used to his silences and sat patiently.

"I don't think any of us will ever see Sister's paintings," Clement said.

"Why not?"

"My guess is that a group of singers have them now, singers who see things the way 'Asdzáán Bítóyiszééyiztał does. But I think the day will come when those singers who are still left will see things differently, after 'Asdzáán Bítóyiszééyiztał's time with us has passed."

"You think they'll destroy them?"

"Hmm." He shrugged. "Or maybe just make sure they can never be found."

"You haven't discussed any of this with Tóya, have you?"

He shook his head. "With no one." He turned his head and looked at her directly now. " 'Asdzáán Bítóyiszééyiztał has survived many hard times, and always deserves to be heard, but she doesn't understand everything. There are other things you don't know. Things I couldn't say before."

Julia sensed that Clement was asking her permission to say them now, but she didn't know if she wanted to hear them. "All right," she said.

"When I came together with you, she told me it was a bad thing to take up with a white woman."

It stung Julia like a backhanded slap. She couldn't help thinking, Was that what he thought, too, now? But she would not demean herself by asking.

"I couldn't do what she thought I should," he said.

"Take another wife," Julia said quietly.

"Aoo'."

Now is the time to leave, Julia thought, and she started to rise, but Clement reached for her arm and held her in place.

"That part of me was empty," he said. "I had no hope that I could ever fill it again. You were not a mistake."

She returned home as dusk was setting in. Sleep immediately claimed but couldn't hold her; her unsettled mind kept surfacing despite her exhaustion. Except for her brief time on Johanna's pallet, she hadn't slept in what seemed like days, not in her bed in Gallup nor on the long ride in the wagon with Johnny Gorman—sleep would come when the task she'd set was done.

She opened her Bible to select verses from Ecclesiastes to honor Owen's mother, and verses from Matthew, for his father. She picked out a passage from I Corinthians for herself. Then, wrapped in a blanket, Julia went out to her veranda and sat looking at the sky. The stars read like a map.

Barely twelve hours ago, striding up Many Springs Canyon, seeing that Clement was waiting for her, Julia still didn't know what she would say to him. Then she reached him, and told him, and stepped into his embrace, pressing into him not with the comfortable coercion of familiar bodies, woman and man—she knew they had left that behind—but to declare her need for his help, offering nothing in return but the request itself.

She wondered now if it had ever mattered to her, as a white woman, that Clement was a Navajo. No, obviously not, not as she'd come to know him over the years. But in another way, yes, and maybe this was what Tóya had also meant about his poor decision—Julia would not condemn her for thinking it—because welcoming Clement into her bed had been without obligations or expectations; no need for her to consider divorce or remarriage or moving into an Albany brownstone or even a nice little house with a picket fence. It had cost her nothing. Not so for Clement or the People, not as Tóya saw it.

Julia had known for most of her life how terrible it felt to be found wanting by the simple fact of her sex, but now she also began to see how devastating the burden of race could be. In that, however, she had a choice; Tóya and Clement did not. Without denying her race or her character, she'd tried to do her best for the Navajo, but *she . . . could . . . leave*, if she so chose, for whatever reason she chose, and that included if she could not live her life subject to another imposition over which she had no control.

When Clement had brought her to the Place in the Mountains the first time, when they had camped for a night and lay in each other's arms, she'd told him that it wasn't her place to enter the ruins. She understood why Owen had thought differently; he'd seen them with a naive explorer's eyes. Clement Yazzie, however, befitting his thrice-conflicted reality, saw them as a place of haunting, of history, and also of duty. And now she'd summoned all three, imposing on him, yet again, because he was the only one who could bring Owen down from there.

THEY STARTED OUT AT FALSE DAWN and then left the buckboard and one horse above Blue Hawk Lake. Yazzie asked Johanna to take the other horse along the trail that he and Owen had followed in December, while Julia and he went on foot by the shorter route, climbing up through a fifty-foot cleft in the rocks that delivered them just below the high plateau. Yazzie carried over both shoulders additional coils of rope; easing Owen's body down over the curved sandstone face below the ruins would require care. While waiting for Johanna to arrive, he would fashion a travois from the saplings he'd cut to shelter the pinto in December.

Yazzie had walked among the ghosts many times, and they had always let him be. Maybe they were so ancient that their powers to intervene were spent, or maybe they'd seen so much human suffering that all they felt now was pity. But he'd left among them a white man whose spirit might still bear all its anger and dissatisfaction and heartache and malevolence, all those damaged feelings that even the gentlest of people held in hidden measure. Still, he was doing this, not because he owed it to anyone, but simply because it was Julia Halley who had asked.

It was a bright day, with a soft wind. The sun was high above as they started across the plateau toward the crowns of the still-bare aspens. When they reached the overlook Julia stood at the edge and wept.

"Oh, Owen!" she cried.

The ruins were gone. Two giant sandstone slabs from the roof of the alcove had come down, obliterating all but a few of the rooms below, at either end of the expanse. Some of the rubble from the collapsed arch and the ruins had spilled over the cliff face into the vale below, leaving a twenty-foot-high pile of stone, splintered wood, fractured masonry.

The wind, sliding down into the canyon, picked up, and the bare branches of the trees responded.

Then Yazzie told her what Owen had said, about how someday the whole overhang would come down but that no one could say when. Tears clung to her eyelashes as she listened, and her nose was running. She drew the sides of her forefingers across her eyes, as children wipe away their hurts and disappointments.

Yazzie was also thinking of his uncles. For their clan the truth of this place was in how their ancestors had arrived here as something less, and had left to become Hopi. In February, in their last conversation, Wellington Katsi had said that the ruins did not belong to the Navajos or the Indian Agency or the people in Washington or any other Anglos. He'd heard what they were doing at Mesa Verde, excavating and rebuilding. That would not happen here, he'd said. But Yazzie told Julia nothing of this. It would all fall into the past.

Johanna arrived, and the three of them stood together at the edge of the overlook.

He was barely even here, Julia thought. By which she meant in these ruins, in the West, on this earth. Words should be said, but her Bible still lay on her dresser back in Many Springs Canyon—she'd seen no need to bring it with her. So she began as best she could remember, as close as anything in the Bible to a Navajo prayer:

"The beauty of the heavenly is not the beauty of the earthly. There is a beauty in the sun, and a beauty in the moon, and a beauty in the stars; and star differs from star in its beauty . . ."

When she was done speaking, and after the silence that followed, she turned to Johanna. "*Tádídíín nihee dahóló?*"

Johanna reached inside the neck of her blanket dress for the small deerskin pouch she always wore. She worked the leather drawstring open and released corn pollen into the wind from between thumb and forefinger.

Here before them lay the inevitable end, dust to dust.

Julia and Clement walked away, but she stopped when she realized that Johanna had remained at the overlook. "I think I'll wait here for Johanna," she said.

"*Hágoshį́į,*" Clement said.

Julia nodded and he moved away. When she looked a few minutes later, he was standing by the horse, a son of the brown, brushing it with his hands and speaking, but she couldn't hear what he was saying.

Julia sat down with her back against a tree. A golden eagle was gliding near the white haze around the sun, silencing any other birds small and hidden and watchful amid the branches and brush. Across the way, the gray wall towered above the reddish brown sandstone cliffs; shattered timbers, wattle and daub, broken pottery, shards of the long ago, lay below, and the clear stream carried its ancient waters away. The oaks were tightly budded. If she sat here long enough the leaves would open, birds would build their nests and hatch their young, always on the alert. Animals would come to drink from the stream, and there would be no people to disturb any of them. She didn't intend to visit this place ever again.

Tom and Johnny Gorman would be finished digging a grave by now—she'd asked them to find a spot near where Owen had pitched his tent. And Carmelita, who had volunteered to make dinner for everyone who might come, would be at work in the kitchen. Win Peabody would be on his way from Gallup in his bright red automobile. Harry Whitaker and maybe Tóya might already have arrived. In truth, though, none of them were doing this for Owen. They were doing it for her, and therefore she needed to rise to the occasion.

She would give them each a shard, a piece of ancient pottery that Owen had found along the mountain trails, to toss into the empty grave, and another piece to take with them as a remembrance. Then they would all sit around her table and eat and tell stories and laugh and maybe even cry a little. She would play on her gramophone the songs Owen had picked for her—"Shine on, Harvest Moon," "Meet Me To-Night in Dreamland"—and she would sing along with anyone else she could gently coerce. Then they would sit in her parlor by her box stove and talk some more while Johanna listened, her pen and brushes at rest.

She was so tired. She closed her eyes . . .

Shádí.

Someone was calling her.

Shádí, k'adish hasht'e'ádiinilyaa? Sister, are you ready?

Julia jerked awake. She had dozed off. How long ago? Minutes, maybe only seconds. She looked up. Johanna was there, her arm extended, and Julia took her hand and rose.

CHAPTER TWENTY-FIVE: Jóhonaá

She watches the wind disperse the corn pollen out over the expanse. Brother warned her that she might feel the presence of those from long ago, but it is another's spirit, full of longing, that she hears:

Paint me a picture, it says. *Paint it bright: deep blue sky, a drift of white, the morning sun, an eagle in flight, red penstemon and yellow-headed birds, sandstone cliffs, a trail in slanted light . . .*

She never questions what she receives. The small rug by the box stove. The pond to wash her hair on a summer day, and the rock where she can sit and let it dry. How to set a table, with knife and spoon on the right, and the serenity of it. How to hold a pencil and pen, and what they can lay bare . . .

Now Brother is gentling his horse. Sister is sleeping, her back against a tree.

This world's sky is boundless and will not be limited by ink or paint. Brother saw how she tried, so 'Asdzáán Bítóyiszééyiztał sought out a Blessingway singer and then brought her north to south and east to west, connecting her once again to the earth, to Dinétah.

Na'ashjé'ii Asdzáá, Spider Woman, has summoned to Many Springs Canyon the women who can teach her. Brother will build her a summer hogan and a loom, and then with her own wool she will bind the paths of the stars to the landscapes she has traveled, true to the Navajo way.

A current rises up over the rim of the canyon and almost lifts her off her feet, and just as quickly leaves without disturbing the leafing trees or Brother or Sister.

She never questions what is given, nor what Nííłch'i, the Holy Wind, may ask in return. To punish the coyotes when in their greed they take too many spring lambs. To alter little things in the sacred sand paintings she imitates for 'Asdzáán Bítóyiszééyiztał—the tint of a bear's eye, the barbs of a feather, the arc of a rainbow—so as not to offend the Holy People—

So when her travels end she will return here, to this Place in the Mountains, and mix her paints, blending in ground stone and ancient shell and crushed pottery shards and pollen and pinyon sap and threads from a shirt and hair from his brush. The Holy Wind will permit it just this once. In this way she will gather his spirit, and then she will put away her pencil and pen and brushes forever, and so she will bring him home.

NOTES, POSTSCRIPTS, ACKNOWLEDGEMENTS

Notes

Many Springs Canyon, Blue Hawk Lake, and the Place in the Mountains That the Aspens Watch Over are entirely fictional, as is the Shaking Aspen Clan and its history.

In general, I've tried to ground the story in established facts, but sources often disagree, even regarding such significant events as the battles of the Cuban campaign in the Spanish-American War. This is especially true when the sources are personal recollections or family histories. That said, any errors are solely mine.

The transcriptions of Navajo ceremonial, personal, and place names of the period, which saw the first systematic efforts to render Navajo in the Western alphabet, vary widely, even in court records and other legal documents. The personal names of the fictional characters in this narrative, most especially 'Asdzáán Bítóyiszééyiztał (Tóya), are purely my invention.

The descriptions of various masks and events of the Night Chant's ninth-night Yeibichei rely on personal observation but also on published sources, particularly Washington Matthews, *The Night Chant, a Navaho Ceremony*, Publications of the Hyde Southwestern Expedition/Memoirs of the American Museum of Natural History (New York: Knickerbocker Press, 1902), and Fr. Berard Haile's *Head and Face Masks in Navaho Ceremonialism* (St. Michaels, Ariz.: St. Michael's Press, 1947). Published descriptions of Yeibicheis vary widely—see James C. Faris, *The Nightway: A History and a History of Documentation of a Navajo Ceremonial* (Albuquerque: University of New Mexico, 1990) for a discussion of Night Chant branches and comparison charts of individual and composite accounts.

The fictionalized details of a Hopi Home Dance in Chapter Twelve and a Zuni Shalako ceremony in Chapter Seventeen are based on personal observation. Here again, any errors are solely mine.

Postscripts

I have fictionalized events in the lives of a number of historical figures. Readers may find the following of interest regarding several who play secondary roles in the narrative:

Lina Hubbell (also frequently identified as Lena) died in Ganado, Arizona, in 1913; she was in her early fifties. *John Lorenzo Hubbell,* having served as sheriff of Apache County, as a member of the territorial legislator, and as an Arizona state senator, died in Ganado in 1930, at the age of 76. The Hubbell Trading Post became a National Historic Site in 1965.

Marietta Wetherill left Chaco Canyon in 1911 for land she purchased near Cuba, New Mexico, in the Jemez Mountains, but she lived several other places before spending her final years in Albuquerque, where she died in 1954, age 77; she never remarried and requested that her ashes be interred at her husband's grave in Chaco Canyon. She maintained to the end that Richard Wetherill's murder was politically motivated.

In 1912, after two years of trial delays, *Chis-chilí Biye'* (Chis-chilling-begay) was convicted of voluntary manslaughter in the death of Richard Wetherill and sentenced to 5–10 years in the penitentiary, but he was paroled in 1915 and lived near Chaco Canyon until his death in 1950.

Bill Finn remained in the employ of Marietta Wetherill until his death from influenza in 1919.

James Robb Church remained in the army after the Spanish-American War. President Theodore Roosevelt awarded him the Congressional Medal of Honor for his actions at Las Guásimas, Cuba, on June 24, 1898. In a distinguished career, he rose to the rank of colonel and was buried in Arlington National Cemetery upon his death in 1923 at age 57.

Having voluntarily returned to active duty from retirement, *Maj. Henry La Motte,* a former Navy surgeon and the chief medical officer of the Rough Riders, was wounded in Cuba and also treated for malaria. He subsequently ran afoul of the War Department for detailing inadequate medical preparations and treatment of the wounded and ill in Cuba, during transport back to the United States, and at stateside hospitals. In November 1898 he testified before a presidential commission established to review the conduct of the War Department; by then he had once again left military service, and soon after retired to Bainbridge Island, Washington State.

Capt. George Newgarden, chief medical officer at the Bloody Ford, survived a subsequent bout of yellow fever, rose to the rank of major in 1905, and retired as a consequence of a service-related disability in 1909.

Dr. Francisco Menocal, who also tended the wounded at the Blood Ford, was later cited by the War Department for his "gallant and meritorious conduct"; a Cuban by birth, he remained in Cuba after the Spanish-American War and later served as director of Cuba's immigration department.

Charles (Charlie) L. Day died in an automobile accident on a muddy road in July 1918, just shy of his thirty-ninth birthday; his brother *Samuel (Sammy) Day Jr.* continued to lead his celebrated Navajo dance team for many years after the events of this novel; he died in 1963 at the age of 82.

Details of famed photographer *Edward S. Curtis*'s visits to Canyon de Chelly in the summers of 1904 and 1906 differ from account to account. Curtis published the final volume of his twenty-volume North American Indian series in 1930 but by then had already sold the copyrights to the Morgan Company. Only 280 complete sets were produced, of the planned 500. He and Clara had divorced in 1919. Impoverished, he died in 1952 in Los Angeles, at 84; a complete set of his opus sold in 2012 for $1.44 million. The brief footage he recorded in Canyon de Chelly of Sammy Day's dance team is included in the 1974 documentary film *The Shadow Catcher*, directed by T. C. McCluhan.

Thomas P. Talle, sheriff of McKinley County (1909–1912), moved to the Las Vegas, New Mexico, area after his second two-year term ended. He remained a prominent rancher until his death from leukemia in 1934.

Acknowledgements

All epigraphs—by Ralph Waldo Emerson, from "Self-Reliance"; Emily Dickinson, Poems 1391 and 341; Paul Laurence Dunbar, "A Golden Day"; and Walt Whitman, "Out of the Rolling Ocean the Crowd" and "Song of the Exposition"—are in the public domain, as is Edith Wharton's *Ethan Frome* (New York: Charles Scribner's Sons, 1911).

In addition to the Matthews, Haile, and Faris books mentioned above, the following were particularly useful:

Edward S. Curtis. *The North American Indian: Being a Series of Volumes Picturing and Describing the Indians of the United States and Alaska.* Frederick Webb Hodge, ed. Foreword by Theodore Roosevelt. Vol. 1. New York: rpt Johnson Reprint Corp., 1978.

Timothy Egan. *Short Nights of the Shadow Catcher: The Epic Life and Immortal Photographs of Edward Curtis.* Boston: Houghton Mifflin Harcourt, 2012.

Kathryn Gabriel, ed. *Marietta Wetherill: Life with the Navajos in Chaco Canyon.* Intro. Elizabeth Jameson. Albuquerque: University of New Mexico, 1992.

Broderick H. Johnson, ed. *Navajo Stories of the Long Walk Period.* Tsaile, Navajo Nation, AZ: Navajo Community College (now Diné College), 1973.

Martin Link. *Navajo Country Pioneers: Four Generations of the Day Family.* Santa Fe, NM: Clear Light Publishing, 2013.

Frank McNitt. *The Indian Traders.* Norman: University of Oklahoma, 1962.

David Grant Noble, ed. *New Light on Chaco Canyon.* Santa Fe: School of American Research Press, 1984.

Robert L. Wilkin, *Anselm Weber, O.F.M.: Missionary to the Navaho 1898–1921.* Milwaukee: The Bruce Publishing Company, 1955.

Special mention must be made of Frank McNitt's *Richard Wetherill, Anasazi: Pioneer Explorer of Southwestern Ruins* (Albuquerque: University of New Mexico, 1966), my source for most of the details of Richard Wetherill's life and death.

Finally, my thanks to my sister Laura Overstreet, whose support and determination led her to read the manuscript for this novel so many times that she probably knows it better than I do.

NAVAJO GLOSSARY

Ahéhee'—thank you

Aoo'—yes

'Asdzání—woman

'Asdzáán—older woman

Bilagáana—Anglo, white person

Chindi—spirit of the departed embodying its negative elements

Diné Bikéyah—the Navajo Reservation (now called the Navajo Nation)

Dinétah—the traditional Navajo homeland bounded by the four sacred mountains, generally accepted as Humphreys Peak in the San Francisco Peaks (Dook'o'oosłíí), west; Mount Taylor (Tsoodził), south; Blanca Peak (Sisnaajiní), east; and Hesperus Mountain (Dibé Ntsaa), north

Gáamalii—Mormon

Hágoshį́į́—all right

Hastiin—older man (term of respect)

Hataałii—singer, medicine man

Hwéeldi—The Land of Suffering; Bosque Redondo, New Mexico, near Fort Sumner, where the Navajos were interned during the Long Walk period, 1864-1868.

Shádí—my older sister

Shich'é'é—my daughter

Shimá—my mother

Yá'át'ééh—hello

Yei—a benevolent male or female spirit, one of the Holy People

Yeibichei (Yei bei chei or Na'akai)—events occurring on the final night of the Night Chant (Nightway) healing ceremony, during which teams of dancers perform outside the ceremonial hogan

Yiskáago—tomorrow

Zhinii (Nakaii łizhinii)—black person, the black race

William Overstreet lives in Western Massachusetts. Before that, he spent four years in Fort Defiance, Arizona, within the Navajo Nation. He has written extensively on international politics and economics, most recently for the Congressional Quarterly Press imprint, but has also published short stories as well as essays, including one on the Navajo Nightway. *Halley's Gathering* is his first novel.